I0761040

No Quarter – Dominium
The Complete Series

No Quarter - Dominium
The Complete Series

By MJL Evans and GM O'Connor

ISBN: 978-1-988616-00-1

Illustrations: GM O'Connor and MJL Evans
Book Production: MJL Evans

This is a work of fiction. Names, characters, places and incidents are either the product of the author's imagination or are used fictitiously, and any resemblance to actual persons, living or dead, business establishments, events or locales is entirely coincidental.

Table of Contents

Dedication

For my father, John Evans, for always believing in me
and
for Diana Marsh, for all her words of encouragement
— MJL Evans

The Hurricane

August 14, 1689

Atia leaned over the railing on the forecastle of the *Aeolus*. She enjoyed being outside. The open air was invigorating. On the crowded main deck below, her mother, Lucretia sat holding Atia's three-year-old half-brother, while her sister Livia chatted to other passengers. So many people about to start fresh new lives; Atia envied them. They didn't have a price on their heads. They didn't have someone hunting them down at every turn.

She shuddered in the Caribbean sunshine. A creeping sensation traveled up her arms and along her neck. The last time she felt the cold was back on Barbados, when a rainstorm pelted the island for almost a week. Now *that* had been refreshing, unlike the past five weeks. Sharing passage in cramped quarters with over a hundred others was hardly ideal, but the journey was coming to an end. They were only hours away from Morant Bay.

From Morant Bay, Jonesy, a lifelong family friend, would smuggle them to Hope Bay, where Atia's father, Cormac O'Malley, planned to relocate them. Thanks to O'Malley's contacts in Port Royal and throughout the Caribbean, they had been transported from Barbados to Saint Lucia, where the *Aeolus* picked them up to make the long voyage. Atia hadn't seen Jonesy or her da for six years. *What did they look like now? Jonesy's hair probably went all silver, while Da's is white as chalk!*

A clergyman in a black cassock climbed the stairs and leaned on the rail beside her. She briefly caught his gaze. "Not long now," he said. "We'll be there by the morrow. Are you getting off in Morant Bay?"

"No, sir."

"You're Irish. How is it you made your way to Saint Lucia?"

"Sorry, sir. Me ma told me never to talk to clergy."

"Didn't mean to pry." The clergyman half-smiled. "Let's just be thankful the journey's at an end. The food here's rancid. It's been causing me Hell's own fury!" He turned to climb back down the stairs.

Atia smirked. *He's right about that, the food's bloody awful!* The wind picked up and the sun sank into the horizon. Atia collapsed her parasol. How she longed to see another sunrise in Hope Bay, a secluded fishing village on the north side of Jamaica beyond the Blue Mountains. She inhaled the salt air, imagining pink and orange hues seeping through the morning mist on the water.

Livia paused beside her sister. "What did he want then?"

Atia shrugged. "Who knows?"

Side by side, they were both beauties. At twenty, Livia towered over her sister by almost a foot. She had piercing pale blue eyes and deep chestnut hair. While seventeen-year-old Atia could pass as her mother's twin with flaming red hair and dazzling green eyes.

"Supper's soon," Livia said. "Are you gonna come down?" She gave her sister a doubtful look.

Atia grimaced. "I'll try." The passenger hold reminded her of the times she'd been locked in a closet by Hansel Crisp.

Livia squeezed her sister's arm before returning to the main deck.

A mantle of charcoal clouds stretched for miles across the sky and the wind rocked the small barque. Atia's body stiffened. A gust whipped the linen coif off the top of her head, unleashing a mass of curls. *Damn, another one gone!* The embroidered cap stitched by her ma spiraled into the dark mass forming behind the ship.

The supper bell sounded.

"That's seven," an officer called. "Supper's on, folks."

Passengers filed down a narrow staircase to the hold.

The deep rumble of thunder echoed in the distance. The sea churned into an angry foaming beast. Atia gripped the wooden rail so hard it almost hurt. Her black boots tapped against the deck as Livia and her mother vanished down the stairwell. *I should be with them. I need to be with them.* She hated being afraid, but didn't know how to control it.

The officer on watch sounded an alarm bell, and the captain emerged from his cabin. "Take in the sheets! Get the passengers inside and secure the hatches!" He ran up the stairs to the quarterdeck to peer through his telescope at the fast-approaching Jamaican coastline.

Atia felt the first of the rain hit her face.

"I'm sorry sir; it just came up on us," the officer exclaimed.

Atia shook. A tremendous crack vibrated the ship and the ocean sprayed her face. Her legs shuffled slowly towards the stairs, and then froze a few feet away. She wished Livia were there to wrestle her inside.

Atia remembered the times when she was regularly locked in the dark attic at Crisp's estate. Livia had loosened a ceiling board over the closet. With a candle to guide the way, Livia crawled on her hands and knees to bring her food and water. They'd pass the hours with stories and Celtic lullabies until Atia fell asleep.

Their secret ritual continued for weeks until one of Crisp's slaves turned Livia in. Cold dread consumed Atia when Crisp himself came to drag her sister from the attic. In the dining area of the slave quarters, he stripped Livia, hunched her over the table, and bound her hands and feet. Each slave took a turn at the whip. Atia screamed as she was forced to watch. Sometimes the sound of the whip haunted her dreams, intermixed with Livia's cries.

The cold broke Atia's train of thought. Tears flew off her face beneath a mighty gust of wind. She clutched the rail of the forecastle. Someone grabbed her arm.

"Atia," Livia said.

"Liv," Atia replied. "I can't go down there!"

"I know, Atia. But it's not safe up here. We must get below." Livia tried unsuccessfully to peel her sister's fingers off the rail.

The thought of the dimly-lit passenger quarters and people herded together in the shadows sickened Atia. The stale air reeked of perspiration, foul breath and worse. *I'd rather die than go down there!* She glanced over at the jostling crewmen securing the deck and climbing the ratlines.

Atia heard the yells of the captain shouting, "We're drifting to starboard. Turn her to port."

"Shouldn't we stay on course for Morant Bay?" an officer argued.

The captain raised his telescope. "It's too late for that. We'll be thrown into Folly Bay sure as hell! We make for Port Royal."

Atia met her sister's eyes. "Leave me, go back inside."

"Nay, I'm not leaving you." Livia clung to the rail.

Damn it! Atia cursed herself. The water swelled, causing the ship to lurch upwards and crash down. Another vessel charged from the misty gray, flying a French flag with a gold fleur-de-lis at the stern. It came with such speed she thought they would collide. The men scrambled up into the ratlines and rigging to their stations while the vessel sailed north away from the rocks.

"Please, Atia, we must get below," Livia insisted.

Atia took a few steps along the deck, and then froze, gripping the rail tightly. Nearby, stood the clergyman she'd spoken with earlier. Strange that he'd be outside in the storm.

An officer yelled at them all to get inside.

The clergyman gripped the rail of the forecastle. "To tell you the truth, I have a terrible fear of confined spaces."

Atia faced the growing waves; she had never seen a storm like this before. Her senses churned like the tide and panic burned through her, yet there was no place to run and no place to hide. The ship slammed back and forth while water soused the main deck.

"Atia! Livia!" came a muted voice on the wind.

Atia squinted to see her ma struggle against the gale trying to reach them. "Ma!"

Crewmen screamed. The mizzenmast snapped and toppled over. Flailing lines whipped through the air like blades, tearing a man in two. His bottom half dropped onto the deck while his top half flew over the railing. Red water pooled and the rigging collapsed, crushing several officers.

"Hold on; I'm coming," Lucretia called.

Atia gripped the rail tightly. To her horror, a brutal upsurge clawed the deck, dragging Livia over the side. Shock paralyzed her for several seconds. "Liv!"

The clergyman swiftly reached down. "Grab my hand!" He caught hold and raised Livia up. Before reaching the deck, another swirling swell yanked them both over.

Lucretia patted Atia's arm and they both stared down into the foamy white.

"She's there," Atia exclaimed.

Lucretia reached down to grab Livia and lifted her back up. Manic fear possessed Atia. No matter how badly she wanted to embrace her ma and sister, her arms remained locked around the rail. They were all clinging on for their lives now.

The ship collided against the rocks of Folly Bay. The hull shattered, releasing a loud groan, akin to a wounded animal in the throes of a death blow. Frantic passengers spilled onto the main deck from the hold. They climbed over and pushed one another, until they were finally tossed side to side and slammed over the edge of the ship.

Atia was pelted by flying debris. Her eyes briefly opened to behold a mountain of water as it rolled upon them. There was no air, only the rushing garble of the tide. Water relentlessly filled her ears and nose. Her lips recoiled into her mouth and her teeth clamped upon them. The water receded and she gasped, simultaneously sucking in air and spewing brine.

The rail began to buckle. Before her was a dizzying display of lightning. A short distance away, the rocks flickered and shined. Someone scrambled upon them. She recognized her ma's long hair. The ship's bow, only a few feet away, approached fast. With a potent hit, the front of the ship broke apart and her ma was crushed beneath it. Passengers flew mid-air, some landing in the water, others splitting apart on the rocks.

Atia opened her mouth to scream, but nothing came out. The rail broke loose and she was propelled forward, catching a ride along the spindrift to the stony beach. She landed heavily, her arms still gripped around the broken barrier. The scream finally escaped her throat and she belted it across the landscape. After unhooking her arms, she rose slowly, vomiting mouthfuls of salt water.

Behind her, the ship continued to splinter under the pounding waves. Flames erupted from the hatches of the hold. Unfortunate souls hurled themselves off the vessel to extinguish their clothes, only to be caught in the grinding undertow of the current.

The tide tugged at Atia's feet, toppling her backwards onto a rock bed. A hand grabbed her leg.

"I got you!" said Livia.

"Liv!" Atia clutched her sibling's arm. Together they teetered to land. Another rush of water and curling waves towed them back into a sea littered with corpses. Arm and arm they fought towards the shore.

The water rose, driven by fierce wind. Atia was ripped away from her sister and stumbled over the surf. She reached out to grab at anything. Drenched in waves, her head was sucked under and she felt the brine plunge back into the ears, nose and throat. Momentarily she bobbed back up. Livia was only a few feet away.

Atia reached up and their hands locked. Together they hobbled madly for the beach, towing each other along. The instant the tide subsided they lunged onward to escape its grasp. Several feet away stood a jungle of trees.

Atia lagged, almost succumbing to the pelting wind and rain.

Livia tugged her arm and pushed her forward. “Move it, or we die.”

At the treeline, they found a path. Grabbing at branches, they followed a seemingly endless maze of mud, vines, and roots. They reached a plateau surrounded by dense bushes.

Livia collapsed, rolling in next to the undergrowth for cover.

Atia could see down to the beach. The flames from the ship lit up like a beacon for miles through the murk. Carried on the wind were the screams of injured and dying passengers. They scrambled along the rocks only to be butchered by the waves.

Atia turned away, trapped between horror and extreme exhaustion. Through a break in the trees, she spotted the sails of the French ship caught in the hurricane. Grief consumed her and she lay down to embrace Livia waiting for the storm to pass.

Capitaine la Roche stood on the quarterdeck of his brig *La Lune,* and scrutinized the storm. He was no stranger to hurricanes and stared defiantly into the murk. His vessel was rigged for merchant duty and they carried Cuban tobacco and ten tonnes of sugarloaf bound for Petit-Goâve.

The storm increased in its ferocity and water saturated the deck. The seasoned officers knew how to react, but he wondered how the new crew would respond to true danger. His thoughts turned to the English barque they had passed near the coastline. He tempered his sympathy knowing that death came fast to those who ventured near Folly Bay. La Roche lowered his telescope and turned to his quartermaster, François le Picard.

“North-northwest, Capitaine,” le Picard said. He looked to the boatswain, Martel, and ordered him to check the barometer.

“Dropping fast. It *is* a hurricane. A genius he is, no?” Martel grinned.

Le Picard gave an irritated smirk. “You were right, Capitaine.”

La Roche held out his hand.

“What? I’m good for it.” Le Picard gave a sheepish look. “Besides, it is frowned upon at sea.”

La Roche knew le Picard couldn’t resist a wager. “Only when you’re on account, you cheap bastard!” He watched the men hanging from sails, their bare feet clasping the ratlines. "Lifelines on deck, Monsieur Martel."

"Oui, Capitaine. Lifelines!" Martel ran to the main deck to ensure crewmen roped themselves to the shroud pinrail as the wind and rain whisked over the ship.

"Don't worry. A little rain, no problem," la Roche assured as the sails flapped violently. "No, no! Take in the sheets!" He waved his fist at the men in the rigging. Fighting against the wind they struggled to tighten the lines. "Now make your course due north, Picard."

Le Picard turned to the young, muscular black man at the helm. "Monsieur Delacroix, twenty degrees to starboard. North we sail!"

Delacroix heaved the wheel. "Oui, starboard."

La Roche bobbed his head with a care-free smile. "Looks like it's going west. Just remain on course. Everything will be fine."

Le Picard cocked his eyebrow. "Going west, is it?"

La Roche shrugged. "Well, 'shit we are fucked' is not quite so uplifting! Yet we will try, Picard."

Rain pelted and waves slammed into the ship's hull.

Martel checked the compass. "Heading due north, Capitaine."

Delacroix held the ship's course. *La Lune* pushed through the Jamaican Channel struggling against the disparaging winds.

Martel scanned the coastline through a telescope. "Ship, port side aft!"

La Roche and le Picard raised their telescopes. A flash from a lantern pierced the haze.

Martel squinted. "I think it's a fishing boat."

"A lugger," la Roche corrected.

The signal continued blinking.

"*La Lune de Miel*?" Martel said. "Looks like buccaneers, not fishermen."

"De Kreep." Le Picard sneered.

"That jerk buccaneer who is always sticking up for the Indians?" Delacroix asked.

"That's him!" le Picard snorted. "Probably on his way to attack Port Royal with a fishing boat and twenty guys!"

La Roche paused. His right hand trembled slightly and his throat tightened. De Kreep was as a brother to him and saved his life long ago. He shuddered, not from the weather, but the memory of a doomed raid that ended in the Darien Jungle in '68.

He would never forget the screams of his crewmates, the wet tearing of bloody flesh, and the scent of scorched human meat skewered over a blazing fire. His wrists burned from the rope. He sat within a circle of wooden pikes, next in line to be slaughtered. That's when de Kreep arrived with several Arawak elders. At first la Roche didn't understand why they were there, but soon his life was negotiated for and he was led away. To his shock and amazement, they reunited him with *La Lune*.

"Prepare to come about!" la Roche ordered.

Le Picard closed his eyes a moment in dread. When he opened them again, he gave an understanding nod. "Prepare to come about."

La Lune turned hard to the port side, leaning dangerously, beaten by the gale. Crewmen clung desperately as they followed the flashing light. Officers fixed their telescopes ahead.

La Roche observed the men on the lugger bailing the boat out frantically. "Signal them. No grappling hooks."

"Oui." Le Picard took the signal lamp and flashed the message.

La Roche wiped the water from his eyes and squinted through the viewer. The buccaneers chopped down the rigging and the yard arms. The top sails fell and lastly the bowsprit was broken off the front of vessel and left to sink in the ocean. *Good man, Dashiell,* he thought, keeping his trembling hand in his pocket. *One shot at this – we must get them quickly, and then head to open water. Rocks are everywhere!* The wind and rain hammered the ship. He squinted at crew trying to furl the sails. "Beat them!"

The crewman struck the sails with their fists to purge the water.

Struggling against the elements, *La Lune* slowly fought her way to the lugger. The brig plunged into a large swell, and then propelled upwards, soaring into the air. Crewmen clung on for their lives. She slammed back down, causing an explosion of white water.

La Roche scrunched up his face. "That hurt!"

"This is going to get a lot worse. The storm, she is here. We should not be attempting this!" le Picard said. "Ready ropes and netting. Starboard side. Double quick!"

Martel and several crewmen prepared ropes, while others readied the nets. Men with axes stood alert. "Ready on main!" Martel signaled with a thumb up.

Le Picard turned to la Roche. "Main deck ready, Capitaine."

La Lune came alongside the lugger. The buccaneers leapt off and clung to the netting. De Kreep jumped last, just before the small vessel was sucked beneath the waves. When they reached the top, they hurled themselves over, landing on the deck.

"All aboard, Capitaine!" Martel shouted. "Cut the ropes. Throw it all over!"

"Turn due south for open water," la Roche ordered.

"Turn to port. We head south for open water," le Picard called, and then leaned to the Capitaine. "You know, having armed buccaneers climb aboard is not recommended even in nice weather."

De Kreep staggered up the stairs towards la Roche.

"Permission, Capitaine?"

They shook hands.

"I knew it was you. How do I ever thank you?"

"Even, this makes us." La Roche nodded, and then eyed Martel. "Get these men below, get them rested up."

"Oui, Capitaine!"

"Hold this course for as long as she can take it." La Roche addressed de Kreep, "Take your men below and take it easy. Then join in on the pumps. Martel will show you what to do. It's going to be a long fucking night, uh?"

De Kreep and his men followed Martel inside.

"Where will we put in, Capitaine?" le Picard asked.

"Let's survive the night first. Then if we have to, Port Royal."

Waves crashed over the deck.

"Nice knowing you," le Picard said.

La Roche relieved Delacroix at the wheel, tying himself to it with a pull knot. "If our time it is, *c'est la vie*!" He grappled with the helm. *La Lune* fell upon the back of another potent wave that drove the ship upwards and crashed back down. The sky lit up with brilliant slivers of lightning.

Rain pounded and howling gusts of wind blustered through the trees and bushes. Lightning cracked in the distance. Ma smiled and ran a brush through her fiery red hair. The sun rose over Morant Bay. Ethereal beams of light broke through the mist. Da smoked fish wrapped in tobacco leaves over a small fire. Her stomach grumbled.

Atia's eyes opened sluggishly. The cold damp ground made her body ache. "Ma?" she cried hoarsely and sat up. The hanging sleeves of her dress had been torn away. Atia massaged the cuts on her exposed arms. Her left arm had been branded with an iron cross by Crisp. In retaliation, her ma had ankh symbols tattooed on their arms to cover the scars.

Atia rose to her feet, kneading her bruised ribs. The stern sat half submerged on the beach below. Corpses and wood fragments scattered everywhere. Behind her a field of sugar cane and patches of jungle lay in ruins.

"Ma?" Atia called softly.

Her sister moaned and rubbed her eyes. "Atia?"

"Where's Ma?"

Livia rolled onto her side. "She's in Elysium. No more harm can befall her."

Atia turned to face the sugar field. Wherever home was, it had been swallowed by the storm. *If I had just reached out my hand to grab her, she might be here with us now.*

Livia whimpered, trying to stand. "Bloody hell!" She vomited salt water, doubling over in pain. "Can't…breathe."

"I'll find clean water." Atia hoped rainwater was trapped within the cane. Lifting long broken leaves, she managed to suck back small mouthfuls. When she had her fill she brought over a few stalks for Livia.

Atia braced her ribs with one arm and knelt beside her sister, trickling water down her throat. She cradled Livia's head and gently brushed hair away from the gash on the side of her face. From behind them footsteps sloshed through the wet mud. A voice said, "I hears something!"

The splashing and rustling drew nearer. A group of emaciated slaves in torn rags emerged with their ankles bound in shackles. A short, portly white man covered in dirt pushed his way through, whip in hand.

"What is it? Who's there?" He grinned through yellow teeth and rubbed his hands together. "Well, lookie here, tasty little morsels. And who might you be, me lovelies?"

Atia trembled. "Please help us, sir? We've been put through the mill."

"Irish as four-leaf clovers too," he jeered. "Immigrants? Indentured pikeys?"

"We was on a ship," Atia explained. "It broke up."

"Ah, the shipwreck. You could fetch five hundred pounds apiece! Who needs crops when ya got pikeys, eh? Bring 'em to the ship!" he shouted at his slaves and then kicked at their chains.

The slaves grabbed at Livia, who screeched with pain.

Atia pushed them. "Get away from her!"

The slaver struck her across the face. Atia recoiled, touching her split bloody lip. She reached for her sister's arm.

A slave pointed at Livia. "This one's hurt."

"Of course she is, ya imbecile!" the slaver bellowed. "Bring 'em. She only need live long enough for sale." He yanked the chains and the slaves hauled Atia away. She tried to fight them off. The slaves lifted Livia as carefully as they could and the girls were transported through the field down towards a small dock, where a weathered lugger sat. Upon its missing nameplate at the stern, a mossy stain formed the name *Sweet Dreams*.

"Ready to make sail!" the slaver hollered to the workers aboard, who were in the midst of repairs. "We're going to Port Royal." He pointed at the slaves before heading towards his house. "Put them in the hold!"

Atia stumbled along to the dock. A short distance along the beach sat a village with a dozen storm beaten cottages and a stable. Fishing boats sat tied up at a wharf. *We could escape on one of those boats.* Atia glanced back to the house, where the slaver entered the front door.

One of the slaves stopped. "No one is watching. Go now, run."

Atia rushed to Livia's side and tried to lift her.

Livia writhed in agony. "Go on Atia, leave me!"

Atia tried to lift her sister again. "No! I'll not leave you."

"Save yourself, Atia," Livia insisted.

She wouldn't leave her sister. They always watched over and protected one another. They survived the worst kinds of trouble because they stayed together. One such instance was back on Barbados when they carried out their cleaning duties on Crisp's boathouse. After removing weeds and overgrown vines from outside, they swept the interior and polished the windows.

Crisp arrived to criticize and hassle them. Atia was grabbed by the hair and tossed to the floor. It gave him great pleasure to remind her that she was breeding stock as he raised her skirt and spread her legs. She didn't hesitate for a second and clawed his face with her nails.

Livia joined in with a boat-hook off the wall and lunged at Crisp. She managed to gash the side of his head. He fell, clutching at the wound. Livia grabbed Atia's hand and they ran for the door. Their retaliation was short lived however when they came face to face with Crisp's slaver captain who stood over seven feet tall and wore barbs on his knuckles. Atia and Livia were soon locked up to await punishment.

Atia knelt on the dock beside Livia. "We go together or not at all."

One slave motioned to the others and they lifted Livia down the beach towards the village.

The dirt covered slaver emerged from the house with a bottle in his hand and two ruffians at his side. "Ya ungrateful savages!" His thugs seized the chains. The slaver approached Atia, uncorking the bottle and pouring in the contents of a vial. "Just don't know when to quit, do ya?" He revealed his yellow teeth and forced the bitter liquid down her throat. "We're all going to Port Royal now."

ATia
GO
2014

Port Royal

Capitaine la Roche gazed through the window of his cabin aboard *La Lune*. The morning sunshine cast an orange glow on the English city of Port Royal. It was a miracle they made it with the sails in tatters and wreckage spread all over the deck. He fell in and out of consciousness fused to the helm all night. Only when he saw blue sky with seabirds floating overhead had he realized that they survived. He remembered Martel releasing the rope and de Kreep helping him to his cabin. After suffering a headache and waves of nausea, la Roche woke hours later, almost recovered.

His bluish gray eyes studied the many fishing boats and Turtle Crawls, where the city's turtle supply was farmed in two large pens. Four years it had been since he set foot here and everything appeared the same. He however was now in his forties, his dark hair marred by silver streaks and he bore many more scars.

He finished buttoning his shirt to conceal purple bruises on his torso from being pinned against the wheel. After slipping on a respectable dark blue jacket and black trousers, the finishing touch upon his head was a black wide-brimmed hat. The leather belt around his waist held a cutlass and a Spanish stiletto. It would only be a matter of time before people realized he was back. Known by many names, he was Gator Gar and El Capitaine when he raided the Spanish, le Sage to the buccaneers of Hispaniola, and La Salle when he was sent to England with Henry Morgan to be tried for piracy. He managed to keep his true identity secret; after all diligence was paramount, enemies were everywhere.

The interior of the cabin was simply furnished with a writing desk, chair, corner-bed and a royal blue banner on the wall with gold fleur-de-lis and a faded family crest, given to him by a friend on Cayman Brac Island. Christened Jean-Paul la Roche, he never knew his family. They had been killed long ago. He grew up in a workhouse and escaped before the age of ten, and later served aboard a galiot called *Rascal*.

A knock sounded. "Oui," he said and le Picard and Delacroix entered.

Le Picard seemed refreshed and wore a simple black suit with gold buttons, and black leather bucket boots. He removed his felt hat decorated with an ostrich feather. François le Picard served as quartermaster and sailing master. In his late thirties, he was the youngest of three brothers. His eldest sibling Pierre was a privateer, with the reputation of a fierce pirate. François had tried his hand at pirating, which had failed miserably, resulting in many deaths.

Delacroix wore his usual leather vest and cut-off trousers. Being young and ambitious, Delacroix fell into disappointment when his only task was to help transport sugar. Even so, la Roche had the look of an experienced pirate, with elaborate tattoos on his arms. He gave the impression that there was more to him than being a simple merchantman.

"Crew's making repairs, Capitaine," le Picard said, glancing down at the gold longsword on the desk. "The sword? Someone's getting promoted or killed."

La Roche smiled scathingly. "How did you make out?"

"The harbormaster will let us stay for two days. They're unloading supplies for us at the end of the north dock."

"Take whatever they lay down but clear away when she's loaded and find a spot in the harbor out of the way." La Roche admired the weapon glistening with rubies and emeralds. "It's time I gave you both more responsibility. I'm taking shore leave. Broke my balls, this trip did. Command is yours for a couple of days, Picard. Congratulations."

"Thank you, Capitaine, but if I had a hundred men and fifty pounds of coca leaf powder I couldn't do it in time." Le Picard strapped on the belt housing the longsword.

"Then your new master's mate will help you." La Roche watched Delacroix's face light up.

"Me?"

La Roche nodded. "I'm promoting you. Congratulations. Find some place out of the way. Work fast, but do it right. Remember, hostilities are growing. We could find ourselves in an enemy port at any moment. Keep on your toes. Get to work on the mainmast first."

"Oui, Capitaine!" Delacroix rushed excitedly from the cabin.

"See? Enthusiasm and youth will see us through."

"Enthusiasm and youth? Are you jesting?" Le Picard shook his head.

"I know you prefer Martel, but I've known him a long time. He's a good man but he's not meant to lead. He walks with his head down sometimes and even crashes into people."

"Oui, he does," le Picard agreed. "I know. But Delacroix? Fucking, that's all that kid knows. I for one don't want a bunch of women swimming after the boat!"

"He'll be fine. Stop your bitching." La Roche laughed and they walked from the cabin up the stairs to the main deck.

"Being back here, someone will recognize you."

"Don't worry. Nothing will happen." La Roche held out his arm and a large dark gray parrot mounted his shoulder. "A quick drink at the Swiftsure, things will be fine." He befriended the bird many years ago and trained him to carry messages. La Roche always make sure there was a supply of dead insects around to keep Minuit motivated.

Le Picard's face sagged. "Attracting too much attention you are and the Swiftsure Tavern of all places!"

"No one is going to recognize me, trust me." La Roche rubbed his chin. "I'm yesterday's news." He took a dead cockroach from his pocket and Minuit snapped it up. "Okay. Go stretch your wings." The parrot took to the air, soaring over a mixture of new and old buildings.

Arrow approached the harbor – a thirty-gun frigate with a walnut-colored hull and red and gold trim. White sails with mauve border fluttered in the breeze. The ship listed to starboard. Captain Arthur Valentine, a former privateer and now the top shipper of Port Royal, better known as Bleedin Art, stood on deck like a scarecrow inspecting the harvest. Art picked at his large teeth with a silver toothpick. Not only did he have a head for business, he loved the arts, particularly writing poetry. Art even had the audacity to write a letter to the Earl of Rochester when he was alive, telling him he was an over-indulgent drudge who wouldn't know true poetry if it gave him syphilis. Later, a reply came on parchment: F.Off.

"Gun cay due east, Captain," his first mate Ginger noted the landmark indicating the route to Port Royal. "Ready for the turn."

Art peered through his telescope. Gusts of smoke rose over the city. Hundreds of ships congregated in the harbor. "They ain't here. I can see every bloody mast all the way to Ligania and they ain't bloody here." His was a sinewy English accent. He retracted the viewer. "And where the bloody hell is the pilot boat?"

"She may be sunk. Looks like Port Royal got a piece of it herself."

Cupid, a red Cuban Macaw, circled the vessel, landing on Art's shoulder. Art grinned painfully. "Why did I buy those caravels?"

"I said those ships were too old."

"Did I blame you?" Art stared at the sea. "Bloody hell!"

"Bloody hell!" the macaw agreed.

Ginger tilted his head. "You can always blame Rook."

Art nodded. "Aye, I can blame him. Ya just wanna see Coggshall cut his balls off, you ruthless prick! Nay, it's me own damn fault this time. The investors are gonna be pissed."

"Ruthless prick!" Cupid screeched.

Ginger pointed across the water. "*Diamond Dog*. She's sailing in ahead."

Diamond Dog was a pretty two mast Shnyava with grayish blue sails, and an oak-stained hull patterned with diamonds. Being a light reconnaissance vessel, it was similar to a brig, but much smaller. It reminded Art of his days as a young privateer aboard the *Falmouth* in '59.

Royal Rook, known also as Lieutenant Marquess Castle, was recently hired by Art for added protection and for his previous experience as a privateer who once served the city. Rook's mission was to escort Art and the slave ships to Port Royal. At this point however, the storm may have swallowed the lot.

Art pounded his fist on the rail. "Oh, Jesus Christ, we lost it all!" How he longed for the good old days of simple pirating and pillaging! He despised the slave trade. His wife's family made their fortune in it, thus the only reason for his involvement. *If I could only commandeer a Spanish treasure ship and have a wild drunken spell in Tortuga, I'd be a new man.*

Cupid landed on the taffrail next to a swivel gun. "Bugger it!"

"You shut it! I don't need any of your beak." Art aimed his pistol and the macaw took off, shitting on the deck as it went. He took a deep breath and thought of his favorite writer, Shakespeare. "Shoulda stayed out the picaroon racket, bugger it! True is it that we have seen better days. You know the way, Ginger, take us in." He snarled at Port Royal. "There's four months down the bloody hatch!"

Diamond Dog made her turn at Fort Walker, sailing into the inner harbor and around Fort James, heading to the King's Wharf to dock. Royal Rook peered through his spyglass. "Ah, bloody hell, no sign of them caravels." He lowered the viewer and rubbed the back of his neck. His fingers glided along a diamond-shaped tattoo on the left side of his throat, the result of a drunken, rowdy excursion to a pirate haven known as the Blarney Stone on Cayman Brac Island.

His quartermaster, a wide hulking man named Tiny McAllister, stood at his side. A former crewman of the *Falmouth* under Bleedin Art, Tiny met Rook during a pirate raid. "Any sign of them?"

"Nay," Rook spoke with a stodgy accent.

"Shall we dock?"

"Aye, take us in." Rook whistled. A brown and gray Mascarene parrot named Checkmate circled above.

"I preferred piracy to this lot, mate," Tiny said.

"Aye." Rook screwed up his face. "What the bloody hell did I get us inta this time?"

The ship coasted alongside a sizable wooden dock, where other vessels assembled to be inspected by the harbormaster. Rook, Tiny, and eight crewmen jumped off to secure the *Diamond Dog* with rope. Checkmate swooped down, landing on Rook's shoulder. Waiting for them on the dock stood two of Bleedin Art's cutthroats.

Rook hated dealings with thugs. Things had a tendency to go awry. He took a deep breath and faced Pikestaff, a typical pirate with a patch over his left eye, simple clothes, and a blue and yellow Martinique Macaw named Gibbet. Beside him was Jag'd Jayne, a run-of-the-mill thug, early twenties, broad shouldered, and dressed in plain black trousers with long boots and a brimmed hat.

Gibbet eyed Checkmate, initiating a staring competition.

"Mr. Coggshall would like to know why yer here and the merchandise ain't?" asked Pikestaff.

Rook gritted his teeth. "We lost them."

"I warned him. Stay away from wanna-be privateers." Jayne smirked.

"You lost them all?" Pikestaff folded his arms.

"Art packed the whole lot inta two old caravels." Rook removed his hat and ran his fingers through his hair. "Wasn't my call, mate."

"Not yer call? Be sure to tell Mr. Coggshall that when he cuts off your balls."

"I was hired by Bleedin Art and it be his own damn fault they went down. When he arrives I be expecting payment."

"Aye, be sure to tell him that when he gets here." Pikestaff lit his pipe. "Art may lose a ball or two himself!"

"*Arrow* coming in, sir," *Diamond Dog's* lookout called, pointing to the ship rounding Fort James.

"Better duck, Lieutenant, it be aiming for you," Jayne said.

"Oi, clear the docks, you lot. Official business only!" The stern voice came from Harbormaster Jonathan Pepys, a graying man with a clay pipe poking out of this mouth.

"Say hello to your little songbird for me," Jayne added before walking off with Pikestaff.

Katie Evans. Rook flushed a bit as he thought of the girl he hadn't seen in ages. A pang of guilt tightened his chest. He had left when Coggshall took over the slave industry. Rook despised both equally and didn't want to work with either. He promised to return and take Katie away. *Whether I'm paid or not, I'm taking her away this time.*

Further along the inner harbor at the dock of Waterman's Wharf, another ship landed, a sloop named *Bloody Mary.* A true beauty, with dark red sails and a rosewood-finished hull. Captain Alfonse Slazerelli named her after Mary Rose, a whore he mutilated in Belize. She'd been a work of art that Mary. He slit her throat and watched the blood drain. Next, he severed her limbs and strung up her entrails on copper wall sconces. Captain Slazerelli licked his lips and lit up a pipe before stepping down the gangway. He'd earned the name Slasher Al – the demented, the twisted. *The artistic genius.* He grinned to himself.

He'd seen *Diamond Dog* and *Arrow* come in and decided it was high time to apply for Bleedin Art's position. Al disembarked, wearing his red dress suit and black leather vest that concealed a dozen sharp knives. They whispered to him softly, craving blood. "There, there, me beauties. Soon, very soon." He patted the vest like a truly impulsive madman.

He sashayed towards the Crooked Compass. Upon his shoulder sat Lash, a female macaw of Dominican green and yellow, her wings clipped. His loyal thugs followed. Big Fred was six and a half feet tall, and his talents included crushing heads with his fists and eating live reptiles. Then there was Dogfish, who filed his teeth down to sharp points and reveled in biting the flesh of his enemies. Good men, good cutthroats, not afraid to get their hands dirty.

Al followed a quaint stone path to the tavern. Slave trader Heins Burghill stood on the terrace staring into Cherry Red's Boutique at the erotic activities inside. He sucked on a fat Cuban cigar and drank heavily, until his cheeks turned a festering red. The sound of broken glass snapped him from his daydream and he marched inside.

Al stepped through the entrance and meandered towards a table near the window, avoiding glass fragments. Big Fred and Dogfish followed, grabbing a table on the terrace.

"Clean it up, idiot!" Burghill yelled, throwing an empty bottle at one of the male slaves.

Al sat down.

Burghill glanced over briefly, grabbing a fresh drink before he took the seat opposite Al.

"Fatima!" Burghill yelled. "Fan!"

"Yes, Mr. Burghill." The beautiful young African girl fetched a large bamboo fan and initiated a steady breeze.

"What can I do for you, Captain Slazerelli?" Burghill grimaced.

"I believe ale is in order."

"Ale," Burghill barked, signaling to a slave.

"Word hath made its way that you have lost them both, Mr. Burghill."

"What do you mean, lost? Who says?"

"My sources say *Arrow* and *Diamond Dog* left Barbados with two caravels and five hundred of your property." Al paused, staring at Fatima. *Gagged and bound with rope – she'd be perfect!* "Them ships be in the harbor but there be no caravels."

Burghill chewed on his cigar. "He lost them?"

"I can't help but ponder the idea that had I been trusted with this venture, things may have turned out favorably for all involved." Al puffed his pipe, and then grabbed the mug of ale off a tray from the slave. He took several large gulps and gawked at Fatima again.

Burghill stood up and paced, patting his greasy forehead with a silk handkerchief. "So we have hundreds of buyers and we got no new slaves or whores. He bought caravels? That cheap ass son of whore. This is a disaster!" He collapsed into his chair.

Al sneered at Burghill's distress, but really couldn't blame him.

Caravels were an outdated design that ignored the influences of wind change in favor of social hierarchy. Upper class passengers would stay in the elevated cabins at the bow and stern of the ship, while the lower classes stayed below, all the while sailing nowhere fast.

"I'll have to tell Coggshall. We need every piece of shit slave and whore we can scrounge up." He glowered at Al. "Don't touch Cherry's girls. Not yet."

"I was promised two harlots meself from our previous venture and I intend on collecting."

"Well, it's gonna cost you more 'cause ya never return them. We can only hope Coggshall has some…"

"Fresh meat?" Al grinned maniacally and Lash released a loud shriek. His eyes darted to Fatima. "I'll give ya two hundred pounds for her."

Burghill's face crumpled up. "She mends wounds and speaks eight different languages. She's worth ten times that!"

"A bit expensive for me taste. But perhaps as a signing incentive."

"Play yer cards right and anything's possible." Burghill puffed on his cigar and peered out at the water.

Fort James guarded the entrance to the inner harbor. Cannons lined three sides. On the top level, next to the flagpole, Acting Lieutenant Governor Dorcas Dewar strolled along with a silver walking stick, dressed in a lavish purple suit, feathered hat, and heavily polished buckle shoes. His companion Chief Judge Lord Lawrence Llewellyn was decked out in a finely woven long coat and feather trimmed tri-cornered hat. They walked around the slaves cleaning up storm debris.

Following them was the Governor's advisor, Mason Sleemans, dressed in a dark doublet and matching trousers with a tri-cornered hat.

"Splendid idea, Larry! Splendid!" Dewar clasped his hands together.

"Seems the appropriate thing to do after a hurricane."

Sleemans's eyebrows pointed up. "Pretend to give a bloody damn?"

"Oh, you're so right. For spirit at the very least. That's politics for you, it's all about the people." Dewar shook his head. "Bloody sods!"

"My thoughts exactly, sir." Llewellyn shook his pen, a newfangled invention nick-named the 'Pepys' pen, inspired by Samuel Pepys, cousin to the harbormaster. "Why won't this work?" He tried to write on parchment.

"You turn it. The ink's inside," Sleemans explained

"Supplies may be short, so we may have to dip into the reserves just a bit." Dewar lifted his thumb and forefinger.

"Of course, sir. No problem. The audit is my responsibility, after all." Sleemans bowed, exhaustion permanently etched on his face.

Dewar paused. "A hurricane is a disaster and that's what the disaster fund is for, right? We'll call it the I Survived the Hurricane Ball."

Llewellyn clapped childishly. "Excellent choice, Your Grace!"

Dewar breathed deeply. "I love when you call me that."

Sleemans glared at Llewellyn. "Shall we impose a curfew for the lower classes?"

"Absolutely." Dewar clapped his hands together. "We don't want the riffraff spoiling our fun." He watched a pair of city officials emerge from the top of the stairs. "Here comes the I Want, I Want Brigade!" The city's engineer, Bill Chitty, and Councilman White charged forth. "Councilmen, what is it?"

"Ya wanted the damage report, sir," Chitty replied.

"Ah, of course. Let's have it."

"Thames Street to High Street from the King's House to the Admiralty Court is flooded," White said, clad in a white suite, with a white wig and an ivory walking stick. "My house as well. I'm thinking of renting out the basement as a bath house."

"The bridge to the Palisadoes is out again," Chitty added. "We'll need to appropriate funds from the disaster bank for a new bridge – a proper bridge."

Dewar shook his head. "I'm afraid that's impossible, funds have already been appropriated."

"What?" White demanded. "I haven't seen anything about that. You better not be planning another ball at our expense!"

Sleemans interjected, "If I may, gentlemen. There's currently not enough in the disaster fund to cover a new bridge. However, I suggest a sufficient amount be withdrawn to cover the cost of a temporary replacement."

"Which will disintegrate in the next hurricane." Chitty folded his arms.

“But for now, it will have to do.”

“Where will we make up the difference?” White queried.

“Well, you’re council chair.” Dewar gave an encouraging smile. “Sit on it for a while. You have until next season.”

“We also have extensive damage to the streets. Cracks and fissures have opened up,” Chitty said.

“Well, why aren’t the streets paved?” Dewar played with handle of his walking stick.

“They can’t be paved; they are filled in each time they’re damaged. The ground’s too soft to get a solid foundation without major excavation.”

“Use some kind of interlocking stone,” Sleemans suggested.

“This is unacceptable! We’re English, damn it, we know how to build things where they shouldn’t be!” Dewar bellowed.

“I suggest taxes be raised on the lower classes to cover it,” Llewellyn said. “We’ll call it Chitty’s Infrastructure Tax.”

“Perhaps I can think of a more suitable name,” Sleemans reproved.

Harbormaster Pepys approached the gathering.

“Very well. Fix the bridge, Chitty, and no lollygagging,” Dewar said.

“Ah, Pepys!” Llewellyn began. “This is an ingenious invention!” He held up the metal pen. “How does it work?”

Pepys turned it and scribbled against the parchment.

“Ah, there it is. Marvelous!” Llewellyn snatched the pen back. “Thank your cousin for me.”

“You’re welcome. If you need it refilled take it to Pope’s Tobacco on Honey Lane.”

“Splendid.”

“Pepys, I noticed a lot of foreign ships in the harbor today.” Dewar cleared his throat.

Chitty and White took the cue to leave.

“Two Spanish pinks and a French brig. They each entered under a white flag and subjected themselves to inspection. They all be civilian ships with extensive damage and wounded. We couldn’t refuse them,” Pepys said.

Dewar tilted his head. “Of course not, that wouldn’t be very Christian. We’ll charge them a fee.”

“I think a large fee would be appropriate,” Llewellyn added.

“Quite right. Have them each pay, uh…” Dewar trailed off,

confused by all the currencies being phased out in favor of the new monetary system. “Do they still use doubloons these days?”

“I believe so.”

“Have them each pay four gold doubloons.”

Pepys frowned. “Four doubloons?”

“You think it should be more?” Dewar did not want Port Royal’s hospitality to be taken advantage of. “Well, let’s say—”

“Four will be fine, sir.”

“Oh, hurrah!” Dewar’s sight stopped on a ship with decimated pale yellow sails near Turtle Crawls. “What ship is that over there?”

“*La Lune*, sir. A French brig loaded with sugar. I’ve given her two days to make repairs.”

“Well, he looks like he can afford it.” Dewar mused. “You can start with that Frenchie. Get your men on it right away.”

“Aye, sir.” Pepys departed.

“Commanding, sir, very commanding. If I may say so.”

“Oh, you may. It’s up to us to make the important decisions, Larry.” Dewar’s eyes widened. “It should be a costume party.”

“Dress as your favorite natural disaster?” Llewellyn’s eyebrows perked up.

“What a good idea. See to it immediately, Lord Llewellyn!”

“Right away, sir.” He gave an exaggerated salute that imitated the mating dance of a bird of paradise.

SlasherAL
GO
2015

After the Rain Comes Good Weather

Admiral Christian Goddam cursed under his breath. Atop the tower at Fort Charles, he stared through his telescope at the dozens of wounded ships gliding into the harbor. In its thirty-year existence, the city had seen its share of war and suffered frequent attacks from the Spanish and Dutch. Now under threat from their former ally, the French, the five forts lay waiting to see action again. "My God, look at them all! We should let them all drown," Goddam huffed. The threat was imminent now. His adversary across the chess board was none other than the famous Dutch privateer, Laurens de Graaf. Not only a military genius and working for the French, Laurens had successfully sacked Vera Cruz in the last great pirate raid of '83.

Lieutenant Lance Thorne stood beside him. He spat into the harbor.

"We're outnumbered ten to one and that idiot Dewar thinks we're perfectly safe. I feel like Priam watching the Greeks arrive at Troy!" Goddam barked. "I know they think I'm a fear monger, but the city could be taken at any time." Under the current government, the city's defenses had been sorely neglected. The five forts were manned on a voluntary basis, leaving the cannons plagued with dirt and overgrown weeds. Also, he only had two ships at his disposal for the defense of the city: *Falcon*, a sloop with a dozen guns, and *Drake*, a small frigate with eighteen guns.

"What's your count, Lieutenant?"

"Four more French, one Spanish," Thorne said. "Most of them are merchant vessels and can hardly float."

"Don't be fooled. This is the kind of opportunity Laurens waits for. You never know when the enemy will strike!" Goddam glanced up just in time to see an ugly dark bird fly overhead and shit on him. "See? That's what I mean, caught off guard. We're sitting ducks out here!" He used a handkerchief to wipe it off, but instead made the mess worse.

"It is said to be good luck, that." Thorne pointed.

"Aye, the best of luck, Thorne, thank you," Goddam growled. "Shoot that bird!"

Thorne raised his pistol and shrugged, indicating that it was empty.

"Move *Drake* and *Falcon* to the middle of the harbor and remain at battle stations."

"Aye, sir." Thorne saluted.

"I want every militiaman on double duty, and cancel all leave. We're on the brink and no French Trojan horse is penetrating this man's defenses, not while I'm alive!" Goddam clenched his fist and sneered at the vulgar dark bird as it glided over the fish market.

Throughout the Turtle Crawls market and along Fisher's Row, merchants unloaded barrels and crates. The oily pungence of fresh fish wafted from the merchant stands. Scaly delicacies included snapper, mackerel, tuna, marlin, and grouper. Seabirds skulked around and stray cats wandered among the wooden planks and between crates seeking scraps.

La Roche and de Kreep paused at a stand for a quick meal of smoked tuna skewers and boiled shrimp. They washed it down with a pint of ale from the Three Crownes Tavern and continued to walk until they reached the top of Lime Street.

De Kreep had changed out of his storm-beaten clothes into a brown leather vest and dark trousers. He wore a long musket on his back, his cutlass and dagger on a leather belt. Messy dark hair gave him a youthful appearance despite the fact that he was in his thirties. With a mixture of Arawak and African roots and a sprinkling of French, he had developed an exotic reputation among the brothels for his tribal tattoos and piercings. He used the alias de Kreep to protect his true identity, Dashiell Dupris. "*Après la pluie, le beau temps*." He marveled as everyone picked up the pieces and carried on. "I leave you here, Capitaine. I'm going to go find a whore."

La Roche shrugged, lighting a pre-rolled cigarette. "When in Rome."

"Find a whore!" Minuit squawked, stalking them overhead.

"They are called strumpets here," la Roche said.

"Strumpets here! Strumpets here!" Minuit screeched.

La Roche tossed a dead beetle in the air. The parrot caught it, and perched upon a wooden post above a torn sign indicating NO…UMPING. "The good ones are on Thames Street, yes?"

"Well, I can afford Lime Street, no," said de Kreep.

They shook hands.

"Give the gang my best."

"I owe you a debt of gratitude, Capitaine."

"Even, this makes us." La Roche turned down an alley leading to Lime Street. Within seconds de Kreep vanished. Like a truly experienced buccaneer he knew every pathway, secret shortcut, and available escape route.

La Roche cringed at the thought of sticking it anywhere near Lime Street. He ambled along the lane, lost in thought. A young blond woman in a low-cut dress approached him. "If yer lookin' for company sir, I be exactly what you be needing." She smiled, and flopped out a breast.

He tipped his hat and walked by. Granted, he hadn't had a woman in a good long while. He had an incurable penchant for redheads that stemmed from his youthful liaisons with the fiery Jacquotte Delahaye. They lived happily enough until their differing views caused them nothing but misery. She took off with a group of pirates to start the Freebooter Republic near Santa Catalina. La Roche cut across to New Street, where a skinny prostitute with dirty hair accosted him. "How about a bob for a bob, mate?" She grinned with missing teeth. He raised his eyebrows. *Enter at own risk, huh?*

A wherryman trundled by, and la Roche jumped onto the back of the carriage.

The vehicle turned up High Street and halted at the great brick wall of Fort Rupert. La Roche leapt off and paid the driver. He crossed a makeshift bridge to the Palisadoes – a little village with a cemetery near the water's edge.

Although compelled to pay his respects to his fallen comrades, he felt very alone wandering around headstones. La Roche and the Brethren of the Coast had a falling-out long ago. He had been implicated in the disappearance of Roc Braziliano and two thirds of the loot from a Panama raid. Since then, only two other Brethren members remained alive.

At the foot of a monument, he knelt and cleared away wildflowers, branches, and storm debris. "So, this is what it's like to be almost extinct." He gazed at a skull and crossbones headstone with the words:

Barbadosed
Here Lyeth ye Body ye Sir Henry Morgan, 1635-1688

It was the first opportunity he'd had since his banishment to pay his respects. La Roche removed a bottle of rum from his jacket, uncapped it, drank deep, and poured the remaining contents on the grave. "Drink well tonight, *mon camarade.* Say hello to the boys, Ed, Diego, Davy, and Jamie."

Minuit perched upon the grave stone and said, "*mon ami*."

La Roche smiled appreciatively and tossed him another dead insect.

The parrot snapped it up. His overly large beak seemed to smile back. Then his dark wings spread and he was off, soaring back towards Fort Rupert.

Minuit glided all the way down High Street over the Meat and Produce Market. He landed near the aptly named Bird's Alley across from the Merchant Exchange, a triangular layout of numerous buildings stacked side by side. All the major merchants in Port Royal assembled with over a hundred shops joined together by pathways and staircases. One could easily get lost for hours within ladies' apparel, men's shoes, pastries, books, jewelry, children's toys, pipes, tobacco, and the Wine and Spirits Shoppe which offered liquor from Italy, France, Africa, and London.

From the northwest corner of the exchange, Dr. Sander Strangewayes strolled towards Sea Lane. He wore a burgundy long coat and black breeches, his brown leather medical bag in hand. As he passed the bakery, the aroma of imported apples and cinnamon swirled through the air. He inhaled deeply through his crooked nose and continued across the lane where he approached his assistant, Miles Gladstone, a stocky man with brown skin.

The doctor had adopted ten-year-old Miles on a trip to Barbados, and brought him up in the apothecary trade. Miles grew to know basic chemistry, healing arts, and was critical in running the doctor's business. More than thirty years later, Gladstone remained a faithful assistant and trustworthy friend.

"Oi, why are you dropping that here?" Gladstone asked, watching slaves pile wood debris.

"It's all being moved to the top of Thames Street, sir."

"What for?"

"Bonfire fodder for the governor's ball."

"Not another one. He burned down the orphanage last time!" Gladstone smirked, and then turned to the doctor. "Thames Street is all cracked up and flooded. They shouldn't bother to fix it and just call it Canal Street."

"Quite right. Any news?"

Gladstone scratched the back of his head. "I'm afraid so. A Frenchie reported a barque going down off Folly Bay. Fishermen say there's bodies all over the place. Women and children."

"Any word of survivors?"

"In Folly Bay…?"

Almost a year ago the doctor was contacted by an old friend, Cormac O'Malley, who needed help to smuggle his family away from the slave trader Hansel Crisp. O'Malley knew the doctor's true business of smuggling slaves with a perfect success rate. His business was so cleverly clandestine that none suspected he was anything other than a concerned doctor and the town's chief surgeon.

Strangewayes's concern grew. "We should head out there."

"But the fayre?" Gladstone reminded. "It's tomorrow night."

"Oh shit, I almost forgot."

"The girls are counting on ya. How about I head out to Folly Bay and find out if it was them? It's better you stay here and let me take care of this one."

Strangewayes patted him on the back. *Ah, good old reliable Gladstone!* "Then you must head out there straight away. Let me know as soon as you find out."

Gladstone paused. "What if it really was the *Aeolus*?"

"Then I'll be giving the O'Malley's some bad news."

NO

Giving a Bloody Damn

At the corner of High and Lime Street stood a Tudor-style building with a steeply pitched roof and chimney. It was a quaint design with timber framing, brickwork, and diamond-shaped windowpanes with lead casings. Waiting outside the main door stood silver-haired Mrs. Abigail Beazley.

Strangewayes climbed the steps to let her in, realizing what day it was. "Good day, Mrs. Beazley."

"Good day, Doctor." She smiled. "Is now a good time?"

"Yes. Let's get started, shall we?"

The doctor put the closed sign out in the window. They marched upstairs to the study, where stacks of disorganized papers buried the desk.

"Good Lord, I have my work cut out for me!" Mrs. Beazley sat down to skim the insurmountable stack. After an hour of collectively flipping through information, the weary doctor retreated to a window seat. "I'll never get used to this new money system," he sighed and glimpsed down at the busy street below. Pedestrians and carriages shifted along, while strumpets and beggars persisted in their trade. Behind him, Mrs. Beazley prattled on regarding his bookkeeping and finances.

"Yes, Mrs. Beazley, I understand." He leaned his head against his arm with all the enthusiasm of a student being scolded by his teacher.

"If you don't stop robbing Peter to pay Paul, you're going to go broke. It's that simple!" She shook a piece of paper at him. "So much for keeping inventory. You keep giving things away like you're the only doctor who—"

"Gives a bloody damn?" Strangewayes tilted his head.

She lifted an empty vial off the table. "You gave away the last of the laudanum? Or shall I chalk this one up to personal use?"

The doctor flushed. "Another fisherman lost an eye. I had to give him something. Besides, I didn't know a hurricane was coming. Hurricane prediction is not listed on the sign."

"But you need to sell it to them. You're not going to survive in the new-money world if you keep giving things away. When the tax collector comes you'll have nothing to show for it. They will clean you out."

"Yes, well, that's what I have you for, isn't it? To help me survive in this money world. You worry about what it says on paper and I'll worry about where it comes from. I didn't vote for this pestilent system, so why should I have to bloody live in it?"

Twenty-four years ago, the doctor had been forcibly relocated to the Caribbean so that his radically advanced and non-Christian views would no longer burden England. "I have a new batch of laudanum in the supply room, capped this morning." His eyes strayed down to a carriage halted in the alley beside the apothecary. A woman in black emerged, and his heart palpitated. "Goodness me, this is a first!" He slipped on his best long coat with a hibiscus flower pinned to the pocket and patted down his hair. "I'm sorry, Mrs. Beazley. As much as I value your sage advice, we'll have to pick this up later."

"A paying customer I hope and not a debt collector?" Mrs. Beazley gave him a critical glance as she held up a piece of parchment and a Pepys pen.

"Don't worry. I'm on a winning streak." He paused to sign the paper before descending the staircase.

The storefront bell rang for a second time. The doctor opened the door to Esmeralda Belford. She was a blond beauty with the most enchanting hazel eyes. For the longest time he thought he was in love with her. Long ago, when he was a ship's surgeon, he'd sailed with Rowdy Belford, her late husband. He witnessed firsthand her strength and kindness. Gossip among the pirates earned her the nickname Easy, which fueled many daydreams. Today was the first time she came calling outside shop hours.

"Doctor, I'm glad you're here."

"What can I do for you, Mrs. Belford?" He admired her curls.

"I'm afraid you're needed at the Smith's Alley landing," she said. "That horrible little Magott has slaves in the hold of his ship. They appear to be sick and Sheriff Tellam won't let them out."

"Damn! Didn't Coggshall ban him from selling slaves?"

"Evidently not."

"One moment, I just need to gather a few things." Strangewayes grabbed his large brown medical bag, stuffing it with extra supplies.

"And they call me Widow Bell now, Doctor, haven't you heard?"

"Yes, I know." He followed her outside.

"We'll take my car," she said, leading him to the white and gold horse-drawn carriage. "When I go deaf they'll be calling me Dumb Bell." She pursed her lips into a faint smile.

Strangewayes smiled too, climbing aboard.

"Sorry to kidnap you like this, Doctor, but these people look like they're dying." She released the brake.

"No, not at all. Thank you for alerting me." Their eyes met for moment before she snapped the reins and the carriage took off. They wheeled down Queen Street, past King's Ground. After making a left down Smith's Alley they pulled up near the common area by the water, where a small lugger christened *Sweet Dreams* was anchored.

Strangewayes could already hear arguing between Sheriff Tellam and Johan Magott.

"For the last time, no! I'm going to have to confiscate your ship and cargo until it's been inspected by a doctor."

"Nobody's confiscating nothing. They be special delivery for Mr. Coggshall."

The doctor helped Widow Bell down and they advanced.

Tellam shook his head. "Fine, then we'll ask Coggshall when he gets here."

"He's paying five hundred pounds each for the whities."

"What whities?"

"Two of them, girls."

Tellam leaned over the hold. "What's he want with them?"

"I hears he was paying big fer pikeys." Magott shrugged. "As fer the Indians, I figured I'd sell them. Me crops are gone anyway."

Strangewayes's eyes widened. *White girls? Pikeys? I must look in the hold! Perhaps O'Malley's family survived after all?* As he and Widow Bell drew closer, a carriage arrived, tailed by a wagon that pulled up right next to the docked ship.

Councilman Bernard Coggshall in his finest clothes was the first to step down, his hair covered by a felt hat. Burghill followed, dressed in a mint green ensemble with matching woolen cap. From the wagon emerged Coggshall's newly hired cutthroats – Slasher Al, Big Fred, and Dogfish.

Tellam tipped his hat. "Mr. Coggshall, sir."

Coggshall knit his brow, noticing Widow Bell.

She charged forth in a huff. "Coggshall, you disease-infested carrion, yer behind this!"

The cutthroats laughed and Strangewayes tried to restrain her.

"You again?" Coggshall sickened of her thorn in his side.

"This don't concern you, Mrs. Belford," Tellam said.

"The hell it don't. Magott is banned from selling slaves in Port Royal. You agreed to it yerself, Coggshall!"

Coggshall peered into the cargo hold. He came straight away when word reached him that Magott seized pikeys. It had been many years since he'd seen Crisp's property, but the hair of the two girls, flaming red on one, deep chestnut on the other, was unmistakable. Coggshall practically trembled; he was certain it was Atia and Livia Crisp. The day finally arrived and now Crisp's balls were in a vice! He'd use the girls as a bartering chip or cash in on the price on their heads. *Soon I'll be the wealthiest slaver in America!*

Strangewayes approached the hold. "Disgraceful! As Chief Surgeon of Port Royal, I am responsible for the health and safety of the public; I therefore confiscate these people in the interest of public health."

"Mr. Coggshall has final say in this matter," Tellam said.

Coggshall tried to contain a smile.

"We've been over this. This boat breaks several recently passed laws. For heaven's sake, I can smell the feces!" The doctor's nostrils directed him to Magott. "Unless that's you?"

"You ain't taking me slaves. I got a God-given right to sell slaves. If Mr. Coggshall don't want them, then they goes up fer bids."

"Well your God-given boat invites something we in the science community refer to as disease. Please, Sheriff. All of these people need to be in my care right away."

Tellam covered his nose with a handkerchief. "Do something with them; they're stinking up the harbor! And get those poor girls out of there."

"Bring them up!" Magott called.

"Them Indians aren't fit for sale," said Coggshall. "But I'll take them girls though!"

The door to the hold swung open. Atia and Livia were dragged out by Magott's thugs. Both women slipped in and out of consciousness, sick, drugged, covered in mud and filth.

"See their clothes," Widow Bell gasped. "They're not even slaves!"

"They must be shipwreck survivors," Strangewayes insisted.

"That's right, shipwreck survivors. I finds them and that gives me salvage rights!"

"Salvage rights don't apply to girls, you product of inbreeding and rotgut!" the doctor yelled.

Atia came to for a few moments. "Where's Ma, Livia?"

The sweet sound of victory! Coggshall rubbed his hands together. "Strangewayes can have the Indians. I claim ownership of the girls."

"These girls aren't slaves if they're shipwreck survivors," Widow Bell said.

"Crisp of Barbados reported a missing family of Irish indentured servants bearing his name. They escaped his custody," Burghill explained. "Mr. Coggshall's got a lien on all Crisp's property due to an outstanding debt." He handed a document to Tellam. A letter of recovery signed by Lord Spotswood entitling Mr. Coggshall to seize any property belonging to Crisp.

Tellam inspected the document. "The redhead said 'Livia.' There's a Livia Crisp on the list."

"That doesn't prove anything!" Strangewayes protested. "Sheriff, at the very least, for your own safety and the safety of the people of the city, I beg you."

"It's settled, Doctor," Tellam said.

"What's settled?" Widow Bell was exasperated. "No it isn't!"

"Absolutely not. These people are under quarantine and under my charge," the doctor argued.

"Mr. Coggshall has proof of ownership," Burghill said.

"This isn't over," Widow Bell said. "I demand a hearing be convened!"

"A hearing on what?"

"A hearing to determine if you can still be considered a man when you have such a small prick!" She flipped up her middle finger.

Slasher Al and his men snickered.

"Mind yer tongue, woman, or I'll cut it out!" Burghill took the dagger from his belt.

"Like you did to little Katie?"

"You mean Mute Katie?" Burghill huffed.

"You cowardly troll, these are human beings. Unlike your kind, the sludge of the gutter!"

"She needs a lashing, Mr. Dogfish." Coggshall grinned; it was truly a great day.

Al's thug removed a whip from his belt and struck Widow Bell across the arm and face. She fell into the doctor's arms.

"Oh, that be unfortunate." Coggshall shook his head. "Best be off with ya before we have another…accident. Do we understand each other?" He eyed Al. "The lady needs attention. Escort her and the doctor to the Apo-thery. We'll have the slaves sent on presently."

At blade point, Strangewayes and Widow Bell were hastened into the carriage. The horse snorted and the vehicle took off with the doctor at the reins.

"What ya want done with them?" Al asked.

"For now take the car. Keep them pinned down at his place. Let them know who's boss." Coggshall put a fat cigar in his mouth. "You can have her later."

Al flashed a frenzied grin. "Aye."

"This one's just yer type." Coggshall pointed to the red-haired girl. "Too bad she's spoken for."

"There's the matter of me signing incentive."

"Just be there tonight and you never know."

Al climbed into Coggshall's carriage. "Oi!" He signaled Dogfish and Big Fred. Soon they were on their way to the apothecary.

Coggshall turned to Burghill. "Have Valentine's surgeon inspect the Crisp girls. But, first things first, join us for a drink at the old ship, Sheriff?"

Tellam tipped his hat. "I'd be delighted."

"What did you want done with the Indians?" Magott asked.

"Give them a lethal dose and drop them off at the Apo-thery as promised and go get cleaned up. You can afford it now. I have a room for ya at the Swiftsure." Coggshall entered Tellam's carriage.

Widow Bell held a handkerchief to the side of her bleeding face. It wasn't the first time her views landed her in trouble. She'd been sent to Bridewell Prison once for being part of an anti-slavery group. Pardoned by Governor Dewar himself, whose exact words were, "your husband was a Port Royal hero and you have nice tits, oh, hurrah for tits!"

The carriage pulled up alongside the apothecary and Strangewayes jumped down hurriedly.

“Think I’ll continue home if you don’t mind, Doctor.”

“I think it best you come inside, quickly now.” He reached for her hand.

Slasher Al charged into view.

“Shit, they followed us! Dog sodding bastards. What do they want?”

Widow Bell climbed down and Strangewayes ushered her inside, where he double-bolted the door.

“Let me see.”

“I’m fine.” She held her face.

“Yes, of course you are. Come with me.” He guided her to the parlor.

Mrs. Beazley joined them with a tray of medical supplies and a bottle of rum. “By the looks of it, I’d say a drink is in order?”

Widow Bell laughed. “Please.”

“Thank you for your expert commentary. Now, we need to prepare for patients,” he replied sharply, dipping some cotton in alcohol. “And there are unfriendlies outside, so please stay in and keep the doors locked.”

“Good day to you, Mrs. Belford.” Mrs. Beazley retreated to the examination room.

“And to you, Mrs. Beazley.”

Strangewayes knelt beside Widow Bell and gently brushed her hair behind her ear. “I don’t believe I’ve had the pleasure of your company in my establishment before.”

“There must be something we can do.” She gazed into his striking blue eyes. “I can’t believe we’re sitting here while those poor people are detained.”

“This isn’t over. I promise you.” He dabbed her wound.

“A lot of good we’re doing from in here.” She flinched.

“I’m sorry. I was a little outnumbered.”

“That’s not what I mean. I have nothing against you, Doctor. On the contrary, my husband and I always respected you. I know you sailed with him, though he never spoke of it.”

Widow Bell came to Port Royal at fourteen with her parents, Peter and Annabelle Bartaboa. Her father was a famed carpenter who built the gallows outside the Marshallsea Prison. One day her mother and she stopped in at the Swiftsure Tavern to pick up a couple crates of apple cider. When they tried to leave, pirates accosted them. Slasher Al and Roc Braziliano were among them.

"Let me help ya with that?" Al leered.

"No, thank you," Annabelle said.

Another pirate blocked their path and Rowdy Belford stepped in. "What's the problem?"

The bartender pointed. "These two are hands off by order of Mansvelt. She's the town carpenter's wife, she is."

"He don't tell us what to do. Fuck the Dutchman!" another pirate yelled.

Al grinned. "You can if ya must, but I'd rather fuck these little tarts meself."

Braziliano stepped in as brawling began. "Come now, we're all gentlemen here. My men act like degenerates sometimes ladies. Come have a drink with me. Let me make amends."

"Nay, sir. We're needed at home," Annabelle said.

Braziliano never took kindly to being refused a drink with any woman. "Now that ain't friendly. A drink is all we was askin' for."

"The ladies said no and they be under protection of the Dutchman," one of the French pirates opposed.

Braziliano reached for his sword and unsheathed his blade. "Ya dare to talk back to me, lousy toad!" His cutlass swung through the air cutting off the pirate's head and slashing Annabelle's throat.

Widow Bell would never forget the expression of complete shock on her mother's face. The crates of cider dropped and the glass bottles shattered on the floor. Blood spurted from the gaping cut. She clasped at her mother's throat, trying to stop the bleeding, but blood jetting through her fingers. Soon the lifeless body of Annabelle dropped to the ground.

Possessed by grief and anger, Widow Bell grabbed one the broken bottles and lunged for Braziliano. She managed to slice the side of his face before being punched down. That's when Rowdy and his men stepped in with raised swords.

Widow Bell gazed at the painting of the brig, *La Lune de Miel*, sailing into the north dock with Fort Walker behind it. A dark gray parrot stood guard on a post. "I know that ship. Which one did you sail with, l'Olonnais or the Capitaine?"

"Both." Strangewayes smiled reservedly. "Shall I prepare a bandage?"

"No need, Doctor. At this point in my life I couldn't give a shit about a couple of scars." She rose and glanced out the window to see

Slasher Al. She frowned. He noticed her straight away and made obscene gestures with his forked tongue, grabbing at his groin.

Strangewayes clasped her hand. "No, please don't go outside just yet. It isn't safe."

"You're right about that." Her hand entwined with his. "I've treated you coldly over the years, haven't I, Doctor?"

"Not at all. You've always been very polite."

"To tell ya the truth, I never knew if you were so nice because you genuinely care, or if you just wanted to get into me goods." She gave him a coy stare.

"Perhaps a little of both." The doctor's eyes gleamed. He flushed, and then began to manically tidy the counter. "Where has that Mrs. Beazley gone?"

"Coming, Doctor," she called, entering with a tray of tea and biscuits. "Sorry, I should have left something for you to clean." The women glanced at one another.

"I miss the pirates," Widow Bell professed. "Not the current lot of scallywags, but rather the old crowd."

"I know who you mean." Strangewayes peered out the window into the golden orange sky. "And yes, we could certainly use their help right now."

"If I only had the means to eradicate them all, believe me, I would."

"Indeed," the doctor agreed. "That would be ideal."

Widow Bell
GO
2015

Man-of-War

A battered man in a black cassock limped down High Street. To the casual observer he was either very drunk or had been beaten senseless, tossed down a flight of stairs, and then smashed over the head with a barrel. Whoever he really was, he had been known by several names including Ballock and Dirk. Currently he was called Skean. Agonizingly, he dragged himself through the square of Admiralty Court and hammered on the door. His arrival was met with no response and timing was critical. A light flickered from the window upstairs.

He huffed in a lungful of air, preparing for the climb up by unstrapping the leather case from his shoulder and removing its contents. Contrary to appearances it contained only a scroll. With a broken arm he latched onto the stone crevice and willed himself up, hoping that by the end of the ordeal he'd be rewarded with a brandy and a chaser of laudanum. He grunted, reaching the outside of the chamber.

Inside, he could see Admiral Goddam preparing to call it a day, downing a glass of booze and removing his jacket. Goddam unbuckled his sword belt, setting the rapier on a table. In the reflection of the mirror, Skean knew he'd been spotted. Unintentionally he crashed through the frail glass of the window and slumped onto the floor. He stretched out his hand to deliver the scroll.

"Good God!" Goddam knelt beside him. "Take it easy, son." He examined the scroll, popped open the red seal and scanned its contents which declared:

Orders to the Admiralty, new government to preside
over Port Royal. Military units are to stand down.
Place local authorities under house arrest:
Lieutenant Governor Dewar and Lord Llewellyn.

The Admiral's eyes bulged. "Oh, bloody hell!" He leapt up and pulled a bell cord until a knock came at the door. Lieutenant Thorne marched in, saluting.

"Send word to the forts immediately to stand down," Goddam ordered.

"Sorry sir? Stand down?"

“Aye, that’s the order! Get it out to all the forts double quick. I don’t want any of the lookouts to raise the alarm. Tell them all to stand down.”

Skean breathed a sigh of relief. With his orders delivered, his mission was now complete. His eyes rolled into the back of his head, and he passed out.

Major Thomas Paine neared the harbor on his galiot, *Rascal*. A small swift ship with furled sails, it was the size of a wasp compared with the vessel it towed, *Relentless*. The colossal man-of-war overshadowed everything in its path. Over one hundred and eighty feet long, armed with seventy-eight guns, it was the size of a small city with multiple levels and ornate carvings painted red and gold. The figurehead was that of a golden lion holding the English coat of arms.

Paine glanced back at his charge, awestruck to be in its presence. In his fifties, he had over three decades of service to the Crown as a privateer and dozens of pirate raids under his belt, having served with Henry Morgan, Gator Gar and Roc Braziliano. He dressed simply in faded black with a deep scar burrowed into his left eyebrow. “Detach,” he ordered, aiming his telescope at the city. “Let her run.”

Crewmen axed the ropes that towed *Relentless* and the galiot raised its oars. *Rascal* glided into the fish docks of Turtle Crawls, letting the larger ship drift to the short arm of the north dock.

Paine jumped from the ship’s edge carrying a blunderbuss, a wide-barrel shot gun capable of inflicting devastation at short range. He held the barrel with his three-fingered left hand and glimpsed around suspiciously. All was clear. He turned his head in surprise, recognizing *La Lune* off the long arm of the north dock. *That’s the last ship I expected to see in Port Royal!* Signaling *Rascal’s* captain, half a dozen crewmen leapt off to secure the galiot.

Two men disembarked. Judge Harold Goblet, no more than four and a half feet tall, terribly stout with a round head and big lips that gave the impression that he was always pouting. Beside him stood a man with a chalky white complexion, white hair, and pink eyes. Goblet removed a bag of coins from beneath his judicial robe and handed it over. “For your services, Major Paine.”

“Secure Fort Carlisle and await orders,” Paine instructed, stuffing the payment into his jacket.

"Aye, sir." The captain saluted. The crewmen jumped back aboard, while the oarsmen pushed the ship off.

Paine escorted the judge towards the north dock, while the pale man took off into the night. His first task was complete.

Across the water at the long arm of the north dock, *La Lune's* crew loaded supplies. Le Picard and Martel stood in the rigging to observe repairs to the mainmast, while Delacroix managed the deck hands carrying sail cloth. Le Picard was disappointed they couldn't find it in yellow.

Delacroix looked across the water and his mouth dropped. The massive warship silently approached in the darkness. "*C'est pas vrai*! Oh, capitaine?"

"Oui, what is it?" Le Picard turned to look and almost fell backwards. "Look at the time! All hands prepare for departure."

"*Merde*!" Delacroix trembled.

Le Picard and Martel swiftly climbed down. Once on the main deck they went downstairs to get their jackets and weapons.

"Oh, I'm yesterday's news, he said…nothing can go wrong, he said!" Le Picard scowled, securing his sword belts before tearing back upstairs. "Get her ready to sail. We are going to get the Capitaine. Wait here," he ordered Delacroix.

"For how long?"

"Until we get back," le Picard snapped and pushed Martel along. "Come on, we must get to the Swiftsure." They ran down the gangway.

Upon the short arm of the north dock a crowd gathered beside *Relentless*. Pepys the Harbormaster, Major Paine, and many others stood in awe.

Le Picard and Martel slowed, trying to slip by unnoticed.

"Blow me down! That's a man-of-war!" a dock hand said.

"Blimey, it is!" another gasped. "What's she doing here?"

"You mean *he*," said another.

"Rather hard to miss that," Pepys said. A pipe hung from his mouth and wafts of smoke billowed around his head.

"She is here to transition a new Lieutenant Governor by order of King William." Paine removed a scroll from his jacket. "I hereby commandeer the harbor and these docks by order of Lord Spotswood of the Leeward Islands. Clear the area and order that ship away." He glanced at *La Lune* and addressed the dock hands. "And she's a ship; the captain is the man of war."

"Aye, sir, right away," Pepys agreed.

Le Picard and Martel almost cleared the crowd. Martel tripped over his quartermaster and ended up with an elbow in the gut.

"We must not be seen," le Picard whispered.

They escaped the area and entered the city, racing towards the Swiftsure Tavern.

Relentless crept forward, a silent monstrous beast. Her captain, a titan of a man, perfectly matched to her ferocity. Known to pirates as Big Dick, Captain Richard Longstaff was six feet tall with broad shoulders and dressed in a royal blue jacket detailed with gold stripes and black buttons. His sight set on Port Royal, and he gestured to his first officer, James Fishhook, who manipulated a signaling mirror to contact the vessel *Incorrigible.*

"*Incorrigible* is in position, sir. The harbor entrance is secure."

Standing on the bridge, Longstaff inspected the city, his eyes on Major Paine, and the cigar he held remained unlit.

Unlit. The city is not secure. "It looks quiet," Longstaff said. The last time he had been here was after the battle of Roatán in '85 where he served under Paine. It had been a blood-soaked skirmish that all but wiped out the buccaneers. Longstaff was hired by Paine to escort the Whigs to their new official duties in Port Royal.

Longstaff felt the eyes of the King William's Whigs. They loitered behind him. He bore nothing but the utmost disdain for their arrogance, lack of battle experience and their ridiculous powdered wigs. "The city is not secured."

"Why is it unsecured?" Acting Lieutenant Governor Peter Piper frowned beneath a vast silver-blue wig. Beside him stood Magistrate Harry Mold, who wore an equally large adornment in a dark brown. "Where are Admiral Goddam's men?"

"The man on the inside must not have completed his mission," Mold speculated.

Longstaff retracted his lens. "Or, he may not have arrived at all. Captain Bentley?"

A man in a blood-red waistcoat stepped forth. "Aye, sir?"

"Ready your men. We're going ashore on time."

“Aye sir, we’re ready.” Bentley saluted.

“Very well.” Longstaff turned to the Whigs. “Gentlemen, it hasn’t gone as smoothly as I’d hoped. Seems I will have to go ashore after all. If you’d care to wait on board?”

“If it’s all the same, Captain, I still have confidence in your plan. We’re going ashore,” Piper said.

“Aye, Your Lordship.” Longstaff nodded. “Stand behind us at all times; there may be pirates in the city.”

The gangway lowered from *Relentless* onto the north dock. Scores of Red Royals, special marine soldiers, disembarked to form a perimeter led by Longstaff and Bentley. Piper and Mold followed to meet with city officials who arrived by carriage.

“Admiral.” Longstaff saluted.

Goddam shook his hand. “Dick.”

“Admiral Goddam, what kept you?” Piper asked.

“We only just received word tonight, Your Lordship.”

“Have the forts been ordered to stand down?” Mold pressed.

“The forts are all secured, sir.”

Judge Goblet approached with the mayor.

“Giblet, where is your wig?” Piper glowered at the short man’s partially bald head.

“Goblet, sir. It’s being powdered, it gets so sticky here.”

“You’ll wear your wig and you’ll wear it with pride! Do I make myself perfectly clear?”

“You do, sir. I beg your pardon.” Goblet’s bottom lip threatened to quiver. “Captain Longstaff, may I trouble you for a handful of men to accompany me to the courthouse?”

“Captain Bentley, see to it.”

Bentley saluted and ordered his lieutenant to the task.

The mayor stepped forward, dressed in a tailored suit of deep green and a pleated waist coat of black velvet. He held a walking stick with a silver lion perched on the handle. “Welcome to Port Royal, Your Lordship.”

Piper stuck his nose in the air and gestured to Mold. “You may address Magistrate Mold with matters of government until my staff comes ashore.”

“Wake all councilmen. There will be an emergency session this morning to proclaim the new government,” Mold ordered.

“Yes, sir,” the mayor replied, “but most live on plantations.”

“They’re all ex-pirates and they’re all here. Wake them!”

“Captain Bentley, move your group into the city. We’re going to secure the King’s Ground as a temporary headquarters,” Longstaff instructed.

“Aye, sir.” Bentley and his men marched to the causeway.

Longstaff turned to Fishhook. “Jim, take your men and secure the King’s warehouses.”

“Aye-aye, sir.”

“Very good. We should press on,” Piper insisted, pushing past the officials on the way to the carriage.

Major Paine
GO
2015

Lonely at the Top

The Black Dog Inn, although rough at times, had its charms. The interior walls were nicely appointed with black walnut panels and you'd never see a finer collection of Elizabethan oak wainscot chairs with pin wheel carvings. Upon its floor lay a red carpet accented by a blue arabesque border.

Dr. Marcus MacAskill finished his sixth round of whiskey and was now acceptably drunk. He came to Port Royal in '55 on the *Torrington*, the same ship that brought Bleedin Art. They became instant friends and worked together ever since. Meeting Nadele happened ten years later. His eyes lingered on the table near the fireplace where he'd proposed. She died giving birth to his son, who also perished. From the start, there had been trouble. It had been too late in Nadele's life for her to have children, but she had been just as stubborn as he. After that he couldn't bring himself to attend births ever again.

That's when MacAskill developed his reputation for being a rabid reptile and an ill-tempered Scot who should be deported. Now, in his early sixties, his gray hair was long and wildly out of control. Traditionally he wore a faded black coat with matching breeches, weathered long boots and a gold band on his finger to commemorate his wife.

"Right, let's move out!" MacAskill ordered the newly hired lackeys he drank with.

One was Mace Scarcliff, in his early twenties; he wore basic cotton trousers, a vest, and a brimmed hat. The other two hires looked the part of greasy thugs; unkempt with clothes so tattered, not even the poorhouse would have them. Ironclad and Stutters climbed onto the driver's seat of the doctor's red coach with two large black wheels at the back and two smaller ones at the front. Twin horses snorted at the crowd.

Pedestrians swarmed in the direction of the north dock.

"Now what the bleeding hell is going on?" MacAskill snarled at the commotion. Huge masts over-shadowed the rooftops and a new English flag flew at the stern. "It's King William's forces. Holy Father's rain o'shit, it's a man-of-war!" He jumped into the back seat. "Get us to the captain's house, now!"

Stutters honked the horn. "G…g…get…"

"Get out of the way!" Ironclad finished.

"Charity week, is it?" MacAskill looked at Scarcliff. "He's hired lepers too, no doubt?"

The carriage sped up High Street to Valentine Mansion.

Bleedin Art sat on a large couch propped up by plush cushions, bathing in heat from the roaring fireplace. The Inferno Room was his own private sanctuary and the only place where the ache in his rheumatic knees would let up. He took a long drink of rum and gazed nostalgically at the ornate carvings of ships and sea battles on the wall. *Can one desire too much of a good thing*? He enjoyed the company of Burghill's European strumpets.

"Oh yeah, that's it, right there!" Art said. A woman's head bobbed up and down in front of him. Natalia was a pearl. Young, voluptuous, brunette, and adorned in the finest German fabrics. Her cleavage bounced up and down as she massaged his knees. Catharina, on the other hand, was tall and regal with porcelain skin. Her light blond curls strayed over her shoulders, a crown to the extravagant Românian gown she wore. Her fingers firmly pressed on his neck, washing away the tension.

Art's precious few minutes in Elysium were snuffed by a knock at the door. He patted Catharina's arm. "Get that, would ya, love?" She opened the door to MacAskill. "I wanted one bloody night to meself! What's so bloody important?"

"King William's forces are here!" MacAskill grimaced. "They've taken the city."

Art exposed his huge teeth. "Right bloody now?" He signaled the strumpets to move away and set the rum bottle on the table.

"Aye, right bloody now. A man-of-war has taken the north dock. What the bloody hell are we gonna do?"

"Jesus Christ on a fiery knipple!" Art unrolled his pant legs and stood up. He strained his knees putting on his long boots and turned to the lovely ladies. "You girls make yourselves scarce." Limping over to the coat on the door, he grabbed a coin bag. "Here, take a couple of days off."

"Mr. Burghill will be cross." Natalia stuffed the bag into her bodice.

"You don't worry about it. I'll talk with him. You two just stay home." He escorted them to the door. "And stay away from Slasher Al; I mean it! You don't wanna know him." Art gulped back some more rum before calling, "Stinger, get in here!" A secret passage opened beside the fireplace and a thug emerged. "The timing's bad, is all. They'll be calling for Dewar's arrest."

"Better him than us," Scarcliff said.

"It all ties back to us. He knows too much." MacAskill folded his arms. "We'll have to kill him."

Art's eyes widened. "Kill Dewar?"

"Kill Dewar!" Cupid the parrot squawked from a perch in the corner.

"Aye. Send Pikestaff, tell him it's on Coggshall's order."

"He wouldn't buy it. And besides, it's too late to *do* Dewar. But Coggshall, on the other hand, they'll think he was done by his own cutthroats. We'll never get a better chance." Art pointed at Scarcliff. "You and your men, get over to the Swiftsure. Kill Coggshall before the Whigs get to him."

"Coggshall's kid, too?"

"All of them, damn it! Then go to the Crooked Compass and do Burghill. Call it a structural reorganization. Oh, and have me wife sent to the beach house in Ligania."

"Ru…ru…ru…" Stutters replied.

Art eyed MacAskill. "What the bleeding hell's wrong with him?"

"Maybe you should have asked him when you hired him."

"Right, we'll take care of it," Ironclad finished.

Art scrutinized their shabby clothes. "Get yerselves cleaned up and presentable for the new government. Get the pirates out of the city before all hell breaks loose and keep it orderly! All of ya get a move on." Art slipped on his dress coat and tidied up in the mirror beside the door. He shrugged, disenchanted.

The thugs dispersed and soon the doctor and Art were alone in the Inferno Room. Both of them lit up cigars. "Gets lonely at the top, does it?" MacAskill puffed.

"You know it." Art gulped back the rest of the rum.

At the King's House, a celebration was in full swing. Costumes ranged from simple masks and cloaks to storm debris strapped to one's body. The night's musical entertainment was the local group Trinity, comprised of a fiddler, guitarist and flautist. Giant kegs filled with signature ale from the Swiftsure Tavern sat beside tables lavished in food. Savory sausages wrapped in pastry, miniature meat pies, smoked snapper, cheeses, and imported fruits lay on silver trays.

Governor Dewar practically stomped his feet when called away to the study to attend some outstanding business. He sat tapping his feet against the side of an enormous mahogany writing desk, reviewing documents. Slaves fanned him with large feathers while Sleemans handed him another parchment. "Fine, this is the last one. Then I'm getting back to the party!"

"Or, you could just leave the seal with me and I could sign them all for you."

Dewar eyeballed him suspiciously.

"This is to appoint Mr. Binge as postmaster," Sleemans explained.

"But, he's black, isn't he?"

"Technically, five-eighths black, sir."

Dewar's face contorted. "Oh, no, no, no. That simply won't do. He's at least three shades too dark for public office."

"Not according to your current amendment."

"I told you, damn it, we need a color chart! What happened to Mr. Brooks?"

Sleemans sighed. "You had him killed, remember?"

"I did?" The governor cocked his head to one side.

"Yes. He was arrested for dumping shit out a window onto the street and executed. You made dumping shit in public streets a capital offense."

Dewar nodded. "We had him arrested, of course. That's filthy. What are we, French? But I never said to kill the man!"

"But that's what a capital offense means, punishable by death. I have his arrest warrant right here."

"I know what a capital offense is! But I would remember giving an order like that." Dewar skimmed the document. "Oh, balderdash, I'm using the wrong stamp!"

An assistant entered. "Lord Llewellyn to see you, sir."

Llewellyn entered wearing a stylish black satin corset, with pieces of fish netting draped over his shoulder. Katie Evans stumbled in, shackled to his arm. She accommodated his lordship's fetish by wearing tattered slave rags and pinning up her long dark hair in a masculine fashion.

"Ah, Larry, how's the party going? Have you got them all warmed up for me?"

"The British are coming!"

"We are the British, you corked port!" The governor wriggled his nose at the odor of booze emanating from the pair. "What? Did you lose the key again? Well, I don't have it. Oh, try the linen closet upstairs." He waved at the girl. "Hello, Katie."

An extremely drunken Katie snorted, her face turning bright red.

Dewar continued to shout. "Nice to see you!"

"No…King William's forces, they're coming for us!" Llewellyn gasped. "The Euro-strumpets just told me."

"Oh Larry, you've been getting into the absinthe again."

"Well, of course. Not as much as her tonight, obviously. But this was overheard firsthand from Dr. MacAskill not ten minutes ago."

Dewar's eyes widened. "British, my booty! It's a bloody Dutch invasion, that's what it is."

"British, Dutch, what's the difference? They're taking over the city!" Llewellyn hyperventilated, flailing his arms. "Shit! What shall we do?"

"We have a plan," Sleemans interjected coolly.

Dewar stood up. "Bloody traitors! Shit, what'll we do?"

Another assistant knocked on the door. "This just came from Constable Blower."

Dewar's face lit up. "Ah, good old Blower." He read, not comprehending a single word, before handing the note over to Sleemans. "What does this mean, then?"

Sleemans skimmed over it. "You've been accused of exceeding your authority and charged with high treason. You're to be returned to England immediately, where you'll be hanged before King William."

"Well, that's a bit of rotten luck," Llewellyn said.

"Both of you," Sleemans clarified.

Llewellyn looked up in disbelief. "Me? But I'm so wealthy!"

"Exceeding my authority? It's not my fault if the bloody pigeons didn't make it back!" Dewar argued. "My God it gets lonely at the top. Everyone wants a bloody piece!"

"The militia will surely be on their way here," Sleemans said. "We do have a plan."

"We should give ourselves up and blame it all on Cardinal Grimaldi. We'll say he used God's powers to sway us," Llewellyn suggested.

The governor marched back and forth. "That's good. By the time they track him down in Germany, King James should already be back on the throne."

"Yes, well he's *in* it, not on it." Sleemans shook his head and addressed the wall. "It boggles the imagination."

"Are you sure it's a good idea speaking in front of…?" Llewellyn nodded towards Katie.

"It's fine, she's mute. I wish they were all mute." Dewar paused. "We'll attack the invaders. Send the slaves first!"

"It'll have to be slaves; the militia will side with the Whigs. I'm surprised they haven't shown up already," said Sleemans.

"No military?" Llewellyn bit his lip. "Then we'd better send a lot of slaves. Maybe we should arm them?"

"Armed slaves? Are you mad?" Dewar's eyebrows shot up.

Sleemans clapped loudly. "Not to worry, sir. We planned for this, if you remember?"

"We did?"

"Yes. Operation Fuck Off."

Dewar's face lit up. "Ah yes, good thinking, Sleemans!"

"What's that?" Llewellyn asked.

"Well it's simple, you fuck off." Sleemans pointed to the door.

"What'll we do about you know who?" Llewellyn whispered.

"She fucks off too, just not with us."

Dewar turned to shout at Katie again. "Can you fuck off by yourself, Katie?"

Her eyes narrowed as she rattled the chains.

"Oh, right." Dewar opened his drawer and removed a stiletto. "I'm afraid for the good of society, we have no choice."

"You wouldn't." Llewellyn was ready to weep.

"Of course not. Don't worry, Katie, we're only going to cut off your hand!" Dewar considered the freshly upholstered furniture and Persian rug. "Well, not in here, of course."

Katie looked horrified. "Fuh oo!"

Sleemans sighed and picked the lock with a silver toothpick.

"Don't worry, Katie, we're professionals!"

"And we're insured," Llewellyn added. "You'll make a hundred pieces of eight for that hand."

"For a strumpet's hand? A couple o'bob maybe? Does anyone know how to tie a tourniquet?" Dewar asked.

"Your mental defect hasn't quite been categorized yet." Sleemans continued with the lock and the shackles fell away.

Katie retracted her hand quickly.

Dewar was pleasantly surprised. "Ah, just the thing!"

Katie gave them a disgusted pout and rushed from the room, her middle finger pointing straight up.

"Goodnight, Katie!" Dewar roared. "Oh, what's the use? Poor girl can't hear me anyway."

Dr. MacAskill
GO
2014

One and Thirty

Inside the Swiftsure Tavern, people drank, laughed, smoked, and played cards. Glenda the barmaid, a strikingly robust woman in her mid-thirties, served up wine and ale to sailors, merchants, and tradesmen. “Oi, Nessie! Ales on the speed rail.”

Nessie grabbed a tray and dashed over to the big table.

Coggshall briefly eyed her. He didn’t remember hiring her; he usually left that kind of thing up to Glenda. He drank a mouthful of ale and gazed heatedly at the stack of gold bars, doubloons, and silver pieces of eight in the middle of the table. *What a haul!* Coggshall slipped a cigar from his jacket pocket and lit up, puffing heavily.

“Over to Mr. Coggshall. Stick or have it?” Theodore Binge asked, elevating the card deck gracefully. He was a tall slender man with black skin and long, silver-brown hair tied back with a silk ribbon. Binge dressed in an extravagant purple suit and shuffled the cards stylishly, like a true seasoned artisan.

Coggshall slid another gold bar across the table.

“Ah. Have it, it is,” Binge said, laying down another card.

Coggshall flushed. *There’s no way I can lose!* That’s why he kept Binge around. It kept the gambling lively.

“And you, Captain Slazarelli?”

“I feel lucky tonight. Have it.” Slasher Al grinned, sucking in tobacco from his clay pipe, adding more gold to the pile. Lash sat on his shoulder watching intently.

“Aye, yer doing better than me tonight, I’ll give you that.” Binge turned his head. “And you, Magott?”

“Aye, have it.” Magott patted his brow with a new silk handkerchief, and then stuffed it back into his tidy jacket pocket.

“We’ll have to cancel.” Burghill ran his fingers through his matted hair. “Without new slaves we can’t go forward.”

“This event is going forward, damn it, regardless. Plenty of those ships brought in by the storm are carrying produce that’ll go bad soon. Make them offers, they won’t have any choice but to sell cheap. Buy it all up for the fayre.” Coggshall signaled his thug Johnny Shipwash.

Shipwash stepped forward. “Is that the ‘more cigars’ signal or the ‘bathroom’ one?”

Coggshall grimaced. *Why the hell'd I hire this one again?* "I want big signs all over town."

"Right, big signs, right."

"This town is going to party if I have to round up every rancid whore and slave in Jamaica to do it!"

"S-sure. That don't go on the sign, do it?" Shipwash cocked his head.

Coggshall pointed at the door.

"Right." The thug left quickly.

"Ya do know he's illiterate?" Burghill sneered.

"Then *you* do the bloody signs. Unless yer illegible too?" Coggshall snarled.

"Stick or have it, Mr. Burghill?" Binge asked.

"Have it." Burghill tossed in three more doubloons.

Binge dealt one last card to Burghill and himself. "Dealer sticks. Last discard, gentlemen."

Each man scrutinized his hand and tossed a card.

"What-cha got, then?" Coggshall gazed around the table.

Each man showed his cards. The top three hands belonged to Slasher Al, Magott, and Binge – all totaling thirty each. Burghill laid down a hand totaling less than twenty.

Coggshall coughed up his own cigar smoke, having a hand in the low twenties. He growled at Burghill. *Thought he had the bloody ace!* The two men retreated to the table by the fireplace.

"Thought ya had the one?" Burghill asked.

"Jesus Christ, yer the fucking bookkeeper!"

"Next hand, One and Thirty?" Binge queried, ready to shuffle for the tie-breaker.

Slasher Al and Magott nodded.

"Nothing too fancy there, Binge!" Coggshall called.

"Whatever you say, Mr. Coggshall. Your bet, Captain Slazerelli."

Al's grin stretched ear to ear, accentuating the scar that ran horizontally across his right cheekbone. He took another gold bar from his pocket.

"Getting too rich for my blood." Binge dangled a gold watch and Al nodded. He set the watch on the table.

Coggshall frowned. "Christ! Where's he getting his wealth from? How much of an incentive did you pay him?"

"I ain't paid him yet," said Burghill.

Al eyed Magott. "Ya can't match that; show us yer bet."
Magott shrugged, looking over at Coggshall.
Coggshall elbowed Burghill. "Time to bring in the bait."
"Thought we were saving her for later?"
Coggshall peered around suspiciously. "Now's as good a time as any." If the pirate Gator Gar was here, the sacrificial redhead would draw him out.
Burghill waved to his two thugs, and they vanished up the stairs.
"I'll be covering Mr. Magott's bet."
Al's eyes lit up. "Let's see."
Two thugs dragged a young woman along by the hair, her hands and mouth bound with rope. Atia Crisp trembled, her face flushed with tears.
"Just the way you like them." Burghill raised his mug. "Tenderized."
Al seemed astonished. "Hello again, lovely." He licked his lips as his parrot released a vicious growl.

Capitaine la Roche took a mouthful of ale, tipping his hat to cover his face in shadow. From a dimly lit booth he watched. He tapped his fingers against the mug and gazed at the girl. A lump formed in the back of his throat. The assembly of spectators grunted and cheered. She was pushed out for display. Despite the bruises and rope, her beauty was haunting, hair like flame and eyes like emeralds. His stare shifted to Al. The bastard grinned maliciously, already contemplating which way to cut.
"Show us her bubbies!" a spectator yelled, and everyone cheered.
Binge shuffled the cards, peering up at her sympathetically.
The girl eyed the room, stopping on la Roche. They shared a prolonged stare. His attraction instantaneous, he lost himself heart and soul. *I won't let anything happen to her! Will Theodore back me up after all this time?* Back in the day they'd won many games together and made a lot of gold very quickly. There was only one way to find out if they were still on the same side. La Roche set down his mug and in an act of bravado yelled out, "I am in." He stepped forward into the light and tipped his hat to look Al in the eye. "Deal me in."
Binge's jaw dropped.
"Well, well, well. See what the gales blew in." Al sneered, taking a shot of rum. "Capitaine le Gator Gar."
La Roche lit a pre-rolled cigarette and approached.

Al motioned him to sit. “I heard you was in town.”

“What is your bet?” Binge queried.

La Roche took out a coin bag, withdrew five gold doubloons, and tossed them in the pile.

“Deal him in,” Al said.

Binge dealt left to right. After three cards each, they all pondered their hands.

“Time hasn’t been good to you, has it, Gator Gar? So where’ve ya been hiding, eh?”

La Roche mused. “Just as kind to you, *fils de pute*.”

“Well, I’m out.” Binge threw down his cards, glancing at la Roche.

“That was quick!” Al said.

“Stick or have it?” Binge looked at Al.

“Have it.”

Binge turned to Magott. “Stick or have it?”

“Have it.”

Then finally to la Roche, “Stick or have it?”

“Have it.”

Al snickered. “So, Gator Gar or El Capitaine or whatever you’re calling yerself, did the storm bring ya in? Or do you just want to have it off with the redhead?”

La Roche studied his cards. “I’m surprised they let you in here, uh? Class this place had.”

“Stick or have it?” Binge asked.

“Have it.” Al grinned.

“Stick or have it?” Binge looked to Magott.

“Have it.”

La Roche took one more card from Binge.

Big Fred and Dogfish wormed their way closer to Slasher Al.

“I raise.” Al’s eyebrows pointed up. He withdrew another bar of gold from his jacket.

La Roche glared at the gold. *Merde! Where’s he getting his wealth?* To his surprise, le Picard approached with the gold-handled sword.

“Your sword, Capitaine.”

La Roche took the weapon smugly and set it on the table. The crowd stirred. “I bet the sword of Don Juan Pérez de Guzmán.”

“Henry Morgan gave you that sword.” Slasher Al admired the sharp glistening edges and nodded to Binge.

"Yeah, after I won it from him. Get your history straight, uh?"

"Stick or have it?" Binge asked

"Stick," Al replied.

Magott patted his brow with a handkerchief. "Stick."

La Roche tilted his head. "Stick."

"Last discard," Binge called.

Magott threw his cards down and yelled, "out!"

"Bugger!" Coggshall's temple pulsed.

Al laid down his hand, the nine, ten, and jack of clubs.

La Roche laid down the ace, king, and queen of hearts.

"Imagine that." Binge pointed. "He has the One and Thirty!"

The crowd cheered and groaned in unison, while the girl looked on uncertainly.

"No bloody way." Al clenched his fist. "Yer a bloody cheat!" Lash tried to flap her clipped wings, but hopped away instead.

"You are free to examine all the cards and my sleeves. I have won fair and square. Not my problem if you're sore about it. She's mine and so is your gold."

Al drew a broad dagger. "Ya bloody cheated, ya'll not be taking her neither."

Binge and Magott cleared away from the table, while Coggshall and Burghill stood behind the bar.

"Fatima, get over here." Burghill waved to his slave. She backed away from the fight.

"Aye, we've lost enough money for one night," Coggshall said.

Everyone reached for their weapons. La Roche pulled a stiletto from the leather sleeve attached to his belt. He flicked the gold sword to le Picard, who caught it and spun around to defend the flank. Martel was slow on the draw to get his sword, but improvised effectively by kicking a thug in the groin.

"Good timing," la Roche said. "You are due for a raise, oui?"

"You should have stayed in your cave, Gator Gar. You ain't getting outta here alive!" Al hissed.

"I should have killed you a long time ago, *connard*!"

The adversaries lunged for each other. Their hats spun to the floor and their blades deflected, lightly grazing each other's flesh. La Roche slipped by his opponent to gain better footing. Al winced as a point pierced his thigh and he fell off balance toppling the table. That's when Dogfish and Big Fred moved in, jabbing swords with le Picard and Martel. A barrage of blades chopped through the air. One cut la Roche's arm. He dropped the stiletto and took out his cutlass. The three Frenchmen arranged themselves in a defensive triangle.

"Ya want her so bad? Ya French swine." Al staggered, putting all his weight on his good leg. "Kill the bitch!" he yelled at Coggshall.

La Roche turned to her, mortified. *I don't even know your name.* One of the thugs raised a knife to her throat. Time seemed to slow down.

Atia closed her eyes. She was exhausted and in pain. Death didn't seem like such a terrible fate. However, the regret of never seeing Livia or the rest of her family confounded her. *Thank you for trying, good sir, my Capitaine.* Atia drew a deep breath and braced herself for the end.

The thug slumped forward. A strong, dark-haired man removed his knife from the back of the villain's head. Streams of blood pooled on the floor. Two more men killed the other thug.

"Okay girl, I got you." The dark-haired man caught Atia just as her legs collapsed beneath her.

"This isn't over. Mark my words." Al hobbled to the door with Lash on his shoulder. Dogfish helped him along.

A nasty piece of work, him. Atia remembered Al leering at her and Livia. He described in great detail what he had planned for her. She'd never been so grateful to be caged.

"Flog me, uh? You petty thug!" the Capitaine scowled.

Big Fred remained, hovering over him like an impenetrable brick tower. "Come on Frenchie, let's go."

The Capitaine leaned over to pick up his stiletto. Reflexively, he sprang back up, propelling his cutlass through the air, slicing into Big Fred's head. The colossal man toppled to the floor, blood gushing from his skull. Her champion yanked the stained weapon out of the corpse and pointed it at the crowd. "From now on, my protection she is under. You know who I am?" He slipped the stiletto back into its sleeve.

"Um, no," Burghill uttered.

Atia shivered, watching her other defender.

The striking man with extremely dark rumpled hair gazed at her kindly with warm brown eyes. He returned her to the ground and cut her bonds. "My name's de Kreep. You'll be well, Mademoiselle."

She slid her arms around him, kissing his cheek. "Thank you!"

"You've got some nerve, Gator Gar. Get out of my place." Coggshall sneered.

Atia turned and spat in his direction. "Bloody bastard."

He rose, ready to throttle her. "Yer as good as dead, little girl."

The Capitaine stood between them with his cutlass. "She is mine! I will kill anyone who touches her. Anyone."

"Fine. Keep her the hell outta here. I won't have no thieving pikey in my place anyway!"

The Capitaine pointed his sword at a young African girl. "You there. Pick those up."

Fatima wrapped the coins and the gold bars in the head kerchief that held back her long, dark hair. Placing the winnings in his hat, she handed it over.

"*Merci, jeune dame.*" He stuffed the winnings in his coat and put on the hat.

"*Mon plaisir, monsieur,*" Fatima said.

"Let's go." The Capitaine clasped Atia's hand. They left through the front entrance, followed by de Kreep and the others. One of the Capitaine's men lingered behind and grabbed a lantern hanging from a metal bracket. He smashed it just outside the door and a fire broke out, barring everyone inside, while they ducked into an alley.

"*Connards,*" her champion yelled back. "Shitty fucking dive that place turned into."

"Thank you. Thank you so much!" Atia gasped, hunched over, the pain in her ribs increasing.

"Thank me when we're not in a heap of shit." He lifted one of her arms, while de Kreep took the other and they ran across the street. They passed a wrought iron gate and turned down a path between two properties that led to a sizable yard. Manicured shrubberies and hedges decorated the lawn. Stone pathways lined with exotic flowers led to a pond.

De Kreep gently lowered Atia onto a stone bench and she massaged her side.

"Where do we go, Capitaine?" one man asked.

"I'm thinking! Am I the tour guide?"

De Kreep stroked Atia's hair. "What's your name?"

"Atia, sir. Atia Crisp."

The Capitaine budged in beside her, hastening de Kreep away. "I am pleased to meet you, Mademoiselle Atia, I'm Capitaine Gator Gar. I have won you and you are safely under my protection." He slid his arm around her.

Atia rested her head on his shoulder. He didn't smell entirely unpleasant, a blend of tobacco mixed with ale. She was glad to have a moment of peace. "I don't know how to begin to thank ya." He caressed her back, sending a pleasant chill up her spine. For the first time in days, she felt safe.

"No problem." He kissed her eyebrow. "Let it come naturally, uh? I am curious though, what is your thing? Lick or fuck?"

Atia's jaw dropped. She pulled away, unsure whether she should be angry or amused.

The Capitaine waved his hand. "No, no! You misunderstand. I don't mean *now*."

With her mouth ajar, Atia slapped him hard across the face, wondering if all Frenchmen were this cracked.

He retreated, smirking slightly. "Ah, *le masochisme.* Not my thing."

"Sorry, I don't speak French." She glared at them wearily, crossing her arms over her chest. "Are all o'ya scoundrels then?"

They all shrugged and began to nod.

"Yeah, pretty much." The Capitaine laughed.

A mob with torches approached.

"Everyone get behind the hedge. Keep quiet," one of the men ordered.

The group ducked, keeping to the shadows. Atia limped away slowly, unconvinced of the Capitaine's usefulness. He followed and took her arm gently. "I did not mean to offend. If it will make you feel better, you can hit the other side so my face looks even." He smiled. "Everything will be fine. Please, come with me." His hand reached for hers.

Atia smiled faintly, scrutinizing his face. His eyes smoldered, breaking down her resistance. *Yer* a *charming bastard.* A rough exterior perhaps, but handsome by moonlight with an accent that made her heart palpitate. "Where are ya taking me?" Her hand slid into his and they stared at each other, reliving the intensity of their first glance.

Moments passed before la Roche could breathe. Her eyes kept meeting his and her perfect mouth curled into a little smile. Nothing compared to her loveliness. "Someplace safe where you can rest. You seem a little, how you say, worse for wear?"

"Thanks." She sneered, trembling at the night air. "Hurricanes and slavers'll do that."

"I will look after you." He removed his jacket and draped it over her shoulders.

"Where will we go? *La Lune* is not going anywhere," le Picard said.

"Do any of you live here?" Atia asked.

"Cherry Red's, is it still here?" la Roche said.

"What? Now?" Le Picard scowled.

De Kreep nodded. "Oui, it is."

"Then we head there."

"Where?" Atia asked.

"Cherry Red's. It's a brothel," de Kreep explained.

"Nice place?" Her voice teemed with sarcasm.

"Oui, very nice." He gleamed unabashedly.

"Food, water, shelter is what they have. Let's move out!" La Roche led them along another dark path which came out in an alley riddled with drunkards. They passed a house where a singer and two lute players serenaded a woman in a window with "Man is for the Woman Made". They entered a front yard, pausing beneath the shadows.

"Good luck with that shitty song," la Roche whispered.

"Might as well be "Troll the Bowel"," de Kreep snickered.

A drumbeat grew fast and loud through the air. "Hear ye, hear ye!" the town crier began, "Pirate Gator Gar seen in town. Five hundred pounds for his arrest. Arrest the pirate Gator Gar and his men on sight. Five hundred pounds for his arrest."

"Safely under your protection, uh?" Le Picard cocked his eyebrow. "You go. We'll create a diversion."

"Oui. Cut back across Queens and we will lead them back to Thames," de Kreep added.

Le Picard tapped Martel's shoulder. "We'll lead the rest to High Street then head back to the ship."

"Get her ready to sail as quick as you can," said la Roche. "Leave me if you have to, but protect the ship."

"Oui, Capitaine."

Le Picard and Martel cut down an alleyway.

"Buccaneers with me!" de Kreep said and shook la Roche's hand. "Always a pleasure, Capitaine. We have to stop meeting like this, people will start to talk."

"*Merci.* You saved our lives back there." La Roche smiled, gripping de Kreep's hand.

Atia lost her balance and was caught by both of them.

De Kreep felt her forehead. "You should get her outta here. She is not well and you have looked better too."

"Thank you." Atia kissed de Kreep on the cheek.

He leaned in to capture her lips before backing away. "That's how you thank me, Mademoiselle."

As torchlights and the mob drew closer, the buccaneers snuck away.

"This way, keep your head down." La Roche took Atia's arm. They crossed a misty street near the harbor and slipped along the waterfront. Everything was quiet. The pair reached a black door. Atia leaned against the wall. He knocked twice, then added a third. They waited. He knocked again, but nothing happened.

"Do ya know where we are?" she asked.

La Roche pounded the door with his fist. "Ah, she changed the fucking code!"

From inside a voice emerged, "Keep yer pants on, I heard you the first time." The door opened and high-class strumpet Cherry Banks came into view. She was a lovely woman in her mid-thirties with long mahogany hair covered by a transparent black veil. Her lavish dress was deep purple with a black petticoat and around her neck sat a strand of pearls. Her arms crossed her chest as she stared at them. "Aye, what do ya want?" She glared for a moment and her jaw slacked. "As I live and breathe, Capitaine? I ain't seen you in these parts for years. Why are you knocking on the black door?"

"*Bonjour*, Cherry."

"I didn't recognize you without the beard."

"Oui, a long time it has been."

"Should have shaved it off sooner. I'd have been wet as the moors." Cherry scrutinized Atia. "She'll fetch a pretty penny. A little young for yer taste, ain't she?"

“We need a place to hide.” He slid Atia’s arm over his shoulder. “Please, *merci.*”

“It’s good to see you too.” Cherry held the door open and they entered. “What’s this all about, then? Who is she?”

“Me name’s Atia.”

“A pikey eh?”

Atia frowned. “Sorry?”

“A Roman?”

“Aye, my da says we’re Romans, descendants of Pikemen.”

“Aye, a pikey,” Cherry said.

They shuffled down a candlelit corridor lined with fluted fan-shaped brackets made of copper. Stylish fabric lined the walls with a bird and floral motif blended with gold, pink, and blue thread work. A pair of oak Tudor chairs sat at the end of the hall.

“A place to lay low a while, that’s all we need,” la Roche insisted.

Cherry laughed. “Not by the looks of it!” She glanced down at his bleeding arm.

“Help me get her cleaned up and maybe into new clothes, uh?” He stopped by the kitchen door and grabbed her by the shoulder. “Please, Cherry? For me?”

She smiled. “Anything for you, Capitaine.”

The kitchen was less than glamorous. Pots and pans scattered across the counter and moldy bread sat on a wooden board. Dirty plates and cups piled high. “Sorry about the chaos. Housekeeper only comes once a week.” Cherry grabbed a glass bottle filled with water and handed it to Atia. “So, where’d ya find her?”

“I took her away from Coggshall and Slasher Al.”

Atia slumped on a chair and gratefully guzzled the water. “They still have my sister.”

“Sister?” La Roche entertained the notion that he might have two stunning redheads under his protection.

“And you be needing a place to hide?” Cherry eyed Atia. “Don’t be drinking so much of that. It’s bad for ya.”

He grabbed the bottle away. “Where is the clean water?”

“That is the clean water.”

La Roche took a mouthful and winced. He took a swig of rum to lose the taste.

“Cleanest I can afford. We’re out of the stuff Strangewayes drops off. Right, let's go." She guided them from the kitchen and down the hall, straightening la Roche's collar. "This way, simple scrubber."

"I dunno what that means. Do ya care to repeat it?" Atia challenged.

"She's got fire, she does. Did you swindle her?"

La Roche tipped his hat. "As a matter of fact, I did. Oui."

"Good man! A festering disease Coggshall be!" Cherry opened the door to a well-appointed parlor. In the center of the room, an elegant oak table sat next to a chaise longue bound in a sky-blue brocade with brass fibers. Beneath it, a lush slab of Persian carpet embraced an otherwise plain floor. But the crowning jewel was the whitewashed stone fireplace with a gothic-style mantel.

"Business is good, uh," la Roche said.

"Indeed it is, Capitaine," Cherry boasted. "Maybe I don't have twenty-some-odd girls like Johnny Starr, but this is a first-rate bordello. The place was bustling earlier." She stood at the foot of an ornate staircase. "Lilly! Violante! Come here, quick!" Footsteps thudded against the floorboards. "I'll get Dr. Strangewayes, shall I?" She pulled a handkerchief from her bodice. "Not on the carpet, please."

La Roche wrapped the handkerchief around his wounded arm.

A blond strumpet galloped down the stairs. She wore a pale pink bodice with matching skirt. She eyed Atia. "She ain't sharing my room. I earned it." She observed la Roche. "Why hello, good sir. What be yer pleasure?"

He tipped his hat. "*Bonjour*, Mademoiselle. I have not made your acquaintance."

"They ain't customers, Lilly. They're hurt."

"Oh. Nice to meet you anyway, sir."

"Go heat up the pots and fix this one a bath." Cherry pointed at Atia.

"Aye." Lilly nodded and ran towards the kitchen.

"A pleasure, Mademoiselle," la Roche called after her.

"Vie," Cherry bellowed.

Another beautiful strumpet entered the room wearing a black, low-cut witch dress complete with broomstick. It accentuated her voluptuous figure and protruding nipples. She too examined Atia. "Good lips for polishing."

"Polishing?" Atia's eyes narrowed.

"Go fetch Dr. Strangewayes, will you? It's urgent."

"Pleased to meet you, Mademoiselle." La Roche tipped his hat, ogling her curves.

"I be late already, but I'll let him know on the way." Vie adjusted the pointy black hat that matched her long dark hair.

"Mum's the word, Vie," Cherry insisted.

"I'll fly." She winked at la Roche before going to the front door.

"Cardinal Grimaldi has a weakness for witches. He leaves for Germany tomorrow, so she wanted to surprise him." Cherry patted his back.

"She can ride my broomstick."

"You've been at sea too long, haven't you, my dear?"

"Hmm, three long days," la Roche lamented.

"Come with me, darling and we'll get you cleaned up." Cherry motioned to Atia. "Care to join us, Capitaine? Or are you going to wait down here?"

"It is tempting, but I think I will bleed down here in case the doctor arrives."

The two women climbed the staircase and la Roche sat down on the chaise longue, stretching out his legs. "So many beautiful women, I hope there's enough blood left tomorrow for my prick to work!"

Theodore Binge
GC
2015

Laudanum and Hallucinations

In his study, Dr. Strangewayes sat in a rocking chair beside the window, writing notes in a leather-bound book. For a moment he looked up to see the silhouette of a witch on a broomstick glide by. His eyes opened widely and continued note-taking. "Long term use of laudanum leads to hallucinations." He put down the quill and massaged his eyes. "Time for sleep, old chum." He set the book aside. "Come along, Boots." A large marmalade cat napped, sprawled out across the width of the desk. "Oh, never mind."

From the back door came three knocks. "Oh, shit." The doctor reluctantly headed downstairs. After monitoring the events outside when mobs roamed the streets with torches, he feared he'd meet his end with a pitchfork. He passed by the examination room and down the hall to the back. He held up an oil lamp and opened the door cautiously.

The doctor paused, stretching for the appropriate words. "Well, I must say, this is a switch, you knocking on my door for a change."

Vie stood there boldly, broomstick in hand.

"Are you quite well?" His gaze stumbled onto her pointy hat and costume. "My dear girl, if you get caught dressed like that, the best solicitor in the world couldn't get you off."

"You don't know how right you are, Doctor." She adjusted her hat. "Cherry needs you. People are hurt. One's been cut and he's bleeding pretty good. The other's a girl. She looks like she's been through a hurricane."

"Well, we did just have one." The doctor smiled. "You'd better come inside whilst I get my things."

"Thanks Doc, but I must fly. Just passing on the message is all." Vie turned and slipped into the blackness of the back yard.

"Lucky broom." Strangewayes closed the door to grab his medical bag and changed his clothes.

Down near the waterfront at the Crooked Compass, drunken patrons broke into a chorus of "Once, Twice, Thrice". Upstairs in Burghill's sitting room, Slasher Al lay sprawled on a plush sofa, his injured leg propped up beneath a mound of pillows. Tending to him was Dr. MacAskill, who tied a loop and finished stitching the gashed leg.

"No, stop! Yer killing me!" Al protested.

The doctor's eyes narrowed. "Oh, ya big baby. I've seen bigger wounds than this at a Bris."

"I'm so tired; he must have got the artery."

"If he had, you'd be dead by now. But ya lost a shit load of blood, so shut the fuck up!" the doctor instructed with all the concern of a galliwasp munching on its prey. He'd seen enough carnage from this maniac.

"Jesus!" Al cried, clutching the edge of the sofa.

"I don't cure lepers." MacAskill finished the bandage. "You'll need to stay off it for a while."

"How am I supposed to get around then?"

"I don't know. What am I, yer fuck'n mother? Try riding a wheelbarrow for Christ's sake!" *I could get away with it,* MacAskill thought. *I could say he bled out.*

"Can ya give me something for pain at least? Laudanum?"

"That shit leads to hallucinations." The doctor grabbed a bottle of rum. "Here, take two of these and fuck off." He rummaged through his medical bag. There sat a bottle of laudanum and a bottle of poison in a small vial. He eyed Al again. *Time to do the world a public service - ya sick bastard!*

To the doctor's dismay, Pikestaff with Gibbet on his shoulder entered with Jag'd Jayne and Mike, another of Art's thugs. They immediately paused at the bar to fetch a drink.

Fuck'n hell, another missed opportunity! MacAskill snapped his bag shut. "I thought you were supposed to guard Coggshall?"

"He had me guarding the other pikey." Pikestaff stuffed tobacco into his pipe and struck a match. "Just who is this Frenchman anyway?"

"Gator Gar it was," Al hissed. "I'll have his liver for this!"

"And you're certain it was him?" MacAskill stared at Al doubtfully.

"Who?" Jayne interjected.

"A pirate who used to serve under Henry Morgan. A Frenchman," Mike said.

Jayne grabbed a rum shot. "With all the buzz, I thought it be someone important."

Al took a swig of rum. "Gator Gar is in town. Believe me that is important. There be a lotta pirates who'd like to have a chat with him."

"Jesus Christ on sweaty Palm Sunday, not one of ya's got the brains to find the chamber pot under yer arse! We got bigger problems than Gator Gar. No one's seen him in nearly four years. Those are King William's forces out there." MacAskill pointed.

"Whoever he was, he ain't worth causing a panic." Jayne poured another shot.

"Was? Careful, laddie, Gator Gar's killing total is higher than you can count up to. If it is him, he's not to be messed with." MacAskill turned to Pikestaff. "What the hell were you thinking sending mobs into the streets without checking with us first?"

"Mr. Coggshall wants them found." Pikestaff puffed his tobacco.

"Mr. Coggshall wants 'em found," MacAskill imitated and cleared his throat. "Ya work for Bleedin Art, not fuck'n Coggshall. And don't ya forget it, unless ya want to find yerself on a slave galley bound for the Barbary Coast!"

"Look what he done to me," Al snapped, finding some solace in the rum. "There's a bounty on him and I'm the one collecting! Coggshall is personally granting a letter of reprisal on account of me attack. I won't be denied what's due me! I want his liver!"

"Or I could open this back up and let some air in," MacAskill offered, wrenching Al's leg, causing him to scream. "If Gator Gar is here, we'll find him. Quick and quiet before the Whigs do."

"Aye, sir, we'll find 'em," Pikestaff assured. "Quick and quiet."

Inside Cherry's posh bedroom, Lilly dumped a large kettle of hot water into a copper bathing tub and lit the wall-mounted oil lamps. Steam rose and the entire room transformed into a sensual sanctuary. Silk flowers sat in crystal vases and luscious velvet curtains hung from a brass rail over the window, matching the drapes of the canopy bed.

Atia felt dazed by the grandeur. She was steered towards a large oak wardrobe, where dozens of dresses, skirts, petticoats, overcoats, bodices, and corsets all hung from wooden hooks.

Cherry patted her shoulder. "You'll be needing to get changed. Take a gander, see if any of them tickle yer fancy. The Capitaine's buying." She checked the progress of the bath. "That's almost got it. Just needs some of this." Cherry sprinkled scented flower petals into the water and leaned in close to Lilly. "I admit it's a shock to see him."

"He's the Frenchman ya told me about?" Lilly asked.

"The very one."

"Kinda old, ain't he?"

"It ain't the age; it's the size that counts! And Lilly dear, he counts."

Atia draped a couple of choices over a chair. First, a nightdress of creamy satin, sleeveless with thin shoulder straps accompanied by a regal blue robe. The other was a deep forest green bodice with gold beading and a matching petticoat.

Cherry rested her hands on the edge of the tub and eyed Atia. "And her, she's a double for Jacquotte. Just his type."

"I have to go. I must find me sister." Atia trembled, and her limbs felt like they were trudging through cold wet sand.

"The Capitaine will find your sister. We need to get ya cleaned up." Cherry waved her over. "Well, get undressed, girl. I can help wash yer hair if you like."

Lilly left the room to refill the kettle while Atia approached the tub shuddering fiercely. She tried to unlace her dress, but her fingers lost their strength.

"Let me help you, you're shaking like a leaf."

Atia nodded.

Cherry assisted and Atia soon sunk into the hot water.

"Vie's just gone to get the doctor for you, so you just relax now." Cherry brought out a tin cup and a bar of soap. She saturated Atia's long red hair before working the bar gently through. "Well, yer too civil to be one of his usual picks. 'Course I haven't seen him for years. He is a bit more seasoned than I remember."

"That smells pretty." Atia closed her eyes, drinking in the sweet flowery air. It reminded her of the small wildflower garden her ma kept when they lived in Hope Bay.

"Thank Dr. Strangewayes when you see him. He makes special soaps with honey and herbs. Clever man, he is."

Atia massaged some on her face and all over her body, washing away the filth of the past few days. "I think met him. Seems nice, he does."

"He is that. When did you meet him?"

Atia splashed water on her face and remembered hanging onto the rail of the *Aeolus*. A strange tingling started at the base of her neck and made her head throb. "When we was…" her eyes enlarged. "We was caged." She gasped for air – her lungs felt as though they were closing. "Livia? Where's Livia?" Her eyes rolled to the back of her head and everything went black.

Cherry pulled Atia's head from the water. She lightly slapped the girl's face with no response and brushed a strand of hair from her eyes. "Bloody hell! He goes away for four years without a word, and brings back a stray that faints! Are ya okay?" Cherry smacked Atia's face again. "Hello in there? Help, Capitaine, Lilly!"

Seconds later, footsteps could be heard on the staircase and in the hall. Both the Capitaine and Lilly burst into the room.

"What is wrong?" He stared down at the water.

"She passed out, said something about a cage, and then fainted. Help me lift her out."

The Capitaine rushed to Atia's side to lift her body from the water.

"She don't look so good," Lilly said.

"Thanks genius, give us a hand!" Cherry grabbed Atia's legs. All three carried her from the tub to the canopy bed.

The Capitaine propped Atia's head against a pillow and stared longingly at her bare body.

Cherry shook her head. "She's just your type, too."

"Redhead?" He grinned.

"No, unconscious and naked."

The Capitaine smirked. "That was one time! I didn't know she'd been drinking wormwood wine. I thought she was a virgin!"

Cherry batted her eyes. "A virgin in these parts? A likely story, you scoundrel."

"Just because I was conscious doesn't mean I was any less drunk than she was."

"I don't want to know." Lilly handed him a blanket.

A knock came at the door and Dr. Strangewayes materialized. "Don't mind me, I'm just playing follow the blood."

"Evening, Doctor. Thanks for coming so late." Cherry took his hand warmly.

"Well, you know what the Christians say about the wicked? I hope you don't mind, but I let myself in. Vie had to fly."

"Not at all. We got wounded and fainted here."

"I see that." The doctor did a double take when he beheld the Capitaine. "Oh, good God!"

"No see, long time, uh?"

"I heard you were back. Hence the mobs in the streets." Strangewayes leaned over Atia, opening each of her eyelids. "And she only just fainted?"

"Just now in the bath," Cherry said.

The doctor felt Atia's pulse before examining her neck and chin. "Hmm, delayed shock."

"Will she be well again?" The Capitaine stroked her hair.

"Yes, I should think so. Her color's good aside from the bruising. Probably hasn't eaten in a long time, poor girl. She's been through a terrible lot. Has she been drinking water?"

"She drank a lot when she got here. Not the clean stuff, though. We're all out of that." Cherry leaned against the bedpost.

"I'll have more delivered in the morrow. I don't want her getting dehydrated. For now, just keep her warm. Now, let's see that arm." The doctor cut away the bloodied fabric of the sleeve. A large curved gash ran from bicep to his forearm. "Well, sorry if I seemed startled, Capitaine. It is good to see you again. What winds blew you back in? Was it a hurricane, by chance?"

"Oui. Not my choice."

"We're going to need more hot water and plenty of booze for disinfection."

"Right-o." Lilly ran out the door.

"I could go for a good disinfecting right now." The Capitaine winced. "Whatever that means."

"You're lucky. It's only a flesh wound, but I'm still going to have to clean it before stitching it."

"It's clean enough, just stitch it."

"Oh, don't be a baby." The doctor took gauze and a meager supply of alcohol from his bag. "Where did you find her?"

"She wandered in one day, looking for food and a place to sleep," Cherry began.

"Not Lilly, Sleeping Beauty here." He motioned to Atia and dabbed the wound.

"*Merde*! Funny story. I won her in a card game from Coggshall and Slasher Al."

"Well done, old chum."

The Capitaine stroked Atia's hair. "Beautiful, she is. A certain look there is in her eyes. Now she is mine."

Cherry crossed her arms over her chest. "Careful, Capitaine. Your heart's throbbing worse than yer cock!"

Strangewayes put down the gauze and readied a needle and thread.

Lilly arrived with hot water and a new bottle of alcohol.

"Good timing. We're both going to need some for this part." The doctor smiled.

"Will Russian vodka do?" Lilly asked.

"Oui, nicely, it will." The Capitaine eagerly uncorked it with his teeth to take a mouthful.

"Did she say her name at all?" Strangewayes grabbed the bottle and splashed some on the wound.

"*Putain*! Her name is Atia."

"Ah yes, that would be Atia Crisp."

"Familiar with Coggshall's girls, you are, Sander?"

Strangewayes's eyebrows peaked. "My goodness, no. You're completely wrong. This girl is not one of Coggshall's." He took a swig of vodka and handed it to Cherry. "Why, she's a shipwreck survivor. I saw her earlier today with her sister."

The Capitaine's mouth dropped. "Folly Bay is where she was found?"

"Yes, the ship broke up there. She and her sister may be the only survivors, if Livia is still alive." Strangewayes held a lantern over Atia to reveal the bruises on her face.

"I saw that ship, but nothing I could do; straight into Folly Bay they were headed." The Capitaine lifted the blanket to inspect the heavy bruising to her arms and ribs.

"You didn't notice those?"

"I hadn't got around to undressing her yet. But it's normal for around here, no?" The Capitaine shrugged, replacing the blanket. "I thought she was a prostitute. I feel kinda bad."

Cherry took a swig of vodka. "How did Coggshall get her?"

"Thank Magott and the sheriff." The doctor began to stitch up the arm.

"Who's Magott?" the Capitaine asked.

"A local sugar farmer and slave trader. He sold them to Coggshall and our town sheriff declared it legal."

Cherry shook her head. "If they're indentured, then it was legal. Poor girl, her sister be as good as dead."

"She's right. Slasher Al always cuts up one of Coggshall's girls whenever he's in town. It's his way of protecting his investments, offering up a lamb for slaughter." Lilly sucked back some vodka.

"Strange as it may seem, Atia's the lucky one. I myself would be willing to pay handsomely if anyone could find her sister, before it's too late," the doctor said.

"I think we can find her for ya, Doc. We could ask Edmund; he's a stand-up gentleman. He ain't like his father at all," Lilly insisted.

Strangewayes appeared horrified at the prospect.

"She's right. He's different; one of them scholarly types. He's always a gentleman to the ladies and I know you won't believe me, Doc, but he don't mistreat slaves either," Cherry said.

"He's probably the best chance we got to finding her. If I hurry, I might catch him before he locks up," Lilly offered.

"Well then, I think it's a superb idea. What do I know?"

"Go on, then. But don't say anything to anyone about the Capitaine or his pikey, right?" Cherry pointed at Lilly. "Not a word."

"Lilly, if by some chance you're able to find her, send word to me straight away at the apothecary. If I'm not there, inform Mrs. Beazley. She'll know what to do."

"Aye, Doc." Lilly smiled and departed.

"She's a good girl," the Capitaine said.

"Yes. Her heart's in the right place," the doctor agreed.

"All me girls are good people. I don't want nothing to happen to them." Cherry eyed the doctor. "We should tell him."

"Moi? Tell me what?" The Capitaine blinked slowly, clearly drunk.

"The real reason Al is here is to kill me and my girls."

"A mutual friend informed us. Coggshall plans to kill all of Cherry's girls and replace them with his own," the doctor said.

"It's his way of competing with Johnny Starr's brothel and we're not waiting for them to come to us," Cherry added.

"Coggshall and his men are all thugs and creeps," the Capitaine deduced.

"Indeed," the doctor agreed. "They now run the city."

"No kidding? Those knuckleheads? This place has gone to shit."

"Well, to put it frankly, you lot all died off, whilst the wolves were left behind to guard the sheep." Strangewayes finished the last stitch on the wound and sprinkled it with sulfur.

"What a day this turned out to be. What are you planning to do?" the Capitaine slurred.

"We're going to *do* Coggshall and Burghill too. He's the one who cut Katie's tongue out. Magott, Bleedin Art and Pikestaff."

"You were going to take them on by yourselves? They may be stupid thugs, but there are many of them, professional killers. We'd better kill them all, right down to the last one. Including Art and his men. We should attack by force right away. My buccaneer friend is in town. I could find him and we can teach these thugs a lesson." The Capitaine collapsed beside Atia.

"We? You haven't lost a thing, Capitaine." Cherry felt a flicker of adoration. "However, ya ain't going anywhere tonight in the state you're in. We'll talk about this in the morrow."

"Yes, Capitaine. You must rest now, and I must prepare the apothecary." The doctor packed up his medical bag.

"What do I do with them?" Cherry glanced at the Capitaine. He stroked Atia's hair, doting over her like a pet.

"Make him drink clean water, lots of it. Let her sleep as much as she needs. Give her water and food when she wakes up. Someone should stay with her; she shouldn't be left alone."

The Capitaine put his hand in the air. "I will care for her."

"When she wakes up, she will be in a lot of pain." Strangewayes set a small bottle of laudanum on the bed table. "Do you remember that stuff, Capitaine?"

"Ha!" His face flushed red. "Not really, no. Well, yes. Don't you have any opium tablets?"

"This should be more effective for her type of injuries; no doubt more will manifest. Only a few drops."

"Thank you, Doctor, I remember. She will be fine. *Merci*, my friend."

They shook hands.

"At least Atia has landed someplace safe, for now."

Cherry escorted the doctor out, glancing back at the fugitives in her bed. Jealousy raged within her, especially when he caressed Atia's face and uttered, "I will look after you, *ma chérie*." *Not a bloody word for four years! Not even a note!* Once downstairs, she stomped her feet. "Bloody hell! This changes everything! Ya know what they'll do to us when they find out he was here?"

"Please take a deep breath," Strangewayes soothed, massaging her arms. "On the contrary, somebody had to make the first move."

"Right, well, whoever makes the first move is usually the first casualty."

"That's not always the case." He cradled her hands. "Our next steps are critical. The hurricane bringing buccaneers here may have tipped the scales back in our favor. Don't give up hope, especially now that help has finally arrived."

A thin layer of sea mist covered Thames Street. Members of the mob disbanded, leaving only a few men standing guard with torches. Le Picard and Martel raced along, keeping to the shadows. The north dock soon came into view.

La Lune's crew busily prepared for departure. Harbormaster Pepys argued with Delacroix, while Major Paine observed from behind.

"French shipmaster, you must leave straight on. Make way," Pepys said.

"Oui, we are leaving," Delacroix called back, "but we must wait for our capitaine!"

Le Picard and Martel arrived but were blocked by Constable Blower and two city guards who came storming from the King's Ground and onto the long arm of the north dock.

Le Picard held his breath while he ensured the handle of the gold sword was hidden beneath his coat.

"They might mistake you for your brother," Martel said.

"I don't want my relation to be a problem, you be the Capitaine." He pushed Martel in front of him.

"Me?" Martel pointed to himself.

Constable Blower charged towards *La Lune*. "I want that ship stopped. Search every crack in her stinking French hull!"

"I already did that." Pepys turned to Blower. "This ship's been ordered to leave."

"On whose authority?"

"On my authority, if ya please," Major Paine spoke sharply.

“A wanted pirate was seen in the city,” Blower huffed. “The Frenchman Gator Gar.”

“Gator Gar? Ya don’t say. Well, ya won’t find him on that ship.” Pepys lit his pipe. “I searched that ship meself. She’s loaded to the gills with sugar and carrying minimal weapons.”

Paine lit his cigar. “Don’t sound like your man.”

“They paid their fee in gold dust from a locked chest,” Pepys said.

“Then it’s a merchant vessel,” Paine explained. “Regardless, we want a peaceful transition and all ships are allowed to leave, pirate or otherwise.”

Blower snorted with irritation. “Where’s her captain?”

Le Picard nudged Martel in front of him and hid his own face behind the rim of his hat. “Just don’t mess this up!”

“I am capitaine of this ship,” Martel declared.

“Aye, you’re free to go, Captain.”

“Oui, *merci.*” Martel swiftly led them forward along the gangway. “*Au revoir.*”

Le Picard patted his brow once they reached the deck. *How the hell did we get by again? Surely Major Paine is more diligent than this?*

“Thank God, you are back!” Delacroix exhaled deeply. “Where’s the Capitaine?”

“Let her go, fore and aft,” le Picard ordered.

“Long boats away. Prepare to make sail!” Martel shouted authoritatively, and then bumped into a crewman on his way up to the quarterdeck.

“*Mon dieu.*” Le Picard shook his head while the men scrambled to get the ship mobile. “The Capitaine is not coming. Prepare for departure.”

“We can’t leave without the Capitaine!” Delacroix looked shocked.

“That is an order, Delacroix!” Le Picard gazed back at Port Royal. “I told you it wasn’t a good idea, Capitaine. No one escapes the clutches of the wickedest city on earth.”

The Whig Invasion

Torches lit up the streets and alleys near Fort James in Port Royal's inner harbor. The mob searching for Gator Gar – the elusive pirate who, until recently, had been thought long dead, had been disbanded by the city guards. All that remained were curious spectators gathered around King's Ground – the common area before the King's warehouses. Red Royals under the order of Captain Richard Longstaff set up a perimeter around the buildings.

"A new Whig government has arrived. Governor Dewar and Lord Llewellyn are to be arrested for treason forthwith!" the town crier said.

Longstaff stood at the main entrance to the King's Ground contemplating which brothel he'd visit. Rumor was that all the beautiful strumpets had been killed in the five years since he'd last been here. Cherry Banks still remained, however. She'd have a couple of pretty ones for sure.

Piper's aide Sydrack Taliare and two assistants dragged out a wooden podium to create a makeshift stage.

These Whigs love their pomp and circumstance. Longstaff remained silent. The corner of his mouth twitched. Admiral Goddam stood nearby, ready to pounce on anyone suspicious. *The old boy will retire soon and his job's as good as mine.*

Piper's aide approached with a case of documents.

"Ah, Trainor, what kept you?" asked Piper.

"It's Taliare, sir. Just a bit seasick is all." He took out a journal.

"What time have you got, Harry?" Piper turned to Mold.

Mold glanced at his pocket watch and rolled his eyes. "I'm still on London time, sir." He checked the mechanical clock housed in a small wooden structure overlooking the grounds. "Quarter past eleven of the clock, sir."

"Note the date and time," Piper ordered and then raised his walking stick as he addressed the crowd. "I am Acting Lieutenant Governor Peter Piper. By order of Governor Spotswood of the Leeward Islands, I hereby claim custody of Port Royal in the name of King William."

"Which king's that, then?" a bystander called out.

"In the name of King William." Piper's face twisted. "Port Royal belongs to the Orange Party."

“Ain’t that a fruit?” a spectator heckled.

“Whigs over Port Royal!” Mold shouted.

“I liked the other one better,” a man grumbled.

An elusive smirk formed on Longstaff’s lips. Frankly, he didn’t care who ran the city. Everyone would eventually contract syphilis anyway. He’d made a bet with Fishhook that this government wouldn’t last two months before being eaten alive. They weren’t the least bit prepared for how things were run in Port Royal.

Piper addressed Longstaff, “Continue the search for Lords Dewar and Llewellyn, Captain. We’ll take charge here.”

“Aye, sir.” Longstaff returned to his carriage where Lieutenant Lance Thorne stood waiting. *Thorne, what a prick! Family wealth got him where he is. He never commanded a ship in his life and certainly doesn’t command any respect in the ranks.* “Leave two squads here,” Longstaff said. “The rest come with me. Move in and take the city.”

“Aye, sir.” Thorne rallied a team of Red Royals.

Longstaff’s carriage sped off into the city.

Behind the courthouse stood a small building of stone and wood. Heavy metal brackets gripped large torches illuminating the city’s hall of records. Slasher Al and Dogfish led six men with lanterns and stormed the front entrance.

Al leaned on his musket as a walking stick while his parrot, Lash clung to his shoulder. His stitched leg dragged behind. “Watch what yer doing!” he barked when his men practically squished him through the door.

They were met by a night guard, who trembled at their approach. “What do ya want?”

Slasher Al aimed his pistol and squeezed the trigger. “Yer silence, assured.” He cracked his neck and limped forward to get closer look at the blood dripping down the guard’s forehead. *Not me best work, but it’ll do.* “That’s eight shots without a miss. Mark it up.”

Dogfish nodded. “Yeah, yeah. I’ll mark it when we get to the ship.”

Al motioned to his men and snarled. “Search every shelf. Just do it alphabetical. Search ‘A’ first for the name Albemarle.”

“Take anything with the word Ablemayer. Do it ala-betical,” Dogfish said.

“Thanks, tuna head. And don’t repeat my orders, we’re not on board!”

The men scoured the room.

“What do ya want ’em for?” Dogfish asked.

“It means us having the records is a binding contract that Coggshall can never break.” Al sneered at Dogfish. “Coggshall worked for two of the last governors, Modyford and Molesworth. They two ran an indentured servant business with the late Duke of Albemarle along with Molesworth’s advisors Dorcas Dewar and Larry Llewellyn. Get it?”

“Aye.” Dogfish nodded blankly.

“These records are worth more than gold.” Al clenched his fist. “These records are real power.”

“Like, magic powers?” Dogfish revealed his pointy teeth.

“Nay, ya fucking idiot! They be the only documents tying them all together.” Al eyed his men. “Search every corner.”

The whole thing was reminiscent of the last time the government of Port Royal fell. Pirates and slavers weren’t getting along, yet most of them had a hand in both trades. Coggshall and Crisp used their contacts in Africa to bring in huge shipments of slaves at rock bottom prices. They ran Modyford and Molesworth’s indentured servant business into the ground. Coggshall bought them all out and replaced them with his own shipping line. Slaves, whores, and indentured servants were all under the rule of Coggshall and Crisp. To distance himself from the pirates, Molesworth fired the last government and replaced them with his men, Dewar and Llewellyn, before he was sent back to England for treason.

Al’s men returned with pages and folders. “That’s all of them?” Al asked.

They grunted and nodded.

“Right, let’s go!” Al’s men picked him up and crushed him through the entrance. “Christ! Yer all real heavy drinkers, ain’t ya?”

They ran back through the alley out to Thames Street.

Militiamen closed in, calling, “You pirates, stop!”

Dogfish drew his pistol and fired, causing them to scatter behind barrels and corners.

Al recognized Fishhook. “It’s Big Dick’s Number One. Back the other way.”

Militiamen were ready to fire. “No, let them go,” Fishhook said. “All pirates are allowed to leave.”

Al winced as he was carried away. The wound sustained from the fight with Gator Gar earlier that night, made his thigh sting like a mermaid’s severed tail. Down a narrow pathway, he saw the bodies of two murdered strumpets who lay with ropes around their necks. “They’ll blame me for that too! Crude it be, I be far more inventive than that.”

Bloody Mary came into view; she was fully loaded and ready to sail. The harbor behind her lit up with lanterns from hundreds of sloops and ketches fleeing the city.

“Get her underway, Dogfish,” Al ordered.

“Cast off, fore and aft,” Dogfish said and crewmen took in the lines. “Set sail for Rio Cobre.”

Once in the captain’s cabin, Al sat at his desk and opened a drawer. He’d have given his left nut for a bottle of laudanum from Dr. MacAskill. *That rabid old Scotsman!* Al took a swig of rum from a silver flask.

Along the Palisadoes, a churchwarden’s carriage sped along the dark, bumpy road leading away from Port Royal. Sleemans sulked across from Governor Dewar and Lord Llewellyn. All were disguised as slaves, dirty with soot.

Sleemans arranged for his carriage to be waiting in Sweeting Lane, just beside the King’s House. Things had gone mostly according to the escape plan, apart from Dewar and Llewellyn leaving three slaves naked in the street after stealing their clothes. Sleemans reluctantly changed into slave attire; while Llewellyn just slipped it over the corset from his liaisons with the strumpet Mute Katie earlier that evening.

“Excellent disguise, sir. They had no idea!” Llewellyn said.

Dewar furled his eyebrows. “Why did we bribe them?”

“It’s customary nowadays, isn’t it?”

Sleemans slapped the side of his head. They got as far as the gate of Fort Rupert, where they encountered two drunken city guards. One winked at Llewellyn, ogling his cleavage before waving them through. “Oh for Christ’s sake, you didn’t fool anyone. The guards didn’t take you for slaves. They thought you were off to do something kinky in the graveyard!”

"W-why would they think that?" Llewellyn squirmed.

Dewar bit his thumb. "Well, it wouldn't be the first time we've dealt with that accusation."

Sleemans peered out the window into the pitch black. "Fortunately for us, the Fort was given conflicting orders. Someone did us a favor."

"It's always good to have Big Dick and Major Paine in your pocket." Dewar winked.

"Aye, you were right. Having Big Dick comes in handy," Llewellyn said.

"Well, I need a piss." Dewar banged on the door. "Pull over, driver."

"Sorry sir, I gave the driver strict instructions, no stops," Sleemans spoke smugly. *Next time I do the books, think I'll give myself a raise.*

"What am I supposed to do, piss out the window?"

"It wouldn't be the first time you've done that either," Llewellyn added. "Sorry we had to leave the wives behind."

Dewar's nose wrinkled. "Well, I couldn't very well let them see us like this now could I?"

"But they could give away our location."

"Don't worry. They know nothing. They're women."

"Yes, well, even so." Sleemans sneezed soot from his nostrils. "I was careful not to let on where we're going."

"Ah, good thinking." Dewar nodded. "So, where are we going?"

The Swiftsure Tavern was closed for repairs. Smoke lingered in the air while slaves toiled, sweeping and scrubbing. The fire earlier that night had reduced the front door to ashes while leaving scorch marks on the walls. A pile of broken tables and chairs sat in a corner being repaired by a carpenter. New curtains were already being hung and new panes of glass had been installed. Coggshall wanted everything ready for the morning rush.

Heavy footsteps slammed against the floorboards in the office upstairs. Coggshall rifled through a small mountain of paperwork on his desk. He gulped back a shot of rum and hurled random scrolls on the floor. "Gator Gar slipped right through our fingers! But the trap was perfect!"

Burghill tried to gather up the documents. "Not only was he there, he went for the redhead, just like you said he would." He took a sizable parchment to the head.

"Gator Gar's biggest flaw is he's predictable." Coggshall reached for a box.

"Predictable? I thought he was dead." Burghill massaged his temple where he sustained a paper cut.

"Well, he's predictable when he's alive anyway, and thanks to Harbormaster Pepys, we had the jump on him!" Coggshall removed a Cuban cigar. "What went wrong?"

"Simple numbers. Pepys says he didn't know about the buccaneers."

"Now the bloody Whigs are gonna get him!" Coggshall pummeled the desk with his fists. "Did Slazerelli get away with the Albemarle records?"

"Aye, he did. My sources say he's already on his way."

Edmund Coggshall sauntered in.

Coggshall's head darted upwards, still puffing the cigar. "Don't you ever knock?"

Edmund dressed in a light brown suit, which added the illusion of height to his short stature. Bearing some resemblance to his mother, his son had bright blue eyes and the same dark hair. Edmund's mother had passed away giving birth to him.

"I was under the impression all this will be mine one day," Edmund said.

"Right, right. What do you want?"

"I hear we bought slaves from Magott; two Irish girls."

Coggshall wondered what shenanigans his son was concocting. "Gotta craving for pikey, do ya? A couple o'no-good trulls! I lost one of them too, swiped out right from under me."

"Is the other one still alive?"

"She is for now, but she's sick." Coggshall drank in the pungent tobacco. "What do ya want with her?"

"I'll give you six hundred pounds. Where is she?" Coggshall choked back a laugh. "Six hundred for a sick pikey who mightn't survive the night and you think I'm gonna let ya run things. You can wait till I'm dead!"

"Didn't you pay a thousand for the pair? How about seven then?"

"She's in the upstairs bathroom. Doc MacAskill wants her quarantined. Besides, she ain't for sale; I got bigger plans for her. She's my only chance on recouping on this deal."

Burghill peered through the window down at Thames Street. "They're here!"

Coggshall drove his fist into the desk. "This ain't the time for this shit; the government's been overthrown. The streets ain't safe; I'm leaving Pikestaff in charge of the Swiftsure tonight, so yer staying at the Wild Orchid with Shipwash until this all blows over. Now get out of here and leave me to me business!"

Edmund backed away. "Not to worry. I'm sure the new government will be just like the last."

"You better bloody hope so. And don't you go near the pikey, ya hear? She ain't none of your concern." He eyed Burghill. "Pack up what you got and let's get the hell outta here."

The street glowed with torch lamps and the night sky above twinkled with a blanket of stars. Port Royal's night scene buzzed with heavy drinking and merriment. Strumpet Lilly Waters loitered beside the front entrance to the Swiftsure Tavern. The repairs were well underway. She noticed men in red coats entering buildings. Her attention turned to Stevens, Edmund's right-hand man, guarding the carriage. Tall and muscular with dark skin, and wearing a charcoal gray dress suit, she thought him quite handsome and blushed when he tipped his hat to her.

From the Crooked Compass, the tavern down the street, strumpet Sierra Lee strolled along, decked out in a sky-blue skirt and matching bodice. Her honey gold hair was neatly arranged into curls. Although timeworn and sporting a scar across her cheek, she was still pretty enough to drum up business from the upper class.

"What's with the red coats?" Sierra Lee began.

"Who cares as long as they're paying!" Lilly smirked. "Say, have ya seen the Irish girl?"

"Nay, not at the Crooked Compass. We would've seen her. Maybe Katie knows?"

"Have you seen her around?"

"She's working the governor's party tonight. Won't be seeing her till the morrow."

"Well, when you see her, tell her to give me a shout?"

Sierra Lee gave her a strange look.

"Ya know what I mean!" Lilly grinned.

"I'll tell her you was looking." Sierra Lee strutted away.

Edmund emerged from the tavern. In his mid-twenties with dark brown hair, well groomed, and with polished manners, Edmund was clearly a gentleman. Lilly folded her arms at his approach, putting on a haughty air. "I hear your father's already got Katie working."

"I swear I had no part of that." He raised his hand peaceably. "You know I would never let that happen if I had any say in the matter."

Lilly smiled and caressed his face. "I know."

"I have word on the Irish girl. She's sick and Dr. MacAskill has her quarantined upstairs."

"Will you help me get her to Dr. Strangewayes?"

Edmund shook his head. "She's being watched by Pikestaff and probably Jayne."

"I know how to handle Jag'd Jayne." Lilly bit her lip.

"I'm sure you do, but I've done all I can."

"Right. But at least we know where she is."

"Come along, I'll take you home." Edmund offered his arm, and she took it eagerly.

Redcoats stormed the street, blocking their path. Lieutenant Thorne stepped forward. He'd been at Cherry's before; Lilly was the only one who'd service him. She couldn't figure why everyone called him a prick, he was more of an arse.

"You there, stay where you are!" Thorne removed a scroll from his jacket. "Who goes there?"

"I am Edmund Coggshall, son of Bernard Coggshall."

"Coggshall?" Thorne scanned a list.

From the opposite side, a squad marched in from Water Lane. Leading them was a handsome man in royal blue ordered, "Secure the perimeter. You four, secure the Wherry Bridge."

"This one's on the list, Mr. Fishhook," Thorne said. "Says his name's Edmund Coggshall."

Fishhook took the list. "Edmund Coggshall?"

"That's correct, sir."

"And you?" Fishhook glanced at Lilly.

She gleamed. "A friend."

"We're looking for Bernard Coggshall," Fishhook said.

From the Swiftsure Tavern, Coggshall and Burghill came out with their hands in mid-air. Coggshall stepped forward. "I am Bernard

Coggshall. I surrender willingly in exchange for protection. This is my bookkeeper, Barrister Burghill."

"Blimey!" Fishhook's eyes widened. "Lieutenant, take these men into protective custody."

"Aye, sir." Thorne signaled an officer. "Have them escorted back to Fort James and put under guard."

The officer approached. "Mr. Fishhook, sir? Major Paine reports Fort Carlisle and Fort Rupert are secured; however, Lord Llewellyn and Governor Dewar seem to have escaped. We have arrested Ladies Dewar and Llewellyn at their residences on Sweeting Lane."

"Have Captain Longstaff meet us there," Fishhook ordered.

"I ask that my son be escorted to Lime Street," Coggshall added as he was led to a carriage.

"I was taking the young lady home," Edmund explained.

"Escort them all," Fishhook instructed. "And start searching door to door. Find Dewar and Llewellyn."

"Aye, sir." Thorne saluted.

Lilly gave Fishhook a wink before drunken hecklers spilled onto the streets. A man in a pink suit and white lace cravat sneered. "You spoiled a wonderful evening."

Fishhook averted his eyes. Troublemakers mooned him and made obscene gestures with empty bottles. "And they wonder why I hate Port Royal!"

Longstaff
"Big Dick"

Truth in a Rumor

Violante Hayze in her witch costume, traipsed the grounds of St. Paul's Church en route to pay Cardinal Grimaldi a visit. She followed a gravel pathway lined with fancy hedges, stone pillars and manicured topiaries. Behind her, swarms of men lit up the streets with lanterns and torches. She moved to a discrete side entrance and tried the handle, but it wouldn't budge.

Vie's body went rigid. Soldiers in red coats came closer. "Shit! This is what I get for making church calls." She snuck away down an alley.

Two men with guns blocked her way.

"Oi, where do you think you're going?" one asked.

"To church. What does it look like?"

"Why ya be dressed as a witch?" The other glared at her.

Vie's nails tapped against the broomstick handle. "Maybe I'm a cleaning woman in mourning?"

"Should we take her to Captain Longstaff?"

Vie straightened her skirt. She'd heard of Longstaff before. Rumors spread like yellow fever about him. He was known as Big Dick, and there was much speculation that he had lovers at every port in the Caribbean. She waved her hand around, as if attempting to cast a spell. "Aye, take me to Captain Longstaff."

The soldiers aimed their guns.

"Hands up you, you're under arrest. We're taking you to Captain Longstaff."

Vie raised her arms in eager surrender.

Along Church Street sat waterfront properties surrounded by ornate wrought iron fences. A tall weathered house on the corner had a four-sided tower with circular windows at its peak. Neatly kept gardens and hedges stretched down to the causeway.

Ellsebeyth, or Bizy Gale, peered out the front widow of Widow Bell's candlelit sitting room. Soldiers skulked around outside brandishing torches and lanterns. They moved methodically door to door, searching. Bizy pulled back her long fair hair. A vicious scar ran down the middle of her forehead to the bridge of her nose. The wound endured in her youth was compliments of Slasher Al, who had raped and tortured her until death closed in. Bizy's discarded body was discovered by her mates and Esmeralda Belford nursed her back to health.

Against the odds, Bizy survived. She'd been involved with pirates and like so many, the father of her children was lost at sea. She was left with Isabella, fourteen, and Jamie, six. They lived as tenants in the house adjoining Widow Bell's.

The soldiers were only a few doors down.

Sprawled out on the couch, Widow Bell, affectionately known by the pirate crowd as Easy, breathed heavily in her sleep, gripping a bottle of rum. Bizy reached over to wake her. "Easy?"

Grumbling, she opened her eyes. "What is it?"

"Soldiers. There are soldiers coming!"

Widow Bell sat up quickly, setting the bottle on the side table. "Soldiers? Whose?"

"I don't know." Bizy snuffed out the candles and looked back at her children hovering in the hall. "You kids stay down."

Both women gazed out. They witnessed Violante being herded up the street at gun point.

Widow Bell squinted. "Is that a witch?"

"I think that's one of Cherry Banks's strumpets dressed as a witch. Who are they? What are they arresting her for, I wonder? Witchcraft?"

"Well, not prostitution." Widow Bell smirked. "They'd have to arrest half the town."

"Bella, take your brother upstairs and lock the door."

"Yes, Mama." Isabella grabbed her brother's hand.

"Do you think it's an invasion?" Bizy whispered.

"Who is it, Mama?" Jamie asked eagerly.

"On your way, Jamie."

Isabella dragged her brother upstairs. "Come on, dog-boy!"

"Stop calling him that!" Bizy looked through the window.

"Look, they're English. There's Beckford, your favorite suitor." Widow Bell winked.

"Oh, piss off!" Bizy had never shown the slightest interest in Beckford. After the death of her lover, a mercenary named James Deane, Beckford was the one who'd shown interest. When he learned it wasn't mutual, he was none too pleased.

A group of men came up the front stairs.

"Ah, shit." Bizy sneered.

"Wait here. I'll go talk to them." Widow Bell started towards the door.

"You're not going out there alone."

The pair opened the door cautiously. They raised their hands as militiamen aimed their muskets.

"Lower your weapons and stand down," Major Beckford ordered, glancing at Bizy. His sandy blond hair was tied back, exposing his big ears. "Don't fret, Mrs. Belford." He straightened his waistcoat and curved helmet. "Miss Gale, good evening."

"What's going on Beckford?" Widow Bell asked.

"We're under curfew, ma'am. A new lieutenant governor has arrived, and Lords Dewar and Llewellyn are to be arrested for treason."

"About bloody time."

"We're going to have to search your residence. I will personally take charge so as to be less intrusive." He summoned his men up the front stairs.

Bizy folded her arms. "Going to the next house would be much less intrusive."

"Is anyone else at home?"

"Only my children." Bizy reluctantly stood aside.

Beckford's men skimmed the main floor and the basement before moving upstairs. One of the bedroom doors was locked.

"Are they in here?"

"Yeah." Bizy knocked. "Bella, open up." After a few seconds, Isabella peered out. "These men just want to look in the room."

Beckford and his men pushed through.

Jamie sat on the bed playing with a wooden ship. "Are you looking for pirates?"

"Aye son, we're looking for pirates. Seen any?" Beckford smiled.

"My dad was a pirate, but he died."

"Aye, I know." Beckford took a good look around. "Thank you. The room's clear."

Bizy frowned, escorting him out.

"You'd be a lot safer with a man in the house."

"Thank you." Bizy scowled. "Let me know if you see one."

Beckford snorted. "Right, they're not here."

One of the militiamen opened Isabella's robe with the end of his musket.

"Watch where you're pointing that!" Bizy snapped, grabbing the gun barrel. "Don't you dare aim that at my child."

The soldier pushed the gun barrel up beneath Bizy's chin.

"Outside, on the double. NOW!" Beckford ordered.

His men slowly obeyed.

Beckford paused to whisper in Bizy's ear. "A woman needs a man, or she's not really a woman."

Bizy bit her tongue and glared at him.

"Goodnight, ladies." Beckford gave them an unnerving stare before closing the door.

"What did they want, Mama?" Jamie asked.

"It's okay, boy." Bizy squeezed him, and then wrapped her other arm around Isabella. "They're just sanctimonious louts on a witch hunt, is all."

The grounds at the Governor's Mansion lit up with flickering torches. Red Royals skimmed the stone pathways and inspected arches. Large round shrubs lined the wrought iron fence. A crowd gathered on the boulevard. Longstaff and Major Paine arrived amid loud protests from the governor's wife, Lady Margaret Dewar, who was trying to make them go away.

"They left already, haven't they?" Longstaff whispered.

"Aye. They took the long way around to Ligania," Paine replied discretely. "The guards at Fort Rupert were drunk, but they remember them. Apparently, Llewellyn was covered in soot and had cleavage."

Longstaff massaged his temple and Lady Dewar's shrill tones echoed across the estate.

"For the last time, I have no idea where they went! Now let us go, damn you!" she bellowed. "You have no right to stop us." She tried to climb into the carriage, where Lady Lyla Llewellyn sat with her three children and Margaret's five.

"Dick!" Lady Llewellyn called as she saw Longstaff. "Thank heavens."

Longstaff approached. "Lower your weapons." He glowered at the Red Royals. "Good evening, ladies. What seems to be the problem?"

Lady Llewellyn's face was pale. "They're arresting us!"

"Not by choice, ma'am." The sergeant turned to Longstaff. "Orders, sir. They be on the list."

Longstaff reviewed the document. "They are, good work, men."

Lady Dewar put her hand to her chest. "Captain, what is to be done with us?"

"Release them," Longstaff said.

"Aye, sir. Right away." The sergeant saluted.

"Your husbands' left you behind?" Longstaff remembered a similar complaint from the last time he'd seen the ladies. He'd spent a few days in their company, mainly drinking and fornicating.

"Seems I wasn't fast enough for Operation Fuck Off!" Lady Dewar growled.

"Is there anyone left inside?"

She nodded. "He's ordered slaves to fight to the death."

"With kitchen utensils," added Lady Llewellyn.

"Hmm, marvelous." Longstaff scratched the back of his head. "Jim, take the governor's estate."

"Aye, sir." Fishhook saluted, leading the Red Royals towards the mansion.

"Where were you going?"

"We were going to take the wherry to Ligania," Lady Llewellyn said.

Longstaff signaled the soldiers. "Let them go."

"Thank you, Captain," Lady Dewar exclaimed.

"Major Paine, would you be so kind as to escort the ladies and children to Ligania?"

"Aye, Captain, that I can do." Paine turned to the sergeant. "To my ship."

"And, Major Paine?" Longstaff added.

"Aye, Captain?"

"You'll be sailing off into the sunset, I believe?"

"I suppose so, Captain."

"Then smooth sailing to you, Major." The two men shook hands warmly.

"And to you, Captain." Major Paine nodded and signaled for his carriage.

Lady Llewellyn gave Longstaff a familiar wink. "Thank you again, Captain."

"Not at all. When you see your husbands', tell them they will be under my protection when they return. I give you my word they won't be harmed."

"I'll pass the message along, sir. After executing Operation Leave the Prick!" Lady Dewar motioned the driver.

Longstaff and Captain Bentley watched the carriage pull away, just as two Red Royals escorted a very attractive woman in a witch costume through the Old Church grounds at gun point. *What the hell have they done now?* Longstaff thought.

"What the hell?" Bentley said.

"Sir, we arrested a witch!" a Red Royal explained.

"A witch? Superb!" Longstaff snatched the list from Bentley. "Ah, there are no witches on the arrest warrant."

Bentley put the list back into his jacket. "Let her go."

A courier arrived.

"What's your problem? Goblins in the Admiralty?" Longstaff put up his hand. "Don't answer that."

"Sir, Governor Dewar and Lord Llewellyn have fled the city."

"Aye, we know. Thank you," Bentley said snidely.

Longstaff imagined the look on Governor Piper's face. "Sorry, sir. We lost Dewar, but we found you a fucking witch!"

"Apologies sir. What do we do with her?" asked a Red Royal.

Longstaff contemplated the girl. *Port Royal never saw a finer set of curves.* "Leave her with me. You two continue searching door to door and remember, a peaceful transition."

Gunshots echoed through the air. Bentley signaled his men, who took off towards the commotion.

Longstaff turned to another messenger. "Report."

"Mr. Fishhook reports that the city west of the Governor's Mansion has been secured."

"Very well, have them continue door to door." Longstaff eyed the girl. "So, what's your story?"

She gazed at him coquettishly. "Just like ya said, I'm a fucking witch."

"I'll bet you are. Do you happen to know where the Lieutenant Governor and Lord Llewellyn spend their time?"

"The Swiftsure and the Crooked Compass, both down Thames Street."

Longstaff nodded. "Re-check the Crooked Compass and Swiftsure Tavern."

"Aye, sir." The messenger saluted and hurried away.

The girl folded her arms over her protruding nipples. "I'm afraid the sea air seems to have got the better of me. Have you got a coat for a lady?"

Longstaff removed his jacket and draped it over her shoulders. More gun shots filled the night sky. "Stay close." He glanced around. "What's your name?"

"Violante Hayze. People call me Vie."

"A pleasure, Vie." He tipped his hat. "Well, there's nothing to worry about here. This is just a peaceful transition of government."

"I don't concern meself with politics, sir."

"Good for you. They're all a bunch of cunts anyway." Longstaff turned to see the glittering expression she wore. "Where are my manners in the presence of a lady?" He bowed. "Allow me to introduce myself."

"You're Captain Richard Longstaff."

"Have we met before?"

"You've quite the reputation around here, Captain." She leaned back against the carriage and bit her lower lip. "I've been curious to meet you meself."

"I'd be happy to satisfy your curiosity." He admired her pretty face and dark hair. A spark of desire stirred between his legs.

Another courier arrived, out of breath.

"What news from the front, Marc Anthony?" Longstaff jested. "What was that shooting?"

"Captain Bentley's men ran into some resistance. Pirates and cutthroats in the alleys. He said not to bother you."

"Have Captain Bentley issue a proper report on the double."

"Aye, sir." The courier saluted.

"And notify Captain Bentley and Mr. Fishhook that I'm returning to King's Ground."

Vie gave him a sultry gaze. "People have seen me with you. I wouldn't feel safe being on me own tonight. Can I have an escort home?"

Longstaff slid an arm around her. "You better come with me."

Vie stepped up into the enclosed carriage and slid across the seat. Longstaff tucked in beside her and closed the door before banging the roof. The carriage took off. They sat in silence for the first minute rolling down High Street. Vie hesitated at first. *What if the rumors were true?* There was only one way to find out. Casually she dropped her handkerchief on his lap. When she fetched it, her hand slipped between his legs. "So, it is true." Her interest piqued.

Longstaff leaned over to whisper in her ear. "Imagine that. Truth in a rumor."

Vie crushed her lips against his. The faint scent of herbal cologne and perspiration drove her to the point of wanting to straddle him.

The carriage halted.

"Damn, just when things were starting to get engaging." He sighed and jumped out. "Wait here."

Two men with large powdery wigs stood at the entrance to the King's Ground. They congratulated him on a job well done and asked about her.

"A recruit. She was quite helpful," said Longstaff.

A man with a silvery blue wig nodded. "Then she is to be rewarded."

"I will see to it, sir."

"I'm sure you will, Captain." The other man laughed.

"Return to *Relentless* and get some rest. Stand by at the north dock and wait for orders."

"Aye, sir." Longstaff returned to the carriage.

"Are you taking me to yer ship, Captain?" Vie asked.

"My dear, you shall get the grand tour."

The carriage wheeled across the courtyard to the north dock. Within minutes they boarded. Vie gazed up, straining her neck to see the full length of the masts and the furled sails. The vessel was a colossal floating metropolis. The bosun's whistle sounded and Longstaff guided Vie along the main level.

"Captain on deck," an officer announced.

"As you were, Mr. Cook," Longstaff said. "Welcome aboard, my dear."

"This is *Relentless*?" Vie's mouth dropped open.

"Aye, ma'am, *Relentless* is her name and her demeanor; the finest ship in the Royal Navy. Nothing smaller can take her and nothing larger can catch her. Isn't that right, Mr. Cook?"

"Bloody well right, sir."

Longstaff led Vie down the deck. "She's taken on first-rate warships and taught them a thing or two about English resolve. We'll stay awhile. Remain at general quarters, Mr. Cook."

"Aye, sir."

Vie felt Longstaff's hand grope her waist, guiding her across a chamber to the captain's cabin. Once inside, she spun around, taking it all in. His cabin was twice the size of her room at Cherry's. There was a heavy oak desk, a corner bed, and naval artifacts hanging from the walls.

Longstaff clicked the lock to the door, and then went to his desk. He set his hat down and removed a bottle from a drawer. "I want to thank you for your help." He uncorked the rum and took a swig before handing it to her.

"Sounds like fun." The rum slid down her throat, warming her insides. "When would you like to do that?" Mounting herself upon his desk, she playfully trapped his leg between hers. "Isn't there a Mrs. Longstaff back in Nevis?"

"You're very direct aren't you? Aye, there is, in fact."

"It's true then. All the good ones are already taken," Vie lamented, gulping back more rum.

Longstaff removed his sword and gun belts. "A captain is only really married to his ship. His wife must adapt to a life of loneliness." He caressed her neck, causing a pleasant chill.

"What does a captain do when he gets lonely?" Vie put on his hat and took another mouthful of rum. This time she let it dribble down her chin and she licked her lips slowly, before setting the bottle down. "Now I'm the captain and you have to do as I say. What are ya gonna do about it?"

Longstaff tore down her corset and they kissed fervently. "What are your orders, Captain?"

Vie bit her lip hungrily, and anticipation made her insides squirm.

Bizy
Gale
GO
2015

Something Like Scarlet Fever

Morning sunlight crept into the room, causing la Roche to stir. He opened his eyes to find Atia curled up beside him. At first, he thought he was still asleep, seeing the woman of his dreams beside him in the flesh. He rubbed his eyes and stared at her, pale and peaceful in the morning light. Slowly he slid his hand free and leaned in till his mouth met hers in a purely blissful moment. *What joy it would be to be mounted between her thighs and feel her flesh against mine!* He briefly tongued her perfect lips before wandering down the stairs.

He entered the kitchen to find a chamber pot beside the window. Once his morning wood subsided, he undid his trousers and peered out the small warped window. *La Lune* sat in the bay, tied up just beyond Waterman's Wharf. "*C'est quoi, ce bordel*?" He pressed his face against the cracked window. "Ah, great place to hide idiots! No one will think to look for me here, uh?" He buttoned up and ran from the kitchen to peer out the back door.

A dozen red coated soldiers marched to the wharf. They were led by Lance Thorne and followed by Harbormaster Pepys. *What a prick!* La Roche had known Thorne as a talentless midshipman who'd landed a position on Captain Goddam's ship because his father was an admiral.

La Roche closed the door quietly and retreated to the bedroom, where Atia was still asleep. He rifled through his coat pocket to find his whistle and then went to the window. Redcoats approached his ship.

"Ahoy, Captain," Thorne shouted.

Le Picard supervised the crewmen in the rigging, while Delacroix and Martel stood on the deck, leaning over the rail.

"Ahoy, where is your captain? Captain Jean-Paul la Roche," Thorne bellowed.

Martel looked up at le Picard for a moment and cleared his throat. "Oui, I am Capitaine la Roche. How may I help you?"

"Is that Gator Gar?" Thorne addressed Pepys.

"Nay, it ain't him." Pepys looked as if he'd been awake all night.

Behind la Roche, Atia stirred and called out, "Ma?"

He put on his best maternal tone. “Back to sleep,” he crooned, scribbling a note on a piece of parchment. His parrot Minuit landed on the windowsill.

“Back to sleep,” Minuit said.

La Roche slid the note into the parrot’s leg bracelet. “Go!” He signaled, and the bird flew for the ship, landing on a ratline near le Picard.

“Captain, you must leave Port Royal forthwith,” Thorne insisted.

“We have many repairs to make before we can sail open water,” Martel said.

Thorne tapped his foot. “Regardless, by order of the Whigs, you must leave English territory immediately.”

“May we have time to finish loading provisions?” Martel asked.

“Nay. Leave now.”

“We must secure the mainmast,” Martel argued.

“Nay! You’ll be arrested if you’re not underway forthwith.”

“Oui, we will go now, *connard*!” Martel nodded. “*Au revoir, merci*. All hands departure stations.”

Le Picard took the note from Minuit’s bracelet, read it, and wrote a quick reply before sending the parrot back.

Thorne gazed up at the bird, grimacing as it went by. “Well if that ain’t the ugliest crow I ever seen!”

Minuit returned to the windowsill and la Roche unrolled the parchment. Le Picard’s message indicated the ship would return to Petit-Goâve to make repairs and send word from there. La Roche darted downstairs, leaving Minuit to guard Atia. Through a crack in the kitchen door, he watched the activities until the handle slammed into his face. “Ah, fuck!”

Theodore Binge the card-shark entered. “Clever disguise. I would never think to look for a Frenchman hiding at a brothel in front of his own bloody boat.”

La Roche rubbed his nose. “What are you doing here?”

“What am I doing here? What are you doing here?”

La Roche grabbed a bottle of rum. “I missed the *ambiance*. What do you think?” He observed *La Lune* as she pulled away.

“Well, there goes your ride. Do you have alternative arrangements?”

“Not on me.”

“I hope you came here to get fucked, ’cause ya are.” Binge glanced around. “Where’s that pretty little thing we saved last night?”

"Upstairs. Oui, *merci*. I owe you for that."

"No, you don't. I ain't letting them cut up another girl if I can help it. We won a few games like that in the old days. It's good to know that time hath not taken the magic touch."

"What are you doing hanging around with those petty creeps and thugs? And that *connard* Coggshall?"

Binge waved his hand. "Oh, he's the *connard*, "rectard", and "collard" all rolled up into one! But he and his thugs are now the richest men in the Caribbean dealing in slaves and women."

La Roche pulled a face. "And you do business with them?"

"Don't you dare judge me. I'm doing what I can to survive and right now and that ain't enough. Do you know what it's like being a black man in a slave's world? The whites hate me, the browns hate me, and the reds hate me. Hell, if there were greens here, they'd hate me too!"

Cherry entered from the hallway. "I tried to tell ya last night, Capitaine, you ain't dealing with thugs anymore. The slave trade runs everything now. They have hundreds of men and dozens of ships. They own Port Royal."

"Port Royal doesn't fare well in times of peace, as you can imagine." Binge smiled at Cherry. "Morning, Miss Banks."

Cherry winked. "Morning, Mr. Binge."

"Feel the earthquake this morning?"

"Another one?"

"A good one too. Another big crack in Thames Street."

All three gazed out the kitchen window. Soldiers in red coats headed in the brothel's direction.

"Quick, duck!" La Roche dragged Binge down by the shoulder next to a large butcher block.

Cherry grabbed the water jug and shook her head. "Why are *you* hiding?"

"Impulse of repetition?" Binge smirked.

La Roche eyed Binge. "Why did she call you that? Someone called you Binge yesterday too."

"Remember Old Man Binge?"

"Oui."

"He always wanted a son, so he bequeathed his estate, name, and custody of his daughters to moi!"

"Because he wanted a son?"

"And because I saved his daughters when the house burned down."

"Were you not also screwing his daughters?"

Binge grinned, eyebrows pointing up. "Why do you think I stay in Port Royal?"

Sunshine flooded Cherry's bedroom. Dust particles whirled about in the air floating around the canopy bed where long panes of deep plum fabric partially blocked the light. Atia's legs twitched and kicked beneath the bed sheets.

Warm rain pounded the deck of the Aeolus *and a strong gust of wind snatched crewmen into the air. They grabbed the rope but the wind yanked their legs above their heads. They hung upside down freezing in mid-air against a vivid golden sky. Bright orange lightning pierced the dark water below. Livia's pallid corpse climbed backwards over the rail covered in seaweed. Her ma's voice echoed like thunder.*

Atia's leg jolted up and she stirred. Tears trickled down her face. She brushed them away before opening her eyes. After some deep painful breaths, she lifted her head towards the light, trying to focus. A peculiar creature stepped into view.

"*Bonjour*, Mademoiselle." A bird with dark reflective eyes stared at her.

"Hello, who…what are ya?" Atia asked.

"Hello," it replied.

"What kind of bird are ya?" It had an overly large beak that appeared to form a strange smile. The dark feathers almost shimmered in the sunlight and an adorable tuft stuck out the top of his head like a crown. She reached out her hand to pet it.

The bird shuffled up to her shoulder and nudged her. "*Ma chérie*," it said, and nibbled at her hair.

Atia lay back down on the pillow. "Ah, a French one." Her eyes drooped and she fell back asleep.

Steam filled the kitchen. Tea was brewed and plates of cured fish, dried bread, and apple tarts sat on the table. La Roche stuffed his mouth with fish while watching *La Lune*, she had almost cleared the harbor.

Cherry poured a cup of tea. “The soldiers are all gone now.”

“So is my ship.” La Roche scowled. “What’s with the Redcoats? They can’t all be after me?”

“You haven’t been keeping up with current events. Those are King William’s forces,” said Binge, tucking into an apple tart. “They’ve taken over the government. There’s a big man-of-war looking mean over at the north dock. Most of the pirates have fled and it’s only a matter of time before they start going after all King James’s supporters.”

Cherry filled the large copper kettle with more water and set it over the fire.

“Coggshall had the previous government paid off and he’s got the three biggest pirates in Port Royal in his pocket. But now—”

“Everything’s changed,” said Cherry.

“No, it hasn’t,” la Roche assured.

Binge stopped chewing.

Cherry patted his shoulder. “’Tis okay love, the Capitaine knows; we filled him in last night.”

“Then you know that Coggshall plans on getting rid of the competition?”

“Oui, I heard.”

“But maybe now ain’t the best time?” Cherry bit her thumb.

“It’s the perfect time. Most of the pirates are gone and those who stay are killing each other off. You’re having second thoughts ’cause yer scared is all.” Binge looked at la Roche. “And you, stick or have it?”

“Oui, I’m in. What else am I going to do?”

Two knocks came at the black door, which was normally reserved for non-white or illegal customers. Dr. Strangewayes entered carrying a large brown medical bag. A broadside was rolled up under his arm. “Good morrow.” He saw la Roche and frowned. “Capitaine, I thought I just saw your ship leaving.”

“Oui, she did.” He took a bite of apple tart.

“Oh, I’m sorry.” The doctor addressed Cherry, “Miles will be by with fresh water this morning.”

“Yer too kind, Doctor.”

“Did you find Atia’s sister?” la Roche asked.

“Sister? There’s two of them?” Binge was surprised.

“Lilly says she’s at the Swiftsure. Alive, but not well.”

"Then let us proceed to the next task," la Roche said.

"Excellent! Good to have you aboard. Well, I see most of our murderous conspirators are here. How is our other shipwreck survivor doing?" Strangewayes set his bag on the counter.

Cherry patted la Roche's shoulder. "The Capitaine's wee bonnie lass is sleeping upstairs."

"She's Irish, not Scottish, dear." Strangewayes winked.

"Well she's sleeping like a baby!"

"Good. I'll check on her in a moment. I brought teas, dressings, and laudanum."

Cherry clapped excitedly. "Yay, laudanum!"

"Yes, well it's not for you, is it?"

She stuck her tongue out at the doctor and he unrolled the broadside, flattening it on the table in front of la Roche. "Since you are still here, you might want to see this." The paper read:

Wanted for Piracy, Sodomy, and Murder
Gator Gar, 8000 pieces of 8

"These are going up all over town right now."

"Sodomy?" Cherry scoffed. "A likely story!"

"Since when's that a crime in this town?" la Roche quipped.

"All prerequisites for admittance to this city anyway. I do hope your men got away in time, Capitaine." Strangewayes re-rolled the document.

"A bunch of kids! They'll be fine. Picard knows what he's doing."

The doctor looked up and Lilly entered. "Ah, there you are."

"Yeah, thanks for waiting," she snarled, setting another medical case on the table.

Cherry started to pace the kitchen. "I think we should wait. It's too dangerous right now with all the soldiers in town."

"Are ya serious? After what they done to Katie? Ya saw what they did to the Irish girls!" Lilly fumed.

"They won't do anything to us with the new government here."

"Don't count on it. Slasher Al ain't afraid of Whigs and he didn't come here for the view," Binge said.

"Slasher Al left this morning." Strangewayes opened his case. "But he'll be back; count on it."

"Oui. You can't hide from them. And if you are going to kill them, you must wipe them out. Every one of them, or they will come back at you." La Roche felt a twinge of excitement, as though he were planning a raid. Henry Morgan had valued his keen sense of strategy, and had hired him for all major attacks.

"Are they going ahead with the slave fayre tonight?" The doctor looked at Binge.

"Yup, as far as I know. They're setting up all around Swiftsure, all big and fancy-like despite the bit of...fire damage." Binge nudged la Roche.

"I did not mean for Picard to torch the place."

"Well, that was always his forte."

"You said all the pirates left; Slasher Al too. That means they'll need all their remaining men there tonight for protection?"

"Most likely."

"Then that's where we do it. We hit them tonight at the Swiftsure while the rest of the pirates are away," said la Roche.

Strangewayes nodded. "All the top dogs at once. Coggshall plays One and Thirty there every Saturday night. We stand a good chance of taking out the top dog himself."

"But...with what?" la Roche pondered. "We are short on muscle. Our buccaneer friend might be able to help."

"Our buccaneer friend also left before sunrise, I'm afraid." The doctor rummaged in his case. "However, I have just the thing right here." He cocked his head to one side and removed a handful of vials containing dark liquid. "Especially if it means sending the gutter rats back into the slime. I think a selective outbreak of scarlet fever is in order. Or rather, something that closely resembles it. Coggshall and his associates could all suddenly contract the disease."

"What is it?" Cherry reached for a vial.

"Belladonna, otherwise known as deadly nightshade, with just a hint of pennyroyal oil." The doctor admired the unassuming liquid. "It's quite remarkable. The best part is there's no cure." He sighed deeply. "I've often dreamed of the day I could look into Coggshall's eyes and say, 'Sorry, old chum. There is no cure'."

Binge smelled the contents. "How do you plan on poisoning them all?"

"It's best poured into wine or mead."

"But will they taste it?" Cherry inspected the poison.

"Apparently it has a sweet taste, but I have yet to try it myself." Strangewayes handed a vial to la Roche.

"After a few rounds they won't notice the taste."

"The real question is: how do *you* plan to get close to their drinks? Us ladies will take care of this lot," Cherry said.

Lilly's face lit up. "I can get it in their drinks, sure as shooting! Natalia and Catherina too." She slipped a vial into her top.

The doctor frowned. "I'd prefer not to involve them."

"Nonsense, this is our fight." Cherry stuffed a couple vials down her bodice. "You want it in their drinks and in their drinks is exactly where we'll be putting it!"

"Make sure you give them a good unhealthy dose." Strangewayes handed her two more.

"We should test it first." Binge grabbed a vial from the medical case. "I have the perfect candidate." An evil grin formed on his face. "Magott's at the Swiftsure right now. He's staying there for the fayre."

"That's like hearing your favorite song for the first time!" Strangewayes beamed. "Excellent idea. If we could poison him within the next hour that should give us enough time to test its effectiveness. Who'll do the deed?"

"I will. I've been looking forward to this." Binge put the poison in his breast pocket. "I'll meet ya back here after."

"I'll go with you," Cherry offered.

"Are you kidding? I can't be seen with you. My stepdaughters would have my nuts!"

"I'll go. I have an idea." Lilly looked to Cherry. "Got any olive oil?"

Binge advanced to the black door while Vie limped in, her hair in disarray wearing a raincoat. "Morning all," she began.

"There you are!" Cherry exclaimed.

"Morning, Mr. Binge," Vie said. "Sorry, I'm plumb tuckered out."

"Good morrow, Miss Vie." Binge held the door open and Lilly rushed out. He followed enthusiastically.

"When you didn't come back, I thought something happened to you. Are you well?" Cherry asked.

"To tell you the truth, a little sore." She noticed Strangewayes. "Doc, might I trouble you for some of that special ladies' cream?"

"Yes, of course." He took a small jar out of his bag.

Cherry gave him an odd look. "Ya brought some with you?"

"A good doctor is always prepared."

"Thank you. You're a Godsend!" Vie winked and ambled gingerly down the hallway.

"Wore you out, did he?" Cherry called.

Vie leaned against the wall for a moment. "The man has a god between his legs. An absolute god! I'm in love." She continued her delicate journey.

Cherry shrugged. "I didn't know Cardinal Grimaldi had it in him."

"Well, I think I'll check on our lovely Irish patient." Strangewayes started down the hall.

"Oui, I'll come with you." La Roche's face colored. He followed the doctor, eager to gaze at his revered redhead.

Minuit stood guard beside her and snapped his beak at their approach.

"What the?" La Roche retracted his hand. "Get away!" Minuit reluctantly perched on the headboard.

"Can you change these for me?" La Roche opened a bureau drawer and took out four gold bars. There were more inside, including a gold watch, formerly belonging to Binge.

"Oh my. Are these from the card game?"

"Oui."

"It shouldn't be a problem, although Mrs. Beazley will probably hit me with them." The doctor stuffed the bars into his coat.

"Kicking still, is she?"

"Yes, harder than ever." Strangewayes examined Atia. "We have to get this girl and her sister out of the city. You swindled one; now how do we get the other?"

La Roche slipped his hand into Atia's. "We need a plan."

"Her father still lives on the north side of the island. Delightful man, I know you'll get on with him straight away."

"Dangerous. The English will be watching him." La Roche kissed Atia's forehead amid Minuit's beaky protest. "We'll have to find a place to lay low first."

"I have the perfect location for laying low, just a few hours' carriage ride from Ligania." Strangewayes inspected the bruises on her arms.

"Is she good to travel?"

"I don't like the idea of moving either of them just yet, but it's for the best. Once Livia has been recovered, my assistant Gladstone will take you."

"You are not coming?"

"I'm staying for the aftermath. Port Royal is going to have to pick up the pieces and I intend to see them put back right."

Atia's leg twitched and she took a large mouthful of air. Her eyes opened to see the Capitaine holding her hand and a heavyset man with a crooked nose looking her over. "Hello," she said hoarsely.

Above her the peculiar bird sat staring down. "Hello," it replied.

"Morning, *ma chérie*," the Capitaine said.

"How are you feeling?" The heavyset man began, looking as though he just rolled out of bed.

"Like I been beaten senseless by a bloody hurricane." Atia tried to sit up. "Oh, a lot o'pain." She met the bird's stare. "Thought I dreamt that. Who are you and where's Livia?"

"I'm Dr. Sander Strangewayes, Chief Surgeon of Port Royal. We know where your sister is," he said. "We'll reunite you with her just as soon as we can. But for now, you're going to have to trust us. We're going to move you to a safe place."

"Can I have some water?"

"Of course. I'll go get Cherry to boil some and see if there's any broth around too."

"Why boil it? Takes too long to cool down." The Capitaine poured a shot of rum and reached for the laudanum bottle.

"Because…" Strangewayes paused at the door. "It's bad for you."

"Yeah, yeah, next you'll say the lead pipes are bad for us." The Capitaine shook his head, dispensing a few drops before handing it to Atia. "This will take care of the pain."

She gulped it back, cringing. "That's awful!"

"If it tasted good, it would be an epidemic." He set the empty glass on the table.

"Well, I feel…better." She beamed, glancing up at the bird. "I don't think we've been properly introduced."

"That's Minuit; I've had him for many years now."

"Hello, Minuit."

“Hello,” he squawked.

She was silent for a moment, admiring the Capitaine’s striking black shirt. “Ya look nice.”

“*Merci*. Cherry gave it to me.”

“How’s the arm?”

“It’s good, *merci.*” He smiled.

“Liar.” She knew it throbbed like hell. “Was a deep cut that.”

Strangewayes returned with a glass bottle filled with water and a cup. “Found some clean stuff, here we go.” Atia could barely grasp the cup so the Capitaine held it to her lips. “Cherry is just mixing some broth with cured fish in it for flavor. She’ll only be a moment.”

From the kitchen, a keen ear could hear Cherry bellow, “Yeah, now I’m the bloody cook!”

“Thank ya, you’ve been very kind.” Atia took more water.

“Kind nothing, I’m astounded by how well you’re doing. After you’ve had a bite to eat, we’ll find you something to wear.”

Atia’s eyes darted down at the bed sheet barely covering her. She yanked the sheet up to her chin, catching the devious gleam in the Capitaine’s eye.

“Then we’ll get you standing up and stretching as you’re going to get pretty sore. Then back to sleep for you, it’s going to be a long and difficult ride.”

Atia eyed her champion. “They’re after ya, aren’t they? For helping me?”

The Capitaine’s arm slipped around her. “Not for you to worry about.”

Worrying was second nature to Atia. “How many times have I heard that before.” She knew Crisp and his slaver captain too well not to fret. *They’ll be coming.*

M.E. '15

Back to Business

La Lune glided by Fort James, her oak hull glowing in the morning light and the repairs fully visible. The cracked mainmast was reinforced with plenty of rope. The torn sails were patched with sections of white canvas and the vessel glided with a lean.

"What heading do we take, sir?" Delacroix looked to le Picard.

"We'll head southeast for a while and put some distance between us and Port Royal. The Capitaine knows where we are going. We take what's left of the cargo to Petit-Goâve, get paid, and make repairs."

Martel nodded. "He would expect no less than one hundred percent from all of us regardless if he were here."

"This is not the first time the Capitaine has taken shore leave, Monsieur Delacroix." Le Picard glanced back at Cherry Red's Boutique.

"No, sir," Delacroix said.

"Shore leave with five large forts and a maximum-security prison?" Martel smirked.

"Six forts now. Weren't you counting? The Capitaine has known Port Royal since it was a sandy beach the English named the Cagway. He knows that city from the ground up. Every alley, crook, and cranny."

"Why did he not send the bird back?"

"He didn't need to. I got the last message."

"What was the last message?" Delacroix asked.

"He says, 'I'm keeping the bird'." Le Picard strolled to the stern of the ship to look back at the city. "*Au revoir, mon ami. Mon Capitaine*." It took almost an hour to clear the harbor. The last place they passed was Morgan's Line. Just beyond, next to the storehouses, was a large brick house nicknamed Henry's Loft.

Back in '78, le Picard and the Capitaine had spent five years there protecting Port Royal from the Spanish. They lived like kings – given free drinks and food in every tavern in town. At night they made a point of visiting all the best brothels and attending only the most exclusive gatherings.

When Grammont's Flibustiers or de Graaf's Samaná Bay Buccaneers came into town, there was always a huge shindig at the

Swiftsure Tavern. One evening after much drinking, the Capitaine reunited with Cherry Banks, a strumpet he'd known for many years. She worked for Starr's Palace and they'd screw every time he visited Port Royal.

Times changed however, and the English made peace with the Spanish. It had been too good to last. The Capitaine was furious when his investors dropped their contract. It meant a quick return to pirating, this time under Laurens de Graaf. The Capitaine had been contracted to represent the interests of the English in a raid on Vera Cruz.

The night before their departure, le Picard, the Capitaine, and Cherry went on a rum-fueled night out involving a quick stop at the King's House with a bucket of hot tar and a large brush. The Capitaine climbed up to the hanging sign above the main entrance. "How do you spell arsehole?" He reached for the bucket in le Picard's hand. "Ah, fuck it." He wrote: Thomas Lynch takes it up the ass.

Back on the ground, the Capitaine admired his handiwork. "There! Lynch can suck my indentured cock!"

Cherry laughed. "Sorry love, that's my job."

"And gifted you are too." The Capitaine kissed her forehead before peering in the window at a fully stocked liquor cabinet. "We should have broken in and stole the booze first." He signaled le Picard. "Let's go before the guards come back."

"What could they do? You are the Capitaine." Le Picard laughed.

"This is the English. They cut off their own king's head to make a point." The Capitaine slipped his arm around Cherry and they left the grounds.

Le Picard looked back at Martel, who was overseeing repairs. *He's right. It's Dante's Pit now! This wretched city could change its mind and send in warships at any time. As for* La Lune, *she is far too wounded to protect herself.* Vulnerability crept inside le Picard like a sickness. He had never felt this under the Capitaine before. *We must reach Petit-Goâve with all haste.*

A churchwarden's carriage arrived in the sleepy town of Ligania, across the harbor from Port Royal. It passed houses, stables, trade stores, and a general market. The townsfolk took little notice of the car. Farmers transported their crops to the wherryman's wharf, where they were packed into crates to be transported to Port Royal. Barreled water shipments arrived at the smaller wharf and were rolled into town for distribution.

The Cagway Inn and adjoining shops stretched over an entire block. Curved archways accented the inn's front walkway, which was lined with potted trees. The inn itself was built with tens of thousands of limestone bricks. Its multilevel red clay tiled roofs baked beneath the morning sun and many of the slatted windows were open to the intermittent breeze coming off the water. The large central archway led to a stone courtyard and the main entrance.

The churchwarden's carriage halted beside the archway. Dewar, Llewellyn, and Sleemans stepped down.

"No, I'm pretty sure hearing nothing means mute," Dewar said, feeling quite confident.

"People are just calling her that as a joke, Mute Katie can hear just fine." Sleemans looked around. "So much for not being seen."

The three men strolled through the courtyard. They passed a large black anchor commemorating the *Torrington*, a ship of the line. *Torrington* had led the English invasion fleet that first took the sandy beach that became Port Royal. Surrounding the anchor was a bed of wildflowers and prickly bushes.

Dewar stretched his hands above his head before shaking out each leg. "We got out of the city. That was the plan."

"Yes. Also part of the plan, nobody knowing where you are, hence the fuck off," Sleemans replied.

"Don't think your little inu-endums are going unnoticed."

Major Paine stepped through the inn door with a cigar jutting from his mouth.

"There's the major. Perhaps they got something right," Sleemans said.

"Your families are inside," Paine began. "Right this way, if ya please."

The walls of the main floor were lined with a silk brocade of reddish brown and gold, forming spade-like patterns. The varnished floors shined, and the brass wall sconces gleamed with candlelight.

Dewar looked around at other people lingering in the main entrance. *Ah, they all must be in on Operation Fuck Off!* "Fuck off!" He gave them a thumb up and a wink.

Patrons gave him a peculiar look and hurried away.

"Where did you sail from?" Sleemans asked Paine.

"Nevis, with four ships. Two are still in Morant Bay."

"Then why the hell didn't we find out sooner?"

"The Whigs wanted absolute secrecy. We couldn't risk being exposed." Paine turned to Dewar and Llewellyn. "Your families are upstairs under Captain Fokman's charge."

"Ah, excellent, good old Fokman. We can all relax now, right?" Llewellyn asked. "Perhaps I'll just step into the tavern first and secure us some provisions shall I?"

Dewar nodded. "Good thinking. It's a long ride to the house."

"It's a ten-minute trip," Sleemans said.

"Right this way." Major Paine guided them up the foyer stairs. The sound of children arguing could be heard from all the way down the hall. Dewar opened the door to the room as debating continued. The bickering children and Lady Llewellyn didn't even notice.

"And who's Fokman?" Dewar muttered as he looked at all the children. "Nice to see you too. Sometimes I wonder which ones are mine and which ones are yours."

"Well, as long as they're fed." Llewellyn shrugged. "Dorcas Junior is getting as tall as Laura."

Dewar sighed. "Ah yes, Dorcas. Margaret insisted that the name be passed along." Dewar resented his parents. "For whatever reason they wanted a girl and when I popped out, they christened me Dorcas anyway. They say that the biblical name is equivalent to Tabitha in Aramaic. I would have preferred Tabitha. People could call me Tabby, far more refined. None of this Dorcas nonsense!" He eyed Llewellyn. "Every family ends up with a tall blond one. Don't ask me why. The Lord has mysterious ways, he does. Guess he likes tall blond children." Dewar inspected the ghastly room – it was simply furnished. A walnut table and two Baroque armchairs sat in the corner. The upholstery and curtains were green velvet. "Take that Captain Longstaff for example, he must have broken his mother's box on the way out." He turned and waved to his son. "Yo anchor-head, where's Mummy?"

"You mean Grandma?"

"No, imbecile! Younger Mummy."

"Mother isn't with us."

"Oh, you are gifted! I see that. Did she go on ahead?"

Dorcas shrugged. “She didn’t say. But she took her case.”

Lady Llewellyn approached. “Lady Dewar took the wherryman’s carriage on ahead.”

Dewar nodded. “Ah, good for her.”

“Did she say why?” Sleemans asked.

“It’s not my place to question the governor’s wife,” Lady Llewellyn said.

Dewar patted Llewellyn on the back. “She’s gone to get it ready. See? She’s coming around. You’ve just got to condition them right. Marriage is a lot like being indentured.”

“With less whipping, of course,” Llewellyn speculated, gently slapping his wife’s bottom.

“Speak for yourself.” Dewar’s eyes widened. “Sometimes a little whipping goes a long way!”

Captain Fokman entered and saluted Major Paine.

“Are we ready to move out?” Paine asked.

“Aye, it’s clear to the Retreat. We should leave now.”

Sleemans clasped his hands. “Your Ligania retreat will serve as our headquarters until we’re ready to return to Port Royal. You’ll be able to relax there.”

Llewellyn smiled. “All the comforts of home, because it is home.”

“This is going to sound unedu-cerated, but why so close?” Dewar asked.

“Longstaff is commanding the soldiers, and the militia in Port Royal are kept busy by the return of Gator Gar,” Paine explained.

“Nice touch with the Gator Gar bit.” Llewellyn winked.

“Touch nothing; he was there when we pulled in.”

“Refresh my memory a bit. Are we friends with Gator Gar?” Dewar queried.

“We’d all took him for dead till now.”

“So that’s a ‘no’ then? I’m glad I’m not the only one. Thought I had him confused with other buccaneers.” Llewellyn rubbed his chin.

“They are good at that. Like a game of mimes, who are we this week – Capitano Froggo!” Dewar laughed. “Well, never mind, let’s get going shall we?” He looked out the window towards Port Royal. “My beautiful city, I’ll save you from the Whigs yet!”

The Aeolus *crumbled beneath the brute force of the storm and churning waves. The ship broke apart into small fragments on the rocks. Upon the beach, bodies washed up with debris and flames engulfed the remainder of the hull. The water was terribly cold and brackish.*

Daylight penetrated the window and the pain in Skean's arm caused him to stir. He lay on a cot in the Admiralty Court in Port Royal. Relief rattled from his lungs, he'd never been so glad to be away from the water. A burning shot down his arm. It had been splinted and bandaged.

Judge Goblet entered with a cup of steaming tea. "How are you feeling? The bonesetter said you are able to keep the arm."

Skean flinched. "Not sure I really want to."

"Are you well enough to answer a few questions?"

Skean tried to sit up but could scarcely move. "Yes, sir."

"Why were you late?"

"I followed the lead to Saint Lucia. There wasn't time to inform you before I left. When I received your orders, I boarded the next ship to Port Royal. The *Aeolus,* unfortunately."

"Damn it," said Goblet. "Why didn't you send for a pick-up? The nearest mission was only a day's sail."

"I couldn't risk being exposed. Bleedin Art's men were there too."

"Bleedin Art?"

"Sorry, sir, that's what they call Captain Valentine here. To many people he's still just a pirate. His men were all over Saint Lucia. Seems I wasn't the only one interested in the *Aeolus*." Skean sipped the tea, felt his nose and lungs soothed by the steam.

"And was it as you suspected?"

"Strangewayes paid the passage for one of the families on board."

"But no slaves?" Goblet's round face scrunched up as if he were suffering from severe constipation.

"I got the impression that some were indentured, but it was not a slave ship. Perhaps Strangewayes is not involved?"

Goblet paced back and forth. "He must be. There is no question he's involved to some degree, and obviously Valentine thinks so too."

"It's a shame they all died. I wish I'd known where they were going."

"I'll have Strangewayes's plantation checked; we must leave no stone unturned," Goblet said.

"Understood."

"Are you capable of continuing your mission?"

"Yes, sir."

"Good." Goblet handed him a dossier. "I hope you don't mind being clergy again?"

"Thy will be done."

"I know the timing's bad, but we need you on it straight away." Goblet departed.

"Yes, sir." Skean rose slowly. "I'm here to serve."

Spiral topiaries in stone pots, well-trimmed hedges, and lush hibiscus plants in a multitude of reds and oranges dressed the grounds of St. Paul's Church. At its center a small water fountain babbled peacefully.

Father Parker Alcocke sprawled out on a wooden chair wearing only a small pair of blue tinted spectacles and a towel over his groin. Once famous for performing clandestine pirate marriages in Ye Old Marriage Shoppe for over twenty years, he had been forced to sell his business when new marriage laws were enacted. Under the guise of regular ministerial duties, he still ran a lucrative marriage business when he was not baking like a great round cat in the sunshine.

A shadow fell over him.

"Blocking a man from the warmth of the sun is the first sign of oppression," Alcocke said flatly.

"Oh, I'm quite sorry," replied a clergyman dressed in a black cassock with his arm in a cotton sling. "Can you tell me where I can find the churchwarden?"

"Who wants to know?"

"I'm Brother Gideon, sent by Bishop Eromenos. I'm here to replace Brother Gregory."

"Then that would be me. Around these parts I'm referred to as Churchwarden, Parish Priest, the Hand of God, and Alcocke. Pleased to make yer acquaintance, Brother Gideon. Rotten luck, huh?" Alcocke pointed at the injured arm. "I didn't think Bishop Eromenos would be keen on sending someone to replace Brother Gregory so soon, but I certainly could use the help."

"What is it you are doing?" The clergyman's face contorted.

"It's called basking in the sun. It turns you brown."

"You want to turn brown on purpose?"

"Ain't too used to the sun, are ya?"

The clergyman patted his perspiring forehead. "No, sir, it's rather too warm for me down here."

"Things are done a little differently in the Caribbean. You just gotta flow with it." Alcocke draped his arms over the chair and spread his thighs to tan the lighter undersides.

"Sorry?" Covering his mouth, the clergyman averted his eyes.

"Adaptation, my son."

"If you don't mind my asking, why did Brother Gregory leave so unexpectedly? An emergency, perhaps?"

"He heard his calling."

"From God?"

"No, his printer. He ran off to write a book on the sins of Port Royal. It's called Confessions of a Confessional. From diaconate to capitalist is one easy step." Alcocke released a large yawn and closed his eyes. "It's good to have ya aboard, Brother Gideon. You'll find lodgings all ready at the Old Anglican Church. Perhaps you may consider applying for churchwarden yerself. The old church could use a fresh face." He pointed up the road. "Tall stone building, looks like it's sinking, can't miss it. I'll be up later to help you get settled."

"Aye, thank you, Father."

"Don't mention it Brother, my son." Alcocke spread his thighs a bit wider. "Now if you'll excuse me, I must continue to bask in the Lord's warm glow before beginning the daily chore of saving wretched sinners from the clutches of Hell."

Next to the Admiralty Court stood the courthouse, where the town crier and his drummer pitched a commotion. A crowd began to gather. The drum aggressively vibrated the air.

"Thank you, enough." The town crier plugged his ears. "Stop!" The drummer halted and stood at attention. "Bloody hell!" The town crier massaged his ears. "Hear ye! Hear ye! Pirate attack on Barbados!" He unrolled a scroll. "Admiral Hewetson's ships were attacked in the Port of Barbados. One frigate destroyed; exploded in the harbor right next to the flagship. The entire fleet has been damaged or destroyed. Admiral Hewetson's Pacific expedition is officially canceled. Governor Spotswood declares all English ports to be on full alert. No foreign vessels are permitted to land under any circumstances. Those already in port are to be seized immediately! This message brought to you by Merry Maker Rum, supporting your local press gangs since 1670."

Goblet pushed through the crowd to the courthouse, where Constable Blower assisted the printer in nailing up wanted signs to the side of the building.

"You there! What is that?" Goblet grabbed one of the signs, which read:

Wanted for Piracy, Sodomy and Murder
Gator Gar, 8000 pieces of 8

"A wanted fugitive is in town," Blower said.

Goblet pursed his lips. "No, this won't do at all." He crumpled it up. "I want all of these destroyed immediately. Where are they being printed?"

"My shop is at the Merchant Exchange," the printer replied.

Goblet frowned. He forcibly shoved the crumpled sign into Blower's hand and snatched a new one. Laying it on his ledger, Goblet used a piece of charcoal to make corrections. "I want you to have these re-printed with haste. Make these corrections and redistribute them. I'm going to make myself perfectly clear; I'm Chief Justice now and you will do exactly as I say."

"Aye, sir."

"Gator Gar should have stayed under his rock!" Goblet continued inside the courthouse to the top floor patio where Acting Lieutenant Governor Piper and his entourage sat basking in the sun.

Goblet cleared his throat. "Sir, we're ready to begin the tour."

"Ah, Gobbles!" Piper looked over, pointing to the nooses secured around the necks of five men on the hanging platform at Gallows Point. "So, what's this lot, then?"

"Goblet, sir," the judge corrected. "Those are vagrants."

"Excellent, always a good place to start," Mold said.

Piper gave the signal and the vagrants dropped to the ends of their ropes. The bodies twitched and swayed in the breeze. "Good view from up here!" The governor stretched out his legs, draping them over the arm of his chair. "Seems like such a waste. These are the most impressive gallows I've seen in the New World."

"Indeed. Named Oliver, by the late town carpenter, Peter Bartaboa.

We'll hang the real criminals tomorrow," said Goblet. "Hopefully Governor Dewar and Lord Llewellyn will be on their way to a similar fate in London."

"Nay, that won't be possible at this time." Piper looked to the harbor. "Gentlemen, the economy is extremely fragile and we cannot risk any civil discontent. We must ensure that maintaining stability is of utmost importance during the transition. God knows that a collapse in stability leads to anarchy, plain and simple. Take this down."

"Sir." Taliare brought out parchment and ink.

"As representative of His Majesty and the Orange Party, I pardon Lords Dorcas Dewar and Lawrence Llewellyn of all charges."

Goblet felt his bottom lip start to quiver. "Those charges include fraud, conspiracy, and treason."

"Furthermore, they shall keep their appointments to City Council. Dewar shall be made Council Co-Chair with Mr. White."

Sheriff Tellam coughed back a laugh. "Mr. White is not gonna like it."

"Too bad. He's just going to have to shove over or step aside." Piper waved his hand. "And I want Llewellyn reinstated as Judge of the Court."

Goblet cringed, as though someone had repeatedly stomped on his testicles. "But that's absurd!"

"We must lure them back somehow," Piper said. "They'll go for it." He lifted a paper off a table. "Have you seen this?" The Port Royal Daily Gazette indicated that the pirate Gator Gar had been seen in the Swiftsure Tavern. "I'd prefer to find this information out from my people, not from the local paper."

Goblet grimaced. "A surprise to me, as well. I thought he was dead."

"Evidently not. He was brandishing the sword of Don Juan Perez de Guzman. Doesn't sound very dead to me," Mold said. "What's his real name again?"

"No one knows. Not only is he Gator Gar, he's also El Capitaine, La Salle, le Sage, and others. Buccaneers change their names more often than their clothes. He was one of Henry Morgan's captains until England banished the pirates in '85. We had a falling out with the Capitaine and helped the Spanish take him down in Yucatán bay with Laurens de Graaf."

"There's a bounty on him now, so it's only a matter of time before we bring him in," Tellam added.

"Yes, eight thousand from the investors in Port Royal. Add to twenty thousand from both the Dutch and the Spanish and he's worth a bloody fortune!" Goblet couldn't help but contemplate luxury retirement in a remote Jamaican villa.

Mold's eyes nearly sprung from his head. "Why so much?"

"They think he's the only one alive who knows the true identity of Roc Braziliano. The Spanish have a two-hundred-thousand-piece bounty on Braziliano, as well as one hundred thousand from the Dutch investors who lost huge when Braziliano disappeared with two-thirds of the loot from Morgan's Panama raid."

"So Gator Gar is the key to a potential bounty totaling over five hundred thousand pieces of eight?"

"Exactly," said Goblet.

"Why haven't the Brethren of the Coast collected on him? And why would no one know their real names? Someone knows; we just have to look in the right place." Mold turned to Piper. "Five hundred thousand could solve all our problems."

"More importantly, Henry Morgan's pirates were not only employed by King James, they followed him. That is something we cannot allow," Piper asserted.

"If he is here, it could be due to the storm," Mold said.

"I'm fairly certain he's gone," Goblet speculated. "A French brig was here after the storm and was released. Gator Gar sailed under l'Olonnais on the brig *La Lune de Miel*. The brig that left this morning was called *La Lune*. I request we send ships to intercept her and bring them in for questioning."

"Taylor, draft a charge for Admiral Goddam," Piper ordered.

"It's Taliare, sir."

"Whatever. Send *Relentless* and *Incorrigible* at once to capture the French brig *La Lune*. After the fayre, however; I want Big Dick there tonight as a show of force. He can depart in the morrow."

Goblet cleared his throat. "There is another pirate that needs to be dealt with, Captain Valentine."

Piper put up his hand. "Coggshall's problem not ours."

"Coggshall and others have invested substantially in Captain Valentine. Almost all of Port Royal's exports are going through his shipping company," Mold explained.

"That is my point." Goblet reddened slightly. "They've almost completely cornered the market. Not just in exports, but in the slave trade as well. Do we want Coggshall and Bleedin Art having control of so much of the Empire's money?"

"Coggshall and Captain Valentine will have to remain exactly where they are for now. It's a necessary evil." Piper looked over to the bodies being dragged from the gallows.

Smoke wafted about the room. Coggshall sunk into the seat behind his desk with a Spanish cigarro protruding from his mouth. Pikestaff joined him in an over-stuffed arm chair with Gibbet roosting on his shoulder. Agitated footsteps thudded towards the office and stopped just outside the door.

"Come in, Mr. Valentine." Coggshall's imperious tone was normally reserved for his son.

Art plowed through the door. He signaled his thug, Jag'd Jayne, to wait in the hallway before slamming the door. "It's Captain to you. And since when do you summon me like one of yer dogs?"

"Don't think me stupid, Art. I know what you were planning!" Coggshall snorted smoke from his nostrils.

"What are ya talking about?"

"Your man Jayne had all the strumpets in Port Royal under your protection while you were gone. Did you know that?"

"Aye. MacAskill told me. He said Burghill cut Katie the Swallower's tongue out just after I left."

"All the strumpets! Starr's, Cherry's, and mine. He had no right! Damn near started a war!"

"I'm one-third owner. I left him in charge and she *was* under my protection. One of my lieutenants fancies her."

"Well, thanks to him, not a single strumpet has been killed in Port Royal in months."

Art felt a sense of pride. "That's unheard of. The boy must have shown real metal."

"We had an agreement. I thought you and MacAskill were going to fix the syphilis problem. Now the bloody strumpets think they own the goddamn place!" Coggshall thrust a document in Art's face indicating a letter of reprisal.

"I have a personal guarantee from the Whigs that me business is paramount and must not be disrupted and *you* betrayed me."

Art glimpsed at Pikestaff, and then shot a glare at Coggshall. "It goes around here from time to time. I did everything like you said. Jayne ran things the way I told him. 'Tis business."

"He was thinking with his prick and you know it! Now you're gonna help me recover me losses. You're gonna set a trap for Gator Gar."

"Gator Gar? Desperate, ain't we?" Art's eyes narrowed. "Even if he was here, he's long gone now."

"I have it on good authority that he plans to come back for the other pikey."

"Then he's a fool."

"Tonight, I want all your men on guard. If Gator Gar shows up anywhere near the fayre, take him in alive!" Smoke practically billowed from Coggshall's ears and his face felt hot and sticky. "Pikestaff here is in charge of his capture."

Art's lips curled back, exposing his sizable teeth. "Pikestaff? He can't find the cunny without a map and a sponge."

Pikestaff jolted, accidentally toppling Gibbet off his shoulder. "Sorry, mate!" He made clicking and cooing noises to coax the parrot back up.

"True as that may be," Coggshall said sharply, motioning Pikestaff to stay put, "ya be old and tired. You no longer command the respect of the ranks. If you want any piece of the pie from now on, you'll mind your place." His finger wavered in Art's face. "Now, if you want to keep yer tired old bollocks, I suggest you go collect what's left of your men and get them situated in and around the Swiftsure." Coggshall leaned over his desk, dropping cigar ash everywhere. "This be your final warning. You belong to me and so do your men. Otherwise, Pikestaff here gets the dual honors of yer castration and replacement."

Art clenched his fist. "You can have him when his contract is up, but not before. I own one third, signed and legal. If you offered him a commission, then it comes out of yours."

"He don't get a commission and he answers to you until his contract is up. We're agreed?"

Pikestaff nodded.

"Now get out." Coggshall growled. "The sight of yer lanky old carcass makes me sick to me guts."

"Nothing worse than a soft pirate." Pikestaff patted Gibbet's head and made a cooing noise. "Is there, mate?"

Art swallowed hard and retreated through the door in silence. *If you wrong us, shall we not revenge?* A knot formed in his stomach and melancholia washed through him. Was he really so old and downtrodden? Art pondered. He'd sailed with famous pirates and shared in raids that had been commemorated in song. It was cruel to know that his wife would agree with Coggshall about minding his place.

Art and Jayne marched from the Swiftsure Tavern across the street to a black and red coach to climb aboard. Dr. MacAskill waited inside.

"Aye, I'll take all the blame. It was my call. I thought it's what you would have wanted," Jayne explained.

Art nodded, rather impressed in spite of himself. "You're not afraid to make decisions, I'll give ya that. A quality you're gonna need when I make you captain. Don't sweat it none. You did good."

"So, how are the whore saviors of the New World today?" MacAskill asked.

"Aw, cork it, Marcus! Get us the hell outta here." Art shuffled across the seat.

The doctor banged the side of the vehicle and they rolled along. "I tell you, it was a big mistake not doing them all when we had the chance."

"Coggshall hasn't got the men or the guts to take us on," Jayne said.

Art sneered. "That little bitch Pikestaff lined himself up to be Coggshall's number one. He thinks we're gonna answer to him when his contract's up."

MacAskill's face contorted into a half snicker. "Don't make me fuck'n laugh!"

"Do ya see me laughing?" Art massaged his knees. "They're setting a trap for Gator Gar and we're all supposed to show up."

"Gator Gar!" MacAskill roared. "What? They think they can cash in on Roc Braziliano?"

"Aye, that's the plan."

"Well, it's a big waste o'time. Roc Braziliano must surely be dead or Gator Gar would have cashed in on that bounty himself."

Art shrugged. "Even so, Gator Gar's long gone. He ain't stupid enough to stick around here. Not over a couple of pikeys."

Llewellyn
Dewar
GO
2015

The Poisoning

Cherry padded down the hall. She balanced a tray in her arms and stood outside the bedroom door. It was open a crack. The Capitaine lay beside Atia, who twitched from nightmares.

"Shhh. You are safe." He spoke softly, his mouth brushing against her lips.

"Liv?"

"I will find her. Try not to worry." He stroked her hair.

There was a time when Cherry would have given anything to be looked at the way he looked at the pikey girl. The look of unyielding love. It was back in '73 when she'd first met the Capitaine at Starr's Palace.

"I'm married," he said after their first sexual encounter.

Cherry was well aware of his wife. Rumors of Jacquotte Delahaye's fiery temper swept through the Caribbean like the tide. "To Jacquotte, I know. Don't worry lover, I'll never tell a soul. I don't want her mad at me."

His smoldering gaze snagged her straight away. "I want to see you again."

She smiled. "When?"

"Whenever I'm in town."

Her hand slid between his legs. "Now that's what I wanted to hear. I be getting kinda partial to this here organ."

"I'll see you when I'm in town, and I might ask a favor now and then."

There's always a catch, ain't there? When '78 rolled around, the Capitaine had been hired as a privateer to protect Port Royal. He lived in the city for almost five years. The sea occupied most of his time, but when he was in port they continued their affair and became good friends.

When the English made peace with the Spanish, the Capitaine resumed a life of pirating. Cherry soon learned that he disappeared at sea. She was shattered, not even able to look at the items he'd left behind in a secret compartment of her room at Starr's Palace. One day she decided it was high time she moved on. When she opened the loose floorboard beneath her bed, she saw gold bars and silver coins with a note:

> In case I don't come back for a while, take care of this for me. Use it to start your boutique, but don't overdo it. If you need anything, call on L.C. Baldran Shipping out of Cape Francois.
> You will always be my Cherry

Even in death, he laid it on thick! She now had enough to lease her boutique and establish her brothel. As it turned out, the Capitaine hadn't died. He paid her a visit soon after, looking for a hiding place. Cherry owed him a lot and she was grateful, but she never attained what she truly desired – his love. His exact words to her were: "I cannot love in the way that you want."

She took a deep breath to quell the stone rising in her throat. "Capitaine, it's time for her to eat. Doc's orders. Rise and shine, girly." Cherry entered. "I brought ya some too."

"*Merci. Ma chérie*, time to eat."

Atia stirred. "Any word?"

He slid pillows behind her until she could sit up. "We're going to get her back tonight. I promise." He took the tray to prepare a dose of laudanum.

"Ain't it a bit early for that?" Cherry gave him a nudge.

"Not for me."

She laughed.

"It's going to be a long night." He put a few drops on his tongue, cringed, and then passed the bottle to Cherry.

"Please and thank you." She took a few drops and winced at the bitterness.

Atia devoured the soup. "When are we leaving?" She took a mouthful of bread and eyed up the plate of apple tarts.

The Capitaine kissed her forehead. "After dark. Be patient."

"We're waiting to hear back from a friend," Cherry added, setting the bottle of laudanum on the table. She left the room to pace downstairs, unable to bear watching them. *This plan must work; it simply must.* She invested everything in her business. It was all she had. Staring out the window she brushed a couple of tears from her eyes. *I'd give a red-haired pikey to be with Mr. Binge right now!*

Around elevenses, Theodore Binge entered the Swiftsure Tavern. Everything was almost back to normal. A few tables and chairs were still being repaired, but no one would have suspected that the place had been on fire the night before. Binge wore a deep burgundy suit with black buckle shoes and held a pewter-tipped walking cane.

Behind the bar, Glenda polished the glasses with a rag. Her apprentice Nessie, a young Scottish girl, bled the tap to the large kegs.

"Grip it hard love!" Glenda instructed. "Give it a good yank!"

"Like trying to get it off, ya mean?"

"Naw, mo'like it's personal!"

Glenda turned to Binge.

"Good day, Glenda."

"A little early for you isn't it, Mr. Binge?"

"Just here to deliver a message. You haven't seen that creepy little Magott, have you?"

"Smell him is mo'like it! He's out back." She pointed. "Not the sort of company you used to keep."

Binge grinned. "The price of success, my dear." He straightened his collar. "Much obliged." He tipped his hat and moved coolly towards the patio.

Magott's voice traveled. "As fortunes come and fortunes go, I told ya I'd be back, didn't I?"

"Yeah, I hears ya, stick or have it?" one his thugs replied.

"Don't rush me." Magott frowned, eyeing his cards. "Stick."

Binge advanced leisurely, admiring the view of the harbor before stepping forth. "Mr. Magott, sir?"

"What do you want, Negro?"

"Sorry to disturb you at elevenses."

Magott ate his cheese and sausages. "Oh, it's you."

The two thugs glowered at Binge.

"Relax, gentlemen. We're business associates."

"What do you want?" Magott took a mouthful of wine.

Binge leaned over the table, his back to the thugs. "Excuse me, sir, but if you want first table in tonight's One and Thirty, you gotta pre-stake."

"Pre-what?" Magott revealed his yellow teeth. "What the bloody hell are ya saying?"

"Mr. Coggshall's rules, sir. He's calling tonight's stakes. He's afraid of dead beats at the big table with all the strangers in town. Are you in?" Binge glanced over the railing, his eyes bulged. "Wow, look at those tits!"

All three men got up and leaned over the barrier to ogle Lilly's bare breasts. She stood on the lower deck of the building next door.

Binge slipped five drops of poison into Magott's wine.

"My gawd!" One of the thugs leered. "They point up!"

Lilly drizzled olive oil on her skin and massaged it in.

Binge put five more drops into another mug.

"Oh, sweet Lordy!" the second thug exclaimed.

Lilly rubbed the oil around in a circular motion and Binge tainted the final cup.

Magott licked his lips. "Who is she?"

"That's one of the girls who'll be working the bar tonight. If you came here for a stiff drink, yer one letter off!"

Magott's attention was so focused on Lilly that he handed over a small bag of coins. "Put me down for the big table."

"This will definitely cover it, sir." Binge nodded, putting the coins in his pocket. "I'll reserve your favorite spot."

"And I want that little tart brought up here right now."

"Sorry, sir, she's one of Mr. Coggshall's girls. You'll have to ask him. I'm sure he'll be in a generous mood tonight."

"Leave them diddeys out sweetheart!" the first thug yelled.

Lilly glanced up, covered herself, and ran indoors.

Magott shook his head. "Little cock tease." He turned to Binge. "Piss off – it's elevenses!"

Binge tipped his hat. "'Til this evening Mr. Magott. Have a pleasant afternoon, gentlemen." He slipped back inside. "Have a pleasant afternoon, ladies." He tipped his hat to Glenda and Nessie before scurrying out the side entrance to the alley.

Binge hopped into his shimmering black carriage complete with a handsome steed named Pénombre. A few meters down the street, Lilly darted out of a pathway. He extended his hand to help her up.

"Did you do it?" she asked.

"Damn right. I got three of them! And I couldn't have done it without you." He took out the bag of coins. "The stupid arse even gave me these. You earned them!"

Lilly drummed her feet excitedly and stuffed the satchel down her bodice. "I can't believe it. We actually did it!"

"If it works, we'll do the rest of them tonight."

Lilly gave him a sultry gaze. "Was I ok?"

"Are you kidding? You were great. I'll be stiff for weeks thinking about it!"

"Not if I can help it." She lifted her skirt and shifted onto his lap before thrusting her tongue into this mouth.

Binge caught his breath while the carriage swerved. "What? Whoa!" He regained control of the reins and sped down Thames Street. She bounced up and down on his manhood until it grew painfully stiff. He scrambled to undo his trousers. Lilly thrust her eager wetness onto him and both of them released a loud sigh.

"Go down, Mr. Binge," she gasped, gyrating exuberantly.

"Can't, I'm driving."

"Down Queens, it's bumpier!"

Queens Street bustled with activity. Supplies were unloaded from the storehouses onto wagons and transported to the Merchant Exchange and all across the city. Many tradespeople made a good living including blacksmiths, coopers, carpenters, shipwrights, and sail makers.

Acting Lieutenant Governor Piper waved to the common people as his tour of the city continued. "Now this is what I like to see – order and stability."

"A peaceful transition, just as we planned." Magistrate Mold smiled smugly. "Where to next? The Fish Market or Turtle Crawls?"

Piper wrinkled his nose. "Both of them stink."

"We'll tour the Merchant Exchange."

Pedestrians scattered for cover as an uncontrollable carriage swerved around the corner. Everyone witnessed a pretty blond woman bobbing up and down on a black man's lap.

"Good God!" Piper stated. "Stop them! I want them arrested."

"Sir?" Tellam queried.

"It's hard to drive when you're doing it," Blower said. "I've tried."

"And the roads are a mess," the mayor added.

"They should be arrested!" Piper yelled.

“There’s no law against fornicating in a carriage or on a public street,” Tellam explained.

“Well, it’s a traffic violation at least.” Piper’s eyebrows furled. “Wait a minute that man is black! Surely that’s illegal?”

“No, sir,” Tellam said. “Mr. Binge is five-eighths black. He’s a landowner and has a white family, making him legally allowed to fornicate with a white woman in a carriage.”

“Well, it’s illegal *now*, damn it!” A look of putrescence set in on Piper’s face. “Jesus Christ, what is the world coming to?”

A copy boy dusted himself off and yelled, “nice ride, mate!” He limped to his stack of papers and gathered them. “Get yer Port Royal Daily Gazette, only a penny. Shipwreck survivor found alive! Read all about it! Care for a Port Royal Daily, Yer Lordship?”

“Ah, that’s showing initiative! Good for you, lad!” Mold tousled the boy’s hair.

Goblet removed coins from his pouch. “I’ve got a penny, kid.” He handed the boy the money and whispered instructions in his ear.

“Jolly good, sir!” The boy ran off up the street.

“Good form, Judge Gibble. Good form.” Piper patted him on the back.

“Anything for city spirit, sir.”

Magott
GO
2015

Worth Seven Years' Bad Luck

Inside a dark narrow hallway of the Black Dog Inn, two Red Royal guards gave each other peculiar looks. Loud panting and grunting transpired from the room they watched. A loud bang resounded, and then the thump and crash of something being knocked over.

Longstaff's yeoman marched down the hall and hammered on the door. "Captain Longstaff, sir? I have urgent orders."

"One minute," Longstaff called and a loud feminine moan continued. There was another loud thump and the door opened. Violante Hayze clung to Longstaff, her arms locked around his neck. She continued to vent all her sexual desires. He reached out his hand. "Pass it here."

Longstaff read the parchment swiftly and handed it back. "Give this to Mr. Fishhook immediately. Tell him I'm on my way." The door slammed shut. Vie's amorous wailing intensified and he held her against the wall, thrusting into her. The mirror beside them unhinged and shattered on the floor. *She's worth seven years of bad luck. Hell, she'd be worth seven years in a gibbet.*

Longstaff spun her around, pinioning her down on the bed. She was insatiable; he could feel her insides quake again hungrily, as she writhed and panted beneath him. Her tongue plunged into his mouth, her flavor sweet, like mint. He consumed her lips, losing himself in the moment before sliding off her and grabbing his clothes from the chair. "I have to leave in the morrow." Longstaff grabbed a bag of coins and set it on the bed table.

Vie sat up, folding her arms below her plump breasts. "Is that still all I am to you?"

Never in his life had he considered having only one woman until now. "There's enough here for six months' rent and provisions." He put on his boots and fixed his trouser legs. Her face flushed beautifully as she rose from the bed. "I want you to take some time off. No more working the streets."

Vie's eyes lit up. "Are you saying you want me to wait for you? Am I yer girl, Captain?" She groped between his legs and they kissed rapturously.

"Will you be at the Swiftsure tonight? I want to see you before I go."

"Aye, I'll be there." Vie beamed. "How long are you going for?"

"Not long." He caressed her face. "Promise me you'll stay off the streets and wait for me?"

"Forever and always, my love." She pressed her mouth to his.

The window of the upper room in the Anglican Church had a perfect view. The curtains to the room at the Black Dog Inn were not drawn when Longstaff entwined with his new love interest. Skean looked through his spyglass and jotted down several notes in his ledger. He bided his time, compiling evidence to later engage in blackmail.

"Excuse me, sir, are you Brother Gideon?" a boy began.

Skean looked over. "Why, yes I am, my boy. What can I do for you?"

"Justice Goblet asked me to give you this with his compliments." He handed over a Port Royal Daily Gazette bearing the headline: Survivor of *Aeolus* Shipwreck Found Unconscious in Folly Bay.

"Thank you, son. Very kind of you to deliver this." Skean set the paper on his desk.

"Aye, sir. He said to give it straight to you."

"Indeed." Skean reached into his pocket and withdrew two silver coins. "Here. Perhaps in the future we may count on your services again?"

"Thank you, sir!" The boy smiled and ran off.

Skean took one last look through the spyglass. Longstaff's liaison had finished, and the young woman got dressed. Skean skimmed the gazette article. *Excellent. Perhaps the crewman can answer a few questions.* He stuffed the paper into his ledger. *Hopefully he hasn't blabbed. Technically, I don't exist.* Always a strange concept to grasp; each new assignment required the utmost discretion and tact.

A shiny black carriage turned onto Water Lane and pulled up behind Cherry Red's Boutique. Pénombre squealed, annoyed at the passionate moaning. Binge and Lilly were wrapped around each other, rocking until both released a loud sigh.

Lilly climbed off Binge's lap, staggering down to smooth out her dress and fan her face. "Thank you for the ride, Mr. Binge."

"Thank you, my dear!" Binge hopped down to adjust his collar and trousers. "And I must say I enjoyed the pleasure of your company immensely." He suddenly thought, *I hope the girls weren't out shopping today!*

"The pleasure was all mine, sir." Lilly winked and they ventured into the kitchen.

Inside the boutique, the Capitaine sharpened his stiletto, dagger, and cutlass against a block, while Cherry cleaned and loaded pistols.

Cherry looked up. "Well?"

Lilly nodded. "We did it."

"We certainly did." Binge's eyebrows peaked. "We got three of them. Now we wait for news."

"Sander said it should look like scarlet fever," the Capitaine said, his attention on the knives. "A few hours, maybe longer?"

Two short knocks came from the black door, and Strangewayes entered with another sign rolled up under his arm.

"Do you have a crystal ball I should know about?" Binge asked.

"I caught a glimpse of you turning onto Queens. My apothecary has a perfect view, perhaps too perfect at times." He gazed at the weapons. "You look like you're ready for a war."

The Capitaine looked up. "War it is, Doctor. We must prepare for anything."

"Quite. This complicates things, however." Strangewayes unrolled the broadside:

Gator Gar wanted Alive for Piracy, Sodomy, and Murder
50,000 pieces of eight

"Another one?"

"Hey, you're worth a lot," Binge exclaimed.

Cherry's eyes narrowed. "That *is* a lot."

"Ah, water off a duck's back," the Capitaine scoffed. "They want you to turn on me."

"Tempting, to say the least." Binge grinned. "Did I say that out loud?" *If I haven't turned him in over the last thirty years, I'm not gonna start now. But shit, he's worth a lot.*

"It is meant to make us turn on each other, which we mustn't do," Strangewayes reminded. "The rumor going around is that you left on a French brig this morning."

"Why do they want him so bad?" Lilly asked.

"The Whigs see Henry Morgan's men as followers of King James. Since you are a wanted man, Capitaine, I'm afraid you'll have to stay behind."

The Capitaine clenched his fist. "*Va te faire foutre*!"

"I was so looking forward to him seeing me in action tonight." Cherry pouted, pushing her way onto the Capitaine's lap. "I want him to come."

"We can disguise him," Lilly suggested.

"What a good idea! I got the perfect one." Cherry whispered in Lilly's ear.

"This I gotta see!" said Binge.

"Oh well." The doctor shrugged. "I lived to see sixty; that's an achievement."

It was late afternoon. Skean strolled along High Street and turned left at the Admiralty Court. The sun baked the bricks and stones at Fort Carlisle. Even the water seemed ridiculously hot and great beams of light burst against the wrought iron gate leading to the infirmary. Skean patted his forehead and followed the path inside, where it felt slightly cooler. He swiftly scanned the rooms until he came across a battered patient.

"Can I help you, Brother?" a thin, balding doctor began. "Good Lord, are you quite well?" His eyes paused on the bandaged arm.

Skean smiled, detecting a strong scent of rum. "Yes, thank you. Thames Street is a right bloody mess; I shall certainly speak to city officials about compensation." He looked to the *Aeolus* survivor. "Oh, the poor fellow. What an ordeal he must have been through. I'm Brother Gideon. How is the patient doing?"

"It's in God's hands now. He could go at any time."

"Has he been able to say anything?" Skean pressed.

"Poor fellow has been unable to speak since he was brought in. I've been asked to get a statement out of him, but so far nothing."

"I'll sit with him a bit, then, if you don't mind?"

The doctor leapt at the opportunity. "Not at all. I'll stretch my legs." He staggered down the hall and into the sunshine.

Kneeling beside the patient, Skean ensured that his broken arm was comfortably situated. He took a vial of hartshorn from his pocket and twisted the cork with his teeth. He placed it beneath the survivor's nose, causing him to stir.

The officer jolted awake, aggravated and gasping for breath. His eyes were bloodshot and wild. He glanced around frantically. "W-what?"

Skean spoke in a soothing tone. "Take it easy. Everything is going to be fine." He re-corked the vial slipping it back into his pocket.

"The pain," the officer wheezed. "So much pain."

"I can give you something for pain." Skean pulled out another small bottle from his pocket. "What can you remember about the voyage?"

"Voyage?"

"Yes. Where was the Irish family going?"

"We was to meet a ship in Port Morant; they were getting off there. A doctor paid for them. Then we was to sail for Port Royal."

Skean uncorked the bottle. "Which doctor?"

"I never knew his name."

"Were they indentured to him? What did he want them for?"

"The pain. Please?"

"In a minute. What did he bring the Irish over for?"

"I heard some of them say they was starting a colony, a Pagan colony." The officer looked up suddenly. "Say, I know you, you was on board."

Skean stuffed the bottle into the officer's mouth and watched as he jerked and twitched for about ten seconds before drawing a last breath. "Dear Lord, please accept this gentle soul into your warm embrace."

Violante Hayze

Time to Up the Stakes

Glenda reached for her rag to polish more glasses. Occasionally she glimpsed Magott and his lackeys. They sat at the table in the far corner playing cards. Magott coughed and scratched his neck. His men looked pale and blotchy. They seemed to get worse with each passing minute. She snickered to herself as Magott toppled onto the floor. He doubled over and a burbling noise escaped his throat before he vomited down the front of his suit.

Glenda turned to Nessie. "Quick, you better go get Dr. Strangewayes. He could use a good laugh."

"Aye, I reckon yer right." Nessie took off out the front.

Glenda watched for another minute or so before deciding that she should inform Coggshall of the situation. She exited towards the Wherry Bridge. A crowd gathered to watch the Le De'va Band perform the classic tune, "Wine Does Wonders". Overseeing the entertainment was Jarvess Coxenspit, otherwise known as Monsieur De'va. He owned the local haberdashery and two peacocks that drove his neighbors mad with their screeching. His attire for the evening consisted of an enormous dark curly wig, gold satin waistcoat with matching breeches, white leggings, and shiny black shoes.

Glenda was a frequent customer of De'va's Delightful Haberdashery. She had a substantial collection of fine hats and assorted frilly accoutrements decorating her room above the Swiftsure. Hers was a simple, homely space, part of her compensation for being the head barmaid for the past nine years. She pressed through the crowd, watching Coggshall and Burghill chat up potential buyers. *They'd tug it off with both hands to make a sale!*

"I promised you the best slaves in the Americas, and I always keep me promises," Coggshall boasted.

"I thought you lost them all?" a buyer asked.

"Four hundred or so. You didn't think I'd risk my best stock to Bleedin Art and a couple of old caravels, did you?" Coggshall motioned to two new Mediterranean galleys rowing in off of Fort James. "May I present the two newest members of me fleet: *Friendship* and *Companion*." Everyone gawked at the oddly-shaped vessels with angled sails and long oars manned by slaves heaving in unison.

Burghill fluffed up his doublet. "Similar to the Barbary slave ships but with larger lateen sails. Up to thirty guns on each as well, and a greater capacity for crew and slaves. They fit five hundred easy. Half rowing, half below deck lying horizontally for maximum capacity. Sustainable for short distances."

"I like to keep me best at a safe two hundred," Coggshall said. "I guarantee you, gentlemen, on those ships is the finest stock of Negro slaves I've ever had. More expensive, aye, but well worth the investment."

Glenda snuck a word in, "Mr. Coggshall, sir?"

"What d'ya want, wench?"

"It's that rancid little Magott, sir. He's puking his guts all over the tavern."

"Again?" Burghill grimaced.

Glenda already dreaded the clean-up job. It wasn't the first time Magott had made a mess. Whenever he came into a bit of money he'd get intoxicated, puke, and then keel over. He looked awfully sick however, perhaps this was the last time he'd sully her tavern.

After gathering supplies, Dr. Strangewayes followed Nessie to the Swiftsure Tavern. The fayre had begun. Merchants set up their stands and colorful banners and lanterns decorated the street.

"Right this way, Doctor, quickly!" Nessie ushered him through.

"Yes, I don't want to miss this." He'd been waiting for this day for many years and found it difficult to contain his delight. Magott was crumpled on the floor beside his thugs. "Oh my goodness me, don't we look like shit?" The doctor's hand covered a laugh.

"What is it? What've they got?" Nessie asked.

Strangewayes paused. "Looks to me like scarlet fever."

Magott struggled to speak. "Do something, help me, damn it."

"Sorry, Mr. Magott. There's no cure."

Magott writhed in a furious frenzy, blood spewing from his mouth onto the floor. "You did this, ya quack!"

"What the bloody hell is going on in here?" Coggshall approached, but kept his distance.

"It looks to me like scarlet fever. They should be quarantined immediately," said Strangewayes.

"Find Valentine's surgeon before you make any judgments," Coggshall insisted.

"Well, whatever they got, it's bad for business. Get them outta here!" Burghill pointed to a couple of slaves. "You there, get them out of here."

"Take them upstairs to Magott's room." Coggshall hid his mouth and nose with a handkerchief.

"They must be kept away from other people." The doctor watched as the slaves lifted Magott and his men and carried them up. He addressed Coggshall, "Everyone who came in contact with them should also be quarantined. Those slaves have been exposed; they'll need to come with me."

Coggshall yelled out, "someone find Doc MacAskill and clean up this mess! We have a party tonight, damn it!"

Strangewayes proceeded upstairs where the slaves dropped Magott on his bed and the thugs on the floor.

"A bit poetic, isn't it?" The doctor smiled while Magott vomited more blood, succumbing to the poison. The two thugs already died. The doctor clapped his hands together and looked at the soon-to-be-freed slaves. "So, who wants to leave town?"

Strangewayes guided them down the servant staircase that led to a side door into the alley leading to Thames Street. The deep auburn glow of the sunset cast the city in partial shadow. Vendors lined the streets, selling produce, parrots, turtles, rum, food, and articles of clothing. The crowd thickened.

The doctor directed Coggshall's slaves to an unmarked delivery car where Gladstone napped on the driver's seat.

"Please take this lot to the Snapper Shack right away."

Gladstone jolted awake and the slaves filed into the carriage.

"If anyone stops you, tell them that these people are under quarantine for possible scarlet fever. I know it's not part of the plan."

Gladstone rubbed his eyes and smacked the doctor's back. "Don't you worry, Doc, improvisation is me best quality. I'll be right back." He snapped the reins.

Binge returned home to find one of his stepdaughters, Henrietta, crocheting a pillowcase beside the bay window in the sitting room. She gazed out at the sea view, her fair hair loose over her shoulders. Today she wore a blue bodice with matching skirt and shiny laced boots. Her eyes shifted at his arrival.

“There you are.” She glared at him. “You weren’t by any chance giving a young blond girl a ride down Queens this morning, were you?”

“Listen, you have to leave right away.”

“What?” She rose from her seat. “Why?”

“There’s a scarlet fever outbreak. I need you and your sister to get out of town tonight. Where is she?”

Henrietta’s eyes widened, and she reached for his hand. “Scarlet fever! What do we do?”

“Everything will be fine. Where is Gerty?”

“And what did you get up to this morning?” Gertrude, another beauty, entered the room. She wore a frilly gown that matched the pale-yellow color of her hair. “Another one of your strays?” She stood with her hands on her hips.

He turned to put his arm around her. “I need you both to go to the house at South Point Lagoon. You’re leaving tonight – there’s a boat waiting.”

“The lagoon house?” Henrietta’s nose wrinkled. “It stinks!”

“That’s a week’s sail, are you mad?” Gertrude moaned.

“I know it stinks.”

Gertrude’s eyes narrowed to defiant slits. “Why aren’t you coming?”

“I have to stay and help the Chief Surgeon.”

“There’s no way you’re getting me to that disgusting island!” Henrietta scowled. “The lagoon’s full of caiman.”

“Scarlet fever, my fanny! You and Strangewayes are up to something.” Gertrude snarled. “What’s going on? Tell us the truth.”

“Well.” Binge pondered for a moment. *Why is it I can pull off swindling cards, but I can never fool these two?* He shrugged. “Coggshall plans to kill Cherry Banks’s girls, so me and the good doctor are on our way to try and kill him, Burghill, Art, Jayne, Pikestaff…”

The sisters looked at each other briefly and left the room.

“We should take high collar bodices,” Gertrude suggested.

“Hmm…cloaks too,” Henrietta added.

Binge wiped his brow. “That went better than expected.” After kissing them goodbye, he watched them hastened away in a carriage before going upstairs to get ready. Donning a purple suit with intricate stitching and gold buttons, the finishing touch was a black velvet vest that concealed small, sharp knives within the lining. He poked his arms through a fur overcoat and grabbed his sword, artfully disguised as a walking stick. "Time to up the stakes."

Carriages lined up, taking turns depositing fayregoers in front of the Swiftsure Tavern. One carried Bleedin Art and Dr. MacAskill. Art grunted, straining his knees as he slid across the seat. "Bloody hell! What am I supposed to do, jump?"

Scarcliff leapt down to lend a hand.

"You just wanna be carried like a babe on yer ma's fuck'n shoulder!" MacAskill barked, sliding to the edge, unable to go any further. "Oi, Starfish, get over here!"

Scarcliff helped the doctor down as well.

"Park it and man the perimeter," Art instructed.

"Aye," Jayne replied and snapped the reins.

Art and MacAskill entered and were met by Nessie.

"Doc MacAskill, sir," she said.

MacAskill ogled the girl. "Aye, lass."

"Mr. Coggshall needs ya."

"What's he need me for? He's got plenty o'strumpets!"

"There's sick men upstairs."

MacAskill elbowed Art. "Sick men in a tavern; who'd have guessed? You coming?"

"Nay, I've gotta unload a twenty-pounder." Art headed off towards the curtained toilette area.

MacAskill followed Nessie up the stairs, admiring her swaying hips. They walked along the second floor corridor to a room where the remains of Magott and his men lay in a mess of their own blood.

Nessie covered her mouth and turned away.

"Hmm." MacAskill cleared his throat and grabbed a poker from the fireplace. He pried open Magott's mouth and depressed the blue tongue with a small shucking knife. "Christ! And I thought he was ugly when he was alive!" Using the poker, he turned the corpse's neck side to side. "Who left him here?"

"Sir?" Nessie looked as though she were ready to faint.

"He didn't just lie down peacefully on the bed to die, lass. Who put him here?"

"They was brought in by Mr. Coggshall's slaves. They left him there." She covered her mouth with a bar rag.

MacAskill nodded and wiped off his shucking knife. "Right. Where's Mr. Coggshall?"

"In the Red Room, sir."

"Don't say nothing to nobody about nothing."

"Sure won't." Nessie gave him a brief smile.

"Thank ya, lass." The doctor patted her bottom, sending her on her way. *I'll have to come back later for the full tour!* Her tantalizing hips disappeared down the hallway.

Art stood outside the Red Room and took a deep breath. He paused to look at himself in the hall mirror. *Not exactly ship of the line, are you?* His jacket hung off him like a curtain. He listened in as Piper declared, "I've just been informed that the Chief Surgeon has closed the auction."

"Bloody Strangewayes," Coggshall yelled. "He's on the laudanum again!"

Art reluctantly knocked on the door. *'Tis gonna be as fun as a bad case of lice!*

"Come!" Coggshall barked.

Art entered. Normally reserved for exotic entertainment and Morris dancing, tonight the Red Room was a temporary sanctuary to Piper and Mold, who were accompanied by Taliare and two Red Royals. They sat on a couch of thick dark taffeta with embroidered flowers. Bright lanterns hung on the red walls. Piper and Mold sipped brandy in dainty gold-rimmed glasses wearing their ridiculous wigs. Art glared at Pikestaff, who sat like a watch dog in the corner.

"First the hurricane, now scarlet fever. I tell you, it's God's will," Piper insisted.

Coggshall paced back and forth. "Everything's God to you people, ain't it? God's will. God knows all. God, me wig itches!"

Piper glared at Art. "Mr. Coggshall tells me you sent thirteen merchantmen and two escorts to protect the Duchess of Albemarle and her entire fortune."

"That's right," Art said. "She sailed in May."

Mold aggressively advanced. "Did it not occur to you that those resources could be better used in the service of Port Royal? How are we going to make up the lost revenue?"

Art stared daggers. "She and her late husband were major

landowners. They helped found this city. There wouldn't be a Port Royal if it weren't for them."

"They were supporters of King James and are enemies of England!" Mold spat.

Art couldn't believe his own ears. "Enemies of England?"

"You had no right, just because they were friends of yours," Piper said.

"I had every right," Art argued. "She paid for it!"

"Well, fortunately the authorities have arrested the duchess and seized her fortune. Justice has been served upon her." Mold's superior tone beat Art down even more.

"The estate is now safely in the hands of the Orange Party where it belongs," Piper said nonchalantly. "Which brings us to the matter of your taxes."

"What taxes?" Art's face darkened.

"Your income tax will increase by fifteen percent, effective immediately, to cover the losses stemming from your bad judgment." Piper took a sip of brandy.

Art choked back his contempt. "Fifteen percent, eh?"

"Yes. Five percent to His Majesty's government, and ten percent to the local government. Us." Mold smiled.

"How about zero for King William? He can bend over and kiss his own hairy Dutch arse. You can have your ten percent; that's what Dewar got anyway. You can give *King Vilhelm* five percent out of yers."

Piper and Mold looked at each other, amused. "I believe you misunderstand, Captain. This is an *increase* of fifteen percent. You will now be paying twenty-five percent directly to us," Piper clarified.

Art clenched his fists. "You ain't getting twenty-five percent of nothing but the blade of me sword! You come in here like Oliver fuckin' Cromwell with your fancy ships and your fancy wigs with no sodding clue how things work on the front line and start mucking with everything ya don't understand!"

Piper's face ignited to a deep crimson. "You and Coggshall have mismanaged this city to the point of gross negligence! Now this scarlet fever outbreak will bankrupt us for good."

Coggshall waved his fist. "Nobody's saying scarlet fever till we hear back from Doc MacAskill. This fayre is saving our bloody arses, and I won't hear another word about shutting it down."

“Frankly, it’s not up to you,” Piper argued.

“What happens if you cancel the fayre, dullard? Canceling the fayre will kill this city. You stop the slave trade and everything stops, water shipments, trade, and city maintenance. And, what will the people do if that happens? I tell you, they won’t stand for it.” Coggshall pointed through the small widow to the festivities below. “Take it all away from them and those people out there and meself too will take that colossal dead sheep of a wig off yer empty noggin and shove it so far up your pipe, you’d look like a curly gray comet soaring over the Palisadoes!” Coggshall gasped for air as the blood vessel in his neck threatened to explode.

A knock came at the door and MacAskill walked in, followed by the thug, Stinger.

“What now, malaria!?” Coggshall roared.

MacAskill closed the door. “They show all the symptoms of scarlet fever, I’ll admit.”

“Damn it,” Mold said.

Coggshall waved his hand. “It don’t change a thing.”

“Yes it does. A scarlet fever outbreak?” Piper foamed at the mouth.

MacAskill folded his arms. “I said they have all the symptoms of scarlet fever. I didn’t say it *was* scarlet fever. When did Magott first get sick?”

Art looked at him. “A few hours ago.”

The doctor snickered. “Then it’s the bloody scarlet fever outbreak of the fuck’n century.”

“What do you mean?” Mold asked.

“This strain of scarlet fever may have had help.”

Piper’s eyes narrowed. “You suspect treachery?”

MacAskill bypassed Piper and went to Art. “It could be poison.”

“How will we know?”

“He was apparently carried in by Coggshall’s slaves. Find out if they show any symptoms. I’d wager they don’t.”

“So, this could be a deliberate attack from one of the anti-slavery movements?” Piper said.

Art’s mouth curled into a maniacal grin. “Well, we don’t all play nice out here, Mr. Whig.”

“I need an accurate count of how many slaves were dead and dying when they arrived.” MacAskill looked at Coggshall.

"All the records are on me desk. We'll reconvene in ten minutes in me office." Coggshall wiped his forehead. "I need a bloody drink!"

"We'll bring along with the chief surgeon who thinks it's scarlet fever," Piper said.

"We'd be obliged if you left your dog behind." Mold pointed at Pikestaff.

"Then you do the same." Coggshall pointed at Taliare. "Same goes for the fancy red Borgias here too."

"Fine," Mold said. "Ten minutes."

"Wait downstairs with the boys," Art said to Pikestaff. "And you," he turned to Stinger, "find Strangewayes and bring him to Coggshall's office."

Which Way She Blows

A beam of evening sunshine intruded through the cracked window of the uppermost bedroom at the Crooked Compass Tavern. Strumpet Katie Evans lay on a small hay-stuffed mattress atop a rope support. She held her face and rocked herself gently, releasing a moan. Wiping away a few tears, she rolled over when Sierra Lee entered with a bottle of laudanum.

Katie snatched the medication. *About bloody time, I only had my tongue cut out!*

"Sorry Katie," Sierra Lee said. "Thought I'd just let you rest."

Katie managed to get a quarter of the tincture down her throat before it was taken away and prepared properly.

"You remember what Doc MacAskill said? If ya drink it all, you'll get sick again." Sierra Lee diluted the mixture in water, added a cube of sugarloaf and stirred it with a spoon. "Remember, you gotta rinse with salt water too."

Katie massaged her head and continued rocking. Her mouth throbbed fiercely.

Sierra Lee handed over the laudanum concoction.

After gulping back the mixture, Katie raised her thumb.

Mina Jacobs entered the room, teeming with self-importance. "Ya better give her lots of that because she's workin' tonight."

Katie raised her thumb sarcastically.

Sierra Lee looked mortified. "Doc MacAskill said she weren't to get up for days, weeks maybe."

Mina waved her hand. "Not my fault. Coggshall says she's upstairs in the booths with the other strumpets."

Sierra Lee shook her head. "What an arsehole!"

Katie raised her thumb again and the pair started to laugh. What started as a light chuckle turned into hysterics.

"Get her going before I have her flogged," demanded Mina. "And *yer* supposed to be on Thames Street. Now come on, move it!" She clapped her hands before slamming the door.

Both Katie and Sierra Lee forked their fingers. "You was born in the outhouse, Mina!"

Katie's lips curved into an evil grin. She grabbed the laudanum bottle and finished it off before rising to get dressed.

"Shit, you weren't supposed to drink it all!" Sierra Lee rose to leave. "I'll see ya there, then."

Katie signaled with her thumb again before braiding her hair. She slipped into a light blue petticoat and matching bodice, accented with yellow lace. Catharina had given it to her as a farewell gift. After tonight, she wouldn't see Cat or Nat again. After lacing up her boots, she stomped downstairs. *Fine. Time to get on with it!*

On the porch of the Thames Street side of the tavern, Mina and other strumpets flaunted their curves to passers-by.

"Didn't take her long to bounce back," Mina said.

Katie came down the porch steps.

"Oi! Out and about already?" another strumpet heckled. "Might want to avoid polishing for a spell."

"The punishment fits the crime as they say," Mina bellowed. "Serves her right for wagging her tongue where it don't belong."

Katie tried to ignore their existence. The laudanum made her sway as she walked. She smirked and shot her middle finger into the air. She advanced to the Swiftsure Tavern.

"Oi, strumpet!" Mina yelled. "They're all calling you Mute Katie now!"

Well, how ironic, I used to sing. People called me Songbird and I was damn good at it, too. Times do change.

In Ligania, Governor Dewar sat on the stone patio of his oceanside retreat. He listened to Lord Llewellyn's daughter pluck away at a lute, accompanied by the soothing drawl of the ocean sweeping against the jagged rocks. Major Paine, Llewellyn, and Sleemans sat with him, drinking large quantities of Madeira wine. Dewar raised his cup. "It's with heartfelt emotion of some sort, and gratuitous sadness, that I announce the retirement of Port Royal's oldest living privateer – Major Thomas Paine."

They all clapped.

"Hear, hear!" Llewellyn cheered. "Just in time for war with France, he knows when to bow out."

Dewar gulped back the wine. "Indeed."

"The French must be breathing a sign of relief."

"That's 'sigh', knot-head!" Dewar slapped Llewellyn's back.

"He's retiring before he becomes Colonel Paine. How long were you privateering, Major?"

"Thirty-nine years, sir."

"Wow! Thirty-nine years. You are old!"

"But you don't look a day over seventy," Llewellyn added.

Paine took a sip of wine. "I hope not, considering I'm fifty-seven."

"Way to go, mutton mast!" Dewar smacked Llewellyn's shoulder. "Sorry, Major, he's got his ballast aloft."

Paine laughed. "Aye, sir."

"Aye. Thirty-nine years of devoted service to our mighty city, now safely in the hands of the Dutch. There's neither a pirate nor buccaneer who doesn't know and fear the word Paine!" Dewar raised his half-empty glass.

Llewellyn belched. "Hear, hear!"

A slave flipped an hourglass and rang a bell seven times.

"See?" Dewar rose from his seat and entered the dining area. "You won't catch me getting one of those new-fangled clocks. Completely unreliable and bad for the slave trade!"

The inside of the house was luxuriously appointed, with plush red draperies, ornate pillars, and dark walnut furniture. Slaves set large trays of fruit, bread, cheese, and a main course of roasted pheasant on the banquet table.

"Ah. I see Monsieur De'va is missing another bird!" Llewellyn snickered. He turned to his daughter. "Come along, Laura."

"Yes, Papa." She set down the lute and came in.

Dewar, now very drunk, pulled out a chair and collapsed.

"Shouldn't we wait a bit longer?" Llewellyn whispered. "Is your wife not joining us?"

"Nay." Dewar removed a letter from his dinner jacket. "Not according to her latest tantrum ultimatum."

The letter read:

> Dorcas, you are a bumbling pillock of a man with all the charm and determination of a clay-brained codpiece. I wash my hands of you. I am leaving Port Royal and you won't see me again. The children are your problem now, you errant, beslubbering, nincompoop! Margaret.
>
> PS, you won't find Daddy's money, I got to it first!

Llewellyn's mouth dropped open. "She knows about the codpiece?"

"She didn't even have the guts to face me." Dewar finished off the wine and signaled for another. "Damn it! Why did she do this? Think of my image!" His head rolled back. He looked at the mural on the ceiling – a customized rendition of Michelangelo's *Creation of Adam*. God, of course, bore Dewar's likeness, and Adam too displayed a resemblance to Dewar.

"Well, according to this, you're a beslubbering nincompoop!" Llewellyn continued.

"Not out loud, you frothy nut-hook!"

His friend shrugged and passed the note back. "Not to worry. I'm sure she'll be back."

"After all I gave her! All those years and four – five reasonably tolerable children!" Dewar staggered to the window. "It's because I had her flogged, I'll bet." He sighed. "Truly, I thought she'd be aroused."

Major Paine tucked into the pheasant. "Trouble at home, Your Lordship?"

"Yes. Seems I'm exiled from Port Royal. You may have noticed, Major!"

"Apologies, sir," Paine said.

"She said she wanted to try new things." Dewar held out his cup and a male slave poured the wine. Impatiently Dewar grabbed the decanter and shooed the slave away. "If I had known what she meant, it would be a very different fish in the kettle."

"Women!" Llewellyn sat up straight. "If they didn't have their frocks in a knot about something they'd have nothing at all."

"I take offense to that," Laura piped up.

"Oh, piss off! It's not like I said cunt or anything!"

"Papa! My word!" Laura's face flashed red.

"Don't talk to your daughter like that!" Lady Llewellyn threw a crab apple at her husband's head. *Smack!*

Llewellyn rubbed his temple and downed a goblet of wine. "See what I mean?"

Dewar lifted his cup high in the in the air, spilling half its contents. "Tonight's fowl is in honor of our guest. I hope it's to your liking, Major…*Paine*."

Paine cleared his throat and took a sip of wine. "A bit more fanciful than a seaman like me is used to, sir, but I'll manage."

"Yes, indeed." Dewar hiccoughed. "So's a trough." He swaggered back to the table. "I'd like to thank Major Paine for his help, along with Captain Longstaff, for evacuating our families, although Dick couldn't make it this evening."

Llewellyn tried to stand up, but instead fell back into his seat and massaged the tuft of hair on the back of his head.

"Yes, here's to Big Dick and Major Paine! Gotta love Dick! Now there's a real leader, a man of action and principle, a man who's not afraid to get drunk."

"I just wish I'd been notified a bit sooner of our unexpected departure." Dewar gave Paine a rueful look.

"Yes." Sleemans suddenly spoke after swallowing a wedge of mango. "Last month would have been ideal."

"The Whigs had all communications cut off," Paine defended, loading his plate with cheese and barley bread. "There was no way to get word out."

"Nobody had a pigeon?" Sleemans retorted.

"All was under control," Paine replied.

"Well, what I want on the option is tables!" Dewar waved his finger at the major. "Table one, getting my city back! Table two, how are we going to get Port Royal back?" He laid across the armrests with his bottom protruding beneath him.

Paine tilted his head to look Dewar in the eye. "For now, wait for news from Longstaff. He knows the Brethren of the Coast are watching. I promise you, he won't cock it up."

"No, Big Dick never cocks up!" Dewar slurred.

Llewellyn raised his goblet. "That's right; you can't go wrong with Big Dick at your back! There's a real leader, a man who's not afraid to stick it out. Hear! Hear!"

Dewar forked his fingers at Llewellyn. "I was invoking sarcasm."

Llewellyn rose and his legs gave way. "I've injected it myself from time to time!" He looked at everyone blankly and turned to face Port Royal. "Wow, you can smell it from here!"

"But how do we know?" Dewar flailed his arms and legs like a turtle trying to flip itself over. A male slave approached and reluctantly helped him into his chair. "Ah, thank you, Margaret." Dewar fondled the slave's bottom. "As I was saying, how do we know when to make our move?"

"It's Port Royal." Llewellyn shrugged, slipping into a stupor. "Just wait to see which way she blows."

M.E. '15

Walls Have Ears, Doors Have Eyes

A refreshing breeze came from the water, diffusing the intense heat of the day. The brilliant orange sunset cast Port Royal into a mantle of light. Waves of fayregoers crowded the streets and filled the Wherry Bridge. Live entertainment and hundreds of vendors enthralled the masses.

From the alley door of Cherry Red's Boutique, Capitaine la Roche emerged dressed in a dark suit with a tri-cornered hat. A false nose and a stringy ginger beard stuck to his face. Still injured from the shipwreck, he assisted Atia Crisp into Dr. Strangewayes's enclosed delivery carriage. She wore a simple cotton nightdress that clung to her curves, giving la Roche an eyeful.

"Thank ya." Atia flipped her long red hair over her shoulder before massaging her ribs.

"*Je t'en prie.*" He flushed, draping her in a knitted blanket. "You are welcome. Don't worry about anything. Try to stay comfortable." La Roche climbed into the driver's seat and caught his breath.

Lilly Waters wore a pink silk skirt and cream bodice with gold buttons. She sat down next to Atia and withdrew a small brandy bottle from the bodice. Both girls took a generous mouthful.

La Roche steered the horse forward a few feet to keep lookout. He glanced back at them. "Not too much of that, uh? You need to keep your wits about you." Lilly took another sip before he reached back for the bottle. "That's enough! Give me that."

Lilly surrendered it and gave him a dirty sneer. "Oh, fine."

He turned back to the street and finished the brandy. Another delivery carriage neared, driven by Miles Gladstone, Dr. Strangewayes's assistant, who tipped his hat to them. "Ok, this is us." La Roche snapped the reins and they drove up a lively Thames Street. They followed Gladstone to a busy loading bay just off Honey Lane. In a dark stall, la Roche stopped to observe. People bound in chains were dragged off the slave ships.

"What is this?" he muttered.

"The slave fayre, Capitaine." Lilly climbed through the front window on to the driver's seat beside him.

Gladstone approached with Strangewayes. “Aye. To boost support for the slave trade they turned it into a fayre. Ships have been arriving all week from the Americas with dealers and buyers.”

“They’re awaiting the slave ships,” Strangewayes added. “Two of which are overdue and presumed lost in the storm.”

“Lost?” Lilly was horrified. “How many people?”

The doctor shook his head. “Hundreds.”

Lilly and Atia shared a sickened glance.

“It’s not only the driving force behind the economy, one’s status in society is determined by one’s property, slaves included.” Strangewayes snarled. “Our species has and always will be the most loathsome of creatures.” He gazed at Lilly and extended his arm. “With noted exceptions, of course. Shall we, my dear?”

Lilly took his hand and hopped down.

Strangewayes examined la Roche’s costume. “I didn’t know I employed any Rabbi carriage drivers. I approve of your attire, Capitaine.”

La Roche scratched his chin. It had been many years since he had a beard. “First time for everything.”

At the Swiftsure entrance a wherryman’s carriage pulled up, dropping off Violante Hayze. She wore a new dress of rich plum. Gathered panels cascaded over the underskirt, and the gold-buttoned bodice had frilled sleeves. Her dark hair hung in ringlets. She waved to Lilly and the doctor.

Strangewayes offered Vie his arm. “I must say, both of you look ravishing!”

Vie felt her face redden. “Evening, Doctor.”

He escorted them inside. “If you’ll excuse me ladies, duty calls.” Strangewayes smiled before climbing the staircase.

“Whoa! Where’d ya get the fancy threads?” Lilly asked.

“I went to Annabelle at the Merchant Exchange.”

“It’s beautiful!”

“Thanks. You look beautiful yourself.”

Lilly’s face lit up and she leaned in. “So’s it really that big?”

“Biggest white one I ever seen!”

They both giggled.

“I have to go find Nat and Cat,” Lilly said. “I’ll catch you up later.” She kissed Vie’s cheek and took off.

Vie searched around to find a couple of Cherry's day-girls and joined them for a drink.

Patrons filled every inch of the main floor. They drank imported liquors, local brews, and the Caribbean staple of rum. The festivities overflowed onto the sumptuous patio where trellises strewn with flowers and colorful glass lanterns lined the promenade.

Vie and her mates sat at a table behind one of the four large wooden pillars surrounding the bar. The pillars were etched with ships and other nautical motifs. Vie felt a pair of eyes burrow into the back of her head. A quick glance told her it was Constable Blower. He still held a grudge from when she refused him service. He'd been reeking of whiskey and Cherry tossed him out on his arse. Ever since he'd been deliberately rude to her at every turn.

Hoping to lose Blower's glare, Vie excused herself and went to the bar to see Glenda for another honey-wine.

Blower cornered her. "So, it's only the rich old doctors that get your attention, eh?"

"Excuse me?" Vie retorted. "Official Blower, ain't it?"

He sneered. "That's Constable Blower now."

"Well, me ladies and I be having a discussion not involving you."

Blower leaned against the bar. "All the ladies be across at the Four Feathers. There be no ladies here that I can see."

"None that would ever see *you*, I'm sure." Vie eyed Glenda, who tittered to herself and poured another mead.

Sheriff Tellam approached the bar hastily. "I gotta go! Another Gator Gar sighting and two ships stolen from Turtle Crawls. *Tartanas* this time."

"You want me to come?" Blower asked.

"Nay. Stay here and keep an eye on things."

Vie returned to her table, leaving Blower to stew in his hostility.

Theodore Binge entered from the patio and advanced to the biggest table in the place. He removed the dealer's cards from a small wooden box and fanned the deck with flair before picking it up to give it a good shuffle.

Glenda approached with a mischievous grin and presented him with a bottle of brandy. Binge uncorked it and took a swig. "Thanks. What's this for?"

“No special reason. Oh, the auction’s been delayed.”

“Delayed, eh?” Binge took another swig to conceal a smile. “Now that’s a shame.”

“There’s a rumor that the new slaves have scarlet fever. Seems that horrible little Magott and his two goons succumbed to it this afternoon.” Her expression revealed pure satisfaction.

Binge’s eyes widened. “Magott succumbed, really?”

“Indeed. He turned inside out all over the bloody place!”

“Oh, that’s a pity. That would have been entertaining!”

They had a good laugh before Glenda returned to the bar.

Binge noticed the slaver Burghill nearby, arguing with a potential buyer. “There’s no proof of that,” Burghill said. “Other than the ones that were already dead when they got here, no slaves have taken ill, have they?” He sucked on a cigar and waved to his slave Fatima to fan harder.

“Well, no,” the buyer agreed reluctantly. “But why have it at night, unless someone’s trying to conceal something?”

“Strictly for the festive atmosphere.” Burghill inhaled deeply, revealing his stained teeth. “Yer decision would be without merit at this point. Give it time. The auction shall be re-opened. You have me guarantee!”

The patio door opened, and a grinning Jag’d Jayne charged towards Lilly, who swaggered after several shots of rum. Her scream caused everyone to stop and stare. Jayne hoisted her up onto his shoulder before setting her back down to feel her bottom.

Binge stared holes into the floor while his pulse pounded. He dabbed his forehead with a handkerchief before looking around peaceably and straightened his collar. *Easy, man! Almost crapped my best suit!* Absentmindedly shuffling the cards, he eyed the patio. “Well, I’ll be damned!”

Tiny McAllister and Royal Rook entered. Tiny strolled to the bar, where he towered over Glenda.

“What be yer pleasure, Tiny?” She ogled his wide physique.

“Wormwood wine,” he replied in a sinewy voice.

“We got lots of that, sweetie.”

“What have you got to eat here? I gotta eat something. I’m on the verge of going scurvy.”

Glenda batted her eyes. “Well, the smoked turtle’s good. There’s turtle pie o’course and a new bread from Italy called a pizza-pie.”

"Another bread from Italy? That won't catch on. The smoked turtle sounds good, bring me three stones of them."

"Right away, sir." She winked.

Rook approached the big table.

A wide grin formed on Binge's face. "Well, walk the plank! I thought it was you!"

"Blow me down! Theo? Do I believe me eyes? Yer still here?" Rook and Binge shook hands.

"Still here. What happened to never setting foot in Port Royal again?"

Rook sighed. "Tough times, mate. Tough times."

"And Tiny, how's he doing?"

"Him? As always, crazy to be sailing with the likes of me." Rook snorted and scrutinized the card table. "And you? Still playing cards for a living?"

"This is recreation now. Coggshall pays me to deal. It's also the only tavern in town that lets me play."

Rook rubbed his chin. "I heard something like you got a title and yer a landowner now?"

Binge snickered. "Yeah. Well, sort of."

"You still living with the Binge beauties?"

"They're worth staying in Port Royal for." Binge took a swig of brandy and passed the bottle over.

"Yer doing well, mate!"

"So what brings you into town? Not the fayre?"

Rook flushed. "Working for Art now, I am. Protecting his ships from pirates."

"That's unfortunate."

"Aye, that it is." Rook took a drink. "Running slaves for King William's brave new world."

"As opposed to King James's cunning old one? Welcome to Port Royal, the wickedest place on earth. In '56, two thousand Irish children were brought here as slaves. A year later, not one of them was still alive. It don't matter who wears the throne out here." Binge emptied the bottle. "We should talk; I'll get us another."

"Nay for me, thanks, Theo. I'm getting laid tonight, first and foremost." He glanced around. "Say, you haven't seen little Katie, have ya?"

Binge hesitated.

"You know Katie. Mouth like a sailor, tits like a—" Rook paused. "Something happened to her? What then?"

"Burghill cut her. He cut out her tongue."

Rook hung his head. "Ah, bloody hell! I shoulda come back sooner. When did he cut her?"

"Right after Art sailed, though all the girls are under his protection now. Jag'd Jayne to thank for that, he got Katie to Doc MacAskill before she bled to death."

"Bloody bastards! Why'd I leave her here? She was always mouthing off."

"She said something to piss him off. Nobody knows what and she ain't talking."

"Where is she?" Rook browsed around again, gutted.

"She's here somewhere. But between me and you, she may want to take up knitting for a while. They got it in for her. If you was planning on taking her away, I'd say the sooner the better."

Rook patted Binge's arm. "Thanks, Theo. Good to see you. I'll catch ya up later, mate." He surveyed the crowd.

"Stick around, my friend. It's going to get interesting tonight." Binge pondered all the potential candidates for Strangewayes Special Blend.

Cherry sat at the bar, deep in thought. She drank gin with a twist of lime, watching Violante with the girls. *Vie's not getting out of this one, she needs to do her part.* Cherry finished off her third drink in one swift gulp. She tapped Vie's shoulder and pointed to the cloak room. Both women slipped behind the curtains.

"What's up?" Vie began.

Cherry held out a vial of poison. "I need ya to help us."

Vie's face went blank for a moment. "No bloody way!"

"I need ya to do this!" Cherry insisted. "You're a part of this group."

Vie shook her head. "Forget it! I ain't killing anyone. I know how this is gonna end. You're opening a door that won't close till we're hanging from the gallows!"

"Yer as good as dead along with the rest of us if you don't." Cherry felt as though she were scolding a child.

"I finally got me a way out and you ain't taking it from me!" Vie crossed her arms over her chest.

"A way out?" Cherry gave her a sympathetic smile. "Your Big Dick just wants in dear, he's not offering you a way out."

"You don't know that. Just cuz you're content to sit here with yer legs open for every scallywag that comes into town!"

Cherry struck her across the face. "Where the hell would you be without me? Answer me that! I found you in the gutter bleeding out from a gang bang. You'd be dead if it weren't for me. I saved yer fucking life, whore! You owe me!" Cherry shook. Her own harsh tone shocked her and she felt the prickle of hot tears.

"I'll be outta the house by the morrow."

"What?" Cherry's tone softened. *I didn't mean it, Vie!* "Where the hell will you go?"

"Who cares?" Vie sniffed hard and stormed off.

"Vie! Come back! He doesn't love you!" *That's what men do. Even the ones with hearts can't be touched.*

"Can ya be any more discrete?" Lilly entered the cloak room. "Where the bloody hell's she going?"

"To a Cistercian convent; what do you think?" Cherry was silent for a moment and drew a deep breath. "It's just you and me." She removed the vials from her bodice.

"No, it ain't." Lilly stuffed a bottle in her hidden pocket.

Katie walked in and reached for a vial.

"What are you doing here? Sorry Katie, but you couldn't get within fifty feet of them without getting caught," Cherry said.

"You shouldn't even be up and about yet!" Lilly insisted.

Katie snarled and pushed up her breasts. "Aa, uh ah!"

"Fuck you, wait'll you turn thirty!" Cherry hissed.

"No, it's for Nat and Cat!" Lilly exclaimed.

Katie applauded sarcastically.

"What'd ya do, take out an advertisement?" Cherry handed her a couple of vials. "Don't go near them! You'll get us all shackled in irons before we can even get close enough!"

Katie gave Lilly's hand a squeeze and then darted out.

"She's gonna get us killed." Cherry suddenly felt very cold. "Can we do this?"

"Aye, we can and will! Right-o then, time to kill," Lilly said.

Tears streamed from Violante's eyes. She sat on a chair in the third-floor toilette of the Swiftsure Tavern holding a handkerchief to her face.

When she was twelve, Vie's father had given her as payment on a debt to a gang of pirates. They'd dragged her screaming into an alley, where she was held down and raped. She'd passed out after the second assault. Never before had she felt so much bitterness, betrayal and humiliation.

Vie was semi-conscious when Cherry pulled her from the alley, leaving a blood trail. That's when Dr. Strangewayes entered her life. He drugged her, stitched up the wounds, and gave her a place to rest. It took such a long time to heal. She thought she would die from the pain, but the doctor helped her manage. He always made her feel safe.

Cherry took her in and became the only mother she ever knew. She educated and toughened her up. Survival skills were critical for women, especially in Port Royal. Vie learned to defend herself and carried a bodice dagger. She also learned how to remain in control of a conversation, not taking anyone's cheek. Never again would she let herself be hurt or controlled by men. Then along came Captain Richard Longstaff, a man with an infamous reputation.

Vie stared into a cracked mirror. Her eyes puffy and her cheeks red. Was she being used by him, or could it possibly be love? Or was she succumbing to lust for the first time in her life? Her sexual encounters had never been pleasurable until now because of her injuries. Somehow Longstaff had figured out how to handle women tenderly but firmly and he was bloody good at it. *Oh, who are you kidding? Don't be so daft!* She dried her eyes and took deep breaths. When her courage returned, she opened the door to see Strangewayes nosing about.

She was about to speak when Mina Jacobs came out of one of the rooms. Mina was a piece of work – a buxom brunette with a cruel temperament.

"What'cha be looking for, mister?" Mina spoke in a muddy drawl.

"I'm looking for the indentured Irish girl that was brought in yesterday. She's to be quarantined," the doctor explained.

"Ya mean the pikey girl?"

"Yes, have you seen her?"

"Aye. Mr. Coggshall has her locked in the room behind his office, but no one's allowed there without his permission."

"I understand. I'll take it up with Mr. Coggshall."

"Right. You do just that." Mina retreated down the hallway, passing one of Bleedin Art's thugs, Stinger, on the stairs.

"Doc!" Stinger called. "MacAskill wants a word."

"Of course."

"This way." Stinger led him down a long hall to an office.

Vie crept down the corridor, straining to hear raised voices. She slipped into the adjacent bedroom and closed the door. With her ear firmly against the wall, she listened.

Coggshall sat behind his desk, relishing the barrier between him and the Whigs. He finished a shot of whiskey from the bottle in his drawer and took out a cigar. He struck a match and puffed away, listening to Governor Piper carry on like a bemoaning crone and Strangewayes trying to talk his way out of everything as usual. At the same time costing him a bloody fortune!

Piper stared down his nose at the doctor. "You are the man who identified scarlet fever?"

"I'm the Chief Surgeon. Sander Strangewayes, sir, at your service. And yes, they did show the symptoms of scarlet fever."

"To that I agree," MacAskill said.

"You realize we'll have to destroy the entire lot if we decide it is scarlet fever?" Burghill eyed Strangewayes.

"You wouldn't? I'm merely being cautious! Twenty-four hours' quarantine is all I ask. Mr. Coggshall's slaves are under observation and so far, all of the victims seem to be white."

Magistrate Mold's jaw dropped. "Are you saying this disease only affects white people?"

"Then it must be the work of Satan!" Piper added.

Coggshall gnawed on the cigar. *Yes, Satan, that's always the best explanation!*

Strangewayes coughed. "Excuse me, but at this point I'm only saying that the cause is unknown. It could be something in the food or water. The turtles may have some sort of disease we don't know about."

Coggshall scratched his chin. "Or worse, Satan's turtles. Strangewayes here is a nature-ist."

"A naturalist, among other things." Strangewayes addressed

MacAskill. "Incidentally, the other Irish girl will have to be quarantined as well."

"She is quarantined and has no symptoms. Her problems are all injury-related. She does have a nasty case of the flux, but everyone gets it their first time here. Where are the slaves that were exposed?"

"I have them under quarantine at my apothecary."

"You took my Negroes?" Coggshall snorted. "What the bloody hell gives ya the right?"

"As Chief Surgeon of Port Royal I have the authority to detain and quarantine anyone posing a risk to public health," Strangewayes replied. "Can I see the girl?"

"Nay," MacAskill said. "She's my patient, my responsibility."

"There was dead slaves on both ships, what did they die of?" Piper asked.

Coggshall shrugged. "There always are. Some just don't make the trip."

"Twenty dead slaves on the galleys, which is well below the average," Burghill said. "Until you factor in the other ships, of course."

"How many slaves die on an average trip?" Piper asked Art.

"Don't look at me!" Art's eyebrows furled. "I don't even believe in slavery. I'm just out to make an honest living."

"It varies." MacAskill folded his arms. "I've seen losses that range from thirty to a hundred percent. Coggshall's slaves, are they at risk? Do they show symptoms?"

"I don't know. Perhaps if you shine my crystal balls you can see them." Strangewayes smiled politely.

"Like that wouldn't ya?" MacAskill turned to the Whigs. "Gentlemen, the huge scarlet fever outbreak of '89 has claimed three lives. Now I think we can safely move on. In my opinion, Dr. Strangewayes is incorrect. There is no risk to public health and the slaves are cleared for sale."

"You will return Mr. Coggshall's Negroes to him unless they show definite signs of infection," Piper said.

Art tapped Stinger's shoulder. "Send the new boys over to his apothecary to pick them up."

"No need. I'll send my carriage straight away," Strangewayes said.

Piper sighed. "Very well then, re-open the auction."

Coggshall's shoulders relaxed and he marched to the small window and stuck out his thumb. "About bloody time!" A cheer erupted from the crowd outside.

"Now, what's being done about the Frenchman?" Piper asked. "Five hundred thousand should be a high priority."

Vie pulled away from the wall, her eyes huge. "Five hundred thousand! I could start a brand new life!" Someone struck a match behind her and she jumped. Sulfur penetrated the air as Edmund Coggshall lit the wall sconce, and then his cigar. "Hear anything of interest?"

"Mr. Coggshall, I was just seeking the ladies room."

Edmund faintly sneered. "You do look like you're about to piss yourself."

"I wasn't meaning to."

"To eavesdrop?"

Her face felt hot. "I didn't mean to. I was searching for the Irish girl. Lilly wants to know what happened to her."

"She's not here."

Vie swallowed hard. "No?"

"MacAskill had her moved."

"Do you know where?"

Edmund signaled her to be quiet. The men next door entered the hall and shuffled past the bedroom door.

"If those ships can carry five hundred, then damn it, ship five hundred," Piper insisted.

"That's senseless killing!" Art protested. "Most of them would be dead before they got here."

"Then it goes to the insurance company and everybody wins." Mold chuckled.

"We can up it to three hundred with an acceptable loss as long as advance sales can be assured," Burghill's voice carried. Shadows paused at the door.

Coggshall knocked. "Ed, I'm going down to play cards."

Vie clasped her hands together. *I'm going to the gallows when I ain't done nothing! Thanks Cherry.*

"Right," Edmund replied. "I'm staying in. Not feeling all too well."

"Suit yerself," his father replied and the group carried on down the hall.

She sighed. "Thank you."

"That gets me free service for the rest of your life, doesn't it?"

"I guess it does."

"MacAskill's staying at the Clubhouse. He had her moved to the loft so he could keep an eye on her. You'll find her there."

Vie gave him a peck on the cheek before he pushed her shoulders down. He opened his trousers and pushed his member into her mouth. "You're welcome," Edmund said.

Royal Rook
GO

Birds with Bite

Katie glided down the stairs. *Thank you laudanum for controlling my legs!* Lanterns glowed warmly against the fir panel walls and the fire roared within its hearthstone. She scanned the Swiftsure Tavern crowd. Liquor flowed and everyone was relaxed. *It'll be easy to move among this lot.* She wandered, a predator stalking, biding her time.

Cherry made her official grand entrance in a lovely a crimson bodice and black skirt with gold lace, her hair a waterfall of mahogany curls. Gentlemen instantly lined up to kiss her hand and offer her drinks. *A true master of her trade, but arrogant.*

Katie paused behind a pillar near the bar to eavesdrop on a conversation between Pikestaff and Coggshall.

"Yer covered on all sides," Pikestaff said.

"I don't care if Gator Gar shows or not, you *do* Art and that rabid old Scotsman. Then you work for me," Coggshall assured.

Pikestaff nodded. "Aye. Consider it done."

That Coggshall always thinks himself sneaky. Katie could scarcely contain her excitement at the prospect of poison sealing his fate. Coggshall strolled over to the big table, where Binge shuffled his deck. One and Thirty wasn't the only game being played. All Fours, Primero, and the latest trend, *l'Hombre,* governed the smaller tables.

Katie hopped up on a bar stool and slapped the counter.

"Oi?" Glenda turned. "Are ya sure? It's gonna hurt."

Katie threw her hands up in the air. *As does life.*

"Rum it is."

"One and Thirty, straight up," Binge called. "Are we waiting for Captain Valentine?"

"Otherwise engaged, he is. Go ahead and deal." Coggshall lit up a Cuban cigar and greeted Natalia and Catharina who flaunted their elaborate costumes of fine fabric with gold accents. "Those are my special Hapsburg strumpets. Guaranteed, they be." He elbowed a potential buyer. "Come here ladies and say hello."

Katie glared at Burghill. She had been in and out of consciousness when Natalia tried to stop the bleeding. Jag'd Jayne had driven them both to MacAskill's residence at the Black Dog Inn, where she was stitched up. Natalia stayed by her side throughout the ordeal.

Katie boldly stepped forward meeting Burghill's eyes.

"What is she doing here?" He growled. "Go on! Get outta here. This place is too classy for the likes of you!"

Step into my parlor, Mr. Burghill. Katie defiantly knocked into him, slipping past his drink.

"Insolent little strumpet! Sorry, gentlemen, no damaged goods here tonight."

Katie looped back through the crowd, glancing in Cherry's direction. *I can't get close, eh?* Cherry gave her a grinding stare, practically trembling in her seat. Satisfied, Katie took a meandering route through a group of sailors throwing darts at a mounted barrel top. They whistled as she climbed the staircase.

Natalia swallowed hard, lingering beside the buyers. She smiled and patted their shoulders. The meaningless gestures reminded her of her noble family, entertaining faux allies with grandiose dinner parties and lavish dances. The falsity of it made her stomach churn. All this, while their fellow humans were kept as slaves. Natalia thought of Fatima, someone she'd like to have as a friend – keenly perceptive, beautiful and intelligent – and wept to think of her future as Burghill's possession.

Catharina gave Natalia a cautionary glance. She had been against letting Fatima in on the escape plan from the beginning. There were too many risks already. But to liberate someone so intelligent was a duty rather than a choice.

"Fatima, come here," Burghill said.

Fatima stepped forward. "Yes, sir."

Coggshall puffed his cigar. "I'd have thought the Songbird would have learned her lesson by now."

"Some dogs just can't be trained." Burghill handed Fatima the ale. "Drink it. All of it." She guzzled it back and he inspected her. "Go get me another."

"Yes, sir." Fatima hiccuped. "Thank you, sir."

Natalia readied the note she'd transcribed earlier and slipped it into Fatima's apron as she passed.

"Another drink for Mr. Burghill," Fatima told Nessie, while securing the note.

"Oi!" Coggshall motioned to Glenda. "These ladies need rum!"

Binge dealt the next hand. "Over to you, sir. Stick or have it?"

"Stick," a buyer replied.

"And you, Mr. Burghill?"

"Stick." Burghill slid his arm around Natalia's waist. The scent of him was nauseating. She pretended to watch the game, hoping to deflect the stare of Mace Scarcliff, who plunked his drink down on the big table.

"If you say so." Binge's hand slipped past Scarcliff's drink to deal another card.

Scarcliff lit his pipe and continued staring at Natalia.

"She's a little out of yer class, lad," Burghill said.

"Come back in a few dozen doubloons." Coggshall laughed.

Everyone had a good chuckle, including Natalia, who knocked over Burghill's mug. Ale spilled on her bodice and soaked the cigar box on the table. "How clumsy," she exclaimed, thrusting her wet cleavage forward, drawing the eyes of many men.

A buyer elbowed Burghill. "Can't hold yer liquor tonight, can you?"

"Guess not."

Natalia pouted her lips. "I'm very sorry."

Burghill patted her arm. "'Tis free advertising, love, and ya can work off the cigars."

"May I get cleaned up?"

"Aye, ya look like a cheap strumpet," Coggshall said.

"As opposed to a classy whore?" Burghill snorted.

"Aye. If for nothing else, come to Port Royal for the classy whores!" Coggshall chortled, shaking the table.

Natalia slipped away.

"Whatever floats yer galleys, Mr. Coggshall." Binge shrugged. "Shall we pause, gentlemen?"

"Nay, deal on." Burghill shook his head. "It's not my lucky night anyway. I'll go get cleaned up." He summoned Fatima. "Go get me another box of cigars."

"Yes, sir." Fatima took the ruined box. She slipped out the patio, peering over her shoulder.

Natalia made her way to the curtained area of the toilette. By candlelight, she patted her bodice with a handkerchief and made a fanning motion with her hand. It was almost dry by the time Burghill intruded, groping the back of her dress. "Nice trick with the ale. I wanted you wet anyway." He nuzzled her hair.

"But Mr. Coggshall said no."

"What the eyes don't see, the heart don't grieve for."

"What?"

"I must see ya in the third-floor bedroom," he said.

"Yes, sir. But we shouldn't be seen together."

"No, meet me there."

"Yes, sir."

Natalia waited until he was well on his way upstairs before dashing out the alley exit.

The night air was fresh and cool. She took deep gulps of air to clear out the stench of the tavern. Festivities were in full force. Colorful lanterns flickered, people danced themselves giddy and the aroma of fire-roasted meats filled the air. Natalia darted down a path and to Fatima, who waited nervously.

"Fatima," Natalia began. "We're leaving tonight; come with us."

"Tonight?" Fatima trembled. "If they catch me again—"

Natalia stopped her and kissed her hand. "They won't, I promise. We're getting out of here. Are you coming?"

She nodded. "Yes, I'll come."

"Good! Be up at the loading bay at ten of the clock. If we're not there, leave without us. Tell Strangewayes we'll meet you there. Don't be late and don't drink anymore." Natalia slipped back through a rowdy crowd. Monsieur De'va's band began "An Ape, a Lion, a Fox, and an Ass".

The third-floor bedroom was where Natalia and Catharina lived. Natalia knocked and entered the moonlit room. Light from the outside lanterns cast a pale glow and she could make out Burghill's silhouette.

"What kept you?" He rubbed his body against hers.

"I was afraid to be seen."

"I can't stop thinking about you." His face burrowed into her cleavage, lapping at her flesh with his tongue.

Natalia reached for the ties to her bodice and loosened them. He ripped open the fabric to unleash her endowments. Her hand slid to his trousers, where she worked against the increasing bulge. He panted in her ear, "Ya know what I want. Ya know what I need." His fingers skimmed around her neck and guided her head downward.

She stopped abruptly. "Wait."

"Wait?"

"Give me just one minute." Natalia backed away to a curtained washing area.

Burghill sat down on the bed, dropping his trousers to the floor. "I'm gonna free you, just as soon as I can. Would ya like that?" he spoke kindly. "You and Catharina can live at the Crooked Compass in luxury and never have to worry again."

"That sounds wonderful. I've thought about you too," Natalia replied, splashing her fingers in a basin of water.

The curtain shifted and Burghill laid back. A female hand massaged his organ until it engorged. Lips manipulated the shaft until it pulsated. "Oh yeah, suck it. Suck it right off." He gasped and pushed her head down until she took it fully in her mouth.

Outside, loud cheering and clapping filled the air and the music grew lively. The crowd sang "Once, Twice, Thrice."

Burghill lurched forward. "Ouch, careful! What are ya trying to do, bite it off?" Teeth latched on and sunk in. He wailed, thrashing beneath her. She wrenched her head like a wild animal, ripping into him until the final brutal crunch of her teeth. Burghill drove his fist into the side of her head.

Off-balanced, Katie backed away. Blood spilled out of her mouth and down her naked body. She stepped into the moonlight so he could see her spit out his severed remains.

Burghill howled. The only phrase he could muster was, "You whore, I'll kill ya!"

Unleashing the dagger she held behind her back, Katie pounced, driving the weapon into his stomach. She withdrew it and plunged it into his throat. In a final fury, she yanked it out and wedged it in his chest. She stood over his squirming body until it expired. Deluges of blood saturated the bed and marinated the floor. Katie retrieved her weapon and stuffed the torn organ into Burghill's mouth.

Natalia lit a candle and opened the curtain to reveal a full wash tub. She watched the blood streak down Katie's breasts. "We're leaving at ten. Fatima is coming. You should come too."

Katie shrugged, stepping forward with the dagger and dropping it beside the tub. She plunged her feet into the tepid water and massaged the redness across her skin. She felt a perverse thrill at bathing in an enemy's blood.

"I have to get back," Natalia said, heading to the door. "There's nothing here for you but death, Katie. You should come with us."

True enough. Katie couldn't stay in Port Royal, not now. She rubbed away more blood. Most likely she'd be caught and killed. After cleansing herself, she slid on a dress and left the room. *It's only a matter of time before someone discovers the dickless prick.* She went downstairs to the main floor.

Katie noticed Royal Rook navigating through the crowd. *It can't be!* A wave of excitement and fear swept over her. *Didn't expect to see him tonight. I can go with him!* She felt hopeful but it was soon snuffed out. *He'll be blamed too.*

Catharina emerged from the toilette and strolled casually back to the big table, passing Rook on the way. She slid a few drops of poison into the mug he carried. Rook sat down at Tiny's table near the fireplace and readied a toast.

Katie pushed her way through the crowd.

"Kaitlyn!" Rook gawked, reaching out his hand to her. "My sweet girl, are you well?"

She grabbed the mug and poured it down his suit.

"What the fuck?" Rook's mouth hung open.

Katie slapped him across the face before chucking the mug on the floor and knocking Tiny's drink over with her fist.

"Fun evening that was," Tiny said as Katie stormed off.

"Kaitlyn!" Rook ran after her. "Wait!"

Katie marched through the front entrance and was nearly run over by a carriage.

"Watch where yer going, strumpet," the driver yelled.

She flipped up her middle finger before turning down Honey Lane.

"Kaitlyn, wait." Rook followed. "I said I'd come back, but I didn't say when!"

Katie finally stopped to lean against a brick wall. Tears pricked her eyes. *What if I disgust him now?* Sobs overtook her.

"Kaitlyn?" Rook gently reached for her arm. "Don't run, love." She thrust herself against his chest. "I'm so sorry, Kate. By almighty God, I'm so sorry." He embraced her and kissed her forehead. "I won't let them touch ya again, I swear." They held each other. "Come on. Let's go somewhere."

Walking back to Thames Street they flagged down a wherryman's carriage and vanished down the road.

In the back of Strangewayes's car, Atia stirred beneath the blanket, kicking her legs. She thought she heard the Capitaine cursing in French, but she may have been dreaming. Her legs slid off the seat and she sat up, coughing.

The Capitaine turned in the driver's seat to look at her. "How are you feeling?"

"Fair to middling."

"Huh?" He gave a half smile.

"It hurts to breathe." Atia took a sip from a water canteen.

"Oui. It will for a while yet." His eyes lingered on her. "Your ribs are bruised; very painful it is. You take it easy back there; I don't want you getting sick." He glanced back to the street. "Very lucky you don't have a bad cough."

"The doctor gave me something for the cough. He said," she cleared her throat to do her best impersonation, "that should keep the cough at bay for a while, my dear."

"We also gave you something for the pain."

"I know!" she spoke giddily.

"Don't move around too much."

Atia yawned. "I could sleep for a month or two."

"Hmm. You and me both." The Capitaine yawned.

"Where are we?"

He immediately tipped his hat. "Oh, my apologies, Mademoiselle. You are in the city of Port Royal."

Atia smiled. "Thanks. Why are we at a fayre? Is Livia here?"

He cleared his throat. "There's, uh, business that needs attending to. And oui, we are picking her up."

Atia wrapped the blanket over her shoulders and delicately climbed through the window opening to the driver's seat. "Yer gonna kill them aren't you?"

"No. Who says that?" He stalled. "Oui. How do you know?"

"Lilly can't keep a secret."

Her champion smacked his face into his hand, doing a trademark frown. "Idiot! What else did she tell you?"

Atia fondled his leg. "It's my fault, really. I made her tell me. Don't worry. I'm on yer side, remember?" She tilted her head and blinked at him coyly. "I knew something was up. The lot of ya have been sneakin' and plottin' all day."

"Just keep it to yourself."

"O'course." She swept her hair over her shoulder.

Minuit the parrot swooped down and landed on the edge of the carriage.

The Capitaine waved him off. "No! Get away! Give us away, you will."

Minuit squawked and flapped his wings in protest, peering down at Atia.

"No, it's okay." Atia made a clicking noise. "Hello, Minuit."

"He only speaks French," the Capitaine said.

"Hello," Minuit said.

"*Merde*! He'll give us away."

"Oh, like no one has a parrot in Port Royal." Atia gave him a doubtful gaze and held out her arm. The large bird hopped down onto her shoulder and she ruffled the feathers on the top of his head. "Can I ask you a question?"

"Me or the bird?" The Capitaine was unimpressed. "You will be seen!"

"Who? Me or the bird?" Atia snickered. "No one's watching. No one minds." She slid closer to him so their shoulders touched.

His face began to redden.

"Is Gator Gar yer real name? Not to pick yer fiddle or anything, but it's an awful funny name for a Frenchman."

"Oui, we're all named François." He glared until the look softened to adoration. "I shouldn't have given you such a high dose."

Atia wanted to kiss him. She remembered his lips against hers somewhere between waking and dreaming. "Fine – I'll share if you do. Me last name is O'Malley, not Crisp. Crisp is something I was stuck with. Me real father's a pirate."

"If true, then that is not something you want to volunteer." His face twisted into an endearing scowl. "O'Malley."

Her eyes lit up. "Do you know him?"

He watched the front entrance to the Swiftsure. "It is possible. I know a lot of pirates. I knew a man named O'Malley once."

"What was he like?"

"Insane." He examined her face. "Could explain a lot. Fine man, though. Very fine man."

"Now you be knowing my real name. What can I call you? Other than Gator Growls or suchfuck?"

He met her eyes again, his hand hovering over hers. "Why is it important?"

A lump suddenly formed in her throat. "I just figured it was a bit more personal and thought ya must have a preferred given name, is all."

The Capitaine tried to be aloof. "Paul is what you can call me, but only in private."

"Like I was saying, I knew something was up. You're way too easy to read, Paul. Lucky for me you cheat at cards, though."

They stared at each other, unable to look away. She put her lips on his, softly at first. The intensity escalated and his hand slipped behind her neck pulling her urgently to him. His lips crushed against hers in a frenzy; her mouth filled with his tongue. Chills rose on her arms. The rugged scent of him was intoxicating, causing butterflies in her belly and an ache between her thighs. A moan escaped her lips when his hand slid down her neck and probed her breasts.

Minuit pecked at the Capitaine's head, and then retreated to the roof of the carriage, screeching, "*connard*!"

Atia pulled away, rubbing her face. "Whisker burn!"

"*Désolé*! This fucking beard!"

"Contrarily, Monsieur." Her lips grazed his ear while her hand slid between his legs to feel his excitement. "We'll just have to pick this up later without the disguise."

"Perhaps someplace more private?" Gladstone spoke beside them, standing next to the driver's seat.

"*Merde*!" The Capitaine jumped and reached for weapons that weren't there.

Atia climbed back inside.

"I could come back later if it's more convenient." Gladstone's lips curled. "Any movement?"

"No, they are all inside."

"Well, the militia are searching Cherry's as we speak. So stay here and out of sight, and don't go back there whatever you do."

"My hat?" The Capitaine suddenly realized.

"Cherry's got all your things hidden," Gladstone assured.

"And Atia's sister?"

"Sander hasn't found her yet. As soon as he does, he'll let us know, so stay sharp." Gladstone winked and returned to his carriage across the way. "As you were, Capitaine," he said over his shoulder.

The Capitaine shifted uncomfortably, adjusting his trousers and muttering in French. He glanced back at Atia. She blew him a kiss before surrounding herself with blankets. Minuit hopped in through the open window to sit beside her. Her champion shook his head. “Watch it, he bites.”

Mute
Katie
GO
2015

Jalapenos and Coconuts

Merrymaking was well underway all over the Swiftsure Tavern. On the second floor, ship captains congregated around the billiard table, drinking vast amounts of rum as they swapped stories of peril on the sea. Other patrons danced to the tune of a lone fiddler who'd been guzzling Madeira wine all evening.

Lilly teetered, happily intoxicated, while Pikestaff's parrot Gibbet balanced on her shoulder. She loved the Swiftsure; anyone could have a good time. Even old Glenda unpinned her thick blond locks to seduce Tiny McAllister. The barmaid plunked a bottle of wormwood wine in front of him and jiggled her curves before taking a seat beside him.

Lilly laughed, sliding off her chair. She knocked Pikestaff's pipe to the floor.

"Oi!" He sneered, retrieving his pipe. "Go bug Jayne!" Gibbet flew back onto his shoulder.

"That's right, come here and bug Jayne." Jayne patted his thighs. She hopped onto his lap, wrapping her legs around him.

"He's me favorite anyway," Lilly proclaimed. Pikestaff was wound up tighter than a corset. She considered him a stupid bugger as he never tried her before. And his mate, Codface, was really no better, although he did pay her for a suck once – it was like shooting a fish out of a barrel.

"She's in bloody heat again, I tell ya," said Pikestaff, making no effort to lower his voice. "A piece o'eight says they go at 'er right here!"

"I'd go at 'er right here," Codface replied.

"Remember, lads, stay sharp tonight!" Pikestaff said seriously. "Watch for the Frenchman."

Jayne momentarily stopped tonguing Lilly's neck. "He ain't coming. Art says he's long gone."

"They be sending Big Dick after him in the morrow anyway." Codface shrugged.

"All the same, you stay sharp and do yer bloody jobs!" Pikestaff scowled.

Lilly slid her hand down between Jayne's legs.

"See, what'd I tell ya?" Pikestaff muttered. "Does she charge him every time, or is he on account?"

“I don’t think they be keeping track,” Codface said. “He probably owes her a king’s ransom by now.”

“I’d sooner stick it in a crab trap. ’Tis safer!”

“C’mon Lilly, ya know I can’t say no to you. I’m on duty though, ain’t I?” Jayne fumbled with his trousers, unleashing his member.

“You sure are,” Lilly panted in his ear. His hands slid up beneath her skirt, positioning her upon his organ. She moaned and gyrated. His fingers roughly kneaded her buttocks, pulling faster against him. She gasped, feeling him pulsate inside her, filling her. He remained rock hard. Undulating until her thighs quivered, an exuberant orgasm burst forth.

Lilly happily remained on his lap, her head resting on his shoulder, her eyes closed. Jayne was the type who’d go at it all night, that’s why she adored the ones in their twenties. She never understood Cherry’s penchant for the older ones. Lilly opened her eyes to see Cherry seduce Shipwash, Burghill’s thug. *Now that’s more like it – all young muscle.*

Masterfully, Cherry sat on his lap and slipped her hand between his legs. The expression on his face was somewhere between frustration and elation. Each man was the same, but different, acting like it was the end of world unless it went off. Lilly had one customer who even wept afterwards.

Shipwash buried his face in Cherry’s cleavage while she tugged enthusiastically. With her free hand, Cherry removed a vial from her hair, bit off the small cork stopper and poured it into his mug. Soon Shipwash finished, a satisfied expression on his face. Cherry removed a handkerchief from her sleeve to wipe her hand. *Such class Cherry has!*

MacAskill’s thick Scottish snarl thundered from the stairs. “What’d I tell ya? Top notch soldiers? Nothing but a bunch of fuck’n animals the lot of them!” The rabid doctor marched down. “Is this what he’s paying you for? What do you call this?”

“All under control here, Doc,” Pikestaff said as Lilly moaned rebelliously. “No sign of the Frenchman.”

“Enough already,” the doctor barked.

Lilly slid off Jayne’s lap, still wet between the thighs and straightened her skirt. MacAskill appeared the part of a madman, his silvery white hair wild and bushy. Beside him was his dim-witted thug, Stinger. “Take it outside! Pikestaff, you work for us or not?”

"Come on you lot, take it outside!" Pikestaff reprimanded, clapping his hands, rallying them all out the door.

Catharina sat up straight on Coggshall's lap, his arms clasped around her as if she were a dog meant to obey. Being a German aristocrat, she was accustomed to being still and ornamental. The grotesque man wasn't even paying attention to the game; he was drawn to the conversation between MacAskill and Scarcliff at the entrance to the patio. The buyers too were preoccupied with this conversation.

Stinger gazed lustfully at her and she gave a polite smile back before staring at the floor. *As soon as the adolescent looks away, I will poison the mugs.*

Binge continued to shuffle cards.

Catharina glanced up. Stinger had gone to the bar. The only watcher was Binge, who gave her an encouraging nod. She removed a vial from her sleeve, twisted its top, and reached out her hand if trying to grab one of the mugs. Several drops fell into the ale. She moved to another, her hand hovered beside Coggshall's mug. The fool shifted forward slightly, stretching to hear each last little syllable.

She felt her hand tremble with exhilaration, putting at least ten drops of poison into his mug. Swiftly, she re-capped the bottle and was about to stuff it back up her sleeve when it slipped from her hand. Catharina froze. Binge pointed down. She spotted the vial in the folds of her dress. Her body remained still. It was just beyond her fingertips but seemed miles away. Leaning forward, she almost had it.

Coggshall reached for his drink.

The chair tipped and both of them spilled to the floor.

"Shit!" Coggshall said.

Catharina scrambled to retrieve the poison, feigning a cough. She snatched it off the floor.

MacAskill shook his head. "Looking for yer arsehole by any chance, Mr. Coggshall, sir?"

Catharina tried to stand gracefully.

Coggshall climbed back up. "Clumsy bitch, this is my best suit!"

"Well, it's not all bad luck. You didn't spill a drop," said a buyer, taking a drink.

After MacAskill finished laughing, he saw the curtain move to the toilette. "There's Strangewayes now. Finish up here and grab yer men. Go get Coggshall's slaves so we can get the fuck out of here."

Strangewayes left the tavern by the front door. At the same time Natalia came back downstairs. *Thank goodness she's back!* Catharina exhaled as the women squeezed hands beneath the table.

Coggshall adjusted his collar. "Where the hell's Burghill?"

"I don't know where he's got to," said Natalia.

Coggshall took his first mouthful of poison. "Probably gone to get his pecker off!"

Natalia shrugged. "Well, he shouldn't be long then."

On Thames Street, people bustled through the maze of vendors. Hats, clay pipes, leather pouches, smoked fish, pineapples, and dried figs were among the countless items for sale. Monsieur De'va's band entertained the drunken masses as they danced and brawled.

Pikestaff led the group, keeping a watchful eye out for anything suspicious. He struck a match and puffed his tobacco. Jayne was molested by Lilly at every turn. *Why don't he just marry the bitch and shut her up? At least then he'd be obliged to leave the wife at home!*

Lilly stopped in front of a produce stand that sold jalapenos and licked her lips.

"Mmm, hot peppers." She beamed. "I got a challenge for you, gents. I bet I can eat these and you can't."

"She's stuffed worse in there, I'm sure," Pikestaff said.

"These are very hot. Burns for hours unless you rinse out with coconut milk." The vendor pointed to the coconut stand managed by his twin brother, who waved excitedly.

"Good scam," Pikestaff said.

Lilly batted her eyes. "Bet-cha I can eat more than any of ya."

"What are they, then?" Pikestaff asked.

"They be called jalapeno peppers, it's Spanish."

"What are they called in the King's English?" Pikestaff flashed his sword.

"Hot peppers, sir," the vendor replied.

"Come on then? Who will accept the challenge?" Lilly grinned. "How about free polishes for life if you can eat more than me?"

The vendor's eyes widened, while Jayne and Codface grabbed coins from their pockets.

"You do have a talent for the polishing." Jayne adjusted his trousers.

Pikestaff shook his head. "I'd sooner stick it in a bug's nest."

"Bug's nest!" Gibbet screeched.

"That's right. You're a good lad, aren't you?" Pikestaff cooed. He couldn't believe they were actually going to try for it. What a waste of gold.

"Ya must chew or you're cheating. Down the hatch." She popped a jalapeno in her mouth and chewed quickly. Her face screwed into an agonized pose.

Wait a tick, this is getting good! Pikestaff smirked and watched the lads stuff peppers in their mouths.

Jayne's face contorted in torment and he paid the vendor for more. He gulped air into his mouth.

Lilly had another.

"You said chew…chew!" Jayne reminded.

"She looks like she just blew Magott!" Pikestaff tittered.

They all laughed. Lilly swallowed and opened her mouth for everyone to see before racing to the coconut vendor and pointing to the sign. She threw him a coin and slurped back the liquid.

Jayne dangled a pepper in front of his mouth. "I–I can't."

"For life, she said," Codface gasped.

"Aye. 'Tis a third of me rent. I must try! Two more!" Jayne's face turned red after a few seconds.

Pikestaff choked back his laughter, watching a new brand of pain and suffering. He'd have to remember this for future interrogation tactics.

La Roche sat in Strangewayes's carriage as fayregoers enjoyed the various entertainments on offer. He tightened his boots and secured the disguise to his face. He glanced at Atia, wanting to tear away the beard and finish what they'd started earlier.

"It's the ideal time, Capitaine. Lilly certainly has them distracted," Strangewayes said.

"Oui. I'm going in."

"Right. I'll come in the side entrance in ten minutes and meet you on the top floor."

"Thank you, Capitaine." Atia popped up behind him eagerly. "Good luck."

La Roche turned to steal a kiss, and slid his fingers through her hair. "*Merci, ma chérie.* Stay out of sight. I'll be back." They gazed into each other's eyes until he forced himself to turn and climb down. *Focus, damn it. Focus!* They'd have a private rendezvous in his cabin later. Coolly he strolled through the crowd into the tavern.

The atmosphere was heavy with smoke, drink, and sweat. He scanned the main floor and met Cherry's glance. She nodded and left by the side door.

La Roche went for the stairs and climbed to the second floor. Drunken scallywags tried to juggle billiard balls while downing pints of beer and hardened ship captains focused on their card games. Someone waited in the shadows.

"*Bonjour*, Monsieur," a voice whispered. Vie signaled him.

He stopped in his tracks. "How did you recognize me?"

"The shape of yer bulge."

He looked down to his coat buttons. "Huh?"

"I've worn that costume before. You suit it better."

La Roche stepped into the shadows. "What do you want?"

"The pikey girl ain't up there."

"She's not?" La Roche eyed her suspiciously. "How do you know?"

"I overheard them. I know where they took her. Go outside and wait for me."

"Why? Where is she?"

Vie tapped her foot. "I'll take you to her. Now go outside and wait for me. Trust me, they're all upstairs waiting for ya." She slipped away down the hall.

La Roche stood still for several more seconds. Finally, his lip curled into a snarl and he reversed direction.

The Whigs stared impatiently at Bleedin Art. After a very long, unpleasant conversation, they finally wore him down. He removed a Pepys pen from his pocket and signed a parchment mandating a ten percent tax increase. His signature was rather ornate – an A and V joined together to form a broken heart.

Piper admired the pen. "What is that?"

"Mine." Art put it back in his pocket.

Piper signed his name with a quill. "If we have no further business to discuss, I should like to take my leave of you."

“Good night to you, Mr. Valentine,” Mold spoke smugly.

“It’s Captain to you, Moldy, and that’s *fini*!” Art jeered.

Piper moved to the door. “Pleasure doing business with you.”

MacAskill and Stinger entered the room.

“And good night to you, Doctor,” Piper said.

MacAskill slammed the door behind them. “Don’t trip on yer way out.”

“This day can’t get worse.” Art massaged his face, indulging in self-pity. “Where’s Jayne?”

“Outside with the rest of yer scallywags winning fair maiden’s mouth, why?”

“We’re going back to the Clubhouse.” Art rolled up his copy of the document. “I ain’t sticking around this disease-infested hell hole any longer.”

“What about the Capitaine?”

“You really think the Whigs could catch him? Not bloody likely.”

MacAskill shrugged. “Not impossible either. Times have changed. This isn’t the seventies when ignorance led to good fortune, ya know.”

“Nay, tell Dewar his man Sleemans has it wrong. Gator Gar ain’t here; he buggered off with his ship,” Art insisted.

“Aye, but—”

“Do I look worried?” Art sneered. “If Gator Gar falls into the hands of the Whigs, I’ll cuff me nuts to a chain shot and blast ’em off Morgan’s Line. How’s that for ya?”

“What’s the point? They’d only stretch,” MacAskill said.

“Oh, shut it and go get the car.”

“I’m second in fuck’n command, remember? Dough head! Don’t ya forget it!” He pointed at Stinger. “Go get the car.”

“Aye,” Stinger said.

Strangewayes leaned against Gladstone’s carriage. The alluring aroma of food caused his stomach to rumble. He watched for Natalia and Catharina. “What could be keeping them?”

“They’ll be here, don’t you worry,” Gladstone said.

A young girl approached them.

“I wonder who this is, then?” Strangewayes pondered. “I believe I’ve seen her with Natalia before.”

"I think she's Fatima."

"Wait here." The doctor went to meet her. "Excuse me, is your name Fatima?"

She clasped her hands. "Yes."

"My name is Dr. Strangewayes."

"Natalia asked me to say hello if she was late and said she'd meet you there."

"I see." He smiled. "May I offer you a ride?

"P-please."

Gladstone pulled the carriage forward.

"Thank you," Fatima said.

"Thank us when we're all hanging from the gallows," Gladstone added under his breath.

The doctor helped her into the carriage. "Take her to—"

"The Snapper Shack. Right away," Gladstone finished. "I know. I got it under control, alright?"

"You'll write what?" The doctor was befuddled.

"No, alright. It's an expression, like all is right with world."

"You kids and your slang!" The doctor ventured up the street. *Time to see how Lilly's doing.* She stood in front of a hot pepper stand. "Oooh, jalapenos!" He clapped his hands together.

Lilly galloped across to the coconut vendor, while Jag'd Jayne gagged as if he'd just swallowed a box of silver toothpicks.

"Christ, you look happy as a pig in a barrel o'pork!" Pikestaff said.

"Good evening, my dear," the doctor began, giving her a jolt. "I didn't mean to startle you."

She giggled nervously. "Fine this evening. How are you, sir?"

"Here ya go, strumpet." The vendor placed two drinks on the counter.

"I'm well, thank you!" Lilly swaggered.

"Of course, you ordered them *with* rum. Why am I not surprised?" Strangewayes spoke to the vendor, "Those jalapenos over there, are they fresh? The sign says they're from Vera Cruz."

"Well, that's what the sign said when we bought them in Belize," the coconut vendor said. "Ripe they are and very hot."

Lilly glanced over her shoulder before she withdrew a small vial from her sleeve, twisted off the cap and poured half the vial in each drink.

The doctor stood in front of her, acting as a shield. He cleared his throat. “I could use some jalapenos for a cough syrup I’ve been working on.”

“Aye, very medicinal. One of those will cure you.”

“Or empty you out.”

Lilly staggered back to the group, coconut drinks in hand. Jayne’s eyes bulged and Codface rushed for both drinks, guzzling them back.

Jayne waved his hands in distress. “Mmm! Mmm!”

“Let me get you another one Jayne dear,” Lilly slurred. “Not to worry.”

Jayne fanned his mouth and approached the vendor. “I’ll get it meself. This better be worth it!” He handed over a coin.

Strangewayes addressed the produce vendor, “Hello sir. I would like to make a purchase. One basket of jalapenos and these plantains here.”

“You’re killing me, I give,” Codface squealed. He tossed Lilly a small bag of coins.

She plunked herself down on a barrel. “At this point love, I don’t think it’ll make much difference.”

“Slap me with a fucking eel and feed me to the bloody sharks! I don’t think I’ll ever taste anything again!” Jayne handed Lilly a bag of coins.

Pikestaff shrugged. “It’s for the best, me thinks.”

Stinger motioned to them. “Oi! Jayne, Codface! We’re moving out to the Clubhouse.”

“Ya hear? Let’s go!” Pikestaff called.

“Make sail!” Gibbet squawked.

“Pity you got to go.” Lilly blinked drunkenly at Jayne. “Can I get ya one for the road?”

“Nay.” He sneered. “You’ve done enough.”

Strangewayes paid for his peppers and plantains.

“Codface, you go ahead and get a fire going. Check on Mikey and the girl. We’ll get Art,” Pikestaff said.

“Aye, got a fire going meself.” Codface turned down the alley.

Lilly winked at Jayne. “I’ll give ya a free polish anytime.”

He fanned his mouth. “Aye, you will.”

“Go on strumpet, away with ya!” Pikestaff ordered.

“Leave her be!” Jayne scowled.

“Best wait a little while first; you don’t wanna be her next customer anyway.” Pikestaff headed inside.

Jayne followed. "Aye, those lips are gonna be scorchers for hours."

Basket in hand, Strangewayes strolled to the coconut vendor. "One more drink please, hold the rum." Lilly sat with her head between her knees. "Painfully ingenious. You poor dear, let's get you out of here." He administered the coconut milk and passed her a handkerchief. "You know, I do have room for you in the apothecary trade."

"Good." With a revolted expression she hiccuped. "It stings." She hugged him and covered her mouth.

They returned to the carriage, where Lilly passed out on the back seat.

"What's happening?" Atia asked.

"Valentine is leaving. I've got to go in and meet the Capitaine." The doctor slid the basket onto the seat beside her.

"No need." She pointed. "He's coming out."

The Capitaine calmly mixed with the crowd. He narrowly avoided being hit by the carriage delivering Longstaff and Fishhook to the party. Big Dick and his Number One dressed in their finest red wool jackets and smart black pants.

"She's not here," the Capitaine said. "That's what Vie says."

"Art's men are leaving right now as well, along with Art!" Strangewayes spoke in a hushed panic. "Does she know where Livia is?"

"Oui. She's coming out to meet me. Can we trust her?"

"Vie?" The doctor tilted his head. "A tad more than your average Port Royal strumpet."

"What are these, some kinda fruit?" Atia asked.

The Capitaine frowned. "That's not encouraging, any other plans?"

"Feel free to try something unexpected." Strangewayes rubbed the back of his neck. "I'm afraid I'm at a loss."

"We can't miss our chance, but it's not safe. Get Atia out of here." The Capitaine glanced into the back seat. "Did you just?"

Strangewayes turned to look.

Minuit snapped a bite of the pepper.

Atia fanned her mouth. "Bloody hell! What the bloody hell is that?"

"Stay calm! Don't scream!" La Roche waved, laughter brewing behind his eyes.

"Oops! Well, it wears off in a little while." The doctor shrugged. "Try a plantain, one of the black ones, it might help."

Atia rolled her watery eyes and peeled the fruit. "Mmm! Bloody hell!"

"Bloody hell! Bloody hell!" Minuit screeched, taking off into the starry night sky.

Lilly stirred, clawing her way to the window before vomiting an evening's worth of jalapenos, coconut milk, and rum. She lifted her head heavily. "They're going to the Clubhouse." She wretched over the side again.

The Capitaine grimaced. "Oui, good job. Now it's time you called it a night."

Lilly
Auction
GO
2015

Game's Afoot

Natalia sat on the lap of a buyer, anticipation bubbling inside her. Binge dealt another hand, while Coggshall patted his forehead and took large mouthfuls of ale as if trying to kill a putrid taste.

"Go do something for a minute, eh?" Coggshall tapped Catharina's arm and she slid off his lap.

"I'm getting some air too," the buyer said, patting his feverish forehead.

Coggshall gasped, his complexion ashen and sticky.

The two women locked arms, strolling to the toilette in the far corner. In the dimly lit space, an oval mirror hung on the wall and beneath it a water pitcher and a basin.

Catharina squatted over a chamber pot. "It's working, are we done now? We must leave!"

Natalia poured some water in the basin. "Yes, we should get out of here." She vigorously rubbed her hands before splashing water on her face. "By Nerthus, they disgust me so!"

"How is Burghill doing?"

"Decomposing as we speak."

"Did Katie…?" Catharina mimed a vicious chomp.

"She did." Natalia was impressed. "He didn't see it coming."

"Hopefully, neither did she."

They both laughed.

Natalia poked her head out from behind the curtain. "Let's get the hell out of Port Royal, shall we?"

"We'll go out the side door," Catharina insisted and went to wash her hands. "You were fantastic!"

"So were you." Natalia reached over to kiss her lips. "Now, let's get out of here."

Binge shuffled subconsciously. His hands repeated the same gestures with the occasional flip for flair. Coggshall and several buyers appeared sicker and sicker, turning a whiter shade of death. "You're dead, Mr. Coggshall," Binge declared.

Coggshall patted the sweat beads from his neck. "What'cha say to me?"

"Your bet, Mr. Coggshall," Binge said. "Stick or have it?"

A grumbling erupted from Coggshall's stomach and spittle dribbled down the front of his suit. A mixture of disgust and glee formed on Binge's face. "Shall I call for an intermission, sir? Or is there a certain card you were hoping to regurgitate?"

Coggshall gave him a vacant nod before taking great gasps of air.

"A short rest everyone," said Binge. "We'll resume in fifteen." He carefully placed his deck in the small wooden box before wandering to the bar. "A shot of whiskey, please, ma'am."

"Right away, Mr. Binge." Nessie poured a shot. "Say, they don't look so good."

"No?" The whiskey slid down his throat, filling him with fiery delight. "They look all right to me." From the side door to the alley, Natalia gave him a quick wave. "Think I'll get some air. All that talk of scarlet fever going around is giving me the willies!" He casually moved to the patio and took the side stairs down to the street.

In the alley, Pénombre stood alert and nickered with satisfaction at the delivery of a cube of sugarloaf. Binge climbed onto the driver's bench and glanced into the back. "Ladies."

Natalia and Catharina both smiled, wearing travel cloaks. "Mr. Binge."

The reins snapped and Pénombre started forward onto Thames Street. A few meters away sat a Strangewayes delivery carriage. Binge pulled up next to it and cleared his throat. "Excuse me, Doctor?"

"Yes? What can I do for you this evening, Mr. Binge?" The doctor tipped his hat. "And Miss Binge and Miss Binge?"

"Seems there are some sick people in there, Doctor. Mr. Coggshall and two of those nice buyers from the slaving company have taken ill. Could be scarlet fever." He wore a mock expression of fear.

"Oh dear, that does sound infectious."

"Captain Valentine and his party couldn't make the game, however."

"Well, how fortunate. All the same, I think you three should stay indoors tonight."

"Right you are, sir. Good evening to you." Binge nodded and sped off down Honey Lane.

La Roche glanced into the back at Atia. After much contemplation, he recognized her now. He met her before when she was a child. He had done Cormac O'Malley a favor and as fate would have it, he was doing O'Malley another by keeping her safe now. La Roche leaned out in anticipation for Violante's arrival, nothing yet. From the inner pocket of his jacket he removed a satchel filled with gold coins. "Keep this safe for me until I return?"

"O'course." Atia tucked the bag in beside her.

"She is coming," the doctor said, climbing onto the driver's seat.

"Be safe, Capitaine." Atia blew him a kiss.

La Roche tipped his hat to her. "Till we meet again, charming Atia." He stepped down and addressed the doctor, "You should get them out of here. See you at the rendezvous, I will."

Vie pulled up in a wagon led by an aged gray horse. "Come with me, Capitaine. I'll take you there."

La Roche climbed up, glancing back to see Atia give Vie a cautioning glare.

"Don't forget, it's imperative that you be at the meeting point by sunrise," the doctor insisted.

La Roche nodded. "Oui, I'll be there." He tried to contain a smile; it had been ages since a woman grew so jealous over him.

The wagon sped along at an unruly pace and he held onto the side. "The Clubhouse, where is that?" He observed a pistol tucked in beside her.

"Next to Henry's Loft. It's a big house with a lookout near the storehouses for Morgan's Line."

His face shriveled with disgust. "They got Henry's Loft too? I lived in that house! Dirty bastards!"

Vie cranked the reins, turning sharply down Church Street. "What'll we do about Art's men?"

"Let me deal with them." He grabbed her gun before she could react and inspected it. "That'll do." He tucked the gun back. "Have you handled a pistol before?"

She gave him a defiant stare. "Plenty."

"Have you fired a weapon?"

"Once or twice."

"Did you ever hit anything?"

"Nay, I haven't, with neither a pistol nor a carriage."

"Leave the fighting to me, yes?" la Roche said.

"That's my intention."

They pulled up next to a driveway lined with a wall of shrubbery separating homes from storehouses.

La Roche yanked the false nose and beard from his face and buried them in the branches of bush. He rubbed his irritated skin and drew his sword. “Stay behind me and don’t make a sound.” Attached to a leather cord around his neck, he withdrew a small wooden ankh. He briefly kissed it tucked it back into his shirt.

Vie drew her pistol.

“Not unless you absolutely have to,” he said.

“Oui, Capitaine. Lead the way.”

Along the Sea Lane behind the King’s warehouses, several cloaked figures traveled like phantoms along the dimly lit wharf. A fishing boat engulfed in sea mist sat waiting for them. Gladstone ushered the group along to the Snapper Shack, an old wood structure, where they met a fisherman with a torch in his hand.

“Right on time, Snuggles,” said Gladstone.

An experienced seaman and a lifetime member of the League of Olde Fishermen, Snuggie “Snuggles” Maxwell looked as warm and receptive as a sea serpent. His face was deeply scarred by disease, booze, fishing tackle, blades, and a barrel that was once smashed over his head. “As always, mate.” Snuggles shook hands and led the group of now ex-slaves aboard. “Right this way, folks.”

Fatima squeezed Gladstone’s hand. “Thank you.”

“No problem.” He smiled and escorted her aboard. *This is me favorite part of the job, making a difference in people’s lives.* The plantation was a fine place, although a bit overcrowded these days. Everyone would be welcome there. He was excited to see Carlena again; it had been far too long.

Binge emerged from the shadows, arm in arm with Catharina and Natalia. “I know, I know. It’s all my fault. I’m always making women late.”

“Thank you.” Natalia kissed Gladstone on the cheek.

“Yes, thank you.” Catharina kissed the other side.

“Thank him? Do we look so much alike?” Binge scoffed.

The ladies turned. “Thank you, Mr. Binge.” They kissed his lips.

Binge came up for air. “Now that’s better. Credit where credit is due.” He rubbed both of their backs.

"You are very kind and I'll miss your humor sense." Catharina gasped tearfully.

"Well, my humor sense thanks you."

Natalia laughed. "I especially liked your inappropriate, adolescent antics. A welcome change to the stagnant aristocracy we're accustomed to."

"Why, thank you." Binge's eyes widened. "I'll find out what that means someday."

"Don't forget, I brought the boat," Gladstone added and they turned to him.

"I didn't believe anyone would help us. Not in a million years." Catharina sniffed, tears streaming down her face.

"Don't you know you can't cry before getting aboard, it's bad luck!" Gladstone sniffed slightly.

"Thank you again." Natalia grabbed Catharina's hand. "We'll see you there?"

"Very soon. Don't you worry, love."

The women boarded. "Why do you always cry?" Natalia scolded. "You make us look like a couple of whimpering Borgia sluts!"

Gladstone smirked. "I always like being thanked."

"Well, I ain't thanking you like that, so you can just get it outta your head." Binge waved.

Gladstone signaled Snuggles. "We'll be here before sunrise. I hope you can make it back in time. And stick to the plan unless it goes to shit."

"Aye, we'll be back." Snuggles raised the gangway and crewmen untied the bowline. The fishing boat drifted away.

"I'm going back for Cherry and Katie," Binge said.

"Aye, I'm headed back there now. You want a ride?"

"I don't think it's even legal," Binge speculated. "But as it is, Pénombre's gone home to bed and we've got more damsels in distress to save."

In the driver's seat, Gladstone unlocked the brake and untied the reins. "I really do like being thanked." They drove up Thames Street around pockets of people, and halted across from the Swiftsure. Crowds spilled onto the street and down the alleyways. Many screamed, flailing their arms. From afar, the tune "Merry Month of May" echoed.

"Aye, I never liked that song much either," Gladstone declared.

People ran by, yelling, "It's here! Run for your lives!"

"What's here?" asked Gladstone.

"Scarlet fever, it is!" a man bellowed and vanished down a path.

Gladstone tried to hide his grin. "The man's a bloody genius. Scarlet bloody fever?"

"Would you prefer the black plague?" Binge seemed mildly entertained.

"Run, it's scarlet fever?" Gladstone laughed. "That's like saying, shit, I wet me pants!" He stretched out, putting his legs up on the seat. "That's fine, I had it as an infant. Again in my twenties, though at the time I thought it was a bad case of lice."

"Having fun?" Cherry Banks arrived, hidden under a cloak.

Gladstone turned to offer his hand. "Scarlet bloody fever?"

"Would you prefer the black plague?" Cherry tucked into the back seat.

"Aye, he said that one already. Where are the others?" Gladstone asked.

"The doc took Lilly and the pikey girl. I think the Capitaine's gone looking for the sister."

Gladstone sat up straight. "Alone?"

"Where did Art go?" Binge eyed Cherry.

"He's gone to the Clubhouse."

"Wanna bet we'll find the Capitaine there?"

Gladstone released the brake. "Well, let's go for a little ride and see, shall we?" The carriage moved at a turtle's pace through the stream of pedestrians.

Binge shrugged. "Go with the flow; always works for me."

They turned down Honey Lane when Cherry slid in between them. "So, ya wanna hear what happened in there?"

"Aye." Both men nodded.

A smug expression formed on her face. "Well, I peeked into the room with Coggshall and the slavers and they was gasping for air and puking up their guts! They're done like last week's dinner!" She pictured Coggshall's ruddy, spotted skin with blood caked around his mouth. His face frozen in a horrified pose. Then Sheriff Tellam and Beckford arrived.

Tellam covered his mouth. "Sweet Jesus!"

“Sweet ain’t exactly the word,” Beckford said.

“Is he dead?” Tellam asked.

“Aye.”

Red foam burbled from Coggshall’s mouth and his hand reached up.

Beckford stepped back. “Well, ye abouts.”

Cherry tittered. “Then there was gunfire, so I followed Big Dick and his Number One outside.”

“Big Dick?” Binge asked. “Is he *that* big?”

Cherry grinned. “Not by your standards, dear. So we all ran downstairs and we finds the slaver ship captain and his men laying there on the dock with holes in their heads. One of the officers shot them trying to get aboard.”

Gladstone slapped his thigh. “Scarlet fever again!”

“Then people started to panic,” Cherry continued. “We spotted one of Coggshall’s new guys, Shipwash, face down on top of the causeway wall. Monsieur De’va said he just fell off the porch and went splat!” She sighed. “Good times at the old Swiftsure tonight!”

Miles
Gladstone
GO
2015

Tomfoolery and Hocus Pocus

Atia gave Lilly a nudge when they arrived at the apothecary. Strangewayes climbed down and offered Atia his arm. She dismounted carefully, bracing her aching ribs.

Minuit swooped overhead and landed on the roof. He stared down at her with a peculiar smile. "*Bonjour*, Mademoiselle."

"Hello, Minuit."

"Ugh! Right peculiar bird that," Lilly said, jumping down with the basket of jalapenos.

"Don't ya go listening to her, you're a treasure," Atia fussed.

"Right this way, Atia, my dear." The doctor led her up a flight of steps to the side entrance.

"Is this yer apo-cracy?" Atia asked.

"Yes. I couldn't have said it better myself. This is my institution of tomfoolery and hocus pocus." He held out the key. "Lilly, could you please?"

"Sure." She took the key and opened the door.

"You wait here. I'll be back soon," Atia chirped at Minuit.

"Who's a pretty bird?" he whistled back.

"Think I need a laudanum drop," Lilly moaned.

"Not right now!" Strangewayes held up his hand and entered cautiously, peering into the corners of the room.

"Are we expecting guests?" A graying woman appeared holding a lantern. She wore a simple but elegant kirtle with a jacket bodice of linen.

Strangewayes jumped. "Mrs. Beazley!" he said. Then, more calmly, "Very likely."

Lilly set the basket down. "Me mouth burns o'hellfire!"

Mrs. Beazley raised her eyebrows. "I don't think I'll ask."

"Lilly, can you take Atia to the supply room and pack whatever you think you'll need? Within reason, that is." He glanced down the corridor to the apothecary.

"Mrs. Beazley, I need you to prepare for incoming patients."

"You know what happened the last time you said that."

"This is different; I can assure you."

Lilly grabbed a candle from the table and inspected a shelf filled with various bottles and flasks.

"You won't find anything good over there," the doctor said. "There's two new bottles of 'L' in the store room. Take *one* for the trip."

"Sure." Lilly took Atia's arm. "Come along. Second door on the left."

Atia opened the passage and they entered. Lilly shut the door behind them. "Well, ain't this cozy?" She held up the light.

"What'll we need to bring?"

"Let's see what he's got." Lilly grabbed a spare medical bag. "I recognize those." She grabbed two vials of laudanum. Next, she opened a cupboard. "Definitely need these. His honey soaps are amazing." She tossed several in the bag.

"Have you been there before?" Atia examined a jar filled with dark liquid.

"To Strangewayes's plantation? Nay, but Cherry has. She said it was like a dream. Flowers everywhere and green. He's a naturalist. That means someone who knows all about nature and all." Lilly pointed. "That tin there, we'll take it."

"What is it?" Atia detected a sweet peppermint smell.

"It's a skin salve. Put it on your bruises and they should heal right up. You wanna be lovely for your Capitaine." Lilly winked.

Atia flushed, stuffing the salve in the bag. "Mine, is he?"

"You kidding? I ain't seen Cherry jealous before. The way he looks at you has her head spinning!"

"Her and the Capitaine, was they ever married?"

"Nay. They spent a few hours here and there." Lilly shrugged. "Cherry always talked about him. Her bread basket's right bloody on fire now that he's back, I tell ya!" She shoved some bandages in the bag. "He's all yours, darling. Cherry knows it. She's just having a hard time accepting, is all."

"Well, he's a charming bastard," Atia said. She had suspected as much; Cherry's hostility was so palpable it seemed to travel through walls.

Strangewayes anticipated trouble. He'd started the day with a strong cup of tea laced with laudanum and coca leaf powder. Still reeling from yesterday's delivery of half a dozen dead slaves, his judgment was compromised from stress and fatigue.

Mrs. Beazley's eyes burrowed into him even under lantern light. She leaned in close, keeping her voice low. "Any sign of the other pikey?" She looked horrified by her own mouth. "Good Lord, now I'm talking like a Port Royaler!"

"I'm afraid we've lost Livia for the time being, but the Capitaine's gone to search for her. We do have reason to believe she's in fair condition, considering MacAskill's been tending to her."

"Poor child. I don't wish his bedside manner on anyone."

"All the same, if the Capitaine does find her we must be ready. I'll drop the girls off and come straight back." He felt a verbal reprimand coming on.

"Need I remind you that we've only been paid for four. You have to take into account the resources. There have been fourteen births this year. There's no more room at your *fucking* plantation!" Mrs. Beazley grumbled.

"We have the room!" the doctor argued. "And why must you always call it that?"

"How are we going to account for the missing slaves?"

"We'll have to cook the books a bit, that's true. But admit it, you're having as much fun as I am!"

Mrs. Beazley rolled her pearl necklace in her fingers. "If you mean having heart failure is your idea of fun, then yes, quite!" She stomped to the examination room.

The doctor followed, wanting to make peace. He helped her to lay out clean towels, sort out a tray of supplies and set up fresh water in a pitcher. "It may seem rash, I admit, but a move had to be made."

"Rash?" Mrs. Beazley seethed. "Yes, I suppose that's one word for it. You're being downright cocky! Stop and think about what you're doing!" She drew herself up to face him. "Do you realize what will happen if you've started a slave revolt? Any idea at all how many people could die? Friends, neighbors, and the very slaves you've been trying to help. You may have destroyed everything we've worked for. I hope to God it's worth it!"

The clop of hooves and screeching wheels sounded. Strangewayes checked the storefront window. "Our guests have arrived, I'm afraid. You're just going to have to trust me."

"Perhaps this time you should have trusted me." She stormed off down the hall, pausing at the supply room. "There are men here, you'll need to be absolutely quiet."

"Right-o," Lilly said.

The doctor went to the front door. He recognized one of Bleedin Art's men, Scarcliff. He jumped from the car, panting and wiping his brow. Two thugs followed behind.

"Y–you a…all…ruh?" One of the thugs stuttered.

Scarcliff knocked. "Aye, I'm all right. This be the place."

"Coming," the doctor called and unlocked the door. "Welcome, gentlemen."

Scarcliff perspired profusely, his skin chalky white. "We're here for Coggshall's Negroes."

"Yes, of course you are," he replied. "How unfortunate."

"Unfortunate? Not a word I'm wanting to hear."

"This way, please." Strangewayes guided them by lantern light along the front porch to a flight of stairs. "They're out back." He glanced at Scarcliff. "I say, are you quite well?"

"With some haste, sir, if you please," said Scarcliff.

Strangewayes led them to a shed at the bottom of the steps and unbolted the door. "For containment, you understand." He shone the light inside at the corpses clad in white rags.

Scarcliff stepped backwards.

"Wha–, wha–, w–w–w—" the stutterer said.

"What happened to them?" the other thug finished.

"It looks like scarlet fever."

"Oh f–f–f–f—"

"Were you lot at the fayre tonight?"

Scarcliff hyperventilated. "Buggered, ain't I?" Fat drops of perspiration slid down his face.

"Have you started vomiting blood yet?" Strangewayes asked.

"What?" Scarcliff gasped.

"Oh, you poor bastard!"

"Don't say that!" Scarcliff moaned.

"My apologies."

"Is there a cure?"

"Like the old rope said, I'm afraid not. I can brew you tea and give you something for pain," Strangewayes offered.

"Will it help?"

"No, but it'll make your transition to death much less horrifying."

Scarcliff signaled the thugs and they ran up the stairs. "What would be the bloody point?" He followed. "Good night to you, sir."

Strangewayes relocked the shed, chuckling, and went back up. Scarcliff's carriage jetted down High Street.

Lilly poked her head out the door. "Who's in the shack?"

Strangewayes jumped. "Please don't do that!" He caught his breath. "Those poor people were delivered yesterday. Some died in the storm, some were victims of that man you helped eradicate earlier. I believe these people could be Tainos – very few left, you see. This is a very sad day indeed, though not uncommon in this business. Are you sure you're ready for it?"

"Aye, I am."

"Good. Are you and Atia ready to leave?"

"Aye and she's feeling better than I am." Lilly pouted.

"Oh, the laudanum. I told you, that stuff is bad for you. It should never be taken recreationally by anyone other than a trained professional." He gazed into her eyes and smiled. "Okay, I'll give you a drop when we get to the boat."

Lilly beamed and kissed him on the cheek. "Yer the best, Doctor!"

"Quite right," he said. "Atia, my dear, are you ready?"

She nodded. "Can I trouble you for another drop?"

"Unfortunately, taking more right now wouldn't be good for you," he explained.

"Do you have anything else?" she pressed.

"For pain at this point I would normally recommend a couple of puffs from a marijuana plant. But with bruised ribs, we can't risk giving you a cough or the giggles."

Atia laughed, and then grabbed her side. "Oh, ouch!"

He smiled at her. "See what I mean? I'll get Gladstone to make you some special biscuits when you get to the plantation. That should do the trick. Now, we should be off to see some good friends of mine."

"More pirates?"

"Nay, fishermen. Ain't that right?" Lilly replied. "Sea Lane is where the old fishermen hang their rods!"

"Very funny." The doctor climbed into the driver's seat. "The boat should pick you up by dawn."

"And Livia?" Atia asked.

"We're still looking. I promise we'll find her. The Capitaine knows where to find us."

Lilly slid in beside Atia, covering them both with a knitted blanket. “Don’t you worry, Doc Strange never let us down before, and this is a town bubbling with let-downs.” Lilly gazed at the sky, pondering. “I wonder how Codface is feeling about now?”

DR. STrangewayes
I Wont prescribe
Taken Thyself
GO
2015

Over a Barrel

La Roche squinted through the partly open shed door. The air was stuffy, reeking of stale beer and the sewage-like aroma of gunpowder. Avoiding broken barrel fragments, he positioned himself with a clear view of the back entrance to the Clubhouse and the second-floor patio. He left Violante to hide in a bush next to the shed. So far she'd been helpful and seemed honest in her intent.

Codface staggered out back and hunched over a barrel. He sweat copiously and heaved.

Mike glanced down. "Shit, Cod. You look like death. Didn't think ya could get any uglier."

Codface forked his fingers. "Aye, I feel like death. It must be scarlet fever."

Mike grimaced. "Doc'll be here soon and *she* ain't going nowhere. Go lie down a spell."

"Aye." Codface tottered back inside.

"And stay the hell away from me," Mike uttered before padding down the stairs to light up his pipe and admire the old brickwork of the building and the recently trimmed hedges.

The shed door creaked as la Roche slipped out. Mike approached to investigate but found it empty and re-latched it. He turned to star gaze as la Roche plunged a dagger into the back of his skull. Not a sound escaped and the blade was yanked out quickly. The body fell and blood gushed out of the fatal wound, pooling around the head.

Vie stepped forward, holding her hand over her mouth.

"Wait here," la Roche said. He went inside to the parlor where a fire roared. Codface stoked the burning log with an iron, and then wrapped himself in a blanket. The floorboard squeaked.

"Mikey?" Codface beckoned.

La Roche stayed in the shadowy hall and readied a thin leather strap.

Codface investigated. "Who goes there?" He grabbed at his throat, choking until his body went limp. The corpse was dragged out back to join the other one.

La Roche put the strap back in his pocket. Vie seemed anxious, ignoring the dead bodies. She seemed preoccupied by some internal debate. *Oh, now it happens! Greed or desperation,* he thought.

She raised the pistol. "Hold it!" Her hand trembled. "I'm sorry, Capitaine, but put down all your weapons."

La Roche reached to the sky, still holding his dagger. "You disappoint me."

"I don't have a choice," she stammered.

"Oui, you do. And you are making the wrong one, believe me." He stepped forward and put the blade away. "You won't do it."

"Don't move," Vie warned. "I will do it!"

Ah, desperation. Don't force my hand. "No, you won't because you are not a killer. Whatever happened to you didn't take away your soul. You are still who you are and taking me in may get you fifty thousand or so—"

"Five hundred thousand," she corrected.

"Fuck, are you serious?" La Roche smirked. "Five hundred thousand? I'll turn myself in!"

"I don't want to."

La Roche inched forward. "Good, because when you collect all that money and you are sitting on the beach, drunk and covered in jewels, you will think to yourself: no, that's not it. It is not enough. You will still be empty. Believe me; I've been there. You will regret this day for the rest of your life. You'll wish you could come back to this moment and stop yourself from acting like such a stupid bitch." He slowly reached for the pistol. "Come on, give me the gun."

"I won't live like this anymore!"

"Yeah, well, you're about to get your wish." His fingers reached for it. "Come on, give me the gun."

Vie surrendered it.

"Taking me on alone is not a wise thing to do. You should learn who you're dealing with before attempting such a thing." He scowled, tucking the gun into his coat. "I'll let it go this time because I like you." Giving her a very cold stare, he hissed, "But never again point a gun at me. *Never*. Or I will kill you!"

"She's upstairs in the loft, is what they said."

"Coming with me?"

Vie nodded and he motioned to her to go up first.

Beneath layers of blankets, Livia slept fitfully. She was fair like Atia, but with dark hair.

"She survived a hurricane, a shipwreck, and MacAskill, and you think *you* had a shitty day?" he said.

Livia stirred and tried to sit up. "Who are you?"

"We are here to take you to your sister." He gazed into her pale blue eyes. While she was pretty, she didn't have the same vibrant spark as Atia. In fact, there was a somber maturity about her that reminded him too much of himself.

"Atia?" Livia asked.

"You have another one?" He tried to help her up, but she cried out in pain. "Give me a hand, Vie." They bundled Livia up in bed sheets and each lifted an end, trying to keep her as flat as possible on their journey down the stairs and along to the road where Vie's wagon waited.

Once Livia was aboard, la Roche covered her with a horse blanket.

Vie climbed onto the driver's seat, but la Roche stopped as a light up ahead caught his eye. A carriage rolled towards the Clubhouse. "Go, get out of here." He handed back her pistol.

"Now I know what Cherry sees in you." Vie slid the gun in beside her.

"It's not loaded," he confessed. "I'm not an idiot; I unloaded it before we got here; that is why you're alive. Adieu." La Roche crept back to the Clubhouse.

"Good luck, Capitaine!" Vie called after him and the wagon sped away.

La Roche remained hidden behind a shrubbery. The carriage pulled up. It was Bleedin Art and his men. They disembarked only feet away from the bodies beside the shed. A branch poked into la Roche's side as leaned forward as far as he dared to listen in.

"I been meaning to ask you, what's with the Redcoats?" MacAskill slid across the seat. "I thought King William was all about orange?"

"A special training force on loan from Lord Spotswood. He calls them Red Royals," Art said.

"Aye, they're special, all right. Well, the bed boils look a lot like militia to me."

Art took a deep breath. "Mmm, smell that sea air!" He turned to his men. "You know, this is the only side of Port Royal that don't stink."

Jayne climbed down, packing a musket at his side. "I'll never smell anything again."

"Well, yer the one who ate the bloody things! Christ, you'll do anything she tells ya! Don't fall in love with a strumpet. Never works out. Trust me. Stinger, go to the loft and check on the girl. Jayne, open the storm shutters and break out the rum." Art limped inside with MacAskill following.

Yards away at Morgan's Line, two figures gazed up at the twinkling night sky from the gun platform. Royal Rook held Katie, glimpsing into her eyes beneath the light of a shooting star. "There ain't nothing I can say to put it back right, I know. But I'm sorry, Kaitlyn. I really am."

Katie turned to put her finger on his lips. *I still love you.*

"If you'll still have me, I meant what I said. Someday I intend to marry you. This don't change nothing."

Katie laughed silently, feeling hideous. She opened her mouth to show the small stump of tongue left. "Aaaaaaa!"

At first he seemed revolted, but then love overtook and he slid his arms around her. "I don't know what to say. Tell me…" He rolled his eyes, grinning stupidly. "What do you want of me? Revenge?"

Already taken care of, thanks. Katie shook her head, frustrated she couldn't get a single word out, yet so relieved to hear that he still loved her. Tears streamed down her face again.

"I can't tell which way yer nodding," Rook admitted and she gave him a half laugh, half sneer. They kissed and he tried to slip his tongue in her mouth. She pulled away, reprimanding him with her eyes. He grinned sheepishly. "Sorry, I forgot." It was then he noticed the blood in her ear and down the side of her head. "You're bleeding. Are you well, love?"

Katie raised her thumb.

"Don't you remember?" Rook watched the water. "This is where we were first together. Romantic, ain't it?"

She smirked.

"Granted, I paid you to polish me knob, but that doesn't make it any less romantic. Something happened to me that night."

She made a crude swallowing sound.

"Before that. Something happened to us both that night, didn't it?"

Rook kissed the side of her head and pulled her closer. "I promised I'd take you away from here on me ship and we'd never look back. Didn't I?"

Katie nodded, wiping away a stray tear.

"And I'm gonna take you away from here, no matter how many body parts you lose."

Katie rolled her eyes, raising both her thumbs. *Aye, ya fucking idiot!*

"No one'll ever hurt you again, love. I promise. You know, I always wanted to tell you—"

Katie thrust his face into her cleavage.

"Right-o then," he murmured.

Checkmate swooped over, landing on the wall behind them. Another shooting star streaked the sky while starry reflections rippled on the water's surface.

Violante's wagon wheeled down the bumpy street, passing tall buildings that housed businesses on the bottom floor and residences on the top. Already on the move were fishermen who wanted to be on the water before the sun rose. Her nose wrinkled. The scent of fish always lingered in the air. But, she reminded herself, getting Livia to the apothecary was more important. *Strangewayes will be so pleased, I can't wait to see his face.*

Vie turned a corner sharply, coming face to face with Constable Blower's carriage blocking her path.

"You strumpet, stop!" He climbed down. "You was at the Swiftsure tonight."

"Aye."

"Just where you be off to now, then?"

Vie reluctantly stepped down. "On me way home."

"What'cha got in the back?" He cocked his pistol.

Vie felt her face redden. *Curse the Capitaine for taking my shot away!* A moment of perfect timing is very rare, so she was stunned to see Longstaff's carriage. Air gushed from her lungs and the horse whinnied in sympathy.

"Violante!" Longstaff dismounted, glaring at Blower. "What's going on here?"

"Richard, I was on me way to find you." She wanted to thrust herself into his strong arms.

"I was taking her in for questioning, sir," Blower said.

"Were you?" Longstaff gave her an affectionate gaze. "Are you all right, my dear?"

"Aye, now that you're here." She smiled brightly. "Seems I've broken a law of some sort."

Longstaff checked the back of the wagon. Livia stirred beneath the blanket. "State your business with her, Constable."

"There's been an outbreak of what appears to be scarlet fever. Dr. MacAskill suspects—"

"She looks perfectly healthy to me," Longstaff insisted. "I'll assume full responsibility for this one. On your way."

"With respect, sir, I'll need to report it."

"I said, on your way!" Longstaff yelled and Fishhook flashed his pistol.

"Aye, Captain." Blower grimaced. "You navy think ya own everything." He climbed back into his carriage and sped away.

Vie slid her hand into Longstaff's. "Richard, thank heavens! Nessie gave you the message, then?"

"Aye, she did." He checked the back of the wagon. "What are you up to?"

"Richard." She put her hand on his cheek. "If I was to lead you to the French captain, would you be inclined to split the bounty with me?" Vie's face filled with excitement.

"Where did you last see him?"

"At the Clubhouse. He's taking on Art's men alone."

"Alone?" Fishhook asked, his eyebrow raised.

Longstaff smirked. "You never fought the Frenchman." He lifted the horse blanket in the back of the wagon to reveal Livia, pale and shivering.

"My God! Is that the pikey girl?" Fishhook exclaimed.

"He led me to her," Vie said.

Fishhook chuckled. "You're finding just about everyone tonight! Can you lead us to Roc Braziliano?"

Longstaff was silent a moment. "No, but the Frenchman can."

Livia released a rattling cough and groaned.

"I was taking her to Dr. Strangewayes," Vie explained.

Fishhook eyed his captain. "How shall we proceed, sir?"

"We'll have to see if Bleedin Art catches him first," Longstaff said, taking Vie's arm and escorting her to the driver's bench. He slid in beside her, taking the reins. "We'll drop these two off at the doctor first. Then perhaps a bit of pirate hunting?"

Fishhook returned to his carriage.

It was only a short drive to the apothecary. When the doctor opened the door, astonishment lit his face. "Am I hallucinating? Is that Livia?"

"Found her for you, Doc." Vie gleamed, happy to see his excitement.

"Steady, her ribs are broken on the left side," Fishhook cautioned and they lifted her through the threshold. "Other wounds have been mended already."

"She's drugged too," Vie added.

"Thank heavens she's alive!" Strangewayes patted Livia's face. "Whoever she is."

"I believe this is *the pikey* they were using as bait, Doctor," Longstaff said.

"Yes, quite. Right this way, quickly." The doctor led them to the examination room where they set Livia down gently, propping pillows beneath her head, legs and arms.

Fishhook smoothed her hair over the pillow.

Mrs. Beazley immediately brought in a pot of hot water and went to work changing the old bandages.

Longstaff patted Fishhook's shoulder. "Come on." He turned to Vie. "Will you stay here?"

"Aye. I'll see you out." She followed them to the storefront entrance. Longstaff kissed her eagerly before returning to the car. "If Bleedin Art can't catch him we stand a good chance."

Fishhook was already in the driver's seat holding the reins.

"No need to rush, Jim." Longstaff climbed up. "Now that we know it is him and where he is, I know how to bring him back. We'll take his ship as ordered and that'll flush the man out." He waved to Vie and the carriage rolled away.

She stood in the doorway of the apothecary until Longstaff vanished from sight.

"Violante, can you give us a hand?" the doctor called.

Vie returned to the examination room.

Strangewayes checked Livia's pulse. "Good, considering."

"What's he got her on?" Mrs. Beazley opened the girl's eyes.

"Probably just opium tablets. Unlike us, she most likely has a low tolerance." He passed Vie a small mirror. "Can you shine this into her eyes for us?"

"Sure, Doc."

"I have a feeling your captain and I would agree. You made the right call tonight."

She was taken aback for a moment. "I reckon I did, sir."

"Thank you. Now the left eye, please." Strangewayes opened the eyelid.

"Bloodshot, but not yellow," said Mrs. Beazley. "MacAskill knows how to tend a wound when he puts his mind to it."

"Atia?" Livia uttered, barely conscious.

Strangewayes squeezed her hand. "Everything is going to be okay, Livia. We have Atia and she's safe." He and Mrs. Beazley examined her torso and found massive bruising and sections of punctured skin.

Mrs. Beazley shook her head. "She's certainly not well enough to travel."

"You're absolutely right, she'd never make it. She'll have to stay here."

"We'll need more clean linens ordered."

"That shouldn't be a problem, we'll order them from Widow Bell." Strangewayes patted Livia's arm. "Atia's not going to like it, but I'm afraid we have no choice."

Mrs. Beazley sighed. "I'm not going to like it; do I get a choice?"

Vie watched Livia, reminded of the time of when she herself lay on the same table being stitched up. *The pikey girl's in good hands, if anyone can heal her, it be Strangewayes.* Her thoughts turned to Longstaff. If anyone could catch the Capitaine, it's Big Dick. Her lifelong dream of seeing Port Royal fade off in the distance, inched ever closer.

Henry's Loft

Flames licked the old marble pit, saturating the loft in waves of heat. Art entered the Clubhouse parlor, surrendering to the heavenly sensation. He sunk into the couch, where the pain in his knees finally eased.

Jayne lit up a cigar and collapsed on a Wainscot chair near the window. "How much heat do we need?"

"If you're gonna complain, ya can massage the boss's knees!" Art said.

Pikestaff entered. "Ain't it a bit warm in here?"

MacAskill peered around with a cigarro hanging from his mouth. "Where the hell is everyone?"

"We got bodies out here!" Stinger called from outside. Everyone ran out in the direction of the shed.

"Codface?" Jayne gawked at the corpse. "He got it, whatever *it* is."

MacAskill knelt down beside the bodies. "Well, this sure ain't scarlet fever, I can tell you that." There was a sticky pool of blood and bruising on Mike's throat. "Murdered, both of them."

Art kept his distance. "But he's got spots."

"Aye, but he's also been strangled. I guess poison wasn't fast enough."

"Where's the pikey girl?" Art looked at Stinger.

"Gone."

"Well, she didn't do this, that's for sure."

"You sure?" Pikestaff asked doubtfully. "Them pikeys can get pretty mean."

"She could barely walk, ya imbecile!" MacAskill snapped.

"Means someone took her. Now someone's gotta go find her. Start back at the Swiftsure," Art ordered.

"Codface and Mike, poor bastards," Jayne lamented.

They regrouped inside, readying weapons and guzzling rum.

"I ain't going near the scarlet fever," Pikestaff said as he loaded a pistol. "I'm staying right here."

"Fine," Art agreed. "Suit yerself. Cover the back."

An urgent knock came at the front door.

"Who goes there?" Gibbet squawked.

Pikestaff opened the door to find Constable Blower gasping for air. "There's another outbreak! Coggshall and two slave buyers."

MacAskill smirked. “Oh, Jesus fuck’n Christ on Good Friday, they’re sick?”

Blower fanned his face. “All dead! Same as Magott.”

“Okay, that’s a bit unexpected,” the doctor admitted.

“Isn’t it, though?” Art was very pleased. “Where’s Burghill?”

“No one’s seen him for hours.”

“Yer sure those company arseholes are paid up?” The fire light reflected off Art’s teeth.

“Aye, it’s in the vault.”

“If the slaves aren’t sick, take them back and we’ll resell them.”

MacAskill laughed. “Health regulations.”

Blower’s face faded back to its normal color. “I caught a strumpet.”

“Good for you.” The doctor slapped him on the back. “We’ll make a man of ya yet!”

“Nay, I caught one of Cherry’s strumpets a couple of blocks over. She was up to something, but that Big Dick made me let her go. She was at the Swiftsure tonight.”

Art pondered. “Which girl was it?”

“Don’t know her name. The gorgeous one with the great tits.” Blower cupped his hands to demonstrate.

“Violante Hayze,” Art said.

“She is friends with Katie, too.”

“Katie Evans?” MacAskill mused. “Revenge, maybe.”

“She was there at the outbreak. And there are more deaths. One of your men – Scrub Brush?” Blower said.

“Shipwash,” Pikestaff corrected.

“He’s not one of ours. That’s Coggshall’s new man,” MacAskill chuckled. “I guess not anymore.”

“Who keeps doing us favors?” Art was amazed that things were actually going right for once. Then Scarcliff charged through the front door, sickly pale and ready to vomit. “Well, so much for me winning streak!”

Everyone instinctively drew their weapons, ready to blow holes in the newcomer. Scarcliff held a rag over his mouth, choking back sickness. “They’re dead.” A sweaty rash formed on his chest and neck. “Coggshall’s Negroes are dead.”

Art grimaced. “All of them?”

“Scarlet fever, it was.”

MacAskill rolled his eyes. “Jesus fuck’n Christ on the bowsprit crapper, no it ain’t.”

“I have it Doctor, I’m sick,” Scarcliff said.

“And you brought it to me?” Art took several steps backwards. “How thoughtful!”

“I’m telling you, it ain’t scarlet fever.” MacAskill went in for a closer look. “You’re barking up the wrong bloody tree.”

“Tell me why you’re so convinced it’s poison?” Art argued.

Scarcliff’s eyes widened. “Poison?”

“As the sun comes up in the east, I’m sure it *is* poison. Why don’t anyone here have half a brain outside his pants?”

“But who did it?” Scarcliff asked.

“One of the anti-slavery movements. Who else?” the doctor said.

Art shook his head. “Nay, they ain’t organized enough for that.”

“I got it!” Blower bellowed and everyone backed away. “It was Cherry’s girls! The strumpet was hiding something, I’m sure of it.”

“You don’t know that,” Jayne protested. “What about food contamination like Strangewayes said?”

“Don’t listen to that opium-addicted crackpot! I wouldn’t trust him to fix a hangnail.” MacAskill inspected the red spots on Scarcliff’s neck. “How do you feel? Describe your symptoms.”

“I feel like shit.”

“That’s helpful. Thanks for that.”

“It *is* scarlet fever, damn it!” Art snapped. “He’s got the symptoms. Why do I listen to you?”

“Because people don’t stagger in and die like they’re in the final act of a fuck’n Shakespeare play when it’s scarlet fever, got it?”

“I don’t want him here. Get him a room or something.” Art glared at Scarcliff as though he were a leper. “Just get him outta here.”

“I’m finished, ain’t I?” Scarcliff whimpered.

“Whatever it is, it’s too late to find a cure.”

“We could try!”

MacAskill rummaged through his medical bag. “Try this, it’s activated charcoal. It’ll absorb whatever poison you got in yer gut.” The doctor addressed Jayne, “Get him some water, will ya?” He patted Scarcliff’s back. “You haven’t dropped dead yet, so that must count for something. I’ll have someone watch him through the night. You like strumpets, don’t ya?”

Scarcliff groaned. "Not now."

"I'll get him a room at the Four Feathers and pay a whore to look after him. If he lives through till the morrow, he should be through the worst of it."

Art nodded reluctantly. "Right." He turned to Jayne. "Go with MacAskill."

"You sure?" Worry filled Jayne's face.

"Aye. Stinger'll cover the front and Pikestaff the back." Art watched Scarcliff choke back something disgusting. "Find Violante Hayze and bring her in for questioning," he ordered Blower. "I don't care what the Big Dick says; bring her in!"

"Aye." Blower nodded nervously and left by the side door.

La Roche rolled up his sleeves and crept closer to the street. The prickly bushes grazed the exposed skin of his forearms. He unsheathed his cutlass slowly, watching two thugs on the driver's seat of an open carriage. They watched a shooting star streak down to the water and lit up cigarillos.

"D–do ya–ya–th–th—" one stuttered.

"He'll be well. He's tough as blade steel, he is," the other replied. "Besides, if he dies, we all move up in rank. Don't you sweat it."

"I g-g-gotta…"

The other nodded. "Right." The stutterer leapt down to take a piss in the nearest hedge. Once finished, he tied his trousers, stretched, and gazed up at another shooting star. After a lengthy yawn, the stutterer turned just in time to see a cutlass coming towards him. "Shit!" His head rolled into the bush and the body fell to the ground. Blood drained from the stump of his neck.

"What? Stutters?" The remaining thug called.

La Roche skulked alongside the carriage at a crouched angle, readying his weapon. "Psst."

The thug gasped, reaching for his partially severed neck. His head hung too far to the side, eyes still open, gushing blood like a gruesome joke.

La Roche paused a moment before reaching into the thug's pocket to swipe his tobacco, papers and matches. He rolled one and lit up, taking a deep breath. It had been a long time since he killed this way. Making a brief detour to the shed, he grabbed several small rundlets of gunpowder and set them on the seats. Next, he ran a powder trail along the length of the main pathway to the Clubhouse.

La Roche unhitched the horses and threw the empty barrels into the bush beside the shed. That's when Pikestaff came out the back door and lit his pipe. He went over to the shed, where the bodies of Mike and Codface already attracted flies. The moon washed everything in a pale luminous glow and the ocean's surface sparkled with shooting stars.

Gibbet swooped down and landed on Pikestaff's shoulder.

"Scared the shit outta me, stupid bird!" He removed his hat. "Show some respect. Sorry mates, not much of a send-off, eh? Dear Lord—"

"Dear Lord—" said Gibbet.

"Shush you. Dear Lord, we commit these bodies to—" suddenly la Roche charged from behind with his sword, lopping off yet another head. The body dropped with a thud.

"Shit!" Gibbet screeched, flying away.

La Roche finished his cigarette and ran alongside the building to peer in a window. Art strolled towards the study of Henry's Loft. *Ah, he's alone – I can surprise him.*

La Roche struck a match and tossed it at the gunpowder at the top of the main pathway. He skimmed through the side entrance and stole through a secret passage. Before long, la Roche watched Art through a crack in a closet door as he adjusted an oil lamp until the room brightened. Art plunked himself down in a chair and reached into the desk, fetching a bottle. After a large mouthful, he opened a leather-bound notebook and began reading aloud:

Shall I compare thee to a summer's day?
Thou art more lovely and more temperate:
Rough winds do shake the darling buds of May,
And summer's lease hath all too short a date.

La Roche pulled a face. *I'm not listening to fucking Shakespeare; I get enough of that shit from Laurens!* He burst through the door.

Surprise and fear filled Art's eyes. "Gator Gar! It really is you!" He swallowed hard, fixing on the sharp cutlass pointing in his direction. "So, how've you been?"

La Roche remained silent.

"Is it about the pikey girls, 'cause I had nothing to do with it," Art's voice wavered.

"A slaver you are? Kissing up to that *connard*, Coggshall?"

"I'm surviving the New World. You gonna kill me for that?"

"Pay the piper time it is, Bleedin Art." La Roche thrust his weapon.

"Oh, shit." Art shifted from side to side. "Help!"

"Busy, they are. I set a little surprise."

With perfect timing, an explosion resounded, and pungent gunpowder infused the air. The room vibrated and debris flew as the storm shutters splintered. The study door shook and two more explosions blew in succession.

Art cowered behind his chair. "I see you're upset about something."

"*You* sold us out, Valentine." La Roche charged, swinging the cutlass and slicing Art's arm. "It was *you* who led them to us at Roatán."

"Well, okay, that's true. But I was bound to; I was a bonded privateer." Art picked up the chair and attacked.

"As were we all." La Roche fell backwards. "*Merde*!" He regained his footing before running after Art into the parlor. Both men stumbled over broken glass and debris.

Art's arm dripped blood. He drew his longsword to deflect the cutlass, but it was still stuck in his belt. "Let's talk it over."

La Roche attacked again.

"You're right, enough talking." Art came at him swinging with belts flapping.

Jayne stumbled in through the ruined front entrance, his clothes and hair charred. He brandished pistols.

La Roche dove for the back door. "*C'est des conneries*!"

"Get him." Art collapsed on the floor, nursing his arm. "Christ, what a night!"

The pistols fired. Into the smoky night air la Roche ran like hell, down the path between Henry's Loft and a hedge wall.

GO
2015

Dante's Bloody Inferno

Draped in shadows, the causeway wall was the perfect spot to assess the situation. La Roche hunkered down, peeking over a stone barrier. City guards scrambled, heading in his direction. He crept along the ground towards a short fence and climbed over. Nearby, Jag'd Jayne and other thugs scoured the area.

A faint tapping came from behind him. La Roche turned, but saw nothing. It came again, louder this time, tapping out the tune "What to do with a Drunken Sailor". He followed it alongside a house. A familiar face appeared from a basement door.

"*Merci*," he whispered, stepping inside.

Widow "Easy" Bell locked it. Figures approached, trying the door. Moments later they moved on to the next house. She grabbed his arm and led him up a narrow staircase into a hallway. They entered the sitting room at the front where moonlight gleamed through the window.

"I thought it was you. All that fire was a dead giveaway. What the hell are you doing here?"

"Hiding, it would seem, no?" La Roche admired the bric-a-brac on the tables and the old books stacked on the shelves. "Thank you, Madame Belford. I am in your debt."

"Damn right you are. I heard you were in town but I never expected in a million years to see you here."

"The hurricane brought me in." He crouched beside a chair, watching the fire blaze down the street. "Not exactly welcome in this town any longer." Militiamen snooped around the front gate. "It is good to see you, truly. How is your boy?"

"He ran off at sixteen to be a pirate like his father. Thank you for asking." Widow Bell took a case off the shelf.

La Roche winced.

"Last year his name turned up on the manifest of a ship, apparently lost with all hands."

"I am sorry."

"Well, he grew up around pirates. What can I say?" She opened the case to reveal two ornate Spanish wheel lock pistols. "My plunder from Panama, Capitaine. You look like you need them more than I right now." She began to load them. "Considerably less than we were promised. This plot of land and a couple of Spanish pistols."

It was a common complaint regarding the Panama raid. "A big piece of property for Port Royal this is," la Roche said.

"You ought to try managing it." Widow Bell stared at him. "You all came back with stories of conquest and I was left to raise my boy alone with little compensation. You know, after all these years, I still don't know how my husband died. Bravely and with honor. That's the only answer I ever got from Henry." She wiped her cheek. "I just want one of you to tell me how he died. You owe me that."

La Roche took a deep breath. "Collecting ransom from a plantation, Rowdy and his men fled into the jungle with our take, leaving us pretty fucked. When we found him, he had screw-worm maggots coming out of his mouth and eyes, though he was still alive."

Widow Bell paused. "Thank you."

"The stories were bullshit. Nobody got paid what they were promised. The job was a bust." He squinted through the window. "All just a bloodbath…that's all it was. You were better off staying behind."

She squinted, spotting something through the window. "There's a man across the street."

"Where?"

"We both need spectacles. There, behind that wall." She pointed. "That's Strangewayes's man, isn't it?"

"Is it? Who?" La Roche recognized Gladstone's form.

"I'm not stupid. You and Strangewayes are both in on this." Widow Bell reached behind to grab a lantern. "You should let him know where you are." She slipped a silver plate into his hand. "Use this."

"Oui, that will work fine." He lit the lantern and used the plate as a signaling device. "Ah, Spanish silver. Very nice." After sending another flash in response, Gladstone waved back and disappeared.

The fire continued to rage down Church Street. Carriages burned on the Clubhouse pathway and Henry's Loft lay in ruins. Townspeople rushed from their houses with buckets of water.

Bizy Gale, wearing only her nightdress and slippers, organized people into rows, pointing at the nearby reservoirs. "Two columns, one here, and here! Use the wells from both properties!" The crowd quickly followed her direction. Buckets were filled and passed to the front. This wasn't the first fire to threaten the street. Everyone knew that Bizy was good friends with the old Fyre-Master. The buildings were so close together that the flames passed easily from one timber building to the next. Speed was essential.

"Douse the storehouse!" Bizy called. "Don't let it catch fire."

Everyone pitched in beautifully with a few notable exceptions. Father Parker Alcocke sat with his legs sprawled over the arm of a chair on the veranda of St. Paul's Church. He held a bottle, toasting the flames. "Whoa! Dante's bloody inferno tonight!"

From the neighboring building, Jarvess Coxenspit, more commonly known as Monsieur De'va, emerged from his upper floor balcony, dressed in silk nightwear with a matching pom-pom nightcap. Glass in hand, he admired the chaos, and then noticed Father Alcocke. The two men toasted enthusiastically.

Bizy gritted her teeth. Beckford and his militiamen were there, and would have been a great help, but they were more concerned with finding the arsonist than saving the city.

"Go get the dogs!" Beckford called.

Bizy tossed another bucket of water on the storehouses and noticed her son Jamie racing towards her with a small bucket. Panic seized her. "Jamie! Get back in the goddamn house!"

"But Ma!"

"Don't argue!" Bizy hollered.

Isabella chased after him.

"Both of you get back to the house!" Bizy screamed.

Isabella took her brother's hand and dragged him away. "Come on, dog-boy." They were soon watching from the safety of Widow Bell's front yard.

Where the hell are you, Easy? Thanks for all the help. Flames shot out from the fence around the storage sheds. "Keep dousing the storehouse!" she yelled.

Constable Blower, dazed and smoldering, tried to corral runaway horses in a nearby yard. "Someone grab the horses!"

Beckford charged to the front of the line. "On the fire, idiots! Douse the fire!"

"We have to stop it from spreading," Bizy protested, knowing full well that throwing water directly at the flames was futile.

“Don’t argue with me!” Beckford snapped and reorganized the lines.

A bell rang out and drew closer. A Keeling fyre engine with six horses charged down the street. Provost Marshall Nicholas Keene pointed and yelled through a blow horn, “Clear the way! Clear the way!”

Bizy breathed a sigh of relief. Keene was the one man she respected; he was practically a father figure to her. He had been the Provost Marshall, Fyre-Master and Surveyor General since the moment he set foot in Port Royal back in ’55. He’d designed the layout of the city and was in charge of every emergency that Bizy could remember since her arrival twenty-one years ago. People mocked his stern nature, but they soon realized that you don’t make fun of old man Keene around Bizy Gale unless you want an earful. When she was recovering from her injuries from Slasher Al, Keene had hired her to draw schematics. Not out of pity, but practicality; he was impressed by her skills at logistics.

The crowd cleared for the fyre engine. It was indeed a marvel of design genius. When the city acquired a Keeling fire engine from London, Keene took one look and determined that it desperately needed modifications. With Bizy’s guidance, he had mounted it on a large wagon, added a fifty-foot leather hose, reinforced it with iron scantlings, and built a railing around it to resemble the forecastle of a small ship. The finishing touch was an extendable ladder designed like a bowsprit located at the stern. The ladder could reach the upper windows of three- and four-level buildings. When complete, he named it “Bizy” in her honor, as she was not allowed to be a member of the Fyre Brigade.

Keene and “Bizy” had saved the city many times. Three years ago at Binge Manor, Master Binge’s two daughters had been trapped on the upper floor by the fire below. They were rescued by the house manservant, Theodore, who helped them onto the roof. They had been easily retrieved with the ladder.

The engine came to a stop across from the Clubhouse. Keene and his brigade dismounted.

“Fill the tank!” Bizy called. Townspeople lined up to dump their buckets into the engine’s cistern while men prepped the handles. She snarled to see Jamie re-emerge with his tiny containers, waiting to empty them.

The hose now jetted a steady stream and the firemen were ready to aim.

"The storehouses first," Keene instructed. "Stop it from spreading!"

Bizy dashed over, taking Jamie's arm and guiding him away from the crowd. They neared a gated yard, where behind them, Bleedin Art shook the filmy powder off his jacket and Dr. MacAskill looked dazed.

"You all right?" MacAskill's wild hair smoldered.

"I'm great, thanks for asking!" Art growled. "Where's the new guys?"

MacAskill glanced around. "All over the fuck'n place."

Bizy wrapped her arms around Jamie.

Constable Blower staggered over to Beckford. "It's the pirate Gator Gar! Search the streets and yards. He's near."

Bizy's eyes widened. *It couldn't be. He's long dead, I'm sure.*

Art caught his breath. "Half me men are missing heads."

"Aye, that's Gator Gar's calling card." Beckford watched Bizy.

She could barely contain herself. *He's alive!*

"He went a bit twitchy ever since his trip into the Darien Jungle with l'Olonnais," MacAskill chuckled.

"Aye, wouldn't you?" Art grinned painfully.

Bizy's eyes watered from the smoke.

"It's fine, Miss Gale," Beckford soothed. "You're safe now."

"Thank you, Major." She tried to contain a smirk.

A clergyman with his arm in a sling wandered among the crowd. "What's happened?"

"Pirate attack!" a bystander blurted out.

"Guess they never seen a pirate attack before?" Art said.

"Guess not." The doctor noticed something and tilted his head. "Jesus Christ on Wallace's grandmother!"

Bizy saw a hand emerge from under a flipped carriage. The fingers wiggled. "My God! Someone's under there!"

"Can ya help me out, sailor?" a voice mumbled.

"He's alive!" MacAskill exclaimed. "Lift it off him!"

Keene joined Beckford, MacAskill, Art, Bizy, and Jamie as they each took a section of carriage and slowly tipped it.

"Easy does it, tip it back!" Keene instructed.

The carriage landed in an upright position.

"Starfish?" MacAskill called. "He's alive."

They all looked down at the bloodied, bruised Scarcliff who rolled himself onto his side to throw up.

Art cringed. "He's puking up things he hasn't even eaten yet!"

MacAskill helped the poor bastard to his feet.

"Where's Jayne?" Art asked.

Scarcliff moaned. "Aruba, if he's smart."

The militiaman's dog carriage approached. Beckford and Blower flagged it down.

"About time!" Beckford snapped. "Search every house. It's the pirate Gator Gar."

Bizy smiled and took Jamie's hand. Both of them received a pat on the back from old man Keene before he returned to the fire.

"We'll sick the dogs on him." Blower grinned, unlocking the cage. "Those dogs like French meat." The dogs barked ravenously and bolted through the door to run off into the night.

"Maybe if you gave them a scent first?" MacAskill spoke sternly.

"Stupid dogs!" Blower's shoulders dropped.

"You wanna fetch them now?" Beckford pointed the way.

Blower cursed under his breath.

A huge shooting star streaked overhead, catching everyone's attention. Bizy caught MacAskill checking out her curves in the soiled nightdress. Both were embarrassed for a moment.

"Gotta love August," MacAskill said awkwardly, and then turned his attention to more arrivals, including the strumpet Katie. A pretty little thing that Bizy herself had previously hired for personal services. The rumor was that Katie had her tongue cut out. Bizy made eye contact and the sad look she received in return confirmed it.

Bizy guided Jamie back to the porch stairs where Isabella sat.

"I'm proud of you, boy. You did good." She slipped her arm around him. "But next time I say get in the goddamn house, you get in the goddamn house!" She smacked him on the head. "There's gunpowder all over that property, the whole block almost went up! Now get inside and put the water on."

Jamie ran off inside while Bizy paused beside Isabella.

"Thanks for watching your brother."

"But Ma—"

"But Ma nothing!" Bizy growled. "Get in the goddamn house before those dogs come back."

"Yes, Mama," Isabella groaned and marched up the steps.

Widow Bell came out onto the front porch. "Hurry up, children," she ordered. "You know the routine, Bella."

"Yes, ma'am," Isabella obeyed.

Widow Bell took Jamie's coat. "You can use my tub."

Bizy entered the living room and tears welled up in her eyes.

Isabella noted the man smiling awkwardly. "Who's that?"

"A friend. He was hurt in the fire. Now, go on."

"Yes, Mrs. Belford." Isabella took Jamie's hand and led him down the hall. "Come on, dog-boy!"

"Lock the door," Widow Bell insisted. "And stop calling him that."

"Yes, ma'am."

"What are you doing?" the Capitaine asked as Widow Bell shook soot all over the front entrance.

"Throwing off the dogs." She tossed the coat down the basement steps.

"Aw, throw them a bone." He grinned. "Dogs love me."

Tear tracks formed down Bizy's sooty cheeks.

"That is Isabella and James Junior?" he asked.

Widow Bell smiled. "That it was."

"Oui, I have missed a lot."

"We've filled his head with stories about you, too."

"All good ones, I hope."

"They said it was you…I didn't believe it!" Bizy's lip quivered and she rushed to embrace him. "We all but gave up on ever seeing you again." Her expression turned to anger. "Where the bloody hell have you been?"

Widow Bell peered out the window. "We've been through that."

"Occupied, I've been." He took her by the arms. "I'm glad to see you're well. And your boy, he's growing so fast. Sorry I am that I couldn't come back."

Bizy locked her arms around the Capitaine and started to cry. "Why didn't you come back? At least let us know you were alive?"

"Look around, yes? It was better for all of you."

She put her hands on his face and examined him. He was certainly older, but at least he was real. A warm comfort flooded her, reminding her of the good old days.

On the garden path of St. Paul's Church, Cherry Banks hunched among rows of hedges and statues. Her heart raced with anticipation. Binge guided her to a small clearing where the Clubhouse could be seen through whorls of smoke.

Bleedin Art's form was obvious, tall and thin, while MacAskill's hair seemed to blend in with the haze. Cherry squinted, trying to make out the other thugs. Scarcliff fastened two horses to the carriage, and Jayne staggered, trying to secure the reins.

Binge leaned in close to her.

She gave his hand a reassuring squeeze before he readied his silver pistol. "We have only one shot." Cherry inhaled; his rugged scent was invigorating.

Binge aimed the pistol.

"No, let me." Cherry stopped him. "I'm a sure-eye shot."

"We only need to cause a distraction," he reminded. "That thing can't hit anyone from here."

"Oh, yeah? A pound says I can hit one of them."

Binge smirked. Unable to resist, he handed over the gun. "Let's see then, but give Gladstone a minute to get into position."

"Who will it be?" She aimed into the crowd.

The whole thing was Gladstone's plan. Cherry and Binge were to cause a distraction from St. Paul's Church, behind the wall of Morgan's Line, while Gladstone picked up the Capitaine. They waited and watched the Fyre Brigade pack up.

Cherry took aim. "Gladstone must be there by now."

MacAskill spoke with Katie and her loyal old dog, Royal Rook.

Cherry closed one eye, targeting down the barrel.

"Careful. Katie's over there," Binge said.

"I see her." *He's good to a fault, that Mr. Binge.*

"And don't shoot her beau, either. That'd be waste of a good suit."

"The Capitaine himself taught me this," Cherry said. "First, we move it a little bit this way for the wind." She lined up with Bleedin Art. "And then distance." Her aim shifted and the shot rang out, pistol fuming. Someone yelped and a body fell to the ground.

"You hit one!" Binge exclaimed.

"Aww, fuck!" Scarcliff groaned.

"Aye, told you I would," Cherry boasted.

"I don't believe it. Nice shot." Binge took her by the arm and they ducked away.

"I was aiming for Art, but thanks anyway. We gotta get outta here."

They sped up and reached the tall houses of Tower Street.

"This is where we say goodnight, my dear." Binge halted and pointed up the next alley. "You head back to your place and call it a night."

"I'll be your decoy anytime, Mr. Binge." She blew him a kiss and continued on.

In the Swiftsure Tavern's Red Room, Mina Jacobs cleaned up after servicing several clients. Splashing water on her face, she noticed a dark mass in the basin. When she turned up the oil lamp, she realized the mass was blood. The ceiling dripped red. "Someone's having an off night!"

She ran downstairs to get Nessie, who was being questioned by Councilman White.

"What the hell is happening here?" White asked. "I was having a quiet drink at the Four Feathers when all hell broke loose."

"We had a scarlet fever outbreak." Nessie wrung a bar rag. "Mr. Coggshall's dead!"

"Scarlet fever? Where the hell's Burghill?"

"He and his slave went to get cigars and never came back."

A city guard approached. "We just searched the Crooked Compass and there's no sign of either of them."

"Is it Burghill you're looking for?" Mina interrupted.

"Aye, where is he?" White insisted.

"You might wanna check in the strumpet rooms, third floor. Ceiling's bleeding in the Red Room."

Mina followed the procession upstairs. White and the city guard inspected the Red Room first. The blood pool had expanded several feet now dripping persistently over the basin. Mina's eyes rounded, wondering what horror lay above.

"That doesn't look like scarlet fever," White spoke coolly. "Upstairs we go." He tried many doors, each room empty. When he encountered a locked one, he yelled, "open up, strumpet!" No response. He lunged, throwing all his weight against the door and then bounced off, injuring his arm. "Good solid door that is."

Nessie came forward with a key to unlock it.

Inside was too dark to see anything in great detail – just a dark figure on the bed. "Gimme a light," White demanded. With a lantern in hand, his face wilted. "Good Christ!"

"What's that in his mouth?" the city guard asked.

Mina peered inside, recognizing the shape. "His will to live."

"Looks like a grudge to me," White said.

The city guard covered his mouth. "I'd say he bled out."

Mina shook her head. "From the prick or the liver?" The sheer quantity of blood was astounding. *Bugger all, I'm outta of a job!*

"Both." White covered his mouth. "Does it matter?"

A militiaman popped his head in the door. "Morgan's Line is on fire, it's the pirate Gator Gar."

White turned to the city guard, face ashen. "Inform Piper. Recommend he declare martial law. Have Beckford summon all militia to duty. Find and apprehend the pirate Gator Gar. Have Sheriff Tellam block off all the streets and cut off all the exits."

Mina stared at Burghill. "Shoulda listened to me Mr. B. That slag's out fer yer head and she don't swallow no more."

GO
2015

Triumph in Chaos

Down the street from Widow Bell's house, Bleedin Art and MacAskill stormed off in a carriage, while their men galloped over hedges and spread across the grounds of St. Paul's Church. La Roche heard a gunshot minutes ago and soon the militia followed through the maze of shrubberies and pathways.

"That looks like all of them," Widow Bell said. "I'd say you're good to go, Capitaine."

"Oui." La Roche nodded. "Owe you for this and I won't forget it."

"Well, I won't hold my breath."

Jamie returned, wrapped in towels.

Isabella followed. "What's going on now, Mama?"

"Nothing, Isabella. Take Jamie upstairs and lock the door."

"Lock the door because nothing's happening?"

"Lock the door or I'll beat you!"

Isabella huffed and took Jamie's hand.

"Are you a pirate?" Jamie asked.

La Roche grinned. "Can you keep a secret?" He never really considered himself to be father material, but deep down he had always wanted a son. Jacquotte never wanted children; not with him, anyway.

"Aye, I can keep a secret." Jamie's eyes lit up. "My ma said I can keep a secret. Once I saw her and Nanny Bell in the bath and they was playing a game with their feet—"

Bizy and Widow Bell made loud noises and threw cushions at him from the couch.

La Roche bit back laughter. "Then I'm the sugar delivery man."

"Take your brother upstairs!" Bizy hollered and Isabella led Jamie away.

Jamie shook his head. "He don't look like a delivery man."

Bizy peered out the front window. "Here comes your ride."

Both women locked la Roche in an embrace. Bizy patted his chin. "It's good to see you without the beard." She brushed away a tear. "I always imagined you settling down in a house by the sea with some redhead by yer side and that God-awful bird of yours." Bizy kissed him on the cheek. "Don't disappoint me."

"If you only knew," la Roche sighed.

"Here, I packed you a lunch." Widow Bell handed over the Spanish pistols.

La Roche took them gratefully. "Oui, very kind."

"I want them back." She flashed him a look.

He nodded. "Adieu."

"Be well, Capitaine." Bizy reached for his hand one last time.

"Drop in again sometime," Widow Bell added as he dashed out the door.

La Roche heard a deep sigh from Bizy.

"Did you ever cock a leg for him?"

"You mean, you didn't?" Widow Bell replied.

La Roche smiled. *Shame I must leave. A guaranteed ménage à trois, that was.* He leapt aboard the carriage.

"Welcome aboard, mon Capitaine." Gladstone snapped the reins.

"What's the plan?"

"To run from danger as fast as we can without getting hurt."

"I should put you in charge of all my campaigns."

The carriage wheeled up Coal Lane.

"Binge and Cherry are acting as decoys, so we can feel free to call it a night."

"Thoughtful," la Roche said, clinging on as the worn wheels slid along the sandy street. He squinted and caught a glimpse of Royal Rook and Katie the Swallower. *Rook must work for Art now. Merde! A good man, but desperate for employment. He will sound the alarm.* "We've been spotted." A gunshot echoed through the misty night sky.

Gladstone sped up the carriage, reaching Tower Street where a barricade waited. "It's blocked up on the main roads!"

La Roche frowned. "They'll all be blocked in a minute."

"We'll head for the Merchant Exchange." Gladstone cracked the whip and the carriage darted forth.

From the church grounds, Bleedin Art had heard the warning shot. He shuffled uncomfortably in his seat. The Capitaine was nearby. "He's gonna be the death of me!"

"It came from Church Street," MacAskill said.

Bleedin Art drew his sword and pointed it. "Back to the Clubhouse on the double!"

The carriage quickened its pace, followed by Jag'd Jayne on foot.

Royal Rook kissed Katie's cheek before he latched onto the side of the carriage. "He went up Coal Lane."

"Charge," Bleedin Art yelled. "That way Scarcliff, head them off!"

The carriage swerved along an alley.

"He's heading for the harbor side," Art called. "Stop him before he gets there."

"Aye, Captain," Scarcliff said.

They turned up Love Lane and accelerated around the corner. The sky began to glow red and early morning dust clouds whirled around the streets. The Capitaine's carriage was much easier to spot being only two blocks up, turning left onto Cannon Street.

"There he goes." Art pointed with his sword, causing Scarcliff to duck.

"I reckon they're headed for the Merchant Exchange," MacAskill said.

Art grinned. "He's only got one horse to our two."

"We'll get them, Captain." Scarcliff briskly snapped the reins and they gained.

"Aha!" Art bellowed. They were just out of reach, when they made a hard right turn up Risby's Alley.

"Hang on!" Scarcliff matched the turn.

Art pointed his sword again, cutting Scarcliff's ear.

"Ah, fuck!"

"Don't worry, kid," MacAskill said. "I'll fix it later."

"Charge," Art called.

The carriage whizzed by the Cheshire Cheese Tavern, which was famous for its assortment of locally made British cheeses. Drunken strumpets spilled out the front door. Among them was Sierra Lee. She waved.

Scarcliff waved back.

"Just drive, boy," Art snarled.

The Capitaine's carriage approached the Merchant Exchange, while Sheriff Tellam's vehicle swerved out of an alley. One of the city guards attempted to leap onto the fugitive carriage, but missed, ending up face down on the ground.

Unable to slow down, Art's carriage rammed forward, bouncing over the guard.

MacAskill glimpsed down at the mangled body. “I’ll get the coroner to skip that one.”

Art cringed. “Aye.”

Tellam’s carriage made another sweep for the Capitaine’s vehicle. They locked wheels momentarily before the sheriff's driver lost control and the horses veered off, dragging the carriage past the Blue Anchor Inn. Tellam’s head slammed into the great iron anchor fixed to the sign. To everyone’s horror, the sign broke off and crushed the sheriff beneath its enormous weight.

Art squirmed. “Eeew!”

MacAskill gritted his teeth. “That’s a job for Dr. Sober.”

Scarcliff wrenched the reins to avoid the calamity. He made a sudden left up High Street. Everyone jerked, clinging on for dear life. Before the Capitaine could turn into the Merchant Exchange, Jayne and Stinger arrived on foot with their pistols drawn. Shots were fired. Jayne dove behind some barrels and Stinger gave chase, jumping onto the back of the Capitaine’s carriage.

“Good man; go get him!” Art cheered.

The Capitaine aimed a pistol at the boy’s forehead and pulled the trigger. Stinger’s body tumbled off the back onto the sandy street.

Scarcliff teetered in his seat, trying to keep control of the horses. A dog ran right out in front of them. They heard a yelp and the carriage bounced.

“Watch where you’re going, ya stupid fool,” MacAskill yelled.

“You hit a dog, arsehole,” hollered Art.

Scarcliff wiped his forehead. “That wasn’t my fault!”

The offending carriage made a sharp turn down Lime Street into the arched gateway of the Merchant Exchange. Scarcliff missed the turn and the carriage accelerated.

Art pointed with his sword again. “He went that way.”

Scarcliff ducked, narrowly avoiding another wound.

“You lost them,” Jayne gasped, catching up on foot.

“I quit!” Scarcliff yelled.

“Take the next right,” Art ordered.

Royal Rook leapt down from the back to pursue on foot.

Cherry hid beneath a cloak in the doorway between two shops in the Merchant Exchange. The predawn light penetrated the maze of alleyways, but she remained in shadow. Reluctant to call it a night, she followed Binge, knowing full well he'd meet up with Gladstone and the Capitaine. Sure enough, a carriage pulled up.

Binge smiled. "I believe this is your stop."

"Right on time, mate." Gladstone hopped down.

The Capitaine followed, reloading the pair of pistols.

Cherry's heart raced, but it wasn't possible to say goodbye. She had to be satisfied with one last look.

"Take care of him." Gladstone patted the horse. "A big bucket of clean water and extra sugar cubes."

"Got it, man." Binge turned to the Capitaine. "How about giving me my watch back?"

"What watch?"

"The gold watch from One and Thirty."

"Forget it, it's mine. I won it."

Gladstone and the Capitaine ran off through a dark corridor.

Binge sat on the driver's bench, drawing a cloak over his head. "Cheap bastard!" He guided the car to the Broad Street exit.

Cherry followed, sneaking down an adjoining walkway.

Royal Rook approached from a footpath, pistol drawn. "Stop where you are!"

Binge flipped back his hood to make eye contact.

"Theo?" Rook seemed shocked. "Down from there, slowly."

Cherry stepped out, holding a pistol.

"No; don't!" Binge exclaimed. "Don't shoot."

Rook tried to duck, but the shot fired. He was hit through the left eye and collapsed to the ground. Blood streaked down the side of his head and face.

"Damn it!" Binge snapped.

Cherry leapt onto the carriage. "He be one of them."

Binge stared down at the body. "He's a friend of mine."

Cherry shrugged. "I didn't know. I thought he was one of the slavers."

"Aye, he was that," Binge said mournfully. "It weren't yer fault." He snapped the reins hard and accelerated.

Cherry had never done anything like this before. Killing was easier than she thought it would be. *Poor Mr. Binge, he'll get over his friend.* She reloaded her pistol.

Bleedin Art's carriage pursued them through the Merchant Exchange.

Binge passed her another pistol. “Here, use this one too. Those arseholes you *can* kill.”

“Way ahead of you, Mr. Binge.” She loaded it swiftly and readied herself as Art closed in.

They neared High Street when Binge cursed. There was a blockade of militiamen armed with muskets. Frantically, he yanked the reins, but lost control.

Cherry slipped onto the driver’s seat. “Don’t panic; let me drive.” She steadied the horses.

“I’m not panicking. I’m getting in touch with my hysterical side!” Binge insisted and they galloped along Water Lane.

Art’s carriage was so close now, Cherry could spit on it. Excitement pumped through her veins. She secured the hood around her face and handed the reins back over to Binge.

“Shoot the horse!” Art instructed.

“Not the horse,” Cherry said. “Shoot the driver.” She grinned, turning to aim the pistols. Bangs echoed. Scarcliff slumped over, while the other shot went astray. Art and Jag’d Jayne took aim at her and fired. She fell back, but not before witnessing Art’s carriage slam into the side of a building. The horses crashed into each other with a panicked whinny, and then the carriage tipped and rolled.

“Well, that bloody well settled it!” Cherry laughed, clutching her arm.

“You shoulda gone home,” Binge barked. “That was a friend of mine, back there.”

“I’m sorry, Mr. Binge. I thought you needed help.”

He turned left onto Tower Street. “Whoa now, it’s over,” he said calmly to the horse as it slowed down.

Cherry’s arm began to burn and blood dripped off her wrist. She withdrew a handkerchief from her bodice and pressed it against the wound.

“You’re hit?” Binge suddenly realized.

“I’m fine,” she insisted. “Was hoping to lose an inch off there anyway.” She tucked in close to him, feeling her heart rate slow. “Thank you, Mr. Binge. I can’t thank you enough.”

“Yeah, you can,” he grumbled. “Know where I can find passage to New Zealand?”

Cherry remained silent as they drove slowly towards the Old Church. She realized how well he had been concealing his anger.

Water Lane was a right bloody mess littered with a smashed carriage, shattered barrels, toppled merchant stands, and semiconscious people. Shop owners came out to view the wreckage, including the owner of Ching's Chinese Imports, his novelty stand decimated by the brawl.

Art felt his toes move but his legs seemed numb. "I didn't see that coming." He lifted his head.

"I did." MacAskill coughed and slowly climbed from the wreckage. His arm bled badly. "Are you hurt?"

Art felt hard, pointy spikes embedded in his backside. "Think I've been buggered by a wooden snake!" He rolled off a large wooden dragon.

MacAskill staggered over to Scarcliff, who was miraculously still alive. "Those were some fancy maneuvers. Where'd you learn to drive, China?"

Jag'd Jayne limped forward, his head bleeding. "Maybe the post office is hiring?"

The doctor told him to sit down.

Art rolled onto his stomach and slowly pushed his way onto his knees, which cracked horribly. That's when radiating agony came from his shoulder. "Me shoulder's broke!"

"My dragon's broke!" the shop owner cried.

"So's my arse," Art added, grabbing MacAskill's arm.

The doctor examined the shoulder. "It's dislocated. Don't move around much."

"Thanks."

Jayne checked the horses that were tangled in their harnesses. He aimed his pistol.

"Check to see if they're hurt first, ya stupid twat!" MacAskill snarled, unhinging the straps.

"My horses, don't you shoot my horses," Scarcliff moaned.

Once freed, one horse clambered up onto all fours.

"See?" MacAskill turned to Jayne. "That wasn't so difficult. Now go lie down."

Jayne stumbled to the nearest patch of garden and collapsed.

MacAskill checked the other horse, recognizing a broken leg. "But this one on the other hand—" he cocked a pistol "—wasn't so fortunate." He aimed at the horse's ear and a bang echoed.

Beckford, Constable Blower, and the militia came running to the scene.

Art leaned on the shell of the carriage. "*Now* you're all here? Useful, thanks for that." He pointed at High Street. "Well, he's back there, where you came from, sod-knobs!"

Beckford sighed and signaled everyone to turn around. "Search the Merchant Exchange and the waterfront."

MacAskill addressed Art, "That wasn't him."

"Aye, it was a decoy. They musta made a switch. We need to find out where he and his crew are hiding."

"And do what?" MacAskill snapped.

"And go after them before they can regroup."

"This is our fuck'n group," MacAskill barked. "We can't take on his crew, look at us."

Jayne sat up, stunned. "It wasn't his crew."

"What are you talking about?" Art's entire body throbbed. *Rum, laudanum, and a week in the Inferno Room is all I ask.*

MacAskill tilted his head. "Who was it then?"

"Do you smell the perfume?" Jayne asked. "I ain't hallucinating it."

It dawned on Art. "That was Cherry Banks!"

Atia rested on a bench on the dock, trembling beneath a blanket. Not from cold, but from fatigue. She couldn't bring herself to relax, worrying about Paul, her Capitaine. It wasn't until she peeked in his satchel that she truly began to fret. All the gold he had in the world probably. *A man don't let that go unless he knows he ain't coming back!* Atia pulled the blanket tighter.

Dawn broke, igniting the sky into a swell of pink and yellow hues that shimmered the on the water's dark surface. *And Livia, what happened to her?* It felt like an eternity since she'd seen her sister. A fishing boat, captained by the man Strangewayes called "Snuggles" pulled up next to the dock. She frowned.

Strangewayes sauntered along the Sea Lane dock towards her, his expression calm with a touch of self-satisfaction.

"Livia?" Atia asked.

Strangewayes smiled. "We found her, and she's alive."

"Where is she, then?"

"Resting. I'm afraid her injuries won't permit traveling at this time. She'll have to stay here with me for a while." The doctor removed a bottle from his jacket and passed it over. "This will take the edge off the pain."

"Then I'll stay too," Atia insisted. "Where's the Capitaine?"

"You must leave without us."

Desperate to ease her ribs, she twisted the cap off the bottle and took a mouthful, grimacing. "No. I won't go. Not without Livia or the Capitaine."

"Come on, Atia. It's fine, love." Lilly sat down and slipped an arm around her.

"Gladstone will catch you up shortly, and as for the Capitaine, well, to be honest, we may never see him again," the doctor spoke gently. "He's a wanted man. Very wanted, to tell you the truth."

Atia swallowed hard, anguished by the thought of not seeing him again. "Why does everyone call him Alligator?"

"Gator Gar? It's a river fish common to the Americas, with particularly sharp teeth. Colonists have been trying to eradicate them since we came over. The Capitaine took that name as his alter ego." The doctor rubbed his chin. "It's a false identity. Buccaneers are big on concealing their identities; it helps them evade retaliation. He was Gator Gar when he raided with Henry Morgan and l'Olonnais. Then he was El Capitaine when he was with Grammont and Laurens de Graaf."

Lilly helped herself to the rum bottle. "But pirates like to be famous."

"Some do. They get very famous very quickly and then die very famously. The successful pirate is the one who gets away with it. Whether their plunder is legalized by a letter of marque or not, they're still going to have many enemies. By using a false identity, the Capitaine increased his chances of being able to retire in peace."

"He hopes to retire?" Atia was surprised.

"No, he *is* retired. For some time now. His being here has been quite a shock."

"Does he have many enemies?" Lilly handed the bottle back to Atia, who took another cringe-worthy mouthful.

"Yes. Although there was a time when he was Port Royal royalty, back when he was one of Henry Morgan's captains. They protected Jamaica for years from the Spanish and Dutch. They were like kings to the people here, and they're still thought of as heroes by many. He's an outlaw now as far as the British government is concerned."

"Do you know his real name?" Atia asked.

"No. And you best not be looking to find out. People have killed for that information."

A bird whistle sounded and Atia's heart leapt. Along came her champion down the walkway. His disguise gone, he was worse for wear. He stared at her intently.

Gladstone trailed behind, yawning.

"I knew they was coming back!" Lilly shrieked, flying at Gladstone.

"Not unscathed, I see," the doctor added.

Atia rose slowly and walked towards the Capitaine. "I was getting worried." She caressed his face. "Didn't know what happened to you." His arms slid around her waist and he kissed her forehead. She buried herself against him, his scent familiar and comforting.

"We have Livia. Thank you, Capitaine," the doctor said.

Lilly released Gladstone, but not before giving him an enthusiastic kiss.

Gladstone paused to catch his breath. "I always like being thanked."

The Capitaine gazed eagerly into Atia's eyes. "Now let's get you sound and safe."

"What about Cherry and Binge?" Lilly queried.

"Last we saw, they were leading Art and his men away," Gladstone said.

"Both are cunning as cats. Now we need to get you lot away, if you please?" Strangewayes escorted them to the boat. "Now take the carriage from Ligania directly there, no stops." He handed the bowline to Snuggles, who looked hideous in daylight with all his scars.

Gladstone gave a chirpy grin. "We'll be fine. I have done this before you know."

Atia took a seat on the main deck and Minuit swooped in beside her. "You're a good boy. Yeah, ya are."

The Capitaine collapsed beside her and tossed a handful of nuts to the parrot. "A long day that was." After stretching out, he slid his arm around her. A grimy lip print soiled his cheek.

Atia wiped it away. "Vie?"

"No." He closed his eyes.

"You'll be there in no time." Strangewayes waved. "I'll follow with Livia as soon as she's able."

Atia blew him a kiss. "Thank you, Doctor."

"Tell Cherry, thanks!" Lilly called.

The Capitaine started snoring.

The doctor shrugged. "Delayed shock, I should think. Not to worry. Good luck."

"*Bon voyage*," Minuit squawked, and the small vessel drifted away.

Sheriff
Tellam
YE BLUE ANCHOR
GO
2015

Aftermath

Dawn brought intense hues of orange and gold, painting Port Royal in a warm glow. Hundreds of ships sailed in and out of the harbor, some docking for repairs, others heading out to sea. Billows of smoke rose from the bake houses, covering the landscape in soft white clouds. Near Morgan's Line, the large defensive wall on the south side of the city, a row of flags fluttered in the breeze. Adjacent the line of heavy cannons sat a quaint gated garden with stone benches. A young woman in an extravagant light blue gown sat staring at the sunrise.

Katie Evans rubbed her tired red eyes from an action-filled night. She brought her feet up on the bench and hugged her knees. It felt like she'd been waiting for Royal Rook for an eternity. To her left at the scorched Clubhouse and Henry's Loft, the corpses of Codface, Mike and Pikestaff lay beside the wooden shed. She knew she had no choice but to go back to the Crooked Compass Tavern to collect her things. Perhaps Rook would track her down there, if he wasn't dead after the previous night's hunt for the elusive pirate Gator Gar.

Sunlight glazed the weather worn buildings and crooked chimneys. The bells rang out at St. Paul's Church. Katie walked through alleys and hidden corridors until she came to High Street where the town crier and his drummer rallied the masses. The drummer banged for about thirty seconds before the town crier yelled at him to shut up. Next, Royal Rook's parrot, Checkmate, screeched overhead. "For pity sake!" the crier yelled. "Hear ye, hear ye! This be the morning news! Port Royal thwarts pirate attack! French pirates attack the city! Dozens killed!" He cleared his throat. "Firstly, your government wants you know that the slave auction was a huge success despite the health scare and pirate attack. Your investments are safe." A sigh of relief filled the air. "The defense forces of Port Royal have thwarted the French pirate Gator Gar, who poisoned the water supply. Secondly, Acting Lieutenant Governor Piper strongly urges all citizens and patrons to purchase new barrels of drinking water. A bounty has been declared of sixty thousand pieces of eight on the renegade pirate Gator Gar." The town crier opened a broadside with a crude likeness for everyone to admire. "Acting Lieutenant Governor

Piper has vowed to capture Gator Gar and bring him to justice. This morning's news has been brought to you by Strangewayes Soothing Wormwood Formula. If you're not hallucinating, it ain't Strangewayes."

A smile formed on Katie's face. Inducing fear always whipped the general public into a frenzy. Rook told her you could never believe the papers. Most of the time they only printed rubbish to distract people from the real issues. She turned down a passage towards the inner harbor.

Beside the Wherry Bridge, *Diamond Dog* was docked and its crew readied for breakfast. Checkmate squawked agitatedly, perched on the ship's rail. Quartermaster Tiny McAllister paced the dock, eyeing Copes Alley and Water Lane. *This be a bloody unfortunate place,* Tiny thought.

The ship's sailing master Quinton Winter approached from the street. Winter was in his mid-thirties. He was not as battle-scarred as the rest of the crew, but he had one rather impressive scar from a cutlass that ran all the way down his left arm. "No sign of him. He never went back to the Swiftsure." Winter's look of concern grew.

"Nor the Crooked Compass neither," added a russet-skinned crewman called Snapper.

"What about the girl?" Winter asked. "Any sign of her?"

Tiny shook his head. "Katie? Not since last night, if she's still alive."

A cloaked man approached hurriedly.

Tiny recognized the newcomer. "Theo?"

Binge pulled back the hood. "Tiny. Quint."

"What be yer business here?"

"I was hoping *he* was here. He ain't at the infirmary at Fort Carlisle." Binge swallowed hard. "He was shot in the head."

Tiny clenched his fist. "Who shot him?"

Binge winced. "I did. We was on opposing sides."

Tiny folded his massive arms. "Bloody Port Royal. Bloody unfortunate business."

Checkmate shrieked and took off to perch upon a roof along Thames Street. Below her, two militiamen pushed a cart with a body on it.

"That be him, I suspect." Tiny charged forth. "You there, stop!" he thundered. "Let me take a look." He lifted the white sheet to see Royal Rook's body, blood oozing from his left eye.

Winter inspected the body. "My God, Tiny, he's still alive! He needs a real doctor."

"I know a doctor, a good one. I'll go get him." Binge took off.

"Right, let's get him aboard!" Tiny lifted Rook as though he were no heavier than a feather pillow.

It was midmorning when Cherry Banks arrived at Strangewayes Apothecary. She kept her injured arm tucked in beside her and rang the bell. She wondered if it had been worth it, or if the retribution would be worse. It was only a matter of time until Art discovered her involvement in last night's chase around the city. With the Capitaine gone, she felt more vulnerable than ever.

Strangewayes opened the door. "Ah, Cherry. Good to see you." He noticed her frown. "My dear, whatever is the matter?"

Cherry cradled her arm. "Got grazed by a shot last night."

"Oh my, let me take a peek. Come inside. I was just about to have some tea with *kirchwasser*, would you like one? It'll take the edge off the pain."

"Sounds good to me, Doc." Cherry followed him inside.

In the parlor a fire blazed. Cherry sipped tea while the doctor wet her sleeve until it loosened. Next, he cut away the fabric. "Sorry about your dress. This may hurt a bit." He peeled the cloth away, revealing an oozing bloody gash. "It's going to need stitches. In the meantime, I'll add some laudanum to your tea."

Liquor and laudanum mingled in Cherry's empty stomach, making her feel like a rolled-up piece of carpet slumped in the chair. Her arm was tended to quickly and soon came the last stitch. "A few more drops of laudanum?" the doctor offered.

"I'm…quite fine…thank you," she spoke in a slow, deep drawl and leaned against him, slipping her good arm around his waist. "I can't thank ya enough." Her cheek pressed against his belly.

"I'll give you a care package; something to clean it with and a bit more laudanum." He patted the top of her head. "You're showing signs of shock. You need to rest."

Cherry looked up. "Have you seen Vie since last night?"

"I had the pleasure of her company early this morning. She left to see her captain off. Personally, I'd rather she stayed in bed to get some rest, but you kids know best."

"She's a grown woman," Cherry acknowledged. "Her captain's leaving, then?"

Strangewayes massaged his temple. "Preparing to sail as we speak, going after *La Lune,* I suspect."

"You need to relax, Sander, or you're gonna drop dead." Cherry ran her finger over his lips. "I'll be needing more of the poison."

"Oh?"

"I'm gonna finish this meself."

"Alone? That's not a good idea. Give it time."

Cherry's eyes widened. "Why not?" Her hand brushed against his hardening manhood. "O ye of little faith. We almost made it! The Capitaine even said all or nothing. Take them all out or they'll come back at you."

"I see your points." He gazed down at her cleavage. "Well, I'm afraid I'm out of the belladonna."

She unbuttoned his trousers.

"I could whip up some pennyroyal oil for you. That should do the trick."

"Yes, whip it up. That should do the trick." Cherry's mouth moved against him.

"Under a state of shock, y–you could have s–side effects" The doctor grunted. "Oh…of course there is a risk of lock-jaw." He gasped while her tongue tantalized him. "I wouldn't want to end up like Burghill." He grabbed the edge of the chair and she became more aggressive. "Only a small chance, though. Normally someone in your condition should be resting. Oh, you are so good at that. Well, as it is you shouldn't rest with that high a dose anyway…a good polishing might do us both some good. Go ahead and get it all out."

The back door to the apothecary creaked open and Binge called, "hey, Doc!" Footsteps approached the parlor. "Shit, it's like walking in on your parents!"

"Thanks." Cherry collapsed back into the chair.

"But I am glad you're here, Doc." Binge averted his eyes while Strangewayes buttoned his trousers.

"I was almost glad I came," the doctor retorted.

"Royal Rook's alive!" Binge blurted.

"Katie's Rook," Cherry said.

"He's been shot in the eye."

Strangewayes grabbed his medical bag and looked at Cherry. "I should like a follow-up appointment later, but truthfully you need rest. I want you to have some of the tea I've left for you and go to bed."

Cherry waved him away. "I'm fine, really. Don't forget, you need rest too."

"Yes. Well, you know what the Christians say about the wicked." The doctor smiled and the two men left.

Cherry crushed herself against the chair. *Damn, he survived. Good shot that was.*

The Inferno Room inside Bleedin Art's mansion, acted as an operating room in which a thin, balding doctor shook horribly while stitching Dr. MacAskill's arm. Dr. Sober was chronically drunk and the type of surgeon you'd only hire if no one else was available. MacAskill winced, grinding his teeth through another stitch until the thread was tied off.

Art was sprawled along the large couch, watching the procedure. "Where the hell are they?" He rubbed his dislocated right arm reflexively, causing himself to recoil.

"You only sent for them ten minutes ago," MacAskill said. "It's not like we got a work shortage going on!"

"Why are you first? I'm dying over here!" Art snarled.

"Because I can't very well help anyone with my arm spewing like a whore on church day, now can I?"

"It don't make sense. Why now? How could she?" Art pouted.

MacAskill coughed. "That's a fine job, Dr. Sober, fine job indeed." He looked down at his partially bandaged arm. A drunken parrot could do better work. "I can manage from here, Doctor. Thank you."

Sober looked over the spectacles hovering on the tip of his nose.

MacAskill took a coin bag off the table and handed it over.

"Anytime I can be of service, gentlemen." Sober put the money in his pocket and gathered his tools. "Good day to you." He opened the door and saluted. "Long live King James."

Art saluted with his good arm. "Aye, long live King James."

Jag'd Jayne entered. "*Arrow* coming in."

MacAskill grabbed a large bottle of rum. "That's why you named it that, ain't it? So ya could hear '*Arrow* coming in!'" He smirked. "Headed right up yer arse if you're not careful." MacAskill signaled Jayne before removing a mallet from his medical bag. "Come here, boy."

"What about him?" Jayne indicated Scarcliff, who snored with his head pressed against the wall and his legs dangling over an armrest.

"Is he breathing?"

"Yeah."

"Good. Let him sleep."

"I'd like to sleep meself," Jayne grumbled.

"Is it my turn now?" Art asked. "Hate to trouble ya!" He dropped into the chair by the table.

"You'll be wanting a big ole shot of rum." The doctor handed the bottle to Art.

Art took a swig and braced himself. "Don't you got anything stronger?"

"Do I look like Strangewayes? Come on, ya wimp!"

"Be gentle, it's me first time." Art grinned and lay his arm on the table.

"Try to relax, this might sting a bit."

"What's the mallet for?"

"Just in case."

"In case of what?"

"In case you get on my nerves!" the doctor snapped. "If the bone doesn't want to pop back in place, I'll have to force it. Now shut up and let's do this." He shoved a piece of biting leather in between Art's massive teeth. "Ready?" The doctor twisted and jerked the shoulder back into position.

"Fnuckin' 'ell!" Art gnawed viciously on the leather, tears escaping his eyes.

The shoulder popped.

"There, that wasn't so bad, was it? Like setting a mast." MacAskill slid Art's arm into a cotton sling.

"Ya know where you can stick it!" Art took another mouthful of rum.

"Careful, laddie. Any sign of discoloration and I'll have to cut it off. I might anyway, for all the shit you put me through." The doctor took a drink. "Take it easy on that arm awhile."

Scarcliff stirred and released a dull groan.

“G’mornin’ sunshine!” MacAskill said, raising the rum bottle. “Gator Gar and Cherry couldn’t have poisoned them all. Not with just the two of them.”

“Why would Cherry be helping him?” Jayne asked. “That don’t make sense.”

“Unless – it’s the other way ’round. He’s helping her,” MacAskill mused, eyeing Art. “She must’ve found out why Slasher Al is here. I told ya what would happen if Coggshall hired that bloody maniac, and now you’ve got one of your own pulling the same shit!”

Jayne leaned over the table. “What am I missing?” His face twisted to a frown.

“The full frontal lobe!” MacAskill bellowed. “You know who I’m talking about. That Ginger is Roc Braziliano all over again and that’s the last thing we need in Port Royal.” He glanced at Jayne. “Well, boy, you’re gonna get invited to more meetings now. Coggshall hired Slasher Al to get rid of the competition.”

“You was gonna let him kill Cherry’s girls?”

Art looked guilty. “Not the little tart you fancy. But most of them, until you…Captain Cunnilingus came to the rescue.”

“We’ve gotta get a handle on the syphilis problem in this city,” MacAskill reasoned.

“Bullshit!” Jayne roared. “Cherry’s girls ain’t got no siffles. The cleanest in town, they is.” He shook his head in disbelief. “What happened to the vote?”

“The vote’s for show, kid. Get your head out of the clouds,” Art advised. “Here’s what we’re gonna do – Jayne’s gonna go pick up Cherry and bring her here this evening.”

MacAskill burst out laughing. “Good thing she’ll come quietly!” He put his hand on his hip and stuck out his rear. “Sure Art, I’d love to get killed, ’course I’ll come quietly!”

“We want her to think she got away with it,” Art said.

“She can lead us to Gator Gar,” Scarcliff added weakly, barely able to lift his head.

Art nodded and pointed. “There. Someone’s thinking!” He drummed his fingers on the table, and then eyed Jayne. “I’ll bet she’ll play it cool. Don’t let on that we know. Tell her I’m hurt and I need her to run the payroll. She’s done it before; she’ll go for it. But tell her I need to see her.”

"Can I sleep?" Jayne moaned.

"Aye – if ya must. Lazy-arse kids!" Art huffed.

Edmund Coggshall peered down at his father's body in a wooden box. In the coffin beside him was Burghill. Both men had been cleaned up and dressed in fresh suits. They appeared to be only napping. More bodies were laid on the mortuary floor. Sheriff Tellam's crushed bloody remains had been scraped up and deposited in a casket, the lid closed. Stinger, Shipwash, and two slave buyers were stacked in the corner. The coffin maker growled with dissatisfaction, hammering loudly.

Edmund remained silent and lit up a cigar. He wasn't terribly broken up; it was inevitable given their family business. What concerned him was the circumstances of the deaths, and the sheer number of victims. Those who had been decapitated hadn't even been collected from the Clubhouse yet. *What's the true motive here? Am I next?*

The coffin maker set down his hammer and handed some papers to Edmund. "Mr. Taliare dropped off new forms to sign; he needs you to confirm that this is the body of your father. There's a pen and ink on the table."

Edmund signed and dated the parchment.

The front door chimed, and a cart rolled in with more bodies. Constable Blower patted his forehead while Beckford eyed all the cadavers. The newcomers included Ironclad, whose head clung to his trunk by a few ligaments, Stutters, Mike, and Pikestaff, their heads tucked under their arms.

"Where should we put them?" Blower asked.

"With the rest of 'em." The coffin maker pointed at bodies in the corner. "Cover 'em when yer finished." He tossed them a blood spattered sheet. Militiamen unloaded the bodies.

Blower cringed as one of the heads rolled towards him.

The coffin maker kicked it back into place.

Blower gagged. "Mr. Coggshall, sir, sorry for yer loss."

"Thank you, Constable." Edmund glimpsed at two strumpets who'd been mutilated in unimaginable ways.

Father Parker Alcocke arrived, wearing blue tinted spectacles and a robe with a large wooden cross dangling from his neck. "Well, bugger me sideways with the Holy Trinity!" He lifted the lid to Sheriff Tellam's casket.

Blower took one look and heaved. "Goddamn!"

"And the Lord taketh away or somethink?" Alcocke coughed into his handkerchief.

"He had a run-in with the Blue Anchor," Beckford said.

Alcocke slammed the lid back down. "Haven't we all?" He saw Edmund. "Sorry for your loss. I'll perform last rites, shall I?"

Edmund nodded. "Very well."

Beckford leaned over the two mutilated strumpets. "When did these two come in?"

The coffin maker glanced over. "Strumpets came in this morning, but they been dead a full day at least."

"Two dead strumpets? Who cares?" Edmund said.

"Gator Gar obviously didn't do this," Beckford stated.

"Well, they're not mine," Edmund spoke in a disinterested tone. "Do you need anything further from me?"

"Not presently, Mr. Coggshall. We'll be in touch," Beckford replied.

Blower leaned against the open doorway, sucking in the fresh air. "This be all of them for now, unless Bleedin Art's lieutenant comes in."

"Aye," the coffin maker said.

"Think you be needing more coffins."

"Aye!" The coffin maker hammered violently.

Beckford rubbed his chin. "I want Mute Katie arrested for murder and aiding a known pirate, along with her accomplices, Violante Hayze and those German strumpets."

"Aye," Blower agreed. "Straight away."

Edmund handed the papers to the coffin maker and took one last look at the bodies. "I bid you gentlemen a good day."

A dark shiny box carriage waited outside, and its door opened. "Mr. Coggshall, might I have a word?"

Edmund stopped in his tracks. "Mr. Mayor?" He cautiously entered, sitting on the seat opposite. The door closed and the vehicle took off casually down the street.

"My condolences, Mr. Coggshall. I'd like to help you get your estate back. Seems our business interests have become more or less intertwined. Your father's former business partner has seized control of your rightful assets. Well, you see, my businesses are also suffering under these crude social standards imposed by the previous government allowing pirates like Captain Valentine to soil the fabric of our society. We run our own shipping companies and don't need Bleedin Art's protection."

"Always wanting to do my part, sir. What is it you need from me?"

"To fight fire with fire as they say. Though not officially on record, I'm sure your family has employed the services of Captain Slazerelli? Or as they call him in the taverns, Slasher Al?"

"I've heard the name, of course."

"We would like you to employ Captain Slazerelli in the name of reclaiming your family birthright. If for some reason Acting Lieutenant Governor Piper chooses to award Captain Valentine a commission to protect Port Royal's interests at sea, it will open a door to commerce raiding of enemy ships. We have a lot of business partners who would unjustly be deemed enemies. If this happens, our goal is to eliminate Valentine and divide his assets in the interest of protecting Port Royal investments. I will then return all of your family's assets and titles to you."

"I may be able to contact Captain Slazerelli. And, since I would be the one to employ the pirates, it only makes sense that I collect a fee from the sponsors. Fifteen percent should suffice."

The mayor knocked his walking stick on a side panel. "You catch on quickly, Mr. Coggshall. I believe our business venture will prove to be quite profitable."

The vehicle pulled over in front of the mortuary. Edmund's man Stevens stood waiting with his carriage. Edmund opened the door to get out.

"We'll be in touch, Mr. Coggshall," the mayor said, slamming the flap shut.

Katie paused outside the parlor door in the Crooked Compass. She heard arguing from within. One voice was like a rusty nail scrapping against a slate board. Mina Jacob's mouth always spewed rank nonsense and she was aptly called "the great beast". Katie peered through the gap in the door frame. Two other strumpets, Sierra Lee and Lucia Puscat, nattered on.

"But we're still under Bleedin Art's protection, right?" Sierra

Lee's voice heightened. "Even if Coggshall and Burghill are dead, right?"

"I'd say all bets are off," Mina contended. "Wouldn't you? Thanks to chomps, we're on our own now!"

Lucia twirled her hair. "What are we gonna do?"

Sierra Lee shrugged. "Go independent?"

"We'd be cut down in a day!" Mina's anger grew.

"Or work for Cherry?" Lucia proposed. "She got protection."

"Not no more, she don't." Mina scowled, watching the door. "Ah, there's the little Songbird!"

Katie entered, on the defensive.

"Katie, tell them ya had nothing to do with it." Sierra Lee immediately realized her mistake and covered her mouth in embarrassment.

Mina lunged forward. "This be all yer fault! You couldn't leave it be! You had to bite off the cock that feeds ya!"

Katie's defensive impulse got the better of her and she pulled out a bodice dagger and grabbed Mina. The blade grazed the soft, dirty skin just enough to leave a fine red line. "Mmm? Hmm?" Katie growled, feeling Mina tremble.

"Oh, Katie, don't do it; we be friends here," Sierra Lee said soothingly.

Katie stared daggers, pushing the blade a little harder against Mina's skin.

"Katie, she didn't mean nothing by it. Now get off her!"

Katie retracted the blade and ran upstairs to gather her things. She stuffed a large satchel with a nightdress, stockings, and a worn copy of *Romeo and Juliet* that Rook had been using to teach her to read. Through the window, *Diamond Dog* sat anchored at the Wherry Bridge. With her bag in one hand and her blade in the other, she left the room. She heard Mina's angry footsteps in the hall behind her. Katie passed Salty Sally, a skinny brunette with several teeth missing.

"So, did you swallow or spit?" Sally asked.

Sally and Katie laughed.

"Hate ta shit in yer bowl, but yer sailor beau got his brains blown out last night," Sally said to Katie, who stopped in her tracks.

"Really?" Mina smirked.

"Oh yeah. Took a shot right in the eye, he did." Sally grinned crookedly.

Katie's lips formed the word "no". *It's not true. It can't be!* She gripped her bag tightly.

"I sees them wheeling out his corpse just this morning. Right bloody mess they made outta him!" Sally cackled.

Lucia ran up the stairs. "Blower's outside. He's looking for her." Her eyes met Katie's.

Mina charged down to let him in.

"I'll hold them off. You gotta get out of here!" Sierra Lee said. "Good luck, Katie."

Katie fled down the slave stairs at the back and crouched behind barrels stacked in the alley. Militiamen searched the causeway. *Diamond Dog* was so close she could see the men on deck smoking pipes.

Strangewayes inhaled a lungful of marijuana smoke and passed the pipe along. Everyone wore blood-soaked clothes and grim expressions. Rook's surgery had been one of the more gruesome of his career. The shot had gone in through the temple and come out the eye. It was a miracle they'd been able to stop the bleeding. "He'll live or die now. There's no other way to put it, I'm afraid."

Winter cocked an eyebrow. "Never thought I'd see a man's life saved by a red hot marlin spike in the eye!"

"The medical profession is like any other. Sometimes you have to use what you have," Strangewayes said.

Winter choked on a lungful of smoke and something caught his eye. He pointed towards the causeway. "That be the strumpet Rook fancies, ain't it?"

Katie signaled from behind a barrel.

"That is she," Binge concurred.

"Well, *she* is currently wanted for Burghill's murder," Strangewayes added. "I better go get her."

"Prepare to make sail," Tiny called.

All hands rushed to their stations.

Strangewayes looked to Binge. "Then we best be off."

Binge clasped the rail. "I'm going with them. I gotta disappear for a while. Y'know that feeling the little fish gets when all the other fishes swim in the opposite direction? I got that feeling."

"Yes, it's called self-preservation, an old diagnosis. I myself am feeling a touch of what I call ‘peril-itis’.” The doctor shook hands. “Perhaps it’s best I don’t know where you’re going. All the same, Mr. Binge, a pleasant journey.”

“Thanks again, Doctor,” Tiny acknowledged.

“I’ll add it to Mr. Binge’s tab. Good luck, everyone.”

“Be seeing you,” Binge said. “As always, our business relationship proves to be both beneficial and entertaining, though we may have gone a tad overboard this time.”

“Yes, a tad, I’d say.” Strangewayes departed and headed towards the causeway. He slipped off his jacket and dropped it beside a barrel. Katie took it and draped it over her head.

From inside the Crooked Compass, Blower bellowed, “She’s not here. Search around the building!”

Winter and Snapper wheeled a cart down to the causeway and loaded one of the barrels. Katie slipped onto the back and hid by the cask. The men continued to the gangway just as Blower burst through the back door. “Did she not come this way?” He asked one of the militiamen.

“Nay, not out this way.”

“Then spread out!”

Strangewayes loitered nearby long enough to see the cart successfully loaded onto the ship.

Violante watched *Relentless* drift away from the north dock. Captain Richard Longstaff watched her from the rear of the vessel. Her heart leapt and sank simultaneously. It was unfair to be parted from him so soon. His image grew smaller and smaller as the vessel glided from the harbor. Vie turned and walked up Thames Street. She passed a watchmaker’s shop and a produce stand, where she purchased a mango.

A sense of liberation came over her. She had loads of money. Perhaps she’d never have to perform services again! She could triple her gold at the Swiftsure – there was plenty of room at the big table. Or better yet, she could get her own room at the lavish Wild Orchid Palace, the former guest residence of the Duke and Duchess of Albemarle.

As she neared Smith’s Alley, a strange man stepped out before her. His skin and hair stark white, and his cold pink eyes bore into her.

A dagger flashed from his sleeve, thrusting into the fleshy crevice beneath her arm and into the side of her breast. A scream was trapped in her throat until her instincts took over and she ran to the water. "Help me! Somebody help me!"

Spectators spilled onto the streets. Reaching Bird's Alley, Vie yelled at the top of her voice, "What do you want of me?" Blood soaked her dress and dizziness took hold. Her pace slowed as she came to a landing along the causeway. The attacker followed, lunging for her again with a dagger, but she hurled herself into the harbor.

The cold wet embraced her and she tried to stay afloat.

Shouts filled the air above. Someone called, "Murderer! Murderer, over here!"

A splash came a few feet away from Vie. She tried to swim for it, but exhaustion set in and she began to sink. An arm slipped around her waist, pulling her towards a dock. Hands yanked her up.

Beckford stood over Vie's body. "What's going on here?"

"Another strumpet's been cut," a man replied.

Beckford inspected the injury. "It's deep. She'll need to go to the infirmary at Fort Carlisle."

"Is that Katie the Swallower?" someone asked.

"Nay," said Beckford. "It's one of Cherry's strumpets."

Vie opened and closed her heavy eyes. The people around her appeared distorted, and the pressure of Beckford's hand against her wound caused her to scream. A group of militiamen carried her to the infirmary. The semiconscious nightmare continued as bitter laudanum was forced down her throat and a stitching needle punctured her skin. Raw, aching nausea swelled inside. Her eyes flickered to see a thin, balding man sprinkle her with a pungent substance. Scorching pain grew and more liquid was forced down her throat.

Art napped sporadically on the sofa; his injured arm propped on a stack of pillows. The flames from the fire purred. MacAskill slept sprawled in a big chair, while Scarcliff spread over the short couch with the parrot Cupid pecking his head. A burbling snort came from window seat as Jayne snored. Art sighed. *I swear I'm gonna smother him.* He sank back into the sofa. *Nay, that would mean standing up.*

The wheels of a carriage thudded along the gravel path outside and came to a halt. Haughty voices permeated the property. Everyone in the Inferno Room woke, drawing their weapons.

"The Whigs are here," Jayne said, wiping his drool off the window.

Art rose delicately to look out. "Hymen and the Huguenots! What do they want?"

MacAskill yawned. "To stitch a great Dutch wig to yer arse, that's what."

The doorbell sounded.

"Arthur Valentine! Open up in the name of King William of Orange!" Piper called.

"Well, I'm Bleedin Art of Red, so let me bloody sleep! Oh, fine, go let them in." He gestured to Jayne.

"Where is Captain Valentine?" Piper demanded. "I wish to speak with him immediately."

Jayne guided the Whigs to the Inferno Room, where they were immediately irritated by a wall of heat. "The Honorable Acting Lieutenant Governor Piper to see you, Captain."

"Ah, the Whigs over Port Royal. What can I do for you?" Art asked.

"Why wasn't I notified of the pirate attack immediately?"

Art raised a rum bottle. "Consider yourselves notified. Good day to you, Acting Lieutenant."

Mold advanced. "Tellam was killed, did you know that?"

"Aye. I lost plenty o'good men meself last night, so feel free to find yer way out."

"Was it the pirate Gator Gar who attacked Port Royal? And was it a scarlet fever outbreak?" Piper demanded.

Art rubbed his chin thoughtfully. "Well, aye, 'twas the pirate Gator Gar, or the Capitaine as the strumpets call him, who attacked; and nay, that was no scarlet fever outbreak. 'Twas Gator Gar's killings and begging yer pardon, Acting Lieutenant Gov'na, yer men are what we in the shipping industry refer to as ballast." The Whigs seemed perplexed. "Dead weight." Art burped.

"Did you see him yourself?" Mold queried.

MacAskill took the rum bottle. "We both saw him, and it *was* him. He attacked us and fled."

"Then you've seen him before!" Mold said. "Where did you last see him?"

Art flinched and repositioned his arm. "Turning towards the Old Church."

The doctor took another shot. "From there he could have turned anywhere."

"What was his intended target?" Mold continued.

Art gave a carefree wave. "Maybe he just didn't like what we've done with Clubhouse?"

"Maybe he prefers a more Jacobean motif?" the doctor suggested.

Mold scratched beneath his wig. "Could he still be in the city? That's my question!"

"Maybe." Art now felt pretty much numb from the neck down. "Y'know, if I was Acting Lieutenant Governor, I'd be declaring martial law right about now."

"I told ya before you'd make an excellent Acting Lieutenant Governor. I'd vote for ya in a heartbeat." MacAskill gestured with a raised thumb.

The inebriated pair burst into hysterics, relishing Piper's contempt. They halted suddenly, clutching at their wounds.

Art yawned. "Now, if you'll excuse us, I'm bloody tired. Wake me in the morrow."

"The bird is pecking your man's head," observed Taliare.

MacAskill observed Cupid and Scarcliff. "Aye. Around here, he's head pecker!"

Art passed out on the sofa, head lolling to one side.

"Must be delayed shock. It's a recent diagnosis," MacAskill said. "Well, if you'll excuse us, we've had a trying night. Gator Gar is long gone. Do let us know if he turns up, won't ya? Now bugger off, begging yer pardon, the lot of you!"

Piper, Mold, and Taliare shuffled to the door.

"We'll show ourselves out," Piper huffed.

"Good luck with the capture of Gator Gar, Acting Lieutenant Governor," the doctor said.

"Oh, Gator Gar won't get far, I can assure you." Piper slammed the door to the Inferno Room.

Art's eyes suddenly sprang open. "It has a nice ring – Gator Gar, won't get far!" He scribbled on a bit of parchment.

"Oh, by all means, stop to write a love sonnet. We got lots of time!" MacAskill said.

Scarcliff pushed Cupid off his head. "Why does he do that?"

"He's pecking the lice, so leave him be," MacAskill replied.

"You still living in that dump over by the fish market?" Art addressed Scarcliff.

"Aye, but I told him if he fixes it, he can live at the Clubhouse or the loft," the doctor added.

"Good idea. Move in there with Blackmoor and fix it up," Art agreed.

"Right then, O Great Leader of Men, what are we doing about Gator Gar and the pikey? Surely you're not going to let the Whigs find them?"

"That's exactly what I'm gonna do," Art mused. "It'll keep them busy for a while. Gator Gar's long gone anyway."

"There's that echo again!" MacAskill held his hand up to his ear.

Cherry
Banks
GO
2015

Strangewayes Way

Atia flinched, rousing from a sleep fraught with visions of her ma being sucked over the edge of the ship. The air was different – cleaner, with a hazy sweetness. The wheels of the carriage rattled along a dirt path occasionally skipping over a stone or a tree root. The rocking motion reminded her of the *Aeolus*. Fingers stroked her cheek and then gently brushed through her hair.

"We have arrived, *ma chérie*," the Capitaine whispered.

A dark figure flew past as she opened her eyes. The sun's intensity shimmered like flames through the thick green trees. Slowly she sat up, feeling rather dizzy. Was this a wonderful dream or had she succumbed to her injuries and strayed into a strange paradise?

The Capitaine slid his hand into hers. "You were having bad dreams; they are over now."

The carriage trundled casually along a path lined with bushes and hanging vines. Large bright green leaves and vibrant wildflowers spread as far as the eye could see. Birds chirped and swooped overhead from tree to tree. Iridescent butterflies shimmered through the air reflecting green, red, yellow and blue.

Minuit flew in, landing on the back of the carriage. Atia put out her hand and he hopped down onto the back seat. "Hello, Minuit." Her throat was dry and scratchy.

"Hello, hello," Minuit squawked.

The Capitaine opened a canteen and she put it to her lips. "Thanks." The parrot nestled onto her lap and she gently touched the feathers on his head.

Lilly snapped the reins lightly, letting her mind wander in the pristine setting.

Gladstone shifted beside her, lifting his hat. He yawned, stretching his arms above his head. "We're just about there. It's just up ahead, Lil." He pointed to the bridge and the waterfall below. "This is the river where we get the clean water."

Lilly laughed. "The good water you label vinegar?"

"The very same." Gladstone smiled back at Atia. "We always drop off a few barrels for the ladies."

"And we love ya even more for it." Lilly's face lit up as they approached a large green field, brimming with wildflowers and bushes with bright red berries. "Oh, my!" She snapped the reins a bit harder. Just beyond the lake lay tall green mountains. The car picked up speed and Minuit flew off into the trees.

"Welcome, ladies and Frenchman, to the plantation. We call it Strangewayes Way." Gladstone signaled a gray-haired man in a faded suit. "That's Gillis, our gatekeeper."

The carriage rolled through the large wooden entrance and turned onto a dirt road that led across the field towards a large whitewashed house with a newly built wraparound porch. A couple of giant trees guarded it and a jagged border of wild, bright pink bromelia afforded some privacy. Across the lake, a cluster of bungalows sat inside a wooden perimeter.

Atia's jaw dropped. "It's beautiful!"

A black moth with reflective shiny green and blue markings rested on the side of the carriage.

"It will do," the Capitaine replied. His eyes latched onto her. "You should be safe here for now."

"Pull up at the house first," Gladstone advised. "We'll drop off a few supplies before taking you down to the bungalows."

Lilly paused beside the large trees and locked the brake.

Down beyond the house were bungalows, situated at the edge of the lake. "Is that them there?" Atia asked.

"Aye." Gladstone unloaded a couple of crates. "That be them. Your dwelling for the next little while until you get healed up."

"How big is this place?" Atia probed.

Gladstone paused to wipe his brow. "Over a hundred acres. There's the lake, and a river nearby with good fishing, if you like mullet."

Atia hadn't been fishing in years. The last time was with her da. In fact, she recalled that he threw her into the pond to retrieve the fishing rod and the fish.

"When you're a bit stronger we'll head up north to the O'Malleys'."

"How far is that?"

"Two days up the mountains and a day by riverboat."

Her shoulders dropped. "Another boat?"

Two people emerged from the house. A beautiful black-skinned woman stepped onto the porch. She wore a short sleeve pale yellow dress and her molasses hair flowed freely over her shoulders. Next to her was a young African man with a muscular physique, dressed in plain linen.

"This is Carlena, Lady and Empress of our council of elders," Gladstone teased.

"Watch it." Carlena gave him a playful smile.

"And Ekene, her Lord Adjutant." Gladstone turned to Ekene and put on a contrived, stern face. "You there! Get over here and pick up these bags!"

Ekene stared him down, folding his arms over his chest. "I do not take orders from you."

"Right-o then." Gladstone shrugged and began to smile. "Can you take this lot on whilst I unpack?"

Ekene laughed. "Sure, mate. That I can do."

"I'd like to introduce our latest runaways. This is Lilly, Atia, and an old friend of the doctor's, the Capitaine."

The Capitaine bowed to Carlena. "*Bonjour*, Mademoiselle. Capitaine Gator Gar at your service."

She came down steps to greet them. "I am aware of you, Capitaine."

Lilly automatically eyed up Ekene.

Gladstone embraced Carlena and stroked her hair. "Did you pick up our German guests?"

"I did. They are down at their hut, trying to adjust."

"That's all that can be expected. Lilly here has decided she wants to work for us."

"Good, she can help me out."

"We're completely off the map here, Capitaine," Gladstone explained. "The best part is that everyone here is officially dead. We move people and supplies to the fishing villages where we ship them to just about anywhere in the Caribbean."

"O'Malley is one of your fishermen?" asked the Capitaine.

"Not too often. The English keep a close watch on him, so he prefers a certain amount of discretion. Lilly, there's a room for you here at the main house," Gladstone said.

Lilly's eyes sparkled. "Whatever you say."

Gladstone picked up Lilly's bags. "Come on, Lil. Your first job will be to help me have a drink."

"Aye, I can do that!" She darted inside.

Carlena went to the house. "I'll be back in a moment to take you down."

The Capitaine took the seat next to Atia. "No rush."

Atia leaned against the Capitaine and closed her eyes, feeling peaceful for the first time in days.

He lifted her chin gently to behold her eyes. "Care to join me for supper this evening, Mademoiselle?"

Her hand rested on his thigh. "Do you have supper with every girl you win in a card game, Capitaine?"

His lips brushed her forehead. "Only the pretty ones. The rest get scraps."

"O'course I will." She watched the sunlight ripple on the water.

Carlena returned after a few minutes. "I'll take you to your bungalows." She snapped the reins. "You'll be fairly close to the Germans." She pointed to a stout hill. "There are corn fields up there. Farms, a barn, and a stable down this way on the right. And the sugar cane fields and swamp are back that way."

The Capitaine glanced towards the mountains. "You don't get attacked here?"

Carlena shook her head. "No, they leave us alone. We are not exactly friendly, but we have an understanding."

"Friendly with who?" Atia asked.

"Maroons," the Capitaine said.

"The who?"

Carlena clarified, "The Maroons are tribes of runaway slaves. Mostly African and Arawak who live in the mountains. Many Maroons escaped from the Spanish long ago and have lived in the jungle ever since. We are all strangers to them."

They passed through a tree filled area.

"Your living quarters are right through here," said Carlena.

Minuit glided in, landing beside Atia.

"Hello, again."

Minuit whistled. "Hello, hello."

"No, no. Say '*bonjour*,'" the Capitaine corrected.

"Who's a pretty bird?" Atia cooed.

Minuit bobbed his head. "He's a pretty bird!"

The Capitaine rolled his eyes.

They pulled up alongside a double bungalow and disembarked. Atia massaged her ribs and watched the lush green trees. Her feathered admirer landed on the bungalow roof to keep watch.

"There's one side for each of you, or you can open the middle and make it one," Carlena said.

The Capitaine grinned fiendishly and both women caught the look. "What? So I can keep close watch!" He turned to Atia. "Are you going to be content here?"

"I think I could get used to this," she said.

"*Pardon moi*!" Minuit flew off.

Atia moved towards the porch as something enormous darted down the steps. A shiny gray lizard vanished into the bushes, flicking its long tail behind itself. "What was that?" She froze on the spot.

"A galliwasp," Carlena said.

"I see." Atia cautiously went inside. "Hope I don't end up with one them in me bed!"

The golden moonlight sparkled on the lake, while across the water, other plantation residents gathered around a bonfire. Smoke drifted to the open window where Atia stood with her eyes closed. She went to change into something more comfortable. The cream-colored nightdress and royal blue robe slid on easily, letting her ribs relax.

Minuit landed on the windowsill, a dead rat in his beak.

"Shit, bird!" she exhaled.

He dropped the rodent and gazed up, seeking praise. "Who's a pretty bird?"

Atia patted the feathers atop of his head. "Thanks, bird."

A knock came at the door. Atia smacked a mosquito stalking her neck. "Come in." She straightened her robe and pushed up her breasts.

The door opened and the Capitaine stepped in. He had bathed and shaved, and he wore a neat suit, his hair tied back. Her heart leapt.

"Good evening, Mademoiselle, am I disturbing you?"

Atia blushed. "Good evening, Capitaine. Come in."

He presented her with crimson hibiscus flowers in a glass decanter.

"Thank ya, they're lovely…Paul." She set them on the table beside her bed.

"Who's a pretty bird?" Minuit cooed at her.

The Capitaine noticed the dead rat. "No, no. *L'enlever*!" He pointed and waved his finger until the parrot flew away with the prize. "Stupid bird." He flushed with humiliation. "I apologize. He was bringing it as a gift."

"Aye. Some bring flowers, some bring rats. How is a girl to say no?"

"I also brought you something from Lilly." He took a small bottle from his pocket and offered her a chair. "This will help with the pain."

"About time!" Atia exclaimed.

"I think it's laudanum. I better have some to be sure, uh?" He winked, giving her a formidable smile that ignited her pulse. After rolling up his sleeves he opened a cupboard and took out two pewter goblets. He blew off the dust and set them on the table.

Atia used water from a pitcher to clean the cups. The Capitaine's bluish gray eyes studied her. In them she saw an underlying sorrow, mixed with a passion that intrigued and intimidated her. Her experience with men was limited, although she'd been fond of a man back on Crisp's estate – a stablehand. They'd had a brief tryst, but he was sent away as soon as they were discovered.

Atia slapped another mosquito from the side of her face. "So have ya been a pirate a long time?"

"Are you trying to be romantic?"

"When did you become a captain?"

La Roche was silent a moment examining her pretty green eyes. He clearly remembered sailing aboard the ship called *El Diabolito.* He'd been an ambitious young renegade who sabotaged Capitaine le Clercq's balcony. When le Clercq stepped outside for his nightly smoke, the structure fell away into the sea. Le Clercq was never seen again and la Roche became the new Capitaine.

Atia touched his hand, breaking his train of thought. She pointed to his arm. "What do yer markings mean? Is each one someone you killed?"

He glanced down at the thick green scars patterned down his forearm, created by a gunpowder-stained knife. "Oh, no. I wouldn't have enough room." Her curiosity was so sweet and innocent; he had no wish to scare her. But she had always been fearless, even as a child. *Does she not remember that we met before?* "Why do you ask so many questions?" He paused. "Each one is a raid. A Spanish or Dutch city that I sacked."

"Why is that one crossed out?" Atia reached over to touch the last line, which had an X cut over it.

He studied her again, anxious she might vanish if he looked away.

He put several drops of laudanum in each goblet. “Observant, aren’t you? Maybe another time I will tell you about it. But tonight, only pleasant things.”

Atia poured the water.

La Roche raised his cup. “To you. *Ma belle jeune fille aux cheveux rouge*.”

They toasted and drank.

Atia shifted her chair closer to touch the skull tattoo on the back of his hand. He leaned in to catch the scent of her hair and kissed her forehead.

“I’ve got marks.” Atia slid the robe down to reveal a brand of a V on her shoulder. “Got it when I was at a workhouse.”

He reached up to gently brush her hair over her ear. “Why were you in the workhouse?”

“Crisp sent me there when he caught me stealing from his stores.”

“A woman after my own heart.”

“He just wanted me out of the way.” Atia lifted her hair to expose scars on her neck. “These are from Crisp’s monster. A giant slaver with barbs on his rings. He lifted me in the air with one hand and threw me onto the ship.”

La Roche lightly stroked the marks.

“Captain Mandingo is what Crisp called him, but his men called him Kabaka. He used to be an African king, they say. More than seven feet tall.” Atia held her hands a foot apart. “With a thing this big.”

“I’ve heard of him.” He frowned.

“Well, at least I’m not Crisp’s bitch. Can’t say the same thing for Captain Mandingo.”

She showed him her left arm. An ankh tattoo covered a cross brand. “And this one from Crisp himself. He burned a cross into my arm when he caught us praying to…ya know, I don’t even remember anymore. Guess that’s what he wanted.”

La Roche removed a leather cord from around his neck. On it hung a small wooden ankh.

Atia studied him carefully, and suddenly her eyes lit up. “Yer the bearded Frenchman!”

“I have been called worse.”

“And that, it’s me lucky charm!” She turned the carving over to see the letter A engraved on its base.

He gave her a wink. "It's brought me good luck."

"I gave this to you. When did you know it was me?"

"The bird told me," he said. "The other night in the carriage."

She handed it back. "You kept it all these years?"

"It is special to me." He slipped it back around his neck. "You were just a little girl then."

"We was running from Crisp too, and you came to my rescue."

His hand covered hers. "I knew your father from a few raids. He was well liked by *les Flibustiers,* the men I associated with. We all liked your father and when we found out the English were screwing him over we decided to help."

"I still don't know what happened. Ma never said."

"We attacked a slaving station on Tobago in '77 when we heard the English took O'Malley's family. You were chased all the way up the Chippewa into les Gichigami to a place call Baie du Tonnerre, and then all the way back down to Barbados. We helped your father take you away but the English never gave up."

Atia was silent before looking embarrassed. "I pulled you down by the beard!"

"Oui, you did. I have had neck problems ever since."

Young Atia had defied everyone's warning to stay away, but when she came over to him she tripped over her feet. She'd grabbed his beard to pull herself up.

At first, he was furious. "What were you thinking?"

"I want to give ya this." Young Atia took the wooden ankh from around her neck. "For helping us. It's me lucky charm. I want ya to have good luck, since ya brought us good luck."

He knelt down and took the carving. "In that case, *ma chérie,* I accept your lucky charm. I will keep it forever." He glanced over at his men. "I'm just glad it was the beard!" It was then that young Atia leaned over and kissed him. She wrinkled her nose at the roughness of is cheek.

La Roche played with the stem of his goblet as he remembered the young Atia.

"We don't have much luck, do we?" Atia said.

"I guess not. But I still have your lucky charm." His mouth moved to hers. "And being O'Malley's daughter makes you pirate royalty. I'm bound to protect you."

Atia gave him a crafty smile. “You mean all the pirates should grovel at me feet?”

“Let’s not get carried away.”

Atia jumped at a loud knock at the door. She wanted to tell them to go the hell away, but instead politely called, “Come in.” Slipping the robe back on, she glanced at the Capitaine. She now understood why he had seemed oddly familiar.

“*Merde*,” he cussed under his breath.

Gladstone entered carrying a small steaming pot, a round of bread, and wooden spoons.

Lilly trailed behind. “Hope we’re not disturbing you. ’Tis supper time.”

The Capitaine took the pot and set it on the table.

Atia slapped another mosquito on her neck.

“Bugs aside, how do you like it?” Lilly asked.

“It’s lovely. The water is clean and it smells so nice.”

“It does, don’t it?”

“All the same, Dr. Strangewayes insists we only drink the boiled stuff.” Gladstone removed a block candle out of his coat pocket. “Light this. The mosquitoes don’t like it.”

“Thank you. Yer too kind,” said Atia.

The Capitaine took the candle and struck a match.

Lilly whispered in Atia’s ear. “You have to come up to the house! You won’t believe what he’s got up there!”

Gladstone headed to the door. “I’ve asked everyone to let you rest tonight. We’ll have introductions tomorrow.”

“*Merci*.”

“Well, we got more stops to make. Natalia and Catharina are not taking to the bugs so well,” Gladstone said. “You get settled in and we’ll see ya in the morrow.”

Lilly kissed Atia’s cheek before she departed.

After the door shut, Atia sniffed the stew. “Mmm, it looks—”

“Disgusting,” the Capitaine finished.

They laughed quietly and each grabbed a spoon. The first mouthful wasn’t bad, but after the third, the peculiar salty aftertaste lingered, making Atia want to gag.

“It’s interesting, but I dunno what it is,” she said.

"Turtle."

Her eyes narrowed. "Oh."

"Here, have the bread instead." He handed over the round.

Atia ate it gratefully. After supper she slid the robe off, exposing her arms.

"And this one?" He caressed a dagger scar.

Atia shifted closer. "Captain Mandingo again. It matches the one I gave him." She shrugged. "Anyway, it adds character."

He kissed the mark. "Character you have much of and you are exquisite."

She shied away from the intensity of his stare. "What else we got to drink?"

He removed a flask from his jacket. "You could try this?"

"What is it?" She sniffed it.

"Chartreuse Liqueur d'Elixir."

"Sharr-truth-lick her what?" She took a mouthful and screwed up her face. "Whoa! Anything to get rid of the turtle taste."

The Capitaine laughed. "As bad as a hot pepper?" He pulled her onto his lap, clasping her waist.

"About the same, I think." Atia glided her fingers along the thin scar upon his cheek. His manhood stiffened beneath her. She capped the flask and put it into his pocket. "Whew! Strong stuff, that is."

"Lightweight."

She hugged his neck to steady herself. "Yer a famous pirate." She gazed heatedly at him, her desire increasing. "Infamous. Chopping off men's heads. Blowing things up. Do you always try to leave such an impression?"

"I have style, huh?" His humor turned serious. "Truthfully, I have killed many times. Does this trouble you?"

"Ya being a murderer?" She ran her fingers through his hair. "Ya ain't really the murdering type, not a bloodthirsty killer anyway. Rather a man who does what's necessary, a soldier, both gifted and cursed."

"Oui, you could say that." He laughed ruefully.

She poked his chest with her finger. "A noble quality, but it will get you killed one day. And then who will be there to swindle me away from the sharks?"

Their eyes locked transfixed, his thumb slid over her lips. She tongued it playfully, and then took it in her mouth, sucking gently. He gasped and crushed his mouth against hers. She reciprocated eagerly. His fingers glided along her neck and over her breasts. Her nipples stiffened when his tongue probed them through the fabric. Their lips met again. Atia pulled away to catch her breath. She covered his forehead in kisses. "I want you. Follow me."

"Ah, the direct approach." His breath caressed her ear. "Good."

Atia rose, but her legs collapsed on the way to the bed.

He seized her before she hit the floor. "Okay, take it easy. Perhaps a little too much laudanum?"

Atia melted into his arms. "And the Char-whoosh!"

He was amused. "Oui, you're wasted."

"Wasted…a good word for it." She giggled. "I be wasted!"

"I am a bad influence, I think." He set her down gently and propped her head on a pillow.

Atia pulled him down beside her and nestled against him. "Or maybe the other way around, my Capitaine." Her eyes closed as she relished the heat of his body.

He gathered her in his arms. "*Je t'aime*."

A collection of lemon balm scented candles lined the railing to the bungalow. Natalia was tempted to close the window, but the air in the room was too heavy. A bead of perspiration trickled down her neck and she slapped at it automatically.

Ekene wrinkled up his nose as he lit another candle.

Catharina paced. "Thank you, that's very good." She carried a candle in one hand and a bottle of brandy in the other. "You may go."

"Catharina!" Natalia scolded. "Thank you, sir. You've been very kind to us."

"Yes, thank you," Catharina slurred.

A wagon approached outside.

"Got yer grub, Nat and Cat. Hold yer frocks!" Lilly called.

Natalia was entertained. "She has such a keen vocabulary."

"I don't understand a word she says," said Catharina.

Gladstone squinted. "Every bug in Jamaica's heading for Cuba! Don't use too many of those candles; they'll make you sick."

Natalia gave a polite nod. "We'll stop after we've cleared out a few more bugs."

Lilly carried in a pot of stew.

Natalia's nose rumpled. "Oh, that smells wonderful."

Catharina sulked. "It does?"

Gladstone set down two bowls with spoons and dished out the stew before heading back to the wagon.

Natalia accompanied him to the door and gazed up at a myriad of stars twinkling against the darkness.

Carlena approached on foot. "Guards are on watch and everyone has had their supper." She coughed. "You can smell it all the way up to the house."

"How's Fatima doing?" Lilly asked.

"Asleep. Probably for the first time in long while. When you're done here, why don't you two get some rest?" Carlena patted Gladstone's shoulder.

"That's the best idea I've heard today." Exhaustion dulled his face, and he smiled faintly. "I don't know how Lilly's still walking. Come, Joan of Arc, time you got some sleep."

"Aye," Lilly said.

Carlena addressed Ekene, "I'll take the first watch down here. Check the gate before you go to bed? Say goodnight to Gillis for me."

"I sure will."

Gladstone and Ekene climbed into the wagon.

Natalia waved. "Goodnight and thank you!" She shut and locked the door.

Catharina drank large mouthfuls of brandy. Neither she nor Natalia touched the stew. They sat across from one another in silence until Natalia took a mouthful. "Tomorrow, I will ask the French captain how long it takes to get to Caracas from here. He should know," Natalia said, reaching for the brandy to wash away the peculiar salty flavor. "It's not far from there."

"I'm not going to make it. Fever or insects or pirates will get me if I don't end it!" Catharina sobbed.

"Where would that leave me, my lady?"

"They sent us here to die in the heat along with all the Negroes and Indians!" Catharina cried into the stew.

"They also turned out to be completely different from what we expected," Natalia reminded. "We've learned more this year than in our whole lives. The countess was right!"

"Don't look for the bright side."

"We would be dead anyway if we'd stayed. You made it this far." Natalia finished her supper and followed it with more brandy. "Carlena, the woman you were just watching she's putting on a Shakespeare play for the doctor when he returns." She handed back the bottle. "Everything we've been taught about the Western world is all wrong."

Catharina tried a mouthful of stew and cringed. "Oh, this heat! Your heart is much stronger than mine. The thought of never going home again is too much for me to endure."

"It won't be long now." Natalia squeezed her hand. "If it's too hot, then we'll try further south. Duke Helmut has a cousin who founded a colony in Uruguay." She paused for a drink. "Do you know what the *Rio de la Plata*, the River of Silver, is called on the English maps?"

"No. But I'm sure you will tell me."

"It's called the River Plate."

"Why?" Catharina took more brandy.

"Because the English thought Plata must mean plate." Natalia smirked.

"They named it after a plate?"

"Yes, a non-existent plate! Not even a silver one!"

Both ladies burst out laughing.

"Do you know why the natives here are called Indians?" Natalia continued. "Because Columbus, the great discoverer, thought this was India. The Indians here have never even been to India!"

Catharina giggled, finishing the dregs of brandy.

"If this place has taught me anything, it is that the wealthy and powerful are flawed and insane, just like the rest of us," Natalia said. "We'll find our place in the world and things will be better, you'll see. You will have amazing adventures to write to the countess about." Natalia went to the cupboard to get another bottle of rum and uncorked it. "If disease or pirates do get us, then I'll cut open both our throats. You have nothing at all to worry about."

Catharina gave her tearful hug. "Just so we're clear on that."

Natalia took a drink. "We will be fine, my lady."

Gladstone gave up trying sleep in his bungalow. He sat by candlelight at a desk near the window, glancing at Strangewayes's house. He poured himself another shot of rum. The sounds of Lilly and Ekene's amorous activities traveled through the open window. He tried shutting it, but the heat grew too thick, so he became a reluctant voyeur.

"Oh!" Lilly called out. "Oh, yeah!" Intermingled with gasping and grunting from Ekene.

Gladstone sucked back the rum. "Doesn't she ever sleep?"

The door to his bungalow creaked open and Carlena entered. "Doesn't she ever sleep?"

"I doubt it."

She helped herself to rum. "You finally came back."

"Aye. And by the way, we might just have our ship," Gladstone said.

"Sander's out of his mind. The Capitaine is wanted!"

"Can't really argue with you there. But poor old Coggshall and Burghill bit the big one."

Carlena's warm auburn eyes lit up. "What?"

"Well, more the other way around for Burghill. Katie the Songbird gave him his last bites."

Carlena was stunned.

"Strangewayes Scarlet Fever Brand Elixir took care of the lot and a few more good gents too. We didn't know for sure until we reached Ligania, but we got them. I feel a sense of extreme jubilation, like I've done something really important for the world. Also, complete exhaustion; like I just came from the outhouse after three days of the flux," Gladstone mused.

Carlena laughed. "Such a way with words."

Gladstone topped up their glasses and they toasted. More loud moans came from the doctor's house.

"She's too young for you," Carlena said.

Gladstone beamed. "You be jealous?"

"You wish."

"She's too young for me. I be a tad too old for her, too."

"You are not too old for me, I hope?" Carlena stepped forward, unlacing her dress until the garment fell to the floor. Her naked skin shimmered beneath the moonlight. His eyes widened.

Gladstone put the bottle down. "Perhaps a bit stiff—" he groped her smooth round bottom "—but never too old for you, my dear."

A great feast of roast pig lay on the table. La Roche joined Pierre le Picard, Basque, and l'Olonnais in a toast. L'Olonnais knocked over his tankard and laughed.

"Forgive me, gents; I'm merely obeying the law. What goes up must come down!"

They all raised their mugs and cheered, "What goes up must come down!"

"Like the Spanish Empire!" Basque said.

They all laughed. La Roche watched the pig now dripping in blood. Down along the beach, their galleon lay on its side, smashed against the rocks. Don't leave the ship! We mustn't leave the ship! *A storm rolled in, thwarting their desperate attempt to get away by raft.*

L'Olonnais tapped la Roche's shoulder. "Are you well?"

La Roche nodded.

"Take the food," l'Olonnais said, carving a slice out of Basque's arm. Blood spurted across the table, covering the plates and cups.

"What are you doing?" la Roche yelled. Flames erupted all around, engulfing l'Olonnais. Scorched flesh crackled and split in the fire. "What goes up must come down." L'Olonnais's body ripped apart; blood and chunks of flesh flew through the air. Cannibals forced bloody pieces of human meat into la Roche's mouth.

La Roche's arms jolted upwards and his eyes opened. Sweat rolled from his forehead and along his neckline. He retched over the edge of the bed, still tasting the blood in his mouth. *It's over. It's over now. It's over.* He tore off his soaked shirt and tossed it to the floor.

Atia was still asleep beside him; he touched her hair to ensure she was real, and then caressed the exposed skin of her back. Her scent was intoxicating and comforting. He put his arm around her waist and kissed the back of her neck. He clung to her for several minutes before she started to jerk.

Atia thrashed in her sleep. Her ankle wrenched backwards, striking him in the groin. He groaned and she rolled off the bed, hitting the floor hard. She grumbled and grabbed the edge to lift herself up.

"Atia, are you well?" He rubbed his tender testicles with one hand and helped her up with the other. "You were having a bad dream."

She climbed back in beside him, giving him a peculiar look as he released the hand between his legs. "I was holding onto a rail and I could see the rocks coming. They were shiny beneath the lightning. I saw Ma die. I watched her get pulled over and I knew there was nothing I could do."

"I've been there many times," la Roche said.

"You have nightmares too, I've seen it. You grab at the air." She laughed painfully. "Are we both tainted goods?"

He shrugged. "Maybe. But…*c'est la vie*."

Atia put her mouth on his gently and smoothed his hair with her fingers. The fear subsided, defeated by her sweetness. He rested his head against her heart, and she slid her arms around him. An Irish tune softly flowed from her lips, lulling him into a peaceful sleep.

M.E '15

The Waning Moon

Muffled voices roused Violante. Her eyes remained shut, and she listened. The pain in her chest ignited and she rubbed her teary eyes.

Blower and Beckford spoke in hushed tones.

"She's still in and out of consciousness, but Dr. Sober says she'll come around," Beckford said.

"Royal treatment for a strumpet," Blower huffed. "They should hang her."

"Not before she's questioned and not before due process," Beckford reminded. "Judge Goblet's ordered a quick trial. He's going hang this one as an example."

Blower laughed. "I doubt even Longstaff could get her off now!"

"Mind if I have a few moments alone with her?" Came the voice of Edmund Coggshall.

"Sure," Blower said.

"Hold on!" Beckford interjected. "She's accused of participating in his father's death. You think leaving them alone is a good idea?"

"I assure you Major Beckford, my only interest is seeing her get better so she can be processed by the law and punished accordingly."

"Fine, in you go," Beckford agreed and footsteps approached her room.

Vie kept her eyes closed, pretending to be asleep.

"Violante?" Edmund pulled up a chair beside her bed. "Even your name is beautiful, such a waste."

She opened her eyes. "Mr. Coggshall, sir? Where am I?"

"In over your head. You know just how close you came and still are? You are to give evidence as to your involvement with Mute Katie in my father's death. Then you are to be hanged," he spoke softly.

"Edmund, I swear I wasn't involved."

"The evidence suggests otherwise."

"But Richard, Captain Longstaff knows of my involvement. He'll tell you I had nothing to do with it!" Tears rolled down her cheeks.

"There's nothing your navy captain can do for you now. I'm sorry. I could solicit on your behalf?"

Vie gave him a desperate stare. "You will?"

“Of course, but you must tell me everything you know.”

“But I wasn’t part of it, I swear! What could I know?”

“Start with the Hapsburg women, who helped them escape?”

“I don’t know. I didn’t know they escaped.”

Edmund stood up. “Then I can’t help you.”

“The pirate who took their ship, the red beast who works for Bleedin Art, they say he knew the Germans were worth a lot, a lot more than he let on.”

“Are they nobility?”

“Aye, one of them is cousin to a countess in Hanover. She belongs to one of the ruling houses. Lilly said he kept the gold for himself and he kept her title a secret.”

“And the Irish girls?” he pressed.

“I helped the French captain get one to Dr. Strangewayes, they already had the other one.” She sniffed. “That’s all I know. I didn’t mean for any of this to happen.”

He started for the door. “I know you didn’t.”

Her voice cracked. “Please believe me. Don’t let them hang me!”

“I’ll do what I can,” he spoke sincerely. “Not a word of this to anyone. Not a word.”

In the hall, Blower was waiting. “I must say, yer a lot more forgiving than your father,” he said.

“Aye. You’ll need to have a talk with Cherry next and see where Lilly has gone,” said Edmund.

“She’s long gone too, probably with the other pikey.”

“Possibly. And I’ll need the belongings of the two Hapsburg strumpets returned to the Crooked Compass,” Edmund insisted.

“That be evidence,” Blower said.

“Nay, they’ve been exonerated. My father claimed full ownership of them the night before he died, and I’ll need them returned along with all their belongings.”

“They may be missing, but they’re still under Bleedin Art’s protection.”

“I can claim ownership by law, Constable. Give the mayor my best.” Edmund walked away.

A door opened and footsteps rushed into the hallway. “Edmund Coggshall?” Strangewayes sounded surprised. “Is Violante Hayze here?”

"Aye, she is," Edmund said.

"She's just in there, Doc," Blower added.

Strangeways entered the room and Vie reached for him. "Doctor, please help me!"

He placed his arm around her. "There, there, my dear. I promise." The doctor gently lifted the bandage. "Christ, he should take up knitting! I'll find a way, don't you worry."

After a proper dosage of medication, the doctor cleaned and redressed the wound and removed a book from his bag.

"Are you familiar with Shakespeare's *Romeo and Juliet*?"

"Nay, neither," Vie replied, feeling happily relaxed.

"Well, then, you're in for a treat. I'll read you some today and the rest another time." He opened the leather bound book. This is a Welsh version from a French translation, so I'll have to recite some from memory. Forgive me if I curse a bit here and there." He cleared his throat and began.

Mrs. Beazley set the tea tray beside the bed and drew the curtains. Late afternoon sunshine flooded the room. Steam rose from a cup as she poured.

Livia groaned, trying to move. "Where am I?"

"Good evening. I'm Mrs. Beazley. I'll be tending to you for a while. Do you remember what happened?"

Livia's eyes widened. "Where's Atia?"

"Not far. We had to move her and we'll take you to her as soon as you're able. Can I get you anything?" Mrs. Beazley patted her arm.

"No." Livia winced, trying to breathe.

"Now you need to lie still. We'll take care of everything," Mrs. Beazley said softly. "When the doctor returns, which should be anytime now, we're going to wipe you down and clean you up again. I'll give you something more for the pain. And we'll be ready next time; I've sent for fresh linens."

Livia realized she had soiled the bed. "I'm so sorry."

Mrs. Beazley set a clean chamber pot on the bed. "Nonsense. Everyone gets the flux their first time here. Something in the water, the doctor says." She felt Livia's clammy forehead and passed her the tea. "We'll get you some new clothes, too, very soon. Is there anything you'd like? Anything at all?"

“My ma.” Livia felt a tear escape her eye.

“That of course, I cannot do.” Mrs. Beazley moved to the window.

Livia panicked. “The men who took us, are they coming back?”

“Those men are dead, dear, I assure you. But all the same, we’ll need to keep you hidden for a while, just in case. Try to relax; you’re in good hands.” Mrs. Beazley observed the street. “Ah, about bloody time! Was I going to play indentured servant to a wretch all night again?”

“What?” Livia asked, sipping the tea.

“Oh, not you, dear. Now take it easy, the doctor has arrived.” Mrs. Beazley jolted. “Shit! It’s Edmund bloody Coggshall too!” She opened the window to peer out.

“What’s going on?” Livia asked.

Mrs. Beazley signaled her to be quiet.

Strangewayes grew befuddled as Edmund accosted him at the front door. “Doctor, excuse me. Might I have a word?” Edmund began. “Violante, they’re going to charge her with my father’s murder.”

“Violante? That’s absurd! She wouldn’t harm anyone. I’ll post her defense.”

“That *is* complete nonsense!” Mrs. Beazley huffed quietly, leaning over just enough to see the color rise in the doctor’s face.

“No need, Doctor. I’ll represent her,” Edmund assured.

“You will?”

“Certainly. The poor girl’s innocent. You said so yourself. Well, maybe innocent isn’t the word, but I’m confident the real killers will be brought to justice.”

“Oh, by the way, about your father, sorr– no, that’s not it. Well… you know.”

Edmund put up his hand. “And about the Irish girls—”

“Irish girls?” Strangewayes was taken aback.

“Yes. At least one of them is with you, isn’t she?” Edmund glanced up.

Mrs. Beazley stepped back from the window.

“I have one of the indentured Irish girls under a fever quarantine,” Strangewayes said.

“Like you, I’m only interested in what’s best for the girls.” Edmund paused. “May I have a word with Livia?”

"Livia? She's not here."

Widow Bell's carriage pulled up across the street. "Oh, shit!" Mrs. Beazley turned, accidentally bumping the bed.

Livia moaned.

"I'm so sorry, dear, I'll be right back."

Mrs. Beazley slipped downstairs and cautiously approached the front door. Edmund and Strangewayes were still talking.

"Well, she's here, yes, but she can't be disturbed. I can assure you, she's not going anywhere," the doctor said.

Mrs. Beazley checked the side door and found Widow Bell with fresh linens.

"Here you are." Mrs. Beazley took coins from her pocket.

"Good day to you," Widow Bell acknowledged and ducked away.

Mrs. Beazley crept to the front door.

"Do with them as you see fit, and tell Livia I hope she's feeling better soon," Edmund said.

"Thanks very much. I'm sure she'll be thrilled. Good day."

"Let me know if there's anything she needs."

"I will, Edmund, thank you."

Mrs. Beazley watched young Coggshall through the front door window. She let the doctor in as Edmund boarded his carriage.

Strangewayes lifted the bags and set them inside. "How's our patient doing?"

"Mrs. Beazley?" Livia called.

"Be right there!" Mrs. Beazley replied. "Jesus Christ!" She marched up the stairs.

Strangewayes followed close behind.

Livia clutched her ribs. "I'll have that shot now, if ya please."

Mrs. Beazley sighed. "Good idea; let's both have one!"

Strangewayes lifted the bottle of laudanum on the dresser and began mixing.

"How'd the little bastard know she was here?" Mrs. Beazley pondered.

"I thought the other girl said he helped me," Livia said.

"Violante?" Mrs. Beazley asked.

"Yes. Well, he may have played a part, but some things are best left under lock and key for now." The doctor smiled, administering the laudanum.

Candlelight illuminated a large copper washtub where Bizy Gale and Widow Bell sat opposite each other. Swirls of steam rose as their legs intertwined. Widow Bell's blond hair was draped over her shoulder and one could see why she had earned such an infamous reputation in her twenties.

"Strangewayes has the poor girl over at Mrs. Beazley's house," Widow Bell said.

Bizy massaged some of the doctor's honey soap into her arms, it felt good on her skin after washing linens all day. "Hence the shitty linens and the bastard's son knowing where she is."

"Aye, that's what I can't figure out. No way Coggshall is gonna let something stand between him and his property. That's why Edmund was being so nice. Damn it, what's Strangewayes got himself mixed up in?"

"Now, just you relax and take a load off. Yer wound up like a top!"

Bizy could hear her children whispering at the door. She threw the bar of soap. There came a faint "ouch!"

"Serves ya right!" Bizy scolded. "Remember private time!"

"Yes, Mama," Isabella replied.

"Yes, Mama!" Jamie called.

"Go clean yer rooms!" she instructed, pausing until they ran up the stairs. "Since when do kids *want* to see their mother in the tub?" Bizy grabbed a pipe stuffed with dried weeds and struck a match. After a deep breath she passed it over.

Widow Bell took a large puff. "Strangewayes says it's the lead pipes turning us all into imbeciles."

Bizy belted out a cough. "He could be right."

The front doorbell rang abruptly, causing both women to scramble for towels and robes.

"I'll get it!" Jamie bellowed.

"No, dog-boy!" Isabella yelled. "Get back here!"

"No!" Bizy huffed, running to the bathroom door. She opened it just in time to catch her son and thrust a leg out. Jamie crashed into the wall and then fell backwards onto the floor. "What'd I say? No one answers the door!" She dashed down the stairs, calling behind her, "Remember, I beat ya cuz I love ya!"

"Yes, Mama," Isabella replied.

Widow Bell followed, wrapped in only a robe. The bell rang again, followed by a knock. "We hear you in there! Open up!" Beckford's voice penetrated the door.

"Ah, shit, it's him!" Bizy scowled.

Widow Bell rolled her eyes. "What the bloody hell does he want?" She let her robe fall open and answered the door. "Can I help you, Major Beckford?" Several men stood at the threshold, including Fyre-Master Keene and several of his men. Swiftly she covered up. "Mr. Keene, what can we do for you today?"

"Well, yer doing a mighty fine job of it already, I must say." Keene gave a wide smile. "I almost went out with a bang!"

Bizy stepped into the doorway, while Jamie limped behind her.

"There he is, and his mother too," Keene continued.

"What can I do for you, sir?" Bizy asked.

Keene removed one of his medals. "Young man, don't think your service to the city went without notice the other night." He pinned it on Jamie's shirt. "On behalf of the city of Port Royal, I award you this medal of service. Congratulations, my boy."

Jamie showed off his medal to Isabella.

"And the same goes for you, Miss Gale. You're to be rewarded as well."

Bizy was alarmed. "Sorry?"

Keene's eyes beamed. "It was you who saved the storehouse from catching fire. The whole block could have gone up. I've been Provost Marshall and Fyre-Master since '55 and I've put out a lot of fires. You saved lives and property."

"I did my part," Bizy admitted.

"And then some!" Widow Bell said. "He's giving you credit; take it!"

"I've recommended you for a special citation and Councilman White has approved." Keene shook her hand warmly.

Bizy blushed. "I don't know what to say, Mr. Keene. Thank you."

"There's a ceremony at the King's House in the morrow. Please attend at eight bells."

"I will." She glanced at Isabella, who was overjoyed.

"Then I bid you a good evening and expect to see you first thing in the morrow." Keene tipped his hat and started back down the front stairs with his men following.

"I will be there, sir. Thank you."

Beckford eyed them suspiciously. "Have an accident?"

"Did you?" Bizy replied. "We have clean linens."

"Good evening to you all," Keene called from the street. "I'll expect to see you in civil training when you're of age, lad."

"Yes, sir!" Jamie waved. "I'm gonna be a fyreman! A fyreman pirate!" He whirled down the corridor.

Bizy closed the door. "No running in the hall."

Jamie stumbled into a side table and hit the floor. Tears welled up.

Isabella clapped. "Good form, dog-boy!"

"Now that was your own damn fault." Widow Bell shook her head, and addressed Isabella, "And stop calling him that."

"Lead pipes, eh?" Bizy said, glancing at Widow Bell as she helped Jamie to his feet.

Former Acting Lieutenant Governor Dewar, currently in exile at his Ligania retreat, stuck his feet up on the desk in the study. He hadn't heard from his wife for over two days. Perhaps if he regained Port Royal, she'd change her mind. He pulled a scroll from the drawer for some light reading. The medical report on lead pipes contaminating the water through the city wasn't terribly absorbing, and he found himself distracted by the sunset on the water. Returning his attention to the report, he said, "Strangewayes has a theory that lead pipes taint the water supply. He says there's a direct link to the flux."

Sleemans peered up from his copy of *Confessions of a Confessional* by Brother Gregory, a former Port Royal priest. "Balderdash!"

"Balderdash? That's *our* word, commoner, and Strangewayes has been right before."

"I seriously doubt that. People have been using lead for hundreds of years. I think we'd know by now if it was bad for us. The windows, statues, and altars of every church are lined with lead. Are we poisoning our brains every time we walk into a church? I think not! And why bother yourself with that at a time like this?"

"Because, my not-so-good fellow, when I take my city back, I won't look like a complete twat for not keeping up on current events. Port Royal changes every minute. You must be ready for whatever comes your way."

Llewellyn rushed in with his young slave, who carried various papers. "I have them!" His eyes lit up. "Our link to the outside world!"

"Ah, there he is," Dewar said.

Llewellyn scattered the papers on the desk. "I got *The New World Today*; *Slavery Now*; *Sensible Politics*, and my personal favorite, *Port Royal Times*, or as I like to call it *Who's-at-War-with-Whom Weekly*." He sniffed the paper. "I remember a time when Port Royal prospered."

Dewar flipped through the papers. "Indeed, it's called wartime."

The Llewellyn family arrived with slaves carrying supplies. Lady Lyla Llewellyn and Laura entered the study.

"Ah, the nightly frenzy we call family." Dewar took the cigar box. "Where did you go? Cuba?" He stared at a small fury creature sporting an enormous mustache, cradled in Laura's arms. "What the hell is that? You bought a rat!"

"It's a dog. It's called a Chico; they breed them in Mexico. I named him Chico Gonzales," she replied.

Dewar was mortified. "What's it bred for, eating bugs?"

Laura set down the small dog and it ventured to the wall to rub its backside against it.

"Or perhaps, it's bred to add a special shit-stain motif to the decor?" Llewellyn gritted his teeth.

Dewar pointed at the creature. "Just keep it the hell away from me."

Laura passed a package of matches to her father.

"Thank you, darling." Llewellyn lit a cigar. "Now don't forget to say your prayers before bed."

"Yes, Papa." Laura kissed her father on the cheek before heading upstairs.

"And say hello to God for me, will you? I don't want him thinking I've lost interest," Llewellyn added.

Dewar reached his hands up to the sky. "Oh, how I long for the sounds of Port Royal! Must I wake prematurely to the call of the cock ringing in my ear only to be tormented by Chico the rat-dog as I yearn for sleep in my own bed? A bed being soiled at this very moment by a filthy sheep-sodding Whig! The thought of it pains me so!" He strolled out to the veranda where light rain now misted the air. "Where's the gazette?"

"It didn't come out. Distribution was halted by direct government order," Llewellyn explained.

"Bloody cotton-heads! They can't do that, it's ...what do you call it?"

"Censorship," said Sleemans.

"No, that's cutting off the foreskin, you fool!"

A great ruckus came from the bedrooms above.

"Shut them up, will you?" Dewar and Llewellyn both called. "It's time for bed!"

"It's Dorcas Junior, he refuses!" Lady Llewellyn shouted.

"Dorc Junior!" Dewar scowled. "All of you get to bed! Or Jesus will…" he looked at Sleemans. "What does Jesus do again? Go to bed or Jesus will sod you with his holy cross! A big wooden one!" Dewar noticed the shed, where a slave was hunched over, trying to drag something heavy. Dewar made eye contact with Llewellyn and gestured to the slave's wriggling bottom. Both of them grinned.

"They can't just stop printing the news and get away with it. Those ridiculous swirly hand jobs are too hard to comprehend. Besides, the people have a right to know the information that's vital to them as it is currently relevant!" Dewar continued.

"Relevant information like 'Two-Headed Boy Linked to Interracial Sex?'" Llewellyn asked.

"No, relevant information like someone sacked the hall of records. If it was Slasher Al, then he has the Albemarle records and you can forget about getting your city back because we'll all be hanged," Sleemans explained.

"Well someone has to have them. Better him than the Whigs. We can negotiate with *him*," Dewar said.

"What was the part about being hanged?" Llewellyn asked.

"I knew we should've had a massive fire to take out all the rabble, but no! You and your morality, and all that loss-of-life shit!" Dewar snarled.

"Those records exonerate Colonel Beeston and link us with Modyford and the Duke's treasure hunt," Sleemans replied.

"I thought "Beesty" was supposed to swing for the Albemarle cock-up? We paid good money to send him up the Thames and the plan was foolproof!" Llewellyn huffed.

Sleemans eyed Llewellyn. "Perhaps I underestimated thee."

"Not to worry. There's no problem a good bribe can't overcome," Dewar insisted.

Llewellyn was overwrought. "What if he's not interested in a bribe? What if his motivations are political? If those documents are discovered by English authorities, we will have no hope of escape!"

"Oh, be calm. A good government knows how to handle blackmail. We shall hire Bleedin Art to haggle with Slasher Al, or feed him to the shrimp."

Sleemans gave a dry laugh. "We hired Bleedin Art to solve the syphilis problem. Now the strumpets are all under his protection."

"Good thing for Katie, though. I'd miss that one. Can't sing worth shit anymore, though," Llewellyn said.

The rain pelted down, plunging the horizon into a gray haze. Lady Llewellyn appeared. She saw Dewar and her husband watching the slave outside and gave them a disgusted glare. Finally, the slave succeeded in dragging a heavy fabric awning out of the shed. It became apparent that the slave was in fact male.

Llewellyn blanched, and brought the paper up in front of his face. "Speaking of treasure hunts, the pirate Laurens de Graaf was seen at a galleon wreck off Serranilla Bank, just one hundred and eighty miles south-southwest of Jamaica. What is that in days?"

"He could be here in less than two," Sleemans said.

"De Graaf, digging for treasure? Balderdash!" Dewar grumbled.

"I agree. Perhaps we should send someone to Cayman Brac and check with the Brethren of the Coast," Sleemans suggested.

"True. *We* – as in *you* – should sail right away," Dewar said.

"Me? I can't sail; I'm having my hair done. But I'll find out what he's up to."

"You're having *your* hair done? That should be a privilege for the wealthy elite. We don't want subordinates running around with privileges. You'll fall under the delusion that you're a "middle class," throwing your opinions around like they'll make a difference." Dewar uncorked a bottle. "The time has come to execute my plan to return to the Governor's Mansion."

Sleeman's frowned. "Your plan?"

"Ok, well, *our* plan."

"Suppose the island was taken by King James?" Sleemans suggested.

Llewellyn rubbed his chin. "Yes, and what was the part about being hanged again?"

Evening approached as Cherry was escorted to Valentine Mansion. Despite her aching arm, she dressed whimsically in a low-cut pale pink gown and a hat with a white ostrich feather.

Jayne stopped the carriage and climbed down to offer Cherry his assistance.

"Thank you, kind sir." She took his hand to steady herself.

He gave a large yawn. "This way, Miss Banks."

Cherry eyed him suspiciously. "We can always do this in the morrow if you gents be tired?"

Jayne opened the door and she went in ahead of him. "Nope. Art wants to take care of this right away." Panic seized her in the darkness of the hallway, and she reached for her bodice dagger. She turned to Jayne and a pistol cocked, aimed at her forehead.

"Now you don't want to be doing that, Cherry. Thought we was all friends here?" Jayne said.

"You broke my heart, Cherry. Not to mention my balls and my arm, too." Art's voice came from his study. The door was open and lantern light flooded out into the hallway. His silhouette hung in the doorway.

"What be the trouble, Art? Thought you wanted me to take care of yer finances."

Jayne steered her into the room.

"Polish the silver, girl, it's up!" Art limped to the gun cabinet to unlock it. "Ever heard of a blunderbuss, Cherry?" He removed a wide-barreled shotgun and cradled it in his good arm before passing it to Jayne. "The name comes from a long, Dutch word meaning 'thunder gun' or something."

She stepped back, trembling as Jayne took aim.

"This one can fire ten shots at once and can blow ya clean in half. Well…clean ain't exactly the word."

Cold sweat formed on her neck. "C-c'mon Art. If ya wanted to kill me, ya wouldn'ta brought me here."

"Hmm…smart girl." Art revealed his large teeth. "Now no one's going to blame you for taking out Burghill and Coggshall. They was a couple of arseholes anyway. But Jesus Christ woman, you and Captain Crocodile took out half the bloody city!" He stepped forward.

"They was gonna kill me and my girls and ya know it!"

"I lost five of my boys and someone's gonna pay."

"It was self defense. Violante had nothing to do with it, and she got a knife in the chest!"

"You coulda came to me for protection, and I didn't know nothing about Violante."

"I don't have a cock, Art, so stop trying to jerk me off!" Cherry scowled. "Nothing happens in this town without you knowing about it. I had to take action!" Her voice quavered, half in fear, half in anger.

"Trust, Cherry. We used to have trust. I would never let them do anything to you." Art's voice got louder. "But now the trust is gone. If we don't got trust, then we don't got nothing. Jayne told Coggshall to leave you alone; you was under my protection and that's the God's truth!"

"Bull fucking shit!" Cherry's voice rose above his. "You were gonna let Coggshall kill us all and corner the market. You talk about trust? I was always loyal to you. I trusted you, bastard! We always took care of you and yer boys and you spat in my face!"

"Don't you backtalk me, woman!" Art roared and pointed his finger at her. "I've always looked out for you and this is how ya repay me? Aw, fuck it! Plug her, Jayne!"

Cherry's hands shot out in front of her face. "No! No, wait! I'm sorry! I'm sorry, Art. You win!"

"Too late!"

"I promise I'll be loyal. Please?" She peered through her fingers and their eyes locked.

Art was silent a moment. "That's better, see? You can be sweet as sugarloaf when you want to be. Put it down, Jayne. Cherry's gonna behave." The blunderbuss was lowered. "Now, this is how it's gonna be. You and yer girls belong to me. Yer gonna take Coggshall's girls to MacAskill and clean them up. My men will be on guard starting tonight."

"I don't want Coggshall's scraps," Cherry blurted out.

"Did I ask you what you want? Two of me men will be at yer disposal. Do we have an accord? Or will I be getting the carpet cleaned?"

"Aye, we do."

"Then it be so." Art put cigar in his mouth and struck a match. He puffed for a few seconds, staring her down. "Now, who helped you? You had help, who was it? All of them, Cherry, or you're getting ten new customers right now."

Her eyes lowered. "Strangewayes and his man, Gladstone."

"Yeah, I figured that. Who else?"

"L…Lilly. Lilly poisoned Codface and almost Jayne."

Jayne's jaw dropped. "Blow me down!"

"See? Ya got played, boy."

"Mr. Binge."

Art blew out a lungful of smoke. "The card player?"

"He's friends with the Capitaine and Strangewayes. The pikey girl was in on it too."

"Didn't Coggshall find her in a cage covered in shit?" Art managed a semi-amused frown.

"Aye, but I hear she's hotter than Helen o' Troy," Jayne said.

"Think we'll let that one slide. Anyone else?"

"The German girls."

Art was silent a moment, puffing on the cigar. "Can't say I blame them. What about the Capitaine's crew?"

"He's here alone."

"Right. Now, if you want to live, yer gonna play by my rules. You got that? Okay, take her home."

Jayne grabbed Cherry's arm.

"Oh, and Cherry?" Art added.

"Yes, Art?"

"Next time, you're dead. That's a promise."

"Aye, Captain."

Jayne passed the blunderbuss back to Art.

"Don't ever hold it like that again. Break your collarbone in two, it would," Art cautioned.

"I thought it was more dramatical."

"Well, try not to think. It's not your *forte*." Art sucked in more cigar smoke, watching Cherry be escorted away.

In a carriage outside Fort Carlisle, Judge Goblet fidgeted, reading over an article in the paper under lantern light. He glared out the window at one of his men. The one with white hair and pink eyes. Spook. *Bloody Spook blew his cover!* Goblet had been sitting there for hours observing the main entrance to the fort. First Beckford arrived, then Blower, then Coggshall Junior, and finally Strangewayes. Beckford remained along with his guards. He glared down at the headline of the gazette indicating:

Strumpet Stabbed by White Man!
Port Royalers witnessed the stabbing of a strumpet
by a culprit known as the White Ghost.

"I don't think anyone sleeps," Skean said, sitting beside him. "It may be prudent to devise a new plan."

"Mr. Spook's loyalty is definitely in question." Goblet banged on the roof of the carriage. It stopped several meters from entrance and the door opened.

Spook stepped inside.

"Your cover has been compromised!" Goblet hissed. "You must leave the city today. It's a bloody disgrace!" His bottom lip quivered. "I'm sending you north."

Spook grimaced. "You mean north as in the colonies?"

"No. North as in over there." Goblet pointed through the window. "I want you to assess the plantations around the Blue Mountains. I'm going to ask the Acting Lieutenant Governor to send Strangewayes to Nevis. The hurricane disaster on Nevis is a perfect pretext to remove Strangewayes from the equation while we probe his business more closely." Goblet removed additional documents from his case. "These are Strangewayes's land titles, borders, and a map." He pointed to the border coordinates. "Dr. Strangewayes might want to consider permanent residency on Nevis." Lightning struck in the distance, and the sky rumbled. The waning moon hung above like a sickle. "When he returns to Port Royal, we should have enough evidence to send him to the gallows for theft, fraud, and any other sick things he might be doing up there."

The next day around noon, Atia and Lilly sat on a small sofa in Strangewayes's library, surrounded by lanterns. Outside the sky was dark and cloudy, and thunder rolled. The two girls flipped through books and papers that contained detailed descriptions of contortionist sexual positions, banned writings, and illicit seductions.

Atia's mouth gaped open. "That is positively disgusting! They publish this filth?"

"They're called transcriptions," Lilly explained.

Atia flipped the book upside down to see if it made more sense. "Let me see another."

Lilly tossed her a black leather bound notebook that contained hand-copied poems by the Earl of Rochester. She scanned the writings eagerly, her mouth dropping at the more shocking phrases: *her hand, her foot, her look's a cunt*, and then, *melt into sperm, and spend at every pore*. At the bottom of the page, an afterthought was jotted down. "What's a cunni-gul-what?"

"Cunnilingus?" Lilly whispered the answer in her ear.

Atia's eyes widened. "Oh, wow!" She took out an innocuous medical textbook. Various diagrams of human anatomy were revealed, paying particular attention to the sexual organs. A revealing study on the anatomy of nipples filled one chapter, while the mechanics of female genitalia was detailed in the next.

Lilly flipped through the book until she came to a hand-sketched diagram of an erect penis spanning two pages. She thrust the book into Atia's face.

"Yeah, I know what *they* look like."

"Have ya seen the Capitaine's yet?"

Atia's lips curled into a full blown smile. "Aye, he ain't too careful."

"You've been here a week and that's it?"

"We've played about some! I been in a shipwreck, haven't I?" Atia defended. "It's enough to put ya off moving about a lot, if ya know what I mean?"

"Nay, didn't catch a word," Lilly teased. "Big, ain't he?"

Atia bit her lip. "Impressive." She paused. "Wait a tick, how did you know?"

Lilly made a clawing motion. "She wants it! Relax, he's yours. Me professional opinion, I can tell size by the way it sways when he walks." She turned another page that was stuck together with a waxy substance.

"Can I borrow this one?" Atia eagerly wanted to read more poetry by John Wilmot. She slipped it into her sleeve.

Gladstone poked his head in the door. "Hey, that's not my fault. Doc leaves candles on them. By the way, Carlena wants you to help with cooking tonight, if you don't mind? After yer done getting acquainted with the medical books, of course."

"Aye, I will," Lilly agreed.

"And try to get some rest tonight. I really could use some."

"Right, early to bed tonight. Yes, Pa."

Carlena stormed through the front door. "Miles, come quickly!"

Gladstone ran to her and they went outside, where plumes of smoke rose from behind the western trees. "The Maroons! How soon will you be done?"

Ekene peeked up from where he and the Capitaine were replacing a wheel on the wagon. "One minute."

Atia and Lilly stepped onto the porch with several books tucked under their arms. The atmosphere had grown warm and sticky. Atia hoped it would rain; that would freshen the air. "Are we under attack?"

Gladstone gave her a reassuring look. "No. Well, yes, but it's nothing to be alarmed about." Then the alarm bell rang and residents from nearby bungalows filed towards the Gathering Place. "Well, fine. You can be alarmed, just don't panic."

A silver-haired native approached. He had a necklace made of teeth and claws, and his arms and hands were covered in tattoos. He held a carved spear and wore a dark shirt and trousers. "Move to the Gathering Place, people!" He stopped next to Gladstone.

"Welcome home; how did it go?" Gladstone asked.

"O'Malley will take the Hapsburg women himself. But the Maroons are angered. The trip will be dangerous."

"I'll ask Bilwi to come with us." Gladstone turned to Lilly and Atia. "This is Yaguara, our chief of security."

"More women?" Yaguara said.

"Atia O'Malley," Carlena replied.

"O'Malley? They survived," Yaguara said.

"Two did, with the help of the Capitaine. Her sister will be arriving later," Gladstone explained.

The Capitaine stood up and wiped grease from his hands onto a rag. "Oui, and she is mine."

Yaguara appeared shocked. "Capitaine?"

"You two know each other?" Gladstone asked.

"Oui. Yaguara and I are old friends from Henry Morgan's day," the Capitaine said.

"You knew Henry Morgan?" Carlena asked.

"Henry Morgan was a back-stabbing serpent!" Yaguara scowled.

"Oui, he knew Henry Morgan," the Capitaine quipped.

Yaguara eyed the Capitaine. "You got gray."

"You shrunk," he deflected. "This year's storm season is turning out to be particularly bad."

"Oui. You never know what can blow in," Yaguara agreed.

"What's going on out there?"

"The Maroons sometimes burn down sections of the outer wall. It's a game with them."

"Right-of-passage bullshit, uh?"

"You're not a man till you've broken Strangewayes's fence."

"We're going to have to go fix it," Gladstone said.

Lilly got excited. "Can we come?"

"We?" Atia asked.

Gladstone shook his head. "She can hardly walk and you never seen a Maroon before. When this happens we all meet up at the Gathering Place until we're sure any danger has passed."

Ekene gave Lilly a playful hug. "We're ready to go."

A small group approached. Among them, limping, was a mocha-skinned woman in her mid-twenties with long dark hair and a dirt-covered dress.

"Is it the Maroons again?" Gladstone pressed.

"Again!" The woman snarled. "Five of them. Youths with spears. This time we got wounded."

"Who?" Gladstone asked absently.

"Me!" She uncovered a bloody stab wound.

"Damn it, Tanama! What happened?" Yaguara demanded.

"I'll live," she insisted. "They took us by surprise."

Yaguara helped her into the wagon. "Let's get the girl sorted out first. Atia, Lilly, come with us. We'll drop you off at the Gathering Place."

Tanama gritted her teeth. "Got me right through."

"Tanama let her guard down!" Yaguara scolded.

"Come on, let's go," Gladstone insisted, ushering everyone aboard.

The Capitaine followed Atia and they glanced teasingly at each other. The wagon rolled along, passing the bee sanctuary near a cluster of bushes. Beyond a row of bungalows was the Gathering Place covered in lush grass near a fire pit with tables and benches.

Tanama was carried first to a nearby cabin. "I'm fine now, just felt a little faint is all."

"All the same, go have a lie down," Carlena advised as she assigned muskets, passing them to several men. "Take up position around the perimeter."

"What's going on?" Fatima asked.

"The Maroons." Carlena addressed Lilly, "I have to go. Make sure there's enough food and water for everyone."

"I will." Lilly turned to whisper in Atia's ear and pointed to the Capitaine's trousers.

Atia turned bright red when she realized he was watching her.

"You should be flattered," Gladstone said. "When women point at mine, it's usually followed by a laugh."

Yaguara climbed into the driver's seat of the wagon. "Let's move out!"

Carlena sat next to him while Ekene and Gladstone piled into the back.

The Capitaine followed, but not before giving Atia a kiss and an exaggerated wink that made her laugh. "See you later."

She blew him a kiss. "Yer crack'd!"

The carriage trundled through a shady tree tunnel. Overhead, Minuit glided down to land on Atia's shoulder.

"Traitor!" the Capitaine called.

The wagon continued along a winding tree-lined trail, passing a stable and several vegetable fields. Overgrown clusters of deep orange spiky bromelia were intertwined with bright green bushes covering some of the footpaths. Rising plumes of smoke still billowed from the outer wall of the plantation.

"I've been meaning to mention, we have a job coming up and we're going to need a ship," Gladstone spoke to the Capitaine.

"If you noticed, I left it at home. I will consider it." The Capitaine observed the field of marijuana plants. "Good thing they didn't burn that. So how frequent are these attacks?"

"They weren't very frequent at all. Now they're every three or four weeks, and never in the same place twice."

The Capitaine raised an eyebrow. "That is not a good sign."

"We only want to scare them away. Don't shoot any of them. We killed one about six months ago in a skirmish by the river with another plantation owner named Lord Noell and his men. The Maroons retaliated by killing four of ours that night." Gladstone felt glum.

"And fifteen of Noell's people, including three children," Yaguara added.

The wagon halted near the perimeter's west gate. Several Maroons stood ready with spears. Gladstone fired a shot in the air to startle them. They ran off howling and laughing.

"Wait here, Capitaine," Yaguara instructed, scouting ahead through the bushes.

The Capitaine aimed his gun up into the trees, when Gladstone noticed three natives arriving just outside the damaged gate. It was Bilwi and two Miskito scouts, obviously curious about the fire.

Gladstone was relieved. "Not to worry, Capitaine. That's Bilwi, a friend of ours."

Bilwi shouted at the Maroons, "You trespass here! You are breaking the peace!"

"We do what we can to maintain the peace," Gladstone said. "But sooner or later something bad is going to happen again. Now the Maroons want us to stop the slave revolts. What do we do there? We're damned if we do and damned if we don't. We're going to have to come to an agreement somehow."

The Capitaine lit a pre-rolled cigarette. "Uh, good luck."

"Bilwi here is our ambassador to the Maroons. One of the few outsiders permitted to get close to Ashanti, the leader of the Windward tribe. Like one of your buccaneers, no one knows his real name. The strongest and in my opinion, the wisest of the Maroons. He controls these mountains all the way to the North Shore. The English lose scouts every time they go up there. And it's *King* Ashanti now. From what we hear, he intends to unite the Maroons against the English. All we can do is keep the peace as best we can," Gladstone mused.

"Without looking like cowards," Carlena added.

Ekene smiled. "Carlena's real good at winging them."

Gladstone fidgeted. "But if one of those wounds gets infected, then we've got a voodoo curse on us and the Maroons are real good at making them come true."

"Respect is most important to them," Carlena said.

"Ashanti is wary of everyone," Bilwi warned.

Gladstone assessed the burned-out section of fence. "Well, if we want to be home for sunrise, we'd better get started and chop it all out."

Yaguara returned. "The Maroons are gone. They've headed up the trail."

"I think we're secure here," Gladstone said to Carlena. "Head back and grab a handful of men to help us fix the wall, will ya?"

Carlena nodded.

"Bring saws and spikes too."

Carlena took off on the wagon.

Gladstone patted Yaguara on the back. “How’s that for timing? Your friend the Capitaine gets blown in by a hurricane right when we need him!”

Yaguara wore a doubtful expression.

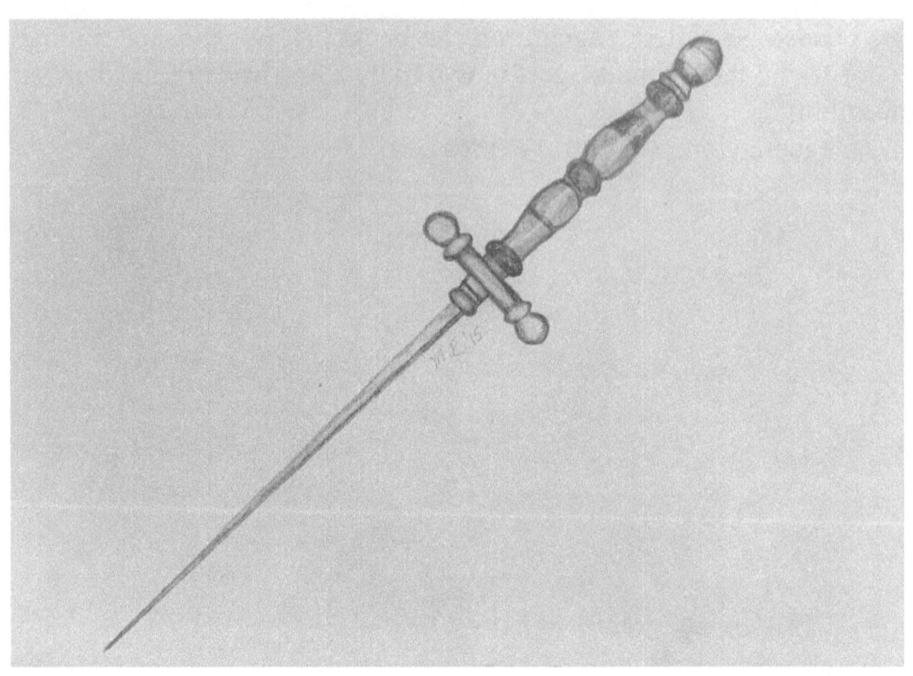

Minuit's Muse

It was evening in the Gathering Place of Strangewayes's plantation. Staked wooden torches illuminated the large grassy area where a makeshift stage had been created, complete with a curtain hung between two trees. Fatima led a group of people in the rehearsal of Shakespeare's *Henry V.*

"Ok. Take it from the top," Fatima directed, and some people gazed up to the sky. "The top of the page," she clarified.

Atia bit back a laugh and strolled past the barbecue pit where men raised a pig from the fire using a giant wooden skewer. Her face furrowed at the stake entering through the mouth and coming out the rear. The supper bell sounded and everyone gathered to the picnic area.

Lilly handed Gillis a bottle. "How's your friend doing?"

"Tanama? She's a strong lass. She'll be well soon." Gillis uncorked it and took a drink of ale.

"Does she need anything?"

"Nay, let her rest."

"Atia's going to need proper rest tonight as well. I'll be tending to her myself," Lilly asserted.

Atia took a seat. "I feel me ears burning."

Gillis began to carve the meat. "Whatever you think is best. I'll be on watch tonight if you need anything."

Tanama approached. "This smells too good to pass up."

Atia waved. "Sit with me, love. This is the wounded section."

Tanama sat down beside her.

"Atia…O'Malley," said Atia. "How's the arm?"

"Hurts." Tanama winced. "Blast those Maroons!"

"Yer lucky it wasn't poison," Gillis called. "They sometimes use frog poison on the tips!"

"Maybe because of the hurricane they're short on frogs?" Tanama speculated. "How are they doing at the fence?"

Gillis filled several platters with sliced meat. "Still fixing it. They'll be a while yet."

Lilly served before sitting with Natalia and Catharina.

"Do you play?" Natalia asked, eyeing a lute.

"Nay, but I play a good organ," Lilly answered cheekily, causing a laugh. "Do you play?"

"A little. May I?" Natalia took the instrument and tuned it before playing an old Germanic song.

"You're the shipwrecked one?" Tanama asked Atia.

"Aye, and then sold into slavery and then rescued. Wait till I get me hands on that traveling agent!"

"I was shipwrecked off the north coast. Yaguara found me when he was out fishing. I'd been on the rocks for three days."

Gillis came over with a plate of food. "The old man thinks of her as an apology from the gods for killing his family."

"Yaguara lost his family?" Atia asked.

"Aye, his son to the pox a long time ago and his wife the same way years later. Then one day he turned up with this young lass on his boat." Gillis took a mouthful. "Hasn't let you out of his sight since, has he?"

"He can get too protective," Tanama said.

Minuit flew in, landing next to Atia. His overly large head nudged her arm and she gave him some cashews. "Yer a good boy aren't ya?"

Catharina watched with fascination and revulsion. "I'm not getting used to your bird."

"Well, he catches a bounty of pests that bird," Lilly defended. "He's a fine hunter."

"Fine hunter," Minuit boasted and stretched out his feathers.

"That he is." Atia tossed him another nut.

"Yes. Thank you, bird." Natalia looked at him. "It does eat a lot of bugs."

"So, did you have to make services on men?" Atia asked Catharina.

Catharina seemed mortified.

"She's asking if we served men in Port Royal," Natalia said.

"They had to service Bleedin Art and Doc MacAskill. They were special hands-off, high-class shit!" Lilly laughed.

"If you call handling Valentine's bony kneecaps and MacAskill's midnight whimpering for his dead wife services, then yes, we had to endure those horrible services," Catharina huffed.

"That's it?"

"I'll die before I do it again!"

Natalia smiled faintly. "We had an agreement with Captain

Valentine. He awaited bribe money from our families and protected us from Coggshall until he lost two ships full of slaves. Then Coggshall seized us in a debt recovery and ordered us to work."

"Bleedin Art told Cherry to watch out for them and if they was in trouble to call Doc Strange and here we all are!" Lilly exclaimed.

"I wonder what happened to Katie?" Catharina mused.

Fatima raised her glass. "Gladstone said he'd find out."

"Then let's drink to her, wherever she is." Lilly lifted her cup. "To Katie, who will not be silenced." They all clinked their cups. "Ya had to service some of them. You was working that night."

"We had a total of three customers. All of whom left very happy and with no memory of what transpired. You and Dr. Strangewayes saved our lives and we wouldn't be here if it wasn't for you." Natalia looked at Fatima. "You're having trouble believing this is real. You made the right choice."

"Where will you go from here?" Lilly asked.

"Mr. Gladstone says he's arranged a ship to meet us on the north side of the island, and then we sail for our new home: Aragua in South America," Natalia said.

Atia gazed around in amazement at the dreamlike setting. "I think I could get used to this right here meself."

"May I?" Fatima reached for the lute and Natalia passed it along. "I just want to play for someone other than Burghill for a change." She played "To Thee And To The Maid".

Lilly whispered to Atia. "I'll be back in a stout. I'll raise ya a proper bath."

Atia's eyes lit up. "Sounds like ecstasy."

Lilly bid everyone goodnight.

Gillis intercepted her. "I'll be manning the front gate tonight. Let Miles and the others know as soon as they get back."

"Aye, as soon as we sees them."

Atia watched the dancing and hugged her ribs. Fatigue set in and she yawned. She propped her head against her arm on the picnic table and dozed off. What seemed like seconds later, Lilly tapped her arm.

"Come with me."

Atia yawned. "Ah, my bath!"

It was late evening when Atia sunk into a copper tub. The water was beautifully scented with herbs taken from the doctor's personal store. All the pain in her body evaporated.

"Here ya are." Lilly dropped in a lump of soap that fizzled in the water between Atia's legs. "The doctor makes these. We call them—"

Atia raised her hand. "Don't spoil the moment." She sat back and closed her eyes. When she reopened them, a dark feathery creature charged past the open door to the porch, chasing a rodent. Atia braced herself for another "gift".

"Ain't birds supposed to fly?" Lilly said.

"I ain't sure he is a bird."

Not a minute later Minuit ran inside with a dead rat in his beak and dropped it on the floor beside the bath tub. "*Bonjour, ma chérie.*"

Atia cringed. "Thank you, Minuit. Good boy."

"Poor little thing…it's because he's the only one of his kind around. He's picked you as his girl."

"Oh, good!" Atia recoiled.

Lilly tilted her head. "I don't know…maybe if ya gave him a tiny hand job or something, he'd leave ya be a while."

"Nay, he's just a dirty little sod. Aren't ya?"

The parrot whistled and bobbed his head. He stared at her with his beady eyes. "Give us a look."

"I wonder where he learned that?" Lilly questioned.

From the front door came footsteps. "*Bonjour, ma chérie.*" The Capitaine entered with Gladstone trailing behind. "We have returned from our dangerous encounters."

Gladstone wore a large smile upon his face. "Oops. Hope we're not disturbing ya?"

Lilly tapped her foot. "Well, you are!"

Both men seemed unable to avert their eyes.

"Saints alive!" Gladstone sighed. "Think I'll go get meself cleaned up." He patted his perspiring forehead.

The Capitaine spotted the dead rodent and pointed at Minuit. "Away with you, bird!"

Minuit took off in a huff, "*Connard*!"

"Gillis is at the front gate alone. He wanted me to tell you," Lilly said impatiently.

Carlena entered. "I'll head up and check on him."

Ekene also stepped inside, his attention fully drawn to Atia. "Wow!"

"G'night all!" Atia spoke sharply.

Carlena pushed Ekene out the door. "Gillis is at the front gate alone. Can you grab some food and meet me up there?" She grabbed Gladstone and the Capitaine by the scruff of their necks and dragged them out.

"Men." Lilly slammed the door. "They always act like they've never seen a girl before!"

"Men have two sides: the arse and the prick. Ours tend to lead with the prick and let the arse follow," Atia tittered.

"And we love 'em for it." Lilly smiled. "You just relax and I'll pop some fresh pillows on the bed."

"Yer too kind. You ain't charging me, are ya?"

La Roche stood outside the bungalow patting his forehead with a rag. Candlelight glowed through the curtains. Naturally, his curiosity piqued.

Gladstone was dazed from exhaustion. "I dunno about you, but I'm gonna go find a cold bucket of water."

La Roche nodded. "I know what you mean."

"Food first, a bucket of cold water, and then sleep," Gladstone said. "Thanks for the help." He started down a path.

"Any time." La Roche entered his half of the bungalow to peel off his soiled clothes. He splashed water from the basin on his face and neck. From a pewter cup he drank fresh water as though it were rum. His eyes lingered on the adjoining door to Atia's room. Muffled voices giggled and chatted.

La Roche washed up and air-dried before slipping on a clean shirt, letting it hang open. He decided against trousers as the breeze from the window cooled his aching legs. He eyed the adjoining door again. No sound. Then a delicate, ecstatic moan and panting.

He knelt carefully on the floor and crawled over to the keyhole. Atia lay naked on the bed with Lilly's head between her thighs. His mouth dropped. "*Mon dieu*!"

Atia bit her lip and writhed. A loud groan escaped her throat and her fingers slid over her breasts.

La Roche looked away for a moment, half torn between jealousy and arousal. He wanted to taste every quiver and joyous spasm in Atia's body. Like any starving man, his eye latched back onto the keyhole for sustenance.

A knock came at Atia's front door.

"Hello? Is everything okay in there?" Fatima called.

Lilly glanced up. "Should we let her in?"

Atia thought for a moment. "When she's older."

"Everything's fine, Fatima. Go to bed!" Lilly hollered, and then dove back down.

Atia's back arched and she moaned, finishing loudly.

"And that my dear, is cunnilingus."

"You can cunni-gush me anytime! Do men know how to do that?"

"Not a whole lot." Lilly emerged, licking her lips. "Careful around here, some men are cannibals."

"What do ya mean?"

"Nothing. Most men don't, so when you get one that does, ya keep him!" Lilly laughed.

Atia reached for her nightdress. Her voluptuous breasts shifted beneath the soft, slippery fabric, while her red curls hung over her shoulder.

La Roche's mouth gaped. Although he was desperate to be with her, her bruised ribs limited their activities. At this point his manhood was achingly erect. There was only one solution; he slid his hand between his legs.

Court of Chancery

Early morning clouds rolled in over Port Royal, draping it in gray. Rain threatened and the wind picked up, scattering wanted signs of Gator Gar down the steps of the King's House. Inside, Piper's slaves brushed the lint off his clothes and re-powdered his wig. Made presentable, walking stick in hand, he strolled downstairs to the study for a smoke and to peruse the papers.

Mold, Taliare, and Councilman White entered.

"Have you seen these? It's intolerable!" Piper exclaimed, waving a paper with the heading: "England Passes Act of Grace Law Forgiving Followers of King James."

Mold shook the paper. "Aw, fuck!"

"Goddamn Act of Grace! Probably Queen Mary's idea, again!" Piper huffed. "I'm calling for an emergency assembly meeting of the Court of Chancery this morning after the ceremony. I read this in the Port Royal Daily Gazette one full hour before receiving official notice from the navy." The title: "Battle of Bantry Bay – French and English fleets do Battle!" "Can someone tell me why I'm learning vital information from a news-letter? Free speech is getting out of hand! These things need to be filtered through the proper channels before reaching the public. The people will lose touch with who they're supposed to be afraid of!" Piper turned to Goblet. "How is it you are not privy to this information, Gilbert?"

Goblet's bottom lip quaked. "We're looking into it, sir."

"Fortunately, we were able to stop distribution before they went out on the street," Piper said.

Major Paine crossed the garden path to the patio door.

Here comes an old relic, Piper thought.

"You wanted to see me, Your Lordship?" Paine began.

Piper signaled Taliare. "We'll be there shortly."

"Before he died, Lieutenant Governor Lynch extended your contract for five years. Is that not right, Major?" Mold queried.

Suspicion formed on Paine's face. "It is, Your Lordship."

"I believe you'll find that under the Christian calendar you still have several weeks on your contract." Mold removed a scroll from his case.

"You're mistaken, sir. My contract is up."

"Due to the pending war with France, that contract must be extended for another five years of service."

Paine stared daggers, his hand near his sword.

"Your pension is withheld and you are hereby charged to serve King William as an indentured servant until the end on the last day of the month of August in the year of Our Lord 1694. I've already sent word to Rhode Island and all your assets and property are being held in trust to the Crown. Don't make us cancel your payments to your family as well. The things women and especially young girls have to endure under financial hardship is most unpleasant," Piper said.

"We all have to make sacrifices, Major. Rhode Island will grant you a full pension and continue payments to your family. What's another five years?" Mold added.

"Win the war sooner and you go home to your wife and daughters, and that windmill of yours," Piper said pleasantly.

"Then what be thy orders, Your Lordship?"

"Confirm the strength of His Majesty's enemies. You'll determine where Laurens de Graaf will strike first: the Leeward Islands, the Bahamas, or Port Royal, and then devise an effective defense reporting to us alone."

Paine accepted the scroll. All emotion drained from his face. "As you wish, Your Lordships."

"God speed, Major Paine," Mold said.

Piper and Mold headed outside for the award ceremony.

"Let's get this done quickly," Piper moaned. "Lord have mercy on us for entrusting the defense of the King's busiest port to the likes of a woman and degenerate scallywags!"

A sudden gust of wind almost knocked Bizy's hat off. She rescued it and jammed it onto her head. She concealed her trembling hands by repeatedly smoothing her dark plum skirt. Her children and Widow Bell stood beside her.

The veranda of the King's House was garlanded with leaves and flowers woven through wooden trellis work. The morning sunshine dazzled the crowd with its glorious golden glow, setting the stage perfectly for the awards ceremony.

Piper stood at the podium, clearing his throat. "For great care and devotion to the city as Chief Engineer, I award the King's Medal of Industry to Colonel William Chitty." The crowd cheered and Chitty stepped up. He gave a brief speech and sat back down.

"Thank you, Colonel Chitty. And now, for thirty-five years of service to this city as Surveyor General, Provost Marshall, and Fyre-Master, we award the King's Medal of Distinction to Nicholas Keene." The crowd whistled and cheered.

"And…" Piper held up his hand. "It is with mixed emotion that we wish him a very happy retirement."

Keene took to the podium. "Thank you, Acting Lieutenant Governor Piper, and thank you, citizens! I am honored to present your new Fyre-Master and commander of the city militia, Colonel Peter Beckford." Beckford rose to accept a scroll, hat, and badge. "Congratulations, Colonel Beckford." They shook hands, and Beckford took the stage.

"Thank you all." His eyes skimmed Bizy. "And with the help of our Lord Jesus Christ, I shall ensure that your city is safe for another thirty-five years and beyond."

Everyone clapped and cheered as Beckford returned to his seat beside Constable Blower.

"You must have undertaken a great deal of effort and training to obtain such a prestigious title," Blower said.

Beckford opened his mouth to reply but was cut off by Mold, who insisted, "Not at all! It simply requires the appropriate accoutrements and perhaps a good soap-down."

Keene started his next speech, "And finally, for service to the community and for her bravery in saving property and lives during our most recent pirate attack and fire – I present the Medallion of Service to Ellsebeyth Gale."

Bizy's children cheered fiercely as she stepped forward. Her face turned bright red when the crowd cheered.

"Congratulations, Miss Gale. I present this award to you along with the honorary title of Acting Corporal and official fire warden of White's new leeward gun battery. I hereby charge you with the defense of this city and confer upon you all of the honors and distinction therein."

Bizy's jaw dropped and the crowd reacted with equal measures of grumbling and clapping.

“Thank you, Marshall Keene,” Bizy stammered. “I pledge to do my part to keep this city and its inhabitants safe. Thank you.” Her children hugged her as she returned to her seat, each wanting to hold the medal.

Mold stood at the podium. “Thank you, Marshall Keene. I’m sure I speak for all of us when I wish you all the happiness in the world in your final days.”

Piper unrolled a scroll. “And finally, for service to the King above and beyond call of duty, I hereby proclaim that the position of sheriff of Port Royal shall be entrusted to Sydrack Taliare.” He removed a new hat from a box sitting on a chair. “Congratulations, Sheriff Taliare.”

Taliare twirled the hat victoriously and slipped it on his head as Blower glared at him. “I’d just like to say, thank you.”

“And you have,” Piper interrupted. “New laws have been posted. They must and will be obeyed. Ignorance will not be tolerated. Port Royal will forever belong to the Whigs! Thank you all for coming.”

“Whigs over Port Royal!” called Mold.

Widow Bell patted Bizy’s arm. “You gave a short speech.”

“They told me to keep it under ten seconds.”

Widow Bell cocked her eyebrows. “Corporal of the gun battery?”

“I know!” Bizy gasped. “That was unexpected.”

“Have you ever even fired a cannon?”

“Not one more than six inches.” Bizy smirked. “I’ll learn.”

Beckford approached them. “Ladies?”

“Beckford,” Bizy acknowledged.

“It’s Colonel Beckford now,” he boasted. “And if you’re accepting your new responsibilities, I shall expect to see you first thing in the morrow at Fort Carlisle for weapons training.” He walked off with a triumphant hop in his step.

Bizy felt dreadful butterflies in her stomach. “Aye, sir.”

MacAskill finished securing the sling for Scarcliff’s injured arm before retiring to the sofa with an early morning pick-me-up of rum. Scarcliff watched the window. His complexion was still chalky white. He gazed down towards King’s House with two bloodshot eyes. “If it was up to me, we’d be killing every last one of them bloody Whigs. And now we be working for them!”

Jayne fidgeted with a clock, pulling the chains and weights back and forth, cursing under his breath. “I just don’t get modern technology.” He tossed the chain aside.

“Then don’t fuck with it,” MacAskill barked. “That should be simple enough for ya. So, what’s he called us here for? Did the strumpets unionize?”

Cupid squawked from her perch in the corner. “Kill every one of those bloody Whigs!”

“Least the bird’s got things worked out,” MacAskill said.

A shrill female voice pierced the air and Mrs. Katheryne Valentine pushed her way through the adjoining door from the study. She was a striking woman in her late forties. She wore an elaborate dark blue gown with gold beading and satin gloves. Trailing behind was her personal assistant, Miss Givings, carrying a stack of papers.

“That bird!” Mrs. Valentine pointed at Cupid. “Know what it did? It shit on me deliberately! Parrots should all be shot!”

“Yes, ma’am,” Miss Givings said.

MacAskill and Jayne bowed.

“Leave the changes on top,” Art called from the study.

“Yes, sir.” Miss Givings set the papers on his desk, tucking them under his blunderbuss.

Mrs. Valentine approached the desk to check the pages and Miss Givings automatically grabbed a wooden chair and dragged it, scraping loudly across the floor.

With pained expressions, MacAskill and Jayne put their fingers in their ears.

“Do I look like I’m sitting?” Mrs. Valentine barked.

“Sorry, ma’am.” Miss Givings put the chair back.

Mrs. Valentine scrutinized the doctor. “Ah! Going out to play war again, I see! Your friends are here.”

“I’ll be right out,” Art said.

“I fixed your spelling mistakes,” Mrs. Valentine added.

“Goddamn it, woman! I spell them like that on purpose!” Art yelled.

Miss Givings retrieved the papers.

Mrs. Valentine rolled her eyes. “Leave the papers. Do it later.” She led her assistant out to the foyer. “Bring the chair.”

“Yes, ma’am.” Miss Givings dragged the chair screeching across the floor.

“She makes my flesh creep,” Jayne uttered.

The doctor leaned in close. "The praying mantis has a kinder demeanor. Check his head for bite marks when he comes out!" He grabbed the top sheet from the paper stack.

Valentine's Love Classics:
Knipples of Love
Blows Like November
Hold Fast, I Think I Love Ya
Smokin' Gunpowder

"What the fuck is this shit?"

Jayne signaled him to be quiet. "He's writing a songbook. You know, like that German at the Merchant Exchange, Bark?"

"Bach, ya imbecile." MacAskill continued reading. "'I'd Walk Thy Plank for Thee'? Good Christ! He'd give his own grandfather a blowjob if he thought he could get a pound for it!"

Jayne waved his arms again. "Shh! He gets real defensive about his work."

The doctor choked back laughter. "Is he fuck'n serious? He forgot 'Blow Me Down, I Got the Itch!'"

Art emerged from his study and snatched away the page. "You wouldn't know true poetry if it bit ya in the arse!" He set the paper back on the desk. "And that Rochester filth gets published!" He was silent a moment gazing fondly at the blunderbuss.

"You know you'll never be able to fire this thing again," MacAskill said, lifting the gun.

"Aye." Art looked slightly melancholy. "Scarcliff, you did good the other night."

The doctor handed the weapon to Scarcliff. "That he did."

"As a reward for your service. Good driving, kid. Use it wisely," Art said.

Scarcliff's jaw dropped. "Aye, Captain!"

Art slid his longsword into his belt. "Once upon a time in a faraway land, there was a handsome prince—"

Jayne clapped his hands. "Yeah?"

"And in the next kingdom there was a beautiful princess. One day the prince went to the next kingdom and asked the princess to marry him. The princess said no. And the prince lived happily ever after."

Jayne scratched the back of his head.

"What did ya want to see us about?" MacAskill asked.

"We've been summoned by Lords Ridiculeeze and Stupidious to the Court of Chancery." With his good arm, Art grabbed the cutlass out of the crest on the wall. "It's gonna need sharpening."

"Did they make it official?" MacAskill relished the thought of legalized piracy again.

"That's what we're gonna find out. Time to go." Art held the blade next to the fire, watching it glisten.

The group gathered at the main entrance of Valentine Mansion, where a new four-door coupe carriage waited. It had a shiny black paint job with wood paneling and freshly upholstered seats. Beside the car stood Blackmoor, rugged and reasonably well dressed. Although only in his twenties, he had several years of henchman experience under his belt.

"Ah, the new hire," Art said to MacAskill.

"Think this one'll live?"

"I doubt it. Nice wheels. Good choice."

"It's an '85," Blackmoor replied. "Practically brand new, delivered to Coggshall's warehouse this morning from London!"

"From London!" Gibbet squawked and landed on Scarcliff's shoulder.

They entered the spacious carriage and took off across High Street.

Scarcliff eyed Gibbet apprehensively. "Why does this bird like me?"

"Gibbet lost his mates." Art patted the bird's head and gave him some seeds from his pocket. "Didn't ya, lad? Anyway, pirates always have parrots. Time I got ya fixed up with a boat, too. Yer gonna need one."

"Boat? I ain't never been to sea," Scarcliff admitted.

"You haven't?" Art and MacAskill spoke simultaneously.

"You haven't?" said Gibbet.

"Nay. I've been across the harbor many a time, but never out there on the ocean."

"Jayne?" Art began.

Jayne nodded. "Aye, train the new man, I know."

"I won't have no landlubbers in my crew," Art said.

"Are ya fuck'n simple?" MacAskill leered. "How do ya live in Port Royal and never go to sea?"

"I was born here," Scarcliff explained.

"Yer ma kicked you out of the nest, did she?"

"Nay, I graduated from the workhouse and was legally free to find work."

MacAskill leaned into Art's ear. "Graduated from the workhouse? Try not to aim too high."

Art leaned towards Scarcliff. "Learn to drive a boat like you drive a car and I'll make you captain someday, boy. I guarantee ya." They came to a halt outside the King's House. "Go back and wait for us."

Valentine Mansion was in plain view across the street.

"Aye, sure thing," Scarcliff said.

Art felt his knees buckle. "Help me down."

Jayne's face contorted. "Me?"

"The horse ain't gonna do it!" MacAskill replied.

Art and MacAskill shuffled inside the King's House. Taliare guided them along an aged walnut wood floor to the study. Piper and Mold sat on overstuffed chairs smoking cigars.

"It is my understanding that you're in business with former Acting Lieutenant Governor Dewar and the late Bernard Coggshall in their slaving enterprise," Piper began. "Funded by the proceeds of the Albemarle estate?"

Art and MacAskill lit up their pipes and sat down.

"I don't know nothing about that," Art said. "All Coggshall's shipping was contracted to my company for a fee."

"A fee of one-third?" Mold asked. "And the Duke's treasure salvage off *Nuestra Señora de la Concepción*, for which you supplied the ships. The English Crown has yet to receive a tax for anything recovered."

"If you could prove any of it was illegal, you would have arrested me by now."

"True," Piper concurred. "But it doesn't change the fact that the Orange Party has seized the Albemarle estate. A letter of recovery, signed by the King, has been issued to both the Royal Africa Company and the West India Trading Company. The same will happen with Dewar and Coggshall which means we will control their shares in time."

Taliare produced a document that they all ignored.

"So, you see, Art, may I call you Art?" Mold continued.

"Nay." Art grimaced. "Coggshall's kid will contest it in court and tie it up for years. His family owns slaving rights."

"Not anymore. Seems someone took the safe from Coggshall's office. Without the will, Edmund has no claim. Therefore, you need us and – obviously – we need you, so that makes us business partners. The only way you're going to make a third of anything is to start shipping for us," Mold explained.

"You want me to run slaves? I'm retired from the picaroon racket."

Mold pouted. "As of when?"

"As of right now."

"The slave trade is vital. We must keep a regular flow coming through to maintain the economy."

"Until when?" MacAskill asked.

"Well, forever. As a silent partner, I could authorize you to assume full charge of Coggshall's and Burghill's land-based businesses, giving you sole title over those properties."

"Brothels and taverns!" Art huffed. "We're knee deep in strumpets and I already own a tavern and an inn."

"Technically, that's your wife's family's money."

"What do we know about taverns and brothels other than drinking and fuck'n?" MacAskill added.

"Precisely!" Mold said. "And you won't have to ship slaves."

"We'll run the slaving, you protect the shipping and if war breaks out, which it will, we'll offer you a full commission. Just keep all our ships safe from attack," Piper said.

"Fine. I get their land and since you're taking Coggshall and Dewar's shares that makes only two of us, so I'll be taking half." Art sat back, getting comfortable. "And if you don't like it, find another shipping company."

"Half will be acceptable," Piper said.

Mold cringed. "It will?"

"Provided of course that shipments arrive intact and on time, and the money continues to flow. The future of the city depends on it."

"I'll be needing one of them new London-built galleys, top of the line." Art grinned.

"Agreed." Piper turned to MacAskill. "Are you familiar with the term junk slave, Doctor?"

"Is that like a Negro stud for breeding?" Art asked.

"Nay," MacAskill replied. "It's buying up sick and dying slaves cheap and trying to recuperate them for resale. If they get healthy again, you can sell them for a hundred times what you paid, more, even! And I'm way too old for that shit, Acting Lieutenant Governor. Ask Strangewayes; he treats slaves."

"We're offering you the position of Chief Surgeon with your own facility. You wouldn't have to treat them yourself."

The doctor raised his hand. "That's Strangewayes's line of interest. Thank you, but no."

The clock chimed.

"Join us in the Court of Chancery, Doctor? For a taste of things to come. This way, gentlemen." Piper strolled into the grand foyer.

Art and MacAskill helped each other out of their chairs.

"You know, sometimes I think yer a fuck'n genius; sometimes I think yer a twat. This be one of them genius times," MacAskill whispered.

A half hour later in the dining room, a great crowd gathered. Gentlemen filed in swiftly as the weather outside grew tumultuous. Slaves fastened the storm shutters and lit lamps. It was midmorning; tea and coffee was served with an abundant tray of sweet snacks artfully arranged on silver platters.

MacAskill and Art positioned themselves as far away from the Whigs as possible around the long table. Piper sat at the head with his group. Around them the wallpaper was peeling, great cracks spanned the floor, and cobwebs hung from the chandeliers.

Councilman White entered and was immediately accosted by Piper. "Mr. White, the state of the King's House is unacceptable. This building is to represent the Crown and should be nothing less than immaculate!"

"Then you can find the funds to keep it up," White said tersely. "And it's Captain or Council Chair to you, Acting Lieutenant." He pushed past Piper and took his seat next to Bill Chitty and Nicholas Keene.

A group of wealthy retired slavers were dressed in patterned

Turkish silks, crimson velvet, and large feathery hats. They immediately bickered among themselves.

"A grim reminder of the trends of the sixties and seventies," MacAskill whispered.

"Aye, fashion has gone to the dogs in Port Royal." Art snickered.

MacAskill privately mused at the eclectic mix.

Dr. Strangewayes looked wrecked on the laudanum again and wore a tattered suit. Everyone else wore brooches, hats, wigs, and scarves. Many were living proof that with the right marriage, even the most incompetent could aspire to the highest ranks of society.

"Slaves, leave the room!" White ordered.

"This meeting is for council members only," Chitty said.

Piper raised his walking stick. "Dr. MacAskill is here at my request as a guest, as is Major Paine."

MacAskill folded his arms. *At least Port Royalers can be counted on to show good manners to newcomers. Yeah, I'm as welcome as a fuck'n leper ship!*

Taliare readied a quill, a pot of ink, and papers. "Ready, sir. They just require your endorsement."

White cleared his throat. "I call this meeting to order! Please welcome the new interim Acting Lieutenant Governor of Jamaica, Peter Piper."

Applause trickled.

"This meeting can only mean one thing," a captain called out. "War with France!"

"There will be no jumping to conclusions," White insisted. "No formal declaration by either side has been made."

"Yet the city was invaded by the French pirate Gator Gar," someone argued. "No doubt under a letter of marque."

Piper waved his hands. "Your government is in full control of the situation."

Several people jeered and made rude noises.

MacAskill took a sugar cookie from a silver platter. *That'll be the day!*

Taliare displayed a broadside:

WANTED!

Gator Gar wanted Alive for Piracy, Sodomy, and Murder

50,000 pieces of eight

"Gator Gar will be caught and hung for his crimes. Good citizens were killed," Piper said.

"Aye, and Coggshall too, they say!" Chitty jeered.

"Fifty thousand! The Spanish and Dutch investors got more than that on him!" another captain called. "Why should Port Royal offer less? We need to bring him in ourselves!"

"Our intelligence is tracking down the French captain. Captain Longstaff is intercepting his ship," Mold assured. "He won't escape the justice of the Whigs."

MacAskill poked Art's arm. "There's one for you. 'Justice of the Whigs,' what a catchy tune that would make."

"Intelligence? You won't find that under a Whig," Art snorted.

Piper waved a copy of the Port Royal Daily Gazette. "According to this, the French and English fleets have engaged in naval combat off Ireland at Bantry Bay. Seems the French were caught providing aid to the armies of King James. This is clearly an act of war."

Strangewayes sat up straight. "This is the first combat between the English and French fleets in a hundred years."

Piper read on. "Notorious pirate Pierre le Picard sailing from Acadia, led the operation."

"We believe this attack was sent to test our defenses," Mold said. "This could be the first step of an invasion."

A wealthy ex-slaver rose. "War between England and France shan't affect us. Saint-Domingue has neither the will nor the strength to take on Jamaica. The very idea of an invasion is preposterous."

MacAskill cleared this throat. "Begging your pardon, but if I was Louis, I'd take Port Royal over England any day. You control Jamaica and you control the central Caribbean. That means the slave trade into America." Suddenly all eyes were on him. "Leave England for James and his supporters to fight over." Many nodded in agreement.

"If the island is under threat, we must act accordingly!" a captain called. "We must authorize privateering."

"Bloody piracy again! I thought we learned that's a mistake we cannot repeat!" Keene yelled.

"It's not piracy, but legitimate privateering," someone corrected. "America was built on piracy!"

"Really? I thought it was slavery," Strangewayes added. "Letters of marque are illegal on all sides for a reason."

"Privateering is legal under His Majesty's government under certain circumstances," Mold defended. "If the council agrees the threat is legitimate."

"Not without formal declaration of war!" Strangewayes argued. "Opening Pandora's box is what you're doing. What if Roc Braziliano comes back or someone like him?"

Art tapped MacAskill's shoulder. "Remind me to stuff his head up Pandora's box!"

"If the French declare war our defenses are inadequate!" came another complaint.

"If ya want to protect Jamaica, start with the bloody Maroons!" a landowner said. "They've been attacking my plantation every day!"

Strangewayes pursed his lips. "That's because you shoot at them, turning it into a game for their adolescents!"

"Haven't you been attacked as well?" Chitty asked.

"That part of the river is on neither my land nor yours. I'm sure a peaceful solution is possible," Strangewayes said.

"Order!" White yelled.

"Gentlemen." Piper waved. "We are not here to discuss the Maroons, although they are a problem. The immediate question is what will be done to protect Jamaica from invasion?" He eyed Beckford. "What's your strength, Colonel?"

Beckford's face went blank for a moment. "W-well, I am more the supervisory type."

MacAskill contained a smirk. *He tries hard, for an idiot.*

"How many men do you have?" Mold asked.

Beckford's ears reddened. "Port Royal currently has one hundred volunteer militia and another fifty in Spanish Town."

"Your government has increased military presence for your protection," Mold continued. "You've all seen the Redcoats. A two-hundred-strong special forces unit under Lord Spotswood. He calls them Red Royals. With musketeers, an engineering battalion, and armored dragoons. Lord Spotswood plans to present them to King William to test their effectiveness. They're currently under the command of Captain Longstaff, with the charge of protecting the shipping lanes from Jamaica to the Bahamas."

White massaged his eyes. "And how is Lord Spotswood expecting payment for these special forces?"

"Payment has already been provided to Lord Spotswood by the Orange Party, so it need not concern you, Captain." Piper turned to Admiral Goddam. "What is our naval strength, Admiral?

"Currently in the seas around Jamaica, we have four of His Majesty's naval ships. *Relentless* and *Incorrigible* are currently in pursuit of the pirate Gator Gar, heading for Saint-Domingue. The light frigate *Drake* and the sloop *Falcon* are guarding the harbor."

"What about the ships to the south and the west?" Piper pressed.

Admiral Goddam's face turned scarlet. "Sunk. *Foresight* struck a reef while looking for food off Corn Island, and *Expectation* ran aground off Hope Bay."

"A third-rate man-of-war and a couple of frigates and sloops?" Piper's face shriveled.

"Du Casse's fleet was defeated by the Dutch off Suriname," a captain added. "His own flagship, *Dauphine*, was sunk off Cayenne. Also, Laurens de Graaf is retired and treasure hunting off Serranilla Bank."

Mold folded his arms. "Right! I'm sure he's just hanging about on the rocks!"

Disdain darkened Admiral Goddam's face. "Laurens de Graaf, retired? Never! You of all people should know that, captain. You employed the rogue! He'll die privateering; it's in his blood. Du Casse still has an effective battle force commanding from the *Hazardous*."

"*Hazardeux*," corrected Major Paine.

"Bless you," Admiral Goddam snapped back. "Now Captain Longstaff can be offered a full commission. Our ships can defend the city without hiring privateers."

Mold gave him a doubtful look. "Really, Admiral? Are you expecting *Expectation* to resurface sometime soon?"

White turned to Major Paine. "You have contacts in Tortuga and Saint-Domingue. Are the French prepared for war?"

"They are, sir. War with Saint-Domingue, preposterous? They'll go after merchant ships, supplies, and settlements first. Next, plantations, where they'll rape, murder, and pillage. They'll strangle the city into surrender while your loved ones are defiled. Our former allies in Tortuga refer to us as *les goddams* – without soul. And they mean it. France has better ships and more of them – five to one. And they have the battle-hardened buccaneers. Look what a small band of them did to your city."

"Are you trying to scare us, Major Paine?" asked a landowner.

"You should be terrified by what's coming your way, My Lord," Paine said.

A great gust of wind rattled the house, making everyone shudder. A knock came at the door and Lieutenant Thorne rushed in with a letter for Admiral Goddam. He scanned the note in silence, leaving everyone in suspense.

"Should I look at that, or shall I wait for the next Port Royal Daily Gazette?" Piper queried.

The admiral handed over the letter and Piper read. "Du Casse attacks the Leeward Islands as we speak." Silence filled the room. "He's taken St. Kitts with a large force."

"Then we could be next!" the mayor called.

"In Nevis, Lord Spotswood has declared a state of emergency for the Leeward Islands and calls for immediate aid."

"Does he want his Red Royals back?" MacAskill scoffed.

"Hewetson's wounded *Lion* is en route from Barbados with a small fleet. What could be worse than this?" Piper dropped the letter on the table.

Mold dropped his head in his hands. "We could be finding this out tomorrow in the Port Royal Daily Gazette?"

"Sending ships to Nevis will leave us dangerously weak," said one of the captains. "There can be no further debate. We need protection!"

"Captain Valentine's ships are capable of carrying out the king's mandate," Piper assured. "Is that not true, Captain Valentine?"

Art rested his elbows on the table. "Aye. My ships are capable of taking it to the French. At yer service."

"Immediate action must be taken." Piper dipped a quill in ink and signed documents. "I hereby call on the council to vote on issuing letters of marque to allow privateering – thus exercising my powers to protect Port Royal from imminent danger."

"Not without approval of the other landowners," Chitty argued. "Where are Lords Dewar and Llewellyn?"

"Dewar would be yelling 'oh, hurrah!'" someone called, triggering hysterics.

Mold rose from his seat. "We sent word to former Lieutenant

Governor Dewar and Lord Llewellyn offering new positions and titles if they were to return. He sent the pigeon back with a small wig stuck to its head."

"Cutest thing you ever saw," added Taliare.

"I believe we have the majority. Motion carries." Piper moved things along and Taliare prepared more pages. "I'm hereby authorized to grant letters of marque for Captain Valentine and all captains under his charge."

Strangewayes raised his hand. "With at least three noted objections, I must add."

"Four!" Admiral Goddam sulked.

"Captain Valentine is a landowner," Chitty remarked. "Is he hiring himself?"

"A valid point, Chitty." White raised his eyebrows. "It does demonstrate a conflict of interest." He turned to Bleedin Art. "Perhaps if you were to liquidate some of your shares?"

"Don't think for a moment I'm giving up my interests over to you." Art glowered. "I'm one of the founders of Port Royal. I was there in '55 and spilled blood taking Jamaica from the Spanish. There's more of me in Port Royal than Henry Morgan himself. What's mine is mine."

Grumbling arose from the crowd.

"You can't run your interests from the sea," Mold said.

"My wife will undertake the role of general manager in my absence."

"A woman!" the men gasped. "Impossible!"

"Legal as long as she has signed permission as a feme-sole," White said. He acknowledged a local priest. "It is not however, condoned by the church. The objection is noted. She is barred from engaging in politics or closed-door meetings."

"Captain Valentine, you may keep your business operations," Piper continued. "When will your fleet be ready to sail?"

"Immediately. The city's gotta breathe and eat."

"Captain Valentine, you are hereby authorized to wage war against the enemies of England. You will report to Admiral Goddam and have the full support of the government."

Art's large teeth appeared. "If you want this war won, stay out of my business. The sea is my domain and I hire the captains, not you."

"Hire as many captains as you see fit but you will command them under – and you yourself will abide by – English law." Piper gave a cautionary glare.

"Aye, on my word. You are making a wise choice."

"Then, Captain Valentine." Piper collected his things. "Assemble your fleet and, by the grace of God, capture or sink all the ships of thy enemies. Thank you, gentlemen. Thank you, Councilman White."

"This meeting is adjourned," White said and everyone rose to leave.

MacAskill smiled smugly. "I thought you were supposed to talk about important stuff at these things?"

The Four Feathers

The Terracotta Terrace occupied the top floor of the Four Feathers Tavern and was a popular spot for low-key gatherings and lively celebrations. Owned by Mrs. Valentine with her ancestral money, every facet was controlled by her. It had a nicely appointed terracotta tile floor and a balustrade of carved acanthus leaves along the patio edge. At its center sat a water fountain surrounded by tables, chairs, and benches.

Art glared at his cards.

MacAskill didn't bother to look up. "I'll raise."

"You'll raise?" Art teetered. "You got five aces, do you?" He tossed down his hand. "I'm out."

Jayne and Scarcliff did the same.

"And he still won't leave a tip!" Art jibbed. "Consider it an advance; Cherry needs help. I need you to take over Coggshall's operations as general manager."

"Yer shitting me! You want me to run the brothels, too, I suppose?" MacAskill laughed.

"Well it can't be too hard. The girls do most of the work, don't they?"

MacAskill clapped his hands together. "Oh, great! Come on down to MacAskill's Fuck House! If the strumpets don't do you in, the haggis sure as fuck will!"

"Where are we puttin' up Violante Hayze?" Scarcliff asked.

"Here probably. There's a lot to do at the Clubhouse," Jayne replied.

Art finished his mug of wormwood wine. "Aye."

"Can't believe she was stabbed in broad daylight in front of the whole city. She knows something, and the sooner we find out what, the better." MacAskill took a drink. "And who's this white-haired goon? You know every low-life cutthroat in the Caribbean—"

"Thanks!" Art said.

"Well, who is he then?"

"A killer Whig!"

"Besides, you're the Strumpet Saviour of Port Royal, remember? You gotta keep up appearances!" MacAskill slapped Art on the back.

Art turned to Jayne. "Violante's in your charge. No one gets to her until Captain Dickhead shows up."

"Aye. I got men watching her."

"You happy now?" Art asked MacAskill.

"Delirious." The doctor finished his wine. "You know the strumpets all keep a wood carving of yer likeness by their front doors."

"They do?"

"Aye, it keeps the birds away!"

Across the terrace, a man slipped from his chair onto the floor. It was Major Paine. He tried to climb back up and released a large burp.

"Christ, he's drinking like Henry Morgan," MacAskill exclaimed.

Art gazed at Paine sympathetically. "That's the pot calling the cauldron black. And I would too if I was him. The bloody Whigs indentured him for another five years."

"Those fuck'n pricks! Mace, go give him a hand, will ya?"

Scarcliff went over to assist.

"Unhand me or I'll run ya through, scallywag!" Paine threatened.

"Port Royal's most famous privateer washed up like a fish on the sand," Art scoffed. "Join us for a drink, Major?"

Paine rose slowly, clutching Scarcliff's arm. "You know, this place used to be mine? I leased it in '72. Then I passed it on to his wife." He pointed at Art. "Where is the old battle axe?"

Mrs. Valentine sat with a group of friends in the far corner of the terrace. She gave Paine a dirty sneer.

"Another round for these fine gentlemen!" Paine called and sat down.

"Which means on me!" Art signaled the barman.

"Then I thank you, Captain! And you, Mrs. Axe!" Paine incurred a wrathful stare.

Art leaned over the table. "What's this crap about Laurens digging for treasure?"

"Aye, and the Capitaine blowing in accidentally at the same time? Jamaica's next, I tell ya! Lorencillo is running a salvage operation off Serranilla Bank in the big galleon that hit the rocks a while back. I hear he's even got diving dress," Paine replied.

"What's that?" Scarcliff asked.

"For breathing under water," MacAskill replied. "And I treated Lorencillo after the Battle at Roatán. His injuries were career-ending; he's in worse shape than you!"

The barman arrived with a tray of fresh drinks.

Art raised his glass. "We were right about Gator Gar too. Governor de Cussy's ready for war, and Chevalier Jean du Casse just took St. Kitt's and Laurens de Graaf ain't gonna miss out. I say Gator Gar was checking Port Royal's defenses."

"Undoubtedly, for attack or for our counterattack?" Paine mused.

Jayne's eyes widened. "They could never take Port Royal, not with five forts!"

"Six now," Art corrected. "White's getting his own line on the leeward side, but that don't mean nothing. Laurens took Vera Cruz and that was the most heavily fortified city in Mexico." He leaned against his arm. "De Cussy's got his aim on the area from Saint-Domingue to the Leeward Islands. It's their back door they gotta worry about."

"That's just what the Spanish thought in '55," Paine said.

"De Graaf, de Cussy and du Casse. Sounds like an African rhythm section!" MacAskill stretched up his arms and clasped them around his neck. "Or a solicitors' firm?"

Paine slapped his thigh. "I suppose my French name would be du Paine!"

Art glanced over the balustrade for a moment. The gray sky was starting to clear and faint streams of sunlight broke through the cloud blanket above. Meanwhile, below in the harbor a merchantman's crew was unloading military equipment, cannons and several horses. Red Royals stood guard over the merchandise. "Nay, Port Royal is secure. It's our shipping lanes they're after."

Paine took off his hat and massaged his head. "Take it from me, the French can take us anywhere they want. Buccaneers are here; that proves it."

"What have you heard?" Art asked the barman.

"Word has it that settlements are scared on Hispaniola, the Spanish and French. The buccaneers are wanting to settle ownership of that island once and for all. They say Governor de Cussy is gathering them in Petit-Goâve and the Spanish added three war galleons to Saint-Domingue."

Paine propped his head on his hand. "Why do I pay spies when all I have to do is go into the Four Feathers and ask? I'll have to stop by Petit-Goâve and have a look for myself." He met Art's eyes. "You're gonna be outnumbered here. How are you gonna defend the city if they do attack?"

"We'll use the convoy system like we did with the Duchess. It works for the Spanish treasure ships. No one goes near them."

Paine rose. "Then with this fine city under your protection and guidance, Captain Valentine, I must bid you good day, gentlemen." He staggered off inside.

Art addressed Jayne, "Find out where he goes."

"Well." Jayne counted off his fingers. "The Catt and Fiddle, the Black Dog Inn—"

"Not in general, ya twat! Right now! Tonight!" Art clarified.

"Oh, aye!" Jayne nodded and grabbed an inebriated Scarcliff, guiding him to the exit.

"Lord help us!" Art shook his head. "I wanna turn those Mediterranean galleys into attack ships to defend the city and escort the convoys."

MacAskill tapped the side of his mug. "The Whigs won't allow it. They'll overrule. The slave ships will have to be sent back to Barbados for restocking. I guarantee you, they've got that greedy glow."

Art leaned forward. "The plantation owners and merchants aren't gonna be buying slaves if they can't sell their goods. Now that they own their own ships, there's no organization between them. Let them get wiped out by the French. My ships will keep the city alive, and they'll all be paying me for protection sooner or later."

"That's my philosophy. You can't please everyone, so yer best option is to sod them all!"

The barman approached. "Word has it that a third galley was sent from Lord Crisp in Barbados; it never showed up. Now it's been spotted south of Hispaniola heading northwest. They say her captain is a giant who eats people. A slaver from the Barbary Coast called Mandingo."

"Aye, they call him Kabaka over there." Art took a coin from MacAskill's pile and tossed it to the barman.

MacAskill glared. "I've done worse things than shoot a man for taking a coin from me pile!"

"Aye, you operated on them! So, where do you think that third galley is headed? And why does he want the pikeys so bad? He wouldn't send it all this way over a couple of Irish girls."

"Crisp? Sure he would. He's got the temperament of a pit bull terrier."

Art scratched the back of his neck. "It's something personal, I bet. Heading northwest, hmm? I want that third galley."

"Then you'll have to send a pirate to go get it."

Ginger and the navigator, Spider, entered the terrace.

"We leave for Rio Cobre, Captain," Ginger said. "Ready to sail."

"It's across the fuck'n harbor and yer taking a frigate?" MacAskill snickered.

Art grinned. "Yer timing is impeccable, Mr. Ginger, as always. There's been a change of plan. If ya don't mind sailing in bad weather, how would ya like to head 'round the north side of the island and do a spot of fishing?"

"Like I says, Captain. Ready to sail."

Art scribbled a note on a piece of parchment and handed it over. "Once more unto the breach, dear friends, once more."

Bleedin' Art
The Slaver with a heart
GO
2014

La Lune

In the vast blue of the Jamaica Channel, the brig *La Lune* glowed beneath the brilliant early-morning light, its shadow stretched like a great hand across the sea's surface.

Le Picard sat in the Capitaine's cabin at the writing desk.

There was a knock.

"Come!" le Picard said.

"You wanted to see me, capitaine?" Delacroix asked.

"Oui. We are not making enough speed. How many men do you have on repairs?"

"The whole crew is working on repairs as fast as they can. We've had two accidents already."

"Then we have had too many. Clear a space for music players and pull them from duty."

"Playing music will speed up repairs?"

"I don't want the men tripping over each other. Besides, it will boost spirit. I'll see you on deck shortly. We must get this ship moving," le Picard said.

"Oui, capitaine."

Later that morning upon the main deck, crewmen worked tirelessly, balancing on yardarms – horizontal spars up in the rigging – and repaired sails. Two deckhands played a three-stringed fiddle and a Spanish guitar.

Le Picard worked on stitching a tear in the foremast topsail with a large needle and leather palm on his hand. "How bad is it up there?" he called.

Up on the mainmast, Martel replaced the rigging. "It runs the entire length."

"Let me know when you're done and furl up the spanker tight. We won't be using it again."

"Oui."

"I hope the Capitaine can wait," Delacroix began, splicing strands of rope on the quarterdeck with several other crewmen.

"You know the Capitaine, he could be there by now waiting for us," Martel called.

"Oui," Delacroix said.

"Don't anyone worry about the Capitaine. He's taking shore leave, that's all," le Picard interjected. "It's not uncommon for him to disappear for months at a time."

"Years, if he meets a redhead," Martel said, inciting laughter.

The ship's cooper, Beaumont, a dark-skinned Haitian youth, passed good rope upwards to Martel. "Capitaine, if you don't mind me asking, are you related to the pirate Picard?"

Martel's eye widened. "Oh no, it *is* the pirate Picard!"

"In his dreams," Delacroix scoffed.

Beaumont smiled. "I was just curious."

"Monsieur Beaumont wants to know if you are related, capitaine?" Martel continued.

"Oui, he's his brother," Delacroix said.

Beaumont's mouth dropped. "I thought so!"

Whispers broke out among some of the crew as le Picard stood silent for a minute, staring at the sun. "We haven't spoken in years."

"What's it like having such a famous brother?" Beaumont pressed.

"I don't know." Le Picard scowled. "What's it like being a knucklehead? Hard to put into words, uh?"

"Oui, capitaine."

A dark haired man with large side burns and a thick mustache peered down from the mainmast. "Then did Capitaine la Roche sail with him? He *was* a pirate?" Boatswain Blanc asked.

"*Was* he?" Martel casted doubt.

"Come on, look at his arms," Beaumont said.

"I owe my life and the life of my sister to les Picards and to Capitaine la Roche," Martel explained. "I've fought with them in battle, and I can tell you firsthand that François is a better sailor than his famous brother."

"Better than Capitaine la Roche?" Beaumont queried.

"Oh, not at all!" Martel said.

"Will you tell us of it?" Blanc challenged.

"I'll tell the tale over dinner," Martel offered. "Or you can hear it in gossip tomorrow."

Le Picard tied a knot and cut the line before peering into the sun. "That's enough for today. Good work. Start packing up." He panned the horizon through his telescope before climbing down to the forecastle.

Inside the Capitaine's cabin at sundown, crewmen gathered around a wooden table laid with a bottle of wine and a pot of turtle stew. Le Picard sat at the head, joined by Martel, Delacroix, Blanc, Beaumont and the badly scarred ship's gunner, Poivre. Everyone brought their own bowls, cups, and spoons, and were soon feasting.

"I see she's not using the spanker," Poivre began.

"The mainmast broke. I have half a mind to throw it over, but we mustn't stall. How are things below?" Le Picard took a mouthful of wine.

"The water's out. Now we got drowned rats to collect."

Delacroix stared at his spoon. "Turtle stew again?"

"It's all there is, so make do until we reach Petit-Goâve!" le Picard reprimanded.

Poivre licked his lips. "I got some rats, if ya like?"

Delacroix sighed. "Oh, Petit-Goâve. I knew a girl there; she was so beautiful. Her name was Jessabelle. I hope she got better. She was sick the last time I saw her."

"Sick of you," le Picard goaded.

Beaumont took a long drink of wine. "I'm curious to know why Petit-Goâve is in such a hurry for sugarloaf."

"Governor de Cussy likes Jamaica sugar and he likes it in a hurry." Martel smirked.

Le Picard stuck his spoon into the bowl. "Capitaine la Roche has made a promise to his customers. He will make three hundred miles a day or he'll eat the cost."

"No way!" Blanc almost spat out supper.

"The shipping business is very competitive."

"What made you go into commercial shipping when you have a famous pirate for a brother?" Beaumont probed.

Le Picard's shoulders sank. "Oh, him again? I hardly know him. Like I said, I haven't spoken to him in years."

"Monsieur Martel said you fought in battle together?"

"Oui." Martel removed a head kerchief to show a sizable scar running down the side of his head. "When I was a small boy my mother and I were run down by a carriage. My sister had the unpleasant task of caring for me. In '59, the Spanish attacked the settlement where we lived in the Bahamas and drove us out. Our ship was damaged so we stopped in Tortuga."

"It was there we met Jean-Paul la Roche when he was just a wet-behind-the-ears indentured servant. And this scoundrel was his mate." Martel motioned to le Picard. "I was one of the very few people who believed his stories of a famous brother. Not very many people did. We became friends and the Capitaine and my sister were, uh…"

Le Picard rolled his eyes. "Fucking morning, noon, and night. Anywhere and everywhere, in and on anything they could find."

Martel elbowed him. "You were also fucking everything you could get your hands on, if I remember right?"

"Oui, so far your memory is holding up. If he starts talking about the Kraken again, run!"

"Once the ship was fully repaired, we sailed for Guadeloupe. La Roche promised to follow us, and he and Jacquotte planned to get married when it was legal." Martel paused for some stew.

A nostalgic grin formed on le Picard's face. "They sailed for Guadeloupe and the Capitaine was a moping adolescent on a mission of drink and opium when we heard pirates were gathering. They were going after the ship, led by the evil corsair Juan Corso. Corso was famous for his policy of "no quarter". They planned to strike once the ship crossed into Spanish territory."

Martel put down his spoon. "Corso and his Sloop of War, *La Serpiente*, attacked our ship, taking us by surprise. They held us captive at Monte Cristi. Corso declared us invaders of New Spain and ordered every one of us killed. They lined people up and shot them. People panicked as they were herded, killed for pleasure. We escaped, my sister and me – we were the only ones. Men, women, and children, were hung on spikes along the coast as a message to the French to stay out of the Spanish realm. We hid in a nearby village, but they read the manifest and they knew we were still out there. They tortured people to find out where we were. Eventually they cornered us when out of nowhere, my friends la Roche and Picard came to rescue us."

"Word reached Tortuga of the murders just as the famous privateer l'Olonnais returned from a raid. One of his ships, *El Diabolito*, was the first to arrive. The people of Tortuga wanted revenge, but the capitaine of the *El Diabolito* refused to sail. So la Roche led a group of men, myself included, on board. We took over the ship and sailed for Monte Cristi. We sailed in under a Spanish flag, passing by the scores of dead people. All the stories were true. We wanted to drink blood, we were so angry. The Capitaine sailed us upriver, where we hid the ship in a swamp," le Picard explained.

Martel gestured excitedly. "It was amazing. The most heroic thing I have ever seen! Outnumbered twenty to one, they attacked like demons and we fought with them, both my sister and me, hand to hand until we were quickly defeated."

Le Picard nodded. "Oui, they beat the shit out of us."

"But as were all about to be put to death, Hell's own fire swept through the town. Corso's ship exploded! L'Olonnais's fleet arrived with his flagship *Mars* and the famous Pierre le Picard." Martel raised his cup. "They captured the town and the surrounding villages from all sides at once with amazing timing and took their revenge, killing Spanish townspeople. Corso and his officers fled inland. The Mayor of Monte Cristi met with l'Olonnais and Pierre le Picard to negotiate. Picard took off his head with a cutlass and l'Olonnais made a pledge right there to la Roche and little Picard to buy their freedom."

Le Picard frowned. "He never got around to it, though, cheap bastard."

"And the famous pirate turned to his younger brother and said?" Martel patted le Picard on the back.

"He said 'I will no longer give you a purple nose.'"

"No! What else did he say?"

Le Picard shrugged. "Nothing."

"He said to all of us that we were as brave and skilled as any of the Brethren of the Coast he had served with."

Blanc pointed. "But you never became a pirate yourself?"

"Who says I didn't?" le Picard said.

"Whatever happened to Juan Corso?" Beaumont asked.

Martel jumped right in. "He was last seen chasing after the famous El Capitaine, deep into the jungles of Mexico in '85 and neither was ever seen again."

Beaumont looked suspicious. "The rush trip to Petit-Goâve? I have always suspected and now I'm certain, Capitaine la Roche is El Capitaine, is he not?"

Everyone around the table fell silent.

"Impossible!" Blanc scoffed.

"It stands to reason he also is the pirate Gator Gar," Beaumont said.

"Capitaine la Roche? He's too nice!" Blanc insisted.

"I will not speak for Capitaine la Roche, but this ship is going to be refitted for war in Petit-Goâve. He plans to offer you jobs but that is all I'll tell you for now." Le Picard wanted to end all speculation then and there.

The alarm bell rang, and there was a knock at the door.

"Capitaine, a ship has been sighted off the stern. She's approaching at high speed."

Everyone quickly gathered on deck.

"Sail ho! Off the stern!" the lookout called. "Man-of-war!"

Le Picard raised his telescope. "Sound general quarters, battle stations!" The approaching vessels appeared as tiny flakes of gold dust kissing the horizon. One with red tinted sails.

Martel peered through his viewer. "It's *Relentless* and a frigate!"

Fear swept over Delacroix. "Are they coming for us?"

"They are not just passing by, imbecile!" Le Picard scowled. "Cut the lines! Ready for evasive maneuvers! Signal lamp ahead and call for help!"

"Maybe we can make it to Dame Marie?" Martel suggested.

"No, it's too late." Le Picard shook his head. "Turn north, stretch every sheet! We need to pick up speed!"

"The mast?" Martel asked.

"We'll make do without a spanker and hope she holds."

Panic filled Beaumont's eyes. "They have no right to stop us!"

"Be sure to tell them that when they get here." Le Picard gritted his teeth. "Get extra men up on the sails. We'll make use of the crosswinds ahead!" He raised his telescope again at the fast approaching vessels. "Run, *Luna*. Run!"

A fading blanket of stars and a bright moon reflected on the sea. *Relentless* had all but caught up with *La Lune*, like a ruthless predator chasing down its exhausted prey. Martel took the wheel and checked the compass.

Le Picard watched the encroaching ships. "I want men on brace winches and trimming sheets."

Beaumont studied the enemy vessel. "She's red like the fires of hell."

"Red is harder to see under moonlight. She's a night hunter," Martel replied.

“They’re better by a third, capitaine,” Delacroix said.

“Oui, not nearly good enough.” Le Picard pointed to a pile on the main deck. “Sort through that shit and find us some more staysails and get them up!”

Up in the masts crewmen stood on yard arms, pulling sheets to adjust the topsails, angling the pitch. Next, they hoisted triangular staysails between the masts.

“We need to stretch her to the limit!” le Picard yelled.

“They’ll have us within the hour, capitaine.” Martel spoke morosely. “It was a good try.”

Relentless flashed a signal.

Delacroix read. “They order us to surrender, capitaine.”

Poivre approached. “You wanted to see me, capitaine?”

“Oui. They’re almost on us. I want you to light the torches and open the gun ports at sunrise.” Le Picard summoned Martel and Delacroix. “At sunrise we turn to port. We’ll make it look like we’re going to fire. The English captain will not allow his ship to be shot. He will turn to shoot and when he does we swing to starboard and run north again. This should break their momentum while we run away before either ship has time to shoot. It should buy us enough time to reach the Windward Passage. Do not allow any guns to be fired. We don’t want to give them an excuse to destroy us.”

“Oui, capitaine,” Poivre agreed and rushed below deck.

“I want to appear like we’re ready to fight. Have the men beat and furl the course sails when we turn,” le Picard ordered.

A burst of red rose on the horizon. *Relentless* and the frigate closed in. Le Picard retracted his telescope. “Now thirty degrees to port. Open gun ports!” Two shots flew past *La Lune* causing crewmen to hit the deck.

“Another surrender call,” Martel gasped.

Le Picard bit inside of his cheek. “Any minute now.”

From off in the distance, the frigate ignited its weapons.

Le Picard’s mouth dropped. “What is this?”

“Chain shot, capitaine!” Martel looked physically ill as the sails ripped. “Long range guns!”

Le Picard clenched his fist. “That worked for the Capitaine! She was supposed to turn and fire! He said they always turn and fire!”

“Now what do we do?” Martel pressed.

“She was supposed to turn! Is this guy English or what!” Le Picard yelled out, “That’s not right, you big dick!”

The frigate’s secondary guns sent everyone on *La Lune’s* deck scrambling for cover. Chain-shots blasted through the rigging and sails, decimating all the repairs.

Le Picard inspected the damage.

“Shall we return fire, capitaine?” Delacroix asked.

“I’m sorry men, it’s over. There’s no escaping this.”

Delacroix shuddered. “Are we to be taken prisoner?”

Le Picard glared. “I would say that is a very good guess! Nothing we can do. They have us.”

“We’ve done nothing! They have no right!” Beaumont yelled.

“Raise the white flag,” le Picard ordered. “We surrender.” *I warned you, Capitaine, no one escapes Port Royal.*

le Picard
GO
2015

Dragons and Dungeons

Moonlight penetrated the fog which lay thick over the sea surface, concealing *Arrow's* presence. The frigate was slowly being towed by longboats into Antonio Bay. Ginger, Bleedin Art's first mate, peered at the sea through a spyglass. He was hunting *Plutus*, a Mediterranean galley captained by an African giant the pirates called Mandingo.

"There she is." Ginger grinned.

The vessel was dark and deserted, like a ghost ship resting in the depths of the misty bay.

"Sleeping like a baby." If everything went well, he'd have wealthy pockets by the end of the day. He signaled the six longboats to get into position. "Turn us to starboard and ready to light the torches. Pirates ready to disembark."

Suddenly a drumbeat sounded, echoing across the water. It was followed by chanting. Lamps sparked to life on the galley and it stirred like a beast. The vessel's sixty oars emerged from the hull, manned by over two hundred slaves, rowing in perfect unison towards *Arrow*.

Ginger dropped his spyglass. "Battle stations. Get her lined up!"

Spider cranked the wheel. "Hard to starboard. Ready to fire on the lee!"

The crew scrambled with the ropes.

"Why aren't we turning?" the gunner yelled. "Line her up."

"Fire!" Ginger hollered and the pirates aimed their muskets and swivel cannons.

A flicker of fear sparked in Spider's eyes as a dragon's head lit up at the bow of the vessel. "What is it?"

Ginger gasped. "It's a bloody fire-ship, it is!"

"Oh, shit!" Spider knit his brow at the scorching gold flames.

Ginger almost fell over the rail as he leaned over to wave down the longboats. "Abandon the longboats. Now!"

The galley aimed the dragon head downwards. From its mouth spewed a jet of slick bright-orange flame. Antonio Bay lit up as the longboats were devoured by fire. Charred men flung themselves into the water only to continue burning as the oil clung to their flesh – dissolving it.

Spider rallied the crew on deck to ready their muskets.

“Fire!” Ginger yelled and a barrage of gunfire flew towards the enemy. Only two crewmen fell. The galley hoisted a red flag: *no quarter*. The banner glowed like an omen of death as the sun rose.

Ginger could only watch as the dragon aimed at the frigate. A collection of fierce Barbary Janissaries stood on deck. Rumors fueled Captain Mandingo’s reputation for sheer cruelty and mercilessness; he stood on the deck like a king, seven and half feet tall, dressed in red and gold silk, wearing gold chains, brandishing an axe and two Nimcha swords.

“Abandon ship,” Ginger shouted and leapt off the quarterdeck with Spider close behind.

The dragon’s breath assaulted *Arrow* with an all-consuming blaze that sent remaining crew hurtling to the sea. Once the fire reached the gunpowder barrels, the whole ship exploded into a massive fireball, mushrooming up into the sky.

Port Royal’s inner harbor drew an early morning crowd. People swarmed to the causeway at the news that *Relentless* and *Incorrigible* were returning with the French brig *La Lune*. *La Lune’s* patched yellow sails glowed in the sunrise and her crew was shackled and lined up on the deck to be ridiculed and taunted by spectators. People jeered, pelting the crew with rotten food and empty bottles. The brig was dragged along to Fort Carlisle to be confiscated, while the crew faced immediate incarceration.

Outside the King’s House, Acting Lieutenant Governor Piper and Magistrate Mold prepared for a ceremony.

“This is what the city needed,” Piper remarked, pleased with the turnout. “Let’s make this a speedy conviction.” An hour later, a crowd gathered in the main garden to welcome Captain Longstaff and his crew.

“Welcome, Port Royal’s pirate hunters,” Piper exclaimed.

The crowd clapped and whistled.

“Law and order under the Whigs.” Piper basked in public approval for several moments before something occurred to him and he turned to Mold. “How come none of them are wearing wigs?”

Mold’s head jerked. “Aw, fuck!”

Piper scowled. “They may as well have shown up in their nightshirts.” How were they to uphold the image of the Orange Party without wigs? He hoped no one else would notice.

After the ceremony, Piper and Mold were driven to Marshallsea Prison to check on *La Lune's* crew.

After descending the stone steps of the prison, they followed a lengthy corridor with glowing torches and old English tapestries on the walls. Screams thundered, followed by the sizzle of a branding iron and more shrieks. The pair passed by cages with floor spikes and impaling devices that left nothing to the imagination. In the far corner stood the pride and joy of the dungeon, a custom-designed metal cabinet lined with spikes fashioned in the likeness of Queen Elizabeth I.

"The old iron maiden never looked better." Piper admired his wig in the polished surface.

"Yes, indeed." Mold nodded as they passed an old version of the Royal Banner comprised of lush red tapestry with three embroidered gold lions.

Piper paused to admire it. "That's when they knew how to design a banner."

"It gives the place a homely feeling," Mold replied.

Guards marched by, dragging a prisoner by the armpits. Bloody and beaten, he was luxuriating in blissful unconsciousness as his body was dumped in a vacant cell. The bars slammed and the door was locked and bolted. The guards saluted and marched away to interrogate another prisoner.

Piper and Mold paused next to a holding cell where Lieutenant Thorne interrogated a prisoner.

"Is this one Gator Gar?" Piper asked.

"He claims he is, but Captain Longstaff identified him as one of the Picard brothers, Your Acting Lordship."

Mold glowered. "And what have we learned so far?"

"Well, they're not pirates."

"How do you know?" Piper eyed the prisoner, who was strapped tightly to a wooden chair. Blood streamed down the side of le Picard's head. His clothes had been shredded and the skin beneath had shallow cuts, which were wet with a recent treatment of salt water.

"The crew are all green. None of them have any scars and the darkie's got a lock box key," Thorne explained.

"So?" Mold shrugged.

"Locks ain't permitted on pirate ships. It's against the code."

“What about the sword of Don Juan Pérez de Guzmán?”

“Nowhere to be found,” Thorne said.

Piper roughly lifted le Picard’s head with a handkerchief. “And this bloody fool says he’s Gator Gar? Obviously covering for the real one.”

Thorne readied another cup of brackish water and doused the open wounds on the prisoner’s chest and legs. “Where is he?” He brandished a broadside.

Le Picard’s face filled with defiance.

Piper removed a leather whip from a bucket of salt water and whacked the insolent Frenchman. “Which one are you, then? The youngest, I presume. The little brother who never amounted to anything.”

“The crewman Delacroix confirmed he’s not the Capitaine. We have a sworn statement,” Thorne said. “Don’t blame him, though. He’s a right bloody mess.”

“So, where’s the log book, Picard?” Piper demanded.

Le Picard remained silent.

Mold folded his arms. “I think he needs more salt.”

“Which wound?” Thorne asked.

“All of them,” Piper said coolly. “You will talk, Picard. Sooner is in your best interest. We play rough from here.”

“I think I’m going to enjoy this much more than you are.” Thorne lashed le Picard’s raw knees, rubbing salt into them.

Le Picard’s screams sounded down the hallways, filling every room of the prison.

Dragons & Dungeons/
PLutus
GO
2015

Liabilities and Bribes

It was morning at Fort Carlisle. After the raising of the new English flag, Constable Blower completed his duties by unlocking the gunpowder shed. All rundlets accounted for, he exited, straightening his clothes and tucking in his shirt. He had to appear his best; there was an execution to attend. Goblet had given him orders to do away with Violante Hayze. A smirk of satisfaction filled Blower's face as he collected his guards. They marched to the infirmary, where they were met by two militiamen manning the entrance.

"Violante Hayze is to be hanged immediately. Open up!" Blower insisted.

One militiaman turned to his colleague. "Go get Colonel Beckford."

Blower unrolled a scroll. "By order of Judge Goblet himself, this must be done with all haste."

"Aye, but Colonel Beckford said no one gets in but him."

"You'll learn who your betters are. Stand aside!" Blower demanded.

The militiaman opened the gate slowly and halted, pointing down the hall. Blower turned to see Beckford and Captain Richard Longstaff march down the corridor.

"Constable Blower," Beckford began.

"I have signed orders to—" Blower spoke defensively.

"You will address me as Colonel, Constable, and I have not yet completed my investigation."

Blower held up papers. "I have orders from Judge Goblet."

Longstaff yanked the orders from his hand and read them. "She is to be hanged immediately?"

From just beyond the gate, Goblet appeared, clearly irritated. "I wasn't aware of any investigation, Colonel Beckford. Please enlighten me."

"Another strumpet gets stabbed and *he* wants an investigation!" Blower huffed.

"One hundred and seventeen strumpets were killed this year in Port Royal. Many of them mutilated. The manner of this attack was different."

"She chose to be a strumpet," Blower said.

"This one was involved in a murder and has been ordered to face justice." Goblet looked Longstaff in the eye. "I fail to see how this has become a navy issue."

"The Port Royal Daily Gazette claims she was a victim of a white-haired assassin. I came for a further description. Perhaps I know the man."

"Civil authorities have the situation well in hand, Captain." Goblet summoned Longstaff down the short corridor beyond the gate. "Our control of the city isn't going to be compromised by a strumpet. Lord Spotswood will be humiliated to find that his own captain can't contain his own, Dick!"

Blower wrenched his neck to watch.

Longstaff met Goblet's stare. "I've followed my mandate to the letter. We're much further ahead than we'd planned and she's been an asset, which is what I will report to Lord Spotswood. I'll expect to see her when I'm in this port or I won't be staying in this port at all. I'll sail for the Bahamas tonight."

Goblet's eyes narrowed. "You wouldn't."

Longstaff gave him a cold stare. "Bet me."

Goblet suddenly glared at Blower. "As it is, these orders were to be carried out at dawn, and tardiness by His Majesty's servants is intolerable!"

Blower's mouth gaped. "But—"

"Edmund Coggshall has not filed formal charges. I have no further reason to hold her." Goblet motioned to the guards and they unlocked the infirmary door.

"If I see the white-haired fellow, I'll run him through," Longstaff vowed.

"Violante Hayze is released. Get her out of there."

Beckford and Longstaff went down the hall to the holding cells while Goblet pointed to Blower. "Constable," he growled. "This order was to be executed at dawn."

Blower could feel his face turning a purplish red color. "I had to wait for the flag to be raised."

"You were beating off in the rundlet shed!" Goblet said. "Be bloody thankful I don't lock you in a room with Mute Katie!"

Blower walked away, humiliated. *That strumpet will get what's coming to her, I'll guarantee it!*

Violante heard the infirmary door open and sat up on the bench carefully. Her arm and chest throbbed; she would have given anything for some more Strangewayes Special Brand Laudanum. From behind the cell door, she thought she could hear Longstaff and Beckford.

"For your services," Longstaff said and there came a rattle of coins. "Was she tortured?"

"Not terribly," Beckford said.

The clang of a key and the click of a lock sounded, and the door opened. Longstaff was handsome in his deep blue suit, and his eyes locked on hers.

She rose and went to him. "Thank God, Richard! Have you got a smoke?"

"Of course. Let's get you out of here first."

She suddenly became conscious of her dirty skin and dress. Her hair probably looked like a bird's nest. Longstaff's strong arm clutched her waist, and he guided her from the prison to his carriage outside. The air smelled pleasant aside from the fishy fragrance.

Longstaff's yeoman hastened them to the Black Dog Inn.

She entered the same room they'd shared over a fortnight ago. A fresh bouquet of flowers sat on the table and a new gown with loose-fitting sleeves hung in the wardrobe. It was a pretty garment of peridot green with gold trim. Longstaff helped her to sit on the bed and he signaled the guard in the hall to close the door.

"It's beautiful. Thank you," Vie said.

"I'm glad you like it. You can try it later and see if it's comfortable. We can always get it adjusted."

Vie paused a moment, trying to relax her arm. "I don't suppose you could have someone stop by Strangewayes Apothecary?"

"Yes, of course."

Suspicion sat like a stone in her chest. "How come you haven't asked me about who stabbed me? Or what he looked like?"

"He was a white-haired man with pink eyes; I saw it in the report."

Vie's trust and confidence was snuffed. "Someone said he arrived on a ship with a judge, the night you arrived."

Longstaff sat down beside her and placed his arm around her carefully. "You're safe now. He won't be coming back." He caressed her cheek and kissed her forehead.

Tears were teeming behind her eyes. “He works for the same people you do, doesn’t he?” Her voice cracked.

“Yes, he does,” Longstaff spoke frankly. “But, you’re under my protection now.”

“I’m sorry if I don’t seem grateful Richard, but the men you’re working for cut me real good.” Tears streamed down her face. “I’m safely under your protection *now*, or do you really mean *for now*? I have to wonder if I’m safe with you.” She sniffed hard, trying to contain the emotion building in her chest.

He checked under her bandages and the wound was seeping a bit. “I promise. I swear on the Holy Mother Mary; I will never let anyone hurt you.” He stroked her hair. “Now you stay here. There are guards outside but all the same, stay away from the window and I’ll be back.” He rose and went for the door. “I’ll go see your witch doctor for you. What is it you wanted?”

“He’s got laudanum called Strangewayes Special Brand.” Vie managed a brief smile.

“I’ll take care of it. Trust me, you’re safe here.” Longstaff gave her an encouraging wink before departing.

Vie stared at the wall for several minutes. *My new prison*, she thought. The pain from her wound radiated – she knew deep down it would never fully heal. The scar would be with her forever – damaged goods. Something inside her snapped as she tore away the bandage and fought to remove the dress that still stank of a prison cell.

Once naked, she shuffled to the window and opened it wide to breathe the thick smoky air tinged by a hint of the sea. A trickle of blood traveled down over her breast and landed on her thigh. “Well then, here I am.” Vie challenged the elusive forces that stalked her. She would not show them fear.

Bleedin Art arrived at the Clubhouse with MacAskill and Jag’d Jayne. Captain White followed separately in his carriage. Smoke rose from the chimney; Scarcliff was in. As they approached, grunting and moaning could be heard.

Art knocked the door with his walking stick. “Oi! Stud-clap! We’re coming in.” He eyed Jayne. “Didn’t you tell him we was coming?”

“Musta slipped me mind,” Jayne said.

They entered and Scarcliff rose quickly from the sofa, tying his trousers. Strumpet Sierra Lee straightened her skirts.

"My compass hasn't pointed north like that since '55," Art said.

MacAskill gawked. "I thought yer wife had it drawn and quartered."

Sierra Lee rushed out the back door.

"Drawn and quartered!" the parrot Gibbet squawked from his corner perch.

Art and White sat opposite each other at a table beside an open window. Before them was a clear view of the construction of the cannon battery along the causeway. White took papers from his case.

"I'm sorry to inform you, Captain Valentine, but the Acting Lieutenant Governor declined your request to keep the Mediterranean galleys here. You'll have to find alternate ships as he wants these ones sent back to collect more slaves."

Art frowned. "Then what are we supposed to protect Jamaica with, our good looks? My sloops are still protecting the lanes." He pointed at White. "You tell that sheep-wearing bastard from me that we all better start learning French if we leave even the smallest crack in the island's defenses!"

MacAskill leaned in. "I see the Whigs approved your plan for a new line, Captain White."

"Only six cannons. My initial plan with Mr. Chitty was to have a battery line from the Governor's Mansion connecting with Morgan's Line. But the Acting Lieutenant Governor overruled."

"Well, as soon as His Lordship's new residence is torn a new one from a French cannonball, he'll see in yer favor, I'm sure."

White flipped through pages. "Aye, of that I have no doubt, Captain. Now to business." He handed Art a page before taking out a pouch filled with coins.

Art lifted the small bag, assessing his down payment. "Aye, in return, all your ships will be protected from here to the Bahamas or right through to the colonies."

"Very well, I leave protection of our merchant fleet to you, Captain." White rose, putting papers back in his case. "And I bid you gentlemen a good day. Oh, and I'd like to keep my carriage here whilst I inspect the new line."

"Of course, Captain. My place is yours, I'll even have Blackmoor tend your horses," Art offered.

"That won't be necessary, I'll not be long." He headed towards the new battery.

Art gazed around in disgust. "You got work to do," he said to Scarcliff. "I like what ya ain't done to the place!"

"I got materials coming this morning, sir."

"If the sloops are protecting ships going to the Bahamas, how are we gonna protect the other lanes?" MacAskill asked.

"Ginger will be back shortly with Crisp's third galley. We'll rig her for escort duty in less than two days and fit her with a crew."

MacAskill gave Art a wry glance. "And who's going to drive it? The Virgin Mary? We've got fewer men than whores in church!"

It was afternoon in the Old Church when Cherry Banks entered, dressed in a plush burgundy gown with a black veil over her head. Kneeling in the third pew she meditated, waiting for Dewar's advisor, Mason Sleemans. Sure enough, he arrived and sat beside her, his greasy dark hair combed back. He crossed himself.

"I have news—" Cherry said quietly, passing Sleemans a bible. "—for the right price."

The bible was hollow inside and Sleemans was able to place a satchel of coins within. He passed it over, not speaking a word.

"Laurens de Graaf is running a treasure galleon salvage at Serranilla Bank."

"What?" Sleemans hissed. "Everyone knows that."

"They say he's raised her largest cannons and cleaned them, ready for du Casse's fleet, coming their way. Laurens is calling for more big ships from Petit-Goâve."

"Where is the Capitaine?"

Cherry handed back the bible.

Sleemans cursed and put another bag of coins inside.

Cherry retrieved the book and hid it beneath her cloak. "The Capitaine and his little pikey are guests at Strangewayes's plantation in the hills."

"I see." Sleemans paused. "Is that it?"

"What more do ya want?" Cherry scoffed.

Sleemans rose and walked casually down the aisle.

Cherry made the sign of the cross and secured her veil. She left by the front entrance and opened her parasol. Along High Street she walked by the wrought-iron gate of the Governor's Mansion. Dr. Strangewayes stormed out the main door, cursing under his breath. Acting Lieutenant Governor Piper and his entourage followed behind.

"Don't turn your back on me and your country!" Piper demanded. "I'm Acting Lieutenant Governor of Jamaica!"

"I'm not acting pissed off!" Strangewayes huffed.

Father Parker Alcocke trailed behind Piper, fidgeting with his wooden cross. "Well, I got no medical skills or equipment. Besides, sea air makes my skin crack."

"We mustn't let Nevis fall into enemy hands," Mold said.

Cherry passed the Governor's Mansion and turned the corner. She stopped to peer around the brick wall at Strangewayes and his followers.

"But I'm Chief Surgeon!" Strangewayes protested. "Port Royal has a fine lot of graduates from our own school."

"Three of them and they all just graduated to ship's doctors," Mold replied. "The Port Royal Daily Gazette reports half the people on Nevis died from the hurricane. The other half are living in bedlam. The situation is so bad the poor souls are turning to the savages and their outlandish religious practices for help!"

Piper tapped his walking stick against the steps. "We shall send ships to Nevis with doctors and medical supplies with all haste. God's wrath will rain down upon us if we allow this to continue. Dr. Strangewayes, you are charged with overseeing and executing the Nevis aid mission and you will carry out your orders. You will organize relief and escort ships will be assigned."

Strangewayes looked aghast. "I'll have to gather supplies from my plantation. I'll need at least a month."

"You'll have a week to prepare."

"I will not be able to perform my functions here."

"Dr. MacAskill will be appointed Acting Chief Surgeon in the interim," Piper called. "One week, Doctor!"

Strangewayes slammed the gate behind himself. He peered around expectantly. "Of course, it would help if I'd brought a carriage!"

Cherry waved to him. "What's got you all in a huff?"

He gave her a strained smile and walked over to meet her. "I'm sorry, my dear. I'm afraid you caught me at a rather bad time. I seem to be suffering from Irritated Whig Syndrome."

"That's fine, Doctor. You still need to get some rest you know."

Strangewayes shot a hostile glance back at the Governor's Mansion. "Hmm, tell *them* that!"

Cherry offered her hand. "Walk with me a spell?"

He squeezed her hand a moment. "No. I really must get back. I have things I must deal with. I did, however, manage to stop by and leave you a little present under your pillow."

"I found it. Thank you."

Strangewayes leaned in close. "It's an especially strong mix, if you should find yourself in Art's proximity. But wait for me if you can. It's better we tackle Art together. And please, not a word to anyone. Not even Violante."

"Course not. Mum's the word, Doc."

Strangewayes advanced down High Street.

Cherry continued en route to the Crooked Compass, where she'd assume her new responsibilities of cleaning up Coggshall's scraps. This lot wouldn't be easy. She already had to take measures; some strumpets were unredeemable. "Saints alive, I'm certainly glad I went to church today!"

Cherry climbed the steps to the Crooked Compass and opened the door to screams. In the foyer, Lucia and Sierra Lee cowered in the corner while Mina grabbed a sword and pointed it at Salty Sally. Sally's skin had turned gray and a blue hue tainted her lips. She crawled on the floor as blood dripped from her mouth.

"It's the scarlet fever!" Lucia screeched.

Cherry stared down, unworried. "Looks blue to me. I heard of blue fever; it's like scarlet fever, only bluer." She disarmed Mina, returning the sword to the wall. "Yer gonna take on the fever with a sword? You're a daft cunt, just like they all say. You'll stay Number One Daft Cunt as long as yer useful."

Mina was taken aback.

"And yer pretty. Pretty fat mind you, but still pretty. Better hope it stays that way." Cherry surveyed Sally, who was choking on her own blood. She turned to Sierra Lee. "You like fucking that Scarcliff stud, don't ya?"

"Aye. I do."

"Well, do it again for under twenty shillings and I'll break yer fucking face! Got it, sweetie?"

Sierra's Lee's eyes grew large. "Aye. Sure do."

Cherry knelt beside Sally. "But you, you're old, unwanted, and used up. There's just no room here for you anymore."

Sally reached up, tears streaming down her cheeks. "Please!"

"You can scarcely pay for yer room and you're always borrowing. Is that gonna get better? Are you gonna wake up pretty tomorrow?" Cherry taunted. "Sorry, old Sal, consider yerself dismissed." She climbed the stairs and leaned over the railing to glare down at them all. "You guessed it, ladies. I'm queen bee now. You just do what yer told and be fucking pretty all the goddamn time and you'll work out fine." Her lips curled into a half snarl, half smile. "Cross me and you'll find out Coggshall and Burghill were fucking saints."

Sally expired at the bottom of the steps, releasing one last gasp. Strangewayes formula had proved to be successful. Cherry was anxious to try it out on anyone who pissed her off.

The sky outside was deep orange and before long, shadows fell across the city. Stars surfaced overhead and the street torches were lit. The heat of the day was dissipating, but upstairs in Mrs. Beazley's guest room, the stifling air was driving Livia to distraction. Her broken ribs hurt beyond all measure and every breath suffocating. She missed Atia and her ma desperately. Tears welled from her eyes and her chest heaved.

Mrs. Beazley arrived with a tray of tea. "Good evening."

"Good evening?" Livia huffed. "You try breathing with fifty bricks on ya!"

"You're trying too hard. Breathing is going to be an inconvenient part of life for the next while, that's certain." Mrs. Beazley set the tray down. "You just stay quiet and rest. You'll be happy to know your sister is well and looking forward to seeing you very soon. Now, would you like something to eat? Supper's on."

Livia shook her head.

"I can give you something for pain. Just a few opium tablets," the old woman offered. "You must eat something."

"No, I'm not well," Livia insisted. "Can I have a mirror?"

"Mirror?"

"Aye, a mirror. It's shiny and you can see yer face in it!"

Mrs. Beazley sighed and took a mirror from a drawer.

Livia checked her face to see some cuts and bruises. She groaned, slamming the mirror down on the bed. "She's in trouble, I know it. She's always in trouble!" A frustrated, painful scream escaped her lips as she tried to hoist herself up.

Mrs. Beazley held her down.

"Let go! I've got to go. I need to find my sister!"

"That would be rather difficult, wouldn't it? The pain would be too much for you. You'll flop about crying all over the place and where will that get you? Further from your sister than you are now!"

A heavyset man with a crooked nose knocked at the door. Dr. Strangewayes entered with a kindly expression, medical bag in hand. "Good thing you're not overdoing it. What's all this about, then?"

Livia released a heavy sob that shifted her rib cage.

Mrs. Beazley put two drops of laudanum on a square of sugarloaf and handed it to the doctor.

"Here." Strangewayes put the cube to her mouth. "This will help. A minimal dose, I assure you."

Livia took the cube and chewed it back without further ado. She winced slightly at the bitter aftertaste. The doctor fixed her pillow and passed her a cup of tea with a few more drops of laudanum. "I just know she's in trouble." Livia sobbed.

"We're doing everything we can, dear. You must be patient," Mrs. Beazley said.

"As it is, we're leaving in just a few days' time," Strangewayes added.

Mrs. Beazley was surprised. "You are?"

"Yes. I'm afraid I've been ordered to head the relief effort on Nevis."

"That's absurd! You're Chief Surgeon."

"I've been over it with the Whigs. Dr. MacAskill is going to be appointed Acting Chief Surgeon in my absence."

Mrs. Beazley folded her arms. "Preposterous!"

"Nonetheless, I must gather supplies from the plantation for the journey. Livia will accompany me."

Livia wiped away her tears. "I get to see Atia?"

"Yes, my dear. She's anxiously waiting for you. However, it will be a painful journey. You must take it easy and rest up if you plan on coming with me."

“I can make it,” Livia asserted.

“Yes, just like your sister, I’m sure you will,” Strangewayes affirmed.

Burning torches flickered against the evening sea breeze. Wavering trees guarded a large estate built upon a bed of rocks about half a mile from the beach. A cluster of pirates drank and sang around a raging bonfire on the sand. One played a three-stringed fiddle, which inspired drunken dancing. Slasher Al’s ship *Bloody Mary* was tied up nearby.

Contempt creased the corners of Edmund Coggshall’s mouth as he approached his family’s private estate near Rio Cobre. His ship, a one mast *tartana*, glided into port. Edmund wasn’t alone; he had his right-hand man, Stevens and Port Royal’s mayor as company. Once tied off, they ventured to the house to find all the lanterns lit and Dogfish guarding the front door.

“Go on in.” He grinned through pointy teeth. “Captain’s been expecting you.”

Edmund guided everyone inside. “I hope so,” he uttered under his breath. “It’s my house.” Inside they found Slasher Al basking in the sunken sitting area beside a flickering marble fireplace. His dirty boots rested on the fine furniture as he drank from an extravagant brandy bottle. Slasher Al took out a fat Cuban cigar, the ones his father, Bernard Coggshall, had been so fond of.

“I understand you gentlemen are seeking my services?” Al relaxed his wounded leg over a small mound of pillows.

“By all means, make yourself at home.” Edmund masked his disdain.

“May I offer my sincere condolences on yer dearly departed father, young Mr. Coggshall.”

“My father and Mr. Burghill, God rest their souls, spoke very highly of you, Captain.”

“Horseshit,” Al said.

“They also hadn’t squared up.” Edmund removed a pouch of coins from his vest and tossed it to Al, who gleamed as he felt the weight. “That’ll put us back right, I expect.”

“You expect right, young Coggshall. I’d say that opens negotiations.”

Edmund eyed Stevens. “Make us a couple of drinks.”

Stevens went to the liquor cabinet and filled pewter cups.

"Since you have the books, I assume you've had a chance to read them over?" Edmund and the mayor sat opposite Al.

"Aye. Especially the part about Beesty Bill's fake records."

Stevens brought over drinks on a tray.

"Unfortunately, my father kept his business dealings from me until such time as I could prove myself a ruthless cunt. At the time of his death, I had failed to accomplish that. Clearly my father misunderstood me."

"As it is, Captain Slazerelli was there, Edmund," the mayor added.

Al took the cup of rum and guzzled it back. "Nine years ago, Port Royal's top two privateers, Bleedin Art and Beesty Bill, had their letters of marque recalled. Beesty Bill was given a commission by Governor Lynch to serve Port Royal with a promotion to colonel and a seat on the council, but old Bleedin Art just got sacked after twenty-five years of service to the Cagway and not even a parting gift from Henry Morgan.

"Old Art was headed for Tortuga to find for work when he heard of a Spanish galleon leaving Santiago de Cuba carrying a fortune in gold, silver, and tobacco, special order for the king of Spain himself. Bleedin Art turned to piracy. The dearly departed Coggshall agreed to employ his services in the taking of this Spanish prize. I was not yet employed under this enterprise or things would have turned out differently. Art shadowed *Nuestra Señora de la Concepción* for days. He had rounded Guantanamo to the Windward Passage when three French ships gave chase from Tortuga. The big galleon fled north where she hit the rocks east of Crooked Island and went down." Al turned to the mayor.

The mayor finished his drink. "Enter the Duke of Albemarle in England. He received a letter from Henry Morgan telling of *Concepción's* demise and fronted an expedition to salvage the wreck. The Duke left the hiring to Henry and of course that meant bribes. Coggshall would supply the slaves and Bleedin Art the ships. But Morgan's rival, Thomas Lynch, refused to allow salvage rights unless his own staff – Lords Dewar and Llewellyn – were in charge of accounting and dispersal, and unless Beesty Bill commanded the expedition. Captain Slazerelli was employed to patrol the seas around Crooked Island and to protect our interests."

“Is that when my father first hired you, Captain?” Edmund asked, signaling Stevens to refill their cups.

“Aye. He hired me to watch their backs while Beesty Bill dug up the wreck.”

“Where was the French Captain Gator Gar during all this? I thought he was Henry Morgan’s top man?”

Al snorted with disgust.

“In those days, Gator Gar was raiding the Spanish Main with the Flibustiers under the name El Capitaine and he was pursued by Morgan’s pirate hunters,” the mayor replied.

“Aye.” Al nodded. “And Mr. Mayor may also remember that Port Royal banned pirated booty and made it difficult to sell cargo, so Hispaniola once again became pirate central.”

“Saint-Domingue.”

“Call it Hades for all I fuckin’ care!” Al pointed northeast. “Next island over, Tortuga, Port-de-Paix, and Petit-Goâve became the ports to go to. Port Royal was in the gutter and they needed this treasure salvage to save the city.”

The mayor met Edmund’s eyes. “Your father was a great man who made bold decisions to save our city.”

“If it paid well, he was a man of business.” Al raised his cup and he and the mayor toasted.

Edmund tried not to choke on his drink.

“Lord Llewellyn put up the money for the latest in diving dress and the salvage was underway.” The mayor finished his second drink. “Poor old Malherbe.”

Al laughed. “Poor old Malherbe.”

“Who?” Edmund asked.

“The former chief judge. The very man who made selling pirated goods illegal. The city named him auditor, making him responsible for keeping it all legitimate. When the ship manifest revealed much of it was unaccounted for, he and Beesty Bill were arrested and charged. Poor old Malherbe, his replacement was Lord Llewellyn. A man who’s known for swift justice. Malherbe hanged on the gallows right after Sunday mass,” the mayor explained.

“There ain’t nothing swift about Lord Llewellyn. Beesty Bill’s still on trial in England. They said Bill’s account don’t match the ship manifest or the Duke of Albemarle’s treasure list,” Al illuminated.

“Beesty Bill marked every last silver toothpick on the salvage of *Nuestra Señora de la Concepción.* I know he did ’cause I saw him. That means Dewar, Llewellyn, Coggshall senior, and Bleedin Art lied to the crown and framed him when things didn’t add up in England.”

Edmund’s interest was piqued. “Then you also know the Duke of Albemarle testified to the authenticity of those records and their counterparts in England?”

“Dewar probably burned the real ones along with the orphanage. And they all let poor old Malherbe swing and Beesty Bill got shipped up the Thames. Kinda makes you lose faith in yer fellow man. Seems to me Governor Dewar and Bleedin Art would do just about anything for these.” Al flashed the papers from his jacket.

“Which I trust you will keep safe until such time as they are needed,” Edmund said.

“Aye, as you wish.”

“I’m certain Lords Dewar and Llewellyn and Bleedin Art will be more than eager to negotiate once our common enemy has been expelled. And we’d like to offer you a share, under the table, of course.” The mayor gave a polite nod.

Al shifted slightly, repositioning his leg. “Heading into war you’re gonna need me to hire pirates. They don’t come cheap and they’ll want to see coin up front.”

“That’s all I have for now,” Edmund said casually.

“But that ain’t enough, young Coggshall,” Al said.

“A credit of fifty doubloons was paid to the shipyard on your behalf,” the mayor added.

“That pays for the boat, not the men.”

“The Hapsburg women were nobility. They’re worth a fortune. More than Bleedin Art was going to get for them. A German privateer was sent with a payoff but he never showed up,” Edmund explained.

Al sat up alertly. “See? There’s yer down payment. You’re catching on, young Coggshall. Where did the Hapsburg women go?”

The mayor shifted uncomfortably. “They already escaped. Besides, we must be careful not to add to tensions with the Hapsburgs. We’re going to need them as our allies against the French.”

“I’m getting tired.” Al raised an eyebrow. “Contact me when you grow a pair.”

Edmund leaned forward. “Dr. Strangewayes helped them escape.

He has dealings with fishermen on the north side of the island. He must have arranged transport."

"Fishermen like Cormac O'Malley?" Al asked.

It dawned on Edmund quite suddenly. "Yes. The red-haired pikey went with them. That's where they're going!"

"Then we triple the ransom and split it three ways with the good mayor here as a silent partner," Al said. "That covers yer crew and ship and I get the redheaded pikey for me own bonus."

"Agreed." Edmund rose, ready to shake on the deal. "How soon can you sail?"

Al turned his empty cup upside down. "When my gracious host has filled my belly with food and drink and I'm content to do so."

Edmund motioned to Stevens to refill the cups.

"Then let's drink to war, gentlemen." The mayor toasted. "Port Royal's most profitable game."

Al licked his lips. "I just want to sink my teeth into that little pikey!"

"Then consider her all yours, Captain." Edmund raised his cup.

GO
2015

The Lake Monster

Atia enjoyed a perfect moment of tranquility beneath the morning breeze perfumed with wildflowers. She sat on the wooden wharf readying a fishing rod while the sunshine shimmered on the lake's surface. A pang of sadness hit her at the realization that this was her last day at Strangewayes Way. Yet she longed to be reunited with her da, uncle, and brothers.

Fatima sat beside her, baiting a hook, while Minuit perched on a post nearby.

"Maybe he scares ya a bit, but he's a good bird. You can thank him for the lure." Atia attached the remains of a large moth to her hook.

"He wouldn't scare me so much if he would just stop jumping out at me all the time!" Fatima exclaimed. "So, this is how your father taught you to fish?"

Atia signaled her to stand back before tossing her line into the lake. "One of the ways."

"Was that far enough?" Fatima asked.

"Well, I'm wounded, don't forget. We'll let the current take it." She tapped her foot impatiently. "If there is a current."

"Maybe you didn't throw it far enough?"

"I threw it out plenty," Atia insisted. "Okay, maybe a little further." She reeled it back in and handed it to Fatima. "You give it a try."

Fatima tossed the line out several feet further but it still didn't budge.

"May we join you?" Natalia called from the shore.

"Aye." Atia waved. "I'm just teaching young Fatima here how to fish."

Fatima gave a skeptical look. "Are you?"

"Shouldn't you throw the line out further?" Natalia said.

"Do you fish?" Fatima asked.

"Never," Catharina said, turning her attention to a large black butterfly with iridescent green and pink coloring. "By Nerthus, it's the most beautiful butterfly I've ever seen!"

Minuit promptly snatched the insect in midair and took it back to his wooden perch.

Atia's mouth dropped. "I hate it when he does that!"

Natalia and Catharina sat down on the wharf and rolled off their stockings to dangle their feet in the water.

Minuit made short work of his meal and then hopped down beside Atia.

"Who's a pretty bird?" he whistled.

Atia pointed. "He is!"

"He's a pretty bird," Minuit agreed and flapped his wings.

"They share the same brain," Catharina spoke quietly.

"How long have you had him?" Natalia asked.

"We recently met. It's the Capitaine's bird."

Minuit gave her a dejected squawk and flew away.

"I didn't mean it like that," Atia said.

Fatima jolted, struggling against the fishing line. "We got one. What do I do?"

"Here, give it to me." Atia pushed past her to take the line. She bumped Natalia, who lost her balance, threw her arms upwards and slammed into Fatima, who fell into the water. "Ya didn't have to go and do that. I got it, love." Atia reeled in the line.

Fatima's head bobbed above the surface for a moment. "I don't swim!"

Atia looked at Natalia. "Do you swim?"

"Yes, of course," Natalia said.

"Then go get her," Catharina replied.

Atia yanked the line and its hook snagged Natalia's arm.

Natalia recoiled and banged into Catharina, who screamed, falling into the lake.

"She swims too," said Natalia. "I hope there isn't anything down there that can eat her."

Catharina cursed in German and flailed at first before she swam to Fatima and dragged her to the wharf. Natalia and Atia leaned over to help them both from the water, when suddenly the wharf tipped up, dropping them into a pool of mud. All of them thrashed about trying to grab hold of something. The wharf broke free and drifted from the plank on the shore, which also collapsed, dropping into the mud below.

Catharina was the first to climb aboard the renegade wharf, where she yanked up the others. A scowl formed on her face as they all caught their breath. "You are surrounded by water on this island and you don't swim?"

Atia patted Fatima on the back. "Not to worry. Someday I'll show ya how to swim like a fish!"

The wharf now floated in the middle of the lake. The four women unleashed a series of curse words.

Finally, they swam back to the shore and waded through the mud. Sloshing along the dirt path back towards the bungalows, they met Carlena, Ekene, and Lilly, who were carrying fishing rods and gear.

Carlena gave them a rather satisfied glimpse. "Ah, seems like our guests have already been fishing. We're about to fetch supper. Would you like us to bring you back some?"

"Ha, ha." Atia grimaced, wringing out her skirt. "While yer at it, catch the one that swam away with the wharf."

"Yes," Catharina added, squeezing her hair. "I've never seen such a creature."

Carlena's face sank. "Are you serious?"

Lilly pointed. "In that lake?"

"Be careful," Natalia cautioned. "It must be twenty feet long with whiskers."

"Maybe we should get the guns?" Ekene suggested.

Carlena nodded and they headed back to fetch weapons.

Lilly stayed behind. "What did it look like?"

"A giant catfish," Natalia explained.

"Right." Lilly winked.

Atia combed her fingers though her hair. "So, Fatima, why can't ya swim?"

Fatima seemed embarrassed. "I just never did! I never been in the water before, other than in a bath."

They squished along the path to the Gathering Place.

"That's a shame," Catharina replied. "In Hanover we lived beside a big beautiful lake, so I've swam many times."

Fatima pulled a face.

"What are we gonna wear?" Atia asked. "There's a dearth of dresses!"

Catharina was on the verge of tears. "I miss my dresses!"

"We have a trunk of Shakespeare costumes up at the hut," Fatima suggested.

Natalia's face revitalized. "We can have a Shakespeare costume ball for our last night here."

"Your bright side is all wet," Catharina grumbled.

"The dresses are dry, and that is reason enough for me." Natalia saw Gladstone at one of the tables. "Mr. Gladstone?"

He grinned. "Did a spot of fishing, did ya?"

"We need the costume trunk from the hut moved to Atia's bungalow. After you've eaten, please?"

"Let me guess: *The Tempest*?" He laughed.

Carlena drew near, holding a blunderbuss. "You heard her!"

Gladstone put his head on his hand. "Somewhere I lost control. Are you wanting to dress up as Shakespeare?"

"The day I wear a fancy dress is the day you put me in a box."

"Where are you going?"

"I have to kill a monster in the lake."

Gladstone puffed up his chest. "Oh, that was just me. I was swimming naked again."

Carlena tittered.

"Oh, right. You've seen it," Gladstone said. "Be careful." He rose. "Let's get these fair maidens some dry clothes."

"Thank you, Mr. Gladstone," Natalia said.

Atia slogged along the path, lifting her dress up to her knees. "I ain't never been to a costume ball before!"

"I get to be the fool!" Lilly followed excitedly.

They all nodded in agreement.

La Roche squinted through the bushes suspiciously; his hand hovered over a pistol. His instincts told him someone was there, but there was no movement, no sound, not even a breeze. The back of his hand grazed a nettle and he was reminded how much he disliked the sting. A whistle came, signaling Yaguara's return. *Good,* la Roche thought. *The last thing I need is start a fight with an adolescent Maroon.*

They met up along the pathway through the trees.

"South is clear," la Roche assured.

"Southwest is clear. Thanks for the help, Capitaine," Yaguara said. "We can head back."

They followed a dirt trail towards the bungalows near the lake. Clusters of bloodwood trees provided much-needed shade, while the air grew thick with flower pollen. La Roche swatted a mosquito from his neck. “Will Ekene patrol this side again in an hour or two?”

Yaguara shook his head. “No set times. The Maroons watch for regular patterns.”

“So, this young girl is yours?” la Roche asked.

“Yaguara found Tanama while fishing. She helps out here and is like my own daughter. Yaguara thought Atia was Jacquotte. Is she related?”

“No. She is very much like Jacquotte. Only she’s Irish, and younger, and kinder. Redheads, they’re fun and feisty when they’re young, but they get mean when they’re old. You just have to know when to return to sea.”

Yaguara scanned the trees. “Has the Capitaine seen the boy in his travels? Yaguara hasn’t had word for months.”

“I saw him recently.” La Roche wondered where de Kreep ended up. “He’s well. We had a laugh at the Swiftsure.”

“Damn kid, he should stay out of Port Royal taverns!”

“Oui. Him and me both.”

They arrived at the bungalows to see Gladstone staggering up Atia’s steps with a big trunk.

La Roche looked at Yaguara. “Should we help him?”

“Be my guest. What do you have there, Miles?”

“Ladies’ fashion.”

“If Miles exercised more, he wouldn’t have breasts.”

“It’s strictly for the comfort and support,” Gladstone assured, barely able to lift the trunk inside the door. “Good to know there’s no slavery around these parts.”

“I thought you were just doing your duty as a man,” Natalia said.

He gave them a good-natured glance. “I’ll go now. I’m sure there’s lots of hard work out there for me to do.”

Lilly kissed his cheek.

“That’s more like it. I always like being thanked.”

“Love ya, now get out. Have fun doing some men’s work for a spell why we get fixed up,” Lilly said.

La Roche gave Atia a full on kiss on the mouth before she vanished inside the bungalow. He watched the closed door longingly. “Why is she all wet?

"They did some fishing," Gladstone replied. "There's a monster in the lake. Carlena's gone to check it out."

La Roche watched the bungalow window, blissfully remembering Atia's silken bare skin. "It torments the soul." He turned to Gladstone. "Where are you off to?"

"I've been ordered to do something manly."

"Like get drunk?"

Gladstone nodded. "I was thinking that!"

"You coming?" la Roche asked Yaguara.

"Yaguara is busy, he has to hunt a monster in the lake." He started down a trail.

"I have rum." La Roche headed to his half of the bungalow. The room was simple: a table, bed, and a chair with clothes hanging over it. A good pair of black boots sat next to a cabinet housing rum and one last bottle of Chartreuse Liqueur d'Elixir.

The female voices next door grew rowdy. Gladstone eyed the crack in door and peered through. "It's a nasty crack, this. You should get me to fix it for ya sometime."

La Roche filled his silver pocket canteen. "No rush. What kind of man needs to peek through a crack anyway?"

Gladstone turned away. "Exactly, I agree. Absolutely."

La Roche toasted. "Especially when the keyhole has a much better view."

Gladstone's eyes widened, checking it out.

La Roche peeked through the crack. "What are they doing?"

"They're getting undressed."

Both men ogled for several minutes before strolling back along the porch.

"Ever have that perfect moment in time that you wish you could relive over and over again?" Gladstone sighed and sat down on the bench near the door. "That was that moment!"

La Roche lit a pre-rolled cigarette, savoring each puff. He skulked to the open window, admiring the view between the swaying curtains. Atia tried on a black velvet dress with long sleeves and a gold-buttoned bodice that accentuated her voluptuous breasts.

"That's gonna drive the Capitaine beyond madness!" Lilly insisted.

Natalia eyed Atia. "The Capitaine, eh?"

"Aye. Where have ya been?" Lilly smirked. "He looks at her like she's the last drop of rum on Drunkard Island!"

Fatima sighed. "You could be Lady Macbeth."

"Don't she die?" Atia speculated.

"It's Shakespeare, they all die!"

Natalia passed a shimmering green dress with gold inlays and a gathered skirt over to Fatima. "Try this one."

"I love the bells!" Lilly placed a three-pronged red velvet fool's cap on her head.

"You are all beautiful," Natalia said, helping a depressed Catharina into a white and gold gown with a large gray stain.

Atia ran a brush through her hair. "What was your home like?"

Natalia pondered a moment. "Big white mountains in winter, wildflowers in spring, and clean water in summer."

"We didn't want to leave," Catharina said. "But it was necessary. Duty and honor and shit."

Atia offered the brush. "Where are you from, Fatima?"

Fatima took it and worked on her thick long dark locks. "I was sent to work for Burghill when I was very little. I don't remember much, but I do remember that men attacked our village. They killed my mother and father and took all the children. I was on a ship for a year and then sold in Port Royal." Fatima turned towards the curtain and stopped to listen.

At Fatima's approach, la Roche and Gladstone panicked. They pretended to check the integrity of the window frame and hinges as she drew back the curtain to reveal them.

La Roche smiled. "*Bonjour,* Mademoiselle."

"I can fix this, you know." Gladstone grinned.

"*Très bien*!" Minuit called from the rail behind them.

Fatima shut the window abruptly.

La Roche glared at his parrot. "You're a wood softener. Go bug someone else!"

"I've got one of those really good ideas. Well, they usually turn out to be really bad – but you gotta take the good with the bad, don't ya?" Gladstone said.

"Does it involve more drinking?"

"But of course, Monsieur!" Gladstone led the way to the Gathering Place.

By late afternoon, they were taking shots of rum at one of the wood tables while around them decorations were put up. People draped fabric over tree branches and hung colorful paper lanterns. Lilly in her brilliantly colored fool's costume pranced around jingling her bells, sprinkling flower petals over the tables and grass. A sawn barrel filled with water, rum, and chunks of fruit made a makeshift punchbowl. Lilly dumped another bottle of rum into the mix, giving it a stir with large wooden spoon before tasting it. Her eyes rolled upwards. "Whoa, it's good!"

Minuit soared in to land upon a nearby branch. La Roche took the cue to look for Atia. Sure enough, she was strolling along the grassy area in the alluring black velvet gown, drawing many gazes.

Yaguara joined them, frowning. "What is this?"

"We're having a celebration," Carlena answered. "A Shakespeare ball."

"Yaguara will be on watch. He doesn't go for Shakespeare's balls."

Tanama patted his shoulder. "You've been on watch for days and Maroons don't usually attack when we have festivities."

Yaguara gave her cynical stare.

"Just come. You'll have a good time."

"Did you find the creature in the lake?" Gladstone asked.

"Oui. Yaguara offered him a doubloon for every white man he eats."

Gillis the gatekeeper arrived in a wagon that carried barrels of ale.

"This will be good for spirit," Gladstone slurred. "You know how important it is to the troops."

Yaguara remained stoic. "A celebration? Go ahead. The English are poking around the north side of the mountains and as Tanama says, the Maroons won't be around tonight."

Gladstone slapped his thigh. "Hey, let's ring the alarm bell and confuse the hell out of everyone!"

"A bad idea, let's not," Yaguara scolded.

"Y-you're right." Gladstone hung his head. "Bad idea."

After fetching a mug of ale, Yaguara sat down and watched Tanama have a good time.

La Roche joined him. "She's very beautiful. She reminds me of Fufu."

"In some ways, maybe. Yaguara knew Strangewayes would take her in so he brought her here."

La Roche smirked. "He taught her English, did he?"

"It shows." Yaguara took a drink. "You know, when we arrived, the Maroons had overrun the place. Strangewayes was being nice to them, the old fool. They had him tied up and gagged and were gonna kill him, so Yaguara kicked them out and stayed on for a while."

"That was in '85?"

"Oui, it has been a while. Yaguara heard you found Atia much the same way."

"Coggshall had her."

"I heard about Coggshall, the man was a pox! How could someone like that gain so much power? It confounds me."

La Roche shrugged. "He had ambition; enough to make up for lack of intelligence. That's all you need these days."

Yaguara drank his ale. "We leave early tomorrow. Cormac the pikey will be pleased to see his daughter."

"You saw him?"

"Cormac is a fish on the sand now."

Minuit chased something into the trees above. Moments later Natalia wiped powdery insect wings off her dress.

Yaguara watched. "She is interesting."

La Roche raised an eyebrow. It was the first time he'd seen Yaguara show interest in a woman since Fufu died. "Oui, be nice to dock in her port sometime, uh?"

Yaguara pondered. "If Natalia had the power Coggshall had, what would she do with it?"

"She'd try to rule the world. Joan of Arc with the Holy Roman Empire behind her," la Roche mused. "No wonder they shipped her off to the Black Lagoon! I would too." He rose and tipped his hat to Atia. "*Bonjour,* Mademoiselle. You are divine this evening."

Atia blushed prettily and pressed her lips against his. "Thank you, Monsieur."

La Roche offered her his arm. "*Ma chérie*, there are no words known to man…"

"You said that one already."

"How do you know?" He put on the scowl he knew she adored. "Maybe I was going to change it up a bit?"

Lilly staggered over to them, spilling some punch on Natalia. "Oh, sorry, love!"

"That's fine. It feels nice, actually."

"Yer pretty easy for a rich girl. Rich girls in Port Royal woulda had me flogged!"

Natalia patted her dress with a handkerchief. "For this? It's just a garment, a thing. I intend to leave the world someday as I came into it."

"Screaming?"

"No. I mean I'm not taking any dresses with me."

Atia leaned to Lilly. "A bit on the morbid side, ain't she?"

"I understand her even less than I do you."

Minuit whistled from the tree. "Mademoiselle."

Natalia took a sip of punch. "Is your bird coming with us?"

Atia eyed la Roche and Gladstone. "Is he not coming?"

Gladstone raised a rum bottle. "He can come, but it's not my fault if he gets shot down by Maroons."

"He's a good bird, he'll do what he's told," la Roche said.

"The bird is coming?" Catharina seemed revolted.

"The bird will warn us of any danger; I'd feel safer with the bird," Natalia professed. "Besides, he does wonderful tricks."

"Tricks?" La Roche laughed. "He's trying to mate with you."

The plantation residents gathered, drinking and feasting. Many of the women draped colorful fabrics over their regular dresses and used flowers to accent their hair. Ambitious youngsters brought out makeshift percussion instruments of coconut shells with seeds inside.

Atia kissed la Roche. Her mouth tasted of fruit and rum. He brushed lustfully against her, slipping his hands around her waist and groping her bottom. "How about 'your eyes are like emeralds?'"

"You said that one."

"Well, words cannot describe—"

Atia pressed a finger to his lips. "I get yer point, Capitaine."

"Ha, you said that one too! My beautiful Atia, Helen of Troy is not worthy to wipe your backside."

She slipped her tongue into his mouth. The intensity increased and she groped between his legs, agitating his desire. "As I recall," she whispered, "you asked me a question when we first met. The answer is – both."

His eyes widened. "Oh really, can you?"

She held her ribs. "Perhaps I should retire for the evening. Care to escort me to my room, Monsieur?"

"Of course." He offered his arm.

Lilly danced nearby with a cup of punch in her hand. "Mmm. Yer cannon's loaded, Capitaine!"

"I gotta get off me feet right quick," Atia insisted.

Lilly winked. "And onto yer back?"

"Tired I am as well. Ladies and gentlemen, adieu," la Roche announced.

The pair retreated to their bungalow, where they danced badly through the front door to Atia's room. Their lips met again languidly, savoring every second. She reached back to the lacings on the gown. "Undress me."

"Oui," he said eagerly, slipping the laces away to reveal the soft skin of her back. "So very pretty." His fingers glided down her flesh and she shivered beneath his touch. The gown dropped to the floor and once she stepped out of it, she was dressed only in a plain linen chemise. La Roche crushed his lips urgently against her.

He guided her to the bed and laid her down gently, propping pillows beneath her before slipping the chemise down past her thighs. He lay next to her, planting delicate kisses around the bruises on her ribs.

Atia reached down to open his trousers and gripped his manhood. He drove forward instinctively, grunting. They were cheek to cheek, his mouth caught hers in between loud unabashed gasps until his whole body vibrated, finishing against her. "My beautiful Atia," he whispered, nuzzling her ear.

He lightly caressed her breasts, before probing the depth between her thighs. He stroked the wet tangle of pubic hair, and his fingers delved inside her. She moaned and met his lips with force. Atia undulated until her passion was spent and they fell asleep in each other's arms.

Natalia and Catharina sat together on a bench, nursing cups of punch. They watched everyone with fascination. Such a mixture of people from so many places all intermingling. From dancing, drinking, and laughing to men throwing horseshoes, there was such harmony to it all.

Natalia watched Yaguara's precision with the horseshoes and was quite impressed. He wore a ceremonial shawl and his braided hair was accented with a beaded headpiece sporting bright red feathers. He seemed far more relaxed than he had been earlier.

They caught each other's eye a few times. Natalia's cheeks flared, and her smile lingered even after she looked away.

Tanama approached Yaguara. "You are dashing."

"Yaguara is dashing," he agreed. "Dashing?"

"Tanama thinks the old man looks good," she rephrased.

"Yeah, that's much better." He tossed a final horseshoe.

Lilly approached with more punch for Natalia and Catharina. "How come you always say 'Yaguara' all the time anyway?" Lilly asked. "Why not just say 'I'?"

"The English say 'I' too much," Yaguara explained. "Aye, aye, I lost me eye! You sound like fowl mating!"

Lilly pointed at him. "There ain't nothing foul about my mating, mister!"

"I hear you're helping Carlena now," Tanama interrupted.

"I'm Second Lieutenant Assist'n Man'ger!" Lilly slurred.

Yaguara watched the trees. "When did Ekene last check in?"

Tanama pointed. "He's fine. His lantern is just over there."

The land and sea lit up beneath a sparkling shooting star. Everyone stood in awe as it streaked towards the northern sky and vanished. All that remained was an eerie red glow.

"Beautiful!" Natalia glanced at Yaguara.

"Sure glad I don't live up north," he said.

Ekene emerged from the trees. "I wonder what that was?"

Lilly gave him a kiss. "Where have you been all night?"

He groped her waist. "Working. The wharf is repaired."

Carlena came up to him with a gun by her side. "Good. Go get some supper." She teetered, finishing a cup of punch. "I want another shot at that monster in the lake!"

Lilly grabbed a lantern. "A giant catfish. I want to see it!"

Ekene went over to the food table.

Carlena gave Catharina a challenging stare. "Care to show me where you saw it?"

Natalia interceded, not wanting Catharina to appear as a coward. "Perhaps we'll sit this one out."

"No, we'll come with you. It's an excellent night for fishing." Catharina marched over to get more punch.

Natalia grew nervous and looked around uneasily. She turned to Yaguara, who was already watching her. "Mr. Jaguar is not coming?"

"No, Yaguara's is doing well." He tossed another horseshoe. "You'll be fine. I'd be more concerned about Lilly with the lantern than Carlena with a gun."

Natalia beamed in return, and she and Catharina strolled down the path leading to the lake. Above them, stars twinkled brilliantly and to the north, the sky remained an intense red. "It's a midnight sunrise!"

Catharina was clearly drunk. "What are we doing again?"

"You said you were going to show me where the monster was," Carlena said.

Catharina waved. "Oh right, lead on."

They arrived at the repaired dock.

Catharina pointed down at the calm moonlit surface. "It came from over there."

Lilly held out the lantern and all of them watched. A dark form rose from the water, growling. Catharina and Lilly screamed at the top of their lungs and ran away.

Natalia watched the scaly thing with mild interest. It was clearly Ekene wearing the remains of a galliwasp lizard, splashing and snarling with enthusiasm. "There was a catfish in '75 in the Rhine three times that size, over twenty feet long. They found two children in its belly. Their names were Hansel and Gretel." She gave a polite nod. "Thank you very much for a lovely time. I'm honored. Good night."

Natalia followed the path back towards the bungalows and found Catharina hiding behind a tree. "It was a fake, you aristocratic coward," she spoke in German.

Behind them, Carlena huffed, "How is it she always manages to spoil the moment?"

Carlena
GO
2014

Into the Blue Mountains

A scorching pink sunrise crept into Atia's bungalow, where she and the Capitaine slept side by side. A quiet tapping at the door briefly woke Atia, who moved closer to her lover and dozed off again.

The Capitaine shifted and rose to answer the door. It was Gladstone, come to remind them that it was time to leave. Reluctantly, Atia got up to finish packing.

When Atia emerged from the bungalow in an ugly pair of brown trousers, a wagon was waiting. She had never worn men's clothes before; the shirt and trousers were less than desirable. She glanced at Natalia and Catharina, who appeared to feel the same way as they walked awkwardly along the path.

Once the luggage was loaded onto the wagon, Gladstone ran them through a final check.

Fatima squeezed Atia's hand. "Good luck in the jungle."

"Jungle?"

"Yes, we have to cross the mountains," Natalia said.

Atia's eyes narrowed. "Maybe someone could've explained that better!"

"It's all right, oui? It's no problem. You ride your own ass all the way up," the Capitaine said.

Atia gave him a defiant look. "But won't you get tired?"

"Ha, ha," he replied.

"Yaguara is going to need to talk to Ashanti, Chief of the Maroons, to get permission to pass unharmed," Yaguara added.

"Thank you. That's comforting," Atia said. "Maybe we shoulda booked ahead?"

"The Maroons are very unpredictable; you just gotta be ready for anything." Gladstone seemed drained from too much merriment the night before. "Now, we'll ride mules up the trails and be there in a few days, no problem!"

"Don't worry. Where you go, I go, *ma chérie*," the Capitaine pledged.

Lilly rushed over, mixed emotions all over her face. She handed Atia one of transcripts from the works of the Earl of Rochester. "I want ya to have this, to remember me by in case you don't ever want to come back."

Atia took her hand. "I'll come back."

Lilly sniffed. "We was best friends for a spell." A few tears rolled down her cheeks.

"And we still are!" Atia gave her a warm hug. "It's not far. I'll see you again, I promise."

"You better!"

Yaguara finished loading guns onto the back of the wagon and secured a cover over the top. "Remember to wear your pants tucked in tight to your boots, and don't wear things that dangle, they will snag."

Atia checked her trouser legs and took a deep breath, unsure if she was ready to face the jungle. "Thank you. Are you coming with us the whole way?"

Yaguara nodded. "Stay close to the Capitaine and Yaguara, and you will probably live."

Gladstone waved. "And me!" He released a loud burp that reeked of stale ale. "Oh, sorry. Overdid it a bit last night. Well, we got a long day ahead. Good thing I won't be feeling the aftereffects for hours yet."

Minuit flew in and landed on the back of the wagon. He regurgitated the remains of a moth, causing Atia to gag.

"If that excites you, I could try?" The Capitaine gave her a droll look.

"Maybe another time."

"Make sure you all have cashews and extra water canteens. We're gonna need those," Gladstone said slowly.

"And your own smokes." The Capitaine stowed his tobacco inside his jacket.

Gladstone staggered.

"Are you well?" the Capitaine asked.

"I took a few drops of Dr. Strangewayes's potion to wake up. Just a little one, I thought it would help. It was only a few drops." Gladstone hiccuped. "What could be the harm in that?"

"Miles should know better!" Yaguara reprimanded.

Natalia and Catharina said their goodbyes to Lilly, who gave them a hug before they boarded the wagon. Atia embraced Lilly once more before climbing up. The next goodbyes took place at the west gate, where Carlena and Gillis manned the entrance.

Carlena waved. "Good luck, ladies."

Natalia gestured back. "Thank you, Carlena. You make a good captain."

"Aye," she agreed.

The vehicle nudged forward down the long dirt road that led to the Blue Mountain foothills and deep into the heart of Maroon territory.

By midday, Minuit had made a game of scouting ahead and then flying back to be rewarded with cashews. They continued until they reached an old barn along the Jamaican hillside. A splendid view of the sea could be seen through the patchwork of trees. The wagon halted and everyone got out to stretch.

"Where shall the ladies…relieve themselves?" Natalia asked Gladstone.

"There's bushes behind the barn." He pointed. "Give us a minute to check it out first."

She rushed forward. Before she could reach the door, it swung open and a native man emerged. Startled, Natalia screamed and jumped into the bushes.

"Everyone," Gladstone began, "this is Bilwi, our guide through the Blue Mountains. He has a good rapport with Ashanti of the Maroons."

Bilwi wore a loincloth with a leather pouch around his waist and a belt over his shoulder that held his machete. He led seven mules out of the barn and lined them up. "Traveling in style, Mr. Gladstone? You are right on time." He glanced at Yaguara. "Warning signs up ahead. The Maroons are getting restless. You might want to reconsider."

Gladstone took a drink from his canteen. "We don't have a lot of choices."

"Bilwi should go on ahead and contact Ashanti. Tell him we're coming," Yaguara said and began packing the mules.

Bilwi nodded. "I will meet you at the mountain pass."

Gladstone clasped his hands together. "Once we've had a rest we can all ride our asses up the hill."

Natalia stumbled out the bushes. "Sounds charming, Mr. Gladstone."

By late afternoon, Atia felt the heat and was content to linger beneath the shade of the trees. The mule trudged along as though it had walked this route a hundred times before. In the sky above, a flock of Jamaican Macaws drew Minuit's attention and he chased after them.

The group ventured up a steep embankment with a river streaming below. At the top they reached a clearing with bright colors of red, blue, and yellow littering the ground.

"That's pretty!" Atia pointed. "Oh...no." The field was littered with the bodies of hundreds of dead parrots scattered and dumped in piles.

The Capitaine frowned. "Oui, welcome to the New World."

Catharina's mouth dropped. "Did the Maroons do this?"

"No," Yaguara said. "This is the white man's legacy. The birds are considered a nuisance."

"The farmers kill them because they eat seeds and crops," Gladstone added.

"It's a terrible waste. You people waste everything and respect nothing," Natalia admonished. "Nature herself is just an inconvenience to be wiped out!"

Atia chirped and Minuit perched on her shoulder. "Don't worry, lad. Yer too smart to end up like them."

"What this place must have been like before the plague of Christianity!" Natalia said. "I imagine lush green trees and parrots playfully prowling about their branches."

Yaguara gave her a fond gaze.

"Don't blame Jesus. He didn't do this!" Gladstone opposed.

"Sleeping tonight is better without hostility," said the Capitaine.

"He's right, we shouldn't argue," Catharina agreed.

"Oh no, get it all out now," the Capitaine insisted. "Once we go up those mountains we need to be focused and calm."

"I live by a code of Christian values!" Gladstone defended.

"Tell me, what exactly are Christian values?" Natalia asked.

"That's easy," Atia replied. "That's how much the church says yer worth."

Thunder rolled in the distance, sending vibrations through the muggy air. Yaguara peered through his telescope. Before them sat a bushy treeline with steep crags.

Gladstone patted the perspiration from his brow. "The women are getting tired."

Yaguara pointed out a clearing at the top of a cliff. "We camp up there for the night."

Once there, they strung up tarpaulins for shelter. Gladstone lit a block candle to help repel the insects. Once a fire was lit, everyone gathered around.

"What's the plan for tomorrow, Mr. Jaguar?" Natalia gave him a friendly smile.

"Bilwi will meet us at the pass and we'll cross the mountains."

"That's Maroon territory up there. We're gonna need to ask permission to pass." Gladstone stoked the fire.

"Didn't you already get permission?" Catharina slid the insect candle closer.

"We do." Gladstone didn't sound confident.

"There are many different tribes of Maroons," Yaguara said. "Scattered people being hunted by the Christians for living in harmony with the natural world."

"Why is everyone picking on Jesus today?" Gladstone bemoaned. "Atia, help me out here?"

"Sorry love, my ancestors fed you lot to the lions. They must have had a reason."

"Ashanti is trying to unite them against the English," Yaguara added.

"Is there a way we can go that don't go through the Maroons?" Atia asked. "Just a stupid question."

"Let us do all the talking. We've dealt with Ashanti before and he knows us," Gladstone said.

"If anyone wants to go back, speak up now. Once up there, there's no going back." Yaguara's eyes met Natalia.

Atia glanced at the Capitaine.

"Do you want to go back? Truthfully?" he asked.

"I wanna see my da, if you don't mind."

Natalia and Catharina whispered to one another.

"We must press on," Natalia confirmed.

Yaguara addressed Gladstone, "Miles can finish getting them settled here." He tapped the Capitaine's shoulder. "We'll scout up ahead."

Gladstone gave a crooked grin. "How come no one ever asks Miles?"

The Capitaine headed off in one direction, while Yaguara went the opposite way. Meanwhile, an exhausted Gladstone found a place under the tarpaulin to lie down.

"Your people sent ya here. Why?" Atia asked Natalia.

"It's a long story, but mainly because they suspected we're Pagans."

Catharina spoke up, "Also our family has been forced from the council. Our Duke Helmut voted against allowing slavery in Hanover and is hated by the other houses. After decades of protecting Europe from the Ottomans, they all turned on us and called us witches."

Atia unbuttoned her shirt to reveal her ankh tattoo. "I think this is Pagan. Or my ma was."

Natalia examined the symbol. "The mark on your arm is an ankh, a symbol of life from many different cultures going back thousands of years."

"Well, my ma put it there for life. I was little when we used to take off our clothes and dance around a fire, but Crisp wouldn't allow it. He burned a cross onto each of us. My ma tattooed over the scar. He never saw our arms again as we had to be covered for shaming him."

"The symbol she put there is meant to protect you from the evil that put the scar there to begin with," Natalia explained. "The dance you were doing, depending on when it was, was meant to encourage fertility, in people or for a harvest, or maybe just to please the gods. There's nothing shameful about it. If we have time before we sail, I say we strip down and I'll teach you our midsummer fire dance."

"I'd like that."

"So would I!" Gladstone made the ladies laugh.

"You said pirates took yer ship and then ya were sold to Coggshall?" Atia continued.

"Close. The pirates were working for Coggshall. He would find out through his network where our ship was going to be. Under a Hapsburg flag, we were not allied with England but apparently there is an English law saying they can stop and search any ship in international waters. We were seized by ships from Port Royal," Natalia said.

"I couldn't stand the heat and the smell belowdecks anymore," Catharina complained. "We were on deck when they attacked."

Natalia took a deep breath, recalling the event. "They rowed up in canoes under an English flag and our captain fired a shot to deter them, but it just angered them. We then realized they were pirates. They took their revenge on us for resisting. They beheaded the captain and officers before our very eyes."

“Although we’d already surrendered,” Catharina said.

“Their leader, the one they call Ginger, was the most terrifying of all. Even his eyes glowed red. I’d never been so scared, and I’ve been around war my whole life. Fortunately for us, his captain arrived and I was able to come to an agreement with him. He told us the women and children would be released.”

Gladstone sat up. “Don’t you worry none. Cormac O’Malley is connected. He’ll have you safely in your new home in Aragua. You’re dealing with professionals now.”

The crack of a branch echoed in the distance, along with a barely audible “*merde*!”

Atia gazed into the vast wilderness. “That’s me da they’re talking about. He’s been trying to find me his whole life.”

Natalia jolted forward and waved her hands at the back of her neck. At the same time, Minuit swooped in to attack something long with a multitude of legs. Natalia screamed. “Ow! Get it off me!”

Gladstone leapt up; his dagger drawn. “What, what is it?”

Minuit thrashed his prey about, while Natalia kicked her feet. “Scared me half to death! You stupid bird!” Her hand reach to her neck. “He bit me!”

The Capitaine and Yaguara returned.

Gladstone skewered the piece of twitching creature on the ground with his dagger. “He may have scared ya half to death, but yer lucky to still be alive.” He lifted the large centipede for everyone to see.

“Deadly, those are,” the Capitaine said.

Yaguara examined the back of Natalia’s neck.

“The bird bit me, didn’t it?” Natalia asked, terrified.

“Please say it was the bird.” Catharina was equally scared.

“Don’t panic. Natalia must remain calm,” Yaguara soothed. “Capitaine, your knife please?”

Yaguara took the blade and placed the tip in the fire. He then took a small bundle of weeds out of his pouch. “Chew on this and don’t swallow.” Natalia complied and Yaguara took another knife from his belt and made two small incisions on either side of the bite.

“What are you going to do?” Catharina’s eyes were wide with panic.

Yagaura took the blade from the fire. “This will draw out the poison. The bird probably saved Natalia’s life.” He pressed it onto the back of her neck. “Yaguara’s seen worse.”

Natalia bore it well, gritting her teeth on the weeds and shaking a bit.

"Why did you use my knife?" the Capitaine asked.

"Yaguara's blades are very fine. It would be a shame to damage them."

Minuit swiped the other half of his prize from Gladstone.

"I didn't know," Natalia mumbled through clenched teeth. "I suppose I owe the bird an apology."

Minuit squawked, turning his back. He carried the trophy to Atia, who patted his head. "Thanks, but you can keep it."

Natalia continued to chew. "And the weeds?"

"The weeds will be Natalia's bandage, so keep chewing."

Catharina brought her knees up to her chest. "Are there any more of these kill-o-pedes around?"

"If there are, we'll find them." The Capitaine looked at Minuit. "There, you have proved your worth to the women. A fine job."

"Aye, a fine job indeed, Minuit," Atia said.

Everyone shook out their blankets thoroughly and tried their best to settle down for the rest of the night.

Atia slept dreamlessly until dawn crept through trees. Everyone rose grumpily and packed up the mules. After a brief breakfast of nuts, fruit, and smoked meat, they pressed on.

"It's dangerous up there, remember that," Gladstone said.

"Dangerous?" Catharina asked apprehensively.

"Miles means keep your wits about you from here and your mouths shut. All of you," Yagauara said.

"Very encouraging," the Capitaine sneered. "Shall we go?"

"How's yer neck?" Atia asked Natalia.

"My head is—" she began, but stopped herself, eyeing Yaguara. "I cannot complain. Let's move out."

They mounted the mules and headed up a narrow trail.

The Capitaine blew his bird whistle and Minuit dove down, landing on Atia's shoulder. "He goes in here." The Capitaine took a sack.

"I'm not putting him in a bag," Atia protested.

"It's okay, he goes to sleep. He's too unpredictable. He'll get killed or get us killed."

Atia reluctantly placed the sack over the poor bird's head. He struggled at first, cursing, "*connard*!" until Atia took him in her arms and hummed an old Irish folk song.

They rode along a dirt path beside a series of rock formations that cascaded downhill. A waterfall gushed over, causing a fine mist to blanket the air. The natural churn caused soft white foam to gather at the base of the waterfall, diffusing into a tempting cool blue pool.

La Roche scrutinized the narrow passage ahead, sensing eyes upon him. He offered to refill Atia's canteen and added three drops of laudanum. When he handed it back, she took a large mouthful. Within minutes she seemed almost sleepy as she softly sang and slipped nuts into the sack for Minuit.

Bilwi waited for them further along the trail. Yaguara signaled to him and then motioned for the group to stop as figures shifted through the wilderness, appearing and disappearing at will as though they were comprised of the vast forest. The dizzying array of shiny dark, light, and yellowish-green trees, bushes, vines, and shrubs surrounded them like titans, guardians of the domain.

Atia glimpsed around, rubbing her eyes. "I think we're being watched."

As figures emerged from the shadows, the group found themselves surrounded by Maroons covered in leaves and mud. They were dressed in simple loincloths, and a few of them wore animal skins over their shoulders. They brandished handmade spears, and weapons created from the bones and teeth of large animals.

Yaguara stepped ahead.

A sizeable Arawak Maroon in his twenties leapt forward. "Yaguara has brought the white devils on us."

"Ashanti has given us permission to pass. Why is Hijo del Cimarrón stopping us?" Yagaura responded.

Bilwi joined the confrontation. "Hijo del Cimarrón claims this mountain. He says he rules, not Ashanti."

"Then Bilwi has explained to Hijo del Cimarrón the white women are only passing through to the north shore," Yaguara said.

Cimarrón assumed an attack posture. "Bilwi has also betrayed Cimarrón's trust."

Maroons began to wave their weapons and holler.

La Roche glanced at Atia, who still seemed placid from the laudanum. Natalia and Catharina on the other hand, trembled. "Stay calm," he soothed. "They're trying to start a fight."

"Stay calm," Natalia echoed, clutching Catharina's arm.

"Hijo de Cimarrón risks war with Ashanti," Yaguara's tone roughened. "And Yaguara will fight Hijo del Cimarrón for the right to pass."

Adolescent Arawak Maroons asserted their ground by yelling and flourishing their weapons. One had an animal bone piercing the bridge of his nose. He raised an axe, glowering at Natalia.

Yaguara grabbed his machete. "Yaguara will fight Hijo del Cimarrón now!"

Cimarrón drew his spear. "Then prepare to die!"

"Who's first?" La Roche drew his pistols and aimed, first at the adolescent with the axe. "You?"

"Who dares defy the order of Ashanti?" A voice boomed and a tall African Maroon stepped through the brush carrying a musket. He wore a red and gold headband and a beaded collar. "Ashanti's word is law!" he bellowed, keeping the Arawak Maroons at bay.

Gladstone climbed off his mule. "Great Ashanti, do we not have your permission to pass?"

"Yaguara said he was taking slaves to the north. These are not slaves! Where is the Strange Man?"

"I bring greetings from Dr. Strangewayes and humbly ask passage." Gladstone's voice remained steady. "We are taking our friends here to a boat which will take them to their home far away. They are enemies of England and were prisoners until recently."

Cimarrón shook his head. "They are English. No longer will Cimarrón's people be friends with the Strange Man. Now more English will come! They are spies. Why should we trust them? We should kill them all now!"

"Ashanti will not break the peace with the Strange Man," Ashanti replied.

"Strangewayes has always respected Cimarrón's people," Yaguara said.

Cimarrón was infuriated. "He is helping too many runaway slaves. Now the English will come in larger numbers. They will mount an assault and Ashanti is the cause. Ashanti's fault!" He glowered at them, his gaze coming to rest on Yaguara. "Your people were warned to stop intruding and Ashanti has brought your stain on all of us!"

Ashanti advanced, at least a foot taller than Cimarrón. "Ashanti rules these mountains! If Hijo del Cimarrón has a challenge, let it be known. A king will be decided today!"

Everyone stared, not daring to move. La Roche's hand hovered near his cutlass. The safety of the women was paramount. He eyed Yaguara, who remained still but ready. If a fight was coming, they would make it worthwhile.

"So, can we pass, then?" Gladstone pressed politely.

"The English cannot be trusted. It has been proven their spies are everywhere. Cimarrón will not abide them!" Cimarrón hissed.

"That is not for you to decide!" Ashanti roared. "Ashanti has given his word they will be allowed to pass and Cimarrón's people will obey. The Jaguar and his friends will pass unharmed." He eyed the bushes. "Togo!"

A young Maroon with a spear stepped forward.

"Togo will ensure their safe passage," Ashanti declared. "Take two of the young warriors with you and see the Jaguar and his friends down river to the north."

"Cudjoe! Quashee!" Togo summoned two pre-teen warriors with spears drawn. "They are guests of Ashanti and we will guard them to the North Sea."

Atia was still dazed. "Who are the little boys, then?"

"Our escorts," la Roche whispered.

Both warriors negotiated until an agreement was reached.

"Cimarrón's warriors will make sure they leave our lands as agreed," Cimarrón said.

Ashanti eyed him with suspicion. "On the word of Hijo del Cimarrón, they will reach the north unharmed."

Cimarrón nodded. "Cimarrón's people will allow them to pass unharmed. Cimarrón will keep his word."

"We will continue," Yaguara confirmed.

"Thank you, Great Ashanti!" Gladstone looked as though he were ready to faint.

La Roche leaned close to Atia, squeezing her hand. "Are you okay?"

She laughed nervously; her green eyes glistened, matching the lush forest. "Next time, put *me* in the sack."

Natalia swallowed hard. "Now I really do need to wash." She

brushed the sweat from her brow and inadvertently patted the back of her neck, cringing.

Yaguara turned to her. "We're going to the river for clean water first. Keep it together. Natalia's doing fine."

Ashanti studied Gladstone. "Now you may go with Hijo del Cimarrón."

"Thank you—" he nodded "—I think."

La Roche glared at the sun. It was afternoon and the day was at its hottest. They continued their journey until they reached a clearing beside a pond. After collecting more water and quickly rinsing their arms and faces in cool liquid, the journey continued.

"From here, we go downriver?" Natalia asked Yaguara.

"We have boats down there." He pointed to the bottom of the cliff.

After braving the steep embankment, they arrived in an area that overlooked a lush green valley. At the edge of the lake, two long river boats waited for them. Everyone transferred their belongings and were soon ready to leave.

Atia carried the sack Minuit slept in. "Should we let him out here?"

"Not yet. Let's get out of here first." La Roche cautiously eyed the Maroons.

"I guess we'll see you on the way back?" Gladstone looked uneasily at Bilwi.

"I'll meet you in three days."

"Aye, thanks."

Bilwi nodded. "When you come back, take the untraveled road by carriage and I will meet you on the ridge."

"We will." Gladstone climbed into a boat.

Once everyone was settled, they took off in silence. The water along the Jamaican Rio Grande was the color of deep indigo. The only ripples came from the boats as they darted along the surface.

Atia opened the sack. "Do ya want a stretch?"

Minuit released a long squawk before flexing his wings. "*Bonjour.*"

"Hello, Minuit," said Atia.

He took off after a dragonfly.

They soon reached a series of rapids and the boats sped up to such a degree that everyone had to hang onto the sides. The Maroons steered them through without incident. Once reaching the bottom, they coasted into another calm body of water before paddling to shore.

One of the Maroons glared at Natalia and Catharina.

"That one may be a problem," la Roche whispered to Yaguara.

"That's Delabra, Cimarrón's second in command. Oui, he will be a problem."

"We stay here for the night," Cimarrón said, rallying the Maroons to set up camp.

It grew dark early within the confines of the forest and soon the only light came from the campfire. They roasted chunks of fish on long skewers over the flames. Everyone sat within their own separate groups.

Natalia turned to Atia. "You held your composure very well today. You were an inspiration to me."

"I did?"

La Roche smirked. "I slipped her some laudanum. She missed it."

"I didn't. Fascinating people, Maroons."

"You wouldn't by chance have any more?" Catharina still trembled.

Delabra gave Natalia a stern stare.

"That one has it for me," she whispered, avoiding all eye contact.

Yaguara positioned himself beside her. "Yes, he does."

"What are they saying?" la Roche spoke quietly.

Yaguara gave Natalia a comforting look. "Do not be alarmed. The Maroon is speaking of war with Ashanti, enticing the others to follow. He says they will follow Cimarrón when war erupts. This one is speaking of starting a war tonight."

"Why is he staring?" Natalia leaned in close to Yaguara.

"The Maroon speaks of the white devils and refers to Natalia and Catharina as Devil Women."

"Am I to understand that we are being protected by the infant with a stick?" Catharina scrutinized the boy.

"We're being protected by Ashanti's word. The kids are symbolic. Ashanti and Cimarrón both know they could take them down any time they want. It's a game of trust," Yaguara explained.

"Clearly Cimarrón wants to be in Ashanti's place," Natalia said.

"Ashanti and Cimarrón must be united against the English. A fight between them would result in disaster for all the Maroons. Hijo del Cimarrón must know that." Movement caught Yaguara's attention and he turned in time to see Delabra nod and Cudjoe ready his spear. "Young Cudjoe is about to make a serious mistake." The spear flew in Catharina's direction and she screamed. Yaguara deflected the spear using his machete before punching the side of Cudjoe's head, knocking him down.

La Roche drew a pistol and his cutlass, positioning himself in front of Atia and Gladstone. A wave of panic and aggression flooded his veins. Various arguments erupted in mixed languages including Arawak, Miskito, and Spanish. He'd die to protect Atia, but if he had to kill her so she wouldn't be raped and tortured, he would make it quick and painless.

Delabra charged at Natalia, but he was repelled by Yaguara.

A shriek escaped Catharina's lips as she waved her arms. The Maroons imitated her. She collapsed to the ground, crying. Cimarrón and Togo returned from gathering firewood and arguments broke out.

"Don't scream. They're trying to make you panic," Yaguara ordered.

Natalia pulled Catharina aside. "I didn't get bit in the head by a kill-o-pede just to give up now!"

Yaguara lunged forward. "Stop! This is not allowed, Hijo del Cimarrón! You gave your word to Ashanti!"

"Are you animals or people?" Catharina yelled.

"Don't show fear, damn it!" Yaguara snapped.

"Enough of this!" Catharina demanded, grabbing Natalia's arm. "End it! End it now!"

Natalia drew her dagger and was ready to plunge it into Catharina's chest. "Help me to go with her, Mr. Jaguar?"

Yaguara shook his head. "Don't be afraid." He turned to face Cimarrón and their eyes met. "Is this the sworn word of the Cimarrón? She is ready to die!"

Atia pushed past la Roche. He called after her as panic gripped him. "Atia!" He remained in his spot.

Natalia put her hand out. "Atia, save yourself!"

"You're right; we didn't come all this way to give up now!" Atia exclaimed. "Tell me about yer fire dance?"

Natalia thought for a moment. "I said I would show you."

"Then show me the fire dance, like you said," Atia spoke fearlessly and the women locked hands, dragging Catharina to her feet.

Delabra grabbed at Natalia's top, tearing it.

Yaguara hauled him away.

"Fine! You want this?" Natalia tore off the shirt and threw it. She slid off the trousers and stood completely naked. “Take off your clothes,” she instructed the other two women.

La Roche paced, convinced this would be the end of them all.

“What are you doing?” Gladstone gasped. “You’ll only make it worse!”

“Dance with me, Atia, through the fire!” Natalia encouraged.

Catharina removed her shirt and trousers. “You don’t want to jump through fire with your clothes on.”

Atia followed and soon all three were nude dancing around the flames. “Do as I do,” Natalia said. She folded her arms over her chest. “We use symbols and gestures to please and arouse the gods.” A Germanic tune poured from her lips.

The Maroons responded favorably, gathering up the torn clothes.

Atia and Catharina stretched their arms towards the fire, and then above their heads. Like curvaceous deities, their hair flowed long and free. They twirled around the fire, their bodies undulating wildly as they kicked up their heels. Their provocative movements entranced all the ogling males.

La Roche watched the Maroons carefully, but they seemed pleasantly distracted, except for Delabra, who tried to lunge at Natalia. He was halted of course by Yaguara, whose devotion to her was now very clear.

“You must jump through the fire!” Natalia leapt over the flames, causing a cheer, before her arms made a gathering motion. “The God of Fire will make you fertile.”

“And trim the quim,” Gladstone said to la Roche.

Catharina chanted in German, jumping over the fire. “Let the spark of life up into your womb, Atia. Jump through!”

Atia leapt over the flames like a natural goddess, landing with her legs a foot apart upon the earth. She too made gathering gestures with her hands, and then swirled about seductively. The flames made her hair glow and she made eye contact with la Roche, stirring his desire for her.

“Throw something up to the gods, Atia, some good feelings or a happy thought.”

Natalia continued throwing her arms up above her head.

Delabra was unimpressed by the display. He lunged forward, hitting Natalia in the face. She staggered back as blood began to drip from her nose.

Yaguara caught her. "May I have this dance?" He lifted her chin.

Delabra was getting ready to strike again, but this time it was Natalia who lunged forward, startling him. He fell backwards, landing on the ground, while the other Maroons pointed and laughed. Catharina and Atia continued to dance. Cimarrón led his men away with Delabra reluctantly following.

"You too, go with them!" Yaguara instructed Cudjo before catching Natalia, who passed out. Scooping her up in his arms, he ran into the bushes away from the camp.

La Roche signaled Gladstone. "Bring the blond and I'll get Atia."

"What the hell, improvisation is me best quality." Gladstone charged forward, gallantly lifting Catharina, his legs buckling beneath the weight as he carried her off.

The remaining Maroons cheered, convinced it was some kind of mating ceremony. La Roche scooped Atia into his arms and ran as fast as he could into the wilderness. After a few minutes of stumbling through the woods, he paused to catch his breath, setting Atia on her feet.

"Halfway to China. He doesn't stick around for confrontations." His awareness of Atia intensified and his fingers glided down her naked back. She was pressed right up against him. He could still see a flicker from the campfire and hear Yaguara and Gladstone from afar, perhaps thirty feet away, but in this spot, they were alone. "We should be safe for now." He slipped his jacket over her shoulders.

La Roche searched around to find a soft patch for them to sit. Atia sat between his legs, using him as a cushion.

They sat in silence at first, until Atia began, "So, who was she?"

"Who?"

"Your redhead."

"You don't know her. I hope."

"So ya were, once?"

"Married? Oui. Once. When I was young and stupid. Red like fire, her hair was."

"Has she passed on?"

"No, it faded out and went gray." La Roche grew thoughtful, wrapping his arms around her and massaging her cold hands. "We grew apart. I'd been with her since we were young. Her father was killed in a Spanish attack and left her and her brother with me. We lived the pirate life until we couldn't stand the sight of each other anymore."

She tilted her head. "Where is she now?"

"Living somewhere on a beach with the Freebooters, popping out little Freebooters. You know too much about me now. What about you?"

"Me? No marriages or betrothals. A shit load of adolescent sweethearts. Made a few boys jump off cliffs to their deaths, but nothing serious." She paused. "Crisp never let us out of his sight. The bastard loathed us but at the same time had to have us, like prized possessions. Maybe I was waiting for me bearded Frenchman to return." She nestled closer to him. "Perhaps we was meant to meet again, my Capitaine."

He caressed her ring finger. "Your interest should be in someone else."

"I don't take kindly to being told where me interests should lie."

"It's just, you are so young and beautiful. And I am…well, less young and beautiful." Realizing life would be miserable without her.

"You've got yer good points." She smiled. "I follow me instincts."

"What do your instincts tell you?"

"*Mon amour*," she whispered and crushed her mouth against his so intensely it paralyzed him. He then buried his face in her gorgeous hair. Soon her body went limp against him. He carefully tried to reposition them both into a better sleeping posture and soon they were side by side.

When Atia was deeply asleep, he felt for his cutlass and slid it in close beside him. Next, he grabbed his pistol, keeping watch. Dozing periodically, he heard the occasional crack of a branch or rustling of the bushes. In the predawn he napped for about an hour, and then at first light he stirred to find Atia pressed against him, wearing only his coat. She rolled over. Her flaming red hair was an exquisite mess and her jewel-like eyes gazed at him adoringly.

"Morning," she said.

"*Bonjour,* Mademoiselle." He helped her to stand.

"I could go around like this?" Her breasts jutted out.

"You get no objection from me." He led her through the trees.

"Capitaine? Atia?" Gladstone called.

"Oui," la Roche said, and they were soon reunited with the rest of the group.

Natalia was partially clad in Yaguara's shawl, resting in his arms. Her face bloody and her eye purplish black.

"Makes ya wonder what we did last night, don't it?" Atia sat beside them on a large rock.

Natalia stirred.

"Wow, do *you* ever fart in your sleep," Yaguara began.

"Do I?" She was too stunned to challenge that one.

"Do you remember last night?"

"Yes, unfortunately." Natalia sat up and rubbed the dried blood beneath her nose and on her chin.

Quashee, one of Ashanti's child warriors, joined them. In his arms were the remnants of the women's clothes. Yaguara thanked him and the women pieced their outfits back together while the men packed up the boats.

Yaguara stood on guard, his machete back in its leather sleeve, but his dagger close by. Cimarrón and Togo emerged from the trees. "We're leaving now. Hijo del Cimarrón has proven that he can't be trusted," Yaguara said.

"No one has been harmed," Cimarrón argued. "You will be escorted down river."

"You allowed Delabra to injure our woman!" Yaguara raised his dagger. "Yaguara will kill him if he comes near her again!"

Cimarrón nodded peaceably. "Hijo del Cimarrón will honor the agreement with Yaguara and Ashanti."

Along the shoreline of the Rio Grande, two rowboats waited for them. Once aboard, they pushed off and glided along a deep blue crystalline surface. The thick of the jungle hung along the beach – a vast green façade hiding the danger and majesty within. Multicolored dragonflies buzzed over the water, their wings dazzling beneath the sun's rays.

Minuit dove down, capturing one in his beak.

"There's me boy!" Atia exclaimed.

La Roche was pleased to see the parrot. The buzz of insects and chirping of birds filled the air. He closed his eyes briefly, succumbing to sleepiness.

Catharina yawned. "It's so sticky here…so very hot."

"Almost there, won't be long now," Gladstone said.

"Maybe we could stop for a swim?" Atia suggested.

“Uh, not this far downriver,” Gladstone said. “Nasty things in the water down here.”

“Leeches, lizards, snakes,” la Roche added.

“Kill-o-pedes?” Natalia said.

“Oh yeah!” Gladstone’s eyes widened. “Big ones. Three, four feet long with fangs, huge fangs!”

Atia nodded. “Okay, thanks. I got it!”

The boats continued downriver for about an hour, their view of the jungle punctuated by explosions of golden yellow, scorching orange, and vivid white flowers. They landed on a bank about a hundred feet away from a cluster of bungalows belonging to a small village. After gathering their things, Cimarrón and Togo returned to their boats and headed back from whence they came.

“Am I ever glad that’s over with,” Gladstone exhaled, leading them towards the village.

La Roche felt himself relax slightly. Atia rolled up her torn sleeves and sat down on an old stone bench surrounded by veiny wildflowers.

“I’ll find us a ride in town. We gotta come back this way anyway,” Gladstone said.

La Roche sat down beside Atia. “We’ll stay here.”

Yaguara led Natalia and Catharina forward.

“Aye, see you in a bit.” Gladstone caught up to the others.

Minuit swooped in and landed beside them. Atia tossed him a cashew and he caught it in his enormous beak. She then tossed a cashew to la Roche, who caught it in his mouth.

“What is this place?” she asked.

“Leftovers from the Spanish occupation. These are stables. This was a plantation at one time.”

Atia rose and strolled through the tall grass until she reached an ornately carved archway. She vanished from his view.

“Uh, don’t go too far,” la Roche called. Receiving no response, he followed, uttering a few curse words beneath his breath. Inside the monument were stone tables covered in overgrown vines. Pale sunshine streamed into the ruin, giving it an ethereal glow.

Atia sat on one of the tables. “Someone put a lot of work into this. All for naught.”

“Whoever owned this was rich and powerful.”

“Not rich or powerful enough, I’d say.”

La Roche smiled. "No one ever is."

"In the end nature wins." Atia wrapped her legs around him and removed her shirt. "Ya know, it was a fertility ritual last night." She stood up and untied her trousers. "We should really appease the gods."

Her earthy sweet scent ensnared him, and he kissed her forehead. Memories of the erotic fire dance fueled his arousal and soon his sex throbbed. He disrobed and kissed her urgently. La Roche's fingers probed the wetness of her depths, igniting his hunger. He ached to the point of eruption. Eagerly, she pushed him down to mount him on the ground.

Unabashedly she straddled him, flinching at first, and then every inch of him penetrated her. His entire body tingled against the softness of her breasts and the sweetness of her mouth. Her hair lashed against him teasingly, kindling his excitement.

Atia sighed and la Roche sat up gripping her against his chest, while her arms grasped his neck. His hands fondled the smooth round slope of her bottom causing her thighs to quiver. Feasting on her orgasm, his mouth intertwined with hers as their flesh undulated in unison. Soon, every bit of him was spent inside her.

The air was dizzying, and a shroud of exhaustion enveloped them. He gathered her against him. Irrefutable love swam through his veins. "I love you." He kissed the lobe of her ear.

"And I you, my Capitaine."

His fingers slipped into the wet gulf between her legs and her body conformed against his. He closed his eyes, knowing he could hold this course for an eternity.

Homecoming

After a few hours' carriage ride along a winding path, a village came into view. Fishing docks floated in the harbor with a few boats tied up and a ramp bridging land and sea. Wooded houses sat in clusters, separated by paths, bushes, and sections of rickety fence. A grassy field sat at the center of the village with a stone barbecue pit, a couple of wagons, and a stable.

Anticipation filled Atia's stomach. She was home, yet pieces were missing – Livia and her ma, Lucretia. A red-haired man in his mid-thirties chopped wood. It was Lucas, her older brother! He had a ginger beard and a pipe hanging from his mouth. Nearby was Uncle Rourke, gray with a walking stick. They watched the approaching carriage.

Lucas rushed forward. "Ma? It's Lucretia!"

Rourke's eyes widened. "On Mercury and Mars, we was told you were dead!"

"Hello," Atia called.

"Not Lucretia, young Atia!" Rourke exclaimed.

Her half-brothers emerged, Rourke's twin sons, Elias and Aedan. They were in their early twenties, both tall and dark-haired.

"They said you shipwrecked? Everyone was lost at sea?" Deep emotion stirred in Rourke's eyes.

Atia climbed down. "We were. Me and Liv are the only ones left."

Rourke seemed dazed as he wrapped his arms around her. He smelled of old pipe tobacco. "Livia's alive," he stated with relief. Atia buried her face against her uncle's chest and wept.

"Aye. Two broken ribs, but she's going to be fine," Gladstone added as he helped Natalia and Catharina down. "And these are the Hapsburg ladies, ready for a *bon voyage*."

"Welcome." Lucas tipped his hat.

Catharina nodded. "Thank you."

Rourke inspected the bruises on Atia's arms. "You look like ya been through Hades and then went back for seconds."

"We have." Gladstone patted his forehead. "The Maroons almost had us this time. Our guests could use a little rest and relaxation."

"Not to worry, ladies, we got just the thing to help calm the nerves." Rourke caressed Atia's face. "It's a gift from the gods you survived, an absolute gift. We was happy when you escaped from Crisp and then devastated to find out the ship went down. But we already mourned for the dead. Tonight, we celebrate life."

"My little sister!" Lucas gave her a hefty squeeze that knocked the wind out of her. "I can't believe you're here. Ya look just like Ma!"

"The spitting image!" Elias rushed over.

"Aye, that she does," Aedan added.

Atia was trapped in a triangle of embraces for the longest time. She wiped a few tears from her eyes, forgetting about everyone else.

Rourke eyed the Capitaine.

"Who might ya be?" Lucas asked.

"This is a close friend of Dr. Strangewayes," Gladstone said.

"He's my Capitaine." Atia put her hand into his.

"The same Capitaine from Maracaibo and Panama," Rourke stated. "Cormac's talked about you."

"One and the same. He helped us rescue Atia."

The Capitaine nodded. "Oui. I won her."

Gladstone began to unload the carriage. "Best game of One and Thirty in years and I missed it."

"He saved me, Rourke. He saved me and Liv from a man named Coggshall," Atia said. "And another one called the Slasher."

Elias, Aedan, and Lucas all nodded approvingly.

Rourke limped towards the Capitaine. "Then we owe you a debt of gratitude. Coggshall's a festering boil." They shook hands.

"Consider that boil lanced." Gladstone smirked. "We gave him one of the good doctor's special remedies for inflammation of festering boil."

"Scarlet fever, it was," Atia said.

"Good. Now tell me all about—" Rourke's eyes widened "Well, fuck me with a rusty cutlass! Your da might be wanting to know yer here!"

"Pandora's bleeding box!" Elias gasped. "Uncle Cormac."

"Poor bastard's been dying of grief since we got the news," Lucas said.

"And beating us like runaway slaves," Aedan added.

"This way. I'll take ya to him." Lucas pointed at Elias. "Get that big ole pig up at the stable, he's overdue for retirement as it is and Mars and Mercury are hungry. Throw him on the spit." He turned to Aedan. "Take the young ladies to their rooms and find some of Lucretia's clothes for them to try on."

Aedan bowed. "Right. If you'll follow me, ladies?"

Natalia and Catharina staggered along.

Natalia caught Yaguara's gaze. "Are you coming with us?"

"Someone has to watch the village. You're among friends now. Go on," he replied, giving her an inscrutable expression as he climbed back into the carriage and headed off.

Natalia seemed on the verge of tears as she grabbed Catharina's arm and followed Aedan.

Atia trailed Lucas down a path with the Capitaine in tow.

"He's out back," Lucas said.

Rourke limped, walking stick in hand. "He's been in a right bloody state. Maybe I should go first; he may be armed."

"He'll be overjoyed," Lucas assured.

"He'll lose his bloody mind," Rourke whispered.

They neared a small house surrounded by lush green trees. A man hammered angrily away at a new slat on the roof, cursing to himself.

"Cormac, you have a visitor!" Lucas called.

Cormac continued battering the roof.

"Oi, Cormac! Someone's here to see ya!" Rourke yelled.

"I'd tell ya to go fuck yerself Rourke, but you'd take it literal!" Cormac spotted Atia on the ground and dropped his hammer. "Well, Pan's a prick and the Devil sucks him! I don't believe me eyes!"

"Hello, Da!" Atia looked up, her eyes wet with tears.

He stared in astonishment. "Yer alive! And your mother?"

Atia shook her head. "Just Livia, and she's in Port Royal."

Cormac stumbled to the ladder.

"Yer gonna fall and break yer bloody neck. Would ya watch what yer doing?" Rourke said.

"Right. Wait inside the house. I'll be right down."

Atia entered the sparse interior. It certainly lacked her ma's flair. There was a small living area with a fireplace and a couple of swords mounted above it. Between two wooden chairs sat a table with an old leather-bound book upon it. Atia opened the cover. It read:

Atia heard footsteps. "Da?"

Cormac entered the living room. He had silver and white hair and several scars across his face. His intense blue eyes studied Atia and he gave her a sturdy embrace, not saying a word.

"Hello, Da." Atia hugged him, wincing.

He held her at arm's length and sniffed. "Let me look at you. Shit, ya look like yer mother. Like ya stepped out of Hades' own sulfur pit, but alive and in one piece."

Atia extended her hand. "Da, this man rescued me. My Capitaine."

"I must be seeing ghosts!" Cormac said.

The Capitaine tipped his hat. "O'Malley."

"We was told you died in the hurricane? That yer ship went down." Cormac rubbed his temple.

"And then she was sold to slavery in Port Royal. Shitty day, that was, uh?" the Capitaine continued.

Atia nodded. "Aye, the Capitaine fought for me. He saved me."

"From who?" Cormac growled.

"Coggshall and then we poisoned him and his men."

"It's a shame I missed it. You came by land. Were you followed?"

"If anyone had, the Maroons would have killed them," the Capitaine said.

Lucas entered. "They brought the Hapsburg women with them. One's pretty badly beat up."

"Still, you got them through. Ya haven't lost too much, Capitaine, I'll give you that." Cormac squeezed Atia's hand. "And Atia has come back from the grave. I don't know about the rest of you, but I think celebrating's in order. Lucas?"

"I was wanting an excuse to get drunk!" Lucas clapped his hands together. "This be a stupor night."

Emotion built up in Cormac's face.

"Well, don't start crying a flood!" Lucas goaded.

"Aye, not now." Cormac smacked him on the shoulder and walked over to a trunk. He opened it to reveal a dozen bottles of homemade rum and handed one to Atia.

"Can't say I'm fond of yer Caribbean rum."

The Capitaine took the bottle. "I'll have hers."

Cormac gave her another bottle. This time it was well-aged Irish whiskey.

"Well, if ya insist, that be more like it!"

"That's me girl! Me and you have a lot to talk about." Cormac took a swig of rum. "A drink to yer mother first. If I do it later, I'll cry like a flock o'seagulls."

After getting cleaned up and changed into one of her mother's dresses, Atia collapsed into the hanging chair on her da's porch. She nursed the whiskey bottle on her lap.

Natalia and Catharina emerged from their bungalow, and gingerly walked the path to Cormac's house. They too had cleaned up and were clearly relieved to be back in dresses. They collapsed on the steps of the shady porch and gave Atia brief smiles before staring at the water.

Exhaustion overtook all of them.

"Maybe the gods have decided to take pity on us?" Natalia massaged her neck and shoulders.

"No." Catharina rubbed her feet. "They're having too much fun at our expense."

The Capitaine and Cormac stood at the porch rail to watch Lucas tend the spit, rotating the pig.

"This be what I was paid by Morgan," Cormac said. "This piece of land, legal title. Three dozen acres by the Rio Grande. Not exactly what I was promised, but it's a home. We heard the captains fared much better."

The Capitaine appeared irritated. "And me, I deliver groceries, uh? You are crying to the well. I got a brig and Don Juan's sword, that's what I got."

Cormac nodded. "I know that sword. That's a nice sword."

The Capitaine suddenly laughed. "Correction! Le Picard currently has both *La Lune* and the sword. So, crying to the fucking ocean, you are." He took a swig of rum.

"Pierre or François?"

"François. Pierre's pissing off the English near Acadia."

Elias and Aedan arrived in their cleanest, finest clothes, pulling a cart of bottles.

"What are those?" Natalia asked.

Gladstone handed her a bottle. "I thought you could use a little of the strictly medicinal – and very flammable – O'Malley's famous memory wiping formula!"

"How do you like yer humble dwellings, ladies?" Elias said.

"Just fine, thank you." Natalia opened the bottle, sniffed, and wrinkled her nose. She took a small sip and passed the bottle to Catharina, who took a large mouthful and crossed her eyes in disgust.

Aedan winked. "Good, ain't it?"

Lucas bowed. "I believe proper introductions are in order?"

"Everyone," Gladstone began. "This is Natalia and Catharina of the kingdom of Hanover. Nat and Cat, these creatures are referred to as O'Malleys. A strange breed of over sized leprechaun from a faraway island in the northeast."

Cormac swaggered. "Have I died? This must be Elysium, for no mortal woman could look as perfect as you women here tonight." He kissed each of their hands.

Atia shook her head. "O'Malleys are charmers, ain't they?"

"Charm does run in the family," Elias insisted.

"Though more prominent in some than others." Aedan bowed to Catharina. "Maybe you'd like to see the river later?"

"Hmm, he's got all the charm of Thor," Atia teased.

"Stop tormenting the poor girls!" Rourke ordered. "They've had enough. Make yourselves useful and tend the pig!"

The twins moaned all the way to the blazing pit.

"Forgive our rudeness. Pleased to make yer acquaintance, ladies," Rourke said.

Natalia smiled weakly. "I'm honored, Mr. O'Malley."

Cormac slapped his brother's back. "I'm Cormac and this urchin is Rourke. We have the pleasure of escorting you on the last leg of yer journey, if it's agreeable with you."

Catharina nodded. "We thank you."

There was a sudden flurry of flames from the pit as the twins poured just a little homemade rum over the pig.

"If there is one thing O'Malleys are good at, it's celebrating!" Gladstone toasted.

"Stop showing off!" Cormac growled at the twins. They feigned innocence, but soon lost their resolve and laughed.

"Why is it when I'm hung over that I start the whole thing over again?" Gladstone took another mouthful of rum. "Going to be in terrible pain tomorrow. I'll just have to make sure it's worth it!"

Lucas eyed his brothers. "I've never seen them so happy."

Rourke sighed. "Two of them. Two women. They're counting on getting their rocks off tonight."

"You'd think they never saw a woman before! Now they've gone soft in the head!" Cormac watched as they rotated the pig. "Make sure they don't do anything stupid!"

"Give the lads a bit of credit." Rourke defended.

Aedan and Elias toppled the pig into the flames, nearly falling in with it.

"That was a close one!" Aedan chuckled.

Rourke's eyebrows shot up. "Well, get it out, ya shitehawks!"

Cormac elbowed his brother. "Makes it nice and crispy like that, anyway."

Lucas intervened to help them drag it from the fire. Elias rubbed his hands, trying to shake off ashes. Aedan patted his twin on the shoulder, leaving a black handprint.

Atia took a mouthful of whiskey and rocked in the swing chair.

Cormac glanced over at her. "I can't get over how much you resemble yer mother. You'll be crushing hearts between yer toes!"

"Who says I already ain't?"

"Aye." He took another swig of rum. "Just like yer mother!"

The sun kissed the horizon, plunging the sky into deep orange and pink hues. The scent of wildflowers intermingled with the freshness of the sea filled the air. Everyone gathered around the fire pit, ready for more drink and food.

A feast was set on a large wooden table. A tray of mangoes, pineapples, plantains, and coconuts sat beside a mountain of bread and cheese. Slices of charred roast pig sat on a platter with a side of spiced mustard for glazing. A seemingly unending supply of rum was stashed beneath the table.

Atia ate some cheese with bread and it was delicious. Everything tasted better than it ever had before. Perhaps it was the heat or, more likely, the company. With food on the brain, she craved a fish fry, something she hadn't had in ages. She eyed her uncle. "I hear the fishing is good here?"

Rourke nodded. "We'll have to take you fishing."

"I did once. She didn't like it." Cormac crunched on an apple between gulps of rum.

"Ya pushed me in!"

"It was an accident. You were gonna lose it; I had to do something. Anyway, it was a pond, not the bleedin' Atlantic!"

Atia crossed her arms over her chest. "Ended up head first in the water, but I got the damn fish!"

"Got the fish? Ya bloody stabbed it a hundred times screaming bloody murder!"

The Capitaine and Rourke both laughed.

"Word of advice." Cormac leaned to the Capitaine. "Don't ever scare her. You'd never seen a fish so terrified as that poor bloody grouper!"

Minuit swooped in to perch next to her.

"There's me boy!" Atia watched his beak. "You don't got any bugs in there do ya?" He lowered his head until she rustled his feathers.

"That mangy thing was at Maracaibo, wasn't it?" Cormac asked.

"Oui. Maracaibo, it was," the Capitaine said.

"Oui, Maracaibo," Minuit agreed.

"Basque sent messages to l'Olonnais who was down in Lake Maracaibo, in the little town of Gibraltar. When Basque died, he decided to follow me around."

Cormac stared at Minuit. "What kind of bird is it, then?"

"I saw one like that in Madagascar, but it was dead," Rourke added.

"Bullshit!" Cormac turned to his brother. "You've never been to Madagascar. Liar!"

"Have too!" Rourke argued. "'78 or '79. I didn't see you for fifteen fucking years; do you really think I spent all that time sailing down to the Caribbean? There was a bird like that'd been killed by a fisherman in Madagascar."

"When? You never sailed the seven seas. Bullshit!" Cormac shook his head.

"He may be right," the Capitaine added. "I remember Basque saying he'd been in Madagascar."

"Well, the one I saw was shot for being a pest. The villagers there all said it was the last one of its kind." Rourke pointed at Minuit. "Yer bird might be the last."

Minuit peered sadly at Atia before he stretched his wings and took off towards the moon.

"The birds are a bloody nuisance," Cormac grumbled.

"They make excellent target practice," Elias said.

All the women around the table gave him a disgusted look.

"Think ya just blew yer chance of getting laid, boy." Cormac finished off another bottle of rum.

"Yeah, real charmers." Atia turned to her uncle. "Do ya know what kind of bird it is, then?"

"Aye, they called it a broad-billed parrot," Rourke replied.

Atia couldn't quite get her drunken tongue around it as it came out, "a bra bill part?"

"A board bull part?" Gladstone was dazed on moonshine.

"A bra bill part," Atia repeated. "Are you having trouble with yer own language?"

"No, just a slight barrier is all."

"Oi, Rourke, ship coming in," Elias alerted. A ketch glided in, and the crew roped it to the dock near the ramp.

Rourke wore a confused smile. "It's Jones. He can't be outta weed already?"

"Jonesy!" Atia's face lit up. "All me mates are here tonight!"

"Oh, go on then, bring him in," Cormac said.

Atia rushed down to the dock.

Alban Thomas Jones was a silver-haired Welshman. He was dressed in royal blue trousers and a white silk shirt with the sleeves rolled up. His swift ketch had a blue and green dragon figurehead. The name *Cymru* was carved into a plank at the bow. He'd been a friend to the O'Malleys' for as long as Atia could remember. She waved and ran to him with a giddy, wounded gallop, jumping into his arms as he spun her around.

"It is good to see you!" Atia flinched.

"Take it easy." He patted her shoulder. "Are you hurt?"

"It was worth the hug."

"I can't tell you how much it pleases me to see you." He noticed the welcoming committee. "I heard a rumor that the most beautiful woman in all the world was seen in these parts. I wanted to see for myself if it was true."

Atia's face flushed.

"And sure enough it is. Hey, I'm real sorry about your ma. Lovely lass, she was. But to see you alive, I can't tell you how happy it makes me."

"And Liv."

"Livia's alive too?" Jones grinned in a happy daze. "Your da's gonna blow my head off. I'm the one who told them you all died in the wreck. No doubt my credibility's shot to hell, but I don't mind one bit."

Atia passed him a bottle of rum.

"Oi, she's getting better looking every minute, too!" He uncorked the top and took a drink. "Ahoy, maties!" Jones waved at everyone.

Cormac charged forward. "I outta blow yer fucking head off! But I'm too happy!" He shook hands and gave Jones a hug.

"What brings ya in? Not that it's not good to see you, but the crop's a bit wee just yet," Rourke advised.

Jones noticed the Capitaine. "Bless me with the Black Death if I ever tell a lie, it's Capitaine El Cocodrilo!"

"Oui, no see long time."

"I didn't recognize you without the beard." Jones shook the Capitaine's hand warmly. "Still breathing, so I can't complain. It's just as well you're here; we should talk."

"Why don't you all feast with us?" Rourke offered.

"Nay, another time." Jones shook his head. "We're heading into the village for a few pints. Thought we'd tie her off here for the night, if you don't mind?"

"Course, anytime," Cormac said.

"Right, lads," Jones addressed the crew. "Head on up and I'll join you in a spell." His men grumbled happily as they moved up the shore. "And try not to get us kicked out before I even get there." He turned to Atia. "Oi, kids, do you mind if I have a word with your da for a moment? Arr, pirate talk!"

"What am I, five?" Atia sneered. "Yeah, sure. Race ya boys up?" She eyed Aedan and Elias. The twins' eyes glistened with competitive spirit, and they were off like dogs after a stick.

Atia shook her head slowly followed.

La Roche waited until Atia cleared away. Jones arriving was no coincidence; something sinister was up. Perhaps they had been followed after all?

"I'm glad to have caught you first, Capitaine," Jones said.

"What is it?" Cormac asked.

"Crisp's Mandingo showed up in Antonio Bay with a big galley and blew Bleedin Art's frigate all to hell with a fire breathing monster head."

La Roche's face betrayed his nerves. "A fire ship?"

"Aye," Jones said. "That guy's mean. Everyone and their cousin's cousin cleared out, including me. My wife sailed out the moment he appeared. She has a keen sense of these things. I'll come home one day to find a note saying 'dinner's on the rack and, by the way, yer surrounded by now, so save some for later.'" He pulled a parchment from his pocket. "I wasn't pulling strokes when I said I knew Atia was here. Your likeness went up the same time they rowed in."

"Bloody hell," Cormac huffed. "But you weren't followed."

La Roche frowned. "Not by land, no. Your men, they know we're here." He eyed Jones with uncertainty for a moment.

"Don't you worry about my men. They don't know nothing and they don't say shit."

"We've gotta get her out of here," Cormac insisted.

"What'll we do with her? She can't go to Aragua," Rourke replied.

"We'll take her to the Caymans for now."

"I'll let you think that through yerself," Rourke said.

La Roche's pulse began to race. "I'll take her with me."

Cormac's expression was less than favorable. "I was afraid you'd say that."

"Her safety is my main concern," la Roche assured. "We'll need a ride."

"Aye, say the word. We'll take you anywhere ya wanna go," Jones offered.

"I'm grateful for my little girl's life, gentlemen." Cormac choked back emotion. "And I ask you to keep her safe once again."

"She is my goddaughter, after all," Jones said.

"I will protect her, I swear it," la Roche vowed.

"Is Crisp's monster still in Antonio Bay?" Cormac asked.

"Aye. I got him watched. They're loading provisions tonight and we'll know the minute he leaves. I've got a man with a signal lamp out on the point," Jones said.

"That is one advantage," la Roche added. "He gets poor mileage. He cannot take food for long voyages."

They turned and strolled back to the bonfire where the feast awaited. A breeze blew in from the water and the stars twinkled against the blackish-blue sky.

"Cooked to perfection!" Gladstone stuffed his mouth full of freshly boiled shrimp.

"I see you still got that bloody bird." Jones pointed. "What kind is it again?"

"What was it again?" La Roche watched Atia, waiting for the twisted pronunciation, which came out, "bra-bill part."

"Come again?" Jones smirked.

Atia appeared mystified that no one understood her.

"Well, he's the only bad-balled pirate I ever seen!" Jones beamed, and then turned his attention to Natalia and Catharina. "Bless my heart, ladies, did I die and go to heaven?"

"Yeah, that never gets old either." Atia shook her head. "Jonesy, this is Natalia and Catharina from Hanover."

He kissed their hands. "Charmed, tickled, and thunderstruck all at once, I am. Pleased to meet you, ladies."

La Roche stared at Atia. It had become a game they played: he'd look away when she made eye contact, and then he'd meet her gaze until she averted her eyes. Silly though it was, he wouldn't have it any other way. Calling a truce, he tucked his arms around her waist.

"What can we do for ya, Alban?" Gladstone asked drunkenly.

"A couple of tons of Strangewayes's medicinal herb plants and some of his ginger ale. God, that stuff's good!"

Atia rested her hands on la Roche's arms. "I thought it was Mrs. Beazley's ginger ale?"

"For marketing purposes, it just sounds better coming from a man," Gladstone said. "I'll put you down for a few crates."

Jones signaled a thumb up. "Stupendous!"

Rourke and Cormac both raised their bottles.

"To Atia and Livia!" Cormac took a swig.

"Returned to us from the sea. Thank you, Poseidon!" Rourke tossed a handful of shrimp on the fire. "We're very grateful that they were delivered once again to their proper home and loved ones. May they always return safe and sound."

Everyone clapped.

"Wait, I got another!" Cormac belted. "May they live to be old and rich!"

"Old and rich!" Jones raised his bottle.

"I ain't done yet," Cormac continued.

"Oh, Jesus Christ! Sit down and have another goddamn drink, O'Malley, you're making me dizzy!" Jones yanked on Cormac's shirt, and then turned to Catharina. "Pass the butter, would ya, love?"

"I haven't had butter since home." Catharina handed it over, savoring the bread.

"It don't last long in the tropics. Not much does."

Atia raised the whiskey bottle and took a mouthful before passing it to la Roche. He drank deeply, satisfied that he would be the one to take her away.

"So, why are ya called Mad O'Malley, Da?"

"I often wondered that myself," Jones added.

La Roche snorted. "He's mad."

"It's a serious question," she said.

"Oui. That is the correct answer. He is completely mad."

Cormac shrugged. "It was a perfectly sound attack."

"Well, are you gonna tell us?" Atia challenged.

"All right, I will tell you why he is called Mad O'Malley," la Roche replied. "Cormac's Pikeys were first on the beach at Sainto Domingo and the Cagway, and they were behind enemy lines at Maracaibo under Henry Morgan."

Cormac leaned forward. "We're supposed to be talking about me and he brings up Morgan!"

"I'm getting to you. Cormac's Pikeys were already famous and when we attacked Maracaibo."

Cormac raised his bottle. "The Capitaine planned that one!"

"Oui. We sailed right into Lake Maracaibo under friendly flags and landed his men behind the city," la Roche continued.

"We had the Spanish believing they were being attacked from the land," Cormac interjected.

"I was telling the story!"

"Then tell it right! They moved all their big guns against us while the main force was hiding down in the lake. Four larger ships and nine sloops. We caught them with their trousers down when we sailed up around San Carlos Island with seven hundred men!" Cormac burst out laughing.

La Roche drew a diagram in the sand. "But the weather went bad on us and a storm came down this way and blew the ships deep into the lake. We couldn't reach the city in time. Henry's ships were too far behind and the Spanish had time to call for help. Admiral Campos's armada of four big war galleons came down from the north. They pinned us down and took up position further out, waiting for us to try to break free. They had the wind and surrounded us. We were dead." La Roche pointed at Cormac. "So, *he* takes a handful of men out in longboats with a white flag, yelling truce. And one of those fat galleons, *Magdalena*?"

Cormac nodded.

"Big ship. She came over to pick them up and then *boom*! His boat exploded, killing the boarding party."

"We was alongside in the water dragging rafts weighted to the waterline – pure genius!" Cormac exclaimed. "The boats were filled with straw-stuffed decoys with a grenade shoved up each one's arse sitting on top of six barrels of gunpowder each!"

"Panic broke out on the galleon," la Roche scoffed. "They didn't know what hit them! We could see Old Campos himself hopping up and down, screaming his head off on the deck of his flagship! Then we saw O'Malley and his men appear up on the other side of the *Magdalena*. They killed everyone on the quarterdeck."

"And then the poop deck, where we took the captain hostage!" Cormac jeered.

"Then the flagship came alongside. What was it called, again?"

"*Nuestra Senora de Aronzazu y San Lorenzo*."

"Yeah, yeah. So, Campos's soldiers swarmed the deck and took the ship back. And then *boom*!" La Roche thrust his hands in the air.

"A bloody work of art if I do say so meself!" Cormac roared, almost falling over. "We demanded they lead us to the prisoners and the bloody fools fell for it. They led us below and we set all the gunpowder ablaze. We jumped out the gun holes while they boarded the ship. Then o'course, *boom*! Both ships went up in flames!"

"The other two galleons thought they were outclassed or something." La Roche shook his head, grinning. "I don't know, but they moved off."

"I willed them away with the power of me mind!" Cormac boasted.

"Oui, whatever. So, we call him Mad O'Malley. Everyone gets a nickname and it was better than Paddy O'Toole."

"Personally, I liked Miracle O'Malley. But it didn't stick."

"Years later he was with us at Panama, but fortune was against us," la Roche lamented. "History tells it as a great victory."

"I lost half me men to disease and exhaustion." Cormac finally sat down after swaggering about. "The Spanish trampled down the rest with a cattle stampede. Granted, they got us good there. We didn't see that coming." He turned to Jones. "How about you? When did you sail with the Capitaine?"

"Curaçao."

"Oh, that one. Another time, maybe?" La Roche rubbed the back of his neck.

"What happened at Curaçao?" Atia pressed.

Jones leaned forward. "A fucking hurricane. You know all about them."

"Aye, I do." Atia gave a good-natured smile.

"We lost half our main force when we hit the reef. The troops turned back and went home. The few of us that were left carried on wounded. We went on to take the Spanish in Caracas." Jones eyed la Roche. "Remember those crazy Germans they had guarding Caracas? Reiters, I think they were called, all wearing armor."

La Roche shook his head. "No, doesn't ring a bell."

"I think they were guarding a settlement called Aragua?" Jones continued. "I was there at Île-à-Vache when Henry Morgan's flagship exploded. The Capitaine was on that ship."

"Oui," la Roche said reluctantly. "I think I passed over your ship on my way out of the bay."

"You flew pretty far; I'll give ya that."

"We were having dinner, all the captains on the quarterdeck of Henry's flagship the *Oxford*, when she blew up into a million pieces and all of us with her." La Roche noticed Atia's astonishment. "All the new captains died and many good friends."

"I picked Henry out of the water damn near a hundred feet away off the stern." Jones made a pulling motion with his whole arm. "He was never the same after that. The bottle became his best and only friend."

"Your adventures are fascinating!" Natalia said.

Atia's mouth hung open. "I'll say, I never knew you were all so daring!"

"They're not all adventure stories." Cormac's face darkened. "I heard you went into the Darien Jungle with l'Olonnais in '68. I often wondered if what we heard was true?"

La Roche was silent for a moment. "The silver train blew up in our faces."

"What's that?" Atia asked.

"It's the shipments of gold and silver collected from all over the Spanish Main. Loaded on mules they're shipped to the major ports in time to meet the treasure fleet. The Spanish set a trap for us and l'Olonnais took to cutting hostages into pieces." La Roche paused. "He lost his mind."

"Who is l'Olonnais?" Atia queried.

"One of the most famous and ruthless French privateers, although he was never a pirate," Jones explained.

"The flagship ran aground and we ended up in the longboats. The wind took us south. What few of us were left went down into the jungles of the Darien region seeking food, and it turned out to be us. We were captured by head-hunters and taken back to be slaughtered one by one. They were all ripped apart. I was there," la Roche said.

"And those who were alive had to eat those who weren't?" Jones asked.

"Oh no, often we had to eat who was still alive and sometimes kicking." La Roche would never get the taste of flesh and blood out of his mouth.

Atia gasped. "By the gods!"

"People ask me what l'Olonnais was like. I say, salty." He laughed mirthlessly. "Could use some tenderizing. Does that make me a second-generation cannibal? L'Olonnais once ate the heart of a Spaniard."

"Was good shrimp, that." Gladstone covered his mouth.

"I never ate a man per say. But that's a whole other subject." Jones winked at Catharina. "Well, I'm gonna head off to the village and find out how much trouble my men have got me into. You'll know what I know when I know it."

"I know," Cormac said.

"I'll walk you out." Atia latched onto Jones's arm and they ambled down the trail past the bungalows.

"It disturbs you that I have eaten the flesh of a man?" La Roche met Catharina's eyes.

"By Nerthus, no, try living on the Ottoman front."

"War drives men mad," Cormac stated. "They do things they don't normally do."

"War is an excuse for men to be mad. They become savages, bloodthirsty monsters," Natalia insisted.

"Yes, it's how men form relationships," Catharina added.

Laughter erupted among the tension.

"It's true!" la Roche agreed. "It creates a band of brothers like that Shakespeare play says."

Rourke grabbed his fiddle and cranked out "The Wild Rover". The twins ushered Natalia and Catharina to their feet for a dance. When Atia returned she joined her brother Lucas for a twirl until her ribs could handle no more and she went to la Roche.

"I cannot stand to see a woman in pain," he professed, removing a tincture of laudanum from his pocket. Mixing a few drops in some water, Atia drank it back gratefully.

"Not too much of that!" Cormac reprimanded. "I've lost good men to that stuff!"

"The doc says it's a low dose and if helps me pain, then what's the harm?"

"You just make sure ya stop taking it when yer healed."

Catharina swaggered towards la Roche. "Capitaine, until I met you, I thought all pirates were bloodthirsty, evil men who would betray anyone for a price. But I believe you to be an honest man."

La Roche raised his bottle. "Oui, you are very perceptive."

"Are you coming with us to Aragua?"

"There's been change of plan on that," Rourke interrupted. "Me back is getting worse. So, you and the lads will have to do it. I'm in no shape to be piloting a boat."

"Us?" Aedan's eyes widened.

Elias looked suspicious. "You never let us go anywhere."

"It'll be good for both of you and it's a fast run."

The twins stared at each other. "Ya hear that? We're going to Aragua," Elias exclaimed.

"Yer sure?" Lucas pressed.

"Very sure. Yer sailing out at first light, so be ready, lads." Rourke patted Lucas on the shoulder. "You'll all do just fine."

Cormac turned to the bonfire to hide his face.

“How long does it take from here?” Natalia asked.

“I’d estimate two to three weeks.” Lucas took a swig of rum.

“Not long to wait now,” Rourke comforted. “And me boys will get you there in one piece.” He picked up his fiddle and played an upbeat jig.

“Gets hotter down south, it does,” Lucas said.

Both Natalia and Catharina pouted. “Hotter?”

Atia enticed la Roche to dance and soon they were in each other’s arms.

“You should be taking it easy,” he said.

“I am easy.”

“I know.”

Rourke shook his head. “Aye, just like her mother.”

“Spitting fucking image is right!” Cormac wiped his eyes. “Well!” he said loudly, “I’m turning in. Mind if I have a word with yer Capitaine?”

“Sure.” Atia went to the bonfire.

“We thought we’d be learning French by now. Saint-Domingue promised an invasion.”

“Well, here I am,” la Roche said.

“I sent for my family with the understanding that the English would no longer rule the island. What went wrong?”

“When you find out, you can tell me. And why didn’t you send for me?” La Roche wondered. “I could have brought your family here!”

“I thought you was dead.”

“That never stopped me before.”

“I didn’t want to ask Bartolomeo Portuguese.”

“The Brethren of the Coast owes you, not the other way around. I shall never let anything bad happen to Atia.”

“Better not. And I don’t wanna know if ya fucked her, either.”

La Roche nodded. “She’s a lot like her mother.”

“I said I didn’t want to know!”

“She will be safe with me, I swear,” la Roche said.

“Me ears are burning!” Atia called. “In some cultures that’s considered rude, including mine.”

“Me girl should be resting up – we’re going fishing in the morrow. This time I won’t throw you in.” He gave her a smile. “Good night, everyone.”

"Good night, Da."

"We're going to bed as well. Good night, everyone." Natalia waved, helping to steady Catharina.

La Roche searched for more rum, but alas it was gone. "I will return." He took the short path to his bungalow. Inside he refilled his silver canteen with the remains of his only bottle of Chartreuse Liqueur d'Elixir.

"What ya doing?" Atia spoke suddenly, standing in the doorway to the bedroom.

La Roche jumped. "Sneaking up on a pirate is a good way to get killed!"

She approached him coyly.

"I was looking to refill this." He recapped his canteen and stuffed it back into his jacket.

Atia slid her hand between his legs. "Well, I was just looking for these." She kissed him urgently and untied his trousers, grasping at his organ.

La Roche grabbed at her delectable rear. "Be careful. You must finish what you start." He gave her a fiendish grin and backed her up against a chest of drawers. Lifting her onto the edge, it was easy to access the delicious wetness between her thighs.

"So, let's start so we can finish." She hiked up her dress and wrapped her legs around him.

Henry
Morgan
GO
2015

Precious Cargo and a Giant Mullet

Atia was summoned for a very early breakfast with the entire O'Malley family at Rourke's bungalow. There was something odd, yet satisfying, about their reunion. She dreamt of being with her family again for so many years, and now it seemed unreal. Her brother, Lucas and her half-brothers, Aedan and Elias were in good spirits, excited about their journey to Aragua. They heckled each other, making her uncle laugh. Rourke gazed at them with pride and an underlying sadness. Her da was quiet throughout the meal; something weighed heavily upon him. When they finished, her da squeezed her hand and said it was time see their guests off and get fishing.

Atia took some provisions to Natalia and Catharina for breakfast. Gladstone showed up to collect the few bags they had. Soon they strolled down to the ramp beside the docks. The Capitaine caught up with them and admired Cormac's swift ketch.

"Now, promise you'll write?" Gladstone said.

Natalia seemed depressed. "Of course."

"If yer looking for Yaguara, he said he was gonna scout the coastline. He told me to give you this." Gladstone removed a ceremonial shawl and a jaguar claw necklace from his bag. "He said ya didn't have much in the way of clothes for the trip down and thought you might want it."

Natalia took it, genuinely grateful.

Catharina kissed Gladstone's cheek.

"I always like being thanked."

The Capitaine examined the ship's nameplate. "*Rover*?"

"Aye," Cormac said.

The Capitaine caressed the rail. "She was *El Diabolito* when I knew her. Lost her to the Spanish at Maracaibo, I did. You know, I always wondered what happened to her."

"I took her from the Spanish at Maracaibo. She was beached and they couldn't get her loose, so we took her."

"This is the first ship I ever captained. There's nothing faster that touches the sea. I'm glad to see she is in good hands."

Cormac watched Lucas give orders. "We take good care of her."

"She prefers leeward, for some reason."

"Aye, you noticed," Cormac said.

"Thank you, Capitaine." Catharina swallowed her emotions. "Thank you for all your help."

Natalia threw her arms around Atia. "This is not goodbye."

Atia could feel the tears prickling her eyes. "I know."

"Every time you see Mars flicker red, you say hello from me and I'll be thinking of you."

Catharina sniffed. "Take good care of yourself, Atia."

"Oh, Mr. Gladstone?" Natalia removed a dagger to sever a long lock of her hair. She tied it with a ribbon. "Can you please give this to Mr. Jaguar when you see him? Tell him to make something nice out of it if he wants to remember me."

"Will do." Gladstone placed the hair in his satchel.

Natalia slid the jaguar claw necklace over her head so it hung beside her heart.

Aedan grabbed the wheel and Elias directed crewmen on the main deck. Those remaining returned to the dock and the gangway was removed. Everyone waved goodbye.

"So, how much do you get for them?" the Capitaine asked.

Gladstone grinned. "Twenty thousand doubloons."

"Each," Cormac said and they all moved back along the ramp to the shore.

"I'll take thirty percent. I delivered them over the Blue Mountains," the Capitaine said.

Cormac grumbled a bit. "Fine."

Business is business, Atia thought and she watched the coastline. "Yaguara is nowhere to be seen."

"He's here. Keeping an eye out," the Capitaine said.

Gladstone released a wide yawn. "He's always on the alert, that Yaguara. Though, I'd love to stay and chat, I think sleeping the day away might be more medically sound. I'll catch you up later." He went back to his bungalow.

The Capitaine scanned the horizon with his telescope. "Oui. That sounds like good advice."

"We're going fishing. Care to join us?" Atia offered.

"No. Like Yaguara, I'm always working." He winked at her and she blew him a kiss.

Atia stared at her da. "As long as ya don't push me in."

"I would never! Well, never again," he corrected.

She followed him down to some older docks deeper in the cove. *Rover* sailed out behind them.

"I couldn't sleep last night," Cormac professed. "Kept hearing yer mother's voice and she told me what she wants me to do."

"We'll bring her back in one piece!" Elias called from the ship.

Cormac waved. "Remember PC, boys. Hands off!"

"PC?" Atia queried.

"Precious cargo."

"But what if my charm and charisma proves to be too much for them?" Elias hollered back.

"Remember to alternate hands, left and right, so yer prick doesn't get bent!" Cormac said.

Atia followed her da to a dock where fishing gear was already laid out. Minuit and couple of sea birds inspected the area for fish. She scanned the trees and noticed the remains of a fishing boat jammed into the branches above from the recent storm.

"See, I even built you a tree house!" Cormac boasted.

Minuit whistled at Atia.

"Those birds are a bloody nuisance." Cormac scowled, picking up the fishing rods.

"A nuisance?" Atia grumbled. "This is their home, not ours. Yer a good boy, yes you are!"

Minuit whistled. "Who's a pretty bird?"

"They're all scavengers, and they'd peck yer eyes out soon as look at ya, they would."

"Bent prick!" Minuit screeched.

Cormac's eyes widened for a moment, and then he attached bait to his line. "Now be mindful of where the hook goes. This is where eyeballs fly out because someone's being stupid." He passed her a rod and cast his line out. "Drop it out and let the current take it."

Atia threw her line out near his.

"Good, but not so close though. You don't want to tangle them." Her father watched the lines drift by for a moment, and then coughed. "So, do you love…what the hell's his name? It was Gator Gar or El Capitaine."

Atia laughed. "I just call him the Capitaine."

"But you do love him?"

"Aye, I do."

"And yer wanting to marry him?" He watched her face. "I can see it in yer eyes."

Atia's pulse quickened. "We was married the moment our eyes met."

"He's a wanted man. He can't stay here, you know that. The two of you'll be off with Gladstone."

She felt wounded. "Am I to make a choice?"

Cormac patted her shoulder. "No, it's for your own good. Crisp sent his mercenary after you. I wasn't gonna say." He lifted her chin. "I love you, but it's not safe here."

"If it ain't safe, then why are you staying? We can all leave together."

"Then we'd be hunted down. I had it all worked out, but yer dying and all messed us up a bit. We're gonna need to find another place and start over. I've been here forever, and it's you they're seeking. You stick out some. When it's safe we'll start over, just like we've done before."

"All we ever do is start over." Atia gazed at the water and reeled in her line. "I remember this bay, and I dreamed of the day I could come home to it. We've been on the run our whole lives. He took everything from us." Her head sank.

"Not everything." He lifted her chin. "It took me too long to get you back. For that I'm sorry. But we'll have to wait a little longer."

Atia nodded. "We knew you was coming. We never gave up hope, even after you was arrested for piracy. Figured you'd be late though, being sentenced to death and all."

"A last-minute pardon from the governor kept me from the gallows. A deal that I would remain here for the rest of me days and never again challenge Crisp's claim on you. A deal that I'll never keep." They threw their lines back out and Cormac observed the Capitaine scanning the coastline in the distance. "I'm not saying I approve of yer choices either, but fatherly advice don't sound right coming from a pirate. Still, right now, you're safer going with him. Yer sister was always the sensible one. That's why I never believed she was related. Yer gonna need to look out for her now, too."

Atia cracked a painful smile. "Me? Look out for Liv? You don't know what yer asking!"

They watched *Rover*. Its mainmast unfurled to catch the wind.

"Sometimes you gotta pick up and start over. This time we'll do it right. This time you'll have a home for good." Cormac wrapped his arms around her.

For over an hour they fished until Cormac accepted defeat. Atia held up a giant mullet, comparing it to the miniature one in her da's hand. She whistled victoriously as they strolled back to the bungalows.

"Don't gloat." Cormac scowled. "It was my lure anyway. Ya catch one fish and yer Jesus fuckin' Christ!" He opened the door to his house and lay the fish on the table in the kitchen.

"How are we gonna cook them?"

"We'll wrap 'em in banana leaves and pop 'em on the fire."

Atia's stomach was already growling. "Mmm!"

"While I gotcha here, there's something you need to see." He led her to the main sleep chamber and dragged a case out from beneath the bed. "Got these for your mother. They should go to you." He opened it to reveal two sharp silver stilettos with finely adorned handles.

Atia eyed them with admiration and picked one up.

"Think of them as a birthday gift. One for each decade I missed," he mused. "She could throw these things, ya know."

She examined it, feeling the tip with her finger. "Ma always liked shiny sharp things."

"I mean it. She was a natural. She wanted to join a traveling variety act as their female knife thrower, but accidentally killed the owner at the audition."

Atia rolled her eyes. "That ain't true!"

Her father raised his right hand. "True as the Virgin Mary. Spanish silver, they are."

"They're lovely, thank you."

Her father pushed the bed aside to reveal a hidden door in the floor. "Just one more thing you gotta see – the crawl space." He took a pry bar from a shelf and lifted up the floorboard to reveal a hole in the ground below. He reached down and cleared away dirt until he found a latch and opened it. "As much as I respect the man, this ain't for yer Capitaine. It's for you alone. This is the family insurance policy."

"You have a secret stash?"

"All pirates got secret stashes and caches, even me. None of you will ever find it, though." He set a chest on the floor and unlocked it. Inside, gold coins, bars, and jewelry glistened. "Don't tell yer Capitaine, but some of us fared better than others after Panama. I meself took a few trinkets for sentimental reasons. Rourke knows I'm showing you. If anything happens to me, there's plenty for all of you unless you turn into squabbling arseholes." He handed her a map and she opened it.

"Yer kidding me! A pirate treasure map?"

"Where the hell else would we keep it? You can't trust a bank!"

"Why don't you keep it?"

"Because Rourke and me know where it is. Lucas has the starting point, a day north of Cayman Brac, and you got the map, so everyone gets a share. It's not the Incan fuckin' treasure, anyway."

He withdrew a velvet drawstring pouch and handed it to Atia. She recognized it as having belonged to her mother.

"Open it. This'll tide you over for now."

Startled by the weight of the bag, she opened it to discover ten gold doubloons and four gold bars. "This is real gold?"

"For you and Livia. You'll need it to start over and lay low, someplace safe."

"But," Atia stammered.

"You're welcome."

"I didn't come for gold." She tucked the pouch under her arm. "I'll take it, don't get me wrong, but when will we finally have a home and be together?" Tears rolled down her cheeks.

Cormac put his arms around her. "Home is where we already be, for bad or worse. You'll not go from me sight, only from me view."

Atia sniffed. "What the hell does that even mean?"

"Maybe you gotta be drunk to fully appreciate it." He shrugged. "You'll have to make yer home where you can for now."

A pecking noise came at the window and Minuit whistled.

Cormac jumped. "There is something unholy about that bird! Maybe the bloody Christians had a point with this one."

Atia peered out. "I guess the Capitaine wants us."

Cormac replaced the chest in the cavity beneath the floor and led Atia outside. The Capitaine was there, speaking with a sleepy Gladstone.

"Why are we summoned by the bird?" Cormac growled.

Atia tilted to one side with the weight of the velvet satchel under one arm and the stiletto case under the other.

"Don't look too obvious, uh?" The Capitaine handed the telescope to Cormac. "Anyone you know?"

Cormac looked to the north. "Nobody I know, and she ain't fishing."

Jones drew near with his crew and Yaguara.

"I lost contact with my lookout." Jones caught his breath. "We're heading out."

"To the ships!" Cormac called. "Can you spare some men? *Lucky Charms* will cover your back."

The Capitaine gave her an urgent gaze. "You must come with me, now."

Sadness filled her. "Must I now? Da?"

"Aye, you gotta go, love. We'll see you again."

She shook her head. "Don't make me go."

Jones tapped her shoulder. "My dear, it would be an honor if you would sail with me once again."

"Aye, she's ready," Cormac said. "Yer things were already taken aboard."

Atia's eyes welled.

"Crisp will send someone for ya no matter where we go," Rourke said. "We gotta deal with this now."

Atia took a deep breath. "I know."

Cormac gave Atia a hug. "You gotta be more careful. He has associates in every port. Any one of which would love to snatch you up and present you to him. I'm sure yer Capitaine already knows that, so stay away from the cities."

"Goodbye, Uncle Rourke. I'm sorry you didn't get to see Livia." She wrapped her arms around him.

"Give Liv me best, would ya?"

"Aye." She climbed aboard Jonesy's ship, where the crew prepared to sail.

"Cast off!" Jones said.

Atia's legs were numb as she stepped aboard. She felt as if it were a dream. As if she'd wake up in the bungalow at any moment, ready to have breakfast with her family. Gladstone took the satchel and the stiletto case and put them with the rest of Atia's things. She waved back at her da and uncle in silence.

A Game of Cat and Mouse

Atia was unaware of how much time had passed, but the wind had picked up and *Cymru* moved at a decent pace. The sky above was steely gray. "Looks like it's going to rain." Beside her, Minuit sat on the rail and she fed him cashews. Another bird flew by and he took off.

Jones stroked her back before climbing to the quarterdeck. "You best be getting inside, love."

Her hands shook as she gripped the rail.

"I think she's content here," the Capitaine said as he joined her. "This ship here." He pointed to an approaching sloop. "We're going to check her out and make sure she doesn't get too close to our friends there."

Atia nodded. "Aye, let's check them out, then."

The Capitaine met Yaguara, who had a spyglass pointed at the *Rover* – fixed on Natalia. "Did Yaguara make the right choice?"

"No. Yaguara should have banged her all the way to the Yucatán."

"Well, don't breed over her all day."

"It's 'brood', and Yaguara's not watching her. He's watching *her*." He indicated the new ship. "Her speed has doubled since we first saw her."

"She's on an intercept course," Jones said.

Atia could clearly see the triangular sails of the ship closing in on *Rover*.

Yaguara lowered his viewer. "*Rover's* picking up speed, but the sloop had a good run when she came down from the north. They'll catch them in half an hour. I can make out a figurehead. It's *Bloody Mary*."

"Is it someone you know?" Atia asked.

"Slasher Al," the Capitaine said.

Her stomach squirmed. "Slasher Al?"

"Maybe you should wait inside?" the Capitaine said.

"We gotta stop him!"

"Thanks love," Jones replied, eyeing the Capitaine. "How are we gonna stop him?"

"Maybe we could just slow them down a bit. *Rover* would have more time and they could lose them in the rain." The suggestion came from Gladstone.

Jones and the Capitaine were impressed.

"I read a lot of pirate books," Gladstone admitted.

"Lads," Jones said, addressing the crew, "we're going into battle. Intercept course, north-northwest!"

The Capitaine blew his whistle and watched the sky. "Come on, Minuit. No time to play!" He glanced at Atia. "Keep low. When I say hit the deck, you hit the deck."

"Aye."

The Capitaine moved to the quarterdeck. "Permission to come up?"

"What is this, the *Queen Elizabeth*? Stop being so goddamn formal and get yer arses up here!" Jones said. "This cat and mouse stuff is your forte. I'm not real fond of being a mouse chasing a cat, either."

Minuit swooped in beside Atia.

"Peril!" the Capitaine said.

Atia nodded. "Peril!"

Minuit flew away swiftly towards Jamaica.

Be safe, my little friend, Atia thought.

Jones took over the rudder. "Take over as navigator, please, Mr. Yaguara. Man the guns, please, Capitano?"

Atia made for the bow of the vessel to watch.

Gladstone joined her by the rail and took a firm hold. "I'll stay here with Atia for luck."

The Capitaine surveyed the ship's cannons. "Sponges and worms, men. Quickly!" The crew started scrubbing the inside of the guns. "Clean them out good!"

Jones paced. "Are you sure we got time for that?"

"Well, if you would keep them in proper condition I wouldn't have to."

Aboard the green and yellow ketch, *Lucky Charms*, Cormac O'Malley supervised the young crewmen he'd borrowed from Jones. They brought the ship up to speed. He could tell they were getting nervous; this was something they'd never seen before. "Yer captain and my girl are in trouble," he called. "We're gonna do something about it. You with me, lads?"

The men cheered.

Cormac already felt the ship move faster. He was always amazed at what could be accomplished with a little spirit.

"Heading, Captain?" Rourke asked. "What's the plan?"

Cormac pointed his spyglass ahead. He recognized the sloop trying to intercept *Rover*. Slasher Al. The game had changed. "Intercept that sloop at all speed!" His heart began to race. "Ready the bow mortars!" He and four crewmen rushed to the bow of the ship to uncover two huge crab traps.

They lifted and tossed the traps overboard. Beneath were two wide cannons angled up. "Newton's Law, lads." Cormac opened an ammunition crate filled with bombs. "What goes up must come down."

Jones's men worked the ropes while others loaded the mortars.

"Load starboard four-pounders!" Rourke called and men loaded the small cannons.

Cormac knew if they could wound Slasher Al's *Bloody Mary*, then *Rover* would stand a chance of escape. One good hit from a mortar would send the pirates straight to the bottom of the sea.

"Starboard guns loaded," Rourke called. "Now load the portside guns."

Cormac snarled at the encroaching vessel. He'd blow it sky high before he let it anywhere near his family. "Bombs ready to fire! And more stay sail! Get her up to speed!"

A foul noise drifted over on the wind. It began with a drumbeat and progressed into chanting. Crewmen turned to find the source of the sound. A vessel advanced around the point in their direction.

"What the hell is that?" Cormac barked.

Rourke grimaced. "The Barbary galley!"

"It's Crisp's monster, Mandingo." Cormac checked the spyglass. "This could be a long day."

"Her speed's better by half."

"I want at least one good shot at *Bloody Mary* before we run. We need more speed. Stay sails!" Cormac ordered.

Rourke paced the deck. "She's faster than she looks."

"Aye. Laurens de Graaf used to have one. Back then he called it *Neptune.*"

Rourke gritted his teeth. "See that dragon's head! She breathes fire, right from the dragon's mouth. We don't want it catching up with us. Faster!"

"Bring *Bloody Mary* into bomb range," Comac said.

"You see those long galleys more in the east, around Madagascar." Rourke gave his brother a defiant sneer.

Cormac checked the wind indicators. "Ten degrees to port! Trim the sheets and get her up to speed!" The flash of a signaling mirror caught his eye. *Bloody Mary* raised a black flag, ordering *Rover* to surrender or die, while *Cymru* was hot on Slasher Al's trail. "Good man, Jonesy!" Cormac wiped his forehead and watched *Rover*. Lucas was yelling orders and soon they were cutting the lines to make a run for it. He shifted his view to Slasher Al's ship where they were loading two twelve-pound cannons at the bow.

Atia gripped the rail of the *Cymru*. The sea grew crowded at the arrival of Mandingo's ship, *Plutus* – a terrifying juggernaut with oars raking back and forth and a dragon head that breathed fire. She'd love to see that ship go up in flames alongside Slasher Al.

"*Bloody Mary's* got two big guns at the bow, ready to fire," Jones said.

"Those guns are for show," the Capitaine insisted. "It's impractical to have forward guns on a sloop."

A fiery eruption came as cannonballs blasted through the air and slammed into the sea behind *Rover*, causing an explosion of white water.

"Ah, they do work," the Capitaine said.

Bloody Mary fired again, this time at *Cymru*.

"Port side turn!" Jones ordered, and Yaguara pulled the rudder over. The ship leaned as shots soared past, blasting the sea behind them. "Ready to fire, starboard side!"

"Aye, prepare to fire!" the Capitaine called. "Powder." The crewmen packed gunpowder into the cannons. "Right to the end. Pack it in."

Jones smirked. "Next he's gonna fucking inspect them."

The Capitaine pointed. "Move guns into position!"

Chills crept along Atia's arms. She had never seen the Capitaine in action before. His presence was very commanding; she could only imagine him aboard his own ship. As Jonesy predicted, he walked the deck, inspecting the guns on both sides.

"Ready to fire!" the Capitaine ordered.

"Thank Christ!" Jones said.

Crewmen lit the torches.

"Hard to port. Starboard batteries," Jones called.

The Capitaine turned to Atia. "Keep your head down, don't be seen!"

She and Gladstone hunkered down, gripping the shroud pinrail. The ship leaned sharply and Atia could see *Bloody Mary*. Slasher Al sat in a chair on deck, watching them through a spyglass, while his men reloaded cannons. Atia swiftly ducked, hoping he hadn't noticed her.

"Let 'em have it!" Jones yelled.

"Fire!" the Capitaine said and a rain of fire was unleashed, tearing through *Bloody Mary's* sails and rigging. "Reload six-pounders with chain shot." Loud explosions and sulfur saturated the air. "Quoin in." Crewmen placed blocks under the cannons to adjust the angle and the gun ports opened.

"Wind change, four knots, west-northwest," Yaguara said.

"Get us closer!" the Capitaine insisted.

"Starboard, ten degrees. Ready to fire starboard batteries," Jones said.

Yaguara heaved the rudder.

"Aye! We fire on the highest pitch, over the mainmast!" the Capitaine instructed.

The chanting from Mandingo's ship drew closer. Atia felt ill. She'd heard this prelude to death before. She peered over the rail as cannons fired, this time from *Lucky Charms*. "Da," she whispered. Bombs soared through the air and pounded the water beside *Bloody Mary*, showering her with white water.

"Quoin in," the Capitaine said. "Chain shot ready!"

Curiosity drove Atia to stand for a clear view. *Bloody Mary* bobbed up and down on the water in plain sight. "Fire!" she yelled and a crewman torched a cannon. Chain shot flew at the men on *Bloody Mary's* main deck.

The Capitaine cursed in French. "Fire!" The other three cannons discharged chain shot.

Cannon fire from Slasher Al's ship came back at them.

"Hit the deck!" the Capitaine yelled.

Atia dropped where she was. Cannonballs slammed through the deck, smashing the shroud pinrailings. She tucked her head beneath her arms. Debris flew everywhere, ripping over her. After the air settled, the Capitaine's hand touched the back of her head and she looked up. "I'm fine."

"I'm not," Gladstone exclaimed.

The Capitaine was relieved. "Stay down." He faced the crew. "Next time, wait for me."

"She's snaking!" Jones hollered.

"Reload with chain," the Capitaine said.

Atia could see her da's ship in the distance with *Plutus* barreling down upon her. A jet of fire sprang from the mighty dragon's head at the bow of the ship. She clasped her hand to her mouth. The flames singed *Lucky Charms* and it turned sharply towards the coast. The fire ship pursued. The rain blew in, casting everything in a thin blanket of gray mist.

"Take this, *connard*!" the Capitaine jeered. "Ready to fire!"

Atia ran to the Capitaine's side. "Me da's in trouble!"

"I know. It's Crisp's war galley. They're after you."

"It's Mandingo. Can't we fire on the bastard?"

The Capitaine nodded. "Oui. We will." He pointed to *Bloody Mary*. "But he's closer and I hate the son of a bitch."

"Oh, by the way," Yaguara interjected, "she got one."

"She did?" Atia replied.

"Atia's chain shot took off a pirate's head."

"Is that what they're yelling about over there?" the Capitaine mused.

Atia stuck out her tongue at the enemy ship.

"Don't gloat, love," Jones advised. "You kill one bloody pirate and you think you're Henry fucking Morgan."

The Capitaine stuck out his tongue at her and returned to barking orders.

"Come on, we got a battle here!" Jones rallied. "Ready to fire!"

"Oui, ready to fire. Slasher Al is about to turn to starboard. I want to turn and fire at the same time. He snakes back and forth to be harder to hit, but he doesn't realize that he does the same turns over and over. Idiot!" the Capitaine gloated. "Torches ready and *voila*!"

Bloody Mary turned, as predicted.

"Ready and fire!"

Sure enough, the chain shot ripped through the sails and killed another pirate. The Capitaine gave Atia a smug look. *Nothing like a bit of friendly, murderous competition,* she thought.

Lucky Charms raced towards the coast. Cormac stood on deck watching the fire ship gain. "Not too fast, Rourke. Just keep us ahead of her for a while. Let's tire her out a bit with some more cat and mouse."

"I never liked being the mouse," Rourke growled.

Another jet of oily flame shot at them, just scorching the aft and the flag.

"Fire control!" Cormac said. "Upon reflection, I think we can go a wee bit faster, Rourke."

"Aye. Oars!"

Crewman scrambled to deploy the oars.

Cormac clapped his hands. "Let's get out of here. Row like you got a fire-breathing dragon blowing up yer arse!"

"'Cause ya do," Rourke added.

Lucky Charms sped up and they pulled a good distance away from *Plutus*.

"That's it! Keep it up lads! Drinks'r on me tonight!"

"They ought to be plenty tired by now," Rourke said.

Cormac also checked. Slaves continued to pump oil and more flames shot out towards them. Another line of slaves ran along the deck, taking over the oars one at a time. "Did they just do a fuckin' shift change without missing a stroke?" He looked at Rourke. "Where'd they learn that, Madagascar?"

"The Barbary Coast. Told ya she's faster than you think."

Cormac sighed. "Ready for evasive maneuvers. They plan on cooking us for supper!"

The flames almost licked the aft sails.

"Make for Anotto Bay!" Cormac pointed.

"Whoever made this guy a slave should be shot," Rourke exclaimed.

A rainy haze rolled in, thick and hard. *Plutus* seemed to vanish momentarily, although the chanting and drumbeat continued.

"Good. We'll lose them sure enough," Rourke said.

"Well, it's slowing us down." Cormac frowned. "Take us into Anotto Bay and run for the river. We'll sick the twins on them."

"Aye. Thirty degrees to port!" Rourke called. "Beat those sails, get the water off!"

Lucky Charms began to lag. The crew was exhausted, and they scarcely knew their location. They were heading into a shallow reef with jagged rocks.

"Almost there, lads," Cormac said.

"They'll follow us upriver," a crewman called.

"We ain't going upriver." Cormac gave a devious smile. "Ten degrees to port, Rourke. Thought you'd been here before?"

Rourke spun the wheel. "Aye. Ten degrees to port."

"This way, Captain Mandingo, sir!" Cormac said. "Right between the twins!" He and Rourke had discovered the dual coral reefs ages ago; and it had damn near destroyed their ship.

A jet of fire shot out of the murk, catching the sails.

"Don't panic," Rourke hollered. "Damage control!"

Crewman gathered to fight the fire while *Plutus* drew closer, ready to destroy them. However, with a loud crunch, the galley slammed into the reefs. Their hull was breached. Splintered wood fell to the sea. They hit again, and this time their tiller broke off.

Cormac watched with great satisfaction. "Starboard turn, Rourke. Take us out of the bay."

"Aye. Heading northwest."

"She's still a wounded beast, though. Head due north and get clear of her. We'll turn and take her down with bombs."

Nearby, *Cymru* sailed towards them, lining up alongside *Plutus*.

Rourke smiled. "Aye, and take her down we will."

From Jones's ship came four fiery cannonballs that slammed into the bow and blasted the dragon's head to pieces. Oily fire spread all over the vessel and the bow exploded. Men afire leapt into the water and another eruption consumed the rest of the ship, lighting up Anotta Bay.

Cormac turned to *Cymru* only meters away. Atia glanced back at him and waved. He raised his hand.

"Sorry, but she's on her own now," Rourke said.

"Aye, that she is, Rourke. That she is." Cormac addressed the crewmen, "You've done well, lads. Yer captain's gonna be damn proud of you. As am I. Drop us off and then carry on. Lay low for a while."

"But your ship?" a crewman asked.

"Yer holding onto her for us awhile, 'til yer captain gets back." Cormac trained his spyglass ahead, gazing at Atia. She stood beside her Capitaine, waving. Beautiful, just like her mother. He took a deep breath. "*Bon voyage*, my girl. It weren't meant to be this time."

Atia clutched the Capitaine's hand, watching *Lucky Charms* as it faded away. It was the most magnificent explosion she'd ever seen. The *Aeolus* had burst into flame, but nothing like this. She could still see her da and uncle from afar.

"There. You are happy now?"

"Oui, very, Capitaine."

Cymru turned, following the path of *Bloody Mary* as it pursued *Rover*. The Capitaine called out the order to fire again and more shots billowed. Smoke and sulfur hung in the air, while Slasher Al's crew dove for cover.

"Hard to port," Jones said.

Yaguara cranked the tiller, turning the vessel, while *Bloody Mary* shot back at them.

"Hard to starboard," Jones said.

"Man port side batteries," the Capitaine ordered.

Cymru leaned steeply and they all hung on.

"On the up roll, fire!" the Capitaine said.

They blasted another round of chain shot, ripping through *Bloody Mary's* sails.

"Steer north, Yaguara. Get some distance from her. They can't catch us now, love," Jones said to Atia.

"Ready for hard turn," the Capitaine instructed.

"Aye," Jones agreed. "Ready for hard turn."

Atia was confused and met the Capitaine's gaze. "But he said they can't catch us."

"That is exactly why he is going to shoot."

Bloody Mary lined up.

"What did I tell you? Who wants to bet on what he does next?"

"Port ten degrees," Jones said. "Incoming."

Bloody Mary fired, and a barrage of cannonballs screamed past, vanishing into the sea spray.

"Course north-northwest," Jones called.

"Aye, north-northwest," Yaguara echoed.

Behind them, *Bloody Mary* disappeared into the gray.

"Is it over?" Atia scarcely heard herself speak.

"What?" The Capitaine removed cotton from his ears. "Did you enjoy your first sea battle, my love?"

Atia stared at him, barely able to understand. She pointed at her ears.

"You had those the whole time?" Gladstone practically yelled.

The Capitaine shrugged. "Oops." He took the bird whistle from his pocket to signal Minuit.

Yaguara peered through a telescope. "No sign of her."

"Wait thirty minutes and turn due west," Jones ordered.

"What'll we do now?" Atia asked.

"We'll follow *Rover* west for a while until we're sure they're away," the Capitaine said.

"We have to go back for Livia."

"Oui. We will."

"Aye," Gladstone agreed. "We should get back to the plantation and start moving them out."

Yaguara frowned. "We have to move now, but where?"

"We careened near Santa Catalina in the mid-seventies, do you remember where?" the Capitaine asked.

"Yaguara agrees that's the perfect spot, but won't it piss off the Freebooters?" Yaguara replied.

"What can Jacquotte do to me that she hasn't already done?"

Both men laughed.

Atia stared into the murk, hoping to spot *Lucky Charms* again. They were all separated now. "I waited years to see them. *Years*. And now I'm gone again."

Minuit glided in from the mist, landing near Atia. "*Bon voyage*," he squawked.

The Capitaine put his arm around her and she leaned against him. He was her rock in this storm, keeping her safe and grounded. There were no words to express the gratitude, nor the sadness, she felt. They sailed off in silence through the gray haze.

Cormac O'Malley sat on a barrel next to a table smoking his pipe. The view from Rourke's house was pristine. The golden sunrise glistened on the water and seabirds skimmed the surface, catching breakfast. A rainbow flashed off in the distance. All that was missing were the kids and, of course, Lucretia. He had loved her beyond measure, yet forfeited his opportunity to marry her long ago.

He heard her voice plainly. “Not a shadow of doubt it’s yours,” Lucretia had said, informing him she was carrying his child, Lucas.

Cormac insisted he was going back out to sea.

Lucretia didn’t look the least bit surprised. “You don’t love me, then?”

“That’s not true.”

“You just love something more – plunder! Bloody pirates!”

Cormac took her hand. “I’m content with yer booty.” He smiled. “I want to be able to give you a home. I’m considered a penniless gypsy by your da, which is true for the most part.”

Lucretia stared into him with her brilliant green eyes. “Then why don’t you go into the shipping business with Rourke?”

Cormac shook his head. “Takes too long to be lucrative.”

“Yer ambition makes you a fool, O’Malley.”

“Tell Rourke it’s his. He’d go to the ends of earth for ya. He’ll take care of you,” Cormac assured.

“You really want to forgo yer own son? Which I be certain it is.”

He took a deep breath and pondered it.

“You’d better be damn certain. Something like this, you can’t take back,” Lucretia had warned and gave him a fiery kiss.

Cormac never realized the full gravity of the decision until he saw Atia again. He wiped his eyes. Rourke sat opposite him with a bottle of rum in his hand. Across the water, a ship slowly glided around the point. The damaged sloop *Bloody Mary* was on her way.

“Try some cunning and stealth, ya sorry bastards!” Cormac growled.

Rourke took a mouthful of rum. “It’s enough to make ya weep!” He lit a cigar and picked up his cards from the table.

“All right, where were we?” Cormac scrutinized his hand. “Do ya have any tens?”

“You already asked that one.”

“Shit! I’m too drunk to play this one, too. Fives, then?”

“Draw,” Rourke said. “That’s a piece of eight to me.”

“Up yers, it’s a shilling!”

“It was a piece of eight, ya tight bastard! We never bet a shilling.” Rourke took a coin from Cormac’s pile.

“Yeah, well good luck spending it!” Cormac flipped up his middle finger. “Where’d you learn this game? And don’t be saying Madagascar.”

“In a little lagoon called Libertatia, in Madagascar.”

Cormac cocked his eyebrow. “Never mind.” He tossed down his cards and grabbed his rum bottle, toasting. “Even if you didn’t sail the seas, you called this one well enough. Our ma would be proud. We took care of the lads and have the two most beautiful daughters in the world, returned from the dead, no less.”

They clinked their bottles.

“And not too soon, neither. We’re the two luckiest men in the world, you and I. You know that?”

Cormac smirked. “You won’t be thinking that in a few minutes’ time.”

“You know what I mean. Besides, we both fucked the most beautiful woman who ever walked the face of the earth. How many men can say that?”

“Lucretia? Half of fuckin’ Ireland!”

They toasted and took another drink.

“I wish I coulda seen her one more time.” Rourke grieved.

“You woulda yelled at each other the whole time and given us a fuckin’ headache.”

“Aye. But still I’d like to have seen her, to tell her I love her face to face. I never said it to her, ya know.” Rourke wiped his eyes. “A shilling says we live.”

“A shilling, eh?” Cormac sneered. “Like you’d really pay, ya tight bastard.”

There came a rustle of bushes and a snap of branches. A dozen pirates emerged, carrying cutlasses and guns. One pirate ventured up the steps to the front door and signaled others to check the adjacent bungalows. “Cormac O’Malley, Captain Slazerelli orders you to hand over Mr. Crisp’s property or die.”

“What if I was inclined to tell you to kindly kiss yer own arse?” Cormac and Rourke drew pistols from beneath the table. “A shilling it is, then!” In a puff of smoke, the pirate was shot in the head and chest, and toppled backwards down the steps.

The other pirates rallied out front while Rourke gathered a handful of hemp cords, two of which were attached to the barrels they sat on. Cormac lit the cords with a lamp. The brothers dashed for the open trap door in the floor. They slammed it shut. Shots fired and footsteps slammed against the floorboard above. Cormac and Rourke squirmed their way to the hole beneath the back steps.

"Y'know, when I planned this out, I envisioned us being a bit quicker than this," Rourke said.

They staggered out from beneath the steps. Inside the bungalow was a swarm of searching pirates. Two of them noticed Rourke and Cormac outside and charged. A massive explosion shook the cottage and fiery debris flew in all directions. Smoldering pirates ran for the bay where *Bloody Mary* sat, having transported the two people the O'Malley's least wanted to encounter – Mandingo and Slasher Al. A wave of Barbary Janissaries leapt from the ship.

"Full attack!" Al shouted.

Cormac and Rourke had set up decoy hemp cords all over the grounds, which successfully confused many a pirate. Several cords were attached to barrels of gunpowder which all went off simultaneously, scorching the intruders. Debris and body parts soared through the air into the bay.

From the temporary sanctuary of Cormac's bungalow, Rourke dipped into a stash of guns and grenades.

After grabbing a pistol, Cormac positioned himself at a window and peered out. "Looks like five on this side."

Rourke checked the opposite window. "Aye, a little more than that on this side."

"Hate to break it to you lads, but we ain't really fishermen!" Cormac called. "What about the rear?"

Rourke peeked out. "You don't wanna know."

Someone outside yelled, "open fire."

Shots rang and the brothers dove flat on the floor.

"You just had to go and say something, didn't ya?" Rourke scowled.

"Like they didn't know we was here." Cormac lit a grenade. He waited until the fuse went down and tossed it out the window at a cart. The explosion scattered wreckage in all directions. Cormac aimed and took a shot, killing a pirate. "I thought you would be more challenging, lads. Don't know about you, Rourke, but I'm insulted."

"Well, we got the cream of the Barbary fuckin' crop on this side!"

Gunfire pelted the room, mixed with flying glass and wood.

"I think these men mean business." Rourke took a shot through the window. "Easiest shilling I ever made!"

They both laughed.

The back wall of the bungalow imploded, and the ceiling collapsed. Cormac and Rourke were tossed across the room. Black smoke poisoned the air and Cormac reached out his hand to feel broken glass and splintered wood. He also felt a leg. Rourke's leg. He turned his brother's lifeless body over. When the smoke thinned, he found a remaining barrel bomb. "A shilling, eh? You tight bastard." He cut the hemp line and lit it with a smoldering piece of wood.

Cormac collapsed to the floor as the Barbary Janissaries charged in. Another section of roof gave way and left him scrambling for cover. One final explosion obliterated the bungalow.

Lucky
Charms
2015

The Blarney Stone

Thunder boomed and silvery black storm clouds covered Cayman Brac Island. Lightning bolts charged the sky. Theodore Binge watched the harbor from his carriage, reluctant to get out. It had been a fortnight since he and his two stepdaughters, Henrietta and Gertrude, left Port Royal. They were staying at the cottage by the lake on the outskirts of the Brac.

Tonight, with the looming storm, Binge had decided they would stay at the Blarney Stone Inn and Tavern. There would be plenty of company and provisions if needed. In any case, Henrietta and Gertrude had tired of waking up each morning to small caiman alligators hanging about on the front porch.

Binge pulled the hood of his rain cloak tighter around his head. Royal Rook's ship, *Diamond Dog*, bobbed violently in the tide. Binge saw quartermaster Tiny McAllister and sailing master Quinton Winter braving the elements to double-fasten her down. Just beyond, near the larger dock, a tall schooner of gray and light blue bounded into the harbor. Binge recognized Laurens de Graaf's *Cometa*. Things were going to get interesting tonight.

Binge helped the ladies down from the carriage. "Go on up; this is gonna be a good one." He gave them each a quick peck on the cheek.

"Don't be long." Gertrude latched onto her sister's arm before they ran to the tavern.

"Don't be long?" Binge said. "But that's my best quality!" He unhooked the horse and led him into a stall. Binge patted Pénombre dry and fluffed up the hay. After fetching clean water and dispensing squares of sugarloaf, his horse was ready for bed. "Sweet dreams, Pénombre. I'll be back to check on you."

Binge shivered along the path to the tavern. "Bart better have a fire going!"

Along the way he recognized a newcomer who was emerging from a small, beat-up fishing boat. Mason Sleemans, Governor Dewar's advisor, trudged along the dock. "I didn't ask for first class, but some class would have been nice!" Sleemans complained to the boat's captain.

The Blarney Stone Tavern was crowded and dirty compared to the

Swiftsure back in Port Royal, but the booze was abundant, the billiard board new, and the fireplace ablaze. Spanish musicians played guitars as patrons clapped along.

"Permission, Capt'n Bart?" Binge asked, wiping his boots on a wicker mat.

"Granted, Theodore. Come in and be welcome." Bartolomeo Portuguese was like a weather-beaten rock, badly scarred and blind in one eye; this never dampened his spirits however, nor did he ever water down the spirits. For the past twenty years he had run the tavern successfully after retiring from the pirate life. Bartolomeo was one of the founding fathers of the Brethren of the Coast. "What'll it be?"

"Two bottles of brandy for the ladies, to go."

Gertrude and Henrietta warmed themselves by the fire.

"Aye," Bartolomeo said.

"Aye!" squawked Checkmate the Mascarene parrot, perched behind the bar.

Binge took the bottles over. "I'll just say hello for a few minutes and be right back."

Gertrude picked up her brandy. "Meet us upstairs when you're done."

"Don't be too late," Henrietta added.

Binge kissed each of them before they vanished up the staircase. "I won't. Don't get cold, now." He went to the table where Tiny and Winter warmed themselves with tankards of ale, joined by Snapper with his rum.

"Miracles never cease," Tiny began. "They let you stay?"

Snapper clumsily mixed cards. "Deal ya in, then?"

"Sure. One hand for old times' sake!" Binge swiped the deck to give the cards a proper shuffle. "Say, there's a light on in the captain's cabin."

Tiny nodded. "He's weathering the storm with Katie."

"Good to see him bouncing back," Binge said.

"Depends on what angle yer looking from," Tiny replied.

The back door burst open and rain blew into the tavern. Binge recognized the new arrivals, Marie-Anne Dominique du Pres and her six-year-old daughter Marie Marguerite, called Yvonne. Marie-Anne was married to Poilu le Grande, leader of the Freebooters.

"Close the damn door!" Bartolomeo called.

Checkmate screeched, "Close the damn door!"

Marie-Anne shut the door and took off her coat. Her long chestnut hair was a tangled mess. She moved to a table near the fireplace. Yvonne followed and produced a box of tobacco.

"Dry as a bone, *Maman.*"

"Good. Roll a lot. Teeze going to be a long night." Marie-Anne adjusted her loose corset and added, "Not too tight."

"Oui, *Maman*."

"Brandywine, Capitaine Bartolomeo, *s'il vous plait*." Marie-Anne glanced around and noticed Binge. "Monsieur Theodore, they allow you out? Miracles never cease. I should join these strong men for a drink. My husband is out at sea."

Bartolomeo brought her a couple of bottles.

"I think that's my cue to leave," Binge said.

"Why?" Snapper grinned. "Got ya worried, does she?"

"You could say that. She's what gamblers call bad odds."

Marie-Anne eyed him up, pushing her hair over her shoulder and lifting up her cleavage.

"She seems to want ya," Tiny said.

Binge pretended not to notice her. "Well, two's my limit. Besides, she don't go anywhere without the dwarf."

"Did you give her the signals?" Winter asked.

"I don't know." Binge raised an eyebrow. "But I'm getting some awfully strange ones back."

"Her trouble is that she goes into heat every time her man goes out to sea," Snapper said.

"And he ain't someone you want mad at you," Binge added. "Remember, I'm allergic to violence. Gives me a rash."

Snapper shrugged. "I may have compounded things for ya when I told her you took a fancy to her."

"You're jesting, right?" Binge's eyes widened. "Why would you go and say a thing like that?" He wanted to lop his own head off, but it would be a waste of a good cravat.

"You was making eyes at her. I saw it."

"Shit! Yer blaming the compass for pointing north?" Binge shifted his chair as Marie-Anne sauntered over to sit with him. "*Bonjour,* Marie-Anne. Liking the weather?"

She put her foot on Binge's chair. "Oui, I do. I have always liked storms." A high-pitched laugh escaped her crimson-stained lips. "Katie – have you seen her?"

Tiny pointed to the docks. "Out riding the waves."

Marie-Anne slid a bottle over to Binge. "Have a drink on me."

Binge felt his face heat up. "Why, *merci*, that's so kind of you. If my stepdaughters walk in now, they'll beat me to death."

"So, what brought you back to le Brac?"

"I just hitched a ride."

Marie-Anne leaned forward, her breasts straining against her corset. "That is not what I heard. They say it was you who saved Katie and brought her 'ere. And they say it was you who killed Coggshall, but they say all kinds of t'ings, don't they?"

"Oui, don't they?" Binge responded awkwardly.

"*Excusez-moi.*" Marie-Anne left for another table.

Binge glared at Snapper. "Your mother left you on a beach, didn't she?"

Winter grinned. "Welcome back to ze Brac, Monsieur Theodore!"

"Tell me, how is it that you've been with two women for years and yet you have no children? Trouble with the old mast?" Snapper guffawed.

Binge laughed. "You only wish. No, my beauties and I aren't inclined to have children right now, so I do the responsible thing."

"What?" Snapper smirked. "They savor the old maypole?"

"I never speak of my ladies in such a way, but you get the idea." Binge shuffled the cards. "Straight up?"

The main door to the tavern opened and another gust of wind and rain blew in. Mason Sleemans, soaked through and miserable, entered. Binge's interest was piqued.

"Close the damn door!" Checkmate squawked.

"Oh, sorry." Sleemans shut it.

"You know him?" Tiny asked.

"Nay. Thought maybe it was Rook."

Sleemans tried in vain to shake the excessive water onto the wicker mat before wandering to the bar, picking fish scales off his clothes.

"What's your business here, *compadre*? I didn't hear you get permission?" Bartolomeo began.

"I'm solicitor for Lord Longbone of Lancashire from Eleuthera. I'm seeking Captain Bart," Sleemans replied.

"Aye," Bartolomeo gave a dry laugh. "From Lord Longbone of Lancashire, what do you want with Capt'n Bart?"

"I'm to order a wormwood wine and frog's legs. But honestly, the frog legs will make me sick."

"Rank amateur. What's your name?"

"Ben Dover from Eleuthera," Sleemans said reluctantly.

Bartolomeo shook his head and motioned the barmaid. "Take over here." He opened a section of the bar counter to let Sleemans in. "Follow me, Ben Dover from Eleuthera."

Sleemans followed and was handed a towel before being led into a private room.

"He seems important," Snapper said.

Binge passed the deck to Tiny. "He was wearing fish scales. Nature calls. Besides, I promised the horse I'd check on him. I'll check for Rook's light on my way."

"Would ya?" Tiny scooped up his winnings.

"You gents go ahead and get cocksure. I'll be back in a spell." Binge darted past Marie-Anne, catching a wink before stopping at the bar. "Another round for the table on me." Cheers erupted as Binge vanished behind a curtained area. Following a corridor to a pantry, he found a spot where he could hear the goings-on in the private room.

"You can assure Lord Longbone he has the support of the Brethren of the Coast," Bartolomeo pledged.

"Laurens is right off our shore," Sleemans said.

Right you are, Binge thought.

"And what of the Capitaine? He was on Jamaica. The French already have St. Kitts," Sleemans continued.

"They can have St. Kitts," Bartolomeo deliberated. "I tell you, any captain who moves against Jamaica is an enemy of the Brethren and is fair game. If it be true, the Capitaine has no exemption."

"What about payment?" Sleemans pressed. "How do we hire the men?"

"It's best we just send ya the bill."

Binge crept back along the corridor. He took his coat from the cloakroom and headed outside. More spindrift blew through the tavern.

"Close the damn door," Checkmate said.

Binge slammed it shut and followed the path to the stable. A light came from *Diamond Dog* and shadows swayed in the window. "They need me in there like I need a hole in the head." He pushed forward; his face slapped by the storm. Grasping the door to the stable, Binge slipped inside.

Pénombre bleated.

"Easy, it's just a storm. It's been a year for them, that's for sure." Binge sensed the presence of someone in the stable with him. A dark figure with a feathered hat stepped out of a stall, stiletto in hand. Binge readied the throwing knives concealed in his sleeves.

The figure stepped into the dim lantern light.

"Should I be nervous?" Binge asked.

"I don't know." Laurens de Graaf put his blade away. "Did you stick it in Marie-Anne?"

"No."

"Then you got nothing to worry about."

Binge retracted his knives. He'd been passing intelligence to Laurens since the late seventies. "Glad you could make it."

"Anything for the Capitaine. Where the hell is he?"

Binge took a note from his inner pocket and handed it over. "On Jamaica, wondering where the hell everyone else is."

"I told him not to go near that island alone, but you know him." Laurens scrunched up his face and squinted. "Uh, five forts and a hundred men, uh, what the fuck, uh?" He read the note. "Where's *La Lune*?"

"Captured in Port Royal. And it's six forts now and a big man-of-war."

"Yeah? Where's the new line?"

"It's White's line, north of Morgan's line. Six guns."

"Old Whitie gets his own line after all these years?" Laurens smirked. "Why didn't they call it Bleedin Art's Line? That would have been snappier."

"With a snag. They put it right in front of Belford's house." Binge patted Pénombre and gave him a cube of sugarloaf.

"That ain't good timing. But I'll remind Saint-Domingue we want to keep to big military targets like Fort Charles."

"That would be much appreciated."

Laurens paused. "We both got a lot of friends in that city. How are Easy and Bizy?"

"They look well, but we don't hang out in the same places much."

Laurens removed a satchel of coins and tossed it to Binge. He took out a Pepys pen and a bit of parchment.

Binge tucked the coins away. "The Brethren knows about the French plan to take Jamaica."

Laurens scribbled a note. "'Course they do. Things don't stay secret out here, do they? His crew won't know anything, but it's the Capitaine they want, anyway. And poor old François le Picard is getting the worst of it; they won't get nothing out of him but a whole lot of frustration. I always wanted him on my ship, damn it. How could the Capitaine be so reckless?"

"He met a redhead."

Laurens sighed. "And all the pieces fall into place." He folded the note and handed it to Binge. "Can you send this by registered post to Port Royal? Care of Baldran Imports, twenty-one up Bird's on Queens."

Binge nodded. "That I can do, but the Brethren's gonna hang the Capitaine out to dry if he's taken by the English."

"He's on Jamaica now and it's his own damn fault," Laurens grumbled. "I sail for Petit-Goâve when the weather clears. I'll check for the Capitaine on the way." He tipped his hat. "Well, always a pleasure, Theodore. Give my best to the girls."

"I will. And vive la Jamaica," Binge said.

Laurens took off into the storm.

Binge patted the horse. "Maybe we'll rename Port Royal Pénombre. What do you think of that?"

The horse whinnied in agreement.

Laurens de Graaf pulled his coat up against the pelting rain. He passed a handful of his men fighting their way to the tavern. He entered unnoticed, slipping into the cloakroom where he shook his hat and ran his fingers through his hair. The tavern was lively, and he recognized the high-pitched laugh of Marie-Anne Dominique du Pres. He peered out. She sat with Royal Rook's crew, a cigarette in her mouth and Yvonne on her lap.

Snapper was telling a tale. "There's only twenty of us left, and they still got one more fort and three hundred men. Henry had us all running around hollering and blowing stuff up."

Laurens chuckled at the memory of Puerto Bello.

Snapper continued. "Gator Gar and Roc Braziliano walked right up to them, right up to the main gate at Puerto Bello, and Henry says 'surrender' and they all bloody did!"

Laughter erupted.

"Yer cunning and skill astounds me," Tiny said.

Marie-Anne nudged closer to Tiny. "My goodness, we are a big boy, yes?"

Winter looked at Tiny. "Your bet."

"How is this possible?" Marie-Anne felt Tiny's arm. "How did your arms get so big?"

Tiny ignored her and continued the card game.

Laurens smiled to himself and thought, *if ever there was a rival to the Whore of Babylon, Marie-Anne was it. She was worth it though, scarred but very pretty.*

Snapper continued. "Tiny was oarsman on a galley for years and rowed clear across the Atlantic and into the Mediterranean. He was a pirate then."

"I never seen you on a raid. When were you a pirate?" Marie-Anne asked.

"Not around these parts." Tiny studied his cards. "Raise."

"I break your concentration, yes?" She teased, looking down. "Oh, I am making you hard, no?"

"Nay. I raise." Tiny tugged his shirt down.

"You just did," Winter said.

"Oui, you did." Marie-Anne laughed. "Tell me about your galley across the Atlantic?"

Snapper jumped in. "It was in Barbados that Tiny here was an indentured man, rowing on a slave galley just over from Africa. The captain gets word they gotta go back at all speed, so they store as much food as they can and row straight back across the sea through an endless chain of storms. Rowing day and night with no stops, only shift changes, they cross the Atlantic. That's where them arms come from."

Tiny lowered his cards. "In the Mediterranean along the Barbary Coast where the slaves are taken from Africa, they're sent to Barbados or Tobago, or one o'them slave conditioning bases in the New World. We was sent to Malta, where we was told we was picking up a message and heading back to Barbados with no shore leave. I'd had enough and jumped over. Took the whole gang with me. We took fire from the ship, but most of us swam to shore."

"They charge you with piracy for that?" Marie-Anne gasped.

"Nay, me and the lads joined a pirate crew and lived in Madagascar for a year. Even met the brother of Cormac O'Malley.

Rourke, his name was. We took a silk and spice ship off India and came away with a good haul. When plunder was divided I had enough to start a new life and me own business, so I sailed for Port Royal. When I got there, I was charged with piracy sent to Marshallsea Prison. A year later, they sent me back to Barbados on a galley that got taken by pirates." Tiny pointed to Bartolomeo. "His pirates, Royal Rook."

"And me," Winter added, taking a card. "I raise."

The door blew open, unleashing a torrent of rain and wind.

"Close the damn door!" Checkmate called.

"You never know what shit will blow in," Marie-Anne said.

Laurens slipped out of the cloakroom and closed the front door. "Permission to enter, Captain Bartolomeo?"

"Permission granted, Laurens de Graaf. Come in and be welcome."

A hush fell over the tavern.

"Laurens de Graaf?" Marie-Anne scoffed. "Laurens *de connard.*"

"*Diamond Dog* is here. Where's Rook at?" Laurens asked.

"Around," Bartolomeo said. "What'll it be? Ales or spirits?"

"Ales for the men, and I'll take a brandy."

Marie-Anne shuffled closer to Tiny. "Ze number one pirate in the Caribbean, he wouldn't stand a chance against you."

"You wanna bet?" Winter replied.

Tiny seemed very uncomfortable. "Huh?"

"Your bet," Winter said.

"What? I'm thinking," Tiny snarled.

"Not so much ze scary pirate now, uh?" Marie-Anne called over to Laurens. "What do ze Spanish call you now? Lorencillo? Little Lawrence?"

Laurens grinned. "Hey, 'double, double, toil and trouble,' Marie-Anne! I was invited as you were, so let's try not to be little bitches, shall we?"

"Little bitch!" Marie-Anne's daughter Yvonne scowled.

Laurens signaled for a drink. "The apple didn't fall far, did it?"

Checkmate squawked. Royal Rook and Katie entered. They struggled to close the door and shook the rain from their coats.

"Zere you are!" Marie-Anne waved. "Katie! Drink with me, dear?"

Katie waved and helped Rook with his coat.

Laurens pointed. "Whoa! You Christians take your Bible

seriously!" A large black patch sat over Rook's left eye. "Or were you looking for love in all the wrong places?"

Rook sneered. "I thought I saw your *Cometa* sail in. But then I asked meself why a slave-trading weasel like 'du Count-Two-Three' be inclined to set foot in the Blarney Stone."

"Hey, I gotta fit into society like everyone else." Laurens took a bottle of brandy and glanced around. "I love the decor. Clientele could use some improvement, though." Laurens winked at Katie. "Hey, I know you! Songbird! Hey, this girl can sing. Songbird, sing us a song."

Katie opened her mouth to show her stump of tongue.

Laurens was revolted. "Shit! Sorry!" He took a mouthful of booze. "Truly, I am. You had an amazing voice. It's a shame. But then again, Port Royal will do that to you."

Rook put his arm around Katie and guided her to a table. "The lady is with me, mate."

Laurens rubbed one eye. "We all make mistakes." He laughed. "Except me, of course." The barmaid walked by. "Mmm, what's that fragrance?"

"Sweat 'n ales," she said.

"Well, whatever it is, it's working for ya." He winked. "Careful, lovely, the divorce is final. De Graaf's a free man again. *Amor vincit omnia,* baby!"

Rook snorted. "There's a sheep out back for you."

Laurens toasted. "And she said she wants you home by nine, so drink up."

"Aye. Maybe you ought to drink up and be off?" Rook said. "Before someone makes you draw your pretty sword."

"I don't mind the implication so much, but I prefer women, thanks. That eye hole could be a lot of fun, though!"

Bartolomeo sat beside Laurens with a mug of ale. "It was my friend Laurens de Graaf who donated the Spanish galleon they called *el Griffe* in his honor, on this very spot. The aft half served as a tavern and inn, and the grand stateroom was my home until the hurricane of '85. The same one that saw the demise of the Chevalier Grammont. She tore through these islands, and then smashed Cuba and Florida. There was nothing left of *el Griffe.* This is the first time Laurens has set foot in my place since it was built, and he is an honored guest in the Blarney Stone."

Laurens raised his bottle. "Well, I'm honored to be an honored guest, Captain Bartolomeo."

"Why is it called the Blarney Stone?" Marie-Anne asked. "Bartolomeo is not particularly Irish."

Snapper explained. "Cormac's Pikeys built this place a week after *el Griffe* broke apart. Cormac himself made the sign as a joke, the Blarney Stone, and put it on the door. He was expecting Capt'n Bart to change it, but he never did. It's just the Blarney Stone."

Bartolomeo signaled the musicians. "And it has survived two hurricanes since."

Guitarists stepped forth. "Tonight, my friends, we play for you a ballad written especially for our guest, from my home, the city of Vera Cruz." A musician bowed to Laurens. "It is an honor, *señor*." They played "La Bamba."

Katie and Rook took their seats far from the music, with Marie-Anne.

Tiny considered Yvonne, who was passed out next to her mother. "The Brethren's changed some."

"Aye," Rook said.

"How's the head?" Winter asked.

Rook gave Katie a prolonged kiss. "Still throbbing."

Marie-Anne squeezed Tiny's arm and looked at Katie. "You never tell me you 'ave such exciting men in your life!"

"Hey, they're playing my song!" Laurens boasted.

"You paid them to write it," Rook goaded.

"I was at Vera Cruz. They could not 'ave taken it without les Freebooters. I should have my own song," Marie-Anne griped.

Laurens flashed a grin. "You do. It's called 'Ring around the Rosie.' Now let them play."

"You was at Vera Cruz?" Tiny cocked an eyebrow.

"No joke? The last great pirate raid!" Snapper bobbed his head. "Tell us a tale, then."

Marie-Anne leaned in, her breasts resting on the table top. "Grammont hired us for a raid, but no one knew where. We all met up at Isla de Pinos. Us, Laurens and his Samaná Bay Buccaneers, Grammont's Flibustiers, Van Hoorne's Interlopers, and *les Frères de la Côte* with le Capitaine and privateers from Port Royal to make sure all investors were 'appy. They sent us to Laguna de Términos and we all sailed for Mexico." She paused to light a pre-rolled cigarette. "Deep down in the bay they took a big galleon by surprise and sailed west for Vera Cruz under a Spanish flag. Ze galleon led ze way with Laurens in command, looking like a merchant coming home with goods. He called it Operation Trojan Horse. He sailed right up to ze great fortress of San Juan de Ulúa and dropped anchor, claiming his ship was damaged. At night Laurens and his men scaled the towers and took zem by surprise. When he had ze fort, Grammont landed us at Punta Gorda and into ze city. By ze end of ze day Laurens and Grammont met up at ze citadel and declared Vera Cruz ours."

"And then you Freebooters moved in to occupy the city," Winter added.

"Oui. I had a splendid view of ze countryside to watch Grammont trample down their armies with their own cavalry, raiding the hills and farms throughout the night."

Winter tilted his head. "What I don't swallow is why the Spanish call him a hero."

"He wrote in ze contract that no civilians were to be deliberately harmed and he more or less kept his word."

"Pirates rape and pillage, it's all part of the deal," Snapper said. "But he wouldn't let 'em. He even killed Van Hoorne 'cause he was cutting up hostages and slaves. That's why they like him."

"He just wanted the slaves for himself," Rook spoke snidely. "Took every last one of them. For their own safety."

The musicians finished the song, and everyone clapped. Binge returned, took off his coat, and hung it in cloakroom before joining the table by the fire.

Marie-Anne addressed Tiny, "My husband Poilu le Grande challenged Laurens de Crap to a duel for cheating us out of our share of slaves, but ze coward has yet to face 'im. Someday when I have my sword – or better, my gun – I shall confront 'im!"

"I take it you've met? That is the pirate Laurens, right?" Binge said.

"Oui. It is 'im. He is a – how you say?— dickhead."

Laurens raised his bottle and gave her a wink. "And your English is immaculate as always, Marie-Anne."

Everyone laughed and Bartolomeo came over with two bags of coins. "Compensation for yer lost parts." He handed a bag to Katie and the other to Rook. "Under the articles of the Brethren of the Coast, yer both entitled. With five hundred each from Bleedin Art and Larry Llewellyn thrown in for a tip."

Rook weighed the bag in his hand. "Aye. Generous, mate. Very generous."

Bartolomeo patted Katie's shoulder. "I'm sorry for what they done to ya. You got a lot of friends in Port Royal. We square?"

Katie nodded, almost tearing up.

"I invite the captains for a drink in the parlor," Bartolomeo announced and opened a door beneath the staircase.

The captains rose to follow.

Marie-Anne nudged her daughter. "You stay 'ere and roll us some more cigarettes."

"Oui, *Maman*." Yvonne yawned and prepared more tobacco.

Binge shuffled cards. "All right, kid, you in or out?"

"Oui, I am in." Yvonne picked up her mother's cards.

Laurens entered and everyone sat on padded wainscot chairs and drank brandy. Faintly, the music from outside could be heard. The musicians were now playing "La Cucaracha".

"Hey, Marie-Anne, they're playing your song!" Laurens quipped, and received a string of curse words in return. He knew she loved the attention. She always played hard to get.

Bartolomeo opened the meeting. "This is Marie-Anne Dominique du Pres. She's le Grande's number one and booking agent for the Freebooters."

"And who is this with ze sparkling shoes?" Marie-Anne inquired.

"This is Mr. Ben Dover from Lord Longbone in Eleuthera. They have business interests in Port Royal."

Laurens beamed. "How is old Dorcas doing, Monsieur Sleemans?"

Sleemans squirmed. "Fine, thank you, Sieur de Baldran. Or is it de Graaf, or the Count?"

"Now that we're all friends, what does Dorcas want, anyway?" Laurens asked.

"He wants to hire privateers. Pay attention," Marie-Anne said.

"I-I- thought women were not allowed on pirate raids," Sleemans muttered, incurring a wrathful stare.

"We're not on a pirate raid, unless you plan to pillage my parlor," Bartolomeo remarked.

Sleemans again shifted awkwardly, resting his head against his hand, trying to partially cover his face. "Our islands have deep economic ties. War between us would hurt everyone. The English know the French plan to invade Jamaica."

"I don't know nothing about that. I'm retired, ask the Capitaine, I hear he's taking Port Royal one tavern at a time." Laurens laughed, and Marie-Anne joined in. He continued, "I got no problems with no one. I'm retired and know nothing of an attack on Jamaica."

"But you refurbished heavy cannons for the Flibustiers," Sleemans argued. "Cannons to be used on us!"

"A man's gotta live."

"Preparation for an attack makes you equally guilty."

"Guilty of offending the slave capital of the New World?"

"You are a slave owner!" Rook said.

"Owning slaves is an immense responsibility. I treat my slaves better than you treat your crew."

Marie-Anne gave an exaggerated yawn.

"Exactly." Laurens gestured to Marie-Anne. "Let sleeping dogs lie!"

"The Brethren will never allow King Louis to rule Jamaica. That must be clear," Bartolomeo said.

"I have no influence over Saint-Domingue. Governor de Cussy gets his orders from King Louis, and if he and William are poised for war, what can I do to stop it?" Laurens leaned back in his chair, hands behind his head.

"Would Saint-Domingue be willing to discuss peace negotiations if Port Royal were under the flag of King James?" Sleemans asked.

"King James's flag is busy trying to take Ireland. When's he gonna get here?" Laurens quipped.

"He never left."

"A *coup d'état*?" Marie-Anne gave a mischievous laugh.

Sleemans nodded. "A coup in the name of King James."

"And 'ow will King James pay?" Marie-Anne queried.

"His supporters would have to put up a lot of money, and at the risk of high treason." Laurens removed his hat and ran his fingers through his hair. "And Lady Spreads-Her-Wares here is right. Who's gonna put up the bond?"

"Bond or not, I'll give me life for King James," Rook stated.

“I’m sure your crew will be glad to hear that,” Laurens bellowed. “Mine, on the other hand, like getting paid.”

“My captains are full supporters of King James and will wage war in his name to defeat King William,” Bartolomeo said.

Sleemans lifted a case from his feet and removed a scroll speckled with gold-leaf and a red ribbon. He unrolled a letter of marque from the Duchess of Albemarle.

Bartolomeo nodded. “The Brethren recognizes that seal.”

“We ask for the support of Saint-Domingue, the Samaná Bay Buccaneers, and the Freebooters as well,” Sleemans said.

Each glanced at the document.

Marie-Anne nodded. “Oui. I will send your proposal to my husband. We will discuss terms with King James on the condition that you can make it ’appen?”

“I won’t promise nothing, but I’ll discuss it with Governor de Cussy in Saint-Domingue,” Laurens agreed.

Sleemans returned the letter of marque to his case. “If we can unite our forces, the Orange Party will fall. They must all realize this to be true.”

Bartolomeo brought out a green glass bottle.

“This must be love. He’s bringing out the good stuff!” Laurens exclaimed.

Bartolomeo filled each of their glasses. “We have yet to make an official accord, but this opens negotiations. We’ll each discuss this with our associates and benefactors and meet here on December first. We must have absolute secrecy. No one can know what was discussed but our benefactors, on pain of death.”

Everyone nodded in agreement.

Sleemans raised his glass. “Then let us toast to the continued friendship of our islands, and to King James.”

“Say aye,” Bartolomeo said, and everyone did.

Laurens felt a cold stare from Rook.

Bartolomeo rose. “Next round’s on me.”

Everyone took the cue to leave.

Laurens sniffed the Chartreuse Liqueur d’Elixir, savoring its pungency. *Every good battle should begin with a shot of this.* He drank slowly. The liquid burned his throat. *Once more into the breach, dear friends. Once more.*

Katie Evans finished her brandy and considered the bag of coins. It was bittersweet that she had to get her tongue cut out in order to come into money. But she and Rook were set for a long time, and she'd never have to step foot in Port Royal again.

Katie poured another shot as Bartolomeo came out of the parlor, followed by Sleemans. Dewar's advisor was such an uptight, slimy little man; she could never stand to be around him.

"See the bar about lodging, *Señor* Dover," Bart said before addressing Tiny. "McAllister, Captain Castle speaks very highly of you."

Tiny was taken aback.

"The best quartermaster I've ever seen," Rook affirmed. "And the men will follow him."

"*Diamond Dog* needs a captain the men will follow and Rook can't command while he's laid up." Bartolomeo presented a scroll. "Tiny McAllister, I promote you to lieutenant in service of the Brethren of the Coast and give you temporary command of our scout ship, *Diamond Dog*."

"Rook's my captain, sir," Tiny replied.

Rook patted his shoulder. "You earned it, mate. I ain't going no place just yet. Ya gotta play the hand you've been dealt."

Tiny nodded. "Temporarily then?"

"Aye, just temporary," Rook agreed. "Lieutenant McAllister, assemble a crew and make sail when the weather clears."

"Aye."

Bartolomeo handed over a letter. "Your first orders are to deliver a message."

"Aye."

Meanwhile, Laurens and Marie-Anne traded insults. It was a game they played, pretending to despise each other. Katie knew Marie-Anne was sweet on Laurens.

Marie-Anne returned to the card table, where her daughter slept on the empty side of the table.

"Uh, she lost," Binge said.

Marie-Anne woke Yvonne with a shriek and chased her out of the room.

"Women." Binge shrugged. "They never know when to fold."

Rook wrapped his arms around Katie, and she kissed him passionately, catching a glance from Laurens. Port Royal in '83 was when Katie had met Laurens. He was selling goods from the Vera Cruz raid and his favorite haunt was the Four Feathers Tavern. Katie sang in the evenings and Laurens offered to take her away. She declined, insisting she was Royal Rook's girl.

Rook's lips brushed her ear. "If you hear when that arsehole is leaving, let me know."

She nodded and they joined the card table.

Marie-Anne reappeared after a few minutes for a drink. She told another pirate story while Laurens and his men threw darts. Binge continued to deal, a large pile of coins on the table before him. It was definitely his night for winning; Winter, Tiny, and Rook lagged from too much drink. Binge scooped up his haul.

"No, you don't!" Tiny pointed. "One more round."

Binge sighed. "If you say so. I wouldn't want to end up having you all indentured."

"Just deal!" Winter growled.

Laurens won at darts. There was clapping and cheering before he signaled his men to get their coats. "Thank Captain Bartolomeo for his hospitality; I shall retire to this splendid inn." Laurens winked and waved at everyone. "I bid you all a fond adieu."

"You are a coward and snake, Laurens de Graaf!" Marie-Anne heckled.

"Don't let the broomstick give you slivers, Marie-Anne." Laurens headed out into the storm.

Marie-Anne cursed under her breath. "Perhaps another time, my big strong pirate." She patted Tiny's arm and rose to leave. "Good night, Monsieur Theodore." Marie-Anne kissed Katie's cheek.

Katie had known Marie-Anne since before her time in Port Royal. They were like sisters and Katie was happy to share her room.

Another hour passed and Katie grew weary of watching Binge throttle Rook and his crew at cards. They were determined to win back their gold. She tapped Rook's shoulder and pointed to the stairs. He nodded. Katie stumbled up the creaky staircase and down the hall.

Wall sconces illuminated the thick red carpet and threw shadows on the black and white floral wallpaper. She passed several paintings depicting lush trees and rolling grassy hills. One had a quaint cottage with a thatched roof. Katie pictured living in such a place, far away from the piratical world of the Caribbean.

When she reached her room, the door was ajar. Yvonne was passed out on the bed. Moaning and grunting came from behind a curtain. *Marie-Anne uses such discretion!* Katie folded her arms, listening to their conversation in between heated gasps.

Laurens groaned. "Oh, I forgot how good you feel!"

"When are you pulling out?" Marie-Anne asked.

"Oh, baby, never! I'll stay in here forever!"

"When are you leaving?"

"I'll go just as soon as I come."

Marie-Anne panted. "Harder, fuck me harder! Dat's it, oh!"

"Spread the word around. We're going to hit Campeche or Vera Cruz again and they will come."

"Oui! Come, come!"

"We'll meet in Tortuga. Collect as many men, ships, weapons and supplies you can."

"Oh, oui! Oui! Oui!"

The bodies rolled to the floor with a thud.

Katie staggered away, passing a lead-cased window. The rain had stopped, and all that remained was a mild wind. Predawn light seeped through the grayish clouds. She carefully descended the stairs, clutching the rail. By this time all the pirates were unconscious. Some reclined in chairs, some were on the floor, and others snored with their heads on table tops.

Katie stepped around several bodies. Rook slept on the table, drink still in hand. She grabbed his mug and he came to.

"What is it, love?" he mumbled.

She pointed to the door.

"Maybe later, dear." He fell back to sleep.

She slapped him.

"What?" Rook lifted his head.

Katie pointed to her rear and made an "O" with her fingers. Next, she swayed her hand like a sail and waved goodbye.

He rubbed his eyes. "Have ya been into that Strangewayes shit again?"

"No." Tiny yawned. "She says 'that arsehole's sailing away.'"

"Laurens?" Rook shook his head to wake up.

Tiny checked the window. "Aye, crew are getting ready."

Rook kissed Katie's cheek. "You did good, girl."

Katie smirked. *Aye, I know, ya fucking idiot!*

Tiny shook Winter's shoulder. "Oi, he's leaving." Then he bellowed, "Ready to make sail!"

"Ready to make sail," Checkmate squawked.

Winter rose half-drunk to gather his things.

"Just like a dog, eh?" Rook snorted. "Don't get too close and once ya see Saint-Domingue on the horizon, cut 'em loose."

"Aye, Captain." Tiny saluted. "I'll see you when I get back."

Rook put his arm around Katie and she helped him upstairs to his room. When his exhausted body fell into bed, he went straight to sleep. She crawled in beside him, content in the knowledge that they had all the time in world together.

GO
2015

He That Dies Pays All Debts

Buccaneer Dashiell Dupris paced along the dock beside the shoreline of Montego Bay. Known among his men as de Kreep, he'd completed an evaluation of Jamaica's defenses over the past few weeks. He waited for his leader, Laurens de Graaf. His report to Laurens would be that the island's defenses were minimal and could be easily infiltrated. Another disturbing report had come of a battle in Anotto Bay. Cormac the pikey was said to be one of the casualties.

Cometa slid steadily into the harbor. Laurens's large blue glaucous macaw, Henry V circled above. De Kreep did one last supply and weapon inspection. *Cometa* docked.

Laurens was the first to step off his ship, Henry V perched on his shoulder. The shipmaster, Ravenau, followed as the crew tied off the boat.

De Kreep bowed. "Sieur."

"I hear the Capitaine took Jamaica single-handedly," Laurens began.

"He is still here. But, we have word that war erupted at Hope Bay. They say the English killed Cormac the pikey."

Laurens's face darkened. "But Cormac the pikey is under the protection of the Brethren of the Coast! Damn *his* recklessness! Where are the rest of the men?"

Laurens was displeased with the Capitaine, but de Kreep was more lenient. The Capitaine had been his friend and brother for many years. The Capitaine had saved de Kreep's life in the recent hurricane and in turn, he'd helped the Capitaine liberate a red-haired slave girl. De Kreep pointed to the village. "The men are here, ready to sail."

"We sail for Hope Bay, pronto!" Laurens called.

De Kreep whistled, catching Arsenault's attention. Twenty buccaneers rallied to the dock with weapons and supplies.

"Board the ship!" de Kreep ordered and his men jumped aboard *Cometa.*

"Cast off!" Laurens shouted.

"Sails. Take us out," said Ravenau.

They sailed around the point, passing Anotta Bay, examining the devastation. The shoreline was charred, and the scorched skeleton of a ship drifted among the coral reefs. An oily slick shone on the sea's surface, patterning colors of green, blue, and pink.

Laurens peered through a spyglass. "What the hell happened here?"

They arrived in Hope Bay's harbor and anchored. Already present was the ship *Lucky Charms*. Her crew gathered on land, their hats removed, anguish on their faces.

Laurens ordered his crew onto longboats and they rowed to the smoking village. Townspeople gathered, silent and tearful. The heads of Cormac and Rourke O'Malley were mounted on spikes next to a sign that read:

We freed slaves.
This is what happens to those who oppose ownership.

Laurens stepped off his boat, speechless.

De Kreep covered his mouth; grief flushed his face.

Arsenault used his sword to take down the sign.

"Careful, it may be rigged," Laurens said. "Find their bodies. Where are their sons?"

"They sailed away, around the west point," one of Alban Jones's crew said.

"Who did this?" de Kreep asked.

"Slasher Al the pirate. He was under an English flag, but it was him," a crewman insisted.

"And a fire-breathing dragon!" a villager exclaimed.

Jones's man trembled. "A monstrous galley with a dragon's head. It breathed fire!"

Ravenau eyed Laurens. "A Barbary fire ship."

Laurens gave an unhappy grunt. "Kabaka."

"Where did Slasher Al go?" Ravenau asked.

"Last seen sailing west, chasing Jones's *Cymru*," a crewman said.

Buccaneers and a couple of crewmen found the bodies of Cormac and Rourke. The remains were placed on the beach.

"They were Pagans," Laurens said. "We'll have a Pagan funeral tonight."

Ravenau conferred with villagers to organize a procession.

Laurens pulled de Kreep aside.

"I want you to find the Capitaine. Meet me back here and tell the Capitaine I want to see him."

"Oui, Monsieur." De Kreep signaled Coupe la Bite. "Coupe, go to the ship and get the rest of our weapons. We're moving out tonight."

"Oui," Coupe la Bite agreed, and five buccaneers boarded a longboat and rowed for their vessel.

By evening, de Kreep and his men had assembled two barges from kindling and rope. Laurens and his men wore dark ceremonial cloaks as they carefully laid the bodies of Cormac and Rourke upon their final resting places.

Another ship docked nearby. Royal Rook's *Diamond Dog* had been following *Cometa,* but when they saw what had happened, they knew they had to pay their respects. Tiny McAllister, Quinton Winter, and Snapper stood at a distance along the beach and removed their hats.

Laurens read from a book. Ravenau passed him a flickering torch. He stepped forward, chanting a Gaelic prayer. Rourke's barge was set afire and Laurens tossed a handful of salt upon it. He lit Cormac's barge the same way. "He that dies pays all debts."

De Kreep signaled his buccaneers and they used oars to push the pyres adrift into the harbor. Everyone stood still and silent. Laurens continued to chant. Many ships gathered and saluted with cannon fire. Villagers set off fireworks that streaked the sky in a multitude of colors.

The O'Malleys were good friends to the Brethren of the Coast. They would be missed. De Kreep let his mind wander. His grief had to be tempered, for his next task was to find the Capitaine. He would start with the Brethren's contacts in Jamaica. The Capitaine would be in a remote location, probably within the vicinity of the Blue Mountains.

Atia stood on the deck of the *Cymru,* watching the dock drift closer. When they landed in Morant Bay, crewman tied off the ship and it was time to say farewell.

Alban Jones came ashore to give Atia a hug. "Thank you, Jonesy," she said.

"Anything for Cormac's little girl."

"The 'little' part's old, but I love you anyway."

Jones climbed back aboard.

The Capitaine ushered Atia along a path through the trees with Yaguara following.

"We'll meet you in Ligania," Gladstone said.

"Right under their noses?" Jones laughed and looked at the Capitaine. "Hope he knows what he's doing."

Gladstone took a drink from his canteen. "Yaguara likes the plan, and I like the plan. We'll gather our people and disguise ourselves like an aid ship to Nevis, with slaves and building materials. It's brilliant."

"If you all think it's brilliant, then so do I," Jones replied. "I'll be off to check on Cormac and bring back ships. I'll be in Ligania in five days."

Gladstone picked up bags. "Please and thank you, Alban."

Atia glanced at Jones again.

Jones gave a final wave. "You just be there. And keep an eye out for the lass for me." His men pushed off.

Gladstone hurried along the dirt trail to catch up with the others. They all paused in a clearing overlooking a cluster of stone cottages with thatched roofs. There was a barn a little way off, surrounded by overgrown weeds and wildflowers.

"Yaguara and I will find us a carriage," Gladstone said.

"Fine. Miles can go up the road while Yaguara scouts the barn further up," Yaguara confirmed.

Atia sat beneath a tree for the shade. The evening sun was brilliant orange and very hot. She patted her face with a handkerchief and watched the sea behind them.

Minuit darted past, chasing dragonflies.

The Capitaine sat down and passed her a water canteen.

She drank. "Do you think Liv'll be there by now?"

"Oui. She will be. Then we get everyone out."

She recapped the canteen. "I'm afraid for Da and Rourke."

"I know." The Capitaine put his arm around her and she nestled in tightly. "Cormac knows what he's doing. Believe me."

Atia's eyes closed and her head lolled to the side. It seemed like seconds before Gladstone came back.

"Not exactly stallions, but they'll have to do."

"What are those?" the Capitaine asked.

Atia opened her eyes to see four very small animals.

"Donkeys," Gladstone replied.

Atia went over to pet them. "They're adorable! Why are they so small? Are they babies?"

Gladstone patted one's head. "No, I think they're bred this way."

"Oui! For amusement! And I am not entirely amused!" the Capitaine huffed.

They heard a cart grinding along the path, and Yaguara came into view. When he arrived, he glared at the animals. "What the hell are those?"

"Donkeys." Gladstone rubbed his lower back. "Couldn't you find something with seats?"

"This is all Yaguara could find with wheels attached." He passed Gladstone the harness. "And Miles can lead them. He is their king."

Gladstone attached the donkeys. "Alright, don't get touchy."

The Capitaine and Yaguara grew more frustrated as they loaded the bags. Gladstone took the reins. Once aboard, they rolled along very slowly. The pint-sized donkeys shuffled as quickly as they could on their wee legs.

"You know," Gladstone started.

"Miles should be quiet!" Yaguara reprimanded.

Gladstone shrugged. "Aye."

They rattled along at a pace slower than walking. Atia covered her mouth, trying not to laugh. The Capitaine and Yaguara jumped down, cursing. They each took a harness, pulling the donkeys and wagon along.

Gladstone gave a chirpy grin. "That's it! Now we're making good time!"

"We only needed a wagon," the Capitaine grumbled. "It was not a difficult request."

Yaguara flashed a defensive frown. "Next time, the Capitaine can steal the goddamn car."

At daybreak, smoke rose above Port Royal. The fish docks bustled with activity from the morning catch. After roll call at the forts, flags rose and the town crier with his drummer took their stations at King's Landing overlooking Turtle Crawls.

"Now for the morning news, brought to you by Nickle's Lead.

Bringing you the finest in lead piping both interior and exterior since 1667! Remember: in lead we trust." He opened a broadside. "In the news, Scottish Highlanders led by Viscount Dundee under the illegal Jacobite banner waged a brutal offensive in what has been called the Battle of Killicrankie. Acting Lieutenant Governor Piper assures us that the chances of Port Royal being attacked by Scottish Highlanders is very low. No Scottish Highlanders can reach Port Royal without much advanced warning. Also, anyone committing vile acts and waving a Jacobite flag will be arrested as traitors. In other news, the Kingdom of Russia has put a tax on the size of men's beards. No doubt to encourage shorter lengths to reduce beard-related accidents. Acting Lieutenant Governor Piper has stated there is no such law in English courts; however, a height restriction on wigs may be imposed if they keep getting taller."

Cherry Banks stood impatiently beneath the Turtle Crawls docks, dressed in black with a veil over her head. Two thugs in her employ clumsily transported the sheet-covered body of the late Salty Sally on a small cart. "Will you bloody hurry it up!" Cherry insisted, keeping watch. A large fin moving just below the surface of the water caught her attention. "See? Fish are already gathering. Get her in there!"

Cherry crossed her arms. She'd risen early that morning expecting the thugs to arrive when it was still dark. Apparently, the wheels on the cart had broken so they had to borrow one from a cousin who lived all the way across the city. *Un-bloody fucking believable!* Cherry thought. *I'd have better luck hiring baboons!*

"Aye," one of the thugs said, gathering Sally's legs.

The other grabbed the arms and raised her up. The sheet fell away revealing Sally's contorted bluish face. "Oi, what are you looking at?"

Cherry turned to see a young girl standing at the bottom of the ramp, petrified and shaking. The girl stepped backwards and tripped over her own feet. She seemed somewhat familiar.

"What the Jesus fucking hell are ya doing down here?" Cherry glared at the girl. "Yer a pretty tart, what's yer name?"

"Bella Gale."

"Bizy Gale's girl?" Cherry smirked. "Yer growing up fast. You got yer mother's fine long hair, you do."

"Isabella!" Bizy ran down the ramp. She helped the girl to her feet and then glanced at the body. “Come on, Isabella. You got no business down here. On your way.”

Isabella still trembled. “She’s blue.”

“Mind yer business and get back up to the street!” Bizy gave her child a push back up the ramp.

“Yes, Mama.” Isabella hurried away.

Bizy towered over Cherry. “She didn’t see nothing.”

Cherry frowned up at her. “And neither did you.”

Bizy backed away, giving Cherry a cold stare before running after her daughter.

Cherry sighed. “Why did she have to go and complicate things?” She pointed at the thugs. “I said ‘where the body will never be seen,’ idiots! She’ll float by the bloody King’s House in ten minutes!” Cherry gave an exaggerated wave. “‘Oh, hello, Lieutenant Governor, I’m a pretty shade of blue!’”

“Right, right. Where, then?”

“I don’t know!” Cherry stomped her foot. “I should ask a local assassin, he should know. But, wait! You are a local assassin! Shit, I outta just ask you, then!”

The thugs grumbled and dumped the body back on the cart and covered her up.

“Do it bloody right. Get rid of the body and don’t leave it in the governor’s trash!”

“Aye-aye.” The thugs wheeled the body away.

Cherry had to find a more reliable source for eliminating the problem of Bizy Gale and her child. Someone who would ensure they were unrecognizable by the time they were through.

de Kreep
GO
2015

Fate and Fortune

Le Picard's eyes opened slowly; his hands still manacled to a wooden torture chair. He spat out a mouthful of blood. Every inch of his body ached and burned. His head felt decapitated, although he was able to raise it to see *La Lune's* crew chained and herded along in the hallway of Marshallsea Prison.

A guard unlocked his cell to free him from the chair. Next, he was manacled to Poivre, the ship's gunner, and they marched down the hall. It almost felt good to walk, his backside numb from two days of immobility. Martel was bruised and bloody, as was Delacroix.

"They are taking us to be hanged," Beaumont whispered.

"We don't know that!" Poivre snapped. "They have to give us a trial!"

Corralled to the courthouse on High Street, a mob waited to yell and throw rotten food. The prisoners were pressed into a narrow box. Judge Goblet adjusted his powdered wig and motioned for everyone to take their seats. The Whig party took their positions on either side of him.

A fragile looking solicitor stood beside le Picard and his crew, belting out a loud wheezing cough.

Piper clapped his hands together. "Finally, a pirate."

Admiral Goddam stood very upright. "Standing before us is le Picard and the crew of *La Lune de Miel*, once flagship for the rogue l'Olonnais, and a known pirate vessel."

"But as I understand it, this not the famous pirate le Picard?" Piper pressed.

"Not the famous one, no, but a wanted pirate none the less," Goddam said.

"Aye, Your Lordships," the solicitor said in a nasally tone. "Not the famous pirate Pierre le Picard. This is his younger brother, François."

Goblet flipped through a document. "The same pirate who, in the year of our Lord 1687, was foiled in an attempt to kidnap the governor of Panama and his family at Pacheca Island along with the pirate Swan, Marie-Anne du Pres, and Jacquotte Delahaye, resulting in most of the governor's family burning to death on their ship. The pirate Swan went down with his ship, but Picard, du Pres, and Delahaye were among those retrieved from the sea and later charged with piracy. The three managed to escape before they could be brought to trial at Cartagena. François is most definitely a wanted pirate."

La Lune's crew rattled their chains and cheered.

Le Picard tried to wave back.

"Order!" Goblet hollered. "Order! You think this is funny, do you? How do they plead?"

"They plead guilty, by the looks of it, Your Lordships," the solicitor replied.

Le Picard and his men shouted and argued.

"Order!" Goblet snapped. "Guilty it is, the lot of you, and justice shall be swift. Though your association with the pirate Gator Gar cannot be established, Louis Martel Delahaye is hereby charged with association with the known pirate François le Picard and sentenced to twenty years' imprisonment. The crew, for following a known pirate, are hereby ordered indentured into slavery for five years. François le Picard is charged with committing an act of piracy and hereby sentenced to death by hanging."

Le Picard was determined not show any emotion. He stared at a stained patch on the wall.

Goblet eyed the Whigs. "Does the government find the sentence satisfactory?" They all nodded. "François le Picard, you will be held in Marshallsea Prison until Governor Estrada of Cartagena arrives to witness your execution. What have you to say for yourself, pirate?"

"Well, since you are asking, how did you get to be such a round little pig?"

The room erupted with laughter.

"Take the prisoners away!" Goblet demanded and guards dragged them from their box.

"I mean, he looks like be belongs in the middle of the table with an apple in his mouth for all you puritans!" le Picard shouted.

"Lock them all up!" Piper hissed.

"I did nothing! I have a family!" Beaumont called.

Le Picard remained silent on the way back to the prison. He was locked in a small dark room with only a slit with iron bars for a window. His chest heaved and he wondered how the Capitaine could have left the crew as he did. *He damned well better come and get us out of this wretched city!*

In the judge's private chambers, Piper wandered the room. It was full of dusty old books and had a clear view of Fort Carlisle. He finished a glass of brandy and poured another. "Now, about those pikey wenches Crisp is on about. We should have them hanged for all the trouble they've been!"

Taliare passed a document to Piper. "Your execution orders, sir."

"That wouldn't be economical." Mold shifted in his chair. "You own half of them. I have drafted a Letter of Recovery entitling us to any of Crisp's property from his outstanding debt to Coggshall. And Crisp has offered to buy them outright."

"Good idea, unload them while they're healthy enough," Taliare said.

Mold shook his head. "Nay, we're not ready to play that card just yet. Let's see what else is in the deck first."

Taliare sighed. "I wish you wouldn't speak in card terms. You know I have difficulty understanding you."

"What's so special about them?" Piper queried.

"Breeding stock," Mold mused. "Crisp believes them to be of pure Roman blood. He thinks he can create the perfect slave from a Roman female and a Negro male."

"Ah, the miracles of science." Taliare paused to have a drink. "The things we can do nowadays."

"Indeed," Piper said. "Taliare, as sheriff of the city you will be given a special battalion of Red Royals to help you keep the city safe from renegades like the pirate Gator Gun."

"Gator Gar, sir. Thank you, sir!" Taliare bowed. "I don't know what to say."

"Of course not. Well, we don't want to keep you from your duties."

"Nay, sir."

"That wasn't card speak, Sherriff. Shouldn't you be off fighting crime?"

Taliare put down his drink, bowed again, and walked out, closing the door behind him.

Piper lifted a copy of the Port Royal Daily Gazette from the desk. "Now, Gilbert, the pirate Capitaine."

“Goblet, sir,” Goblet replied. “Capitaine Jean-Paul la Roche. We now have information that he’s also the pirate La Salle and the Buccaneer le Sage.”

Piper sat on the desk. “Dear God, he must be worth a bloody fortune!”

“Only if these things can be proven,” Goblet replied.

Mold adjusted his wig. “Why has he not been apprehended?”

“Buccaneers are extremely dangerous. A cautious investigation—”

Mold crossed his arms. “For heaven’s sake, he’s only one man!”

Goblet bowed his head. “We’re still searching, sir.”

“Where are you searching?” Piper asked.

“We’re following a lead in the north as we speak.”

“North, as in, the colonies?”

Goblet pointed to the mountains through the window. “No. North, as in, over there.”

“Stability and strength is what we must show to the people!” Piper’s hands trembled angrily. “We can’t have this Frenchman running around making a mockery of us. I want him brought in, so find him!”

Goblet’s bottom lip threatened to quiver. “I am confident we’re aiming down the barrel now, sir.”

Piper stood at the window in disbelief at all the mismanagement. At least they had *La Lune* and her crew. Along High Street, the manacled crewmen shoveled sand from wagons to fill the large cracks in the road.

Bleedin Art sat on the Terracotta Terrace of the Four Feathers Tavern drinking a mug of wormwood wine, the type that relieved you of your eyesight for a day or so. He considered the cards in his hands before watching his opponents – Captain White and Snuggie ‘Snuggles’ Maxwell, one of the old captains from the League of Olde Fishermen.

White placed a pistol in the middle of the table, where a stack of gold was piled. “It’s Spanish silver, from Panama. I raise.”

They nodded and played the next hand.

“Taken from the personal guards of Don Juan Perez de Guzman?” Snuggles asked.

White removed his wig and scratched his sweaty white hair. “The very same. There were six, originally. This is the only one still known to exist.”

Snuggles rearranged his cards. "What happened to the other ones?"

"Disappeared in '72 along with Roc Braziliano. Most likely at the bottom of the sea," Art said.

Snuggles stuffed his pipe with tobacco. "They're gonna hang the Picard brother."

Art took another gulp of wine. "Isn't François the runt?"

"Aye, they're desperate for hangings. First, they kicked all the pirates out 'cause they didn't want a bloodbath, and now the Whigs are seeking them out," White spoke dryly. "And they wonder where all the pirates went."

MacAskill arrived at the terrace entrance.

Art set down his hand. His knees cracked as he rose. "You'll have to excuse me, gents." He took his drink and followed the doctor to a private booth. He anticipated news of the capture of the Mediterranean galley.

MacAskill wore an unusually sombre expression and handed over a letter.

Art stared at the envelope. "He spelled 'captain' wrong." He removed the parchment and read its contents twice.

"You lost *Arrow*."

Art massaged his face. "My one true love. It can't be!"

"Aye. She went up in a ball of fire."

Art sniffed. "Since the first day I stood upon her sturdy deck, I loved no other such as she."

MacAskill took a mouthful of wine from Art's mug. "We have only three men alive and accounted for."

Art raised his hand. "Shh! Never again shall I gaze upon…No, I already used 'upon.' Dammit! I should have been there for her!"

"Well yer farewell sonnet's gonna have to wait. If ya haven't noticed, we're running out of men and ships."

"They all got heads of fire and balls of glass, anyway," Art scowled. "But my lovely *Arrow,* to hath met such an end!"

MacAskill pondered a moment. "I'll hire a press gang. We'll round up men for the sloops at least."

"More deadbeats and drunkards?" Art frowned. "Calm down. Good leadership is determined by how you recover from disaster. Say, what does a Whig have for breakfast?"

MacAskill did not look amused. "What?"

"The egg it was fitted with."

"I'm not laughing. We should capture Gator Gar and use the bounty to fund a ship and crew."

Art finished his drink. "The forest cometh to MacBeth! You're not far wrong. Send Jayne and Scarcliff to take down the Capitaine."

"Dead?"

"Foolish to try and bring him in alive. Tell 'em to make sure he's good and dead, as he has a habit of coming back to life. And make sure they only hire the best men they can find. This one's dangerous."

MacAskill mumbled, "The best men they can find in a Port Royal tavern, ya mean?"

Art resumed his card game; he needed a distraction while he mourned his beloved *Arrow*. He struggled for the best quote. *Ah, "who ever loved that loved not at first sight?" Yes, that's it.* He would compose his own expression later after more wine.

Art picked up his cards and removed a telescope from his pocket. "It's Spanish silver from Vera Cruz," he said.

They nodded and played the next hand.

Dr. Strangewayes loaded his carriage with a crate of medical supplies, a satchel full of clothes, and his large brown leather medical bag. He was prepared to assist with medical aid on Nevis, but he was transporting Livia to his plantation first.

After a strong cup of tea with a drop of Strangewayes Special Brand Elixir, he drove to Mrs. Beazley's house on New Street. Upon arrival, he saw Widow Bell unloading fresh linens. He straightened his suit and climbed down to help.

After unloading a few bundles, he gave her a giddy grin.

"Thank you, Doctor." She smiled. "Any other man in this city would want something in return."

"Well, as it is, I have to go away for a while and Mrs. Beazley is not fond of cats."

"You want me to take your cat?"

"In a nutshell, yes."

"Aye. The kids will like it. For how long?"

"Oh, not long. Six months to a year. His name's Boots."

Widow Bell's jaw slacked. "Six months to a year?"

"I've been ordered to go to Nevis, you see."

"Oh. Oh, shit, Doctor. I'm sorry. Of course I'll take the cat. Not to worry." Her pretty hazel eyes stared at him. "Is there anything else I can do for you?"

"As it is, yes." The doctor waved to Mrs. Beazley at the end of the hall and turned back to Widow Bell. "Help me get *Mrs. Beazley* to the carriage, would you?"

Livia stepped forward, disguised in an old dress and travel cloak that had gone out of fashion a quarter of a century ago.

Widow Bell nodded. "Of course. Come along, Mrs. Beazley."

Livia looked back at the real Mrs. Beazley before boarding the carriage. "Goodbye," she said.

"Goodbye, dear. Take care of yourself and your sister." Mrs. Beazley eyed the doctor. "You take care of yourself too. And good luck."

The doctor tipped his hat and helped Livia into his box carriage. "Thank you again, Mrs. Belford."

"Bell would suit just fine, Doctor."

Strangewayes shot her a look. "Right. Beauty it is." He removed an extra key from his pocket. "Oh, here's the key to the apothecary. The cat might want it."

"Aye. I'll make sure the cat gets it."

The doctor climbed up to the driver's seat and the carriage drove away.

At the Merchant Exchange, Strangewayes took a shortcut through to Thames Street. The alley was bustling with men loading and unloading merchandise. A crate carrying a shipment of gamecocks had fallen off the back of a wagon. The doctor was stuck behind a line of stopped wagons. A dozen angry birds chased and pecked anyone walking by.

Strangewayes was ready to the turn the carriage around when he realized he'd been spotted by Edmund Coggshall. Edmund stood beside a sign advertising German and Hapsburg dresses for sale.

"Dr. Strangewayes," Edmund called. "May I have a word, please?"

"Oh, dear Lord, not now," Strangewayes muttered. Then, more loudly, "Edmund, what an unexpected—"

His horse defecated without warning.

Strangewayes cringed, noticing Livia peer out through the open window. "Indeed!"

"Doctor, I would very much like an audience with the young lady, if it pleases her?"

"I remember you," Livia said.

Edmund tipped his ostrich-feather hat and tossed his dress cape over his shoulder. "Edmund Coggshall, at your service."

"I'm afraid we're in a bit of a hurry, Edmund," Strangewayes explained.

"I want the young lady to know that she is no longer indentured." Edmund winked at Livia and handed the doctor a scroll. "You and your sister are free."

Strangewayes read it over. It was a declaration of freedom for Atia and Livia Crisp.

"Thank you, Edmund. But, Mr. Crisp?" Livia probed.

"He has no legal hold on you. This is notarized by a representative of the West India Trading Company."

The doctor rolled up the document. "It appears to be in order." He passed the scroll to Livia. "My dear, I think you are free."

Edmund continued, "I pledge my debt to you and swear, you will always have a safe home here, with me, if you ever want it."

Livia looked dumbfounded. "Well, I – I'm grateful, but I must go for now."

The clucking from the gamecocks grew louder. Two charged at a man's leg and he yelped. A burst of feathers filled the air.

"What the hell is going on out here?" Constable Blower yelled, stepping out of the tobacco shop.

"Sir, the city is being overrun by angry cocks!" someone said.

"Yes, well we must be off and leave Blower to his cocks," Strangewayes insisted.

"Thank you, Edmund!" Livia gushed.

The doctor snapped the reins. "Yes, thank you, Edmund, toodle-oo!" He wondered what Coggshall Junior was playing at; it was clearly some kind of ruse. They swiftly arrived at the Wherry Bridge on Thames Street. "I intended to bring you some pillows." He silently cursed himself and helped her aboard. "It's going to be a hard journey for you."

"I'll manage," Livia insisted.

The wherryman tipped his hat.

"To the Ligania dock please, Mr. Wherryman," Strangewayes said.

“Aye, straight away.”

Livia settled in. “We’re off to your plantation?”

“Yes, to the peaceful tranquility of my plantation.”

The doctor hoped it would be peaceful. He could use a short reprieve before venturing to Nevis. There were special herbs that needed cultivating and more supplies to gather. But most importantly, there was a concoction involving frog glands that he wanted to try.

Roc
Braziliano
GO
2015

Carlena's Plantation

Carlena trudged along the path beside the corn field seeking Lilly, who was nowhere to be seen among the sea of green stalks. Carlena dabbed her forehead in the afternoon heat. The sky was bright blue with fluffy white clouds as far as the eye could see. She sighed. She needed her "Assistant Manager" to help her manage the damn plantation. There was honey to collect, the fruit trees needed picking and pruning, washing piled up, and security had become haphazard since Yaguara's departure. Thankfully she had already killed a pig and gathered yams, peppers, and peas for tonight's supper.

Carlena heard raised voices as she approached the tool shed. Preferring to keep her nose out of the business of others, she wanted to bypass it completely.

That is, until she heard Lilly, whose outrage carried across the corn field. "What the hell are ya doing?"

Carlena peered through a space in the shed wall to see Fatima straddling Ekene on the one of the work tables.

Fatima immediately slid off him and stood to face Lilly.

"What were ya doing?" Lilly's fists dug into her hips.

"You said I needed to find more sex!"

"Not with him; he's mine! I work all day, breaking me back, only to find you two havin' inner-racial sex behind me back!"

Fatima crossed her arms over her chest. "You have more than one man. How am I to know which one I can have?"

Ekene scrambled to pull up his trousers.

Lilly stuck her nose up at him. "I thought we had something special!"

Fatima pointed her finger at Lilly's face. "You can find others, you have so many and I have none!"

Ekene looked up. "She does? How many?"

Carlena shook her head and muttered to herself. "Unbelievable! What's wrong with this place?" She tore back down the path towards Strangewayes's house unleashing a chain of Spanish curse words.

Gillis the gatekeeper intercepted her when she reached the road. "Carlena! There are buccaneers here. They came up the river." He caught his breath. "About twenty of them on the south side of the lake."

"Did they say what they want?"

"No one's spoken with them yet. They only just arrived."

"Better get everyone to the Gathering Place. No guards. Tell them all to bring guns and maintain a perimeter."

Gillis wiped his forehead. "Are you going down there?"

Carlena nodded. "It's probably just friends of Strangewayes. You know how he is: 'Oh, by all means, pop by and say *hel-low*!'" She started down the hill to the boathouse.

"You should take a gun!" Gillis called.

"If there are twenty of them, how good a shot do you think I am?" Carlena said. "If I don't come back, you can take that as an indication that they're hostile."

The short jaunt through the shady trees was a pleasant distraction, even if it was to end with potentially unfriendly buccaneers. She would not be able to hold her tongue with Strangewayes. He needed a damn good blasting about a great number of things! The echo of the Gathering Place bell sounded as she neared the boathouse. Two buccaneers stood beside their canoe, smoking pipes.

Carlena recognized the one with long dark hair. "We met once before. They called you Dash the Creep?"

He grinned, and his dark eyes smoldered. "It's Dashiell Dupris. And my Indian name is Little Jaguar. Now we have been properly introduced."

"His men call him de Kreep," Arsenault added.

"Carlena."

"I remember you. You were a lot younger."

"Thank you." Carlena folded her arms to prevent herself from throttling him. "The doctor's not here."

"We're seeking the Capitaine."

"He's not here, either." She gave a polite smile.

"We'll come back in two days. Please tell him if you see him."

"I will." Carlena heard footsteps. Tanama and Ekene arrived with guns. "Stand down, they're friends."

Arsenault's and Tanama's eyes met. "*Bonjour,* Mademoiselle. They call me Arsenault." He winked.

She held his stare. "Tanama."

"We'll see you in a few days, then," Carlena said.

"Oui, *merci*." De Kreep bowed and climbed back into the canoe with Arsenault. They paddled away.

Tanama continued to gawk at them.

Carlena sighed. "Oh, not you too. Is it mating season?"

Tanama shrugged. "I was being polite."

By late afternoon, the sun had shifted, casting Strangewayes's house in a veil of heat. After fetching several buckets of well water and carrying them into the house, Carlena patted her forehead. Her legs slowed as she returned to the well. She cranked the handle. A stream of water sputtered out and began to fill a fifth and final bucket just as a horrendous shriek came from the kitchen.

"It never rains but it pours." Carlena dragged herself up the front steps, and Fatima sprinted from the side door followed by a giant galliwasp. Its light brownish lizard scales shimmered beneath the sun. In its snake-like mouth it dragged a dead pig across the yard before abandoning it in pursuit of Fatima.

Ekene raced out with a musket. Instinctively Carlena grabbed the gun, aimed, and fired. Smoke billowed from the top of the lizard's head.

Fatima stumbled and turned to the dead creature. "That was a good shot."

"You're gonna need to learn to fend for yourself," Carlena snapped. "That was supper! Now you can go kill another pig."

"It came out of nowhere!" Fatima gasped. "Why can't we use that pig?"

Ekene helped her to her feet. "It's tainted. Galliwasps are poisonous. You could have died."

"Dr. Strangewayes says not to kill the galliwasps, but what are we supposed to do with them? Do you want to eat tonight? Go get another pig!" Carlena stormed off.

Strangewayes's carriage rolled down the lane. A passenger was propped up in the back, flinching whenever the vehicle hit a rough patch. *Great, another mouth to feed!* Carlena took deep breaths as the carriage slowed to a stop. "This must be Livia."

"Hello," Livia said.

"I heard a shot." Strangewayes's eyebrows furrowed.

"I killed a galliwasp. The big one. He came right into the house this time."

The doctor observed the corpse. "Yes. Well, I suppose he had it coming." He helped Livia down. "Welcome to the plantation, my dear."

Livia wobbled. "Welcome," she slurred.

"I had to give her something for the pain. Very much against her will, I might add." He propped her up with his arm. "The pain was too much for her and me."

"I'm going to be very upset with you later," Livia said.

"Perhaps we can take you inside and put you to bed first," the doctor suggested. "I assume Atia's been taken to the O'Malleys?"

Carlena followed with the bags. "Yes."

"She made it?" Livia exclaimed. "What'dya know! Atia made it. I owe her a shilling."

They approached the doctor's room. "Good. We'll let Livia rest up for a few days, and then she can join her sister." He stopped abruptly, jolting Livia, who screamed. "Oh, sorry! What's happened to my room?"

"Your bed is broken." Carlena gave Ekene a dirty glare.

"Oh. Well, then, perhaps the guest room."

Livia was transported down the hallway into a small room where an uncompromised bed lay waiting. She was gently lowered. "I'm content to stay here awhile if ya don't mind."

"There were buccaneers here today. Dupris was their leader," Carlena added.

"Yes, he's been around lately. Did they say when they're coming back?"

"A few days. They're looking for the Capitaine."

"You rest up, Livia. We'll be back to check on you in a bit." The doctor went to the library. "Who's been into my books?"

Carlena paused in the doorway. "I saw the galliwasp taking a peek."

Strangewayes poured them both a brandy.

"How would you like to run things permanently?" he asked outright.

Carlena snarled. "I'm going to slap you. And it *is* personal." She drank back the brandy in one gulp.

He gave her an apologetic gaze. "I have to go to Nevis. Not by choice, I assure you."

"We have to leave soon. How long will you be gone?"

"I don't know. Long, though. When Cormac's found a location, don't wait for me. Get everyone out and I'll meet you there, wherever it is."

"If the Capitaine agrees, we have our ship. He must know a place."

"The Capitaine's ship has been captured in Port Royal. Nonetheless, be ready to go when Cormac says so."

"We are ready," Carlena confirmed.

They moved to the kitchen where Strangewayes put the kettle on. He paused at the window. Fatima and Ekene were removing the dead pig from the yard. "Ah. I see Fatima and Ekene are getting acquainted."

Carlena frowned. "Ekene and Lilly, too."

"Oh dear. I may have to introduce them to the word 'herpes'."

Gillis knocked at the front door. "Good day, Doc. Nice to have you back."

"It's good to be back, old chum." Strangewayes and Gillis shook hands.

"Carlena, Bilwi's back. He's brought a clergyman and runaway children."

Carlena rolled her eyes. "How many?"

"Five or six."

Strangewayes returned to the kettle. "If you could take care of it, I have to unpack. I want to finish something, a new concoction from frog glands."

"Another concoction? Right, I'll look after it then!" Carlena hissed. "Where are they?"

"They're at the west gate."

"For the record," she stated, "I don't know how Yaguara does it. The next time he goes away, we need more people on security!" Carlena slammed the front door.

"Objection noted," Strangewayes called.

It was sundown by the time Carlena and Gillis arrived at the west gate by carriage. Bilwi, a clergyman, and five children dressed in rags waited.

Carlena marched up to Bilwi with a sour expression. "Who do we have today?"

"Refugees from a plantation revolt in the north," he said.

"Which plantation was it?" Gillis asked. "We never heard anything."

The clergyman advanced. Although cloaked, wisps of white hair could be seen, and he had peculiar pink eyes. "Brother Bright from the St. Andrew's Mission. I've come to ask the doctor to take them in.

These children fled a slave revolt at a northern plantation. I found them wandering in the hills, searching for food. The good Lord was looking out for them and delivered them into my hands. They haven't eaten for hours." He pointed to a little girl of nine or ten. "They call her Nanny. She takes care of the little ones."

"Fancy that, her name also means 'Daughter of the Queen' in her language," Carlena added.

"None of them speak English," the clergyman continued.

"And the girl doesn't speak at all."

"We won't refuse them. Let's get them some food." Carlena studied the pink-eyed man. "You're a long way from home."

"The Lord's work knows no borders," he mused. "I haven't eaten anything myself. I don't suppose I could impose on your hospitality for one night before heading back?"

"Certainly," Carlena said flatly.

"I can take you back in the morning," Bilwi offered.

"Splendid! Thank you," the clergyman replied.

When everyone was aboard the carriage, Carlena drove them to the Gathering Place. Once fed, the children were given spare clothes. The pig would not be ready for a few hours, but the residents gathered, eating fruit and cured meat.

Carlena returned to Strangewayes's house to find the doctor on the porch having supper, accompanied by a glass of wine made from the plantation's own fruit. He wrote a few notes in the book he kept in his breast pocket.

Carlena came up the front steps.

"Please, sit down." He gestured to a nearby chair.

She collapsed, her tired body aching.

"Wine?"

She shook her head.

"You're not really going to make me drink alone, are you?" He poured her a glass.

Carlena grabbed the cup and took a large mouthful. "I've found rooms for the children at the western farmhouse and a spare bungalow for the monk."

"Make sure it's lights-out early tonight, and no laughing. We don't want the church hearing of anyone having fun," the doctor insisted. "How's Lilly adjusting?"

"She's doing well. She's under the weather, so I gave her the rest of the night off."

Strangewayes topped off both glasses. "Is that better?"

Carlena took another mouthful. "Oh, that's good!"

"It's you who will lead these people."

"Me?" She shook her head. "Yaguara, maybe."

"I'm sure he would be the ideal choice to help you, but it's *you* the people love and admire."

Carlena was speechless.

"I'm setting a bad example by leaving. They'll be looking to you for leadership. It won't be easy, but I have complete confidence in you. You are a strong, capable leader."

Carlena finished the wine. She had never heard him speak this way before. "Just make sure you come back. I'll save you a spot at the table, wherever that table may be."

She rose to retire for the night.

"Good evening." Strangewayes tipped his hat.

"Good night," she said and strolled along the path to her house. Stars twinkled brightly and the scent of the sea wafted through the trees. She would be sad to leave this place; it had been her home for three decades. But they would rebuild and persevere. She would lead them to prosperity.

Nanny
GO
2015

Ponder Field

Lilly sat on the porch steps at the doctor's house. She rolled a mango in her hand but couldn't bring herself to eat. She'd been under the weather for days now; the nausea wouldn't go away. Instead she opened a bottle.

Tanama arrived, her arm still in a sling. "How are you?"

Lilly tried to smile. "The same. How's the arm?"

"It never stops hurting."

"Doc's got stuff for pain."

"Yaguara doesn't like me using Dr. Strangewayes's remedies. They make me sick."

"Is Yaguara like your father, or do ya give him favors?"

"He's very much a father to me. A mentor and a good friend," Tanama mused. "And a bit of a mother hen."

Lilly felt the sting of tears. "Cherry was my mother hen. I wonder if I'll ever see her again." She took a mouthful of rum. "So, I heard you saw them buccaneers? What were they like?"

Tanama reflected. "They were filthy, covered in sweat with muscular arms and legs – halfway between man and beast."

"Make ya wet, don't they?"

Tanama sighed. "Like a river!"

Carlena marched around the house with one of the perimeter guards. "The gate was left open?"

"I thought Bilwi closed it when he left with that monk."

"Damn it! We can't afford to be sloppy!"

"Think I'll head to the Gathering Place," Tanama whispered, taking off.

Lilly didn't blame her, Carlena was increasingly grumpy. Running a plantation was a lot of work, more work than she'd realized. And Lilly being sick didn't help. She missed Atia too, and Port Royal. Especially Cherry.

Ekene brought a basket of vegetables for Fatima, who was working in the kitchen. On his way out, he paused beside Lilly. Jealousy got the better of her as she rammed the bottle of rum into his groin.

Ekene groaned and held his wounded testicles. "You stupid drunk!"

Fatima ran outside and gave Lilly a push. "What did you do that for?"

"Sorry," Lilly slurred a bit. "It's me temper."

Fatima slapped Lilly across the face; Lilly pulled Fatima's hair. The pair scraped it out, clawing and smacking one another.

Carlena charged forth. "What the hell's going on?"

"What's wrong with you?" Fatima screamed.

"You!" Lilly pointed. "How could you? You knew I loved him! You knew it!"

"What?" Fatima pushed her again. "No, I didn't!"

"Stop it!" Carlena roared, separating them. "I've had enough of this shit! Lilly, get in the house and stay there!" She glared at Ekene. "Go see Strangewayes."

"I'm sorry." Lilly sniffed. "Cherry says I can get emotional at times."

Carlena yanked Lilly inside, slamming the door.

Lilly massaged her arm.

Carlena's eyes narrowed. "That was cruel."

Lilly folded her hands over her belly. "He shouldn't have stuck it in her!"

"Are you still feeling sick?"

"Aye, I'm sick. Sick of cock!"

Carlena nodded. "That can be normal for your stage."

"Cherry said I go through stages."

Carlena shook her head. "You are with child."

Lilly laughed a moment, and then saw the seriousness in Carlena's face. "A child! 'Tis not possible!"

"Lilly, you are with child."

Lilly was ready to vomit. "But Doc said that couldn't happen on account of me illnesses."

"As smart as Strangewayes is, he is still just a man. When it comes to the female body, they know naught."

Lilly studied the wallpaper. "A baby? What do I do? I don't know how to have a baby. They're horrible little things! Please don't tell anyone."

"Not a soul."

Lilly felt as though a ton of bricks had just fallen on her. "A baby. I wonder whose it is?"

Carlena patted her shoulder. "That I cannot help you with."

Carlena oversaw preparations for supper while Lilly walked around aimlessly, her hand frequently touching her belly. It was too much to take in. She went down the hall to the library, where the doctor was reading and taking notes. Instead of interrupting, she went to the front door to see Fatima on the porch steps, crying.

Minuit swooped down, landing on the rail beside her. "*Bonjour*, Mademoiselle."

Fatima studied the peculiar bird. "Welcome back, Minuit. I trust you had a pleasant trip?"

"*Comme ci comme ca.*"

"The Capitaine is coming," Fatima called.

"I'm so sorry, Fatima," Lilly wept from the doorway.

Fatima turned away and patted Minuit's head.

"I see them!" Carlena said. "Atia's back. What the hell?"

Lilly's expression changed and she wiped her eyes. Her friend had returned. They had so much to talk about. She didn't know where to begin.

La Roche continued to pull the wagon with Yaguara's help. The strength in his arms wavered and they halted at a cluster of shady trees. The tiny donkeys brayed with relief. A welcoming committee formed on the porch.

Strangewayes came out to meet them. "Atia," he began. "Well, not that it isn't good to see you, but I'm a little surprised."

Gladstone disembarked. "Crisp's slaver captain tracked us down."

Atia looked glum. "We had to fight them off. Me da says it's too dangerous for me there."

"And here," Yaguara added. "We have an evacuation plan. We must prepare immediately."

"Well, you're leaving without me, I'm afraid. I have to go to Nevis," Strangewayes explained.

Gladstone frowned. "Nevis?"

"Yes. I'm meeting a supply ship in Ligania tomorrow."

"Why Nevis? Why now?"

"They were hit particularly hard by the hurricane. They need doctors straight away."

"Yeah, but why you?" Gladstone was dismayed. "You're Chief Surgeon of Port Royal!"

"Yes, that does have me rather concerned, but we must press on." He tilted his head at the donkeys. "Your steeds are a tad small, aren't they?"

"They were taller when we left," Gladstone explained. "Must have been all those caimans we passed on the way here. They was taking little bites."

"What's happening in Port Royal?" la Roche asked.

The doctor grew uncomfortable. "Well, Capitaine, seems we've put you in rather a predicament. You've been officially charged with sixteen counts of murder and eight counts of theft and property damage."

He shrugged. "Not the first time, uh?"

"Capitaine," the doctor spoke gently, leading him aside. "It's worse than that, I'm afraid. The English have taken your ship."

La Roche wandered to the side of the house in silence for a moment. "Damn it, Picard!"

"She's in Port Royal under guard. They gave up without a fight."

La Roche stared at the wood paneling. "His brother would never have given up. I picked the smart one." His pulse accelerated into a terrible rhythm.

"They are being held at Marshallsea Prison awaiting trial. The rumor is that Capitaine la Roche refuses to cooperate."

La Roche's hand trembled as he paced. "Oui. Now the good news?"

Strangewayes cringed. "I'm sorry, that's your lot."

La Roche cursed in French. He could feel Atia watching.

"Who's Capitaine la Roche?" she asked.

He met her pretty green eyes. "I am." He wandered over to the side of the house again to think. Atia was coming towards him when the doctor stopped her.

"Best to give him a minute."

Lilly gave Atia a welcoming hug. "So glad yer back!"

"How is Livia doing?" Atia queried.

"You can ask her yourself. She's inside."

"She is?"

"Yes, in the guest room."

Lilly interjected. "How's Cherry and Vie? And Jayne?"

"They're fine," Strangewayes assured. "He's fine, I think. Miles, may I see you inside with the Capitaine and Yaguara? I need to speak with you all."

"We'll talk soon." Lilly squeezed Atia's hand before wandering off.

La Roche reluctantly followed everyone in. Carlena took Atia to reunite with her sister in privacy. Meanwhile, the others gathered in the sitting room and Strangewayes poured drinks.

"We're all set," Gladstone began. "Ships will meet us in Ligania in four days."

Strangewayes raised his glass. "Well done! With O'Malley?"

"Alban Jones. O'Malley's too preoccupied with Slasher Al and Crisp's slaver captain."

"Well, he knew the risks of bringing them over. How's Jones going to pick you up in Ligania?"

"Staging an aid ship to Nevis. We'll load up in Ligania and Yaguara will lead them to an island only he and the Capitaine know of."

Yaguara stuffed tobacco into his pipe and lit it. "We sail southeast until we're out of sight and then disappear into the Caribbean Sea."

The doctor fell into his chair with ease. "I couldn't have planned it better myself. It's perfect!" Strangewayes eyed la Roche. "This island of yours – whereabouts is it?"

La Roche smirked. "We're not telling you when you're sailing off to Nevis! Give your head a shake!"

Yaguara took a deep puff. "The Capitaine and Yagaura are the only ones who know the location. Carlena can make the final decision to stay when we get there."

"I cannot go with you," la Roche insisted. "I must get my ship and crew back."

Strangewayes's eyes widened. "Yes. Since I wasn't born yesterday, I'll ask. You didn't accidentally get blown in by a hurricane, did you, Capitaine?"

"The French invasion of Jamaica is going ahead," la Roche confirmed. "I was going to ask you for your help."

"Sorry, come again? My help?"

"Laurens and I want to do this without attacking Port Royal, and with as little bloodshed as possible. We don't want any civilians killed or taken hostage. Governor de Cussy asks you to take over as Lieutenant Governor of Jamaica."

The doctor seemed to choke on his own bile. "Why me?"

"Because we know you. You're a good and decent man."

"Good and decent men make excellent puppets until you corrupt them. I shall abolish the slave trade in Jamaica once in power. Will that cause a problem?"

"You wouldn't have that power."

"Precisely my point." The doctor gave a polite smile. "What does Governor de Cussy plan to do about the slave trade?"

"You know Laurens and me are no supporters of slavery. Governor de Cussy is going to appoint Jean du Casse to oversee and regulate it."

"Du Casse is a slave trader!" Strangewayes seemed miffed. "Well, fancy that!"

"By necessity, not by choice and he knows more about it than any of us. You think I would go along with them if I thought it wasn't right?" la Roche questioned.

"Yaguara is disappointed in the Capitaine. Regulate the slave trade? We fought through many adventures together and never has Yaguara heard the Capitaine say anything so utterly stupid."

La Roche always admired Yaguara's honesty. "The slave trade is not going away. There's nothing we can do about that."

"Trying to regulate the slave trade is like trying to regulate the ale tap in a pirate tavern," Gladstone said. "It's not possible."

"It's only going to get the Capitaine in shit!" Yaguara continued. "Why doesn't de Cussy appoint the Capitaine or Laurens as lieutenant governor?"

"The buccaneers are forbidden. This all must be done carefully and legally to avoid civilian deaths."

Strangewayes pursed his lips. "Breaking the rules a bit, then, aren't you?"

Gladstone stepped forward. "But how do you plan to capture Jamaica without taking on Port Royal? That's like stealing from a big man and then hiding in his shadow."

"Capitaine plans to blockade Jamaica. Strangle trade and make Port Royal surrender out of starvation," Yaguara spoke bluntly.

"Then Governor de Cussy can appoint key people in government, kick out the Whigs, and stop the English and Dutch flow of slaves coming into the Americas!" la Roche argued.

"And replace them with French slavers?" Strangewayes shook his head. "Do you really think this will avoid civilian casualties? And the Maroons? What does du Casse and de Cussy plan to do with them? Have them over for afternoon sugar treats, maybe a game of backgammon with the wives?"

"We'll give them land of their own on Jamaica and Hispaniola."

"They've been lied to before. A war will give them an excuse to attack the plantations," Gladstone said.

"I'm afraid my answer is 'no,' Capitaine. I will not support replacing one regime with another when it will only cost lives," Strangewayes spoke firmly.

"Yaguara goes with Strangewayes and Miles. He respects the Capitaine but thinks the Capitaine is being naive."

La Roche glared.

"What's in it for you and Laurens if you're not taking land?" the doctor pressed.

"I can't speak for Laurens but I plan to retire. Someplace secret, some place safe to raise a..." la Roche paused. He suddenly felt absurd wanting a family. He couldn't even keep his own crew safe. "You can even return here, without worry."

"So ultimately our goals are the same, only different. I can't abide a system that allows slavery. I wish you could see it my way," Strangewayes sighed and removed a vial from his coat pocket. "Which reminds me, we should have one 'Last Supper' here, the lot of us, tonight up on the bluffs."

"Packing should be first," Yaguara said.

"One more night. We have four days. How slow do you want them to walk?" The doctor cocked an eyebrow. "They can start packing tomorrow. Give them one night to say goodbye and have some merriment. Some of these people have called this place home for years." He rose from the chair. "Time to make preparations for supper, I say."

All was quiet around the house for the remainder of the day. Atia chatted with Livia for hours until it was time to let her rest. It was evening when Livia emerged in a handmade wicker wheelchair, with the help of the doctor.

Atia evaluated her Capitaine, Paul la Roche. So that was his name, shrouded in such mystery. Everyone had pretended not to know to shield her from the danger of that knowledge. But really, was she in any more danger than she'd been in before? With Mandingo around danger was simply a fact of life.

Atia's thoughts turned to Lilly. Her friend seemed happy to see her, but was acting awfully peculiar and was undoubtedly ill with something. Lilly assisted with the preparations for a twilight picnic. Plates of sliced pork, cured fish, fruits, bread, and cheese were carried to the picnic table on the bluff – what the doctor called "Ponder Field."

Atia sat next to Livia. "So hard to believe our brothers are all grown up and tall as can be. Rourke asked about you, he sends his best."

"The man never paid me no mind me whole life."

"He loves you. He was overjoyed to find out you're alive," Atia assured. "I'm so worried about them. You weren't there when Mandingo attacked. He was out for blood."

"When's he not? Sounds like yer da fought him off well enough."

"He still can't catch fish." Atia laughed briefly. "I don't know. He was different this time. Something's up, but he wouldn't say."

The two sisters looked down at the scrolls declaring their freedom.

"Are they legitimate?" Livia asked Strangewayes.

"Indeed, they seem to be. You have been legally freed."

The sisters slapped their hands together in the air, after which both recoiled in pain.

Lilly came over and patted Atia's shoulder. "Now you can go anywhere."

"Unfortunately, no. Atia is wanted for questioning," the doctor corrected. "Livia can go anywhere."

"Where will you go?" Lilly asked.

"Port Royal, I think."

"Well, anywhere but there, as the saying goes," the doctor said.

Atia grimaced. "Why there?"

"Edmund offered us a future. Our own bloody fathers couldn't conjure that. I want to go back."

Atia was about to mention the gold that her da had given her, and then counted her teeth instead. She was always put off by her sister's stubbornness. "Fine, go back."

"Sorry, but you can't, not there." Strangewayes reasoned, "Not until these people are away. And don't forget, the Capitaine is a wanted man. You'll need to rest up here until we're ready to move."

Livia clasped her sister's hand. "And you too. Edmund's offering you a home. I don't want to see ya turn into a pirate."

"Port Royal smells like shit and smoke. I want to live some place that smells like life." Catching the Capitaine's eye, she knew that's what he wanted too.

"I'll be there when ya change yer mind."

"Why don't ya ever trust me?" Atia huffed. "Ya don't know the man."

"Who, Edmund?" Lilly intervened. "Oh, he's a real gentleman. A man of his word too. He knows how to treat a lady with respect."

"Thank you." Livia sneered.

"And if yer ever in a hurry, just massage it with your tongue and he comes every time." Lilly grinned, making Atia smile. "Yer sister's right, ya don't wanna go back there."

"Watch out for her for me." Livia scrutinized her sister. "She follows her heart and never her head."

Livia surveyed Port Royal in the distance.

"Wow, that's pronounced," Lilly misspoke. "Yer a scholar type like Edmund, maybe ya do belong together?" She approached Gladstone. "So, how long have ya worked for the doc, Miles?"

"All me life. I never really considered it working *for* him, really. More like helping him steer the carriage of life."

"Your whole life?" Fatima pressed.

"As far back as I can remember. Doc says I was about two or three years old when he found me on the beach in Barbados."

"And he took you in?" Lilly asked.

"After two weeks no one claimed me, so he took down the sign."

"How'd ya get yer name?"

"He always said the day he found me, he'd been walking miles and he had a particularly glad stone going, but later I found the documents of a free man who died named Miles Gladstone." He raised a bottle of rum. "To Miles Gladstone, whoever he was!" They all toasted. "Say, anyone see Ekene? I thought he'd be here by now?"

Strangewayes sipped fruit wine. "He is taking some rest time. Had rather a bad injury this afternoon."

"Injury?"

"Yes." The doctor eyed Lilly and Carlena. "Light duties only for at least a month. I'm sure Lilly won't mind picking up the slack."

"Is he alright?" Gladstone pressed.

"Well, he…um, no," Strangewayes said.

Lilly wrung her hands together. "I'm sorry."

"Tell him, uh?" the Capitaine replied, sitting beside Atia.

The doctor ate some cured fish. "Most of us are quite attached to that spot, to say the least."

"Well, I'm very protective of mine. I intend to leave this world the same way I came in," the Capitaine professed. "Between a woman's legs."

Atia groped his thigh. "Mine?"

He kissed her neck. "I can think of nothing better."

Livia covered her face.

Atia kissed her lover square on the lips. "The Capitaine saved me life in Port Royal."

Livia frowned. "So I've heard."

"He killed many men too," Atia boasted. "I'm forever bound to him now."

Minuit joined the group, landing beside Livia, who came face to face with the bird for the first time.

"*Bonjour*, Mademoiselle," Minuit began.

Livia screamed, causing everyone to jump.

"This is Minuit from Madagascar, apparently," the Capitaine said. "Minuit, Atia's sister – Atia's sister, Minuit."

Minuit nudged Livia's hand. "*Ma chérie.*"

She retracted immediately. "I'd be grateful if you kept yer bird away from me."

Minuit was thoroughly dejected and went to Atia for solace. She patted his head. "Oh, just ignore her. I still think yer a treasure."

"Think I'll turn in." Livia struggled to rise on her own.

"I'll help you," Gladstone offered. "I'll get the wheelchair."

"No, thank you. I can manage." She stopped at the table to grab a few mouthfuls, and then fought her way up the trail.

Strangewayes opened his medical bag.

The Capitaine's curiosity was piqued. "What nightmare concoction have you invented this time?"

"The primary ingredient for this one comes from a frog gland. I take it you're in?"

The Capitaine smiled. "Oui."

Strangewayes looked to Carlena, "You're welcome to join us, my dear."

"Not for me, thanks."

"Is there something wrong with it?" Atia asked.

"Carlena had a bad experience once. It can happen, but I assure you, you are among friends," the doctor said.

Carlena sighed. "A galliwasp came out of the bushes and attacked me."

"Yes. Not the sort of thing you want happening when you try hallucinogenic drugs."

Carlena tilted her head. "And they all laughed at me."

"Yes. Well, we did apologize." Strangewayes shrugged. "You see, having no idea the bloody thing even existed, we all thought it was terribly funny. Or that it was a cruel trick or something." He chuckled. "Poor girl. But I assure you that can never happen again."

"Poor girl," Carlena huffed. "I learned to shoot a gun that day."

"Did she ever!" Gladstone grinned.

"Yes, terrible shame about the galliwasp. That was the only male left that I know of. And I discovered that certain birds here rely on the galliwasp dung for food. The partially digested nuts of the —"

"I'll go see how the packing is going," Carlena interrupted loudly.

"Right-o, you know where we are," Strangewayes said.

Gladstone loaded his plate with bread, cheese, pork, and salted fish.

"You might not want to eat too much," the doctor advised.

Gladstone stuffed cheese in his mouth. "Weird drugs or not, I'm bloody starving!"

It wasn't until supper was finished and the moon hung like a golden ornament over the ocean that they all ventured near the cliff. After taking Strangewayes's concoction, the moon cast a spectacular shimmer over the water's surface. It drew closer and closer to the earth while the shadows upon it fluctuated from a giant happy face to an angry sneer.

Atia felt as though her chair floated, her eyes wide, staring up as the moon winked at her. "I can see the face!" She pointed. "How can you not see a face? Look! It winked!"

The Capitaine formed an imaginary telescope with his hands. "It is not a face. See it through a telescope."

"It's a giant plate," Lilly insisted. "A dirty plate."

"Everything is dirty to you." The Capitaine put his handmade telescope in his pocket.

A wave of laughter crossed the field.

"It's God's chamber pot," Gladstone pondered. "You see, sometimes he leaves the door all the way open and the moon is full. Then sometimes he closes the door a bit so Mrs. God doesn't get mad."

A shooting star streaked across the sky, leaving a trail that glowed for several minutes. Gasps broke out. Then more laughter erupted as the clouds changed shapes.

"Why is Mars red?" Lilly asked. "Oh, now it's pink!"

"They were out of blue," Strangewayes affirmed.

Atia watched the Capitaine with extreme fascination and he gave her a crooked smile.

"You're seeing things the Strangewayes Way as they say," he said.

"How come ya look so much like the bird?" She cupped his face and tried to squish his head. "How come your eyes are so far apart?"

The Capitaine laughed. "They're not!"

Atia sat on his lap, still staring at his face. "Yer half fucking bird! Look at yer eyes!"

"I was born in a hurry, uh?"

She wrapped her arms around him and tilted her head up at the ship-like clouds floating by. "We'll have to have lots of little birds, then."

"I am at your service," the Capitaine whispered.

"If you made ships that float on clouds, you could sail anywhere," Fatima said. "Over land or sea."

"Why *don't* we have ships on clouds?" Lilly spun in a circle. "I mean, birds fly."

The doctor stared across the water. "Well, they have wings to help them. Unfortunately, we're restricted by something a man named Newton called gravity. What goes up must come down."

Lilly dropped to the ground, landing on her bottom. "Well, I think it's a fine idea. Sod him and his gravity!"

Another shooting star crossed the sky and split apart into dozens of lights. "Wow!" Atia's eyes widened.

Lilly patted Gladstone's arm. "Go on."

"I didn't say anything. Did you?"

"Nope." Lilly shook her head very slowly.

"What are they all?" Atia asked.

"Faraway places," Fatima pondered.

"Faraway places?" the Capitaine snickered.

Gladstone's mouth dropped open with revelation, and then he sat up straight in his chair. "What else could they be?"

The Capitaine squinted to get a better look. "That's a lot of faraway places."

Atia and Lilly stopped laughing and gazed up intently.

"When you see Port Royal or San Juan at night, way out in the ocean, are they not just a flicker of light," Fatima suggested.

The Capitaine grew alarmed. "*Merde*! A lot of faraway places that is!" He gripped Atia's hand. "They could attack at any time!"

Fatima took a sip from a shiny metal cup. "Some of them must be ports."

Small sparkling birds flew past Atia's head. "Who lives there, then?"

Fatima shrugged. "I don't know. Gods? People?"

"*Merde*!" the Capitaine said.

Another shooting star streaked across the sky with a glowing tail that caused gasps of amazement.

"Ok, what was that?" Lilly asked the doctor.

"I don't know, but he's in an awful damned hurry!" The doctor tapped the Capitaine's shoulder. "Mind if I have a word?"

Lilly peered around. "What is that goddamn noise? It keeps me awake at night."

"Sounds like rusty chains," Atia replied.

Strangewayes rose from his chair. "It's the frogs."

Fatima covered her ears. "Why are they so loud?"

"It's their mating," said Gladstone.

Lilly laughed. "You mean they're all little screamers?"

Gladstone nodded. "Aye, they're all getting their little jollies off."

"I can top them any time," Atia boasted.

"Oui, she can," the Capitaine agreed.

"Aww!" Lilly giggled. "You go, little frogs!"

"Who are you calling little?" the Capitaine said.

Strangewayes summoned the Capitaine. "Mind if I have a word?"

Atia climbed off her lover's lap.

"If I'm not back in ten minutes, you come find me, oui?"

Atia mimed a cross over her heart. "Promise." She observed them curiously as the path devoured their feet. The doctor was now a graying bullfrog in a business suit with a pulsating chin.

"Yaguara is right," the Capitaine said. "They must be ready to leave quickly."

"They'll be ready." The doctor swatted at the air. "Strangewayes Way is a model for a self-sufficient colony and these people have flourished."

Atia rubbed her eyes as the gray bullfrog snatched a dragonfly out of midair with his tongue.

"Now I am getting nervous," the Capitaine said.

The doctor chewed. "What I was trying to do here was to stop the mass extinction of people and animals from lust for greed and power, but it's a battle that can't be won. We have to find a place out of the way. Far away."

"Far enough away that the Spanish, French, English, and Dutch don't want it. Your own private *sérénité*?"

"Yes, that's what it is! Our own serenity!"

The Capitaine nodded. "Oui, the place we picked is all that and more. Very hidden."

The doctor staggered a couple more feet down the path. "Then come with us. You, Atia, Cormac. We can all start over."

"I could get used to the idea of *sérénité*, but the English know I'm back and they won't stop hunting me."

"You disappeared without a trace once. You can do it again. Also, young Atia seems to have fallen for you. I can't see you passing her up." Strangewayes strolled back along the trail. "Sorry we were gone so long," he said to the group.

"You left only a minute ago and you were right there." Fatima pointed.

The doctor massaged his temple. "Oh my, this is going to hurt tomorrow."

Lilly grabbed Atia's shoulder, giving her a squeeze. "Serenity sounds charming! When do we leave? And why are the English and the French at war? They've always been friends."

"Most of Europe is already at war," the doctor explained. "They're calling it the War of the League of Augsburg."

Lilly stretched her arms above her head as though trying to pluck stars from the sky. “What are they fighting over?”

“The Holy Trinity.” Strangewayes counted using his fingers. “Money, power, and religion. The three are one, a trinity. The basic design for control of the world.”

Atia kissed the Capitaine’s cheek. “My Capitaine will stay with me, won’t you?”

“Oui. As soon as I can.”

“Tomorrow I leave for Nevis.” The doctor gave a sad smile. “You’re going to have to settle without me.”

“Don’t you worry, man.” Gladstone patted the doctor’s back. “Improvisation is me best quality.” He raised his cup. “We can do it. We’re ready!”

Fatima raised her glass. “I officially name our future home Serenity!”

“Serenity!” Atia cheered.

“Oui, *Sérénité!*” the Capitaine called.

“Capitaine, you were raised by buccaneers on Hispaniola. Your French is as bad as mine.” The doctor raised his glass. “But *Sérénité* it is!”

Atia couldn’t wait and gazed up at the stars. “So, which one is it?”

Arrivals and Departures

The rattling of trays and plates interrupted Governor Dewar's careful counting of the leaves on the wallpaper. Slaves set up breakfast at the dining table while the family bustled about. Chico Gonzales the rat dog barked while rubbing his backside against the wall. To top it off, a rooster crowed from afar, echoing across the entire Ligania retreat.

Dewar sat with his counterpart, Lord Llewellyn, who held his head.

"This is intolerable," Llewellyn moaned.

Dewar pressed his chin against the table top. "Tell me about it. We're living like peasants here."

"This may be the worst headache I ever had." Llewellyn massaged his temple. "Wish I had some of that Strangewayes Cure-All Formula."

Dewar gazed at his beloved smoky city across the water. "That stuff should be – and probably is – illegal."

"So is everything that works." Llewellyn watched the yard through the terrace door. "Are we setting up to beat some balls?"

"We are. I am lieutenant governor by rights, and we should have a few little pleasures while we're stuck on the other side of the world."

"I'm afraid my head's just not into flogging any balls right now."

Dewar poured his friend a brandy. "Nonsense. Drink up! A good ball-basting is exactly what we need right now." Dewar rose. "I'm gonna beat some balls, damn it!"

Lady Lyla Llewellyn filled her plate. "Are you not having breakfast?"

"Aye, go on without us. We've got our balls to flog," Dewar replied.

Lyla ate a wedge of mango and uttered quietly, "However do these rumors get started?"

Rumors? Dewar thought. *Don't get me started about rumors!* "Pick your color, Larry."

Llewellyn drank back the brandy and stood up. "You know me, sir. I like my blue balls."

"Indeed. I prefer the red!" Dewar exclaimed. "They stand out and say: 'these are my balls, so just look out!'"

They progressed out to the lawn, where slaves had set up a course for pall-mall. A dozen small iron arches were staked in the grass at varying positions. A set of finely crafted wooden mallets stood in an upright case.

Dewar grabbed a mallet and tested its weight. He dropped a red ball and took a practice shot. The ball flew over the cliff. He turned to his slave expectantly. "Well, go get it."

The clop of hooves was heard at the back gate. Mason Sleemans stepped down and paid the driver before retrieving his bag. He opened the wrought-iron entry and trudged down the path towards them wearing only one shoe and covered head to toe in shiny fish scales.

"How much are we paying him?" Llewellyn asked. "He seems to spend a lot on travel."

"Far too much," Dewar said. "Plebs; when will they learn to accept what they've got and be happy without constant handouts from their betters? I mean, why do we pay him? He's poor. Why not just have him indentured? Then we never have to pay him again."

Llewellyn sighed. "We strive for the perfect world, sir."

"Glad you could make it," Dewar scowled at Sleemans.

Sleemans passed Dewar a scroll. "Straight from the Brethren of the Coast."

Dewar used his handkerchief to wipe the scroll off. "Just had to get it slimy, didn't you?" He unrolled it to take a gander. "That's Bart's mark. What's it say?" Dewar passed it to Llewellyn.

"Bart approves of Operation Powdered Whig."

Sleemans read the rest. "Indeed, he's discussed a truce with that whore from the Freebooters, and Laurens de Graaf himself will talk to the French."

"Bloody outside politics getting in the way again!" Dewar huffed. "Why do we care if King Louis declares war on the French? Port Royal is the key to America."

"We shall take back your city, sir," Sleemans pledged.

Dewar hit another red ball, this time landing it in a hedge. "And make haste! I've grown weary of cock in my ear every morning. Not to mention that barking rodent, Chico; shit-stain extraordinaire! I'll go mad another day without my beautiful city. And what about Strangewayes? We can't let him fall into the hands of the Whigs."

Llewellyn continued. "Bart says he'll help us defeat the Whigs, but we're on our own if Beesty Bill comes back." He swallowed hard. "What happens if Beesty Bill comes back?"

"Captain Bart assured me he would not let neither Strangewayes nor the Capitaine fall into the hands of the Whigs," Sleemans continued.

"Captain Bart assured you?" Llewellyn scoffed. "You act as if you belong in a position of influence. It astonishes me that peasants will take a minor appointment and suddenly think they have real power. I mean, what is it with Plebs that always want to have a say in what goes on in the world? Is it not enough that we keep you informed? You have to go and take it personally. You think, hurrah for me; Captain Bart and me are mates now. I'm a somebody!"

"That's sticking it to him, Larry!" Dewar patted Llewellyn on the back.

"Of course, Your Lordship, I'm merely being diligent," Sleemans said, exhausted.

Llewellyn continued reading. "He says the Whigs are going forward with Operation Two Birds and you're to advise Captain Longstaff to initiate Dominium."

Dewar raised his mallet in excitement. "Now we're talking! It's about time we got something out of Big Dick. He cost us enough. We'll tell him to inflict pain!"

"Major Paine?" Llewellyn asked.

"No, excruciating pain! As though he were being impaled by a hundred centurion lances!"

Llewellyn continued to read. "Bart says he'll help us defeat the Whigs, but we're on our own if Beesty Bill comes back." He swallowed hard. "What happens if Beesty Bill comes back?"

"If Beeston is found not guilty, his land and titles will be reinstated with governmental authority. He'll return with a vengeful force and we shall be hanged most gruesomely," Sleemans said.

Llewellyn winced. "There's that word hanged again."

"Gruesomely," Sleemans echoed.

Dewar's eyes widened. "He means Beesty Bill would return particularly beastly."

Horror filled Llewellyn's face. "No! Beastlier than ever with beastly plans of beastliness? I won't have it! I don't want to die by Beesty Bill, the Whigs, or the French Capitaine, damn it!" He began to hyperventilate. "I'm taking a stand. I'm too rich to die!"

“Then it’s time for action, Larry,” Dewar insisted. “Get me my squiggly stamp!”

They all marched inside to the study where Llewellyn scribbled out a note for Longstaff.

Dewar marked it with his signature stamp, rolled it, and sealed it with wax. “You’ll leave at once and deliver this to Captain Longstaff with all haste, speed, and agility.” He gave the scroll to Sleemans.

“But, I—”

Dewar gave a cautionary glare. “You’ll be hanged if you don’t deliver this in time. Tell him to initiate Domin– Domin-iong.”

Sleemans rolled his eyes. “Dominium.”

“Exactly.” Dewar nodded. “That one. The one that means we own all the slaves.”

“Yes, Your Lordship.”

“Also, send word to Bleedin Art to recall his men. I’m taking charge and I’m taking my city back from those sheep-wearers and I’m not losing it to the filthy French nor bloody Beesty Bill.”

“Aye, sir,” Sleemans said. “And I’ll need to be paid for expenses.”

Dewar reached into his pouch. “What’s the wherry now, a shilling?”

Sleemans looked down and wiggled his bare toes. “My wages, sirs?”

Dewar and Llewellyn grumbled with discontentment.

“You still have one good shoe.” Dewar turned to Llewellyn. “You carry the money; you jingle in the bloody bath! Pay the man!”

“Oh, fine.” Llewellyn removed a small coin satchel and surrendered it. “Here. If you must.”

“Be off with you now, and carry out your orders,” Dewar said.

Sleemans gave a quick bow and ran off, scroll stuffed in his pocket.

Dewar rested his mallet on his shoulder. “Bloody peasants running the world. What a state we’re in!”

“You were born to lead, sir,” Llewellyn sniffed.

“You know it, Larry. Now let’s go beat some balls!”

Daylight was seeping through the window when la Roche jolted awake from another nightmare. He had been trapped in the jungle while the screams of his tortured men came from a distance. Gasping for air, he wiped the sweat from his brow. Atia lay beside him, peacefully asleep. He removed his drenched shirt and tossed it to the floor.

La Roche caressed Atia's hair, calming himself. He was safe at the plantation with the woman he loved. He took deep breaths and lay his ear on her chest, listening to her heart. He gently kissed her flesh until she released a sigh. Urgently his lips met hers, and he slid the nightdress up past her thighs.

Atia was half dazed when he mounted her. He pushed her hands above her head until she clutched the bed post. She panted, responding to him enthusiastically. Her legs wrapped around him as he thrust into her. They writhed exuberantly, flesh of each other's flesh. He finished deep within her and then crushed his lips against hers. They remained joined for a long time before he pulled away to get dressed.

Atia gyrated her hips against the bed. "Oh, I can still feel you inside me."

He grabbed a fresh shirt from the chair. "Did I leave it in?"

She laughed and threw a pillow at him. The door creaked open and Minuit charged in carrying a dead rat in his beak.

La Roche put on his trousers. "Ha! You are too late. She is full!"

Atia slid her hand between her legs. "Am I ever. Why, what's he got now?"

Minuit dropped the rodent by the bed and stood beside it, waiting for praise.

"Oh." Atia managed not to gag. "Good boy."

"Oui, have a gift. Here's the Black Death!"

"Why does he keep bringing me dead things?"

"Be thankful it's dead." He tossed the rat and Minuit out the door. "Go on, you."

"*Connard*!" Minuit screeched.

La Roche sat on the bed. "He is enamored with you. As am I." They embraced and kissed again.

Atia clasped his hand. "Promise you'll come with me."

"When the war is over, I will." He kissed the nape of her neck. "I belong to no other, *ma chérie.*"

A knock came at the door.

"You are too late. Try fucking a bird for once!"

"Hello?" Livia began. "I'd like to have a word with my sister."

"Aye, come in," Atia said.

La Roche put his boots on and rose to leave. "Good day, Mademoiselle." He tipped his hat. "I was just on my way out."

Livia scowled at him. "I know you saved my sister, captain, or won her, but it don't mean you own her. Besides, yer a might too old for her, cradle robber!"

"Enough outta you, Liv!" Atia slipped a robe on and closed the door behind the Capitaine. "Girl talk." She turned back to Livia. "I love him. I don't care what ya think!"

Outside the door, la Roche smiled and walked away from the bungalow.

"Atia, yer just like Ma!" Livia yelled. "Spreading yer legs like yer holding up the walls!"

"I owe that man me life!"

"You owe him naught!"

"Bloody hell, Liv. Ya ain't telling me how to run me life. You ain't Ma!"

"No. Ma's dead and we're all we got!" Livia paused. "I just don't want to see you get hurt."

"Yer moving back to Port Royal for Edmund Coggshall. That's cracked!"

"And mixing with pirates and runaway slaves ain't?"

"No! The son of a bloody slaver is *much* better. You just met him, didn't ya?" Atia yelled. "Ya have no idea what yer talking about. My Capitaine's a good man. The finest I've ever met."

Outside, Minuit landed on la Roche's shoulder. "See, it's not all about sex with women. There's a lot of yelling, too." La Roche was nonchalant.

From inside, he heard Livia yell in an old Gaelic dialect. Atia shouted back. Her attitude satisfied him. Their life together after was something to look forward to. He whistled as he started down the path to the Gathering Place for breakfast.

After the quarrel with Livia, Atia got dressed and went to the Gathering Place. A large group was there including Carlena, who was making final adjustments to a carriage. Atia was going to miss Dr. Strangewayes. He had always been so kind to her.

Carlena shook her hand and spouted a colorful blend of Spanish curse words. She tossed the hammer to the ground and cradled her finger. “Bloody hell!”

Strangewayes gazed at her with sympathy. “Are you terribly hurt?”

“Me? I am fine. I always wanted a broken finger.”

He inspected the pin lock on the hitch of the carriage. “It’s secure. That would get us to China and we only need to get to Ligania.”

“I know what I’m doing, I have driven a carriage once or twice!” Carlena snapped.

Atia ate breakfast with Lilly, who was still very pale, but in good spirits. She wore the coveted Shakespearean fool’s costume and the three-pronged hat jingled when she moved. They hugged and Lilly hopped into the back of the carriage.

The Capitaine grasped Atia’s waist. “Where’s Lilly going?”

“She’s posting a letter. The doc said it was fine so long as she doesn’t say where she is.”

“Something’s wrong, I can feel it,” Gladstone professed.

“Don’t worry.” The doctor patted his shoulder. “I have more than enough confidence in you.”

“It’s not me I’m worried about.” Gladstone stroked the horse’s head. “It’s you. It smells like a trap.”

“I’ve been pressed into service, so what choice do I have?” Strangewayes tilted his head. “If they’re watching me, you have a better chance of slipping away.” The doctor addressed Carlena, “Let me see your finger.”

Carlena flipped up her middle one.

“Very nice indeed. Everybody ready?”

“Now…who am I, again?” Lilly asked.

“If we get stopped, I’m the slave and you’re his whore.” Carlena said. “The workhouse markings are a dead giveaway.”

“Or, we can really cock them up and say Lilly’s the Negro and I’m the whore,” the doctor chuckled. The carriage was off. “*Vive la Sérénité*!”

Tanama arrived and went straight to Gladstone. “There are Maroons at the east gate. Youngsters picking a fight. Yaguara’s on his way there. We need someone to check the west gate.”

“I’ll do it,” Gladstone said.

“Oui, I’ll come with you,” la Roche volunteered and squeezed

Atia's hand. "Why don't you head back and rest up. Take the little pecker with you."

Minuit landed on Atia's shoulder and she strolled back to the bungalow. She patted his head, cooing, "yer a good boy."

Waiting for her on the porch was Fatima, who seemed distressed.

"What's wrong?" Atia began.

"Buccaneers are down at the lake. Where's Yaguara?"

"He's at the east gate." A wave of anticipation filled Atia at the possibility of seeing her other rescuer again, de Kreep. She distinctly remembered his extremely messy hair and warm brown eyes. She followed the path to the lake.

"Where are you going?"

"They're friends of the Capitaine."

"Are you sure?" Fatima's voice cracked.

"Come along. I'll introduce you."

Minuit took off ahead.

Six naked buccaneers bathed in the lake. Atia couldn't help but admire de Kreep's physique and alluring manhood that swayed provocatively as he washed. The smell, however, was repulsive, and she covered her nose.

"Ah, Mademoiselle Atia," de Kreep said. "Forgive us, we have been walking for over a day. That is Monsieur la Skunk. He has never bathed; it takes some getting used to."

Atia scrutinized the buccaneer on the shore beside her.

La Skunk chewed on sugar cane. "*Bonjour.*"

De Kreep strode from the water right towards Atia, unabashed. "You are looking so much lovelier than the last time we met." He swept the hair out his eye.

"Nice to see it," Atia blurted out, unable to take her eyes off his member. "You!"

"You are doing much better," another buccaneer said.

Atia tried to avert her eyes, but they strayed downwards. "Thank you. So's yours."

"This is Arsenault," de Kreep introduced. "And Coupe la Bite. L'Amiss and Cliché."

She nodded to each of them, while Minuit landed on a branch beside her. He flapped his wings in protest and muttered something filthy.

"What brings ya here?" Atia asked.

"We are here for the Capitaine." De Kreep's scorching eyes met hers and he slid on his trousers.

"He'll be back shortly. How did you know we was here?"

His dark hair fell back over his face. "Far too easily, I can tell you."

"Are you hung–hungry?"

They grumbled enthusiastically and gathered up their clothes.

"We'll get some food on for ya, won't we, Fatima?"

"Oui," Fatima replied, stepping forth to receive lustful stares.

Atia pointed at them. "Hands off. She's too young."

Cliché grinned. "She is about the right age for me."

"You'd have to go through me first," Atia challenged.

"That wouldn't be a problem." Cliché winked. "There's enough for everyone."

"In yer dreams."

"What wouldn't be a problem?" the Capitaine said suddenly, giving them all a stern stare from the trail.

Atia jumped. The Capitaine appeared different, deadly serious. The buccaneers had triggered something she had never seen before.

De Kreep shook the Capitaine's hand warmly. "Capitaine, *bonjour*. I am glad to find you well." They conversed in French under Atia's curious stare.

"What have you found out?" the Capitaine asked.

"A band of children with slingshots could take this island. The English defenses are inadequate."

"Same goes for the north coast. The Maroons are more of a threat."

De Kreep leaned in close. "We have troubling news. The attack on Jamaica is in disarray. De Graaf wants to meet you in Hope Bay right away."

De Kreep contemplated Atia for a moment, her lovely green eyes on the pair of them. Pain was the last thing he wished upon her. He directed the Capitaine up the path a few feet. His tone changed to a whisper. "Cormac the pikey is dead."

The Capitaine was crestfallen. "Slasher Al?"

"It was." De Kreep swallowed hard. "Do we tell her?"

"Don't say anything. I will tell her when the time is right." The Capitaine slid his trembling hand into his pocket.

“Oui, Capitaine.” De Kreep spotted Yaguara and Tanama on the trail to the lake. He went to greet them.

“Yaguara heard French. De Kreep must tell Yaguara when he and his men are here,” Yaguara reprimanded.

De Kreep eyed Yaguara. It had been a long time since he’d seen his father. He was aging well, having Tanama around as a surrogate daughter was doing him good. “My apologies, Monsieur.”

Arsenault eyed Tanama, delaying the buttons on his trousers until she could take a good look. She smiled lustfully.

Yaguara frowned at the pair. “De Kreep’s men will stay away from the residents. They will not pass the Gathering Place. You may go as far as the barbecue pit.”

“Oui, Monsieur,” de Kreep agreed.

Yaguara paused. “It’s good to see de Kreep is well.”

“Likewise, Monsieur.” De Kreep bowed and summoned Arsenault. “Set up camp here and meet us at the barbecue pit.”

Guilt plainly hung upon the Capitaine and darkness filled his face. Atia watched him with worry. The bond between them was deep. De Kreep hoped it was enough. He had seen the Capitaine unravel from grief before and it led to destruction.

GO
2014

Approach the Precipice

Bizy Gale and her daughter Isabella loaded their delivery wagon with the linens they'd washed the previous day. It was time to start their morning deliveries. The city stirred as it always did. Smoke rose from the bake houses and the flag was raised at Fort James.

Bizy tapped the reins and they headed towards Honey Lane. She had to finish the deliveries early as she was wanted at Fort Carlisle to perform duties associated with her new honorary title of Acting Corporal and Official Fire Warden of White's new leeward gun battery. Beckford would be there to supervise, more or less hounding her.

Business at Pope's Tobacco was already stirring when she and Isabella arrived. Sleemans was there, who Bizy recognized as Dewar's advisor. He seemed to be doing well for himself – his clothes were new and his shoes sparkled. He perused the variety of tobacco leaves and then paused at the counter.

"Morning, Miss Gale," the tobacco merchant said.

"Morning, Mr. Pope."

Sleemans cleared his throat. "I understand you can refill a cartridge pen," Sleemans began.

"A Pepys pen?" the tobacco merchant replied.

"Aye, a Pepys pen. Do you have a refill?"

Bizy recognized the pen from the old pirate days, but this one had a wider barrel. She escorted Isabella to the closet, where wicker baskets of soiled linens waited for them. They took them outside and dumped the linens in the back of the wagon.

When they returned with the clean linens, the tobacco merchant had removed a Pepys pen from a drawer and set it on the counter. "I'll be right with you." He handed over a small cylinder before tending to other customers.

Sleemans hovered over the counter with a miniature key to open his pen. He wrote a small note, rolled it up inside the cylinder, and reassembled the pen. "I think I have it." He left his pen and took the tobacco vendor's, slipping it in his pocket. Sleemans left a card and a doubloon on the counter. "Thank you. Have a fine day."

Bizy and Isabella set the fresh linens on the shelf and closed the closet door.

"And to you, sir," the tobacco merchant called and cleared the counter. He grabbed a handful of tobacco leaves and placed them in middle of a piece of cloth. The pen was placed in the middle of the pile and wrapped up. He rang the bell and his shipper entered from the back room.

The shipper read the directions on the card and rolled a fresh barrel of tobacco out the back onto a cart.

The tobacco vendor rolled out a brand new barrel of dried leaves. Bizy sighed. She loved the smell of tobacco, and it reminded her of James, her late husband. He and the pirate crowd could smoke a barrel or two a night.

Bleedin Art's man Blackmoor entered the shop.

"I got MacAskill's order right here." The tobacco merchant opened a drawer.

The mention of MacAskill's name drew Bizy's attention, as did the passing of the cloth bundle, from which Blackmoor withdrew the Pepys pen to sign for the order.

"Pardon me, sir, but if you're seeing Dr. MacAskill, can you pass on my greetings?" Bizy said. "I hope you both have recovered from the fire."

Blackmoor tipped his hat. "I'll pass on the message, Miss Gale. Good to see you are well." He dropped a satchel of coins on the counter and departed.

"Come on," Bizy said to Isabella. "We got another delivery."

The next delivery, to the Swiftsure Tavern, was certain to be less mysterious. Glenda the barmaid greeted Bizy jovially before returning to her duties of instructing her apprentice, Nessie, and taking a broomstick to the unrulier drunkards. Once the dirty linens had been exchanged for clean, Bizy carried on to Fort Carlisle.

Inside, Bizy and Isabella were accosted by Dr. Sober, who stank of stale rum.

"Yer timing is impeccable." His spectacles hovered on the tip of his nose. "We got burn victims today."

Horribly burned men lay on straw mattresses, writhing in agony. They were Bleedin Art's crew. The ginger-haired one was blistered, his neck and face red and raw.

Sober approached Spider, who had bandages on his head.

Ginger complained, "He ain't first, he's bloody indentured."

Sober looked at Bizy. "You're in the service now, tend to the wounded man."

Bizy dropped the linens in the corner, containing her disgust. She signaled Isabella to stay put and grabbed a fresh cotton cloth.

"About time! I'm in pain!" Ginger growled.

"Give him some laudanum," Sober advised.

Bizy grabbed a vial from a wooden cabinet. "How much?"

"Three or four drops should do."

"Six!" Ginger reached for the vial. "Give it here, you stupid wench!"

Sober tilted his head. "Go ahead."

"Fine, then." Bizy pursed her lips.

Ginger drank back half the bottle and choked. He pointed to the water pitcher. Spider passed it over and Ginger guzzled it.

"Oh, and go get some more water," Sober advised, inspecting another wounded crewman.

Bizy took the pitcher and went down the hall to a stack of barrels. She kept watch over her daughter as she pulled the tap.

Ginger waved to Isabella. "You, come here. Help me to get me pants off."

"I'll wait for my ma," her daughter said.

"Bloody come here now!"

Bizy returned quickly. "I got yer water."

Ginger grabbed it and poured it over his head. He shook off the excess. "You can teach that brat of yers some manners." He removed a dagger. "Bring her here. She needs a lesson."

Bizy stood between them.

"There be no call for that," Sober said.

"I'm a lieutenant in the service and she'll bloody come here as she's told and take what's coming!"

"Keep your place, mister," came Beckford's voice.

For once, Bizy was grateful to see him. Their eyes met briefly.

"Your captain wants a full report," Beckford continued. "And so do I. Since you lost the log, you'll describe what happened in full detail." He glanced at Bizy and Isabella. "Both of you, unload the rest of your linens to the wagons down by the wherry boat. We're sending supplies to the plantations."

Sober cringed at a badly burned crewman. "This one's dead."

"What sort of supplies?" Bizy asked.

"Farm equipment," Beckford replied, giving her a cautionary glance. "You mind your place and get to work. You consented to the position. When you're done with the linens, you can sweep the gun deck before you go. Now be off."

Bizy took Isabella's hand and they ran down the hallway.

"I'll be seeing ya, sweetheart!" Ginger hollered after them.

Outside the infirmary, the morning sunshine beat down. Bizy removed a handkerchief and patted her face. Both women took stacks of linens and headed to wagons near the water.

"That one scares me," Isabella said.

"Me too. Stay far away from him."

"Aye," Isabella agreed.

They placed the linens beside rundlets of gunpowder and dozens of muskets. "Farming equipment, indeed." Bizy took her daughter's arm and headed back. "Let's sweep the deck and go home."

"Yes, Mama."

It was late afternoon when they returned to Widow Bell's house. A pot of stew was on and the whole house smelled of herbs. Once the children were fed, Bizy and Widow Bell sat on the rickety deck off the kitchen to watch the ships glowing against the sunset.

"Christ, what a day!" Bizy poured a glass of rum. "Bleedin Art's man, that ugly ginger-bearded one."

"I've heard of him. He is bad news."

"He scared Bella half to death!"

"Maybe we should talk to Art." Widow Bell took a mouthful of stew. "Make sure he knows. I'm sure he and MacAskill don't want their man causing us trouble."

Bizy nodded. "I'll go see them tomorrow."

"Good. Sooner the better."

Bizy ate her stew slowly. "You know, there's something going on over there. They're loading boats full of weapons."

Widow Bell lifted a broadside page off the table. "Maybe this is it?" The Port Royal Daily Gazette headline read:

Another plantation attack!
Dozens mutilated in heathen barbarity!

Angst filled Bizy's stomach. "War." She sat back in her chair and drank. "We've never been at war with France. I mean, the Capitaine and Pierre le Picard? We've seen how they fight. My life changed the day I saw what pirates really do to people. What if the French really attack?"

A reassuring look formed on Widow Bell's face. "Can you get used to a Governor Capitaine?" She raised her glass.

"Aye, I'll drink to that." Bizy toasted. "To the Governor Capitaine of Jamaica!"

Cherry Banks opened her parasol to shield her eyes from the evening sun. She passed beneath a brick archway that led to Thames Street. Before her stood Fort Carlisle, where she'd find the ideal man for a job. It was all over the Port Royal Daily Gazette: Bleedin Art's frigate was destroyed, and the surviving crew were at the infirmary.

Cherry opened the gate and continued along a passage to a door. Once inside, she straightened her dress and walked with an exaggerated hip sway.

"What do ya want, strumpet?" Dr. Sober asked.

"You just blew yer senior discount, Doc Sob. Art wants Ginger and the navigator put up at the Swiftsure." Cherry paused to stare at Ginger's and Spider's marred faces. "I'm giving them a girl each."

"Always a pleasure, Miss Banks." Ginger bowed his head. "I figured ya might find me the prettiest."

Cherry scrutinized him. "Depends on what you plan on doing with her, Mr. Ginger."

He waved her closer and she stopped just out of reach. "You know Bizy and her girl?"

"Aye, Bizy Gale and her pup."

"Gale, is it?" Ginger leaned in. "I'll have both of 'em. Can you swing that for me?"

Cherry thought for a moment. "She's protected by the word of Morgan himself."

Ginger smirked. "That don't hold much water no more."

Cherry smoothed the frills of her sleeves. "As it is, old Miss Gale and I have a misunderstanding that needs correcting, if yer comprehending."

A vacant expression formed on his face. "You lost me."

Cherry sighed. "I like to keep my investments safe, if ya know what I mean. If you promise not to injure any of my girls, and not a word to Art, *ever*, I'd sweeten the deal with a bar of gold."

"But you said she's protected by Morgan's name. That's a bond honored by the Brethren of the Coast."

"So, you don't want them?" Cherry baited.

"Just means it'll cost more."

"I can do that." Cherry smiled. "If you behave, Mr. Ginger, ya might find a surprise gift at yer door."

As she exited, she heard him say, "I'll eat her too someday. Right down to the toenails."

In yer dreams, Mr. Ginger, Cherry thought. She knew the day would come when she'd have to deal with Bizy Gale. Gale had always looked down on Cherry. *The days are numbered for that haughty cow!*

The sky darkened, and the stars cast a glittering reflection on the water while the city torch lamps warmed the midsummer evening. Gathered at the terrace of the King's House sat Acting Lieutenant Governor Piper, Magistrate Mold and Judge Goblet, who smacked a mosquito from his neck.

"Beautiful day, gentlemen," Goblet began.

"I find it ghastly hot." Mold removed his wig and dabbed his head with a cloth. "I will not get used to the temperature."

Piper signaled for his slave to fan harder. "You'll have to. This will be home for as long as need be. Besides, our families will be here shortly."

"I did receive word that the ships have left Charlestown. They are on their way," Goblet confirmed.

"Splendid." Piper swatted at an insect.

Mold sighed. "If you say so."

"Once we've established a one-hundred-percent impenetrable Whig Capital we can relinquish this mosquito-infested shit-hole and go home to kick the Spotswoods back out of Charlestown."

"Yes, sir."

A warm breeze wafted, and thunder rolled in the distance.

"Of course. Time for our nightly hurricane," Mold griped.

Goblet removed his pocket watch. "I believe it *is* time, sir."

Mold pulled out his watch and checked it against the large clock on the wall. "That it is."

"Very well, give them the green light to go," Piper instructed.

Mold whistled to a group of slaves waiting in the balcony above. They lit a large green glass lantern and hung it from a wrought-iron bracket.

Goblet gazed across the water. Somewhere on the foothills to the Blue Mountains, Captain Longstaff saw the signal. He would ready his men and their weapons for war.

The small town of Ligania came into view, illuminated by city torches. Inside his carriage, Dr. Strangewayes folded his copy of the Port Royal Daily Gazette and slid it into his coat pocket. The dock drew nearer. Apprehension preyed on his mind. Perhaps Gladstone was correct, and it was a trap.

"Even with the aid ships it won't be enough. I may be gone longer," he said to Carlena.

"We'll handle it."

"Things must move quickly. Everyone must be ready to go by morning."

Carlena slowed down, nearing the dock. "Shall I leave you here?"

Strangewayes gave a reluctant nod, peering at the merchant ship being loaded. "There's my new home. Whatever force in the universe did I piss off now? Let's not get too close. Pull over there."

The carriage halted next to a fisherman's shack.

"Take it easy and don't worry about anything," Carlena said. "We'll send the Capitaine for you when we get there."

"Do, please. I could stand listening to French cursing the entire way across the Caribbean if it means joining you sooner." Strangewayes jumped down to collect his cases.

Carlena smiled. "You look like a squirrel who's lost his nuts."

"You just head back straight away and begin your *bon voyage*."

Lilly leaned out of the carriage. "You keep those nuts safe, you hear?"

"See you soon, child. You be good," the doctor spoke fondly. "That is asking a lot." He paused beside Carlena. "I mean it, no lollygagging. Straight back to the plantation. Good luck."

Carlena drove steadily away.

Strangewayes waited until the carriage vanished from sight. Belongings in hand, he paused at the foot of the gangway. From behind came a welcoming committee – or press gang – led by Constable Blower. They cornered him.

"No need, gentlemen. I can find my own way," the doctor said.

Blower wore a snide expression. "But you've been very naughty, Doctor. That ship ain't taking you now. I'm putting you under arrest."

"I have orders from Acting Lieutenant Governor Piper to sail to Nevis."

"We all got orders," Blower replied, and the thugs readied their blades.

Strangewayes panicked. "Are you going to kill me, Constable?"

Blower pointed the way. "Don't make a fuss, and we'll make it quick and painless."

Strangewayes slowly stepped forward. Another group arrived – pirates, this time. A skinny man with a long mustache and a tri-cornered hat charged forth, cutlass in hand. "The doctor's coming with us, gents."

Blower's face reddened. "On whose authority?"

A battle-worn brigantine sailed into the dock. It was the *Blessed William*. The gangway was lowered and a wild-eyed privateer in a deep burgundy coat stepped heavily, his buckle boots slamming against the plank.

"I'm Lieutenant William Kidd. I have a letter of marque signed by Acting Lieutenant Codrington. Dr. Sander Strangewayes is hereby pressed into service as Chief Surgeon aboard His Majesty's brigantine, *Blessed William*." He eyed Strangewayes. "Come aboard if you'll be so kind, Doctor."

Too stunned to argue, Strangewayes complied and moved towards the brigantine gangway. Kidd was a distant cousin to Dr. Marcus MacAskill, and their tavern brawls were legendary, even for Port Royal.

"I got specific orders!" Blower huffed.

"So do I. And yer now interfering with an order from the King's navy, giving me right to have you executed!" Kidd snarled. He was said to be stern and hot-tempered, a reputation he'd earned. "Now off with you and your little men before I run you through." He pointed to his man. "Escort the doctor to the ship, Cully."

"I do have urgent business on Nevis," Strangewayes said quietly.

"Nevis is where you be headed." Cully forced him up the gangway at cutlass point.

"I will report this to Governor Piper," Blower sputtered.

"Do that," Kidd said. "Have your Acting Lieutenant Governor write my Acting Lieutenant Governor, if it pleases you, imbecile!" He stomped back up the gangway. "Yer lucky I'm in a forgiving mood."

Strangewayes stood on the quarterdeck, his heart pounding in his throat as *Blessed William* drifted away.

Blower shook his fists before guiding his men back into town.

"Take us out. Head for open sea!" Kidd barked and the crew raced up the ratlines.

"What about my people? What is to be done with them?" Strangewayes pressed.

Kidd faced the doctor. "I'm taking you on as a favor to Thomas Paine, Dr. Strangewayes. That's all I'm obliged to do. They're on their own now. Take the doctor below Cully, and keep a close watch on him. We don't want him jumping over."

"Aye, sir." Cully grinned, guiding the doctor to his hammock. "We prepared the royal suite for ya Doc, all the comforts of home."

Strangewayes set down his bags. It was now confirmed. Something horrific was going to happen and he was powerless to stop it. He only hoped that the people of the plantation would get out in time.

LT. William
Kidd
GO
2015

All Good Things

Carlena peered out from under a rain cloak, just barely able to make out the lantern light up ahead from a tavern just outside Ligania. She stopped the carriage and told Lilly to be quick in posting her letter.

Clouds soared by overhead and the cold damp crept in. Carlena pulled her cape tighter. “Damn it, Lilly, hurry up!” The ground beneath the carriage vibrated, subtly at first. Then came the faint clop of many hooves.

Lilly exited the tavern, bottle in hand. She had just climbed up when someone far away called, “You there, halt!”

Carlena snapped the reins and the carriage jolted, rushing ahead.

Lilly fell into her seat. “Someone found us! What do we do?”

A brigade charged behind them. To Carlena’s dismay, a convoy lay ahead of them as well. She was forced to slow to a grinding halt. “We may have to run for it.”

Lanterns and torches illuminated the road. Before them a group of Redcoats drew muskets. There was no way out.

Lilly waved. “It’s only Thorne.” She called out, “Oi! We be out for some supplies, is all.”

Lieutenant Lance Thorne drew his sword. “Climb down from there. Hands in the air!”

Lilly pushed up her breasts as best she could in her fool costume. “I know what Thorny toad wants.” She sauntered over to him. “What’s got yer loins in a knot?”

“Lilly!” Carlena called.

Thorne jabbed Lilly through the heart and yanked his blade out. “I’ve been wanting to do that.”

Carlena gasped.

Lilly stared back for moment, stunned. Tears escaped her eyes before she dropped to the ground, landing in a muddy puddle. An involuntary twitch shook Lilly’s body before she passed away.

The Redcoats aimed their weapons at Carlena. She wiped the mixture of rain and tears from her eyes. Instinct told her to run.

“Stop what you’re doing!” someone ordered.

Thorne disobeyed and approached with his sword.

Carlena bolted towards a cluster of trees. A hot burning burrowed into her belly and she landed on her knees. She touched the wound. Blood covered her fingers. *I've been shot.*

"Colonel Beckford said 'stop!'" a man yelled.

"We have orders to take all prisoners!" Beckford roared.

Carlena staggered forth and ran for one of the horses at the side of the road.

"She's getting away," a Redcoat called.

"Stop her!" Beckford ordered.

Shots filled the air. Carlena took large panicked gasps. She heaved herself up onto the horse, who was saddled with weapons. She kicked and it tore into the trees.

Carlena clung to the horse's neck as it galloped through the jungle. Branches and sharp bushes grazed her legs. Her heart thudded and she tried to regain her composure. As soon as she was able to get her bearings, she gathered the reins properly and steered north to the plantation.

Tanama sat with Gladstone at the Gathering Place. They ate slices of roasted wild pig, courtesy of the buccaneers. The torches were lit and the recently arrived children laughed as Minuit chased bugs.

"Are you having something to eat?" Tanama asked Yaguara upon his arrival.

"A Miskito scout told me the west gate was left open again!" Yaguara huffed.

"I closed it!" Tanama defended.

"The gate was left open last night, too. Tanama is spending too much time around buccaneers." Yaguara stormed off.

Gladstone stopped him before he reached the edge of the grassy field. "Where's Bilwi? Maybe it was him?"

"Bilwi went north. We'll talk with him when he gets back," Yaguara's tone softened.

Tanama joined them. "I think Bilwi must have left the gate open."

"Yaguara has to go close it again, whoever left it open."

"I'll come with you," Tanama said.

"No. Stay here and finish your supper." Yaguara patted her shoulder before taking the path to his wagon. "Tanama will know if there's a problem."

Gladstone removed a small bottle from his pocket. "Everyone's so tense. You come to appreciate Strangewayes's concoctions at times like this. This one's called Tranquility." He took a small swig. "Can't go wrong with that."

Tanama read the label. "Says 'one to two drops. Maximum.'"

"Oops."

She rose. "Yaguara wants you to watch the buccaneers, doesn't he?"

"Aye." He grinned painfully. "Born killers and he wants me to play nursemaid to them! Do I seem nervous?"

"Come on then, we'll stick together."

Tanama offered her hand. Gratefully he took it and they traveled the trail to the barbecue pit. A second wild pig was roasting over the fire. *We should have buccaneers over all the time*, Tanama thought. The one they called Coupe la Bite sang a folk song from Hispaniola, while the Capitaine and de Kreep entertained everyone with drunken sparring.

Tanama met Arsenault's gaze. He was undeniably handsome and there was something primal about him. All wild hunters bred to survive conditions that would kill ordinary men. She and Gladstone sat nearby.

Gladstone clapped. "Ah, a match of cunning and skill! We're learning from the masters tonight."

The Capitaine thrust a slapdash jab as de Kreep blocked with a slack parry.

"Good form as always, Monsieur," de Kreep quipped.

"A master of my own sword, oui?" the Capitaine slurred.

Atia arrived fresh and pretty in a black velvet dress. The Capitaine and de Kreep immediately bowed in her presence. *The Capitaine clearly loves her*, Tanama pondered. She'd witnessed it throughout their stay at the plantation, but something had darkened. Something was terribly wrong, eating at him like a sickness.

Atia sat opposite Tanama, next to Fatima on a wooden bench. "It don't look like I missed much," Atia said.

"They are like apes in mating season," Fatima whispered.

They sparred again, trading jabs and blocks, quickening their pace.

"Why a fishing boat?" the Capitaine asked de Kreep.

"What fishing boat?" Atia said.

“In the hurricane they were stealing a fishing boat. Why?”

“We had to find a boat in time to meet Laurens,” de Kreep explained.

“Who’s Laurens?” Atia asked.

“Our boss,” de Kreep replied. “The English sunk all the Arawak boats off Ile de la Gonâve. Since we were going that way, I got one back for them.”

“One fishing boat makes no difference.” The Capitaine’s swordplay grew more aggressive.

“It makes a difference. If you believe in something, you must try every day with everything you do, or you’re not making a difference.” De Kreep gave Atia a playful glance. “I will never give up. Never.”

Jealousy flared in the Capitaine. “The Arawaks have no chance.”

De Kreep attacked and out-maneuvered him. “Not with that attitude, they don’t.” He let his blade hover for a moment at the Capitaine’s throat. “Perhaps a bit rusty, Capitaine?” He gazed at Atia again to see her smile.

“I’m too fucking old to play games.” The Capitaine picked up the rum and took a long drink.

De Kreep wore a sympathetic expression. “Your men, Capitaine. What do we do about your men?”

The Capitaine stabbed the ground. “Can you get a message into Marshallsea Prison?”

“Difficult right now. He is under heavy guard.”

Arsenault took a swig of rum. “They’re trying to smoke you out.”

The Capitaine lingered off to the side of the group, cursing inaudibly.

“Is the Capitaine not well?” Tanama asked Atia.

“I don’t know. He hasn’t said anything to me.”

Arsenault flicked his tongue provocatively at Tanama while Cliché and l’Amiss gawked at Fatima.

Atia squeezed Fatima’s hand. “Let me know if you want me to walk ya home.”

“I’m fine for now,” Fatima said, her curiosity piqued.

Tanama held Arsenault’s stare for several seconds until her stomach filled with a delightful squirm.

The buccaneers lifted the pig from the fire. They set it down on a wooden plank to carve.

La Roche felt ill. A vice seized his chest and squeezed. *Do you think she'll forgive you when she finds out her father is dead? You couldn't protect him. He was under the protection of the Brethren. You think Atia will come with you to Sérénité? You think she'll spend her life with you and give you children? Never. You ruin everything you touch!*

De Kreep approached Atia with his cutlass in hand. "Your turn. I want to see if you can handle a sword."

"She handles mine well." La Roche winked.

"I'm a quick learner," she bragged.

Arsenault offered her his shortsword. "Have you used a sword before?"

Atia held the blade naturally. "I'm more of a stiletto lass. Not bad with a dagger, either. I get that from me ma."

La Roche drew near. "Sit down before you get hurt, you silly girl."

Atia snarled and raised the sword.

Several buccaneers gathered to watch as de Kreep instructed Atia, who caught on very quickly. La Skunk watched too, a little ways off from the others. "You must first learn to defend yourself. Now hold it like this." De Kreep wobbled slightly as he demonstrated.

Atia copied his gestures, and then blocked. "Like this?"

"That's it! Oui! Block it, but force it away, you want to throw your opponent off balance." He slashed from different angles and Atia successfully blocked.

"That's it. That is called a parry."

La Roche grew furious. "It is not a game when someone loses her head."

They continued to duel.

La Roche continued, "It's not going to help you. If a man attacks you with a sword, you run away. Only a foolish woman would attempt to fight back. When we took the farms from the Spanish, l'Olonnais burned them all alive, women and children. In Gibraltar, we did them a favor; we killed them first, quickly, while the farmers begged and cried. Then I cut off their heads, too."

"I've killed Spanish," l'Amiss boasted. "Maybe more than any of you and not just the Mestizos."

Cliché shrugged. "I don't even know how many Spanish I killed."

"None of us have killed as many as the Capitaine," Arsenault added.

"Will you teach me proper technique?" Atia changed the subject.

"I can teach you many techniques, Mademoiselle."

"You are not even listening!" la Roche griped.

"Oui, you were killing Spanish," Arsenault said.

"I was listening, and I'm sickened." Atia's eyes narrowed. "You murdered women and children?" She handed the sword back to Arsenault.

"I was merciful!" la Roche insisted.

Atia sat back down beside Fatima.

"Women are not meant to fight. They are the weaker sex and they need us to protect them," la Roche went on, stuffing his trembling hand into his pocket. He thought back to Gibraltar, when l'Olonnais went on a killing spree. After burning dozens alive, he took a young girl around Atia's age. He bound her naked with rope and was going to let his crew rape her to death. La Roche had slit her throat rather than let her meet such a horrible end.

"Women need to fight for themselves the same as anyone else," Tanama said.

"If I was gonna die, I'd rather die fighting," Atia added. "Especially if I had to defend my home and my children against war-mongering pirates."

"Does she mean us?" Cliché asked.

"No, she said pirates," l'Amiss replied.

Furious tears brimmed behind la Roche's eyes. "You know nothing of war. It's not a game." He finished the rum and grabbed another bottle.

Coupe la Bite toasted. "To the Capitaine!"

De Kreep and Atia made eyes at each other again causing bitter jealousy to well up in la Roche's chest. His cutlass ripped through the air. "You have nothing to fear. I am an expert swordsman. Only a man's strength can make the sword an effective weapon." The blade whizzed by Atia, severing a small piece of her hair.

"You almost cut me, ya bastard!" She rose, furious.

De Kreep caught her arm and pulled her back down.

La Roche staggered to the nearby bush to take a piss.

"He's a brilliant warrior and strategist," de Kreep described. "I was on three raids with the Capitaine. We called him Gator Gar after a fierce river fish which he killed with his cutlass."

"I know the name," Atia said. "I'm beginning to know the pirate behind it."

De Kreep shook his head. “He has seen more war than any of us.”

“Just ’cause it’s war don’t make killing right.”

La Roche staggered to her. She was still the most beautiful woman he’d ever seen. “You are angry because I killed Spanish? We should have killed more Spanish for what they did!”

Atia was outraged. “You burned innocent people alive. Murdered men after making them watch their families die?”

“It was war! Us or them!”

“That’s yer excuse for everything!”

“You have no idea!” la Roche roared. “No idea what the Spanish have done! I should have killed them all!” He swung his cutlass, almost slicing everyone around him.

The blade went whizzing by Atia again. “Who are you?” she pleaded.

De Kreep positioned himself between them.

La Roche was taken aback. *I’m a pirate who once dreamed of being an ordinary man.* “You think I would hurt you?” For a moment he was shocked. He loved her so fiercely he almost detested her for exerting that much power over him. “Never! You are mine!”

“We’re all on the same side, Capitaine,” Gladstone said. He tapped a terrified Fatima on the shoulder. “Perhaps it’s time for us to go?”

She nodded.

“The rum has rotted yer skull, la Roche! Yer not the man I thought you were!” Atia scowled and for a moment she didn’t sound like Atia. She sounded like his ex-wife. She tried to take the bottle away.

“Cunts are for fucking, not opinions. Shut it or fuck off, Jacquotte!” la Roche bellowed. Before he could stop himself, he slapped her.

Atia trembled and struck him upside the head. “Now the other side matches, ya drunken scoundrel!”

La Roche felt warm blood drip from his nose. He wasn’t angry, only bemused. “You hit like a girl.”

Atia grabbed Fatima’s hand, while Gladstone stood alert, unsure of how to react.

“Oh, leave the little girl. I need a good fuck tonight,” l’Amiss said.

Atia wore a furious smile. “Then you can go fuck yerself, all of you!” She marched away, dragging Fatima behind her, with Gladstone and Tanama following.

“Thanks for a fun evening,” Gladstone said. “G’night.”

"Do you have any of that Strangewayes Tranquility formula left?" Tanama asked.

Cliché grinned. "Ooh! How you say? Feisty!"

The buccaneers laughed and drank more rum.

De Kreep smirked. "Pure fire, she is."

La Roche began to follow Atia. "Wait! Come back!" He choked back his anguish.

De Kreep stopped him. "She knows not what we speak of. Let her go, Capitaine."

"She thinks I would hurt her?" la Roche slurred. "I've killed for her and I would die for her." He began shaking uncontrollably. His hand could barely clasp his sword.

"You must rest, Capitaine," Arsenault recommended.

"Fuck you!" la Roche spat.

"Take a walk with me, Monsieur," de Kreep insisted. "Got you unraveling, she does."

La Roche glared at de Kreep. "You could never love her as I do! Leave me alone. I need to think." His breathing grew labored as he staggered to the lake.

Lightning struck in the distance, igniting the air with brilliant illuminations as a light rain spat down and was carried by the sea breeze. Atia stood on the porch, shaking with emotion. Her face stung, although she'd had worse from Crisp.

"He's just being a drunken sod. We'll take your things up to the house," Tanama offered.

"I prefer to stay by meself tonight, if it's all the same."

Gladstone squeezed her hand, giving her a sympathetic smile. "I'd rather ya stayed at the house."

"I'm fine," Atia insisted. "I just want to be alone."

"Do you want me to stay with you?" Fatima asked.

Atia shook her head. "You go with Miles."

"Good. They scare me," Fatima said.

Minuit landed on the rail. "*Bonjour,* Mademoiselle."

"There, see? I'm not alone. Minuit will look after me. You go get some sleep." Atia patted the large peculiar parrot. "I'm getting used to you."

Minuit made a flirtatious growl. "I'm getting used to you," he repeated.

Atia sighed. "Yer as bad as he is."

"You're more than welcome to come up if you change your mind," Gladstone said.

"I know. Thank you." She hugged him, trying not to cry. "Good night to you."

They disappeared up the dark path.

"Good night," Minuit said.

She felt very alone for the first time in a long while. Tears rolled down her cheeks and her chest heaved. "I shoulda stayed with Da. What was I thinking?" Minuit nudged her and she cradled him. The parrot nibbled her hair, making her laugh. "Livia's right again. She's always bloody right."

Suddenly, Minuit sprang onto the railing, staring alertly into the distance.

"What is it?" she asked. "'Tis only a storm. Nothing to be afraid of."

Minuit flew off towards the lake.

"Well, then, good night to you too." She opened the front door. "*Connard*!"

De Kreep appeared at the foot of the steps, smiling.

Atia put her hand to her chest.

"I'm sorry, Mademoiselle. I didn't mean to startle you."

She went inside and held the door open for him. He followed. Atia increased the intensity of the oil lamp on the table.

"I came to apologize," de Kreep continued.

"Why should you apologize?"

"This is all my fault. I should not have brought up the past. He is pained by the terrible things he's seen and done. None of which were under his control."

Atia sat on the chair near the bed, massaging her aching ribs. "I ain't seen him like that before, but it's hardly yer fault."

De Kreep sat on the bed, opposite her. "He can be uncontrollable when he drinks and reminisces. Best leave him alone tonight."

"I can leave him alone for much longer than that."

De Kreep gently held her face, angling it to the light. The flesh around her eye felt swollen and bruised. "Are you in pain?"

"I'm fine." Atia nodded. "I've had worse."

"Oui, I know. But he hit you hard. You should rest."

"I should, but I'd rather get drunk and stupid. Seems to be the thing to do in the New World." She took a bottle of rum from the cupboard and uncorked it. She guzzled it, choking back the taste. "I don't even like this shit. I'd sell me soul for some whiskey."

De Kreep took a mouthful. "You seemed familiar when we met in Port Royal. I saw your mother once, a long time ago. You are like her."

"Splitting image, as they say."

Outside, cracks of lightning and rain intensified. A great boom of thunder vibrated around the bungalow. Atia peered out anxiously.

"He'll be well," de Kreep said.

"Not him." She massaged her face. "I'm worried about the bird."

"He's safely under a tree as well."

"Carlena said your name is Dupris?"

"Dashiell Dupris."

"Dashiell, that's nice. Dash. May I call you Dash?" Atia took another swig of rum.

His dark eyes burned into her. "You can call me whatever your heart desires, as long as you know my heart sings to hear you say it."

"Another charmer. Just what I need." She stared at him. "Why do they call you de Kreep?"

His bit his lip for a moment. "Uh, my mother lost part of her tongue. That's how she says our family name."

Atia burst out laughing so hard it hurt. He joined in. Soon she calmed down and put her feet up on the bed, one on either side of him. "So are ya married, then?"

He looked disconcerted.

"I don't mean to pry. Just curious, is all."

"Her name was Isabeau, we had a son."

"Was and had – that can't end well."

"They were killed in '85 near Roatán when the Spanish and English took us all by surprise."

"I'm sorry."

"Arsenault and I shared her; there weren't many women. Most buccaneers live this way."

Atia thought of her ma. "Me ma, she'd been with the O'Malley brothers for over twenty years. Never married, but she had me and me four siblings. Who knows whose is whose, but what the hell, they be my family."

De Kreep massaged her legs. "My condolences for those you lost. I saw your ship when it sailed into Folly Bay."

"The Capitaine told me you were there." She inched her way closer, her legs wrapped around him.

"*Extraordinaire*! Then we meet again. It must be destiny. Very few survive such peril."

"Mostly luck." Atia slid her arms from the dress, beneath she only wore a thin cotton chemise. "I didn't let go of the railing." She showed him her bruises.

De Kreep leaned in, gently kissing her injuries. He embraced her between the chair and the bed.

Atia closed her eyes to listen to his heartbeat. His scent was so raw and alluring. "Thank you for rescuing me at the tavern. I owe you my life as much as anyone."

He met her eyes. "My pleasure."

"I never got the chance to properly thank you." Atia flushed when her mouth met his softly, but intensely.

"That is how you thank me," he whispered.

Eagerly, she slipped her hand between his legs, grasping his manhood. "I know a better way." The hunger between her legs increased. She'd wanted him since seeing him naked in the lake.

His mouth met hers impatiently and he pulled the rest of her clothing off. He buried his face against her breasts. Soon every inch of her body tingled beneath Dashiell's touch. He pinned her down on the bed. She tore open his trousers to unleash his member. Her legs enveloped him. He drove into her slowly and deeply until her thighs quivered. She thrashed beneath until her insides convulsed with pleasure.

l'Olonnais
GO
2015

Let Slip the Dogs of War

Outside the bungalow, clouds swirled beneath the diamond-like stars. La Roche staggered to the bottom of the steps – through the window, he saw the shadows of two figures. Faintly, he could hear Atia's moaning and de Kreep's grunting. Anger twisted his face. He raised his cutlass, letting the blunt end rest on his shoulder. Anguish poisoned him. Near tears, la Roche turned away. *A wise man would go sleep off this torment*, he thought. Instead he stumbled to the lake and collapsed by its edge.

At least it was Dashiell, his friend and brother in arms. It wasn't like they hadn't shared a woman before, but this time it was different. La Roche stared at the moon's reflection on the water for many minutes. Then, from the corner of his eye, a woman materialized.

Tanama crept to the boathouse where Arsenault and Coupe la Bite sat smoking. Her dress was soaked and clung to her curves. Coupe la Bite patted Arsenault on the back before dragging the boat ropes to a tree to tie them off.

Arsenault took her by the hands. They moved to a tall grassy area as thunder rumbled in the distance. Tanama laid down and Arsenault unbuttoned her dress. His tongue slid across her breasts as he licked his way down to her belly button. She trembled as he lifted her hips, and she spread her thighs.

The rain began again, pelting down. La Roche rubbed the water into his face, and continued to watch. *Dashiell's younger, stronger, and less likely to accidentally kill her in his sleep. I am damaged goods, damaged beyond repair. My Atia. Maybe I love her too much. She has a chance at normal life – a life without me.* He clenched his fist. *No! She is mine as I am hers. Forgive my faults, ma chérie.*

Tanama climbed upon Arsenault, and she rocked back and forth, the rain pelting her bare back. When she finished, he flipped and mounted her.

A faint whistle came from the boathouse; Arsenault stopped and drew a knife. Lanterns flashed off in the distance, floating along the waterway to the lake. Minuit's warning call sounded. La Roche staggered along the muddy bank.

Arsenault released Tanama. "Stay low and get back to the house," he instructed. "You must warn the others."

Tanama crawled away to the trail, while Arsenault entered the boathouse to join Coupe la Bite.

Arsenault saw la Roche. "Capitaine, someone is coming!"

La Roche gave a droll smile. "Oui, I know, *merci*." He crouched down beside the buccaneers.

Cliché crawled out from the bushes with a dagger in his teeth. "There are twenty of them coming down the river. English. Maybe a hundred more behind the west barrier with wagons and guns."

Behind the boat house, la Roche and the buccaneers lay flush with the earth, waiting. Blood would be spilled tonight.

The western farmhouse stood quiet beneath the moonlight. It had stone walls, windows on all sides, and a wood slat roof. The upper level held four bedrooms, two below. There was a parlor and a kitchen with a large wooden table.

Fatima stayed upstairs and it was decided that the children would share the room next to hers. When she went to check on them, they were gone. She searched the whole house, but there was no sign. Fatima enlisted the help of the other women. They all ventured outside into the rain.

"Nanny!" a woman called.

Fatima carried a lantern and yelled, "Nanny!" She knew the children did not want to be there.

The women checked the west gate and found the clergyman who originally brought the children, the peculiar one with white hair and pink eyes. He dragged the children back towards the farmhouse. "Come along, you little heathens!"

"There they are!" another woman exclaimed.

"Baby Jesus gets mad when you run away," the clergyman scolded.

Fatima went to retrieve them.

"I found them by the gate," the clergyman said.

Fatima took Nanny's hand. "What am I going to do with you? You're safer here with us. Now, children, back to house."

They all followed the muddy trail back.

Ekene was waiting on the front porch with a lantern. "Did they run off again?"

"Yes," Fatima huffed. "There are plenty of women here, why should I have to look after them? The one thing I am worst at."

Ekene gave her a playful glance. "Maybe it's good practice for you."

She smirked, feeling her face heat up. "The gate was open again; *they* couldn't have opened it."

"Where's Yaguara?" Ekene asked.

Fatima guided the children up the porch steps. "I don't know. I haven't seen him."

The clergyman followed. "You can never be too careful. They almost got away, but I was able to close the gate in time."

Nanny tugged on Fatima's dress; she spoke in Swahili so only Fatima would understand. She said, "The priest is lying. He was with the red-white men with guns."

Fatima swallowed hard; all the moisture gone from her throat. "She says there are men here with guns, wearing red."

"English soldiers?" Ekene scrutinized the clergyman, who backed away slowly.

"Well, I'll be damned. She can talk." The clergyman clasped his hands. "Oh, Lord." He ran for the trail screaming, "Attack!"

From the cover of darkness came Redcoats and Miskito warriors. They brandished muskets, blades, and spears.

Ekene pushed Fatima through the door. "Get them inside!"

"Alarm!" Fatima screamed, dragging the children. "Ring the bell!"

Ekene yelled, "Everyone to the main house."

Nanny seized the other children and left by the side door.

Fatima was about to chase after them. "Come back!" She was halted by Ekene, who pulled her through the back door and along the path to Strangewayes's house. One of the residents made a move for the alarm bell, only to be pierced by an arrow.

Ekene burst through Strangewayes's front door. Once Fatima was secure, he bolted all the doors and closed the shutters. Next, the gun cabinet was opened, and he began loading.

Fatima's heart rose in her throat.

Livia ventured from the bedroom. "What's happening?"

"The English are attacking!" Fatima replied.

"Where's Atia?"

"She's at her bungalow."

"I have to go get her."

Fatima pointed to the window. "We're surrounded."

Figures moved about the grounds, taking up position among the bushes and trees. From one of the trails, Gladstone helped a wounded Gillis across the yard. Fatima ran to let them in. They were arguing.

"It's not the English, just the Maroons again," Gillis insisted; an arrow in his arm. "They got me right through, the little devils!"

Gladstone examined the arrow. "It may be poisoned."

"It is the English!" Ekene said.

Fatima cut the fabric of Gillis's sleeve so she could tend to his arm. "We saw them; they have red coats."

Gladstone paused, trying to compose himself after an evening of too much drink and Strangewayes concoctions. "We'll break out the guns and get away from the windows. We'll have to run for it."

"I feel strange," Gillis said.

"Maybe it is poison." Gladstone's concern grew. "We have to find a way out."

"Here." Fatima offered Gillis a piece of leather for biting. She grabbed a dagger and a small wood block, cut away the arrowhead, and handed it to Gladstone.

Emotion drained from his face. "This is a Miskito arrow."

Fatima yanked the tail end of the arrow out as quickly as she could, causing Gillis to squirm and groan. "I can only patch it; there's no time to stitch it." She padded the wound with cotton and tied a bandage firmly around it.

"Where's Yaguara and the Capitaine?" Gladstone asked.

"No one's seen Yaguara for some time," Fatima said. "He didn't come back from his watch."

Ekene secured a dagger to his belt. "And the buccaneers?"

"I think they're all still down by barbecue pit."

Gladstone thought for a few seconds. "We'll fire a few shots and get their attention." He took one of the guns.

Fatima trembled, not only terrified of being killed by the English, but of being captured and tortured. She was a runaway slave; she would be held up as an example.

Wind swept through the plantation, when echoes of shots filled the air. La Roche sat, cursing himself. They should have listened to

Yaguara and left when they had the chance. It was too late now. The English soldiers were here, and more were arriving by the boatful.

"We should hit them before they organize. Make them give away their positions while we get everyone out," la Roche whispered.

"Oui," Arsenault agreed.

Shadows passed behind them, and they remained crouched. It was difficult to distinguish friend from foe in the darkness. To his dismay, la Roche could hear Atia in the distance. He used every ounce of strength not to go running to her.

Tanama reached her. "It's the English!"

"How many?" de Kreep demanded.

"Lots."

Shots echoed behind through the trees.

Arsenault called, "attack!"

"Run back to the house!" de Kreep yelled.

"No. I have to find the Capitaine!" Atia cried.

Shots fired again from the English soldiers below, hitting the trees around them.

"This way!" Tanama said.

La Roche heard their footsteps trail off. His hand ached from gripping his cutlass. Once the women were far enough away, he sprung forth swinging. La Roche and Arsenault cut down three unsuspecting Redcoats.

"Open fire!" yelled the Redcoat captain.

La Roche led the buccaneers into the maze of sugar cane. Coupe la Bite was hit in the leg and limped behind. The blades of the Redcoat's bayonets glimmered beneath the moonlight, stabbing at anything that moved. Once the Redcoats were upon them, the buccaneers knocked them down one by one with cutlasses. Shots were fired. A body dropped. It was Coupe la Bite.

"Nothing you can do. Follow me," la Roche said, leading them back to circle around. In the distance, he could see the Redcoat captain raising his sword.

"Surround the sugar cane and prepare to fire!" the Redcoat captain ordered, just before his head was severed by de Kreep.

A Redcoat corporal recoiled and fired a pistol. De Kreep was hit and staggered into the bushes.

A barrage of shots penetrated the cane field. When the smoke cleared, Redcoats cautiously entered the grounds. The corporal's face contorted. "What is that ungodly smell?" A stiletto flew out of the darkness, piercing his chest. The corporal dropped to his knees and la Skunk skimmed past, retrieving his weapon.

La Roche led the Redcoats through another maze of sugar cane. The buccaneers cut them down swiftly. De Kreep hobbled from a bush, alerting his fellow buccaneers to the soldiers' presence. La Roche turned in time to deflect a bayonet while de Kreep stabbed a Redcoat. L'Amiss and Cliché aimed their long guns and fired. More bodies dropped in the field.

A Redcoat in a corporal's sash led his men out on the grassy hill just beyond the cane field. La Roche recognized the corporal from his privateering days. His name was Rodney; he was more competent than most soldiers. The battle had just become more challenging.

"Retreat to higher ground and maintain the perimeter," Rodney called. The soldiers backed away from the field. "Ready your muskets and stay in formation. I shall return with reinforcements." Rodney retreated over the hill and the remaining men reformed the line.

As Redcoats readied their muskets, la Roche and Arsenault guided the buccaneers into the bushes behind the soldiers. They attacked swiftly, waving their cutlasses. At the same time, shots were fired from somewhere near the lake. La Roche squinted to see Gladstone and Ekene leading men in hand to hand combat. More Redcoats arrived by boat and infiltrated the sugar cane, brandishing muskets.

La Roche knew when to hit the ground. "Down!" he said and the buccaneers complied.

Gladstone and Ekene fought bravely. Ekene seized a musket and aimed it at a soldier.

Cliché leapt out of nowhere, brandishing two cutlasses. The surrounding soldiers fell, and blood sprayed everywhere. "Let's get out of here!" he shouted.

Some Redcoats tried to run.

"Don't let them escape!" la Roche ordered.

La Skunk threw an axe that landed in a soldier's back. L'Amiss fired his musket. The buccaneers tackled the English to the ground and stabbed them with daggers. Shots were fired and l'Amiss dropped to the ground, dead.

De Kreep fired before collapsing on his wounded leg.

La Roche ran over to help.

"No, Capitaine, I can't make it. You go. I'll only slow you down."

"We're not leaving you," Arsenault said.

De Kreep loaded a pistol. "You must! Hurry, Capitaine. Your Atia needs you. I'll catch up."

La Roche shook de Kreep's hand.

"She loves you. You are very lucky."

Gladstone arrived. "Ekene and I can carry him."

"No. Load your guns," la Roche instructed. "You have to save your people."

De Kreep gripped Arsenault's hand. "Go with the Capitaine."

La Skunk handed de Kreep a short fuse grenade. "Just in case you are late, oui?"

La Roche summoned la Skunk and pointed to the west. "Reinforce the rear."

La Skunk ran down to the shore.

With mixed emotion, la Roche gave de Kreep one last smile and led the buccaneers up the trail to the houses.

Atia followed Tanama up a short hill to Dr. Strangewayes's house. The interior was lit up on all the floors, already on high alert. Fatima opened the door for them.

Waiting inside was Livia. Atia raced into her arms. Both of them wept.

Tanama bolted the door. "It's the English!"

"We know," Fatima replied. "They have the west farmhouse and they're coming our way. Miskito warriors, too."

"What shall we do?" a woman asked. "Can we reason with them? Does anyone speak Miskito?"

Tanama shook her head. "Is Carlena back?"

"They didn't return," Fatima said. "And neither did Yaguara."

"Then they're not coming." Tanama hid her concern well. "Yaguara always said that when the shit hits the roof, we should go to the Safe House and leave through the tunnel."

Atia released Livia. "Where's the Safe House?"

"It's too late for that," Gillis interrupted, glancing out the window. "They're coming down the hill."

"We have wounded. They'll never make it!" Fatima exclaimed.

"We still have people out there." Tanama slid on a leather strap with weapons attached, including a machete. "I have to try to get them out."

"The Capitaine will come for us!" Atia knew in her heart that he was already on his way.

"And he'll need us to be ready to go," Tanama said. "The Safe House may be our only way out. I'll find the Capitaine and he can lead you out."

Gillis prepared a gun. "Get ready to leave everyone."

Atia met Livia's eyes. "I'm going with her."

Livia gave a half smile. "I know, Atia. I'll catch you up."

Atia gave her a tight squeeze. "I'll come back for you."

Livia ambled to the gun cabinet and loaded a musket. "We're going to get through this."

Tanama and Atia exited by the front door. The only light came from the moon and stars as they followed a narrow passage through the bushes. On the way they encountered a small pocket of panicked people with children.

"This way!" Tanama waved and guided them all to an area thick with branches. She used the machete to chop through. "The Safe House is through here."

Atia and the others followed the maze of prickly twigs for a few yards until they reached a clearing. There stood a stone wall ten feet high with a narrow gate leading to a house. Towering trees blocked out the moonlight, casting the area in extreme darkness. Atia hoped there were no confined spaces.

Livia had just finished loading her sixth gun when the jabbing pain from her ribs began to impede her ability. She wished she'd taken more of that Strangewayes pain remedy. Sitting down in a chair really didn't help, but it was better than standing.

Fatima packed supplies and lined guns along the wall for Gillis.

"Remember to pack water," Gillis reminded.

"Already packed."

Gillis watched the window. "Heads down!"

Livia caught a glimpse of Redcoats assembling in rows to the north, readying their muskets. She carefully slid to her knees and rested her elbows on a chair.

"Ready to fire!" the sergeant called.

The men inside crouched by the windows, aiming their guns. Gillis readied another musket and turned to Livia. "If worst comes to worst, you and Fatima get the women and run for it. We'll cover you."

Livia overheard a Redcoat report: "There are slaves escaping through bushes to the north."

"Then we have no time to lose," the sergeant said. "Take the house! Rear batteries, prepare to fire!"

"Open fire!" a far-off voice echoed.

Livia saw flashes of green and gold from the hills. She put her head on the chair and covered up with her hands. The house erupted. Cannonballs shattered the windows, propelling glass and wood fragments through the air. The floor panels vibrated, ready to buckle. Livia shuddered, reminded of how the *Aeolus* splintered apart.

A voice outside yelled, "Muskets, fire!"

Livia continued to mask her eyes. Through the space of her fingers, she saw Fatima try to reach a woman with a bleeding face, while two men fell down, dead.

Gillis fired a musket and return shots pierced his chest. Blood spurted through his back. He dropped to his knees, and then to the floor.

Fatima's injured woman took a shot to the head and dropped, falling between her and Livia. Livia's first instinct was to go to Fatima to comfort her, but she held back and waited for the gunfire to stop. At the next opportunity, both women hid beside a large wooden cabinet.

The outside was lit up with flames. Panic seized Livia's chest, and her breathing became labored. They had to get out! Cannonballs blasted the house again, and the cabinet they were sheltered beside tipped to the floor.

A voice yelled, "Fix bayonets!"

Sharp pain came from Livia's ribs and she leaned against the wall. Redcoats kicked down the remains of the door and stabbed the injured with their weapons.

A soldier charged at Fatima. "C'mon, Negro." He grabbed at her. Fatima swiftly dug her knee into his groin, and he doubled over.

Livia grabbed a fire poker and took a swing. A swift blow to the back of the head sent her reeling to the floor. Fatima too was knocked down. Soon Livia's eyes closed, and she plunged into darkness.

Tanama
GO
2015

Fear is Not an Option

It was well after midnight when Carlena arrived on an exhausted horse at the plantation's west gate. Adolescent Maroons loitered about and she darted straight by them. She rode towards the bungalows near Strangewayes's house, passing the cornfield where English soldiers sat smoking pipes. Carlena dug her heels into the horse's ribs and kept her head down.

The whirl of a shot flew past her head and sulfur permeated the air. She eased back on the reins after making a sharp turn into the trees. After dismounting, Carlena strapped on the weapons from the horse's cache. Fear was not an option; her home was under attack. She proceeded carefully through the brush. Strangewayes's house was ablaze.

"Think I got 'em," a voice said.

"Nay, I got 'em," the other argued.

Upon further inspection, she saw two wagon cages lined up and filled with several badly beaten plantation residents. A handful of English soldiers kicked down bungalow doors. When they reached Atia's dwelling, Carlena readied a pistol in each hand.

"Anyone in here?" A soldier was ready to jab with a bayonet.

A Redcoat corporal picked up something up from the ground. "Oi, who's got smokes? Which one of you has pre-rolled cigarettes?"

Carlena dove for the bushes. Those cigarettes were definitely the Capitaine's.

"Something's burning in here," a soldier called from inside the bungalow.

"Well then, get outta there!" the corporal ordered.

An explosion sent debris and bodies everywhere. The impact knocked the soldiers to the ground. When the smoke dissipated, the corporal staggered to his feet. "Jesus Christ! No one ever listens to me."

Carlena took aim and fired. The corporal dropped and the other soldiers scrambled for their guns. She fired again, putting another shot into the back of a man's head. After tossing the empty pistols she drew another pair and fired. Next, she stepped out with a musket aimed at the unarmed wagon drivers, who ran off.

Carlena grabbed the keys from the corporal and unlocked the cage door. "Go," she said, pointing to the bushes. "Do you know where the Safe House is?"

"I think so," one of the residents replied.

"Just go to those bushes up there and hide," Carlena instructed. She opened the second cage. Residents poured out, leaving only one inside. She took a closer look. "Yaguara?"

Yaguara gazed around strangely, holding his head. Perspiration dripped from his face. "Away with you, troublesome hallucination!"

Carlena took his hand gently. "Yaguara, it's me!"

"This is why Yaguara hates the word 'me.' Any galliwasp can say he's 'me' and Yaguara still has no idea who the fuck he's talking to."

"It's Carlena," she sighed. "Carlena doesn't need this shit right now!"

He blinked. "It is you! Why are you here?"

"We have to get everyone out. The Redcoats are attacking!"

"You mean the fish people?" Yaguara gave her a mortified look. "Shit. Yaguara's messed up!"

Carlena was reluctant to ask. "What have they got you on?"

"A Miskito poison." Yaguara paused. "Half the plants of the southern continent, I think. What's that yellow one from the Andes called?"

"Will Strangewayes have a cure?"

Yaguara rubbed his eyes. "Strangewayes probably drinks the stuff for breakfast. He may have a remedy. You must leave. Yaguara doesn't know friend from foe."

"Too bad!" Carlena snapped. "Focus. I need you!"

"How will Yaguara know which lizards are eatable?"

"The English are all wearing red."

"That helps." His eyes grew large. "Everything's red."

She grabbed his arm, guiding him through the bushes. They took a narrow path to the Safe House. After several yards of ducking and crawling beneath sharp branches, their destination came into view.

Carlena opened the gate. "Let me go first."

Yaguara glanced around suspiciously. "Good thinking."

Carlena knocked on the door twice, paused, and knocked twice more.

From inside came two knocks.

"Good. Yaguara's in," Yaguara said.

Tanama opened the door. "Thank goodness!"

Yaguara smiled. "Good kid."

"What happened to you?" she asked.

"I don't know, but it's still happening." Yaguara entered the house where dozens of residents huddled together. "What are these land crabs doing here?"

"Those are friends, Yaguara," Carlena said. She noticed relief in everyone's eyes at her presence.

"Yaguara's friends? He has strange friends."

"Is he on something of Strangewayes?" Atia asked.

"Worse," Carlena replied.

"Everyone is either in here, up the hill, or barricaded in Strangewayes's house," Tanama explained.

"They've taken Strangewayes's house. I could see it burning," Carlena said.

Atia gasped. "Livia?"

"I don't know," Carlena said. "Do you know where the Capitaine is?"

Atia loaded a gun. "I don't know; we thought he might be here. Where's Lilly?"

Carlena swallowed hard. "The English have us trapped. They will find a way in. We must lead everyone through the tunnel and into the hills."

"Where's Lilly?" Atia pressed.

"They killed her."

Atia's lip quivered. "I must find Livia." She moved to the door.

Carlena stopped her. "The English will follow us and hunt us down. We have to set a trap for them here. If the English make it through the buccaneer lines, they'll come this way. We have to get these people out."

Yaguara rubbed his eyes. "That's a good plan!"

Carlena took a blunderbuss from a gun cabinet.

Tanama gave her a concerned look. "You're bleeding! Carlena, you've been shot!"

Yaguara inspected the bloody hole in Carlena's dress. "You're red! Don't turn red!"

Carlena loaded the gun and strapped it on. "It's not bad. I have to set the fuses in St. Peter's Den while you get them out through the north tunnel."

"Carlena needs to get them away. Yaguara will set the trap."

"Not in the state you're in." Carlena checked the front of her dress. It was saturated.

"I'll do it," Atia volunteered. "Where's St. Peter's Den?"

"Yaguara and Carlena are the only chance they have of getting away," Tanama said. "We'll buy you some time!"

Yaguara snarled.

"Listen to me," Tanama said. "I'll meet you on the mountain."

"She can be convincing when she needs to be," Yaguara admitted.

Carlena realized how cold her hands had become. "Everyone, come on. We're going now."

Tanama took Atia's arm. "Come with me." They headed downstairs.

"Tanama better be there!" Yaguara hollered after her.

"Let's move out!" Carlena instructed, gripping the blunderbuss. People followed behind her, looking to her for safety. She hoped she wouldn't disappoint them.

Yaguara's head throbbed. He vaguely remembered waking to find a dart in his neck. Sounds were unusually loud, even deafening. He stepped into the northern escape tunnel, through which rainwater drained into the creek. Yaguara arrived as if in a dream – beginning in the middle.

Where was Tanama in all of this? Hadn't he just seen her? That's right, she was off to set the trap in St. Peter's Den – the hollowed-out space beneath the Safe House rigged with crates of gunpowder. What a brave kid; he was so proud of her.

Yaguara fumbled with his weapon straps. They were smooth and slippery, like eels. Flashes of red and yellow danced before his eyes and then exploded into a gold dust cloud. The crackling of thousands of insect legs crawled all around him. He slapped his own face, trying to focus. The noise was simply the flow of the creek nearby. *Yaguara has been in this situation before. The poisoned dart or the combat?* "Who are you talking to?" Yaguara uttered aloud.

"What did you say?" Carlena asked, pushing people forward. "Don't stop, keep going."

"I thought I *was* going," Yaguara said. He checked behind them to see a giant yellow millipede at least twenty feet in length. It followed them with thousands of wriggling legs. “A giant millipede!” He drew his machete.

“It’s friendly,” Carlena assured as they reached a gate in the tunnel. She opened the gate to access a metal ladder built into a rock wall. “This way, everyone. Climb up.”

Yaguara paused. Red and white lights formed behind him and morphed into turtles. A white man’s face grew out of a turtle’s belly and he spoke, “They’re getting away!”

Yaguara put away his machete and readied his arrows and an Atlatl – a wooden throwing device. “Anyone for turtle?”

“Soldiers!” Carlena readied the blunderbuss.

“Yaguara will handle this. Just keep the friendly millipede going.” He drew a long arrow and loaded it onto the Atlatl. “Say!” he called out. “You fellows look red.” He propelled the arrow into a Redcoat’s head and reloaded. “Turtles are so much easier to hit when they’re on land.” He flaunted his weapon. “Yaguara has won championships with this thing!”

Carlena whistled. “Let’s go!”

Yaguara climbed the ladder, following the trail of shimmering hummingbirds as they flitted by. The vibration from their wings sounded flatulent. “That was rude.” He staggered, grabbing hold of the gigantic millipede for balance. The tunnel before him seemed to narrow and morph into the likeness of the female passageway. Yaguara groaned. “This is going to hurt tomorrow.”

Atia followed Tanama into a dark room under the Safe House. She held up a torch to illuminate a small filthy bed. The air was a damp mixture of earth and dust. Tanama dragged the bed away from the wall and ripped the thin planks away to reveal a chamber.

“We’re going in there?” Atia asked uneasily.

Tanama crawled in. “No, I only wanted to show it to you!”

Atia peered inside. “Yer sarcasm’s getting better.”

“Careful with the light and tell me when the English are here.”

Atia was content to do so. “Aye, I’ll wait out here.”

Tanama opened a crate and the stench of sulfur filled the small space. “Pass me the torch.”

Atia did so and after a few seconds, the door to the small bedroom rattled. Someone kicked it. “Oh, they’re coming all right!”

"Check the rest of the floor!" a voice said. "Break the door down!" The blade of an axe pierced the wood.

The blood froze in Atia's veins, yet her heart pounded. It was time to crawl into the small passage. Memories of her worst experiences in dark tight places surfaced. Tanama lit the fuse. There was no turning back now.

Tanama grabbed her hand as Redcoats broke in. "Come on, let's go!"

Atia followed a tall tunnel for a few yards, and then encountered a space with a box-frame entrance, only big enough to crawl through. "Oh, fucking hell! Yer jesting, right?"

Tanama took the torch and waved her through first. "Go!"

Atia took one last large gasp of air and crawled inside. She presumed Tanama threw the torch at the crates of gunpowder. Soon she felt a hand pressing against her rear.

"Hurry!" Tanama said. "When you feel a rope, pull it, it'll lower the door."

Atia crawled along until rope filled her hands. She yanked it and the sound of a wood lid shut behind them. The only light now came from the moon ahead.

"Go!" Tanama urged.

Muffled voices came from behind them. "In here! They've lit fuses. Quick, pass me that torch." Sudden tremors shook the entire tunnel. Atia's fear were realized. The air was ripped from her lungs and she froze. Tanama slammed into the back of her.

Atia was paralyzed and suffocating. A ringing began in her ears and she could taste dirt in her mouth. The darkness lightened and everything drifted away. From far off she heard a familiar voice. It was her da! *Da! What are you saying? I'm over here!* Pain shot through her hand and she was being dragged. *Da!* The pain spread to her shoulder and the night air filled her lungs. She coughed and gagged, spitting out dirt.

Half dazed, she saw a Redcoat looking down at her. "It's a girl."

"Get her out," another said.

She could feel a hand touching her leg. *Tanama!* Atia reached behind and grabbed hold.

"She's stuck!" a Redcoat complained.

More hands grabbed at Atia and set her down on the damp ground. She gazed up at the luminous white moon. Thousands of stars twinkled, and a delicious breeze wafted through the trees. Tanama squeezed her hand.

"You'll not go from me sight, only from me view," her da's voice said. Atia closed her eyes.

The northern ridge was a cliff overlooking the entire plantation. Sections lay in ruin, engulfed by fire. Ignited gunpowder flickered all over the grounds. In the distance across the water sat the long peninsula of Port Royal. Street torches lit the whole city, sparkling against the water. Behind it, the moon hung high on the horizon.

Yaguara led the residents to a grassy clearing that glowed bluish-green. The coolness felt good against his clammy skin. Perhaps the poison was finally wearing off? He glanced over at the giant yellow millipede that hung in the trees. Maybe not.

Carlena was missing from the group. Yaguara looked back at the mouth of the tunnel to see her being helped by two men. In the moonlight, he could see that her dress was completely saturated in blood. "Let them carry you."

"Do you see me arguing?" Carlena was set down.

"Find something to carry her with!" His voice boomed. Yaguara knelt beside her and cut away the fabric around the wound. There was a bloody hole beside her belly button. He removed a section of fabric in the back of her dress. "The shot passed right through." The wound had charred bits of debris clinging to it. He carefully plucked them out. "The bleeding is from running around all night, but you lost a lot of blood." Yaguara handed her his water canteen and a pouch of herbs. "Carlena knows the routine."

"Aye, she does." She took a mouthful of water and began chewing the herbs to make a paste.

A hammock and rope were unpacked.

Before Carlena was lifted, Yaguara applied the herbal remedy. "Keep going." He squeezed her hand. "I'll see you up there."

"You better."

"Don't stop until you're in the mountains," Yaguara said.

Carlena was lifted and carried up an embankment. The residents followed until Yaguara was the only one left standing on the cliff. He had to go back for Tanama. The Safe House was still burning from the explosion. "Where did you go, kid?"

Yaguara ran down the steep peak towards the destruction. He'd seen this happen before, to the village he had once lived in with his wife, Fufu. He had warned Strangewayes that this was coming, and yet again those he loved were endangered and might be lost.

Redcoats directed a wagon train of caged prisoners heading away from the plantation. Movement came from the hill behind them. The bushes and trees seemed to come alive. *No, not the poison this time.* Maroons advanced, flourishing weapons, ready for war.

Yaguara traveled along a path through the trees and stumbled upon the body of a clergyman with white hair. A Maroon axe was buried in the back of his skull. The girl they called Nanny, joined by younger boys, stood around the body. Nanny paused to look at Yaguara before retrieving the axe. Then she led the younger ones up the hill.

"Don't stop until you're in the mountains," Yaguara instructed. "Those were cute little kids." He passed through an area shrouded in smoke. Cannon fire filled the corn field and bursts of light penetrated the haze. To the south there was heavy gunfire. At least he had a good idea where the Capitaine was – in Ponder Field.

Through the smoke, la Roche could see Port Royal's reflection on the water. *Cursed place,* he thought. He remained low as shots were fired again. Gladstone crawled alongside him, out of breath and exhausted.

"See!" La Roche coughed. "I got the idiot in the sheriff's hat shooting at Rodney again. How do you like that? Two times I make him do that."

"Right, you're a genius. I know," Gladstone said. "Wait! You said you knew where we were going. We're back at Ponder Field."

"Oui," la Roche replied. "This area is a bit hazy, as you say. Now stay low and keep quiet. This is our way out." He pointed to the bushy hill where a squad of Redcoats guarded the main trail.

La Roche wiped his grimy forehead. Tired and irritated, he could feel time running out. He had to find Atia! They were going to have to run for the Safe House. He knew Rodney's men would regroup and come quickly from the south. They would have to create a diversion.

"How far can you throw?" la Roche asked Gladstone.

"Far enough."

La Roche lit a grenade for each of them. Both were tossed in different directions at the Redcoats. The air was so thick no one saw them coming. Simultaneous bursts caused more carnage. The remaining buccaneers, Arsenault and Cliché, did the same.

La Roche and Gladstone sprang from the tall grass and sprinted along with the buccaneers to the trail ahead. Cannonballs flew in their direction, causing them to dive for bush cover. Once the maelstrom ended, they crawled in the direction of the Safe House.

Arsenault choked from smoke. "I told you those cannons could reach."

"Now we know, uh?" La Roche spat out debris. "Follow me." He guided them through a thick patch of prickly bushes. Before them stood orange flames. The Safe House was decimated. "Fuck!" He sat up and lit one of his few remaining smokes. *Where is Atia?* He took a long puff, trying to collect his thoughts.

I have to make it to the north ridge in order to reach the main gate. We must travel east. The only thing standing in my way is a battlefield. No problem, uh? He took a deep breath and loaded his weapons. The others did the same and followed him out.

As predicted, Rodney arrived with more men and more weapons. La Roche cocked his pistol and fired.

In retaliation, the order, "Open fire!" was given.

La Roche and his men remained flattened against the earth, taking aim at soldiers who struggled through the bushes. They fired, killing many. The man in the sheriff hat reappeared.

Arsenault nudged la Roche before shooting.

"Oui, take him down. You spoil my only fun."

Arsenault fired and the sheriff fell.

A shaky voice called from the bushes. "I'm okay!"

"There's too many of them," Gladstone said. "I'll lead them away. You try to find Atia and Fatima."

"Wow, that is heroic." Arsenault smiled. "They will shoot you in the ass before you get five feet."

Gladstone shrugged. "I don't know. I can be pretty fast."

"Or they might mistake you for a boar?" Cliché added.

"Thanks," Gladstone grumbled.

They all laughed and fired another round.

"Time to move," la Roche ordered as the enemy drew nearer. "Fire!"

"I'm out!" Gladstone said.

"Last one, I'm out too," la Roche admitted, aiming the Spanish pistol.

Arsenault and Cliché each fired a shot.

"We're surrounded," Cliché observed and drew his cutlasses, flipping and catching them in midair. "It's all in the technique."

"We have you!" the sheriff exclaimed. "Surrender! Capitaine Gator Gar, I am sheriff of Port Royal, Sydrack Taliare. I hereby place you uh—" a spear penetrated his chest.

Rodney and his men stared in shock.

Through the canopy of trees came the Maroons, wearing mud and leaves. They wielded spears and axes. The English quickly tried to organize a defense but were overwhelmed and forced to retreat.

On the trail ahead, Ekene arrived with a dozen more Maroons. One, Quashee, was familiar from their travels over the Blue Mountains and la Roche slashed his way towards them.

A Redcoat stabbed Gladstone with a bayonet. Cliché removed the soldier's head while Gladstone applied pressure to his arm.

Rodney yelled, "Retreat! Retreat!"

"I think I'm due for a raise," Gladstone said.

Arsenault checked the wound. "I've had worse."

"You made friends?" Gladstone asked Ekene.

La Roche approached, wanting an immediate report.

"The prisoners are being taken out on the north road in wagons. Atia, her sister, Tanama, and Fatima are with them," Ekene said.

La Roche briefly closed his eyes when he heard her name. *My Atia's alive.*

"The English set a trap for Ashanti," Ekene continued. "He's on his way here. Hijo del Cimarrón has challenged him to do battle on the open field of the Gathering Place."

Gladstone looked perplexed. "Cimarrón sided with the English? Where is Ashanti?"

"Arriving from the east at dawn. Ashanti knows it's a trap. He will die to defend the Blue Mountains. He says we must all leave now, or we will die as well."

"Sounds clear enough for me, oui?" Cliché smiled.

"We'll concentrate our attack on the Redcoats, and we'll cover Ashanti's back while he fights Cimarrón if he lets us pass to the north to get our people out," la Roche said to Quashee.

Cliché dressed a wound on his arm. "We? Us?"

Ekene and Quashee spoke in Arawak.

Quashee sprinted off.

La Roche addressed the men, "I'm going after Atia. If you want to save your people then by all means, join me."

"Lead the way, mon Capitaine." Gladstone slowly rose. "We have our people to rescue."

Arsenault secured his weapons. "Oui."

Gladstone tapped Ekene's arm. "Good work. Now go down to the lake and take the boats across. Wait for us."

"You don't know how to talk to Maroons. You need me to come."

"Don't argue this time, it's not an order. I'm asking you," Gladstone said.

La Roche motioned to Ekene. "Can you get yourself to the prisoners on the north road?"

"Are you insane?" Gladstone asked.

"Get yourself captured if you have to," la Roche instructed. "It's an old buccaneer trick to get behind the lines. Then find us a way to get to them and signal when you reach the road."

"Signal?" Ekene said.

"Anything will do."

Ekene wore a doubtful expression and took off into the trees.

La Roche and the buccaneers started up the trail, reloading their guns.

Gladstone followed. "Does the expression 'out of the frypan, into the fire' ring a bell for anyone?"

The buccaneers shook their heads.

"Is this Shakespeare, no?" Cliché asked.

Ekene followed Quashee to the waterway outside the east gate that separated Strangewayes Way from its neighboring plantation. Trees came alive with movement and an army of seventy Maroons, a mixture of different African tribes, emerged. Ashanti stepped forth, adorned in a red and gold headpiece and a beaded collar. His Maroons followed in similar attire of greens and blues.

Perspiration formed on Ekene's neck and forehead while his throat was dry. He had seen Ashanti before but never up close, and never during wartime. Ashanti was an impressive warrior with an ornately decorated shield of animal hide, an axe forged from iron with copper details, and a Spanish longsword at his side.

Quashee spoke with Ashanti, who in turn addressed Ekene.

"Your people flee into the hills to the north, but that way is closed now. The English have many guns and soldiers."

Ekene's heart raced. "They're taking the prisoners out the north gate. I must try to free them."

"Strangewayes's people can pass to the lake and to the north without harm," Ashanti's voice boomed. "Buccaneers can take their chance."

Ashanti's commanders relayed the message to their men in various languages. Suddenly, Maroons with painted leopard spots dropped from the trees, blocking the way. Ashanti gave the signal to stop any interference as a tall man with a skeleton-painted face leapt down. Ekene had heard of Loa Wanga, a famous shaman who specialized in potions and curses—someone you should never cross.

Loa Wanga advanced and smelled Ashanti. "Death," he sneered. "A simple trap and Ashanti walks in to die. He gains nothing and we all lose."

"A challenge was made here," Ashanti asserted.

"Hijo del Cimarrón has cursed these mountains for his English masters. We all shall die because of it. Death awaits those who pass."

"Slavery awaits those who live," Ashanti argued. "There can be only sacrifice to save those we left behind. He who is afraid to sacrifice has surrendered himself and his people. The Cimarrón people have dwelled in these mountains for many years and they will not make peace. It will be decided today, and the curse will be lifted."

Loa Wanga summoned his men, "We go to war."

Ashanti held his shield and axe in a series of different positions. The Maroons fanned out into various attack formations. Figures swung through the trees.

Ekene waited for a break in the ranks so he could run ahead. He followed a trail that led beyond Carlena's house, next to a barn and stable. Flares shot up, lighting the sky above the Gathering Place. Loa Wanga's Maroons attacked the Redcoats just as cannonballs began to assault the trees.

Through a thicket, Ekene came to the road where the prison wagons were being loaded. He ducked down as three Redcoats marched by. They held two black men at bayonet point. Ekene tossed a stone into the bushes opposite him. The Redcoats aimed their guns. "Right, who's there?"

Ekene slipped in and stood with the prisoners while Redcoats stabbed at the bushes. His first glimpse of the cage wagons sent chills up his spine. On the slave ship, the quarters had been so cramped he was unable to stand. Many people had died around him and when they reached the conditioning base on Barbados after almost a year, it took months to learn how to walk again.

"It's nothing," a Redcoat said. "An animal. Let's move out." The prisoners marched on to the wagon train. Soldiers stood around smoking. They seemed nervous listening to the battle.

"Ain't it something?" one exclaimed.

A soldier grabbed another prisoner from a cage. "Let's do another one. That'll get yer mind off things." He dragged the prisoner to the bushes and shot him.

Ekene cursed himself for coming this way. He recognized the people in cages. Livia, Fatima, and other women. They had been beaten; their expressions hopeless. Bars rattled, and he looked up to see Atia and Tanama. He'd found the right place, but what to do next?

Skean sat opposite Beckford in the back of a militia carriage wearing a black cloak. His broken arm ached within its sling and he looked to the north. The hills were writhing in flames with glints of cannonball fire. He was not paid to have an opinion on morality, but this was nothing less than a massacre.

"My God," Beckford said.

"God has little to do with this," Skean replied. When he received a strange glance, he added, "Let the heathens fight it out." Skean had momentarily forgotten his assignment as Brother Gideon.

They arrived at a checkpoint manned by Redcoats. Soldiers were digging a ditch near the tree line. Dead bodies were being piled nearby. They were in the process of throwing the corpse of a young woman on top when Beckford leapt down.

"It's as I told you, Colonel. They're killing the prisoners," a militiaman said.

"You bloody bastards!" Beckford yelled.

A Redcoat smirked. "We've been called worse."

"It's Colonel Beckford of the militia," another Redcoat heckled.

Skean stepped down. "Damn it. Justice Goblet ordered all prisoners to Port Royal for questioning."

“Ain’t none of these ones on the list, sir,” a Redcoat said.

“You know not the names of these people,” Beckford snarled. “Many are to give testimony and be tried for crimes before the court.”

The Redcoats didn’t seem the least bit concerned.

“Orders from Lieutenant Thorne, sir. He said ‘no quarter.’ Kill all prisoners, right? This is us doing what we been ordered to do. Right?” a Redcoat replied.

Skean’s mandate was shot to hell. “The church doesn’t condone this action. If these people are to face justice under English law then the law shall prevail.”

“We got our orders,” another Redcoat snapped. “If ya wanna go above Lieutenant Thorne, you gotta see Captain Longstaff.” He pointed up the road towards the front gate.

A little way up the trail, a Redcoat dragged three shackled prisoners. “Where do we leave this lot?”

Skean grabbed a book and a stick of charcoal from his pocket and followed Beckford to a cluster of caged wagons. Skean studied the prisoners, and sure enough he recognized the buccaneer de Kreep. He had been beaten and blood dripped down his face. *What a catch,* Skean pondered. He made a note in his book, which drew attention.

“What’s that?” a Redcoat asked.

“Just a little prayer.” Skean pointed to the buccaneer. “Lock this one up good and tight.” He had spotted de Kreep in Port Royal just weeks ago, right around the time of the return of Gator Gar.

Beckford came over. “A buccaneer. Good catch.”

Redcoats brought more prisoners at gunpoint to the wagons. Skean quickly inspected them. One man’s face he saw very clearly in the moonlight. It was Ekene. “Shackle this one in irons,” Skean instructed.

“How can you be sure?” Beckford questioned.

“He’s been seen in Ligania with Dr. Strangewayes and the one they call Carlena.” Skean came across a young red-haired girl. Atia Crisp, still alive. He couldn’t help but be impressed. She was a strong and resourceful young woman. “The red-haired pikey.”

“Both pikeys, actually,” Beckford corrected. “These prisoners are to be transported to Port Royal with all haste.”

“Red Royals don’t take orders from militia.”

“Or clergy,” Thorne said defiantly, strutting towards Beckford. “What’s the meaning of this?”

Beckford puffed up his chest. “Lieutenant Thorne, I’m taking the prisoners.”

“The hell you are!” Thorne signaled his men and they boarded the wagons. “Take the prisoners up the road to the bridge.” Thorne hopped up on the lead wagon, while his men guarded the train. “Report to base camp, Militia Colonel Beckford. That’s an order.”

“You’ll answer for this, Thorne,” Beckford warned.

Skean folded his arms. “If not in this world, then the next. He’s really getting on God’s wick!”

“Come on, Brother Gideon,” Beckford said. “To the command post.”

Skean trailed him to the driver’s bench of the carriage.

“I’ll be right back with Captain Longstaff, and these prisoners had better be alive!” Beckford cracked the reins. They drove to the main gate and up the road to an intersection where the lane split to a neighboring plantation. Scattered Redcoats set up cannons that looked like barrels aimed high over the treeline.

By the gate was a command base with a cluster of tents and horse-drawn supply wagons. Inside, a line of ten bronze cannons aimed over the trees.

Skean recognized this campaign – Longstaff’s Operation Two Birds. He hadn’t figured out if it was all Longstaff’s or if Governor Dewar and Lord Llewellyn also had a hand in it. They passed through the gate and pulled up alongside Longstaff, who was giving orders. His men moved faster with every word. He certainly commanded respect, Skean noted, which would prove very useful.

Beckford jumped down. “Captain Longstaff. A word, sir?”

Skean shadowed.

Admiral Goddam stepped from the command tent. “Captain? Ah, there’s my Big Dick. Are we on schedule?”

“Of course, sir,” Longstaff replied. “Ready to fire!” His men readied the torches and he gave the order. The cannons blasted huge shots over the trees, leaving trails of smoke.

“Prepare for phase two, Captain.” Goddam returned to his tent.

Longstaff addressed his men, “Ready mortars. Report, Mr. Fishhook.”

“The Maroons are in the field and we have them all pinned down,” Fishhook said breathlessly. “Ashanti is in the center, where he should be. Do we signal the Cimarrón people?”

“No, Mr. Fishhook, we will not.” Longstaff took the amplifier trumpet from his yeoman. “Fire mortars!” A flagman waved and cannons fired. High in the air they flew with mushrooming smoke clouds.

Longstaff and his men trained their telescopes through a clearing in the trees to witness the battle on the hills.

Skean took out a spyglass. The bombs came down mercilessly, destroying people and land. He cleared his throat. “Captain Longstaff, the church demands a conference.”

Beckford’s anger mastered him, and he charged right up to Longstaff. “You bloody bastard! How dare you kill unarmed prisoners of His Majesty’s government!”

“What prisoners, Colonel?” Longstaff was calm.

“Killing unarmed prisoners don’t sit right with me, sir,” Fishhook added.

“Thank you, Mr. Fishhook!” Longstaff said. “I’m following orders, Colonel. And we have the red-haired pikey, therefore the trap is set. I’ve ordered the reserves in as well. We certainly don’t want prisoners killed. Especially not those who can bring us the French pirate Capitaine.”

“You’re using her as bait?” Skean surmised.

“Bloody well right. Isn’t that so, Mr. Fishhook?”

“Bloody well right, sir.”

Beckford fumed. “I follow orders from Justice Goblet.”

Longstaff checked his pistol. “The English Navy doesn’t take orders from Justice Goblet.”

Beckford raised his sword. “I’m under orders to return all prisoners to Port Royal for trial and investigation. All prisoners. Slaves are to be re-conditioned for resale and the smugglers tried and hanged before King and God.”

Fishhook and sailing master Cook drew their weapons.

Skean waved peaceably, nudging his way in between them. “The church strongly agrees. If I may speak with you privately, Captain Longstaff, I have a few words of prayer for guidance. That’s not too much for the Lord to ask. Violante would agree, I’m sure.”

They met just out of reach of the others.

Skean cleared his throat. He was no physical match for Longstaff; his power was knowledge.

"Playing both sides is expected, of course, you being from Port Royal and all. But as the colonel said, Judge Goblet ordered all prisoners returned for trial. I'm not fully sure what killing Strangewayes's people does to protect you and Goddam, but I know Strangewayes ties you both to taking bribes from Dewar to look the other way. Just as you looked the other way while Dewar set Beeston up to take the fall for his embezzlement. Yes, God knows that Goddam was made admiral of Beeston's fleet in return for testifying at the hearing. And you were awarded Captain of *HMS Relentless.*"

Longstaff clenched his fist, practically growling.

Skean held out his cross and spoke quickly. "A ship you captured legally from a French Corsair, and a lawful prize." He took a folded piece of parchment from his pocket. "However, it's your shore activities the church takes issue with. This is the note that was left for Lady Beeston, telling her to meet you at the Blue Anchor. Once there, you took her upstairs." Skean pointed. "There's your little phallic signature 'L' right there. What is a bronco? That's Spanish, isn't it?" He briefly glanced down at Longstaff's trousers. After all, it was practically legend. *Christ! He's bigger than my family tree!* "She's understandably lonely, and it's forgivable as long as she confesses. And with her husband on trial for embezzlement, Lady Beeston's mail is subject to scrutiny. The letters you wrote – to both Lady Beeston and her daughter, Jane – were very inspiring. All of you so certain he'll come back exonerated, you all decided to go ahead and arrange the marriage solidifying your unity with the Beeston family. However, you are already married to Spotswood's daughter. The Spotswoods who just lost the Leeward Islands and had to sail north to Charlestown with nothing but the clothes on their backs. There's rotten timing for you. You'll need a divorce if you're to marry the Beeston girl. Of course, your wife will demand one now that your Port Royal whore's stabbing has been splashed all over the daily broadsheets. A wedding would be years away if someone should send a letter or note to Lord Dewar." Skean put the document safely away again.

"Killing unarmed prisoners, you say?" Longstaff said. "We shall look into it, I assure you. Mr. Fishhook, Mr. Cook, civilians have been killed against the orders of the Whig government. All prisoners are to be sent to Port Royal for trial and execution."

Fishhook stood at attention. "Aye, sir."

“That is correct,” Skean agreed. “You can’t execute a corpse. They tried that with Cromwell and everybody laughed.”

“Yeoman,” Longstaff called.

The yeoman stepped forth with a thin leather case. Longstaff took a document from the case and wrote on it. “Colonel Beckford, I’m giving you a field commission. You’ll retain your civilian rank. Do you understand?”

“N-not entirely, sir, no,” Beckford replied.

Skean smiled politely. *He tries hard for an idiot.*

Longstaff gestured to the Redcoats. “You now outrank all of them. Take Corporal Small’s battalion. Take charge of the prisoners and deliver them all to Judge Goblet in Port Royal with my compliments. He can decide what the bloody hell to do with them. Take the wherry from Ligania.” Longstaff rolled up the order and presented it to Beckford. “Congratulations, Colonel.”

Skean bowed his head.

Beckford seemed stunned at first and leapt to his new duties with enthusiasm.

“If Lord Spotswood can dress up volunteer militia in red coats and call them marines, we can make one of ours a colonel,” Longstaff said.

“It’s only fair.” Skean nodded.

“Jim, Mr. Cook, come with me. Admiral Goddam has committed an act of treason and I’m assuming command.” Longstaff marched to the command tent.

Beside the tent stood a group of Dragoons, a special battalion of armored horse riders with lances and guns.

Skean kept his distance. Inside, Admiral Goddam was reading a map with a couple of irate Miskito warriors. Beside them stood a native translator and Colonel Englehorn Spotswood, brother to the governor of the Leeward Islands and the commander of the Dragoons. Spotswood’s helmet creaked loudly as he tilted his head.

“No deal with Cimarrón was discussed. And if Cimarrón had a deal, why is he being killed?” the translator asked.

Goddam waved his hands. “I assure you, there was never any deal between England and the Maroons. Only interference from the Brethren of the Coast.” He addressed the Miskitos directly, “You have done your people a great service and saved many lives. You have honored the treaty, as shall King William. Send your warriors to the hills after the stragglers.”

The translator did his job and the Miskitos continued to argue as they left the tent.

Spotswood's helmet screeched. "Do they have the Maroons completely surrounded? What's taking so long?"

Goddam patted the map. "Victory is at hand, Colonel. Don't worry; we'll save you some Maroons."

Longstaff positioned himself at head of the table. "Sorry, gentlemen, but circumstances demand I take immediate action. Admiral, I'm assuming command of the mission."

Goddam was aghast. "What the hell are you saying, Dick?"

"You've exceeded your authority, sir, costing the lives of men under your command. I'm placing you under arrest."

Skean advanced. "Your government and your church do not condone your actions in combat."

"You haven't the authority to arrest me," Goddam protested.

"Enough of your Port Royal pissing contest," Spotswood reprimanded them. "We are engaged in battle here. Return to your post, Captain." He turned to Goddam. "Are the Maroons where they're supposed to be?"

Goddam nodded. "Everything is as it should be. Go ahead, Colonel. Finish them off."

"Then what are we arguing about?" Spotswood adjusted his helmet. "Let's hunt Maroons!" He charged out of the tent creaking as he rallied his troops.

Goddam stared coldly at Longstaff. "You fool! Our objective is here. You know what's coming. The fate of English Jamaica is in our hands!"

Longstaff signaled to Fishhook and Cook, who seized Goddam. "Don't make a fuss, Admiral."

A messenger entered. "Captain Longstaff, sir."

"What is it, boy?"

"Sir, the checkpoints are sending the wrong codes. They're just flashing randomly."

"Which ones?"

"All of them!"

Goddam's jaw dropped.

"How did they all get it wrong?" Fishhook wondered aloud.

Panic grew on everyone's face. Things were only just starting to move the right way, and now this. A distinctive war call sounded from the hills. The Maroons were attacking.

Longstaff drew his sword and pistol.

“I warned you that this would happen if you made a deal with the Maroons, Dick,” Goddam said. “You listened to Dewar. That man destroys all he touches, with a laugh and a grin.”

“Does anyone have the latest Maroon census?” Skean sidestepped towards the carriage, clutching his cross. “Never mind. I think I left it in the car.”

Someone yelled out, “Retreat to the stable!”

Skean secured the hood around his head and hurried to the stable. Glancing back, he saw Goddam stagger out of the command tent. The admiral had been shot.

“Protect the cannons!” Longstaff yelled, and then blew a puff of smoke from his pistol.

What just happened? Skean wished he’d turned a second sooner.

A flying axe soon finished off the admiral.

“My brother’s going to hear about this!” Spotswood whined. “Let’s move, Dragoons!” He led his soldiers onward. The Dragoons had just made it to the gate when someone pelted Spotswood with pieces of a bloody dead chicken. He fell from his horse. A Maroon with a skeleton-painted face bounded down from the trees to commandeer Spotswood’s horse.

Skean froze. It was Loa Wanga. The shaman had been documented many times, but never before had there been a confirmed sighting.

“After him!” Spotswood yelled and the Dragoons charged.

Skean decided to find a safe place from which to wait out the pending destruction. He neared the stable and became one with the shadows.

"Arsenault"
GO
2014

Epitaph of a Drunken Scoundrel

By firelight the battle raged on. The hills swarmed with movement and below was the clearing where Ashanti's and Cimarrón's Maroons fought gruesomely. The mortar bombs dropped from the sky, tearing men to pieces.

La Roche lit a cigarette, took a big puff and passed it down the line to Gladstone, Arsenault, and finally Cliché. They checked the cornfield. Redcoats were still battling the Maroons.

"Well, we said we were going east and we're going east," la Roche affirmed, tightening the straps that held his remaining weapons. He cocked his pistol and more cannon fire blasted the trees. "Now."

La Roche crossed the charred ground where the Gathering Place had been. He could still see Atia in black velvet with her flowing red hair. Truly beautiful. Colorful decorations had hung in the trees and the ground had glowed with warmth from the torch lamps. They'd danced, happy just to be together.

Ashanti and Cimarrón were fighting to the death in the middle of the field. Their people cut each other down with spears, arrows, and machetes. An incoming mortar bomb exploded on the field, causing still more carnage.

La Roche and the buccaneers paused by a bush until the smoke cleared. The Maroons began cheering and screaming at the same time. Cimarrón lifted the broken body of Ashanti high in the air for everyone to see.

"The Ashanti man falls!" Cimarrón yelled. "Attack!"

Hell broke loose.

"This is a bad sign, uh?" Cliché said.

"All bets are off." La Roche grabbed Gladstone's arm. "Run for it!"

They ran for the eastern side of Carlena's house, dodging spears and arrows along the way. The stable and barn were relatively undamaged. Above, the rain and wind intensified. Bright silver flashes of light brought coded messages from afar.

"It says 'Capitaine.' It's the signal; it must be Ekene," Gladstone said.

"It said 'capitate,'" la Roche corrected.

"I never said he was a good speller."

When they neared Carlena's house, five Redcoats ran out of the side door and the two teams practically crashed into one another.

"Oh, bloody hell!" a Redcoat said and fumbled for his weapon.

The buccaneers stabbed swiftly with their cutlasses, slicing them down. A shot penetrated Gladstone's arm.

"Let's go; keep moving!" la Roche pushed.

"Leave me, Capitaine." Gladstone writhed in pain. "I'll only slow you down. You have to try to reach them; Atia and Carlena. You have to get our people out, whoever's left."

La Roche indicated the nearby trail. "Get back to the lake. Take a boat upriver as far as you can. We'll catch up to you once we find our people. Don't give up now!"

"You find them, Capitaine. You find them and I'll be waiting." Gladstone headed for the path.

La Roche caught up to the buccaneers behind the house. "Stay down and cover me." He moved towards the stable. There was little activity in this area; it was a strangely quiet oasis in a desert of bloodshed. La Roche inspected the barn. Nothing. Then the main doors swung open with a gust of wind. He raised his weapons.

A couple of Slasher Al's pirates appeared. Dogfish, Little Fred, twirling two stilettos, and a third he didn't know.

La Roche tipped his hat. "Apologies. I was looking for someone else."

"You killed my brother," Little Fred growled.

"If I had a doubloon for every time I hear that one, uh?"

Dogfish raised his sword. "This is gonna be fun."

La Roche fired the pistol at Dogfish, causing him to dive for the ground. "Good Spanish silver, it is." He tucked the gun away and readied his cutlass.

The three thugs came at him, swinging.

In return, la Roche parried.

Dogfish drew a dagger, twirling it in his fingers. "You don't make it easy, Gator Gar!" He lunged.

La Roche deflected and retreated to the stable. "Well, three against one wasn't fair. It is not personal. You are familiar with taking bribes, oui?"

Dogfish and Little Fred backed him into a corner.

Two men burst into the stable brandishing pistols and cutlasses.

La Roche didn't recognize one, but the other had an enormously wide physique.

"The Capitaine ain't going with you, mates," the wide one barked, attacking with a cutlass while shooting one pirate in the head.

"What's wrong, lads?" la Roche's second rescuer said, cocking a pistol. "Ain't ya ever seen the shadow of death before?" He shot Little Fred.

La Roche eyed the newcomers. "Whoever you are, you are hired."

Dogfish tried to run and the wide one clobbered him with the butt of his blade, knocking him out.

From a dark corner came one of Slasher Al's sharpshooters, aiming a musket at la Roche. He thought it was the end until someone blasted the shooter to shards. La Roche was surprised to see Major Paine with his smoking blunderbuss.

The commotion drew the attention of Arsenault and Cliché, who came in brandishing their weapons.

"All friends here!" la Roche called out. "Allow me to introduce Major Paine."

Major Paine scrutinized la Roche. "You look..."

"Younger than you. Now with respect, get out of my way. Cormac the pikey's girls are up there."

"You stand no chance of getting 'em back and very little of getting out alive," Paine warned. "The lake is clear. Get out while you can."

La Roche watched the two men who had rescued him.

"This is Tiny," Paine said, pointing to the wide one.

"Sure he is," la Roche scoffed. "As I suspected, Tiny McAllister. Quartermaster for Royal Rook."

"And this is Quinton Winter, Rook's sailing master," Tiny introduced. "I bring a message from Bartolomeo Portuguese." He opened his coat and handed over a damp scroll.

"It even stinks. How nice." La Roche cringed. "I am in your debt, Tiny and Winter." He turned to Paine. "If he brought the message, why are you here?"

Major Paine reloaded his blunderbuss. "The Brethren will never allow King Louis to rule Jamaica."

La Roche wiped his blade. "*Les Flibustiers* will not allow King William to rule Jamaica and I am Capitaine of *les Frères de la Côte*. You don't tell me what to do."

"My orders from the English Crown are to bring you in, Capitaine," Paine said. "My duty to the Brethren is to see that you aren't arrested. I'm in rather a bind, and I was hoping you'd turn around and take the boat out of here before we have a conflict."

La Roche read the scroll, which confirmed what Paine just told him. Jamaica was off limits to the French. "The end to a perfect night," he said dryly.

"Bartolomeo and I are in agreement. If you try to take Jamaica under a French flag it'll be your epitaph. That be our final word," Paine said.

La Roche inspected his cutlass for damage. "It's only a matter of time before Whigs take over the Brethren, no?"

Dogfish groaned, half-conscious on the ground.

La Roche swung the blade and cut into Dogfish's leg, eliciting a scream. "Anything to say, Dogfood?"

"You won't get nothin' out of me."

La Roche stabbed the blade the rest of the way through the leg.

"For…less than fifty!" Dogfish squealed.

"I don't need you alive, stupid dog. I know who Slasher Al works for – Coggshall and the mayor."

Dogfish squirmed. "They want to take the city in the name of King James. The Flibustiers won't attack Port Royal under a Jacobite flag."

Major Paine cocked the blunderbuss. "And Laurens agreed not to invade, Capitaine."

La Roche loaded the Spanish pistol. "Then I'm leaving and taking Cormac's girls with me."

"Aye, long live King James," Dogfish said. "I can deliver a message—"

La Roche swung his blade again. Dogfish's head rolled past Major Paine. "That is a clear enough message." La Roche wiped the blade again.

Paine leaned against the doorway. "We've seen this view before, you and I."

La Roche examined the hills. Maroons and English still battled. "Oui, good times and bad."

"Well, consider that message delivered." Paine straightened his hat. "You have till noon in the morrow to clear your men out. Now if you'll excuse me, I think I'll take an escort out of here with Tiny. I didn't sign up for a Maroon battle. Your job here is done, Lieutenant. We best be off."

"Aye, sir," Tiny said. "We make for the gate." He went first, his sword and pistol ready. Major Paine and Winter followed. Paine blasted his blunderbuss, sending the Maroons running for cover.

La Roche knelt by the buccaneers, who were both smoking his pre-rolled cigarettes. "Where did you get those?"

Arsenault grinned and tucked them into la Roche's pocket. "You should be more careful, Capitaine."

"Let's move out!" La Roche grabbed a cigarette and lit it. "Unless you want to rest a while, catch your breath? Have a smoke, by all means!"

The three kept low until they reached Carlena's house. Redcoats darted past, chased by axe-wielding Maroons. Then came a squad of English soldiers. La Roche and the buccaneers dove for cover beneath the porch. Once things settled, they would head to the gate where the prisoners were being held. *Atia, I am coming. Stay alive.*

Atia regained consciousness inside a hard, wet, rattling cage. She wiped rainwater from her eyes and tried to focus. In the cage wagon before her were Livia and Fatima, who tried to jerk the pins out of the door hinge.

"Liv!" Atia cried.

Her sister looked back with relief. "Just sit tight."

The wagons came to a bend in the road, where they met up with another convoy of prisoners. This one contained Ekene. There was a loud clunk and a scream. A Maroon stabbed a soldier and rolled the body off the lead wagon. Two more Redcoats fell.

Atia nudged Tanama, who was still asleep beside her. "The Maroons are attacking."

Tanama woke and pulled herself up.

Dozens of Maroons swarmed the cage wagons, jabbing through the bars with spears.

"Oh, Vulcan's flaming cock!" Atia blurted and stood back to back with Tanama. They prepared to grab whatever came at them.

A spear was thrust into Livia's cage. Livia and Fatima grabbed and twisted it from the Maroon's hand. They went to work prying the cage door.

A larger cage wagon stalled beside Atia and she came face to face with a battered de Kreep.

"Atia?" he said.

She scarcely recognized him beneath all the blood. "Dashiell!"

De Kreep smiled. "I was just passing by." He used a small metal pick on the lock. "Hang on, I will be right there."

Atia's relief was short-lived when Lieutenant Thorne marched forth, tailed by two Redcoats. She had witnessed his killings many times that night. Thorne loaded his pistol and shot a woman two wagons away. He charged down the line at Atia. "No way yer getting back alive. Port Royal don't need more of yer kind." He aimed the pistol at Atia's head. There came a whistle and Thorne turned. Blood splattered Atia and Tanama.

Yaguara cut down Thorne and both his men with a machete and an axe. He took the stabilizing pin from Thorne's ammunition pouch and then dumped his body in the ditch. Yaguara picked the lock.

"I knew you'd show up," Tanama said.

"Just keep the door still," he replied.

"Watch out!" de Kreep yelled.

Cudjoe and Delabra descended, tackling de Kreep and Yaguara. Delabra stabbed at the cage with his spear. The weapon grazed Atia's back, but pierced straight through Tanama. A horrible gurgle escaped her throat.

Atia shrieked, covering her mouth.

Delabra yanked the spear out, ready for another jab. Yaguara tackled him and they wrestled on the road. Pure rage filled Yaguara's eyes and his machete met Delabra's throat. Blood jetted everywhere.

Atia cradled Tanama in her arms and put pressure on the wound. Blood gushed through her fingers. "Tanama, hang on, girl!" There was no movement, not even a blink; Tanama's eyes stared straight ahead. Atia gently pushed the eyelids closed.

De Kreep continued to battle Cudjoe on the road. Yaguara threw his axe, chopping into flesh. Cudjoe crawled away, a gaping wound in his shoulder blade. Yaguara helped de Kreep to his feet.

A dozen Redcoats arrived to reinforce the area. They beat the prisoners until many, including Yaguara and de Kreep, were unconscious.

The spear was pried from Livia's hand, snuffing out any flicker of hope she had for escape.

"Lock them up!" came a call and the soldiers loaded more cages.
"Yer all a bunch of bastards!" Atia scowled.
"Yeah? Well, lucky for us, right?" one jeered.
"Move out!"
Atia held Tanama, softly humming as the wagons rolled on. *Capitaine, where are you?*

Longstaff cut down another Maroon with a sword thrust to the chest. Early dawn broke on the horizon in hues of red and orange. What a long bloody night it had been. The stench of sulfur hung thick in the air. Longstaff and his men continued to protect the mortar guns while the Dragoons held their ground over at the adjacent plantation. Even Longstaff's resolve was dwindling.

A sergeant led a handful of bloodied and beaten Red Royals up the road to the command tent.

"Protect the flank!" the sergeant called.

Longstaff met up with him. "Are you here to reinforce us or is it the other way around?"

"We've lost the cornfield battery line, sir," the sergeant reported.

"The cannons?" Fishhook asked.

"The Maroons have them."

Longstaff appraised the remaining supply wagons attached to horses. "Get those wagons. We're taking them into the fight."

Panic filled the faces of both Fishhook and Cook. Longstaff turned to see Maroons, some badly burned, others still aflame, furiously attacking. The leader, Cimarrón, came directly at Longstaff with a machete. The blade cut through his coat and left a gash in his chest. The cold steel burned.

The sergeant took aim at Cimarrón from behind, but he was outmatched and soon cut down with an axe to the head.

Longstaff was in shock. This day was far from being won, but he would not go down without a fight. He struck Cimarrón with the butt of his sword. The Maroon was resilient, a worthy opponent. They tumbled to the ground using fists.

Longstaff's yeoman ran to help but was cut down by a Maroon spear.

Longstaff clawed and kicked, knocking away his adversary's machete. Cimarrón drew his knife. Longstaff tried in vain to reach his sword, but the blade was already at his throat. He grabbed it, both hands trembling to find their last bit of strength. Longstaff felt the cold edge penetrate his skin.

Cimarrón suddenly went limp.

It was Fishhook who hauled the dead body off Longstaff. He'd used the captain's sword on the enemy.

Longstaff held his throat.

"Bloody well right, sir?" Fishhook offered his hand.

Longstaff took it gratefully. "Bloody well right, Jim."

"Jesus Christ! They brought an army!" Fishhook exclaimed. "And now they have cannons."

"Aye." Longstaff's voice rasped. "Who set up who? Jim, get ready to fire the guns and mortars." Longstaff ran to the supply wagons, jumping aboard the front one. "Mr. Cook, you're with me. We'll get our men off that hill."

"Aye, sir." Cook led men onto the second wagon. A few Red Royals joined them, reloading their muskets.

"Adjust your target and take out those guns, Mr. Fishhook," Longstaff ordered and loaded his pistols. "We'll bring some Dragoons with us and secure the twelves first."

"Aye, sir!" Cook replied.

Fishhook rallied more men. "Our guns have fallen into enemy hands, lads. We have to take them out." He pointed. "Directly over these trees. Four hundred yards. Make it azimuth eighty-five."

"At 0700 blow the whole bloody hill to hell whether we're clear or not," Longstaff instructed and drove down the road and into the entrance of the plantation neighboring Strangewayes Way. Dragoons circled the bronze cannons and fought off Maroons. Colonel Spotswood could be seen swinging his sword at anything that moved.

"Oh, Big Dick, thank heavens!" Spotswood said. "Regroup."

Longstaff held his throat with one hand and waved his sword with the other. The Dragoons followed, reorganizing their lines. They fired on the enemy. Another horse darted into the mix, its rider a tall man painted to look like a skeleton. The skeleton rider rallied the Maroons. Loa Wanga was a hundred-pound reward. *If I should survive this day, I shall be a wealthy man.*

"Ship of the line!" Longstaff instructed Cook.

Cook signaled the men. "All hands ready."

Wagons and Dragoons lined up in a row to take aim at Loa Wanga's line.

"Fire!" Cook ordered and a maelstrom of shots burst forth with great success. Only a handful of Maroons still stood.

Loa Wanga reached Cook's wagon and readied a spear. Longstaff pulled up alongside and fired his pistol. The shaman was knocked from his horse and then crawled for his axe. A Dragoon rode by and put him down with another shot.

"Our men are losing the battle for the plantation, Colonel," Longstaff reported to Spotswood. "We must get these cannons and horses into the battle."

"That's what we came here for." Spotswood adjusted his creaking helmet. "Charge!" He galloped into battle.

Longstaff looked back at Cook, who gave the order to charge. They all stormed ahead. Colonel Spotswood blew his trumpet, rallying everyone to their coming victory.

La Roche stared at the gate, only yards away. There had been heavy fire on the other side. Maroons and English were sure to be blocking the way. "Go," he ordered. Arsenault and Cliché followed. The deafening squeak of a trumpet filled the air.

"*Merde*!" la Roche cursed. Every fiber in his body wanted this day to be over and it had only just begun with a golden glow on the landscape. He and the buccaneers ducked when they saw the Dragoons approaching. Hooves pounded and armor rattled.

"It's the Capitaine!" a soldier called out.

"The French Capitaine," Longstaff said. "Take him dead or alive."

Cliché stumbled. Arsenault and la Roche grabbed his arms and yanked him into the trees. Maroons continued their attack on the English, which gave them a small window to progress deeper into the jungle.

"This way takes us back to the bungalows and up the east side to the gate," la Roche explained.

"That gate?" Cliché pointed between trees, where the Redcoats had set up a defensive line.

"They seem tired," la Roche reasoned as a sinking feeling came over him. "Come on."

Cliché tripped again and was helped by Arsenault.

"Cross now," la Roche said and they ran for the smoldering bungalows.

"*Deja vu*?" Cliché said.

La Roche's heart sank at the sight of a squad of Redcoats by the front gate. Their numbers had doubled. He could see the cage wagons. He knew Atia was there. A despairing tear escaped his eye. *Atia. I can't get to you, my love.* "They are going to fire the big guns."

Redcoats and Maroons both opened fire on them. The Dragoon with the squeaky helmet recognized la Roche. "Capitaine!"

La Roche reloaded the Spanish pistol, admiring its beauty. "It has been a pleasure, gentlemen. But all good things, as they say." He handed the pistol to Arsenault. "If either of you live, return this to Easy Belford on Church Street. Tell her I say '*adieu.*'"

"Surround them!" the Dragoon sergeant said.

"Surrender, pirates!" The squeaky helmet one drew his sword. "There's nowhere left to run, Capitaine Gator Gar. It's finished. We have you!" He snorted. "What is that foul stench?" He eyed his sergeant, who shrugged. "What the bloody hell is that?" He removed the squeaky helmet to cover his nose. Just then, shots blasted from the bushes.

The Dragoon riders were shot down in a matter of seconds, their horses running off into the woods. La Skunk surfaced with eighteen buccaneers at his side.

La Roche felt his strength return. "This way! To the front gate!"

Arsenault gave him a regretful look. "No, Capitaine."

La Skunk reached out his hand. "Time to go, Capitaine. Laurens is waiting. Apologies, Monsieur."

La Roche tightened his belt. "I'm going to get my Atia."

Arsenault took him by the arm. "You will, Capitaine, but not today. We must leave."

The words were like a dagger to la Roche's chest and he was completely lost. The buccaneers led him back to the lake. Bombs vibrated around them, sending the English running to the hills. The Maroons' claim to victory was short-lived as cannonballs screamed through the trees and bombs fell from the sky.

La Roche remained silent. So much destruction and loss of life. The plantation had been a sanctuary, a private *sérénité.* Gone. He swore vengeance. He would take this island himself if he had to.

Gladstone waited in a boat, wrapped up in a blanket. La Roche stepped aboard with the buccaneers and they paddled away. Away from Atia. *My Atia.* He could imagine her devastation that he couldn't get to her. *I will find her. She must know that she is not alone.*

The cannon fire went on for what seemed like an eternity. When the earth finally stopped shaking, Skean emerged from a somewhat clever hiding spot within the walls of the stable. Around him was a wasteland of corpses, smoke, and pungent sulfur. He was picked up by a carriage and driven into the battlefield where he rejoined Longstaff.

"The Capitaine is close by," Cook said.

Rodney shouted orders, organizing the last Red Royals into formations. "Search the bushes and the lake. Keep your bayonets fixed. We are victorious."

"God be praised," Skean said.

"Not until we have the Capitaine," Longstaff insisted, his throat a bloody mess. "Keep searching!"

Skean walked around. The carnage stretched as far as the eye could see in all directions across the field. The smell of burned flesh permeated the air and Strangewayes's plantation was completely destroyed. "Perhaps the battle is won, Captain?"

The Red Royals compared trophies, pieces they had cut off the dead.

"Get in formation!" Rodney yelled. "Find the buccaneers!"

"We got something for you, Captain," a Red Royal called. The body of Ashanti was displayed, the corpse riddled with stab wounds, protruding arrows, and scorched patches of skin.

Skean practically choked on his own spittle. "Well, God's calling, Captain. I must get back to Port Royal with the prisoners."

"Aye, you do that." Longstaff gave a disdainful glare.

Off in the distance a small carriage waited. Skean's shoulders relaxed; his transport was here. "I don't believe the government will investigate your use of the 'no quarter' policy. Admiral Goddam had a point. This is only the beginning. The buccaneers are coming. The most ruthless of all the Caribbean's rogues."

Longstaff loaded his pistol. "We'll be ready when they do. We're going to need real soldiers if we are to win, not farmers in dyed-red coats, but marines of the highest quality. Or this fate awaits all of Jamaica."

“I shall pray for it,” Skean said thoughtfully.

“And you can advise your Whig government that they have Dominium.”

“Aye, Captain. I will inform Judge Goblet and Acting Lieutenant Governor Piper that we have Dominium.” Skean boarded the carriage and collapsed in his seat. From afar, the screams and howls of Maroons sent chills up his spine.

Atia clung to Tanama’s body, rocking back and forth. She’d been singing a lullaby her ma had sung. It made her feel safe. Despairing thoughts crept in; she’d be going back to Crisp. This time it would be worse than being locked in a closet. She would be tortured and raped. She’d do herself in before she let any of that happen, and she’d take the bastard with her.

The wagon curved around a bend to a cliff where a clear view of the Ligania plain and Port Royal could be seen. The morning light radiated hues of pink and orange. Smoke wafted like soft clouds over the accursed city to which she was once again being dragged.

Redcoats passed her by, bragging about how many buccaneers and Negroes they’d killed. Atia’s lip quivered. The Capitaine wasn’t coming. He’d surely died. *Of course, he’s dead. And my da? He’s dead too. So’s Uncle Rourke and the boys.*

The wagons made a turn. Atia focused on Livia. At least she had her sister. Livia sang the same lullaby to Fatima.

She saw Ekene in the cage in front of them. He’d been beaten for talking to Fatima. He was either dead or unconscious.

Atia continued to rock back and forth, covered in Tanama’s blood. *When they open the cage door, I’m gonna Mute-Katie the fuckers! They’ll have to kill me to get my teeth off ’em!* Pain gripped her chest as she thought about the Capitaine. He would have gone out fighting. She imagined him getting shot down while waving his cutlass and calling her name.

Further ahead, the back door to the largest wagon cage swung open. De Kreep and Yaguara escaped, remaining low enough to avoid being noticed. They rolled into the ditch, disappearing into the bushes.

Drops of rain fell. The dampness slowly washed away the dirt and blood. *Dashiell will come for us, Tanama. Don’t you worry.* Atia continued to rock and hum softly. From the corner of her eye she caught a glimpse of de Kreep and Yaguara. They dragged themselves into the trees, glancing back with red, watery eyes. *No. They're not coming.*

Atia shivered beneath the hardening rain. Livia was all she had now, and they were going back to Crisp. No one was coming this time. She gripped Tanama tightly and tried to match her sister's singing.

A faint noise came from overhead. It was a whistle and then a playful growl. She looked up as something dark and feathery zoomed by, landing in the trees. "*Ma chérie*," Minuit said.

The End

About the Authors

MJL EVANS wanted to be a writer since she was ten years old and in 2014, she finally got her act together and pursued her dream. She is the author of No Quarter: Dominium and No Quarter: Wenches. A huge fan of Monty Python, Red Dwarf, and other BBC shows, her time is devoted to acrylic, oil and watercolor painting, catering to her two senior cats and of course, writing.
You can connect with MJL Evans on Twitter at @artistmjlevans or noquarterseries@gmail.com

GM O'CONNOR is a huge movie fan, writer and visual artist. A lover of sci-fi and history, half his brain lives in the 17th century while the other half sails perpetually through space. He is the author of No Quarter: Dominium and No Quarter: Wenches. He hopes to one day bring the No Quarter Series to film and/or graphic novel format.
You can connect with GM O'Connor on Twitter at @gm_oconnor or noquarterseries@gmail.com

Audiobook versions of No Quarter: Dominium and No Quarter: Wenches is now available

If you have any feedback/suggestions or would like to sign up to be a beta reader please contact us at: noquarterseries@gmail.com **or follow us on Facebook at:**
https://www.facebook.com/noquarterseries

www.ingramcontent.com/pod-product-compliance
Lightning Source LLC
Chambersburg PA
CBHW020718310726
48979CB00004B/973